THE ENGINEER

A CHRONICLES OF ACTAEON STORY

BY DARRAN MICHAEL HANDSHAW

THE ENGINEER

A Chronicles of Actaeon Story

FOREWARD

THIS NOVEL IS BASED ON a true story that took place in the fictional world of Redemption. Redemption MUSH was once a multiplayer, text-based roleplaying RPG that could be connected to with the standard telnet address and port number – one of the last original games of its kind. The story told within is a dramatized version of the epic story of my character Actaeon as it took place in that world. It is also the incredible story of how I met my wife.

I met her in the digital world of Redemption before we ever met in the real world. Our characters went on amazing adventures together – adventures that are worth sharing with the world. I hope you enjoy Actaeon's story, for, in a way, it is my own story – the story of my own journey and my own Redemption. It is a story of adventure and romance and of triumph against all odds.

Thank you to Stefanie, Pauline, Ben, Jodi, Joanne, Joe, and Heather for allowing me to include your characters in this story. They helped bring the tale to life. You and many others were a big part of the journey told within these pages.

Thank you also to the proofreaders and critique partners that helped make this a more solid story: Stefanie, RoseMarie and David, you were a tremendous help in making this a solid read. Also, a big shout out to Eleanor, Cindy and Zora and all the other members of the SciFi Roundtable for all your comments and suggestions. Finally, thank you to all of the backers that donated to make this project a success, especially the following major backers: RoseMarie Handshaw, Christine and Ramesh Malhotra, and John and Nancy Schlosberg,

The biggest thank you goes to Stefanie Handshaw and Simon Svensson for originally creating the world on Redemption MUSH and for encouraging me to write this story. It is an amazing world – it changed my life. You will forever have my thanks!

Stefanie, this book is dedicated to you – for all the love, wisdom, and especially the patience you have always given to me. Life with you at my side is amazing. You make all my dreams come true, you are my shield in the worst of times, and you give me a home to return to every night. You are my dream come true.

TABLE OF CONTENTS

DRAMATIS PERSONAE

RAEDELLE DOMINION
THE ROYAL FAMILY

Aedwyn Caliburn: Prince of Raedelle, seated at Caliburn Castle

Eshelle Caliburn: the Prince's sister

Aedgar Caliburn: youngest of the royal family

Gwendolyn Caliburn: Dowager Duchess of Raedelle, widow of the late Duke Branwyn

Branwyn Caliburn: Duke of Raedelle, father of Prince Aedwyn, murdered in the Forbidden.

Gawyn Caliburn: Eldest son of Branwyn, killed alongside his father.

Owayn Caliburn: Second son of Branwyn, also killed alongside his father.

Ambrosius the Wise: Elder Advisor to the Caliburn family

Wayd Arbrigel: Warbander & Goader of Raedelle, Caliburn family friend

WARRIORS OF RAEDELLE

Geodric Caider: Companion of Raedelle, in charge of counter-tribal operations

Gorgrian: Companion of Raedelle, bodyguard of the Prince

Itarik Faris: Companion of Raedelle, bodyguard of the Prince

Davil: Warbander of Lakehold

Matt: Warbander of Lakehold

Tarcy Hael: Warbander of Lakehold

Drystan Beiloff: Warchief of Shore

Varisk Conmara: Warband Captain of Incline

Jezail Vren: Warbander of Incline, archer, bard

Pollia: Warbander from Blackstone

Olli: Page from Blackstone

LORDS AND LADIES OF THE CONCLAVE

Hamnin Dafryl: Lord of Lakeguard in Lakehold, acting Overseer in the stead of the Prince

Tridarch Hael: Lord of Bastion in Lakehold

Neryl Vanora: Lady of Whiterose in Lakehold

Jad Perth: Lord of Lakefeed in Lakehold

Aethelred Ackart: Lord of Southward in Lakehold

Gunther Arcady: the Lord Shore, Lord of Blackstone, seated at Blackstone Fortress

Cathaoir Conmara: Lord of Incline in Shore

Julip Tanderly: Lady of Highwater in Shore

Delle Fletcher: Lady of the Western Rim in Shore

Cadmere Blarth: Lord of the Eastern Rim in Shore

OTHERS

Actaeon Rellios: Engineer from Incline in Shore

Ithelie Faris: a Voice, one of the religious leaders of Raedelle

Balin: Smith in the Open Market

Lauryn: Woodcarver in the Open Market

Gritta: a Cutter

SHIELD DOMINION

Indros Immerai Zar: Prince General of Shield

Endira Zar: his daughter and oldest child, the Lady of Amphis' Ledge

Enrion Zar: his son

Shar Minovo: an Adjutant to the Prince General, a young but very skilled soldier

Pierxon Hyk: A farmer in Lazi's Tomb

AJMAN DOMINION

Fenrik Mujarba: Raj of Ajman

Gaemri Ip Monjata: the Raj' Portent

Viyudun sil'Mujarba al-Arshad: The Raj's nephew

Nadiya Ajman: High Priestess of the Ajman Dominion

Calisse T'ra Coletka: Warrioress of Ajman, sworn to protect Nadiya

Maerdia Bazardjan: an Artist

NIWIAN DOMINION

Garizo Fothrakas: Lord Protector of Memory Keep

Agarine Lartigan: a young Niwian Lady

Terchin vor Steubick: a young Niwian Lord

Torot vor Steubick: Terchin's younger brother

THYR DOMINION

Captain Amodeus Jarval: Supreme Captain of Thyr

CZERYNIAN DOMINION

Warlord Kergon: Warlord of Czeryn

Berk: Warrior in a small band in Stormstair

THE ARBITERS

Phragus sof Luep: Sentinel Arbiter

Eisandre sof Darovin: Knight Arbiter assigned to protect Pyramid

Garth sof Belidur: Knight Arbiter, partner of Eisandre

Allyk sof Darovin: Knight Arbiter

Trello sof Allyk: a junior Arbiter in Allyk's training

Kylor sof Haringar: Knight Arbiter

Corvin sof Haringar: Knight Arbiter, a technical consult

THE ALTHEANS

Seraeta: Althean Healer

THE LORESWORN

Sollemnis the Gray: an elder Loresworn

Kryo: a Loresworn leader

Fauntin Comeris: Adept Loresworn

Inditrovalis Jem: a young Adept Loresworn

KEEPERS

Atreena Covellet: Keeper Knight

OTHERS

Trench: Invasion War veteran, mercenary

Wave: Invasion War veteran, mercenary, companion of Trench

Phyrius Ricter: First of the First

Green: Old owner of The End

Oril: New owner of The End

Vez: an Old Carter

Raulf: a Baker in the Marketplace

Markor: unsavory character from the Warrens

PROLOGUE: THE ESCAPE

THE ENGINEER ELUDED THEM FOR hours as he fled across the ruins, but in the end they captured him.

Surrounded, Actaeon knelt upon a large, moss-covered tile and lowered his polished recurve bow gently to the ground before him. Then he raised his hands into the air in a gesture of surrender.

"Gentlemen," he addressed them with cheerful confidence. "It appears we have had a misunderstanding."

Through the lenses of his goggles, Actaeon studied his three remaining pursuers as they closed in on him. The sunlight reflected off their clean shaven pates and their expressionless faces were each divided into four quadrants by a sharp, black cross. They wore boiled leather armor and carried blades fashioned from sharpened shards of debris. One carried a short bow. All of them ignored his friendly greeting.

"If there is something that you wish to discuss; a proposal perhaps? I would be more than willing to-" Actaeon's words were cut off abruptly as one of the cross-faced raiders lowered his bow and kicked him in the stomach, causing him to double over onto his side. The recurve bow he had set on the ground so carefully was kicked unceremoniously aside to be collected by another raider. That same raider also took the time to work Actaeon's halberd free from the body of one of their less fortunate comrades.

"Careful with that bow, it is not designed for such abuse," Actaeon said, earning himself another kick that knocked the wind from him. He grimaced and rolled onto his back where he could gaze up at the raider who had kicked him. He was rewarded with a faceful of sunlight instead and pulled his goggles down over his eyes to block some of the rays.

Just as the Engineer had begun to catch his breath, he was hauled to his feet by the raider that had kicked him.

Actaeon took the opportunity to study his captor's face for any insight. He found there only dull eyes, devoid of all emotion. Without words, the raider pointed north, where the ruins stretched out to disappear over the horizon in a turbulent mess of shattered structures and overgrown debris fields.

"You must mean to communicate your desire for me to walk in that direction," Actaeon responded, as though it were up for discussion. "You would, of course, be welcome to join me heading south towards Pyramid, that is, if you would be willing to reconsider." He was rewarded with a smack to the back of his head.

Actaeon grinned at the raider behind him, "I will take that as the implied negative that it would appear to be." He led the way along then and the three silent raiders followed him closely, letting him choose the path northward.

For hours they wound through the treacherous ruins of the northern Boneyards, not pausing for rest. Their path took them past ancient, flickering luminaries and conduits arcing dangerously with blue tendrils of lightning. They climbed over mountains of scree and archaic rubble, up slides of debris from old collapsed structures and through the framework of buildings that had fallen to pieces long before any of the current inhabitants of the city had arrived. Thorny bushes poked through the wreckage and flowering creepers wound their way through ancient structural supports and tangled wires, soaking up every available inch of sunlight-soaked real estate to feed persistent roots in soil far below the degraded remains of a society lost.

Nobody knew what had happened to the civilization that once had flourished there. When people arrived in the ruined city that had eventually come to be known as their Redemption, there was no sign of those that had lived there before, nothing but ghosts and discarded remnants of technology, dangerous and unknown. All had disappeared suddenly, leaving their once great city to fall to ruin. Actaeon had his theories about what happened. The Ancients had left behind evidence aplenty to help answer the great unknown mystery of Redemption.

It was one of the reasons that, for the second time in his twenty-five years, Actaeon had left the safety of his home in southern Redemption, a hold in Raedelle known as Shore, to explore the ruins of the city. The other reason was the fact that nothing else remained there for him.

The young Engineer was nineteen when he returned home after his first three year excursion into the ruins of Redemption, only to find that his father had been killed in battle and his mother was deathly ill. He'd studied with every anatomist and herbalist he could find, looking for a cure to her ailment – a disease called Rogue's Bane, where the joints would swell and cause tremendous pain. Every case that he had researched he found the same outcome: the lungs would slowly fill with fluid and within a season or two, the victim would essentially drown.

Actaeon had even gone to the gates of Travail after hearing from one healer that they had seen a man be cured by the Loresworn there. Despite his heartfelt request for the knowledge to save his mother's life, they had turned him away. As a child, he had thought to join the ranks of the Loresworn one day – to study the relics of the Ancients and unlock the keys to their technology with them. But the Loresworn kept such artifacts and the knowledge they gleaned from them to themselves, with the declared purpose of preventing another cataclysmic event like the one that had been the downfall of the city. They were protecting people, they said. It was the opposite of everything that Actaeon believed; given the chance, he'd share the truth of that knowledge with the world for the betterment of all.

His mother fought a long battle with the Rogue's Bane at Actaeon's behest, to give him time to search for a cure, but she eventually succumbed to the illness, leaving Actaeon alone and heartbroken. He gave up his studies of healing and started a metal-casting business, having learned that he could cast many different parts of varying shapes and complexities out of dies made from a refined clay. He took orders from across Shore and even traveled as far as Lakehold on occasion to make some part or another for a Lord or Lady of the Raedelle Dominion.

The metalwork occupied him for several years. It wasn't enough for him though; it didn't answer any of the big questions. Once he'd earned enough money to fund another expedition, he ventured out into the ruins of Redemption again. This time his ultimate destination was the Pyramid of the Sun. There he would make sure his plans came together.

One of the raiders gave Actaeon a shove, interrupting his thoughts. By Actaeon's reckoning, they were headed northwest towards Craters, a region in the Czeryn Dominion. He frowned at the thought. The people there liked to solve problems and disputes and all matters political with the edge of a sword or the strike of a fist, not a technique of which he was fond. The Czeryn Dominion was also the one Dominion that permitted slavery. Actaeon had heard the stories of the slavers that would wander the unclaimed regions of Redemption, looking for people to capture and sell to the Czerynians. He wondered if these cross-faced raiders were slavers. That would explain why they went to such extremes to capture him alive instead of killing him. Still, they had lost one of their men during the process and that just didn't seem worth the capture of a single slave. No – these men were after something different.

The moment came nearly five hours into the trek. The raiders were getting tired. Actaeon heard them stumble several times on the debris as they followed his carefully selected path towards Craters. When he came out of the winding path between two foundation walls, he spotted exactly what he had been looking for. Before them a rubble pile sloped upwards at a dramatic angle in every direction. To the left and right the ascent looked feasible, but straight ahead was one of those areas he'd learned about the difficult way: the incline ramped up at a steep, unstable angle.

The Engineer started up in that direction and the raiders followed him unaware. In the next moments, he thought, the precision of his actions would determine whether he lived or died.

Actaeon set a strong pace for the climb, hoping to push the raiders to the limit. As he neared the top, he spotted what he had seen earlier: a large bar protruding from the side of the rubble pile. He paused and looked down at the raiders below. They were breathing hard and struggled to catch up with him; they had yet to realize their mistake.

Once he reached the bar, he placed his scuffed leather boot at the exposed end of the bar, and stepped up onto it, throwing his full weight behind it. Just as he had hoped, the bar acted like a lever and shifted. Below him he heard rubble breaking loose from the steep incline. He gave the lever one final shove before he leapt clear of the debris slide he had started. He scrambled to pull himself up the rest of the pile towards the summit as the ruin fragments below destabilized rapidly in a roaring tumult and a cloud of dust. He heard their cries of alarm and warning and grinned at the thought that this is what it took to get them to finally speak.

The thought was interrupted rather suddenly, however, as the debris beneath him began to lose cohesion and slide down the pile as well. Actaeon's heart pounded hard in his chest as he scrambled upward desperately while the ground came loose beneath him and threatened to catch him in the debris slide. With a great effort, he reached the top of the pile and rolled away until he began rolling down another slope. He stopped and scrambled back up to the summit to look down at his captors.

The Engineer surveyed the scene through the scratched lenses of his goggles. Once the dust settled, two of the raiders were nowhere to be found. The third, the one that had kicked him, struggled to pull free, his legs trapped beneath two large beams that had rolled down atop him. Actaeon pulled himself to his feet and maneuvered carefully down the incline towards the survivor. He had a few questions for his former captor.

When the last cross-faced raider noticed the Engineer's approach, his eyes went wide. He dug down into the rubble with both hands, shredding them on sharp fragments in the process as he searched for his weapon. Actaeon slowed as he grew closer to the trapped raider, prepared for a confrontation.

The raider withdrew his hands and, as Actaeon had anticipated, held up a dagger. However, the Engineer did not expect the man's next move and with one swift motion, the raider drew the dagger across his throat to spill thick, crimson blood down his brown leather armor.

In a moment, the raider was dead and Actaeon sat down heavily, taking the entire scene in. Luck and a carefully calculated maneuver had saved his life today, but he was nowhere closer to an answer as to why these men were pursuing him. It was both fortunate and unfortunate at once, he thought.

At the bottom of the incline he spotted his halberd as its finely wrought, curved blade reflected the growing moonlight. He scrambled down the rest of the way to retrieve it. An inspection of both ends found that the pointed wedge at the bottom of the reinforced shaft was intact, but there was a notch near the end of the blade where it hooked back on itself. "How unfortunate," he said aloud.

That done, he set about the task of digging carefully to locate his recurve bow, with the valuable spotting scope attached to its midsection. It took him the better part of the evening, but he managed to locate it buried beside one of the dead raiders as he worked under the bright moonlight. Everything was miraculously intact and he unstrung the bow before he fastened it back into the special clasp on the left shoulder of his ribbed leather jacket.

As an afterthought, he searched both of the dead raiders. There was nothing enlightening to be found on them, so the Engineer turned and started his way back south across the unforgiving terrain of the Boneyards, named for the gigantic struts of ancient structures that loomed like the bones of an enormous beast and cast long, eerie shadows in the moonlight.

As the early morning sun cast its spectrum of color across the ruins, Actaeon summited one of the last debris piles. From there he could see the sunlight gleam off of the reflective tip of the Pyramid in the distance. An appropriate name, he thought: Pyramid of the Sun. Just a few more hours now. From his vantage point, he could make out the collapsed north face of the Pyramid. The enormous building of the Ancients was full of fissures and crevices on that side. Likely the consequence of some manner of great cataclysm, thought the Engineer, perhaps the same one that formed the wreckage he was standing atop.

The fatigue finally found its way into his joints and bones, so he leaned on the halberd and lowered himself until he was seated on a smooth block of elderstone. He could rest here for just a short while now, with his goal in sight. Everything he had planned depended on whether he could convince the people there, in that Pyramid, of his worth to them.

ACT ONE: BREAKING THE MOLD

PYRAMID

ACTAEON PAUSED TO BRUSH DUST from the ruins off of his heavy trousers, then stepped up onto the Avenue of Glass and leaned heavily upon his halberd. Rather than entering Pyramid through the collapsed facade of its northern face, he approached where he could enter the great, ancient structure from its intact southern face.

To the west the ramshackle structures of the Outskirts clustered around the shattered end of the Avenue as though moths drawn to a light. It seemed to him that the Outskirts had grown in size since last he had been here. It was a good sign of the growing stability between the Dominions that people were investing in building there, he thought.

Down beyond the Outskirts was Blacksands Beach. Distant sounds of the crashing waves could be heard even at this distance. Many a strange artifact that washed up upon its shores to be found and studied by the Engineer during his first visit to this place. To the south of the Outskirts was the blasted plain of the Windmoor, sullen monoliths visible from the ancient Stone Gardens within it. To the north past Blacksands Beach, the haze of the Felmere hung heavily over its pools of dangerous substances and rare plant life; not a place to be traversed lightly.

A glance to the east showed the continued length of the Avenue of Glass, running straight as an arrow from west to east. At the far end of the Avenue, past the southeast corner of the Pyramid, he could make out the colorful tents in the Open Market where all the Dominions brought goods for trade. Many independent merchants had opened their businesses there, and the less successful of them eked out a life in the hazardous slum hidden in the honeycomb of broken tunnels beside the marketplace, a place that was known to the Pyramid elite simply as the Warrens. At the broken east end of the Avenue, he knew, stood the dilapidated assemblage of artifact and debris known as The End, which served as the local tavern for the melting pot of Dominions that had grown in and around Pyramid.

"I am returned," said the Engineer aloud, to no one in particular. With a grin, he turned sharply to the east and began the final leg of his journey down the Avenue of Glass.

Inside the Pyramid he made his way expediently to the Mirrorholds, a great hall made from many faceted mirrors – within the hall were housed the embassies. Even the floors were made from the mirrored material. The overall effect made the chamber appear extremely large, and quite disorienting to walk through for the unpracticed. All of the Dominions, the respective nation states of Redemption, were represented there, each within their own chambers.

The Engineer looked at one of his reflections to compose himself. His blackened leather boots were scuffed and worn from his journey and the rest of his clothing was worse for the wear, but that was alright; he could patch it up. A wide leather belt with a large cast buckle held his heavy cotton trousers up and the scabbard for his companion dagger. A finely-woven, green undertunic was tucked into his trousers. Over that he wore a steel grey vest and a heavy, blackened leather jacket with reinforced elbows and shoulders. He brushed some dirt from his sleeves. The many pockets of the jacket bulged with various artifacts and items he carried and sewn neatly into the back was an arrow quiver with several shafts still protruding from it – he'd have to make some more.

He stepped closer to regard himself with his perceptive, emerald eyes and ran a hand through the disheveled, black hair behind his goggles to try to achieve the look that he hadn't just been delving into the ruins. His hair extended down the sides of his face in crisp lines that ended at his jawline. Satisfied that he didn't look too unkempt, he grinned and continued along.

Saint Torin's Hold stood as a welcome relief from the Mirrorholds, with their endless, dizzying reflections. The reflective walls were in Saint

Torin's also, but the Raedelleans of Lakehold and Shore had covered these walls with a variety of tapestries and other effects telling stories and legends of home. The Engineer blinked his eyes to clear away the residual optical effects of the outer Mirrorholds and paused in the entrance to survey the Hold.

It was much as he had last seen it. The long, wooden tables were arranged in the manner of Raedelle's own great halls and one table at the far end of the hall upon a raised dais designated for the Prince, his honored guests, and closest advisors. Along both walls stood weapon racks that held spears, bows and other weapons. Most Raedelleans went the way of the warband, at least for a time – it was a rite of passage for them to learn to fight and spend time defending from the tribal incursions. And those incursions were frequent and pronounced, given Raedelle's location on the fringe of the ancient city. It was a path that Actaeon never followed, and that stood like a gaping chasm between him and his people. It wasn't normal for a healthy young man or woman not to go through the Trials and join the warband for at least a few years – and everyone knew that the unhealthy usually did not survive for long.

Raedelleans were busy clearing the evening's meal as Actaeon made his way to the table at the far end of the Hold. He stopped nearby and allowed his halberd to rest easily against his right shoulder before he scratched the back of his right hand through the fabric of his fingerless glove. He surveyed those at the table for a moment, but failed to find anyone who met the description of the Raedellean Prince. He cleared his throat and addressed those who remained at the table still talking after the meal, "Good evening. I seek an audience with Prince Aedwyn Caliburn, if he can spare a few moments." That said, he smiled broadly, waiting for a response.

One of the women turned to look at him as he spoke. Her bright blue eyes considered him thoughtfully, staring at him a bit longer than was polite. Actaeon hadn't noticed her a moment earlier – a young woman with short, blond hair, dressed in the grey garb and red cape of a Knight Arbiter of Pyramid. It was rare to see a woman in the role of an Arbiter. They were the neutral defenders of Pyramid and its surrounds. He couldn't recall ever seeing a female Arbiter before. When he met her gaze, a strange sensation rose in his chest.

"I'm sorry, but Aedwyn's not here right now. He might be back on the morrow or the next," said a woman with fiery red hair that stood to address the Engineer.

Her words snapped him out of his thoughts and he dipped his head politely in response, "Thank you. I shall have to check back later I suppose." He began to leave before he turned to face her again. "Ah, if someone could please tell His Grace that Actaeon Rellios of Shore seeks his audience, I would be most appreciative."

The Arbiter took that moment to stand and address the red haired woman, "I should go, Eshy. I will be back when I can."

"Take care, Eisandre," replied the woman, with a warm smile for the Arbiter. Could she be Eshelle Caliburn, Aedwyn's younger sister?

"Actaeon Rellios of Shore," the woman called Eshy repeated, as she turned back to face him. "I'll be sure to pass it on to Aedwyn when I see him. I'm afraid I've a few things I need to take care of at the moment, or I'd help you myself." That said, she retook her seat at the table and resumed her conversation.

"I understand. Not a problem. I will return at a later time to see if I can find him. Have a fine evening," he said with a grin and dip of his head. He received no reply and started back out to the Mirrorholds.

Actaeon was disappointed that Prince Aedwyn was unavailable. It was hopeful that he had been able to speak with his sister, assuming his presumption was correct. If he could reason with the Caliburn family, he may well be able to convince them of his plan.

THE MECHANICAL MAN

I N RETROSPECT, IT MIGHT HAVE been cheaper to find a place to stay in the Outskirts, but the Song of the Sisters located him centrally in Pyramid, where he needed to be. Actaeon inserted the key into the door of his new room and turned it to feel the lock mechanism cycle. It wasn't the normal click of a tumbler lock, but rather a buzz followed by a whirring sound typical of locking mechanisms in artifacts.

He knew from experience that the lock operated using a special type of metal that attracted other metals. In fact, this was the property that allowed his directional finder and metal detection device to operate. It balanced a thin wooden beam with an attracting metal tip at one end upon a needlepoint and that beam pointed towards the nearest attracting metal object of substantial size. When there were no metal objects nearby, the beam would point steadily southwards, which enabled him to better navigate throughout the ruins. It also allowed him to find buried artifacts along the shore of Blacksands Beach.

The Engineer stepped into the room to find what would be his quarters for the next few weeks or months. It was a spartan room but well kept. A chest of drawers and a foot locker stood at opposite sides of the door with a small wardrobe against the adjacent wall. The bed was against the severely slanted window in the eastern wall of the Pyramid's glass tip. The window provided a view of the Open Market far below where he could see the lights of luminaries dancing along at the arrival of dusk. He was also able to see some of the treetops far below where the gardens of the Terrace of the Stars jutted from the eastern side of Pyramid.

He set his halberd against the chest of drawers and stripped out of his jacket and vest. After unlacing his boots, he pulled them off. When he laid down, he let out a deep sigh. It was the first time in a little over a month that he would enjoy a rest in a real bed.

He drifted off to thoughts of his home in Incline. The slanted window reminded him of the rooftop window that he had built above his bedroom. He had been thrilled to show his parents the mechanism he'd constructed with pulleys to open and close the window with the throw of a lever. He remembered the look on both of his parents' faces when he first showed them the invention – it had been one of pride. Unhappy, his father had insisted that he double his archery training, to distract him from such pursuits. Actaeon smiled at the memory and soon was fast asleep beneath the canvas of stars that unfolded above him.

The sun woke him up bright and early in the morning. Actaeon sat up with a start and smacked his head on the slanted window above him. He lay back down with a smart. Roll. He would have to roll next time, he noted. Luckily, the goggles he still wore atop his head had cushioned the impact.

With a grin at his own clumsiness, he rolled to one side out of the bed and began to get ready for his day. There was a lot that he wanted to accomplish, including again seeking an audience with the Prince. Plus, he was quite hungry.

Actaeon donned his gear and descended to the lower level of the Song of the Sisters. This level, built into the northern face of the Pyramid, served as an upscale restaurant for Pyramid's elite. He figured he would do well to pick up something to eat at the communal meal in Saint Torin's Hold instead.

The restaurant only had a few occupied tables at this time of the morning. On his way through, he approached the slanted northern window to gaze out over the ruins of the Boneyards. He could make out the rubble and ruin of the once great ancient city for many miles northwards. There were details from up here that he couldn't have hoped to observe even if he spent weeks exploring the ruins down there. He was able to spot a few different landmarks to help find his most recent route through the Boneyards. Even the location of the small debris slide he had created was discernable, he thought. The texture of the ruin pile looked different, as though it hadn't yet settled.

Actaeon leaned his halberd against the table next to him and unclasped the recurve bow from his back, which he lifted to his face to gaze through the monocular sight he had attached to its frame. He gazed through it and surveyed even finer details of the Boneyards far below. The main thoroughfare up towards Craters had a few dozen Czerynians making the journey with handcarts and baskets. With the magnification of the bow's scope, he could make out their slow progress.

He panned across the wreckage of the Boneyards in search of the location of the ruinslide that he had created. "How interesting," he said aloud, upon locating the area once more. "Vanished." The bodies of the cross-faced raiders were indeed gone. Taken, most likely, by their comrades. He wondered how the bodies had been found so quickly. Either way, it meant there were more of them and close to Pyramid. He would have to be on his guard.

He began to turn away, but froze. He had just panned past something incredibly unusual.

There was a body out there.

"I hadn't realized that vagabonds had invaded the more civilized places in the Pyramid to escape the horrific stench of the Open Market," came the melodic voice of a woman seated at the table to the right of him.

Actaeon lowered the recurve's scope from his eye and glanced over. At a nearby table sat a pale young lady with well kept curls of blond hair cascading down her shoulders and back in one of the current styles. She wore an ostentatious, ruffled dress in the manner of Niwian noble ladies that he had encountered before within Pyramid. Across from her sat another noblewoman that kept her back to Actaeon.

He approached them and inclined his head politely. "Ah good lady, you have my sincerest thanks for the warning. I shall keep a watch out for these vagabonds. It would have been quite the unpleasant surprise to have encountered one unexpectedly. To whom, may I ask, do I owe my gratitude?"

Her eyes narrowed at the Engineer's twist to her comment, but after a moment she straightened and responded with cold courtesy, "You are addressing the Lady Agarine Lartigan." That said, she promptly returned her attention to the table and her companion.

"A true pleasure to meet you, Lady Lartigan. I am Actaeon Rellios of Shore and as I said, you have my gratitude. May the day meet your enjoyment," said Actaeon with another exaggerated dip of his head.

Returning to the issue at hand, he raised the scope back to his eye and swept over the section of rubble that he had scouted earlier. It didn't take him long to find it – though it wasn't a body. At least it wasn't any type of human body. Even through the scope it was still quite small in the distance and the details were hard to make out, but it had an unnatural light to it, almost a silver sheen. It appeared to Actaeon that the object was actually some sort of mechanical man, likely another artifact of the Ancients. "Well now, this is quite interesting," he muttered to himself. He would have to map out a route to the mechanical man. An artifact of such complexity would be an incredible find and might even teach him something about the people that once lived here.

Excitedly, he turned back to the Niwian Lady as he unconsciously scratched his right arm through the sleeve of his jacket. "Excuse me, Lady Lartigan, but would you be so kind as to allow me to borrow your napkin?"

The young lady looked downright appalled and her jaw dropped open to protest the Engineer's request. When her mouth closed, she shook her head, her features crinkled in disgust, "You may have my napkin if you will agree to then leave us to eat in peace." She lifted the finespun cloth napkin from her lap and then thrust it towards him, turning her head pointedly in the other direction.

"You are most kind, Lady Lartigan. Once again, you have my gratitude. I will be sure to speak of your graciousness. One must be careful though, lest it become expected," he said, with a smirk. He relieved her of the napkin and laid it out on the table to his left – he would have to remember to carry vellum with him in the future, but the white napkin would make do in the meantime. He withdrew his sharpened charcoal stick and using his scope for aid, drew a rough map on the napkin to help him reach the mechanical man.

Once finished, he folded up the napkin and deposited it carefully one of his pockets before retrieving his halberd. He made sure to thank the

Niwian Lady one last time before he departed, and he thought he heard her companion giggle, though it was quickly cut short.

Saint Torin's Hold was abustle with activity when he arrived, much busier than the previous evening. The atmosphere was tense, as though everyone was waiting for some unseen axe to fall.

"What is amiss?" he asked one of his countrymen.

"It's Aedwyn... he's been hurt," replied the man. "Hunting accident. Preparations are being made to return him to Raedelle."

The Engineer arched a brow in concern, leaning forward on his halberd's staff, "Will His Grace recover?"

"I think he should – yes, of course he will. Eshelle is in charge in the meantime," said the man, with a gesture toward the dais. The man patted Actaeon roughly on the shoulder and walked brusquely away.

A glance in that direction told the Engineer that he had been correct in concluding that the red-haired woman was the Prince's sister. She stood beside the same table as yesterday, wearing the simple but practical leather armor of the Companions, the sworn protectors of the Prince. Her poise was different now, stiff with authority as she directed people to and fro. When everyone moved off, she took a seat down at the table.

With a slight frown, Actaeon made his way over to her. The wedge-shaped endcap of his halberd's staff clicked with every other step as he approached her and dipped his head politely.

"Eshelle Caliburn, my deepest regrets for what happened to your brother. My thoughts are with him and I hope for his speedy recovery," he said. He lifted his free hand and scratched the one holding his halberd as he searched out her gaze with sympathetic eyes.

Eshelle turned to face him, breaking out of a fog of thoughts. "Thank you. Everything will be all right though. It's just... a short term thing. Yes," she said, as if to reassure herself. Her eyes narrowed before she spoke again, "I'm sorry, but have we met?"

"It is not a problem. I failed to recognize you last evening when I visited the Hold as well. I pieced together who you were afterwards," he said as he held up his hand to forestall her apology. "I am Actaeon Rellios of Shore."

"Ah, yes. The artifact collector. Is there something that you wished to speak to me about?"

"I journeyed from Incline to speak to His Grace, the Prince. You see, I am not an artifact collector but an Engineer. With my skills, I believe that I can be of service to Raedelle. I invent things to solve problems and to better our lives," he explained, his face lighting up at the topic. "There are a plethora of challenges for Raedelle to overcome and I have many ideas that will be able to help –"

"Help?" Eshelle interrupted him sharply. "If you want to help, then go figure out what is causing the Open Market to smell so badly – find it and fix it if that is your skill. I'm tired of all the traders and artisans complaining to me about it. I have much more pressing matters to attend to at this time. Do that and we can talk more about your helping Raedelle overcome challenges."

Her sudden annoyance was a surprise to Actaeon, but he figured she was likely under a great deal of stress given what had happened to her brother. The task she gave him sounded uninteresting and disgusting, but he knew it might be his opportunity to prove himself. And so, he offered her a broad grin. "Of course I will look into it for you. I will give you a report as soon as I can complete an assessment of the situation. I could use some assistants to help me with the surveyance. Is there someone avail–"

"I have nobody to spare. And I don't need any report – just let me know when you fix the problem," said the Prince's sister, dismissively.

"It will be done," said the Engineer, remaining positive despite the rude dismissal. He turned upon his heel, snapped his halberd forward into his hand and strode confidently from the Hold.

THE END

THE OPEN MARKET WAS INDEED afflicted with a most nauseating stench. The humid air hung heavy with it and left the marketplace feeling stifled and rushed. A few of the merchants had already taken to offering scented handkerchiefs and they were selling quite well. Though the shoppers were scarce today and many of the various stalls were closed, most everyone wore the brightly colored handkerchiefs over their noses and mouths.

Actaeon recalled that the Open Market was typically lively with activity – trade wagons and merchants moving in and out, the shouts of buyers as they haggled over prices, auctions amidst the chaos, and the rush of buyers toward the announcement of a sale or special deal. The occasional cry of 'Thief' wasn't uncommon, but usually was not followed by any sort of pursuit.

The Order of Arbiters had authority there, but, while they patrolled the area to prevent general civil disorder and unrest, they did not often chase thieves. Instead, it was the responsibility of the shopkeepers to watch after their wares and the buyers to watch after their purchases. Some of the larger merchants had their own hired muscle to look after their goods, but the smaller merchants had taken to clustering their stalls together with fellow countrymen. Such clusters were frequently looked after by soldiers or guards assigned by their Dominion to protect the business interests of their merchants outside Pyramid.

To the east of the markets the Adhikaran Ajmani merchants had the largest and most systematic of these clusters, protected by its own military force. The Ajmani Bazaar, as it was called, stood out with shops under colorfully dyed tents, topped with flags, that contrasted starkly with the ramshackle wood and metal stalls in the rest of the Open Market.

Were a thief to be caught, there was typically little done to them as Dominions did not wish to risk political consequence by harming a citizen of a rival Dominion. Often, the thieves were just roughed up a bit and left in the Warrens or shown to the edge of the market.

Due to this, the Open Market could be a dangerous place. One had to know how to carry themselves if they walked here alone. Many shoppers would travel in groups or with escorts for safety. However, for those willing to brave the vast tents and stalls of the marketplace, every sort of product was available. Items from the far reaches of northern Shield, to the colonies in the south, and even relics purchased by the unruly tribals at the eastern border of Redemption.

Today would be a poor day for the thieves anyway, Actaeon thought. With so many people avoiding the marketplace due to the unbearable smell, it would be difficult to get away unseen.

This situation was beneficial for him, for he had been able to conduct a cursory survey of the marketplace in a single morning. It was as he had suspected: a drainage issue. The Open Market was assembled inside of a very wide crater that had opened in the structure of the ancient city against the eastern side of Pyramid. The northern end of the crater ended abruptly in a shear wall of compartments and tunnels that had become the impoverished slum called the Warrens; a haven for the poor, the criminals and the location of a rumored black market for more illicit goods and services. A rickety scaffolding clung to the Warrens and creaked in the wind, allowing the lowlifes and thugs that lived there to reach the higher openings. The southern end of the crater sloped upward more gradually to meet the Avenue of Glass.

The Open Market was a constant source of muck and filth from animals being traded and other mercantile wastes, often cleansed by the frequent rains that fell upon Redemption. It washed the waste from the crater and flushed it down the lower tunnels of the Warrens that ran into the ground at an angle, on their way to the under-workings of the city itself.

Waste-filled pools of water had stagnated there and completely submerged all but one of the tunnels.

The Engineer stood before that tunnel now, wrinkling his nose in disgust at the smell of the half circle of stagnant water before it. This tunnel was at the edge of the rancid pool with the top of it jutting free from the water. It was clear to him that the tunnel was completely occluded by some sort of brown gelatinous substance.

He walked around to clear side of the mucky pool and leaned his halberd up against the cracked wall before he started to climb. Moving carefully, he was able to make his way over to the tunnel opening just above the pungent waterline. Carefully, he pulled an arrow from his quiver and used it to reach down and scrape some of the material with the arrowhead. After some resistance, some of the brown goo stuck to the arrowhead when he pulled the arrow away.

While clutching the arrow, he maneuvered his way cautiously back to the dry ground beside his halberd. A quick search through his jacket pockets turned up an empty half-through bottle about half the size of his fist. It was a common artifact found out in the ruins, and useful at that – semi-transparent, milky bottles they came in several consistent sizes and were nearly indestructable. He spun the top of the bottle to uncap it and scraped the substance on the edge of the bottle's mouth to remove it from his arrow. The material was sticky but eventually dropped free of the arrowhead to fall with a plop to the bottom of the bottle.

Whatever this gunk was, it was the cause of the obnoxious smell. If he could figure out how to eliminate it, it might solve the smelly problem. First though, he would have to figure out what caused it. He had a few hypotheses already, but he would require assistance in order to carry out the tests. He wondered who would agree to help with such a filth-ridden and stench-filled problem.

The End was an amalgam of old and new, ancient and eccentric, rusted and shining, all rolled into one - smack at the end of the shattered eastern end of the Avenue of Glass. Part of it was certainly a structure of the Ancients. Perhaps it slid over or had fallen onto what was once the Avenue proper during the event that had ruined Redemption. As long as anyone could recall, there had been a tavern in that structure – perhaps before the creation of the Dominions, but certainly before they claimed Pyramid as their center of diplomacy and trade.

The old tavern had changed proprietors many times, and each one had brought their own sense of style to the structure: new sections were added on, artifacts both useless and inexplicable pinned to the walls and hanged from the ceiling, jagged holes cut with writheblades through the otherwise indestructible building material of the Ancients, glass of various colors inserted into holes to let light in from the outside. The tavern was a collection of the strangest the city had to offer. And this held true right down to the people within.

It was one of Actaeon's favorite haunts, where he would come for an ale and to ponder the original purpose of various items on the wall. It helped when one had trouble deciphering some puzzle, he found, to think about something altogether different for a time. Sometimes the answer would arrive in that manner without even searching for it. There must be some part of a person's brain that worked even when they were unaware of it, he thought.

In the past, he had studied some of the artifacts at the behest of the owner. Usually they were worthless or in permanent disrepair, though once or twice he'd found something useful. Actaeon had made a habit out of bringing any artifact he had no use for to The End in exchange for a few bits or an ale. More often than not, whatever he brought would end up hanging on the wall.

The sign outside had faded over the years, though it was still comprised of a large set of boards with crudely painted words: "You've Reached the End. Might as Well Stop in For a Drink!" The words were painted in gray though, instead of the dark green that he remembered.

With his halberd, he pushed the rickety door open and stepped within. The tavern was busy, and the arrangements were different, but it was still the same old The End.

"Just what we needed, another artifact hunter. I hope ya brought some old relics to buy us a drink with!"

Actaeon grinned at the two older men seated at the far corner table that appeared to be far into their cups.

The bigger of the men was a giant – Actaeon wasn't sure if he'd even seen someone so large. The deep, ugly scar that bisected the giant's face horizontally immediately made him want to look away. He wore a boiled leather chestplate and before him on the table sat a wicked-looking war maul.

The giant's short friend, the one who had spoken, looked almost like a child beside him, with a rogueishly handsome face with long, black hair tied into a neat queue at the back of his neck. He wore a loose white tunic of finespun cotton. As the short man leaned back in his chair, Actaeon noticed the rapier dangling from his swordbelt – its crossguard finely wrought in a gentle curve that shined in the dull light.

"Alas, you two are the only old relics here."

As the two men erupted into laughter, the Engineer approached the tavern's long bar, a broken shard from the Avenue itself that had been hauled inside to make it, its sharper edges covered with dried clay to protect against cuts.

He leaned his halberd against the bar and took a seat in his usual spot.

"What'll it be?" asked a busty bartender with a shock of raven hair arranged deliberately into a giant curl to the side of her head.

"An ale, if you please. Oh, and if you could tell Green that Act says hello, I would appreciate it," he replied with a broad grin.

"Green ain't here no more," came her reply. "Didn't ya see the sign? Ownership's changed. Name's Oril. Yer ale'll be right up."

That said, she turned to pour him a tankard which she slammed on the bartop before him, dark ale sloshing onto the bar, "Enjoy!"

"My thanks," he replied, sliding two copper bits across the bar before he took a sip.

The door swung open behind him and he didn't need to turn around – the clanking of plate armor told him all he needed to know. Keeper Knights. If they were in this place, they could only be looking to make trouble. He kept his head down and took another sip of his ale – he didn't need trouble, especially not with religious, anti-artifact zealots like them.

However, as if reading his thoughts, they clanked their way right over to him and sat on either side. Just his luck. His peripheral vision told him that both Knights had their eyes fixed intently upon him.

The Knight on his left clapped Actaeon firmly on the shoulder with a heavy gauntlet and lef it there, "Allfather greets you, friend."

"A pleasure to meet you, Allfather," replied Actaeon, pretending ignorance, as he met the left Knight's gaze and offered him a big grin. The Allfather was the Keeper's god.

Behind him there were a few stifled chuckles and the Knight's expression turned dark.

Actaeon lifted his tankard as if in toast and took another sip before setting it down upon the bartop. "Oril, two more ales for my friends here."

"Oh that's quite alright, Oril. You see, we don't partake in victuals purchased by blasphemous coin," spoke the Knight on his right side. "All the same, we'll still have our ales, and another for *our* friend here."

"Say, friend," spoke the Knight on the left, whose gauntlet still rested uncomfortably on the Engineer's shoulder, "that's quite the interesting bow that you carry. What is that attached to it?"

"Ah, it is interesting that you ask that actually. It is an assemblage of lenses both artifact and of my own manufacture. Affixed to my recurve bow it can allow me to sight and gauge an arrow shot from a farther distance than I would be able to under normal circumstances. You see, the curvature of each lens element can bend light in a certain direction. I have discovered, with no little experimentation, that when the lenses are arranged in a certain order and with certain separations one can gaze through them and observe objects on the other side with much greater detail than normal. Would you like to see how it works?" asked Actaeon.

Both Knights' breath caught in their chests. The one whose hand had remained on the Engineer's shoulder released his grip and backed away so quickly that his stool toppled to the ground.

Muttering prayers under their breath, both Knights circled behind him so that they stood between Actaeon and the exit.

"We will take that bow. Hand it over now and you can go about your day."

The tavern had gone deathly silent, everyone watching now with interest. Anyone near their location at the bar had quickly backed off towards the wall.

"So you are interested in how it works then. Fantastic! I think you shall find it quite interesting. The possibilities that we can achieve with this technology are still quite numerous and I would be interested in your suggestions."

Both men flinched at the mention of the word 'technology'. One of them let his hand fall to the hilt of his sword.

"The bow – right now."

"Patience, gentlemen. I will show it to you. There is no need to get excited," said Actaeon as he stood and pivoted to face the two Knights. He reached back to undo the clasp on his jacket, which dropped the bow into his other hand. As he lifted it, still unstrung, before him, he reached into his pocket and withdraw a small object.

While holding the bow before him, he slid the baffle aside on his small handheld luminary to allow the bright light to pour free and shine through the lenses of the scope into the eyes of the Knight on his right.

Temporarily blinded, the man raised a hand to his face and staggered back. Then he drew his sword. Hastily, Actaeon swept the focused light over the eyes of the other Knight.

That Knight's reflexes were sharp, and he had already drawn his sword from its sheath. Luckily, the light blinded him and allowed Actaeon to duck beneath the poorly swung blade. He was not as lucky with the Knight's kick however. The heavy boot caught him square in the chest and sent him reeling backwards against the bar, which knocked the wind from him.

As Actaeon struggled to regain his breath, he tossed aside the unstrung bow and snatched up his halberd. Both knights approached him in a daze. They were still half-blinded and blinking to try and clear their vision.

The Knight on the right thrust at the Engineer, who was able to deflect the blow with the staff of his halberd. Actaeon then swung the butt of his halberd against the back of the man's knees, which sent the Knight to the floor.

The other Knight let loose a cry of "Allfather!" before thrusting the point of his sword at Actaeon's throat. The Knight didn't get close though before a tremendous figure rushed from the crowd behind him to tackle and throw him clear over the bartop. He landed on the other side in a clatter of armor.

The hulking figure then turned to the other Knight who was picking himself up from the floor. Actaeon recognized his new ally as the giant who had been sitting at the corner table when he walked in. The giant pulled a large maul from his back and slammed it down on the knight's sword, which shattered it between the floor and the wicked head of the weapon with a crack that resounded through the establishment.

The Knight who had been thrown circled back around the bar with his sword at the ready. In a flash, the small, lithe man from the far corner table rushed to meet him, wielding a flamberge rapier, its wide sinusoidal blade shimmering in the light of the luminaries. There was the clash of steel on steel and in the blink of an eye, the smaller man held both his rapier and the Keeper Knight's sword in his hands.

"That's right, fella. I've got both swords! Be on your way, or else the next lesson'll be quite a bit pointier."

The Keeper Knight turned and looked to his friend who had stumbled to his feet, shattered sword in hand. They stared at one another in disbelief but were interrupted when the giant stepped forward and roared at them.

The pair scrambled over one another as they ran for the door, plate armor clanking and clattering in their hasty retreat.

"Well then, gentlemen," said Actaeon with a broad grin. "It seems I shall be buying you that drink you wanted after all."

The large man went simply by the name Trench and the smaller man had introduced himself as Wave. They were mercenaries for hire – veterans of the Invasion War that had fought and repelled the tribal invasion over twenty-five years ago. Trench's massive proportions and the duo's combat proficiency made them popular hires for those needing protection.

Trench was truly a giant. Standing an arm's length above the average man, he towered over the other patrons at The End. His short greying auburn hair and stubble on his chin bespoke his age. The fact that he was an Invasion War veteran put him in his late forties – an age that few people in Redemption survived to. He wore simple brown boiled leather armor and was armed only with his brutal maul, one side curved while the other terminated in a lethal spike – the weapon slung at his back. A deep scar bisected his face, running from the top of his right brow through his nose and across his left cheekbone.

"I'll give ya a hint why he goes by Trench. Take a look at his facial geography," Wave said.

"That blow seems to have shattered your skull. It is impressive that a man would have survived such physical trauma," Actaeon said.

"Well, thankfully he had me there to hold his face together. Else I suspect it'd have opened and let his brain pour out. At least it improved his looks a bit, wouldn't you say?"

Trench growled in response and an ugly grin tugged uncomfortably at his scar, "Whatever ya say, Wave. I didn't see you there to help when I crushed the man who gave me this scar to a pulp."

"Stubborn bastard... who doesn't at least get knocked out after getting their face cleaved in half?"

Wave seemed the polar opposite in appearance from his companion He stood several fists shorter than Actaeon, his shining black hair tied back neatly in a queue that terminated between the tops of his shoulder blades. With his deep brown eyes, chiseled jaw and the sort of suave looks normally associated with nobility, he stood in stark contrast to his terrifying companion.

"Don't let this bastard's face fool ya. He's the same age as me," Trench said about his friend. "He keeps his looks by sneakin' into young girls beds at night and stealing their youth away."

"There's no sneaking required," was Wave's response. "I only accept open and willing invitations. You're just jealous that no invitees 'open' themselves up to *you*. I told ya I'd find a nice Keeper shield maiden with big thighs for you, but after today I think that plan is off the table."

Actaeon took that moment to change the subject. "You both mentioned fighting in the Invasion War, but not the Sustenance Wars. Why is that? I would have guessed that two seasoned veterans had fought in the Sustenance Wars as well."

Both men's expressions went serious at the topic, and they were silent for a long moment. It was Trench that finally answered, "The Sustenance wasn't a war, it was murder. We ain't murderers, lad. We were soldiers. The Invasion War was about protecting our people and our civilization from outside invaders. The Sustenance was about tearing that civilization apart from the inside."

"Any involvement we had in the Sustenance Wars certainly wasn't soldiering," said Wave.

"That's enough, Wave," growled Trench, his deep scar growing dark as he leaned forward. "So what brings a lone artifact collector like yourself out to Pyramid?"

Over several rounds of drinks, Actaeon told them about his work as an

Engineer, his plans around Pyramid, and his reasons for leaving his home in Raedelle. The men listened intently and interjected comments here and there.

"It sounds like you've been targeted," decided Wave, when Actaeon told them about the raiders. "We've seen those guys with crosses on their faces from time to time in the ruins, but they've always kept their distance. Whenever we've spotted them, they've already been heading swiftly away. They seem to have taken an interest in you for some reason. Did ya sleep with one of their daughters? They're heavily armed too – shows some skill on your part that you escaped."

"Sounds more like luck than skill to me," Trench said with a grunt. "You really should have better protection if yer gonna go wandering the ruins." The giant leaned back in his chair and took a deep draught of his ale.

Actaeon leaned back in his chair too and arched a brow. He glanced between the two men thoughtfully for a few moments before speaking, "You are quite correct, Trench. I shall take you up on your offer. Both of you meet me tomorrow afternoon in the marketplace. I could use your assistance with a bit of a sticky situation."

Trench nearly spat his drink out at the Engineer's words, "I didn't- uh, I wasn't suggesting that. It isn't our usual –"

"Fifty copper bits a day; fifty each that is, full upfront. No games. We'll see you then," answered Wave, cutting off his friend.

Trench slammed his flagon down on the table, sputtering as he cast an ugly glare across the table at his companion, "You really do have manure for brains, don't ya? We make these calls together, after hearing the details. You know that!"

Wave folded his arms and grinned. He winked at Actaeon before he turned and responded to his friend, "Sure, sure... just like the last job, eh? Last I checked I didn't like the way those Ajmani merchants looked at all. Their plan came straight out of a mule's ass and we barely made it out of there with the skin on our backs. No matter that Wave said from the first that he didn't like the look of 'em. Well guess what? I like the look of this Engineer, and it is *my* intuition's turn. At the very least, I don't think he'll be trying to extort gangs in the Warrens. I could always be wrong though.

It could be something worse. By the Fallen though, it's my damned turn to be wrong!"

Trench scowled as he finished his drink but said nothing. He simply grunted his consent.

"It is settled then, gentlemen. I will see you on the morrow when the sun is at its peak," said Actaeon as he dropped a heavy coin pouch on the table. "This should more than cover the first five or so days of your employ. If things go well, I suspect there will be plenty of work in the future. Until then, take care," he said, before he drew to his feet.

The Engineer retrieved his halberd and dipped his head respectfully at both the men before he turned to make his way out of The End. As he pushed open the door, he heard the two of them resume their argument and couldn't help but grin.

It was early evening when he left The End and the sun had descended behind the motley assortment of structures in the Outskirts. The Avenue of Glass gleamed in the dim light – the luminaries along it just starting to flicker to life. The luminaries were a relic from the past – some of them affixed permanently in different locations throughout the ancient city, others found loose, scattered among the ruins. Typically, the affixed luminaries only illuminated during the hours when the sun went down while many of the loose luminaries shed light all the time.

All of them appeared to operate off of some infinite or near infinite power source. Actaeon suspected they had been operating in this way for hundreds – perhaps even thousands – of years since the time of the Ancients. He had dismantled quite a few of the devices in the past in order to identify the power source but to no avail. The luminaries seemed to be filled only with a strange fluid that would glow when encased in the luminary's transparent enclosure and cease to glow once the enclosure was broken open. If one touched the fluid, they would feel a sharp tingling sensation along their arm, but the fluid did not have a use on its own. He had tried placing the fluid back into the enclosure to see if it would resume its functionality, but, once removed, it had lost its efficacy.

It was possible that the fluid itself contained the power source by some method that he had yet to envision, but Actaeon doubted that for one reason. Randomly, every thirty or so hours, in an event called the Darkest Hour, all of the luminaries would flicker and cease to function, cloaking the dead city in a blanket of darkness. Because of the interval, sometimes this occurred during the day, which affected only those using luminaries to light the interiors of buildings or exploring underground. For this reason many denizens of Redemption carried an alternate light, such as candles or torches, for those moments. It was also for this reason that he suspected all of the luminaries were powered by a single, remote source. It operated, he theorized, in a similar manner to how a metal object placed near a fire would heat up through radiant energy from the flames. A power fount, located somewhere in Redemption must be what kept the luminaries lit. He hoped to find it one day to study it and perhaps even learn how to harness the energy for other purposes.

As if on cue with his train of thought, the luminaries along the Avenue began to flicker rapidly, as though in rejection of their very existence. They strobed on and off for several long and disorienting moments during which Actaeon lowered his eyes and leant on his halberd to wait for it to stop. Shortly thereafter, the light died altogether and left the world in relative darkness.

The Engineer waited for his eyes to adjust to the pitch black. Of course, his own luminary wouldn't work either during the Darkest Hour. Far ahead in the distance he could make out a spark as someone attempted to light a candle. After three short sparks, a single flame rose up from that location – the only light visible. Even the stars were occluded by clouds this evening.

After several long minutes, he found that he could make out the edge of the Avenue to his left. He made his way over to it and continued along to the west, following it as he walked.

It would take him a half hour or so to reach the Pyramid entrance, by his reckoning. As he continued along, his thoughts drifted. He wanted to take a look in the Boneyards tomorrow to see if he could find his way to the mechanical man. If he woke early enough, he could do some reconnoitering before he met the two mercenaries in the marketplace. At the very least he could try and find the beginning of a path towards the strange artifact.

The implications were exciting. Perhaps this mechanical man was still functional like many of Redemption's artifacts. If so, then maybe it could tell him something of the Ancients. The thought occurred to him that there was a possibility that the Ancients were even mechanical men themselves. It could be that they ceased to function after the power fount that fed the luminaries malfunctioned. That, of course, would not explain their relative absence from the city. He hoped that finding this mechanical man would give him some of those answers.

Then there was the problem with the ooze-clogged drainage tunnels. It seemed unlikely that the gunk was a by-product of something being stored or sold in the marketplace, though that wasn't outside of the realm of possibility. More likely, he thought, that something in the tunnels was causing the buildup. It could be the spread of some fast-growing fungus to the area. Visitors from all over Redemption came to the Open Market. It would only take a single boot with some of the fungus on it to spread it around. He would have to gather some chemicals from the Felmere to see if any in particular would help break down the material. It did seem biological in nature – at least based on the look, feel, and smell of it.

A rustling sound ahead and to his left interrupted his thoughts and he spotted someone moving in the darkness. Actaeon came to an abrupt halt and brought the point of his halberd to bear, "Who goes there? Name yourself!"

A loud groan answered him as the figure, cloaked in shadow, climbed onto the surface of the Avenue of Glass and struggled to his feet. The figure wobbled toward Actaeon with hands held out in a non-threatening gesture.

"Torin's Hold. Bring me... the Hold. I'm – a Companion," a man struggled to say before he slumped to his side. His head thudded solidly against the unyielding material of the roadway.

The Companions were the personal guard and elite soldiers of the Prince of Raedelle.

Actaeon approached the man cautiously, with his halberd still held defensively. It was entirely possible that this was a highwayman's ruse. When he reached the man, he lowered his halberd to the ground and knelt beside him.

The Engineer reached into the lower left pocket of his jacket and withdrew several half-through bottles. He sprinkled the foul smelling contents of the first bottle onto the surface of the roadway before pouring a viscous substance carefully atop. Finally he shuffled back and very carefully poured several drops of water from the third bottle that caused the entire amalgam to sputter and ignite in a radiant blue flame. A special concoction that he had invented when he was much younger, blue fire would burn hotly for over an hour and water would only make it burn hotter. Although the recipe was normally reserved for the single blue fire arrow in his quiver, it now served well to illuminate the man that lay before him on the Avenue of Glass.

The man was badly injured – his tunic was soaked through with blood from a wound across his abdomen. Actaeon pulled up the garment to take a look. "You are a Companion of Raedelle? What happened to you? What did this?" he asked as he pulled free some bandages to inspect the wound.

The man groaned as he descended into a semi-conscious state.

"You have to stay awake, friend. You have lost a dangerous amount of blood," said Actaeon, and he gave the man a sharp tap on the cheek. He couldn't tell if it was the effect of the blue light or blood loss, but the man certainly looked pale. When he held up his hand in the light it served as a good comparison; the man's skin certainly had a pallor to it.

There were several long gashes along the man's belly and they were slowly oozing blood. They looked to be caused by claws of some sort, and could be judged at several days old based on how the bloodflow had slowed. Actaeon was surprised that the wound showed no signs of infection. A pressure bandage would have a better chance of stopping the bleeding, though it might be best to suture the gashes first.

The Engineer reached into his lower right pocket.and withdrew his supplies: a roll of cloth, several needles in a small cushion, a half-through bottle with some alcohol in it and several spools of different size thread. He laid it out on the smooth surface of the Avenue beside the injured man.

"Listen friend, this is going to hurt quite a bit. I will attempt to suture your wound and then I will take you up to the Hold. I fear that if I fail to do that you will soon die of bloodloss." The man groaned again and Actaeon took it as an acknowledgment. As soon as he poured some of the alcohol along the length of the wound, the man awoke to scream and curse at him.

"I'll rip your pissed-stained heart out, you son of a gods-damned whore, blast –" cried the man as Actaeon held him down. The Companion quickly passed out from the pain.

Actaeon set the bottle aside and selected a needle. He brought it to the bright blue flame where he held it for a moment to sterilize the tip. When the base of the needle begin to feel hot on his fingers, he withdrew it and expertly threaded the needle with some of the heavier thread. His fingers worked quickly to suture the ragged gashes and he spaced the stitches farther apart than he liked to save some time. Once that was done, he covered the wound and gave the man a sharp smack on the cheek to awaken him.

"Time to wake up. I need you to sit up so I can get this bandage in place." As the man shook his head and groggily glanced about, Actaeon wasted no time and pulled him to a seated position. From there, he finished wrapping the bandage around the man's torso tightly, tying it at the small of his back.

Actaeon knew a thing or two about needlework – his mother was a seamstress. As a young man, he'd been interested in his mother's work – at least until he had learned everything he could from it. The clothing on him was of his own manufacture, which allowed him to do useful things like install custom pockets, a built in quiver and craft a vest that could double as a carry bag. He'd stitched a wound or two of his own closed – never this big, of course, but there was a first time for everything.

"Okay, I am going to need your help now. I cannot carry you on my own, I am sorry to inform you," said Actaeon. "You will have to walk with my assistance. Though I doubt that will be a major problem for you considering how far you already probably walked."

"I... can walk," said the man with a struggle. His eyes fluttered as he tried to keep them open. Tousled brown hair framed a dirty face that could be made out in the flickering blue flame.

Actaeon lifted his halberd and used it to lever them both to their feet. The man threw his arm over the Engineer's shoulders and allowed him to lead the way to Pyramid and St. Torin's Hold. If he truly was a Companion as he said, then the people of Raedelle would drop everything to help this man: one of the Prince's chosen protectors.

HE WHO GOES THERE

AS THE SUN MEANDERED ITS way up into the sky for its journey across the day, long shadows were cast throughout the Boneyards. The wreckage to the north of Pyramid was extensive and treacherous, home to secret treasures for those brave enough to face the more frequent dangers lying amidst the rubble. The early morning was a perilous time. Crevices and gaps in debris became more hazardous and required constant scrutiny from wanderers. One misstep into a shadow could turn an ankle or worse – send one tumbling down into a void. To be lost or injured out here was a death sentence.

One such wanderer could be found a good distance from Pyramid's northern descent.

As the Engineer navigated from one spot to another amongst the ruins, a baffled luminary secured in the strap of his goggles helped to illuminate areas still drenched in shadow. It would have been easier to have come at midday when the sun was directly overhead, but there was much to be done on this day and he wanted to get this out of the way early.

Actaeon picked his way carefully down the wreckage of an old collapsed building, skirting around some sharpened metal rods that protruded from the pile he descended. From the top he had been able to map out the best path to the mechanical man that he had seen from Pyramid's pinnacle. It would take him a full day to reach it by his reckoning.

At the foot of the ruined building, he glanced up to find the looming shape of Pyramid in the distance. He set out through dilapidated ruins that housed the forgotten memories of Redemption's Ancient Ones – on his way back toward the towering beacon that stood for civilization amongst Redemption's new arrivals. The partially collapsed northern face of Pyramid jutted forth as a jagged reminder of how fragile civilization could be.

There was much work to be done. He had to resolve the horrible smell in the marketplace quickly, so he could convince the Lady Caliburn to hear his proposal for Raedelle. Actaeon had confidence that he would be able to find the solution. He'd thought about it a bit more last night, although much of his evening had been spent assisting the injured Companion he had brought to Saint Torin's Hold.

The other Raedelleans had recognized him at once as a Companion named Caider and immediately since for an Althean healer since none of the Raedellean cutters had been present.

The Altheans were a neutral order based in Pyramid that provided healing and political advice to the Dominions that accepted it. Actaeon had always found that to be an odd combination.

An older Althean named Seraeta had arrived and inspected the sutures.

"Sloppy work," she said, "but it probably kept him alive. I don't suppose you cleaned the wound first?"

Seraeta insisted on resuturing the wound and cleaning it again. The Engineer remained to watch, which she didn't seem pleased with. The healer used a much finer thread that was easier to work with around the edges of the gash. When Actaeon asked about it, she told him that it came from the fine Boll plants grown in the Shield Dominion.

He had made a mental note to buy some spools of the Shieldian thread when he passed through the Open Market before meeting up with Trench and Wave, in addition to purchasing the supplies that he needed for the smell problem. It was quite probably that some creature or legion of creatures –

"Who goes there?" an authoritative voice called out and interrupted his meandering thoughts. It came from one of the rubble heaps to his right. Memories of the cross-faced raiders leapt into his mind. Trench was right, he really should bring those two along next time he went wandering.

"Brilliant," he muttered under his breath, as his lips curled into a paradoxical grin. He returned the luminary to his pocket and located an area of secure footing in case he needed to make a stand.

A stone came loose under his foot and tumbled its way down behind him, giving away his location. He hefted his halberd and brought the blade to bear over his right shoulder before speaking.

"Well you know where I am then. So if you want to come fight me then that is your choice. I warn you though: I may combust suddenly even if you win and you could die in the ensuing conflagration," he called, before laughing. "Damned rock," he said as he squinted into the sunlight to try and descry any movement above.

"That is a very long name, sir," came the civilized reply. A person came into view then, as they climbed to the top of the heap. An Arbiter, by all appearances, garbed in the traditional neutral grey of the order, including the boiled leather plate and the broadsword scabbarded at her side. A crimson armband with a pair of locked shields, the sigil of the Arbiter order, confirmed his first impression. She was a young woman with short blond hair and brilliant blue eyes. Actaeon recognized her as the same Arbiter that had been in the Hold on the evening past.

She clearly recognized him as well. "Ah, it is you, Actaeon Rellios of Shore. Is there any particular reason we should fight?" she asked with genuine curiosity.

Once the weight of the woman's comment set in, the Engineer burst out laughing. He took a knee and rested the halberd across it as the laughs shook his body. If he was slain now, he thought, it would be laughter that killed him. The thought only amused him more.

With a struggle, he composed himself and levered to his feet with the staff of his weapon. "You are the Arbiter from the other night in the Hold," he said, "Eisandre – if I recall correctly. And unless you plan to try and rob me, or enslave me, or otherwise hold me against my will, then we should not fight. I suppose practice against a halberdier might be useful, but, if that is the case, we could cover our blades and just spar. I do apologize. I am a bit jumpy out in this area. Not the safest of places, especially given its proclivity to bandits and raiders."

"You have every right to be jumpy, especially out here," said Eisandre as she watched him climb up to join her. "Even the shadows seem alive sometimes, whispering of the past. Yes. I am Eisandre sof Darovin, Knight Arbiter. And, you'll be happy to know that I do not intend to try to rob you, or enslave you, or hold you against your will. It's not really my style."

She offered him a faint smile and the slight bow of her head. "It's good to truly meet you, sir. The last time was altogether brief."

"Nicely met, Lady Knight. I had not expected the Arbiters to be patrolling out here. It is rare that I meet up with a face out here that is not trying to trick or kill me, and believe me, it is most welcome."

"I am not on patrol. Please forgive me if I had given you that impression. I was just... walking. I'm not often alone as an Arbiter in the Pyramid, so sometimes I wish to get away with my thoughts. I have been warned against it in the past, but something draws me to this area. It is cluttered, yet so empty. I try to imagine how it must have been long ago." Her eyes grew distant, and she looked out over the vast expanse of the Boneyards.

The Engineer followed her gaze. "Yes, it must have been amazing. Sometimes you can get lucky and find the footing of an ancient structure out here, and occasionally even a partially intact structure. I have estimated that some of the structures I have found may have been hundreds of stories tall, even taller than Pyramid, or Memory Keep, if you would believe it. Out here in the ruins one might find the answers to everything."

"Some answers, however, might be lost forever," added Eisandre soberly. "It seems we are both returning to the Pyramid now. We will be better off if we walk together back to the inhabited area of the city. Will you accept my company for the duration of this journey?"

There was a strange, rare note of chivalry in the way the woman spoke, and she had a decidedly regal bearing. Actaeon was intrigued. He found himself captivated by her bright eyes and wondered what other thoughts and insights she had about this place. Where in so many others there seemed to be a void, in this one there was deep thought and life.

"Aye, we should keep joint company here. Of course I accept your company. In fact, anytime I head out here, you are welcome to join me. As you say, there is greater security with more than just our lone selves out here." They started on their way through the rubble back towards Pyramid. The Engineer comfortably navigated the dangerous environment while Eisandre handled herself well, but had trouble keeping up with the more experienced ruin explorer.

"If you don't mind occasional silence, I would appreciate having someone with whom to walk here from time to time," Eisandre admitted as she descended the pile with some difficulty. "Do you come here to investigate the ruins for the sake of curiosity, or is it some part of your profession?"

"Silence is not a problem at all. I usually do most of my thinking in the different ruins around Redemption. Not thinking about anything in particular for some reason helps me come up with better ideas. There are many different reasons that I venture out here. Curiosity drives most of what I do. I want to know how everything works. Occasionally there are specific items that I am looking for to complete my designs or finish research. Once in awhile, I stumble upon something very interesting, but most of the things out here are too big to take with me for further study. More than a few times I have tried to dismantle artifacts with various levels of success. Often, when I get stuck on a design, I come out here to look for inspiration," he said as he hopped down to a level patch of stone. When he glanced back at the Arbiter, he saw that she was smiling.

"There are so many in Redemption who think with their fists, or who have difficulty looking past the desire for wealth. You must have a keen mind, and one that you actually use. This is a characteristic I truly admire. Do you work for your Prince?"

Actaeon laughed. "Well, I am glad that you admire it, because some certainly do not. Many would say I am wasting my life and potential on such endeavours, but I would daresay it is they who ignore the truth lying all about them —" he gestured to the chaos surrounding them, "— in these bones. I actually just arrived at Pyramid to offer my services to the Prince, in exchange for project funding, a workshop, and a staff — or whatever of the three they can provide. That is why I was in Saint Torin's Hold the other evening. I spoke to the Prince's sister about it and I am awaiting an answer. So we shall see," he concluded as he used his halberd to stabilize himself while crossing over a particularly treacherous span.

Eisandre followed Actaeon carefully, holding out her arms to improve her balance. "Ah, Eshelle. She is wise for a woman who is so young. I wish you good fortune in your endeavours, Master Rellios. I, for one, would be curious to see the development of your career. I realize that I barely know you, but you don't seem the sort to waste any moment of your life, much less your potential."

Actaeon slowed to walk beside the Arbiter as the path began to widen. "Yes, she seems like a clever leader. Unfortunately, I had little time to speak with her before she was pressed with other matters. Your words honor me, Eisandre. It is not often that I meet someone so kind. From where do you hail?"

"We do not often speak of our personal histories, as Arbiters. We strive to remain neutral and unattached, but it is not forbidden for us to share this information. I come from the same land as you do, sir: from Raedelle, which in some ways will always be my home."

"I apologize if I placed you in an awkward position. You can speak to me about Raedelle and your origins if you wish, and I will not share it with anyone. However, if you like I will not ask you any further questions about the past." He paused to point the blade of his halberd toward Pyramid. "Although, I shall be sure to continue asking you questions about your future."

"You may ask me any questions, sir, about my past or future. In Saint Torin's Hold, many know who I am, in any case. We'll just have to try and resist the urge to go shouting about my origins from the top of the Skyspiral," she said with a smile as they grew closer to the crumbled Northern Descent of Pyramid. Distant Arbiters patrolled and guarded the entrance. Traders and travelers alike from Czeryn and Shield could also be seen heading back and forth along the cracked and crumbled stairs that led up the northern slope and inside the ancient structure.

"I should leave you now. Time passes quickly in good company," said the Arbiter.

Actaeon halted then and turned to face her, resting his halberd against his shoulder. "It was a great pleasure to meet you, Eisandre. It will be good to do this again sometime. I shall remain around Pyramid, at least until I hear word from Prince Aedwyn or the Lady Eshelle. Oh, and thank you for the escort, Arbiter. Have a good evening."

They went then in separate directions to very different lives. Actaeon was pleased to have found another kindred spirit in the world.

The marketplace was alive with mid-afternoon activity by the time Actaeon met up with his new employees. Both men wore brightly-colored, perfume-scented kerchiefs over their noses. It had quickly become the new fashion in reaction to the unbearable stench. It was simple to pick them out of the crowd, as Trench towered over every other man and woman there.

"Oh, no. That will not do at all. You have to take those off, gentlemen. In addition to looking quite ridiculous, I fear that you will need all of your senses for where we will venture. There is no telling whether or not a scent might forewarn us of danger," said the Engineer with a grin as he joined them.

Wave pulled his kerchief down around his neck and offered him a skeptical look, "Let me get this straight – you want us to go around smelling the ass of the gods here for whatever off-kilter plan you have come up with?"

Trench roared a laugh and clapped his partner solidly on the back, "Ain't that the smell that describes most of the perfumed functions you always get dressed up for? If yer willing to smell the ass of the gods to get some noble whore in the sack, then surely you can do it to get us paid!"

"Maybe you'd actually be able to join me at one of the fetes if you didn't always smell like a drainage ditch yourself," retorted the shorter man-at-arms as he tugged off his kerchief.

"Bah! If I smelled that bad, I'd fit right in with the rest of the foul nobility!" Trench said with another roaring laugh.

Actaeon grinned at the pair and pointed toward the western end of the Open Market with the point of his halberd. "Follow me, gentlemen. We have much to do," he said as he led the winding way past the various stalls and the hullabaloo of the market.

On the way he paused at a Shieldian stall selling clothing and seamster supplies. In particular, they carried an impressive variety of different threads. He selected one that looked close to what he had watched the healer use on the injured Companion and laid down a few copper bits before he pocketed the spool. One couldn't be sure when that could come in use, and it certainly had done the job more cleanly than the thick thread he had carried with him from Incline.

He stopped before a large circular opening in the western wall of the marketplace. The bottom of the opening was at waist height above the ground and they could see a short distance into the tunnel before it descended into darkness. The diameter of the tunnel mouth was twice the height of Trench. Only the right side of the opening appeared to be partially occluded with the strange brown muck.

Actaeon used his halberd to help lift himself up into the tunnel. Once inside, he pulled out his luminary and placed it in his goggle strap so that it would illuminate the area ahead of him. He then turned to face the two men-at-arms where they stood still on the ground outside. "I hope that you both brought the supplies that I recommended. Let us proceed." Without waiting for a reply, stepped forward and disappeared into the shadows of the tunnel.

The mercenaries glanced at one another and then back at the tunnel opening, both of them at a lack for words.

"Well, you were right, Trench," said Wave as he checked his equipment. He tugged on the coil of rope wrapped around his chest and dug his own luminary out of his pocket. "The lad's not right in the head. I figured he'd just be having us escort him in the ruins while he looked for shiny artifacts."

"I guess we don't have a choice. We already got paid for it. It's your judgement on this one, pal. Let's go," Trench said, before he pulled himself up and disappeared after the Engineer.

Wave stood for a moment longer, squinting as he peered into the tunnel. "By the Fallen, why can't we get some normal work for once?" He scrambled up to catch the others.

When they caught up to Actaeon farther down the tunnel, he had knelt to scrape a strange substance from the floor into a half-through bottle. He stood and gestured at the wall to their right, his luminary revealing long lines of slime of various widths criss-crossing one another as they ran generally in the direction of the tunnel.

"See that, gentlemen? That is one of the signs we were looking for. It demonstrates some sort of intelligence and higher organization. It fits directly with my postulate that some sort of creature or group of creatures is responsible for this buildup. Whatever is leaving these lines here would seem to be the same cause of the buildup at the end of these tunnels," said the Engineer.

Wave reached out and touched one of the wider lines, before withdrawing his fingers in revulsion, "What in cracked Redemption is this? Slime?" He sniffed his fingers and retched, nearly losing his lunch, "Awck! That smells worse than the marketplace!"

Behind him, Trench chuckled and gave him a shove after their employer, who had continued on his way down the tunnel.

"We should not tarry here," Actaeon explained as he made his way deeper into the tunnel. "I would just like to find some more evidence that can aid us in the setting of a trap. Evidence as to what might attract one of the creatures would be beneficial – then we can construct a trap to lure them into it. As we are not sure what we are dealing with, it would be inadvisable to try to capture one ourselves. From what I have heard in the marketplace, in addition to smaller livestock, several large beasts of burden have gone missing over the past several weeks, as has one man. Of course, an alternate theory could be that thieves are using the mayhem in the marketplace to make away with a profit. After all, the Warrens are directly adjacent to our area of concern."

"What sort of creature do ya think we're dealing with here?" asked Trench as he ducked under a section of the brown ooze that had massed overhead. "What could possibly account for the disappearance of a man and several large beasts from the marketplace?"

"An excellent question, Trench," said Actaeon with a pleased glance back at the giant mercenary. He scratched his right hand idly as he continued along, "If the rumors that we have heard are indeed truths, then we are dealing with one of two things: a swarm of smaller creatures, or one very large creature.

"Judging by the trails of slime on the walls and the lack of individualized footprints that would indicate appendages for walking, I would speculate that we are dealing with something similar to a common slug or snail, only much larger and more virulent. Though healthy speculation is a good thing, let us keep in mind that we have no direct proof of this and, as such, should be prepared for any eventuality."

"We always are," said Wave, as he tapped the hilt of his rapier.

They reached a branch in the tunnel then, where another tunnel intersected theirs on the right. The slope of this new tunnel descended downward at an unnavigable angle. Actaeon halted and shook his head, "We should turn back. It would be a mistake to allow our position here to be flanked."

Trench flashed the younger Engineer a broad grin that tugged at his scar disturbingly. "That's what you've got us along for now, isn't it? Go on ahead, Master Rellios. I'll be sure we aren't flanked. Just make sure you don't go too far ahead that I can't hear yer calls." That said, he pulled his big maul from his back, standing at ease beside the tunnel branch. "'Sides, there's nothing can get up that steep an angle anyways."

"Don't be so sure of that. There's slugs can climb up walls all over the place," said the other man-at-arms.

"Wave is correct. Be ready, Trench," said the Engineer. He turned to Wave, "Shall we continue?"

Wave nodded and led the way. "I'll take point."

Soon they came to an area where the tunnel opened up into a large chamber. After making sure Trench could still hear him, Wave drew his companion dagger and started into the open area cautiously, his luminary in the other hand.

Their luminaries shed light on a large circular space with a relatively flat floor and tunnels that converged from all directions. There wasn't a discernable ceiling in range of their lights.

"Some sort of hub. This could have functioned as a great many things in the time of the Ancients. Judging by the size of it, I would guess that it was used for movement of something from one location to another. It is certainly large enough for people to move through, but who knows?" said Actaeon, as he swept the room with his illuminated field of view.

"Maybe, but I'm not sure the Ancients had anything to do with that," said Wave, whose luminary had come to a stop on a pile in the center of the large room. Sharp shards jutted out of some sort of big gelatinous mess.

"Curious," said the Engineer. He approached the large mass without hesitation and poked it with the tip of his halberd. A foul smell came forth and it crumbled apart where he touched it, more long shards tumbling out. "Bones... chicken, pigeon, pig – maybe, and that there looks like a bull cow's skull. This is what we came to find. So it *has* been taking animals from the marketplace; how interesting."

"Interesting indeed, boss. But unless you wanna stick around to fight whatever did this, then I suggest we beat a hasty retreat. It could return at any moment."

"Agreed, Wave. Allow me to get a quick sample and then we shall withdraw at once."

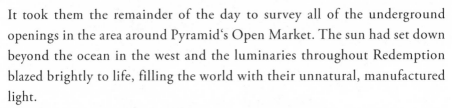

It took them the remainder of the day to survey all of the underground openings in the area around Pyramid's Open Market. The sun had set down beyond the ocean in the west and the luminaries throughout Redemption blazed brightly to life, filling the world with their unnatural, manufactured light.

They had split up to complete the task as efficiently as possible, with the understanding that they would only reconnoiter the tunnel entrances and not enter any alone. They agreed to rendezvous back at the Avenue of Glass when they were done, to share their findings.

Actaeon and Wave both arrived early and waited for Trench to join them.

"It sounds like we have enough locations to start with. The next step will be constructing the traps. I have had some time to think about their design and have formulated some plans in my mind," explained the Engineer.

"There is an old carter named Vez that I ran into. After I told him what I was doing, he agreed to lend us some space and help with deployment. Says that this smell thing's bad for business, so he's got time and motivation to help," said Wave.

"Excellent. We shall be sure not to let the man down. Over the next few days I will need your assistance gathering up the supplies. We will require small cut timbers, twine, material that can be fashioned into spikes, an amount of brick, a bale of hay, salt, some raw meat, and of course we cannot forget the live chickens – a pair in each trap so they are not too lonely. Of course, I am going to require some metal castings to create a trigger mechanism for the release. It would be possible to create a trigger with wood pieces as well, but the metal parts would be more robust in the damp environment that exists down in the tunnels."

"Hold on, let me get this straight: You're gonna shove chickens in these traps to act as bait for a giant snail monster that eats livestock and may or may not be responsible for the disappearance of several missing men, and you're concerned about whether the chickens are lonely? Why should that make a damned difference?"

"Excellent question, Wave. In truth, I am not certain that it will make a difference in the end. However, we are taking these chickens into a strange and dangerous environment that is wholly unfamiliar to them. The added comfort of the presence of another of their kind may serve to provide a calming effect on them. If the chicken is agitated, then the creature we are seeking to capture may be forewarned of the trap and choose to avoid it. Whereas it would not for an otherwise calm chicken. Remember that even though we are likely dealing with a creature similar to that of a slug or snail, it may have much higher intelligence than its garden-variety kin. In fact, that is quite likely if the rumors of men disappearing have any truth to them," explained Actaeon.

"Fantastic. So we're dealing with a smart snail monster that eats people. Remind me again why we agreed to work for you?" Wave complained. He turned towards Pyramid at the sound of footfalls along the Avenue. It was a small Shield delegation making their way along.

"I seem to recall you saying something about lacking familiarity with the sewers below the marketplace. It should be altogether an educational experience for you, Wave," said Actaeon with a grin. "The traps that we will build are a type of deadfall, modified to suit this special purpose, of course. Perhaps you have heard of it if you have done any hunting."

"Aye, of course I know what a deadfall is. Ya can't just go in there and expect to drop a rock on its head though."

"Exactly! Instead of a rock, we can rig together a weighted deadfall assembly, with spikes protruding downward from it. It will attach to a framework that holds our base with our bait on it: the chickens in a lightweight cage along with our soaked hay with salt and raw meat scattered about in it. When the creature catches the scent of the trap and attempts to extract the chickens from it, the base will tip and actuate the triggering mechanism which will drop the deadfall. Additionally, we can design some features that lock the top deadfall platform to the base when it falls so that the creature cannot lift it to escape."

While the Engineer was discussing the trap, Trench climbed up onto the Avenue of Glass in front of the Shieldians. The giant hunched over and tried to wipe something from his eyes.

Wave waved Trench over.

The big man started toward them, but slipped. He lurched backward and stumbled into the Shield delegation as he struggled to regain his footing.

Trench fell and hit the glass surface hard, taking one of the Shieldians down with him.

Actaeon and Wave watched for but a moment before they both ran over to help the fallen man-at-arms.

When they arrived, the Shieldians had already helped their fallen comrade to his feet. The young man brushed off his fine clothes and recoiled from Trench in disgust, "How absolutely dreadful! Not only do you knock over Shieldian nobility, but you smell as though your mother gave birth to you in a pit of sewage!" The man gagged and removed his long overcoat to throw it over the edge of the Avenue, an action which seemed to relieve his nausea somewhat.

Trench climbed to his feet, covered in slime that had evidently caused him to slip. His voice was a growl. "How dare you insult my m–"

Actaeon interrupted him, interposing himself between the mercenary and the Shieldians. "What my friend here means to say is that he is quite apologetic about this unfortunate accident. If he has damaged your coat then we will be sure that you receive recompense."

Trench grumbled under his breath before speaking, "Aye, I'm sorry. If Master Rellios here hadn't had me investigating underground tunnels, then I wouldn't have fallen into the slime clogged opening of one." Behind him, Wave suppressed a laugh.

The Shieldian Lord stepped forward then, regarding the Engineer with a critical gaze from beneath his neat, wavy black hair. He was quite young and Actaeon might have taken him for naught but a young boy if he wasn't clearly leading a delegation, garbed in the expensive clothing of a noble adult, as he flung elaborate words at them. The young Lord marched right up to Actaeon as though to put the Engineer in his place.

Instead, he said, "You really are investigating the stench, aren't you? It certainly smells as such. What progress have you made?"

"Forgive me, my Lord, I have yet to introduce myself," said Actaeon with a polite bow of his head. "I am Actaeon Rellios of Shore. And, yes, we are indeed investigating the cause of the market smell. I have been tasked with solving the issue. These two men in my employ are Trench and Wave. I regret that Trench ran into you in his present condition, but I assure you that the copious amount of sample substance that he has so selflessly obtained will come in great use for our investigation."

The Shieldian regarded the three men once more before he relaxed and took a step back. "You would do well to remember me as Lord Enrion Zar, beneficiary of the Dominion of Shield. Take heed that there is a huge, tentacled monster down below the marketplace causing the smell. I led a squad of soldiers down there to deal with the threat. It killed one of my men and wounded two others before we had a chance to retreat. I recommend that you avoid the issue altogether. What a squad of Shieldian's finest soldiers could not best, three men such as you certainly could not manage."

"Excellent advice, Lord Zar. I will certainly take that into consideration. If there is more that you could tell me about the creature that you encountered down there, then we would be grateful to hear it."

"I am sure that you would be, but alas, I appear to be in need of a bath. The smell took weeks to get off of me the first time I encountered the monster. I am not going to take that risk this time. Good luck with your endeavour, and do try not to be killed in the process," said Enrion, before he turned to lead the delegation back towards Pyramid. The Lord paused for a moment and added, "Oh, and you can bring the compensation for my jacket to the Shieldian Hold – any retainer can then bring it to me." That said, the Lord departed, his delegation on his heel.

When the Shieldians had retreated a safe distance away, Wave released laughter that he had struggled to contain. "I haven't heard such a fine insult in many a year! Your mother birthed you in a pit of sewage – Ha! I couldn't have thought of that one myself. Who would've known? Trench, our very own sewage baby!"

Trench simply stood there, dripping slime and staring at his friend. A hideous grin stretched across his face and tugged at his scar.

Wave laughed again and pointed. "That's it! Watch out, Master Rellios! It's the giant slug monster the Lord Zar spoke of –"

Trench interrupted him abruptly by taking one giant step forward to wrap his friend in a bear hug, and lift him into the air.

When he finished and returned Wave to the Avenue, the smaller mercenary fell to his knees and gagged.

Trench then turned to Actaeon with a big grin. "Anything else you'd like to add, Master Rellios?"

"Oh no, I do believe that Wave has said enough for everyone tonight."

87 A.R., the 52nd day of Arrival
SETTING THE TRAP

T HE FOLLOWING WEEK WAS A busy one for the Engineer. The
acquisition of supplies and assembly of a prototype trap had taken
up most of his time. Many of the items required were easily located
in the marketplace itself and were brought to the staging area that Vez the
Carter had arranged for them. To the old carter's dismay, Actaeon built the
prototype right in the bed of one of the big wagons that the man used to
ferry supplies between Adhikara and Pyramid's marketplaces.

The difficult items were the parts for the trigger mechanism. He didn't
want any false triggers and with the damp, slimy conditions in the tunnels
beneath the marketplace, he dared not use a wooden mechanism. Only a
cast metal part would do for the job. Unfortunately though, all his casting
supplies were back in Shore.

Luckily, he was able to enlist the help of Balin the Blacksmith, whose
shop had suffered largely since the market smell situation had begun. A
short, stocky, bald man with a long bushy beard and a deep, boisterous
voice, Balin was a fellow Raedellean, and when the Engineer told him that
the work was on the order of the Lady Eshelle, he was more than willing to
lend his aid – and more than a few pints of ale – to Actaeon and his team.

With access to a Blacksmith's forge and supplies gathered during a
reconnoitering of Blacksands Beach and the nearby chemical bog called
the Felmere, the cast parts for the trigger mechanism had taken nearly
the full week to prepare. The Felmere was a dangerous arrangement of
chemical pools to northwest – each pool with a different property. It was

extremely difficult to navigate the bog, with its elderstone vats of different colored chemicals, drifting clouds of poisonous outgassing and mutated plant growth. Once the first trigger parts were complete, it was easy to copy quickly.

Actaeon finished each evening in The End, where he treated everyone to a drink or two, which kept Oril in business and the morale of the team high. The latter was quite important, given the foul odors they needed to contend with daily and the generally miserable atmosphere in the marketplace. Lord Zar had been correct: the cloying stench on the pair of mercenaries started to fade towards the end of the week. This allowed the crew to reclaim the corner table that had been the veterans' choice instead of having their drinks brought outside to them.

Wave made several attempts to enter the baths within Pyramid, but each time he was promptly ejected by the attendants there. The idea was even brought up, if only half jokingly, to bathe in one of the foul chemical pools of the Felmere during their visit there. However, the graphic description of the potential outcome Actaeon shared gave Trench and Wave pause. They had to settle instead for using the lower class baths in the outdoor marketplace adjacent to the Warrens.

The smell lingered remarkably even though both men made it a point to bathe several times a day. Whatever the gelatinous substance was that Trench had fallen into must have been absorbed by their skin. Actaeon wondered what health effects such an exposure could cause, especially one that stayed in their bodies for such a long time.

They were quite careful not to touch any of the substance again when they placed the first of the traps in the location they had scouted in the tunnels. It would be best to equip the mercenaries with their own goggles, the Engineer decided. There was no telling what the slime would do to their eyes. Actaeon suspected it would cause permanent damage. None of the tests he had run on the material with different chemicals from the Felmere had yielded any useful information yet.

One morning late in the week, the Engineer sat alone on the bottom steps of the Northern Descent, lost in his thoughts. The first rays of sunlight broke past the horizon in the east and cast a pink hue across the morning sky. Far above him he could hear the appreciative murmur of the small crowd that gathered every day on the steps near Pyramid's northern entrance to welcome the morning.

Actaeon glanced behind him and spotted a lone Arbiter as she descended the steps in his direction, her grey leather cuirass taking on a reddish hue in the sunlight. He grinned at the sight of the familiar figure and used his halberd to leverage himself to his feet.

As the woman drew closer to him, he saw tears in her eyes glinting in the rising sunlight and wiped the grin from his face.

"I'm glad to find you here this morning, Master Rellios," the Arbiter said with a thin but genuine smile. There was no shame or even acknowledgement of the tears on her face as she continued, "Am I disturbing your thoughts, or would you mind some company?"

"Not at all. I have been looking forward to another excursion with you." He gave her a concerned look and asked, "What is on your mind, Eisandre?"

The young Arbiter was conflicted for a moment and she replied with visible difficulty, "You may have heard that Prince Aedwyn of Raedelle was injured this past week. It happened while he was hunting out in the ruins with some of his Companions. His wound has become severely infected. His physicians are unsure whether he will survive. I am very worried for him."

The Engineer's mouth fell open. "That is most unfortunate. I had heard that he was injured, though nobody has been able to tell me how."

"I'm not certain how," admitted Eisandre with a frown. She shielded her eyes against the sun and glanced out over the expanse. "Eshelle Caliburn did not tell me, and the Prince himself was in no mood for conversation. I suspect it was an accident. If it had been an attack, the Companions would be more active. Many places in the ruins are unstable, after all. It is lucky that we encountered each other this morning. Next time you wish for my company, you have but to ask," she said, changing the subject.

"Perhaps not luck. I have watched the sunrise here a few mornings now to see if you would be here. One of your fellow Arbiters told me that you liked to come here in the mornings on days that you were not on duty," he admitted.

Eisandre looked at him in surprise, her tear-wetted cheeks gleaming in the rising sunlight.

"You waited here on several mornings – for me?"

"Well, it is not often that someone cares to venture into these dangerous lands with me. I enjoyed your company last time and remembered that you wished to join me in the Boneyards again. I do hope that Prince Aedwyn recovers. He is a fine leader for our people."

"That he is," she whispered and froze for a long moment. "Wandering the Boneyards gives me a rare chance to be alone with my thoughts. Or in your case, with pleasant company, surrounded by nothing but silent memories. Did you have a specific destination today?"

Actaeon gestured out across the ruins with the sweep of his halberd's blade. "Out there to the east. There were two things that I wanted to investigate. One was a mechanical assemblage of some sort that I think I may have glimpsed from the Pyramid top. The other should be close by, and is a smaller piece of material that I think may have been used in a structure judging by its sectional shape. I believe it can be of use in one of my current projects. You are most welcome along with me if it is your preference. I can keep silent if you want or else we can speak about Prince Aedwyn further if you wish."

"I wish to go with you," Eisandre replied without hesitation.

"Well then, shall we start out?"

Actaeon led the way into the debris field to the northeast. He was careful to select the easiest path. They made their way through the ruins of the Boneyards, with Actaeon pausing frequently for Eisandre to catch up. His progress through the rubble was fast and precarious, though every step found solid footing.

Eisandre moved more carefully and deliberately – slower than the Engineer. She did not have the same level of experience as him when it came to exploring the ruins.

"Too bad really, that we are not heading in the other direction," the Engineer said as he shielded his eyes from the sun's glare.

"It's true that the glare of the sun puts us at a tactical disadvantage," she agreed, "but we shall be aware –"

Eisandre's thought was cut short as she misstepped and slid down the side of an unstable slope. She managed to remain on her feet though and brought herself to a stop by reaching behind her to slow her slide down the rough metal and stone of the pile.

Actaeon was at her side instantly. He dug the wedge of his halberd into a crack in a broken foundation wall and grasped the back of her cuirass to keep her from sliding down any farther.

"Are you alright?" he asked, breathing heavily. "We shall have to modify the soles of your boots I think."

Eisandre lifted her palm to inspect the fresh scrapes along it.

"I'll live," she said with a frustrated shrug. "And you do have a point. My boots are practical for the smooth floors of the Pyramid, but they are not well adapted to trudging about out here. Plus, maybe we can find something that will work as a staff, lest I become more trouble for you than I'm worth."

The Engineer held out a hand to help her back up the slope. She hesitated for a moment before taking his hand to climb to the rough-hewn path they had been walking along.

"I will work on something that you can strap onto your boot that will dig into the rubble more instead of slipping from it. Until then, I would most prefer that you use this," he said and held out his halberd.

"I will not take your weapon, sir," Eisandre stated firmly, but politely. "Perhaps we can find a scrap of something or other as we walk that will do nicely."

"Well then, I can slow my pace. We should be able to find something easily out here."

They continued along in silence for a time, with the young Arbiter careful to place her feet where the path had already been tried. The sun grew higher in the sky and in time the glare became less burdensome to their progress.

"If the Prince is unwell, you will have to seek sponsorship from Eshelle, I suppose. You have spoken with her, since that first meeting, have you not?"

"Aye, I have spoken to her. She was the one you called 'Eshy' if I am not mistaken? Unfortunately, the Prince was already injured by the time I had returned. Though I suppose it went well. I have been given a task to prove my merit and I –" The Engineer paused abruptly as he spotted something down in a pit to the side of the path. "There! Right there. Wait here just a moment."

Actaeon skillfully scrabbled down into the small pit, careful to avoid jagged metal bars that poked out from one side. At the bottom, he found what he was searching for. He inserted the base of his halberd under a large stone fragment and pulled up to roll it aside. It revealed a long metal bar and he knelt to retrieve it. He grinned up at Eisandre.

"It is one of the light ones. Perfect, if not a bit long."

With a broad grin, he took both the bar and his halberd in one hand and shouldered them as he made his way back up the incline. Near the top, he accepted Eisandre's hand to help him the rest of the way and handed her the bar. It was light and easy to hold, standing a foot taller than her with a bend at the top that made it resemble a herdsman's staff.

"Here, try this out. It should do the trick. I can try to modify it for you to make it more comfortable before our next venture out here."

"All these planned modifications, just so I can walk with you in this place. It seems like an awful lot of trouble," she protested.

Actaeon withdrew a short bolt of cloth and tied it around her makeshift staff where her hand would grip.

She tested it by poking experimentally at the ground and putting her weight on it.

"Thank you, Master Rellios," she said. The Arbiter offered the man a genuine bow before they continued along with considerably greater ease.

The following few days were a flurry of activity for the Engineer.

At Balin's shop, Actaeon used the forge to heat up molten metal and manufacture the castings for his triggering mechanism. After only three days, Actaeon had enough mechanisms for a half dozen traps.

Each trap filled nearly the entire bed of the wagon, one man wide and two men deep and taller than Trench when set. They'd have to deploy each one before they built the next. The device comprised of a wide base that supported a series of sharpened spikes of various materials. The base also supported a deadfall platform with its own spikes, which was designed to fall atop any creature unfortunate enough to spring the triggering mechanism. The mechanism itself was Actaeon's custom sand-casted metal assembly and was tied to a bait platform at the bottom and set to release when weight was in the center of the trap. The spikes were arranged to help corral any interested parties into the center to acquire the bait and they were angled so that any creature caught in the trap would farther impale themselves upon the spikes no matter which direction they struggled to escape. When fully loaded, it was heavier than the men could lift on their own, especially once the deadfall stone was added to the upper platform of the trap.

In order to lower the traps into their respective locations, Actaeon built a collapsible stiffleg derrick like the ones that were commonly used to haul supplies up the steep slopes in his hometown of Incline. It consisted of a single pole angled forward that acted as the lift point and three poles behind it that unfolded to support the main pole. He fitted the main pole so it could rotate about the supports so that the traps could be swung around from the wagon and lowered into place. In several locations the traps were lowered onto several cut timber logs and rolled to the position before they were set.

"Wouldn't it make more sense if we built these traps in place right here?" Wave asked while they placed the second trap.

"Aye, it would be more efficient were it not for the danger that these unknown creatures present to us. If we were to spend the hour or two necessary to construct this apparatus, then we would be at a much greater risk. We would also need to haul in the bait, which would leave us reeking of matter that is attractive to a likely hostile creature and down in these tunnels for unnecessarily long periods. It may be more time consuming overall, but minimizes our time in the tunnels."

It took them five days to deploy six of the traps. Some of them were placed deeper into the underground tunnels than others. Actaeon explained that it would increase the chances that they would capture a live specimen.

After the traps were deployed, there was nothing to do but wait. The three men assembled daily in the marketplace to go to the tunnels and check all of the traps, with Trench and Wave spending the remainder of their time – and pay – in The End, and Actaeon spending more time with Eisandre, scouring the Boneyards for useful items.

It was there that the Engineer found himself on one late afternoon, after he'd spent the greater part of his morning checking traps.

The Knight Arbiter appeared atop a fairly treacherous pile of rubble.

"The traction is really quite remarkable. I'm impressed. I would never have thought to do anything of the sort, Master Rellios. Thank you."

Actaeon grinned as he watched her easily traverse the rubble with the new additions to her boots.

"Always make sure the straps hold them tightly before you start out. They rely on pressure from your boot, so if the strap is not tight then they may slide to the side and you will be even less stable. And do not become overconfident," he added. "Every step must still be taken with much care, considering the ramifications of your weight on the debris out here. There are still many areas of Redemptions ruins where even the enhanced traction of that device will not help you avoid a collapse or ruinslide. Perhaps it will now be I who follows you, Eisandre."

"Ramifications of my weight. Are you implying that I'm – Hey, look at that!" she pointed down the far side of the hill to where a little shard of sparkling blue glass glinted in the late day light. She started her way down the hill toward it.

"Eis, wait!" he called after her.

Instead of looking at at the anomalous blue material, he looked at the hillside below her intended path. He grasped her arm to stop her and gestured with the point of his halberd toward a large semicircle of metal at the base of the hill.

"This structure is unstable. See that big piece of debris down there? There is not much holding it in place. I am afraid that if we shift our weight upon this slope too much it will give way."

She froze in place.

"And that is why you will likely never be the one who follows me out here. What do you recommend?"

"You learn to pick these things out after the first few times you are caught in a ruinslide and are lucky enough to live through it. Do you see that long beam over to our left? If we can traverse this pile and gain it, we can then descend to investigate your blue shard."

"We should be mindful of the hour. It is nearly dark," Eisandre replied, though she started on her way across to the indicated beam, a fallen pillar that crossed over the pile at an angle and descended toward the left side of the gulley.

"Sometimes the dark makes strange things stand out here. It is up to you of course. If you would like, we can retrieve it quickly and then start back."

"Might it be useful to you?"

"We cannot really know until we take a look. It could be a lens fragment, or a strange material. Either could be valuable to future designs. Admittedly, I have not seen an artifact like that before."

"As you say, we cannot possibly know more unless we take the chance. Perhaps we will find something useful, or even if it is but a bauble, you might sell it to fund an experiment, yes?"

Actaeon offered her a hand and she paused to stare at his offered hand with doubt. After a moment, she took his hand with certainty, her blue eyes sparkling warmly. Together they made their way carefully down into the gulley.

"Never really considered selling things from out here. Though I suppose you are correct that one could certainly fund a lot of research and design development on a few of these finds. Perhaps I can cut a deal with a collector to sell the things that I find which are of no use. It is just so hard to tell sometimes."

"If you save everything you find, you will run out of space. Besides, if you trade things that might be of use for things that will definitely be useful, it seems to me like you'd be coming out ahead."

"Agreed, though hopefully I will soon have more space in which to store things. The roomkeeper up in the Song of the Sisters has already spoken to me several times about the things I have been storing in my room," he said with a laugh.

Eisandre smiled at his laugh, though she concentrated carefully on the descent.

"You have yet to hear word from Eshelle, then? Next time you go to see her, please let me know and I will join you."

"I will do that. Eshelle has told me that the odors in the market are causing Raedelle a loss of revenue. It is not normally something that I would have any interest in, but I agreed to look into it with the possibility of gaining some funding for a workshop should the market income be fully reestablished. And to my great surprise, there might be more of interest there than at first I surmised."

"I wonder if Raedelle is still steeling itself for a potential war against the Keepers with the rumors that they have entered under Niwian's protection. Although I doubt it, considering Thyr's trade position with Raedelle. Odors in the market, my eye. If, perhaps, you can come up with an invention that would be undeniably useful to Raedelle, or perhaps to the Companions in particular, you'd have a more convincing sales pitch. What about these things that you added to my boots?"

The unlikely pair arrived at the bottom and paused to rest.

"The Keepers as a Niwian Protectorate? That does not strike me as particularly logical. The artifacts and capabilities inside Memory Keep are as legendary as they are secreted – how could the Keepers abide such a thing?"

"It *is* odd, though people say that the Lord Protector of Memory Keep has fallen under the sway of the Allfather."

"That would be quite unfortunate," said Actaeon, his eyes cast down at his boots as he thought about the ramifications of the Keeper fanatics having the power of an entire Dominion behind their cause. "Well, in either case, I should be able to support myself in the vicinity of Pyramid whether or not Raedelle chooses to take me seriously. Eshelle seems genuinely interested, though I do not image she fully understands my capabilities. If I simply demonstrate a few things, say related to the Companions, then my fear is that I will become just that – a dedicated asset to better equip the Companions, or the warbands, or general defense. No," he said, decidedly, "I need to show the entirety of my worth and to do that I must show all of my capabilities. Only this way will I be free to fully exercise my ideas to the benefit of our people. A solution to this market issue might show my ingenuity as well as free up funding for my workshop and staff. And there is also the chance to learn more about a new and strange creature that may be below the Pyramid. I will just have to attempt it, lest I be sequestered into a very specific realm of research and design. Do you follow my logic on this?"

"I do follow your logic, Master Rellios. Forgive me. I think even I might have been in danger of underestimating you, just then," she said with a genuine smile, his hand still held in hers. She frowned then as shadows began to spread along the western edge of the gully. "I think the sooner we see about this glass and move to more solid ground, the better in truth. I don't much care for the feel of this particular place, all engineering-related observations aside."

"It is strange indeed. There is something different about this place. Perhaps it is how low this gulley is with respect to the rest of the ruin and yet not one plant growing here – just these blue shards." He knelt before the shards to examine them. All around them were melted pieces of metal that had fused together in an ugly, blackened mass.

"It looks as if there has been a fire of some sort here, who knows how long ago. What do you make of the glass?" asked the Arbiter.

"Certainly an interesting color. And yes, there does appear to have been a fire here. Good observation. The fire here burned at a great temperature and seems to have inhibited all future plant growth. I have observed similar materials before, but never in this melted condition."

The Engineer took the material in hand and tested its sharpness against the back of his fingerless glove. He grinned as it easily sliced through the outer layer of the material. He bent the material with his hands, which failed to yield it. The final test he tried shocked him: he pushed a finger lightly against the flat surface of the shard and it deformed to take the shape of his finger as he pushed, before it quickly returned to its original shape.

"How fascinating. We shall have to take this with us," said the Engineer as he pulled off his jacket and vest. The vest opened at the neck where he had left a stitch out so the garment could act as a sort of bag. Then he used his bandage roll to wrap the shards before placing them into the makeshift bag.

"I imagine there are all sorts of uses for those that you will come up with. However, it is no longer safe to be so far from the Pyramid," Eisandre reminded him as he finished packing away the blue shards. "Even the two of us together. Although, if that's as sharp as it looks, I'd say you might have found yourself a new dagger."

"This is an incredible finding. Let us take it and return to Pyramid now," Actaeon agreed and pulled out his luminary to place it in the strap of his goggles. He hefted the bag over his shoulder and slid the shaft of his halberd through the arm holes of the vest to haul it. "I certainly owe you one, Eisandre. Shall we depart then?"

Later that week, Actaeon found himself in the Mirrorholds once again. The click of his halberd echoed as he strode along the reflective floors. Even though the Prince's sister had told him that she didn't need a report on his progress with the market smell, he thought that it could not do any harm to give her a brief update.

Eshelle Caliburn emerged from the entrance to the Raedellean hall just as he drew near – three Companions close on her heel. He dipped his head politely.

"Lady Caliburn, I heard that His Grace had an infection. I am sorry to hear it," Actaeon said.

The Lady slid to a stop and narrowed her eyes upon him. "Ah, yes, of course. You're the artifact collector, right? Thank you for concern. He will recover soon, I am sure of it." She started forward again, but the Engineer stepped in front of her.

"You gave me a task many days ago, to solve the marketplace smell. There are some things I would like to discuss with you. And also, I am an Engineer, not an artif–"

"Sandre!" she interrupted him and stepped forward to embrace someone that arrived nearby.

As the Prince's sister released her embrace, Actaeon was surprised to recognize the newcomer as Eisandre. It was unusual that she'd wanted to come to meet Eshelle with him in the first place, but there was clearly a strong connection between the two women.

"Are you okay?" Eshelle asked.

"Worried about Aedwyn, but that can't be helped." She straightened and nodded to Actaeon in greeting. "I know Master Rellios well enough to understand that perhaps you need to discuss a matter of business with him. I do not wish to interfere, but all the same I am presently off duty, and –"

"No, no – you should come along, Eisandre," insisted Actaeon. "You might have some valuable input. That is, of course, if the Lady Eshelle is fine with that?"

"Of course," Eshelle said quickly. "No doubt you know better than I do what he'd like to speak about, Sandre. Let's head to one of the gardens on the Terrace of the Stars."

They made their way out of the Mirrorholds and up one of the winding stairways of the Skyspiral toward the top of Pyramid on their way to the great Althean-tended gardens. The Terrace of the Stars was a gigantic open-air garden that jutted sharply from the eastern face of Pyramid. Nearly every known type of plant life that could be coerced to take root in the freshly imported soil of the Terrace was found there. It was divided into many small gardens, and each one was a miniature arrangement of the different regions in and around Redemption. Pathways of colorful gravel stone wound their way through the lush greenery, past colorful flowing vines and clumps of moss.

From the fragrant, reddish plantlife of the Flamewoods to the east of Adhikara, to the sharp, unforgiving blades and spikes of flora from the barren environment in northern Rust, to the tropical fronds and sparse ground coverings of southern Thyr, and even to the vine-addled, dense jungles of Lakehold, the garden had every common plant and most rare plants that could be found within the boundaries of the lost city of Redemption.

While the gardens stood open to the public and, in fact, the use of them for politic and social discourse was encouraged, the Altheans also used these gardens for the harvesting of many different herbs to suit their medicinal needs as well. It was also thought by some that the compounds from different plants in these gardens were put to use in various tinctures that, when properly administered, allowed the Altheans to influence the decisions of Dominion leaders.

In fact, there were many who did not accept food or drink from the Altheans simply due to this suspicion, and those from Raedelle were especially cautious. Actaeon shared the thoughts of his Dominion on that matter. While all of the other Dominions chose to make use of an Althean attache for political advice, the Raedelle Dominion was the only one that elected not to make use of the Althean service. Such was their distrust of the supposedly neutral organization.

Actaeon thought that it was likely that the Althean's order started with altruistic intentions to provide healing and guidance to the different peoples of Redemption, but that it was inevitable for them to attempt to influence inter-Dominion relations after they had gained such a foothold. Indeed, Raedelle's chief advisor, Ambrosius the Wise, had counseled the Caliburn family on just that point.

"What do you wish to speak with me about?" asked the Lady Eshelle as they wound their way through the gardens. "For the present I speak for Aedwyn."

"Eshelle is a good listener, Master Rellios. Do not be afraid to tell her your dreams," suggested Eisandre as she walked alongside the Engineer. They both trailed the Raedellean leader by several steps.

Actaeon gave Eisandre a smile before he spoke.

"To start with, I am not exactly a collector of artifacts. I do collect them, and study them on occasion, but that is not my primary interest. I am an Engineer. I like to create new things, research new ideas, learn about principles that I have yet to understand, and then apply them to practical designs that can solve problems."

"So you're a builder of artifacts, one might say? Or you're interested in how they work?"

"Perhaps one day I will grasp the answers needed to recreate the artifacts, but I freely admit that I have not been able to reproduce the artifacts that I have found in the ruins of Redemption. I create new devices and structures that are of my own design, on occasion using an artifact or two for their unique and otherwise unobtainable properties. However, and most lamentably, I cannot yet recreate materials or objects with the properties of artifacts."

"Ah, I suppose that would be too much to hope," said Eshelle, with clear disappointment in her tone, and something else – impatience perhaps. "What is it that you'd like to discuss then?"

"I would not underestimate the man's ingenuity, Eshelle, interjected the Knight Arbiter. "Already, in our wanderings, he has modified my boots so that I will not so easily slip when exploring the ruins."

"I thought we spoke about your walks in the ruins," snapped Eshelle in reply. The look she shot back at the young Arbiter was stern and disappointed.

Actaeon spoke again, to bring the attention back to the issue at hand and to distract Eshelle from the nasty look she was giving Eisandre.

"I came to you to speak of my proposal a week past," he said, masking his frustration. "In Shore, I have done well supporting myself with my metal-casting technique. However, it takes up a lot of time and effort that I can spend learning and designing new things. I journeyed here from Shore because I wish to formally offer my services to Raedelle. I can solve a variety of Raedelle's problems with my skills and inventions, and, in turn, that will offer me the opportunity to investigate artifacts, experiment with new ideas, and perhaps even answer some questions that I have about the nature of this city and our world as a whole. I can do my best to provide Raedelle with new inventions to serve as solutions to problems and my research can also put our Dominion at an advantage amongst others. In exchange, I would require very little. Funding for a workshop in the vicinity of Pyramid, a meager staff, and enough to support whichever experiments I am working on at the time. Of course, I can submit for your approval each experiment or new invention and you may choose the ones you wish to fund."

Eshelle shot him a skeptical look.

"So you're hoping for funding for your workshop – which may or may not produce useful things. What benefit is there to Raedelle in this? Materials are expensive. Have you plans that could bring in more coin?"

"I suspect he has more plans than he could tell you in one evening," Eisandre said quietly.

"That's enough, Sandre," Eshelle snapped at the Knight Arbiter.

"I understand your concerns," said Actaeon, though his eyes narrowed upon the Raedellean Lady after she spoke so rudely to his new friend. "Which is also why I propose that my experiments and prototypes must first meet with your financial approval on an individual basis. Of course, it will be my humble task to prove to you why each project should be funded. Different things can always bring in more coin, such as my metal-casting knowledge, but the inventions I can make for Raedelle may help with defense and offense alike, increase trade revenue by leveraging mechanical devices to ease labor on common tasks, and many other things. Any projects that are not approved will be funded on my own. In fact, I am presently funding the project that you tasked me with to eliminate the unbearable stench in the marketplace. I have made some significant progress toward understanding the matter and I have a potential solution in place that should help us eliminate the issue altogether."

"I will certainly consider it," put in Eshelle abruptly. "And I'll speak to Aedwyn about it as well once he's feeling better. It's an interesting –"

She broke off as one of the Companions approached and whispered something in her ear.

"Excuse me," Eshelle said, offering a forced smile to Actaeon. "It seems some business requires my attention. Sandre, you know you can always stop by. Actaeon, I'm sure we'll speak again."

At that, she was off, gone just as abruptly as she had appeared outside Saint Torin's Hold.

The Knight Arbiter came to a halt. It took a large effort on her part before she turned to face Actaeon.

"Eshelle will help you, how she can. She is a good woman – I cannot stress that enough. She could see that I like you, and that just may count for something."

"We shall see. Working with our homeland is the best opportunity to accomplish what I am striving for, and to our mutual benefit, I truly believe. Either way, I will find a way to set up my workshop here. I do hope that I can give back to my homeland, though." The Engineer sat down upon a finely-chiseled stone bench set under a tall tree with many purple flowers. "This week has been a long one indeed."

Eisandre sat beside him without hesitation. "A long week, but a good one, I hope. I can't help but observe that you speak as if there's a different option than to serve Raedelle. Is there no draw of your heart to serve your homeland? Or is it just that your true passion lies in your work?"

The sun began to set over the grand pinnacle of Pyramid, and the insect life in the garden began to buzz to life all about them; a veritable cacophony of sound from insects all over the lost city that had migrated there along with their favorite plants. Actaeon breathed in deeply, taking in the smells of the garden.

"This is my favorite one. It reminds me a bit of home – home away from home – amidst all this ruin. I love my homeland, but my work is an obsession for me. My search for answers might be similar to an addiction to vices for another man, except knowledge is my vice and I will go far and wide to find it. That is why I hope very much that this proposal works out. I want desperately to use my drive to serve my homeland."

"You are different than most men," decided the Knight Arbiter, "than most people, really. Perhaps it's why we get along. There is little I can do, beyond providing a sympathetic ear and being a companion in your ventures through the ruins, but I will help you how I can in your quest to achieve your goals, for however much that might matter."

The Engineer was surprised at her words.

"That matters more than you might imagine. For that you would intend to aid my goals, I am most honored. You have been a fine friend to me since I have arrived here, Eisandre." He reached out and placed a hand gently upon her shoulder. "I can see you are very close to the Caliburn family. Whether you are a relative or a close friend does not matter. It is clear that you are truly hurt by what has happened to the Prince and I want you to know that you can come to me whenever you need someone to speak with.

I can see that you take your role as an Arbiter very seriously, and it seems like it must be quite difficult at times – always trying to exude confidence and reassurance even when there are things that are hurting you inside. Know that I am here, Eisandre, when you need someone to turn to," said Actaeon, before he withdrew his hand from her shoulder and turned to gaze upon the rest of the garden.

Eisandre was left speechless.

"All my life," she began after a long silence. "I have stood in the shadows of the bright stars of people shining all around me. It has become part of my nature, who I am. When I saw you with Eshelle today, I was certain I would fade into the background, that you would see only her – beautiful and radiant jewel that she is – and I would cease to exist. But you are here, still talking to me and offering your presence, your compassion, your thoughts. I am humbled and grateful beyond my ability to express."

Actaeon laughed and nudged her shoulder playfully. "Oh, come now, Eisandre, if you ceased to exist then I would be completely alone during my jaunts out into the ruins. Anyway, the radiance of your compassion and interest in others far exceeds any jewels that I have ever seen. And I have seen many in my travels of this city. Besides, I should be the humbled one here. For most of my life the majority of people I meet find me eccentric and too inquisitive. Yet you listen to me with genuine interest and support my endeavours where many would deem them foolish. To me you shine brighter and more beautifully than the prism atop Skyspiral."

Surprised at his own words, he shook his head and turned back to the Terrace, scratching his right arm.

"Our admiration seems to be mutual, then," Eisandre concluded with her own laugh. She nudged him in return. She was silent for a long moment, as she weighed a decision in her mind before she spoke again, "I think I should tell you that I was born Eisandre Caliburn. Aedwyn, Eshelle, and Aedgar are my siblings. I'm the youngest of them, the outcast, in the most literal of ways, even though there can be no doubt that we love each other very much. I know how it feels to be different. Somehow I don't think you're going to hold any of this against me. Many do."

The Engineer's eyes widened as she spoke her true name.

"Well, I think you should not seriously think yourself an outcast. I would hold you in the highest admiration of all four of you." She opened her mouth to object and he held up his hand. "Wait... allow me to finish. I understand that your older siblings are in positions of great responsibility in the Raedelle Dominion, and, as skilled as I believe they are in their respective stations, it does not fail to escape me that they are not in that station on their own accord but rather by the line they descended from. When I look at you though, I see a woman that has risen to rank and respect among the Arbiters at a young age. You earned that position through your resolve and determination, I am sure. I mean no disrespect to your siblings – I just mean to explain that your position was earned by your personal character and skill alone."

Eisandre was once again struck silent.

"As I said before, I have spent all my life in their shadows," she finally said. "They are great people, Actaeon, and I do believe it to be potential far beyond their birthright. I adore all three of them, and I imagine I'll always be their baby sister, who they will always love and protect, even if I was never fit to stand at their side. But rather than linger all my days in that place where I was small, I work hard to make something of my life. To do my part in making Redemption a better place for everyone who lives here. It is lonely sometimes. I miss my family. And often I still feel like only a part of myself, of who I might be. When we talk though, I feel stronger – like a better person and like the world is more clear. I know we have only met a handful of times now, but I think I should tell you these things, nevertheless. Life is too short, too precious, not to. I must return to my duties now," she said, rising as she suddenly became aware of the time. With hesitation, she lifted a hand and gently touched his cheek. "Thank you. For everything."

Actaeon blushed at her touch and drew to his feet.

"You give me strength, as well, Eisandre, and more. Keep the Pyramid safe, Eisandre Caliburn, and be proud of who you are."

"I am Knight Arbiter Eisandre sof Darovin," she reminded him, offering the formal bow of an Arbiter – a new warmth in her bright blue eyes. "And I keep my Vow and the Oaths for the sake of Redemption. Good night, Master Rellios."

And, with that said, she took her leave.

HUNTERS & PREY

THE FOLLOWING MORNING THERE WAS a crowd of craftsmen and merchants gathered at Vez' staging area in the marketplace. There was a general commotion as everyone shouted at once. The old carter sat upon the warped bench of his cart beside his grandson and was shooing the crowd away as one would a swarm of flies.

That was the situation when Actaeon arrived with Trench and Wave close on his heels. "Alright, alright. Everyone settle down. Tell me what is the problem," called out the Engineer, as he approached the crowd.

One man, a baker with flour covering his brown apron, stepped forward until he was nose-to-nose with Actaeon. "We all've seen what you three and ol' Vez here've been doing. Bringing things down into the tunnels to mess with whatever's down there. Well ya made it mad now, ya did!"

"Aye, we all heard it – the horrific roar," said a plump seamstress, glancing around fearfully as though the creature might ambush her there at any moment. "Whatever you're doing down there, it'll be out for more blood now."

"More of a shriek really," said a young Raedellean woodcarver. "It echoed across the entire marketplace. I heard a lower one late last night as well."

Actaeon nodded in understanding. "I know that you all are nervous about the creature that is down there. It is the same creature that is blocking up the tunnels in the low lying areas and preventing proper drainage."

"This thing's causing the stench, you say?" asked the baker.

"I do believe it is," said Actaeon. "And we mean to put an end to it, whatever it is."

The baker laughed in his face. "Ha! Yer gonna kill it? It's taken a chunk of the livestock outta the pens. Some cattle were four times the size of you. Good luck!"

"Thank you, but I prefer to rely on carefully laid pl—" Actaeon stopped as three women ran up to them, one of them wailing.

"The boys, the three of them are missing — they didn't come home for their morning chores. They've been playing in the tunnels e'en though I've told 'em not to. I know it. Please... please, find them!"

Trench stepped forward and rested a hand on the woman's shoulder in reassurance. "Don't worry. We'll get your boys back." The look he shot back at Wave was a skeptical one though.

The flour-covered baker hefted a rolling pin the size of Trench's maul. "What're we waiting for? Let's go get 'em."

And so, without hesitation, the four of them — mercenaries, baker and Engineer — raced to the tunnel where the roar had been heard. The crowd followed behind.

An Arbiter was already there, sword drawn as he gazed into the tunnel, his crimson cape fluttering in the breeze. He spun to face them as they approached, bewilderment writ upon his features. "Did you hear it? The screaming?"

"No, but there are three boys missing. It might have been them," said Actaeon. He moved to step past the Arbiter and into the dark tunnel mouth beyond but the Arbiter blocked him bodily.

"Hold it. I am Knight Arbiter Allyk sof Darovin. I've been inside those tunnels when Shield's Lord Zar entered them. One of his men died defending him. I saw it — at least as much as could be seen in the darkness down there. His weapons did not even manage to pierce the horror that emerged and devoured him. I can't let you meet that same fate."

Actaeon recognized the end of the Arbiter's name — he must've been trained by the same Arbiter as Eisandre. "Listen, Arbiter Allyk. I understand your fear, but we have children missing and they may well be source of the screams you heard from the tunnel. They will meet the same fate if we do not do something to help."

The Arbiter looked divided, his gaze shifting from Actaeon to the mercenaries behind him. Trench grunted and hefted his maul over one shoulder.

"What're you waiting for? My boy is in there with his friends. Go! Save him! Please!" shouted one of the women from the crowd.

Allyk hesitated, but when more shouts erupted from the crowd, he nodded. "Okay, let's go then. Don't do anything stupid."

"Lads! Where are you?" yelled the baker, before ignoring the Arbiter's order to run forward and disappear into the darkness beyond the tunnel mouth.

"Hey! Get back here!" yelled the Arbiter.

"Ancients! The stench," the baker could be heard yelling from a distance in.

"I said to return at once!" yelled the Arbiter again, but the baker was gone.

Actaeon, Wave and Allyk brought out their luminaries to shed some cold blue light on the tunnel before them. Actaeon stuck his in the strap of his goggles and led the way with the point of his halberd forward. Allyk and Trench were right behind him while Wave took up the rear.

"Stay close together now," instructed Trench. "With the reach of Actaeon's weapon, and the four of us working together, we might be able to fight it off – whatever in cracked Redemption *it* is. Did anyone catch that guy's name?"

"The baker? He didn't give it," said Wave.

They ran along the tunnel quickly, staying close together.

"What are your names?" asked Allyk.

"Actaeon Rellios of Shore," said the Engineer. "And my associates are Trench and Wave."

Soon they reached a fork in the tunnel and Actaeon drew to a stop. He turned his head to cast the light of his luminary down each branch.

"Hail, baker! Where are you? Call to us!" yelled Actaeon. The eerie return echo came back from first one tunnel, then the other. The only other sound they could hear was that of their own ragged breathing from the run.

"We placed a trap down each of these branches. Let us proceed to the closest one," Actaeon said, and led the way to the left at a jog. The others followed him closely.

"Ugh, the smell down here is nauseating," said Wave with a retch.

"I thought you had experience with such smells," said Trench with a smirk.

"I'm surprised you could even fit down here, given your size," Wave said.

"If you were similarly endowed, ya wouldn't need to flee from lasses' beds in the morning to avoid their disappointment."

"The last time I came down here it took me days to get the smell off," said the Arbiter, interrupting the banter.

When they reached the trap, they saw that the deadfall had been released and the spikes glowed in the light of the luminaries, coated with a strange substance. There was no creature caught within, though the chickens had met their demise on the jagged edges of the spikes.

"Excellent. Results!" exclaimed Actaeon. He moved quickly past the trap to illuminate the tunnel beyond, the blade of his halberd pointed forward against the darkness. "Wave, Trench – collect some of that substance, and careful not to touch it. This is good news, the bait must have worked. It is not being snared by the barbs as it may be too lubricious or too gelatinous in form to be held in such a manner." His thoughts were on the problem, but his eyes remained focused on the tunnel ahead.

"I fail to see how you can draw any conclusions from this failed, disgusting trap," said Wave, as he followed the instructions and scraped some of the substance off from the spikes with his dagger and into a large half-through bottle.

Allyk turned to look back at Wave. "What are you doing? Collecting samples? There are boys missing. Let's keep on."

Actaeon spoke over his shoulder. "We do not even know if they are down this branch of the fork. Best we collect these samples now while we are here. It may aid us in deciphering a way to exterminate these creatures in the future."

The Knight Arbiter shook his head in dismay and pushed his way past Actaeon. "Whatever you say. I've got a job to do." He was halted midstep as a yell sounded far back along the tunnel from where they had come. It echoed along ahead of them, again and again, growing fainter and fainter.

The yell was followed by screams.

The screams of children.

The baker had chosen the right branch.

Actaeon turned and ran, pulling his goggles down over his eyes as he did so. He kept the point of his halberd high so that he didn't skewer the baker or children that were somewhere in the darkness ahead. Trench and Wave were right behind him while Allyk followed at the rear.

They made the fork in record time and turned down the right branch this time. While they ran, the screams ahead grew more desperate. Then there was silence.

Actaeon wouldn't have noticed, except that he tripped right over it.

He stumbled forward along the tunnel and managed to arrest his fall by catching one of the sides, tearing the skin from his fingers. The others drew to a stop behind him.

"What in the name of the Fallen..." muttered Wave under his breath.

The Engineer turned and glanced down at the object he had tripped over. It blended in with the muck and debris at the tunnel bottom. Only it wasn't an object, it was a human. Or at least it had been. The head was missing and it took Actaeon a moment to figure out that he was looking at the baker's body. The man was lying belly down and his spine had been ripped from his back, splaying organs in all directions around the corpse. The only recognizable feature that led him to conclude this was the baker was the rolling pin that was clutched in the man's death grip.

The body shifted and there was a groan that made them all jump back.

Trench was the one that stepped forward and rolled what was left of the baker aside. Underneath was a young boy, covered in gore, that couldn't have been more than ten years of age. The boy peered at them in shock, his wide white eyes contrasting sharply with his blood-covered face.

"Help," said the boy, his voice small. "My friends."

Trench lifted the boy in his arms and handed him to the Arbiter. "Go. Get him outta here, Allyk. We'll find the other two."

Allyk hesitated, but then looked down at the young boy. "You're safe with me, little one. Let's get you home." With that he took off at a sprint, back the way they had come.

Trench nodded at Actaeon and the Engineer lowered his halberd once more, starting on his way forward. This time they all moved slowly. There were no longer urgent screams ahead. Wordlessly, the three of them chose caution.

Farther along in the tunnel, Actaeon passed a bone. He didn't stop to examine it. He recognized it as a child's femur. Perhaps he was wrong though. Maybe it was a femur from a calf or another small animal.

The lower jaw told him otherwise. It was polished white by whatever had taken it and it was definitely one of the children's. Actaeon bit back tears as they continued forward, bile rising in his throat.

"Ancients guide us," whispered Trench. Then, "I promise I'll kill whatever did this."

The partial skeleton they came across next took away all hope that they had of finding either of the two other children alive.

Actaeon let loose an audible sob as he knelt before it. Trench's hand was on his shoulder, but everything felt numb.

"Hey guys. We'd better get out of here," muttered Wave, trying to keep his voice low.

Ahead of them there came a violent thrashing and Actaeon was on his feet in a flash.

The light of his luminary revealed the trap they had set farther along the tunnel. Within it was something horrible: writhing, gleaming, shapeless appendages, a bristling array of stalks, and several rows of jagged, razor-sharp teeth that snapped at them rapidly.

Whatever it was, was tremendous.

It suddenly fell still.

"Back off, back off!" cried Actaeon. He shuffled backward, but ran into Trench's bulk.

The thing let out a shrill hiss and several projectiles hurtled toward the party.

Trench threw Actaeon to the floor beneath them and the shiny, wriggling missiles thudded into him and Wave, knocking the smaller mercenary to the tunnel floor.

Trench reached up and wrapped his hand around one of the projectiles that had secured itself to the side of his head – a writhing slug nearly the length of his forearm with an abundance of small tendrils that protruded from its face. Each tendril ended in a mouth with sharp teeth and the ones that hadn't already bitten into the giant's head snapped and sought out a purchase. He crushed it in his hand and ripped it free, taking some of his own flesh with it before he smashed it with his boot and slammed his maul down on another that had bounced off his leather armor.

Wave struggled with another one of the creatures that had latched onto his face. He took ahold of the writhing tail of the creature with his free hand and stabbed it with his dagger, impaling his hand in the process. The mercenary grunted in pain and struggled to yank the slug-like creature from his face.

Actaeon stood and used his halberd to hack apart several of the slugs that had bounced off of the mercenaries. Nearing Wave, he drew his hooked dagger and stabbed through the creature's tail to help Wave yank it free. He pulled and threw the slug to the side, where it landed in a puddle and writhed there as if in agony.

The giant stomped on another slug that slithered toward Actaeon and bellowed a roar that resounded along the tunnel. He rushed forward to charge the large mass in the trap but was halted when Actaeon put his shoulder into him.

"Trench, no! We have what we need to end this. It will not bring the children back," Actaeon said as he held the big veteran back.

"I swear I'll kill that fucking thing!" yelled Trench as Actaeon fought to prevent his charge. The big man turned though, and began to retreat at a run. Actaeon and Wave rushed to keep up as the giant barreled forward through the pitch black tunnel. Only Actaeon's luminary lit the way, secured in the strap of his goggles.

As they ran, Wave noticed something was wrong and reached up to brush his eye, but he found nothing there. His left eye was gone – the socket empty – in the darkness and chaos he'd not noticed it. He stopped and fell against the wall of the tunnel.

"My eye! My fucking eye! That thing took my fucking eye!" Wave clawed at the empty socket and his cheek below, as though that would help the problem go away.

Actaeon slid to a stop beside Wave and Trench joined them a moment later. Wave searched the ground around him in a panic, looking for the missing eye.

There was another shrill hiss and a sharp crack behind them as the trap failed. The Engineer spun to face it.

The creature's reaction was brief – almost imperceptible, but Actaeon caught the movement: it hesitated at the light of the luminary, recoiling for a lifebeat before it started forward with speed that seemed impossible for a creature of its bulk. It was like a garden slug from a child's nightmare: its shiny, black body filled half the diameter of the tunnel and the top of its head bristled with stalks that ended in a hundred tiny eyes. The monster had a mouth filled with several rows of curved teeth. Behind those teeth, like prisoners in a cage were dozens more of the smaller slugs like those it had spat at them. Horrible, biting tendrils poked out randomly from around its mouth and farther back along its body as though it was growing countless more tiny versions of itself. The top frame of the trap was still lodged in the creature's back as it advanced, the spikes coated with a greenish-brown slime that must've been its blood.

"By the Fallen, what am I gonna do about my eye?" Wave asked, unaware of their quickly approaching death.

"Try the luminaries!" said Actaeon decisively. "Wave, forget your damned eye – we will find you a new eye. Get out your luminaries and aim them at that thing!"

Wave calmed at the Engineer's words and stood to face the creature. He pulled another luminary free from his swordbelt and shone it at the gruesome creature. The blade of his rapier appeared in a flash in his other hand, gleaming in the dim light.

Trench ripped his own luminary from a strap on his chest and ran by the other two men. He hurled the luminary into the creature's mouth and leapt toward its maw to slam his maul down upon it.

The creature's tendrils snapped at the luminary as it flew past them and into its mouth. It shrieked when the artifact light landed inside and its entire body contracted. One of the tendrils reached into the mouth, wrapped around the luminary, and squeezed it hard.

There was an ear-splitting crack and the beast exploded in a wave of fire and slime that blasted down the tunnel. Actaeon watched as Trench – still in mid-air – disappeared in a gout of flame. The shockwave threw them back along the tunnel where they landed roughly.

"Unanticipated," said Actaeon as flaming chunks of the creature thudded to the bottom of the tunnel around him. The noxious smell of the burning slime threatened to suffocate him. He blinked to clear his vision from the afterimage of the explosion and saw Trench before him, running to and fro as flames licked at his large frame – the giant ablaze with burning biological debris.

The Engineer tripped Trench with his halberd and pulled off his jacket to wrap it around the flaming mercenary and extinguish him.

Wave helped Actaeon roll Trench back and forth to quell the flames.

When the fire was out, Trench was alive but had suffered severe burns on his arms and face – the boiled leather of his chestplate had protected his chest. They all stunk with the fetid stench of burnt slime and likely would for some time thereafter. A section of the tunnel had collapsed atop what remained of the exploded beast.

"Trench, you okay? What in the name of the Fallen happened to the thing?" Wave asked.

"I think we might have killed it, Wave," said Actaeon, as he regarded the splattered remains of their monstrous quarry.

Trench propped himself up on his elbows with a wince and grinned. "I told you I would kill the damned thing. I always keep my promises."

The three men burst into laughter at that, a mixture of amusement and relief. But mostly relief. Tears of pain streamed down Trench's scorched face as laughter shook his massive frame.

Actaeon and Wave helped the giant to his feet and they collected their equipment and weapons. The Engineer filled the rest of his half-through bottles with slime from the dispatched slug monster and tucked them away in his jacket.

Actaeon tossed Trench a tiny half-through bottle. "Take some of that. It will dull the pain. Better than the most concentrated ale you can find."

Trench drank down the bottle and tossed it aside, sighing his immediate relief.

As the three survivors limped out from the tunnel, they found Allyk.

"No..." murmured Actaeon, as their luminaries shed light on the Arbiter's final moments.

Allyk had fought off two smaller versions of the giant slug that they had blown up earlier. One was neatly cloven in half and farther along – closer to the exit – he had died while fighting the other. It had latched itself to his face, but the brave Knight Arbiter had managed to dispatch it before he succumbed himself. The dead pair were locked in a final pose of combat where they had died. The surviving boy was nowhere to be found.

Trench touched Actaeon's shoulder and pointed. There were bloody footprints on the floor of the tunnel – headed toward the exit.

Wave and Actaeon pulled Allyk's body free of the dead slug and covered his ruined face. They carried him from the tunnels while Trench followed, cringing in pain with every step.

When they emerged from the mouth of the tunnel, Vez was there, sitting astride the bench of his wagon with his arms wrapped tightly around his young grandson. Behind him in the wagon, they were all relieved to see, one of the women clutched her blood-soaked boy. Around him in a wide semicircle the crowd of onlookers stood. They watched in silence as the three men staggered clear. Several people from the crowd rushed forward to help carry the fallen Arbiter.

"Say something, boss. They wanna hear what happened," Wave said, giving his employer a nudge.

Actaeon arched a brow at the mercenary, though he stepped forward to address those gathered. "The baker and the Knight Arbiter died protecting the boy up in the wagon. Without their sacrifice, he would not have made it. I regret to say that the other two have perished."

Wails went up from several in the crowd, most likely the parents of the lost boys.

"Raulf... the baker's name was Raulf," said one of those gathered, the woodcarver.

"Allyk sof Darovin," said Wave. "The Arbiter was Allyk sof Darovin. Let their names be remembered this day."

"And what of the creature?" asked Balin the Smith, who had shouldered his way to the edge of the crowd. He hefted his axe in his hands.

"Three of the creatures that have terrorized this marketplace have been slain. We have information now that we can study in the event that more –"

The cheer that went up drowned out the rest of the Engineer's words and the onlookers rushed forward to congratulate them on their victory.

Trench stepped up beside him and patted him roughly on the shoulder. "Ya did good, Act. Real good."

The Engineer looked up at the mercenary and grimaced. "I did nothing, Trench. If it were not for you and Wave in there, I would be dead."

Late that evening, the three men entered the Pyramid, singed and covered with various wounds. Blood oozed slowly from Wave's empty eye socket and Trench's burns had begun to blister and burst. The lot of them smelled awful and their clothing was still covered in the charred guts and slime of the slug monster. Between them, Wave and Actaeon carried Allyk sof Darovin – the Knight Arbiter's face covered with a hood. Inside the Sun Chamber, other Arbiters noticed them and rushed over.

They relieved Wave and three of them joined Actaeon to carry their brother's body through the Pyramid in silence. As they continued, more Arbiters fell in behind them in a silent procession of crimson-caped guardians.

When they reached the Arbiter Command Post, they lowered Allyk's body gently upon a table. One of the Arbiters that had helped carry Allyk, a young man with reflective goggles, stepped forward and slid the goggles up to reveal strange, red irises. The Arbiter pulled the hood carefully from his lost brother's head and regarded the horror is silence. After several long moments, the Arbiter replaced the hood and turned to Actaeon.

"How did he fall?"

The Engineer touched the dead man's hand respectfully. "I want it to be known that this man saved a young boy from horrendous abominations beneath the markets. Because of his bravery, another's heart still beats. I will remember his name: Allyk sof Darovin of the Order of Arbiters. May he rest soundly now."

"His place is now among the Ancestors. Thank you for returning him to us. We will carry our fallen brother from here."

87 A.R., the 5th day of Hunger's Spur

LIFE GOES ON

THE NEXT DAY THE SUN was out and bright. Its rays warmed the Engineer's face through the sloped windows of his room in the Song. He sat at the small table, a sheet of vellum spread before him with a multitude of sketches scrawled upon it of the approximate layout of the spaces beneath the Open Market – or at least as close as he could approximate. A half-through bottle of greenish brown slime sat in atop the sketch – its cap carefully secured to contain its malodorous charge.

Across from him sat Wave, a black patch covering the socket of his lost eye.

Low moans from Trench filled the room, from where he lay in bed recovering from his burns. The giant was wrapped in gauze coated with some sort of substance the Altheans had brought and heavily medicated.

Actaeon rubbed his eyes – there were flashburned circles around them that matched the shape of his goggles. He winced and lowered his hands, they'd been mildly burned after he had helped extinguish the flames on the giant. He glanced across at his companion and grinned.

Wave was dressed in finely spun cotton and polished leather, despite the new additions of a silken black eye patch covering one eye and a fat bandage wrapped around his off-hand palm. The mercenary had also applied a heavy perfume in a poor attempt to cover up the cloying smell from the slug monster. The perfume's odor mixed with the smell in a way that made the Engineer gag.

"What're ya grinning at? I hoped you've figured out how you're going to get me a new eye already. This is getting old already," said Wave. He tilted back in his chair and took another sip from his tankard of ale.

Before Actaeon could reply, there was a knock at the door.

"Actaeon? Are you there? It smells like you are there."

"Eisandre!" he said, recognizing her voice. He stood up and opened the door. Eisandre stood several steps back from the doorway, carrying a cloth bundle under one arm – her eyes weary. "I am glad to see you," the Engineer said. "Might I express my deep sorrow for your fallen companion."

Both words and smell hung between them for several long moments before Actaeon gestured to a small shelf beside the door.

"I have left some kerchiefs out to filter the smell. I apologize that you have to see me like this." He backed into the room, half expecting the Knight Arbiter to run away from the pungent situation within.

"I'm not sure she is upset to see you, Act. I think she is more upset to smell you." Wave said with a wink with his remaining eye that made him wince in pain.

"He died protecting Redemption – protecting you. I could only hope for such a worthy end myself," said Eisandre as she took a few confident steps into the room, though she did keep her distance – her bright gaze focused intensely upon the Engineer. "I'm glad you're all alive. I brought you fresh bandages, more salve, and some food and extra water so that you'll be sure to have enough. I didn't know what else to do." She set the bundle down upon the table and stepped quickly back. "Is there anything else that you require?"

"You will forgive me if I hope for you to have a different end than brave Arbiter Allyk, but I do thank you for your aid, Eisandre. It is most appreciated," said Actaeon.

"I forgive you," replied the Arbiter with a confused look. "And you're welcome." She took a deep breath and immediately regretted it. "This odor is... impressive. How long do you suppose it will linger?"

"Well, according to both Lord Zar and Wave, who have both suffered the odor previously, it should last about three days. However, they had not been next to the thing when it exploded," Actaeon said.

"Will your friend be okay?" the Arbiter asked with a gesture toward the slumbering giant.

"Trench'll be fine. He's a tough one," Wave said.

"Without him the rest of us might have been dead as well," Actaeon said.

Trench let out a low moan that sounded almost like a growl.

"He is in a lot of pain. Be certain that he drinks plenty of water, even if he gets cranky about it. Do you have enough?" asked the Knight Arbiter.

"I'm alright – it's nothing," Trench groaned in a moment of lucidity. He followed it up with a protracted moan.

"Oh really?," said Wave with a laugh. "We should keep the Knight Arbiter around so you won't moan as loud as you've been doing all morning." He approached the giant's bed to apply some more salve to his burns.

Actaeon laughed at the one-eyed mercenary's comment and shook his head.

"We have plenty of water. Our landlords have been bringing us whatever we ask for all day – they don't want us to leave the room and disturb their other tenants and customers. I shall make sure he drinks as much as possible."

"Poor Trench," said Eisandre. "At least he has cheerful company. I'd stay if I could, but I have another duty shift beginning soon. I did want to come personally and make sure you're all doing okay. And to say thank you, for all that you've done for everyone."

Actaeon grinned and took a few steps toward her, before he remembered the smell and retreated when Eisandre wriggled her nose in distaste and recoiled from him.

"It certainly did not go as intended. I would have preferred to capture and study the creature. Indeed, we shall see if this even solves the market's problems. There may be more creatures and the excrement clogging the overflows may not dissipate on its own."

"You know," she said with a weak smile. "You might actually be able to use that smell if you've managed to collect any of its source. If it's somehow triggered to dump on an intruder, then the person would never be able to escape such incriminating evidence against them."

The Engineer's eyes lit up and he turned to look at the half-through bottle standing on the table. "That is a fantastic idea, Eisandre! If you ever consider a change in occupation, let me know. Yes, yes I see it now. People could even use it as a punishment on lazy employees."

Another groan followed, this time from both Trench and Wave.

"If that is the case, then would only be fair that they spend more time with their boss, making up for a job done poorly," Wave said with a smirk.

"I'll leave you to it, Master Engineer and loyal employees. I hope you all feel better soon. If you need anything from me, you've but to send word," said the Arbiter. She saluted them and backed out of the room into the fresh air beyond.

Construction of the Engineer's workshop commenced the week following the vicious battle down in the market tunnels. Actaeon selected a space in the Outskirts just on the fringes of the small community to the southwest of the Pyramid's base. As soon as the necessary payments were in place and Actaeon had finalized the plans, the construction crew began to set the foundation immediately. They also dug out space for a small cellar.

The workshop was to be made to the Engineer's specifications. He had drawn out exact details, right down to the shape of the keystones at the apex of each of the workshop's five round arches that would support the heavy stone vault. The workshop would run lengthwise from east to west to allow the maximum amount of light in during the day. It was paramount to Actaeon's work that the structural components of the building be comprised only of non-flammable materials that could resist the potentially volatile reactions from his experiments, and so the main structure would be made entirely of stone. A second floor loft with partitions for sleeping areas, a study, and a library, would be framed from heavy timber and planks. If the loft was destroyed in an unfortunate conflagration, it would be much easier to replace than the entire workshop. The plans called for the loft to be positioned between the second and third arches on the west side of the building.

The roof of the building would be the first of its kind. A common problem associated with the experimentation on chemicals and artifacts containing unknown ingredients was that the byproduct of gasses, harmful or otherwise, could easily occur. Such gasses could either sink to the floor or rise to the ceiling, according to their nature, and would pool in these places, thus creating a hazard. On top of this, such gasses were more often than not invisible to the human eye. To mitigate this risk, a ventilation system would be installed at both the floor and ceiling levels in order to release such harmful fumes. Creating these in the floor was simple as the workshop's floor was elevated from the terrain it was built upon. Channels were hewn into the floor at intervals and Actaeon cast slotted metal covers to be laid in along their length. He also cast large grills that were set at the ends of the channels that exited the workshop where the terrain was the lowest. In fact, the location for the workshop was chosen since it sloped away from the other residents of the Outskirts and down toward the Stone Gardens far below. It would not be very neighborly to allow such dangerous fumes to spill from the workshop and pool around other nearby dwellings. The workshop's location would assure its own longevity not just by protecting itself and those within it, but by maintaining a good relationship with the community.

Six such openings at the floor level and six near the vault's ridge would allow for a rapid exit of dangerous airborne chemicals. The horizontal slots in the vault needed to be incorporated into the structure of the vault itself, which required the weight to be distributed carefully around the opening so as to not create a weak point in the structure. Since it would be necessary to close these vents to prevent the entry of unwanted pests; bats, rats and the like, Actaeon designed a system of linkages attached to a crank to open or close the vents at need. These he broke into three sections: the east side, the west side and the center of the workshop, each with its own crank to control the vents.

With the aid of Balin's forge, he was able to cast the various components involved while the construction of the building was underway.

The windows were to be set high in the walls, at the level of the loft, so that significant light could still find the shop floor at all times of the day, but the workshop would not be as vulnerable to theft and vandalism as it would be with ground level windows. The double door entryway in the center of the north wall stood a full two men tall and two men wide so as to accept or let free the largest of apparatus constructed within. The large doors would be securable from the inside with a bar and on one side would contain a smaller door the size of a man (with respect to Trench, Actaeon had made the door slightly larger than average). Two massive stone chimneys extended past the vault on each side of the workshop. The one on the eastern end would serve a foundry and forge setup for Actaeon to continue with his castings, and the one on the western end would serve a laboratory setup with a metal hood with a vent that would direct any fumes up the chimney and out of the building.

The funding of the workshop had been a complicated matter. Following the battle in the market tunnels, Actaeon had monitored the state of the market tunnels closely for the next week or so. The thick gunk that had clogged the ends of the tunnels dissipated in a matter of days and allowed for the market grounds to once again drain normally, thereby eliminating the foul odor. After waiting a few days more, he had gone to seek out Eshelle Caliburn in St. Torin's Hold to give her a full report.

He described in detail how he and his team had designed and set traps that significantly impaired the creature and had discovered that with the correct equipment the slug creature could be destroyed easily. He admitted that the possibility existed that such a creature might either grow there again or return from another location, but assured her that his team would be able to defeat it more quickly this time, before market revenue was significantly impacted.

"Can't anyone see here that I am trying to run a Dominion? When you are through with your trifle you may take your leave so that I might return to more pressing matters," she replied to his lengthy discourse without glancing up from the document before her.

"Respectfully, my good Lady. You had tasked me with this assignment in order that I might prove my worth to Raedelle as an Engineer and I completed it with the understanding that you would be open to a discussion on how a more profitable arrangement might be made for our Dominion with the use of my skillset," he replied, undaunted.

She set aside her quill and shot him a sharp glare. "Understanding, is it? Understanding perhaps that my brother – your Prince – lies ill in bed and that the fate of this Dominion lies fully upon my shoulders? If there is any understanding to be had, it is that one. You had best keep that in mind, because if you anger me further, Shorian, I will have you cast out from this very hall."

"I will certainly keep that in mind, Lady Caliburn. I hope truly that your brother returns quickly to full health and can relieve you of this heavy burden."

With that said, he pivoted about and snapped his halberd forward to make his way out of the Hold. When he was just about through the archway back to the Mirrorholds, a heavy hand landed upon his shoulder and halted him in his tracks.

"Hold on there, brother," came a heavy voice as the hand pulled him about.

Before him, and a half-foot shorter, stood a Companion, donning the fine lion lizard leather armor of his order. Thick and unruly brown hair framed rugged Raedellean features that were further accentuated by the man's rough stubble of a beard. His lips curled up in a broad smile he slapped Actaeon hard on the shoulder.

"Why don't look so surprised! Ya look like you've seen the dead, brother Actaeon, and ya would be if it weren't for your help. Don't tell me you've forgotten your good friend Caider already," said the man as his smile broadened.

Recognition dawned on the Engineer and he grinned in response, though not going so far as to return the slap on the man's shoulder. "Ah, Companion Caider. It is truly good to see you on your feet and not leaking vital fluids everywhere this time. How are you feeling?" he had replied.

"I'm back to full speed about. The Altheans told me to stay off my feet for the time being, but who'd listen to those busybodies anyway? I feel great, thanks to your help. Obviously I won't yet return to full service immediately, but I'm up and about and swinging a sword again – so it's just a matter of time. How 'bout yourself? I hear the rumors abound you know, people are saying that you rid the markets of an enormous acid-spitting creature of the foulest order in a tremendous battle. Tell me what happened, brother."

"The foulest odor is more accurate. And it wasn't correctly a battle – certainly a confrontation, but there was no fighting in the common sense of the word."

"Bah, nonsense! I listen enough to know an Arbiter died in the conflict. And rumor has it one of your team had his eye ripped out its socket. If that ain't a battle, then I ain't been in a battle – and the Ancients know that I've been in plenty. Quit being so humble. You're a hero now. Not to mention you saved my ass too, which counts doubly."

"A hero takes great risks and will stand fast even in the face of great danger," said Actaeon. "I mitigate risk and plan preventative steps for any dangers that might arise. I am no hero, Companion Caider, I am simply an Engineer. The true hero of that day was my man-at-arms Trench – his quick actions saved us."

"If ya say so... hero. Anyways, you can call me Caider. I'll just call you Act to save time."

"Alright, Caider. So what happened to you out there on the Avenue of Glass the other day?"

"A fair question. I'm not supposed to tell much about it, but for you I'll speak of it a bit. There were some tribal incursions deep into the Wall recently and I was sent there by the Prince himself on a deep cover mission to track some of them. To make a long story short, things turned bad. They discovered my position and I was flushed out and had to make a run for it. Some of the tribals – they have trained beasts, similar to our... well, nevermind.

"But one of the beasts they had with them was able to flank me and raked its claws across my belly. Luckily I was wearing my leathers or else I'd have been disemboweled. I was able to lop its head off as I ran and I returned as swiftly as possible to the Pyramid to report to my Prince of what I had found. I had started along through Adhikara under guise because I had been on the northern Wall. By the time I realized I was bleeding so badly, I was too far along to not continue to Pyramid."

The story hadn't made sense to Actaeon. Adhikara was a large country to pass through with such a wound. The Ajmani also would not have let a traveler bleed to death on its roads; it was uncharacteristic of them. Perhaps the Companion had worried about attention or interrogation. Whatever his mission might have been may have been comprimised at that, but it still did not seem worth the risk of dying enroute to Pyramid.

He had learned long ago though that while questioning and searching for the truth was paramount in his life, certain truths only revealed themselves when approached indirectly. Still, the man had wanted to express friendship, and, in this place, one could use all the allies they could get. He would just have to be cautious around this odd new acquaintance.

They ended up talking at length about a variety of things, including the state of affairs in Raedelle and Redemption entire, the plans for Actaeon's workshop, and their explorations in the ruins around Pyramid. Caider made him promise to bring him along on one of his excursions into the Boneyards in the future and they had left it at that.

In the end, although disappointed in Eshelle's failure to compensate him for his work, Actaeon ended up using the coin he'd made from the sale of his home and metal-casting business in Shore to cover the down payment for the construction of his workshop.

It was as the vault was being raised that they showed up. Actaeon was onsite supervising the efforts closely to make sure that all of the small details were lining up correctly. He was up on the scaffolding where he had the best vantage point. Distracted as he was, he didn't notice the strange delegation that marched into the Outskirts purposefully.

Wave did notice them, however, and made his way over to the stack of stones in front of the workshop so that he would be between the delegation and his employer. Once there, he made to casually lean against the pile and missed, nearly falling. He quickly recovered and, feigning nonchalance, he leaned more carefully against the pile and lit a linreed stick as he watched them approach.

That the delegation was an Ajmani one was immediately obvious. A bannerman led the way, hefting high the golden starfield on its crimson red background. To his sides marched several soldiers and behind that three more, all surrounding a royal delegate garbed richly in extravagantly bright colors typical amongst Ajmani. Wave couldn't help but to smirk at the brightly striped red and gold pantaloons of the soldiers. "Careful now, you don't want to rip your pretty pants. This is a construction site after all," he said before taking a long drag of smoke from the linreed stick.

Patently ignoring the mercenary's comment, the delegate shoved his way forward and marched right up to Wave. "I am Portent Gaemri Ip Monjata of his Greatness, Raj Fenrik Mujarba, himself. I will see Master Actaeon Rellios of Shore, Engineer of Repute, at once," he demanded, standing stubbornly before Wave while he waited. The Portent was a small but dignified man, dressed in pantaloons that threatened to swallow him up. His hair was slicked forward with a slick oil to form a lavish pompadour.

"Not if you don't look up you won't. Master Rellios is up on the roof. Finishing the vault, you see," replied the man-at-arms with a gesture back towards the workshop in progress. "If you wish, I could potentially fetch him for you, if he's not too busy."

The Raj' Portent narrowed his eyes upon Wave before flipping the man a coin.

Wave narrowed his lone eye at the man in return, reaching out to catch the coin which fell to the ground just short of his hand. Letting the coin lie where it fell, he smirked and turned to the workshop.

"Oh Master Rellios!" Wave hollered. "There's someone Portent here to see you!"

The Portent scowled momentarily, but wiped the expression from his face as Actaeon approached with Trench behind him. The giant winced – still in pain from his burns – and eyed the Ajmani soldiers suspiciously.

"I am Actaeon Rellios of Shore. How may I help you, gentlemen?" asked the Engineer as he brushed dust from his jacket.

The delegate sketched a graceful bow in reply before speaking, "As I informed your monoculared associate, I am Portent Gaemri Ip Monjata of his Greatness, Raj Fenrik Mujarba, himself. I come bearing great words, straight from the great lips of our most beloved of Raj." That said, he drew silent, head bowed, perhaps waiting for a response.

Actaeon glanced back at Wave, who merely shrugged, before he grinned and spoke, "I would gladly hear these great words you speak of as soon as you would be so kind as to speak them."

That said, Portent Gaemri Ip Monjata cleared his throat loudly and took a knee on the dusty ground of the Outskirts. He cracked his knuckles and held out his hand, into which one of the soldiers placed an elaborate scrollcase. Methodically unscrewing the end, he then let the scroll slide into his free hand while the soldiers retrieved the case and endcap. In a practiced motion, he unrolled the crisp parchment of the scroll and began to read in a booming oratory tone that echoed off the surrounding structures and caused many passersby to stop and watch.

"All pay heed to the words of the Great Raj Fenrik Mujarba. It is with great happiness that the Raj addresses the heroic deed of one Engineer Actaeon Rellios, Master of his trade and a boon to the people of Redemption. With his actions in the defeat of the most malign creature that lurked beneath the depths of the marketplace, he has effectively restored commerce to the people of Redemption and most of all to the One True Dominion: Ajman.

"Commerce is the lifeblood of a civilized people, as all know. Commerce feeds the people, clothes the people and shelters the people of the One

True Dominion. Thus, the Ajman Dominion finds itself in debt to Master Rellios in this matter and as is appropriate fully intends to pay its debts.

One of the soldiers stepped forward then and placed a small chest on the ground beside the Portent.

"In accordance with our intent, the Great Raj himself asks that Master Actaeon Rellios accept this token of gratitude and friendship and employ it to continue his work."

As if on cue, the soldier opened the chest to reveal the silver coins within, filling it to the brim.

It was enough to cover the remainder of the construction costs and then some.

"How would you gentlemen like to work with me on a more permanent basis?" asked Actaeon of the two mercenaries as they stood watching the Ajman delegation retreat back towards the Pyramid. He nudged the chest with the toe of his boot, several coins falling to the earth.

"Aye, so long as the pay is always this good of course," said Trench, his ugly grin tugging at his deep scar.

"Not as though I really have a choice in the matter anyway. Ya still owe me a new eye after all," Wave jested, arching a brow awkwardly over his remaining eye.

"Sounds like you've got yerself some faithful associates, Master Rellios," said Trench, slapping the Engineer on the back. "And you'll save money cause monoculared associates only get half the pay!" He roared with laughter and punched his friend in the arm.

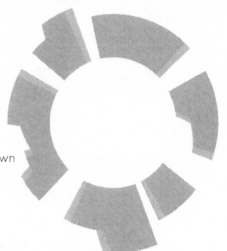

87 A.R., the 15th day of Monsoon's Dawn

THE WORK BEGINS

I N A RARE BREAK IN the rains during the ponderous monsoon season, four people picked their way throughout the rubble of the Boneyards.

"I know I pinpointed it this time," said Actaeon. "If I fail to find the mechanical man again, I will need to swear it off as an illusion." Three prior excursions into the Boneyards to find the artifact had been complete failures. He always ended up circling the area where he had seen it for much of the day with no sign of it. He scanned the broken landscape, picking out landmarks in the terrain to match them to the roughly sketched map in his hand.

Actaeon, Trench and Wave had decided to celebrate their good fortune and recovery from their wounds with an excursion into the Boneyards, a needed break from the constant demands of the workshop's construction. Eisandre had joined them, and Actaeon had also sent word to Caider, who hadn't responded.

"If anyone can spot a mechanical man while standing on top of the Pyramid, it would be you," declared Eisandre as she paused beside him to lean on the walking staff Actaeon had fashioned for her. "And if it's out there, we'll find it. Let's keep an eye on the weather, however. If it starts raining again, it would be best to find shelter and wait it out rather than try to navigate through this mess in a downpour."

Trench and Wave scouted ahead and to either side of them as they spoke, ribbing each other back and forth about missing eyes and slime and size and whatnot. Trench was still smarting from his burns, but the big man couldn't be kept off his feet for very long. The two mercenaries had kept busy with sparring every day, especially to help Wave learn to cope with his lost depth perception.

"Agreed. We do not need anyone to get hurt again. It was nice of you to join us out here today. We have both been busy of late," Actaeon said as he climbed up over one berm of debris. He offered her a hand, which she accepted to help pull herself up.

"You know it's my pleasure to accompany you whenever I can," Eisandre said with sincerity. "I enjoy some time away from the Pyramid and my duties there. It's good for me, I think." She tilted her head back to allow the light misting rain to fall upon her cheeks.

"Sometimes it is good to have a distraction," Actaeon agreed. "Though I am not one to speak on that topic. I rarely accept diversions from my work and even diversions frequently turn into whole projects."

"Ah, and I am notorious for using my free time to immerse myself in frivolous amusements, am I?" Eisandre smiled over at him in amusement.

"Aye. Always throwing decadent parties and succumbing to the vices of humanity. That is the Knight Arbiter Eisandre," said Actaeon with a grin.

"We'd better have some sort of shelter in sight and not let your men get too far away, in case this turns into a downpour," she said in seriousness.

He nodded and paused to point with the tip of his halberd towards a large rise in the distance. "I think if we attain the top of that hill of debris, we should then see it. We can keep an eye out for shelter nearby on the way."

"Find it, Actaeon?" called Wave from atop a shattered wall.

"Let us go ascend that pile of rubble over there." Actaeon gestured again with his halberd.

The one-eyed mercenary nodded. He reached it first and began to climb it easily, his rapier dangling about on his swordbelt as he climbed. When Actaeon and the others reached the pile, Trench looked up and shook his head.

"I'll stay down here to keep watch," said the big man. "Ya know what they say about size and falls. Give a shout if you need me."

"You got it, Trench," the Engineer said. "Stay out of trouble down here."

Actaeon started after Wave, searching for handholds on what he imagined could have been a much smaller version of Pyramid – if Pyramid were built from the collapsed remnant of an ancient building and other associated wreckage.

Eisandre followed, copying the Engineer's hand and footholds. About a quarter of the way up, her foot dislodged a small metal piece that fell and clattered noisily to the ground beside Trench.

"Sorry!" she called down to him sheepishly.

"That's alright, Lady Arbiter. It wouldn't hurt my pretty face too much in any case," Trench called up from below.

Halfway through the ascent the rain picked up and made their climb much more difficult – the handholds became slippery and runnels of water fell down onto their faces, partially obscuring their vision. When they reached the very top, the sky let loose on them with a vengeance.

Actaeon brushed the rain from his eyes and pulled his goggles down before handing his halberd to Wave. He removed the recurve from his back and brought the scope to his eye. "I think we have – "

A roar from below interrupted him. It echoed eerily and thunder erupted in the distance, masking any other sounds from below.

It was Trench.

"You should stay here," said Eisandre, drawing her broadsword.

"Hey Trench! You alright down there?" called Wave, his own rapier already in hand. The man-at-arms let the halberd fall to the ground and swung over the edge to start his descent.

"Wave, damn it! Wait for us, we stay together." The Engineer retrieved his halberd and strapped it to the back of his jacket. When he turned to Eisandre, his eyes held no room for debate. "My man is down there. I must go as well."

Actaeon strung his recurve and put an arrow to the string, using the scope to sweep the terrain below between bursts of rain. "Trench is gone."

The Engineer and Arbiter started down after Wave and by the time they caught up with him at the bottom, any sign of what had happened had been washed away in the deluge. The heavy rainfall severely impaired their visibility.

"Trench!" Eisandre cried.

"Trench, you ugly bastard! Sound off!" Wave yelled, though an even closer thunderclap drowned out most of his words. Mumbling a curse under his breath, he started off in a random direction.

"Hold it, Wave," said Actaeon. "We cannot see a thing in this rain. We need to wait for a sign from Trench lest we lose him or stumble into a trap ourselves."

"Why do you always have to make so much cursed sense?" Wave spat.

"This bodes poorly," Eisandre said. "There is little we can do to find him in this weather, and I fear we may very well be in danger ourselves."

A rush of footsteps from behind them made the three of them turn and bring their weapons to bear. The tip of Wave's flamberge blade found a man's neck and Eisandre's broadsword was brought to the same man's gut. Both had enough control over their thrusts to stay them the instant they realized the man wielded no weapon.

"Geodric Caider. A bit late, aren't you?" the Arbiter said.

"Caider? Is he out here trying to get hurt again?" Actaeon asked with a grin.

"I heard a scream from out here and came to investigate," said Caider, rain-soaked and startled. He pushed Wave's rapier away from his neck. "I got your message, Act – I was coming to meet you all. It is dangerous out in this weather. What are you all doing?"

"Draw your blade, Companion," Eisandre ordered, respectfully. "One of Master Rellios' men is missing and may have been assaulted."

Actaeon had a sudden thought. "Did you happen to bring your whistle, Eisandre? If you blow it, Trench might be able to hear us over the racket of this rain and thunder."

Eisandre reached inside her tunic and withdrew the Arbiter whistle that dangled from her neck with a leather lanyard. She paused then, considering. "He won't be able to reply if he's captured, even if he hears us. And if he were free to return, he surely would have done so already, don't you think?"

"She's right, Act. Blowing that whistle might just bring attackers down upon us. I wouldn't do it," seconded Caider.

"Oh, come on! Who in cracked Redemption would take that big lug anywhere? You'd need a damned oxcart to carry him off. No, he's gone off after someone," said Wave.

From ahead of them came a yell and a crash, followed several lifebeats later by a regular banging of metal on metal.

Wave started off in that direction at a run. The others followed close behind.

"That may not be your man," Caider called out as they ran through the heavy downpour.

"It is him. Hear the pattern of bangs? We decided upon it beforehand in case we should be separated," Actaeon shouted in reply.

The giant came into view through the curtain of rain. Fresh blood dripped from the face of his hideous maul. The party came to a halt and he stepped away from the metal plate he was striking and turned to face them. Before him lay two bodies. One's face was unrecognizable, with an indent shaped like Trench's maul. The other had a gaping red smile across his throat.

Both the bodies were those of cross-faced raiders, with their boiled leather armor. The black crosses dividing their faces looked like targets, one of them struck dead center by Trench's maul.

Wave marched up to his friend and struck him solidly in the chest, yielding no reaction from the giant. "By the Fallen, what're you doing out here? We were looking for you."

"I had to sneak up to them," replied Trench, shaking his head. "They were up to something, sneaking around out here. I tried to take the second one alive, but he took his own life."

They all stood in silence in the heavy rain as it splattering down on the messy scene, washing the blood away.

"There's a lot of noise been made," Caider said, breaking the silence. "Let's get outta here. We can discuss your accomplishments here over a mug of mead in St. Torin's." The Companion looked impressed with the big mercenary.

"I second Caider's advice," said Eisandre.

"There are more about," said Trench. "They were trying to cover this up somehow. I caught one as he dragged his buddy away, but he slit his own throat – like they don't want any evidence left behind of their being here. I bet the one I killed back near the pile's gone too?"

"Aye. 'Tis." said Wave.

"Then let's leave before they return to cover this up as well," said Trench.

Actaeon knelt down to rummage through the dead men's clothing, looking for anything that would provide him with clues as to their goal. Once again, he turned up nothing.

"Agreed, let us get away from this place," said the Engineer, standing.

"Luckily none of us has been harmed." He led the way from the bloody scene and the others followed closely with weapons ready.

Trench stopped in front of Actaeon on their way back to the workshop. It was just the three of them now – they had left off the Arbiter and Companion back at the Pyramid. The big man folded his arms squarely and glared at the Engineer.

"Alright Act, what haven't you been letting us in on? What are these guys looking for from you that they're willing to spill their own lifeblood over?" asked the giant bluntly.

Actaeon drew to a stop and leaned upon his halberd. "The first time I was out around Pyramid when I was much younger, I made the mistake of speaking more openly about my trade to try and find work. I thought that if I had simply gotten the word out about my capabilities and what I could do, that people would seek me out. Alas, that was only half true. People sought me out, but they were not the sort of people I was hoping for. Most people had junk artifacts they had found in the ruins and they wanted me to make them function again. They all expected me to unlock some artifact that would win them riches, or give them an upper hand in battle or at court. Many did not take kindly when I explained to them that it was unlikely that such a result would be obtained. You have heard me say by now that every artifact, material, mechanism or lifeform has a certain potential to it. However, that potential can only be unleashed when the right circumstances of mental exertion, opportunity and probability arise. In other words, someone needs to come to the realization that the artifact, material, mechanism, or lifeform I mentioned can be used in conjunction with other artifacts, materials, mechanisms, or lifeforms in a specific way in order to achieve some task, that task first being realized through the identification of a problem or need – "

"By the Fallen, Master Rellios, please get to the point," said Wave, rolling his eye at the Engineer's typical verbosity.

"Of course. So as I was saying, the wrong sort of people started to find me – the sort of people you want to keep your distance from. They heard I had a reputation for mechanisms and artifacts. One such unsavory man by the name of Markor had me escorted to the Warrens one day to meet him.

It was not a friendly escort. I was stripped of my weapons and supplies, and they were not returned to me even afterward.

"Markor, who claimed to be a secretive member of the Loresworn, said that he wanted me to help him unlock the secret of a certain artifact he possessed. He showed me the artifact, some sort of cylindrical device with rounded ends and lighted symbols upon its body. It reacted to a man's touch – similar symbols to the ones we see all over the structures and technology of old Redemption. When I questioned him about it, he told me that he believed the artifact could make disappear a group of people of his choosing. When I asked him about how he could know such a thing, his answers were vague.

"I examined the device a bit – visually of course. I didn't want to risk activating it if it really did what the man had described. I told him that I needed to do some research and think on it some more. After I had left, I reported the incident to the Arbiters but they were unable to find the man I had described. I was never contacted again by Markor and I have no idea if the event is in any way associated with the cross-faced raiders. There is only the correlation that my encounters with them began shortly after that and have continued ever since. Correlation does not infer causation, so we must be careful drawing such conclusions – though there is a high probability of association there. It is the second biggest mistake I have made – catching those men's attention," said Actaeon with a frown.

"So what's the first biggest mistake then, and who's gonna attack us for that?" asked Wave, throwing his hands up into the air.

"That is not a story I care to relate just now. Perhaps I will tell you some time in the future, over a considerable amount of ale," said Actaeon.

"That's enough, Wave. He's answered my question. Let's go," said Trench, and they continued onward.

Lord Enrion Zar was waiting for them with a small delegation of Shieldians when they returned to the workshop. One held an umbrella over their master, shielding him from a lull in the endless rain that came with start of the monsoon season.

"Master Rellios! I am glad that I did not miss you. Do you have a moment to speak?" asked the Lord.

"Of course, Lord Zar," said Actaeon with a polite dip of his head. "Let us proceed inside – the vault is nearly complete. It will offer us some shelter from this weather."

Wave unlocked the door and pushed it open. The inside of the workshop was dusty and incomplete, but with the vault nearly finished, only some scaffolding remained inside. Much of it had been dismantled and stacked against the walls for use later in the construction of a large loft and workbenches.

"I apologize for the chaos you see here, gentlemen. The workshop is still in progress, although it is proceeding along swiftly," said Actaeon. He dusted off a bench with the sleeve of his jacket and dragged it over, motioning for the Shieldian to sit.

The Lord stared at the bench with no mild revulsion, his youthful features twisting in disgust. "Ahhh... no, that is quite alright. I prefer to stand." he said, composing himself. He cleared his throat. "Actaeon Rellios, Master Engineer from Shore, I am here personally to congratulate you on behalf of my father, Indros Immerai Zar and the entirety of the Shield Dominion for your defeat of the gigantic slug creature that harrowed the marketplace."

The Lord winced and shook the Engineer's hand before he continued, "Allow me to present you with a small token of our appreciation for what you've done." Enrion drew a large pouch from his belt and held it out for Actaeon, shaking it to emphasize the weight of the currency within. "That should help you to complete the construction of this workshop and leave you with some more to spare for your other endeavors," he said as Actaeon accepted the pouch.

"You have my thanks, Lord Zar. This will go a long way toward helping us with our research and construction efforts," said Actaeon, surprised at the gesture. He bowed his head low.

"No, Master Rellios, you have *our* thanks. Now, I do have one more item to discuss with you. I'm sure you won't mind."

"Of course not, Lord Zar. What do you wish to discuss?" The Engineer leaned heavily on his halberd, regarding the young lord with interest tempered by caution.

"My father has assigned me a very important task," began Enrion. "As you might have heard, Shield has invested some considerable resources into the region between Rust and Amphis' Ledge. That region is called Lazi's Tomb."

"After the Shieldian hero Matenko Lazi, who fell to his death while returning to Rust along one of the great bridges, if I am not mistaken," Actaeon interjected.

"That's right," Enrion said, with surprise. "But more importantly, my father has invested in Lazi's Tomb to provide Shield with a better source of food that it would not need to trade for. The land there has been found to be fertile, but it is difficult to reach from either Rust or Amphis' Ledge and passing through the Czerynian Dominion with any regularity is hardly an option. We have had great success there with the establishment of small farming communities and there is interest in continuing to expand Lazi's Tomb. However, the region has been subject to – mostly because of its recent prosperity in matters of sustenance – increased incursions from Ruinic tribals from the east."

"Of course," said the Engineer. "The Czerynians used to pass through that corridor to obtain fresh slaves for their slave markets. Now, without that keeping the tribal forces in check and the additional temptation of your farms, I am not surprised to hear that they are invading more aggressively."

"How did –? Nevermind. But this is where you come in, Master Rellios. Your skills will come in use for us with this situation. My father has tasked me with improving the defensibility of Lazi's Tomb, and with limited manpower in terms of stationed soldiery. The only way that can be done is to provide a means to delay the Ruinic tribals long enough for reinforcements from the Ledge and Rust to arrive to push back such an incursion."

The young lord held out his hand and one of his men placed a scroll into it, which he spread upon one of the freshly built workbenches. Upon it was an old sketch of the surveyed details of Lazi's Tomb, complete with ancient structures and debris.

"There are several choke points that might serve as defensible positions, but they are much too wide to use as they are, especially with the limited force I have available. I need some better ideas, Master Rellios," explained the Lord.

"I shall take a closer look at these surveys for you, Lord Zar. There is always something that can be done – there is just the matter of cost and implementation time of whatever it might be. Also, I will need some funding to send one of my representatives out to the location. These surveys are very rough and lacking in some essential details that will be required. The materials of the terrain and better details of the structures in the area will be of great help."

Enrion looked taken aback, perhaps over the question of funding after so much compensation was just given to the Engineer. But he set his shoulders and smiled. "You will have what you need, Actaeon. When will I be hearing from you?"

"Give me the week, Lord Zar. I will have some better ideas and will prepare an excursion for a detailed survey of Lazi's Tomb," said Actaeon.

"Very well then. We shall let you to your work now. I look forward to our partnership in this."

That said, the Shieldians made their way out. The lead soldier held out the umbrella at the entrance of the workshop to keep the rain from Enrion's head.

Actaeon spent the next morning in the workshop poring over the surveys of Lazi's Tomb. On a parchment beside him he copied the survey and wrote careful instructions about what to look for in each area. He decided that Wave would be ideal for the expedition. Trench would draw too much attention. Hopefully the mercenary would be in agreement.

The construction continued while he worked. The workshop was nearly complete. They had only to install the windows, finalize the roof, complete the outside mortar work and build the remainder of the loft. He glanced about the cavernous space and grinned to himself. For many years he had wanted such a facility to support all his endeavors.

Interest in his services had spiked after word spread of how the marketplace stench was resolved. Some he had to turn away of course – the usual requests to fix a damaged artifact or more menial tasks that failed to capture his interest. One intriguing request came from Kylor sof Haringar, one of the Knight Arbiters that had been present when they brought Allyk's body back to the Pyramid. A serious man with dark skin and red irises, he had arrived and immediately cut to the point of his visit – the baths in Pyramid had ceased to function correctly. They had become exceedingly hot on several occasions throughout the day and had resulted in severe scalds for several Lords and Ladies that frequented them.

The Arbiter's request was a fascinating one. He would be able to investigate the inner workings of Pyramid, as the baths were an artifact of ancient Redemption that nobody understood. The nobility that used them took their operation for granted, but Actaeon was fascinated by them. Somehow the bath water was heated, cleaned itself, and never needed to be filled. The mechanism was unclear, though with people lingering in the baths, there was no opportunity to study it – until now.

Kylor had identified a pattern with the malfunction and reported it to his Order. The Arbiters closed the baths when the water would get too hot and had thus far prevented further injury, but were fearful that the problem would get worse. So they sent the Knight Arbiter with the strange eyes to Actaeon, for further help in the matter.

"A pattern like this certainly suggests a systemic, self-correcting flaw, and you were right to close the baths at those hours," Actaeon said approvingly. He was already impressed with the Arbiter. "However, until we know the cause, we cannot predict whether the periods of intense heat will increase in duration or shift in time. We must implement a method of continuous monitoring to make sure that the situation does not deteriorate and harm someone else," he explained.

Together with Trench and Kylor, Actaeon created several heat measurement devices. They consisted of two long strips of aluminum and copper each, hammered together and riveted at the ends. The resulting joined strip was then clamped lengthwise perpendicularly along a block of wood with a thin rope at the end.

When the devices were finished, he gave explicit instruction to Kylor. "Dangle these in the water of each of the major bath compartments, and the beam will bend toward the copper side. The farther it bends, the hotter it will be. You can put a cut into the wood with a blade to mark the normal temperature and another to mark the scalding temperature. These will have to be monitored by the bath workers constantly. Right now it sounds as if the system has reached a sort of equilibrium based on the details of your report. If it changes again though, these will be the first to detect it, and the baths must be vacated immediately."

He told the Arbiter that he would come soon to investigate the problem directly. Kylor nodded and departed wordlessly after handing the Engineer a folded piece of vellum that had written upon it:

> *Would you by any chance be able to meet me at*
> *the Blacksands Beach later today?*
>
> *-E*

"Quite the verbose fellow there, eh boss?" said Wave of Kylor.

"Now, now, Wave. Not everyone can have the gift of longwindedness that Master Rellios has. No need to insult them," said Trench, as he pulled off his heavy gloves and placed them on a workbench beside the smith's hammer he had used for the riveting.

Actaeon grinned at the two men. "I have nothing to say to that." He was about to put the note in his pocket when Wave snatched it out of his hand and unfolded it.

"A private meeting? How risqué for our calculating Engineer. Will you meet the lady, Act? And with no chaperone?"

The giant laughed and took the note from his friend to hand it back to Actaeon. "I hope yer not offering, Wave. I doubt they want a little one-eyed monster following them around. There'll be enough trouble keeping in line the one that's there, methinks."

The mercenaries doubled over in laughter.

Actaeon grinned and changed the subject. "While you are on the topic of chaperones, Wave, there is something I could use your help with. A different sort of charge, but one I think you can handle."

He explained his plan to survey the region of Lazi's Tomb. After a bit of dissent over the two mercenaries separating, he convinced them that he would need one of them to help him with projects. Wave would have a Shieldian escort the entire time he was surveying. It was decided that the smaller mercenary would depart for Lazi's Tomb in several days' time.

OF SMILES & WHISTLES

L ATER THAT DAY, DURING AN unexpected break in the rains, Actaeon made the long trudge down to Blacksands Beach and found Eisandre where she stood on the black, glittering sand gazing out over the azure sea. Alone she waited, heavy waves crashing upon the shore before her.

Actaeon smiled to himself when he spotted her and took in the scene: the wet black sand sparkled as a few stray rays of sun found their way through the clouds. Eisandre stood with her back to him, her short, blond hair glowing in a ray of sunlight. The sight of her there moved him – this person, who had become his friend so quickly and effortlessly.

"You must tell me how you have found a method to predict the weather," Actaeon said, coming to a halt at her side. "What a fine day to give us a break from the dampness of the rains." He offered her a bright smile and handed her the note he had written in reply to her own.

She read the words and stared at the note for a time, confused:

Sure, and here I am.

-Act

"It is good to see you again, Eisandre. It has been awhile since we have had time to ourselves," he said, scratching his right forearm through the thick material of his jacket.

"It's good to see you as well, Actaeon. I'm glad that you wanted to come. You look well. How do you feel? How goes your work?" she said with a smile.

He nudged her playfully with his shoulder. "You must speak in jest. Of course I wanted to come. I have missed you. Instead I have had to suffer the constant bickering of my two assistants. Most certainly a downgrade from your own company. As for your other inquiry, things are going well for certain. I have found much challenging work after recent events and it keeps my mind occupied. So, is there something that you have asked me out here for specifically or did you simply miss my interminable speculations?"

The Arbiter Knight considered his question seriously before she spoke. "I have taken a vow of honesty, Actaeon. So I am obligated to inform you that I have indeed missed what you call your 'interminable speculations'. I had not realized that you were so busy with your work at present, but I'm glad to hear it. There's another, more official reason why I wished to speak with you. I have been authorized to commission your talents for a project for the Order. But knowing you as I do, I do not think you will find it interesting. I would ask that you feel no obligation to accept work that does not please you or if you have insufficient time, simply due to our friendship."

"Often I am able to find interest in things that seem otherwise dull. So you should certainly run it by me," said the Engineer. "And although I took no vow of honesty, I feel compelled to admit that I might be coerced into taking even the dullest of jobs. Especially one from a good friend."

Actaeon lowered himself down to sit upon the sand. Two birds wheeled overhead and squawked at one another as they fought over some washed up piece of debris. Eisandre sat down beside him and offered him a simple reed whistle.

"You know these are what Arbiters use to transmit messages to each other while in the Pyramid and to summon assistance when required. My superiors feel that it might be possible to upgrade this model to something more durable and efficient, perhaps in metal and with a sound that can be heard from farther away. What do you think?"

The Engineer accepted the whistle and turned it over in his hands to analyze the minute details of it. He raised the device to his lips and blew into it, which made a fine reedy tone that, although being quite loud, was quickly washed away in the pounding of the surf. Next, he lifted the whistle to his eye and looked though its opening to observe the whistle's interior.

"We shall need to displace a larger volume of air, more quickly than this whistle can provide to accomplish this. And this exit port will likely have to be narrower. The problem with metal is that when two unconnected edges touch, they tend to rust, so we would have to figure out a way to avoid that. You can see that if you travel to Rust in Shield Dominion or by dipping any metal device in seawater. Any interfacing edges will react to form rust. That can be dealt with by either making the new whistle from a single piece of metal, or by using a metal and a second, disparate material. There is a metal extrusion technique I use that is quite similar to my sand casting technique. I have never attempted to extrude a hollow cylinder of metal, but perhaps this is just the reason to undertake the challenge. There are a few ideas I have..." he trailed off then, his mind spinning thoughts and ideas. "Yes. I think I can do it. Though the new device will likely be larger than the old. I know not how much larger yet, but I should be able to tell you soon. I may even be able to make it emit several different sounds so that the tones can carry different meanings for your Order. I should be able to do something for you and learn something about acoustic principles. Which is, of course, the major benefit for myself. Sure, I can do it for you," he decided.

"You didn't even ask what we would offer in turn," said Eisandre. "In any case, we would pay you fairly for your time. The Order is not renowned for its wealth, primarily because we have none, but we'll be able to provide whatever materials you require, plus an Arbiter guard while you are working. Also, some coin, or its equivalent in usable materials, should you find that acceptable. We've been using this kind of whistle for over eighty years now, so there will be no deadline so long as you make progress. I imagine you'll come up with a prototype first, and then, once we test and approve the model, we'll need about two hundred of them, in total." She paused and chuckled. "I'm starting to sound a bit like you, going on like that, only in Arbiter terms. Thank you, Actaeon. I thought I was offering you boring work, and you make it sound like the most fun you've had in weeks."

"Well, it sounds like no one will get hurt and unwanted political attention will not be drawn to this project. Truly, I cannot say the same for some of the other various tasks I am currently pursuing. And also, I must say that I could use a project where I can spend some time perfecting a design instead of rushing to a completion. As far as payment goes, it is not so much a concern. If I am paid inadequately, then the project will fail, so no point in worrying over it. If you can supply for me a few of your whistles so that I might compare directly with any new designs, then that would help greatly. And since you mentioned the Arbiter guard that the Order can provide, can I request a specific person for the project?" he asked with a broad smile.

"You can certainly request to have a particular Arbiter assigned as your guard. My superiors will decide whether to fulfill your request." The Arbiter glanced at him suddenly, her blue eyes sparkling. "You know, people might start getting the outrageous impression that I have a social life."

"Well, we cannot have that, can we? Let them know that I would request the Knight Arbiter Eisandre as my guard for the project. She will also prove an invaluable evaluator for the whistles. It helps to have the opinion of an experienced person that will be using these. You may let them know that socialization will be strictly prohibited and that only discussions pertaining to the technical aspects of our shared endeavour shall be permitted," Actaeon said with a wink.

"I didn't say there was anything wrong with having a social life," Eisandre pointed out.

As they spoke, clouds gathered in a dark patch over the water where rain fell in great grey streaks in the distance, moving closer to the shore as the wind blew. All at once, the sky was a light orange and stormy grey, golden rays of sunshine punching through clouds to scatter their light upon the shimmering obsidian sand of the beach. An isolated droplet of rain struck Actaeon upon his cheek.

"I suppose all good things must come to an end – and just as I was beginning to feel like the future ahead might not contain more sogginess." With his halberd, Actaeon levered himself to his feet and reached down to offer the Arbiter a hand that she accepted to pull herself to her feet. "There are some rocky outcroppings back along the beach that we can shelter under. I think we shall not outrun this downpour."

"It may be peaceful to watch the rain over the sea from a dry place, but we'd best make haste," she said.

They jogged along the beach together as large droplets of rain began to fall around them. Actaeon led the way toward a massive stone formation with a large opening that faced the sea. It was difficult to discern whether it was natural or some strange structure of the Ancients.

The wall of rain blew in to envelop them and the sound of millions of raindrops striking the surf could be heard even over the crashing of the waves. They hastened to a sprint to escape the downpour. The Arbiter outpaced the Engineer upon the sands of the beach.

When they reached the structure, Eisandre vaulted up onto the ledge of the opening and offered Actaeon a hand, which he accepted, tossing his halberd in before he hauled himself up after her.

"Still exactly as I remember it," Actaeon said. "This will keep us dry."

They moved deeper under the overhang just as the heaviest of the rain was upon them.

The ledge angled back from the opening into an almost cavernous room that was sheltered by a rocky outcropping that jutted from the back wall of the formation. A smooth wall at the back created a large arc that conveniently blocked the wind which had just arrived, howling. From inside they had a clear view of a large section of beach and the crashing waves beyond.

Actaeon leaned his halberd against the wall and removed his jacket before sitting with his back against the smoothed-out arc. Eisandre removed her swordbelt and placed it beside his jacket before she joined him.

"This seems perfect," she said after she had a moment to look around. "I even have crispfruit." She tossed one of the shiny, fist-sized, green fruits his way, which caught him in surprise. The Engineer snatched it from the air before it hit the ground. He laughed and took a bite from it.

"You always look so happy, you know. Why is that?" asked the Arbiter, with gentle curiosity in her gaze.

Actaeon considered as he chewed. "If life cannot be enjoyed and humor cannot be found in even the darkest places, then I wonder what the purpose of living really is. Of course, the search for truth of our world is something that drives me, but, even so, if I cannot enjoy the life that I am living then it is not worth the different hardships and challenges that one needs to face on a daily basis. The majority of human suffering is brought upon us by those who are not happy with what they have – sometimes even brought upon our own selves in that manner. I have been lucky in my life, though I have faced hardship and suffered at times. No matter how bad things get, I must only close my eyes to see how much worse it could really be. Things I have seen out in the ruins... Well, there is evil in this world, and, as long as I keep a smile upon my face, it will never have the better of me." He laughed then and watched the rain's relentless assault upon the beach.

"For the most part, I enjoy my life," Eisandre said, following his gaze. "I believe in my purpose and my duties and I work with upstanding individuals who feel the same way. But I don't smile as much as you do, that's for sure. Except perhaps, when I'm around you." She smiled at him. "Then it seems like I'm smiling every other moment, simply because you are. I like that. It feels good, actually. Your explanation does make sense in its way, Actaeon."

"Well there is no need to smile outwardly – just be sure you are smiling on the inside." Actaeon met her smile with a grin and reached out to touch her hand. "I am glad that I make you smile. You are beautiful, you know, when you smile."

Eisandre said nothing in reply, but she took his hand in hers and squeezed it lightly. Actaeon glanced over and noticed that her cheeks had flushed red. He grinned and squeezed her hand in return.

Together, they turned to watch the pounding storm outside their little shelter. And there they remained in the peace and strength of their shared company while the remainder of the day's light faded. Oranges faded to reds and then purples before the colors fell from the sky completely, not to return until the morrow.

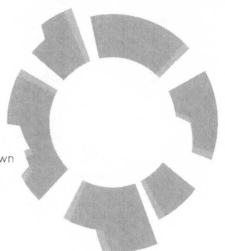

HEADS ABOVE WATER

HE FOLLOWING DAY ACTAEON VISITED Pyramid's baths.
Wave accompanied him, weighted down with equipment, including a heavy crossbow and a coil of rope wrapped around his body.

Actaeon gave him a skeptical look. "Are you expecting to scale the outside of the Pyramid during this trip?"

"You never know when you'll need a rope, Act. And this reeks of just such an occasion. You'll see."

The Engineer had sent Trench off to set some smaller versions of the slug traps that they had built in the tunnels of the marketplace. Nobody had reported any signs of a giant slug creature again, nor had the smell returned – in fact the drainage during the monsoons was reportedly better than ever. However, Actaeon wanted to obtain more of the slug's slime for future experimentation. He devised a series of experiments to further explore the explosive nature of the slug's slimy excretions, and it would require quite a bit of the material to perform the task – perhaps more than he had been able to gather after their battle with the monster.

The slime had the capacity to generate a tremendous explosive energy under the right conditions. Their battle with the slug had proven that much. The luminary had something to do with it – either a component of it or the energy that it contained. A series of controlled experiments would replicate the conditions that created the explosion, if he was correct. After that, he would need to design and manufacture a device to duplicate such conditions and harness the extreme power of the huge slug's excretions.

It was perhaps the most dangerous work he would undertake to date. There was tremendous risk in experimenting with such volatile substances. When he was a young lad, he had searched far and long for a chemical with such properties. During that search, he had discovered the blue fire, but in the process he had suffered tremendous consequences during one experiment gone awry. In his hometown of Incline, his family and friends began to distrust him, drawing distant, and worse yet, someone he had cared about very much had been badly hurt.

It would be different this time, he knew – he had learned the patience and discipline necessary to approach such tasks more safely. The botched experiment from his childhood would never leave the back of his mind though – it never did.

On top of that, there was another risk: the political one. Actaeon was keenly aware that if that particular invention ended up in the wrong hands it could upset the balance of power in Redemption. Projects like helping Lazi's Tomb create a defensible border was one thing, but supplying one Dominion with technology to wipe out the others on the battlefield was on a different level altogether. Part of the progression of his experiments with the slug slime, he thought, must be to determine how to neutralize any possible risk of such an occurrence. It was an atypical thought for him. Usually he sought to share his discoveries, but in this case he wasn't sure there was a safe way to do that.

"– and here we have taken the precautions that you recommended. It has served us well thus far. The forewarnings have prevented further injuries since we implemented them."

Kylor's words snapped the Engineer out of his reverie and he knelt down to examine the device that hung in the water of the many baths.

"You did well, Knight Arbiter Kylor. I wonder if the denizens of Pyramid have any idea how you have kept them safe in this place which they seem to take for granted. Have you noticed any variation in the rate of temperature change then?"

The Arbiter didn't respond immediately, simply staring at him through reflective goggles that hid his red irises. Actaeon found the man's gaze unnerving.

"Yes, Master Rellios," said the Arbiter, finally. "The rate of change has been increasing steadily since we began tracking it."

"That is an indicator that the system is an unstable one. The deviation from normal behavior that the baths have exhibited for almost an observable century is clearly a disruption in a previous longterm equilibrium. I would speculate that it has begun to malfunction. If the reason can be identified, perhaps we could restore the equilibrium."

"Don't ya think it'd be a good thing to keep the noble arses scorched, Act? We don't really want the lords and ladies getting too comfortable now do we?" said Wave with a smirk. He ignored a pointed look from the Arbiter.

"Aye, Wave, I cannot argue with a good scorching, but at this rate they will be cauterized shut and certain matter will flow from a more undesirable location," said Actaeon.

Wave laughed. "A common characteristic of the nobility already. Nobody'd even notice."

The Engineer approached the nearest wall and rested a palm on it before pressing his ear there to listen. "Knight Arbiter, do you know which rooms lie adjacent to this one along this wall? Judging by the layout of the baths and the sounds I can make out, I suspect that the supply is most probably coming from this direction."

The Arbiter offered him that same unnerving stare before replying. "The Sea Lounge is near that wall. Might it be tied to the baths somehow?"

They crossed the Skyspiral at the center of Pyramid along a series of helical staircases that always struck the Engineer as inefficient. Then they made their way down the western tunnel to the lounge. When they arrived there, they found a scene of chaos.

Patrons of the Sea Lounge had begun to pour out from the wide doorway into the gently descending curve of the western tunnel. They were all soaked and determined to exit the lounge – their shrieks of pain and terror emanating through the tunnel as they trampled each other to get out. A half dozen Arbiters were already there, trying to direct people to proceed in an orderly manner. Underfoot, a shallow stream of water emerged from the doorway and made its way down the curve of the tunnel.

Actaeon bent down to touch the stream and grimaced. "It is quite hot to the touch." A glance around showed him that some of the more soaked individuals' skin had turned red wherever it was exposed. "Many of these people have been scalded. You should summon the Altheans at once."

The shrill sound of Kylor's whistle brought a junior Arbiter to his side.

"Trello sof Allyk reporting, sir," said the young Arbiter, snapping a smart salute.

"Go and call on our Althean sisters. Tell them that many here have been scalded, and their skills are needed urgently." As Trello ran off to get the healers, Kylor marched up to two Arbiters that stood within the doorway and requested simply, "Report."

"The water began spraying from the ceiling. We have no idea why. You should not go in there. It isn't safe," said one of the Arbiters, cringing as he emptied steaming water from one of his boots.

Kylor turned his gaze, hidden behind the reflective goggles, upon Actaeon, and tilted his head forward in inquiry.

"We should look inside. It may reveal something important," the Engineer said.

"Master Rellios and his associate will investigate and make a determination. I will be accompanying them. Make sure to keep anyone else out," Kylor instructed the other Knight Arbiters before he motioned for Actaeon to lead the way inside.

The Sea Lounge was in exceptional disarray. Tables and chairs were overturned and food scattered across the floor. A steady spray of water fell from a thin crack in the ceiling behind the lounge's long, wooden bar. Several more patrons lingered within to watch the spectacle but were quickly dismissed by the Knight Arbiter.

The lounge got its name because beyond its three walls were large tanks of water with various swimming creatures, algae, and sea plants within. Whatever the purpose of it was, it seemed to be a self-sufficient habitat. Nobody tended to the creatures beyond the walls of the Sea Lounge. It had become a popular hangout for many of the nobility after the room had been turned into a restaurant. The floor and ceiling were solid elderstone. The pressure to crack such a material must have been tremendous.

The Engineer made his way quickly to the far side of the crack and pulled his goggles down to keep the errant spray from his eyes. It didn't take him long to notice the crack elongating as he watched. The volume of falling water increased with every moment, filling the room with a scalding hot mist that stung his cheeks.

"Collapse is imminent," Actaeon said. "We should evacuate at once and get everyone outside to move up the slope of the – "

As he spoke, a large section of ceiling came loose. It slammed into the bar below and sent splintered fragments of wood in all directions. A deluge of water followed and began to quickly fill up the tiny lounge.

Wave grabbed Actaeon's sleeve and ran with him toward the entrance. Water splashed at their heels and slowed their steps. With Kylor alongside them, they ran toward the entryway, as more sections of ceiling crashed down behind them. They rushed out through the door and to the right where the tunnel graded upward. Wave yanked Actaeon away from the door just in time, as a boiling hot torrent of water exploded from the entryway.

It struck several bystanders and swept them down along the tunnel. The woman closest to them opened her mouth to scream, but a blast of steam seared her throat shut and no sound came out. As one side of her face swelled and burst, Kylor tried to grab her. He was too late though, and the woman fell into the roiling stream to be swept away with the others. Wave and Actaeon pulled Kylor to the relative safety beside them before he would be washed away as well.

The people's screams could be heard even after they disappeared around the tunnel bend as the boiling river carried them to their deaths.

"This is most unfortunate," said Actaeon, at a loss for appropriate words. He watched with horror as the hapless victims of the boiling river were flushed down the tunnel. He'd never witnessed such a grisly scene before in his life.

"That's the understatement of the day!" Wave said, ducking under a blast of steam.

"Kylor, I think it is worth sending a runner to the baths. I believe you might find they have cooled significantly already," suggested the Engineer.

A runner was dispatched immediately on the Arbiter's order. Wave loosened his grip on Actaeon's sleeve and let loose a nervous laugh.

"Collapse is imminent! By the Fallen, Act. Next time can you just yell 'Get Out!' or something to that measure? I don't think that verbosity was the best option in this case."

"Just so, Wave."

"Look! The flow is slowing," Wave said, pointing to the doorway.

Sure enough, the torrent of burning water had slowed to a steady gush, then a stream and then just a trickle.

"Either the volume of water is spent or a safety closed. Let us take a look, gentlemen," said the Engineer. He entered the room, his heavy, black boots splashing as he led the way back into the Sea Lounge.

The creatures and their habitat beyond the walls appeared unchanged, but the Sea Lounge was a disaster. Shattered remnants of chairs and tables were upturned and pushed up against the walls. A section of ceiling that spanned nearly half the length of the bar had fallen down. The solid piece of wood that once served as the bartop was splintered and broken in several places while the intact section was warped severely from the hot water – the end actually bent several feet up into the air. The bar itself had been pushed out by the deluge so that it jutted at a severe angle into the room.

The Engineer made his way behind the bar and looked up, the mercenary and Arbiter behind him.

"Can you get us up there, Wave?"

"How in shattered Redemption d'ya want me to do that?"

Actaeon grinned and plucked at the length of rope that was wrapped around his friend's body.

"Oh... right. Well, the water – and death – was damned distracting. Give me a minute, will you?"

Wave pulled a grappler hook from his belt and tied it to the end of the rope. He set the coil atop the bar and tossed the hook up into the hole. It held on his fourth try, and he pulled the rope taut before he slung his crossbow over one shoulder and began to gingerly, but skillfully climb. When he made it up, he knotted the end of the rope and wedged it into the crack before sticking his face over the edge.

"Not a water goblin in sight. C'mon up!"

Actaeon went next, followed by Kylor. The Engineer pulled his luminary free once he gained his feet and adjusted the baffle to direct the light forward. As he cast the light about, the space they had ascended to became clear.

It was a long cylindrical corridor that, by his reckoning, ran towards the center of Pyramid. The floor had fallen out in one spot – the place where they had climbed through. One end of the corridor was a dead end, blocked by a pile of broken elderstone debris. The other end continued along straight and level beyond the reach of the luminary light.

They proceeded cautiously. With each step, Actaeon tested the floor and ceiling's stability with his halberd. He set Wave and Kylor to search for seams on the walls to the right and left while he searched at the floor and ceiling. They found nothing of interest along the length of the hallway. It was a solid piece of elderstone with the narrow passage carved through it.

It took them ten minutes to reach the end.

There they found a hollowed-out sphere. When they approached it, a large ring suddenly lit up, taking them all by surprise. Within the light ring, nine symbols could be seen, arranged about the circle. They were similar to symbols that one could find all throughout the ruins of Redemption – symbols which were commonly thought to be the language of the Ancients.

Actaeon reached out to touch them and all of the symbols lit up in a soothing blue color as his hand came near. He pulled his hand back and the colors faded away from the symbols.

"Fascinating. It recognizes our proximity. Thus, we can be certain that this is a location that was designed for a person to be within and interact with. I shall have to write down these symbols and study them further."

From his jacket, he withdrew a blank roll of vellum, a charcoal stick, and a measuring slide ruler. These he set down upon the curved floor and started sketching. Once he was done, he drew to his feet and stretched.

"Now let us try to see if we can figure this out," Actaeon said.

He reached out slowly and touched the topmost symbol, which changed its light from blue to green. He proceeded to touch the symbol to the right and it changed as well. When he had changed all of the symbols to green, nothing had happened. He touched the bottom one this time, and it turned purple. Another touch returned it to blue, then green, then purple again.

"It may be some sort of sequence. I will have to study this for some time."

"Hello?" The shout echoed down the corridor from where they had come.

"We'd best see what that is," said Kylor. "We can return another time."

When they arrived back at the Sea Lounge, they found that the runner had returned. The bathwater had indeed gone cold as predicted. In fact, it was ice cold.

The nobility was not happy.

After a long day of study and attempts to affect the sequence of symbols above the Sea Lounge, Actaeon and Wave headed back to the workshop. Despite trying many different combinations, colors, and even activating several or all symbols simultaneously, they had made no progress. A thorough search of the Sea Lounge and Pyramid's baths had also turned up no clues to the symbols at the end of the strange corridor.

Kylor posted a rotating guard at the entrance to the Sea Lounge. This wasn't a problem since the Arbiters monitoring the baths could now be relieved. Nobody was using the baths with the icy water.

There were rumblings about the state of the baths all throughout Pyramid as they made their way out and beyond to the Avenue of Glass. It was unbelievable, the Engineer thought, that they could be preoccupied with such a superficial concern after people had been swept away and boiled to death down the tunnel outside the Sea Lounge. There were even a few clusters speaking about it out on the Avenue, though Actaeon noticed that the tone had changed from one of complaint to one of cynical amusement. The nobles, he supposed, would soon smell like the common people they served.

"Are you prepared for your excursion in two days ?" Actaeon asked Wave.

"Absolutely. I think I'll enjoy it actually. I haven't been to Shield in quite a number of years. The young Lord sent word that an escort would meet me at the workshop just before sunrise, two days from now."

"Very well. Let me know whether there are any additional supplies you require."

"Yes, yes. But more importantly – you'll be joining us at the Monsoon Festival tomorrow evening – right?"

The mercenary arched the brow above his eyepatch as he awaited Actaeon's reply.

"It is an atypical diversion for me," said Actaeon. "Why? Do you suppose there is a reason to monitor the inside of Pyramid during that time?"

Wave laughed and slapped Actaeon's shoulder hard.

"Now now, Master Rellios, I shall teach you about having a fun time yet. The Monsoon Festival is a fine gathering. The noble ladies attend in force, and it would not do for you to miss them. A fine lady during monsoon season, now that's a delicious sight. All that time spent pent up indoors and sopping w–"

A commotion up ahead on the Avenue cut Wave off mid-sentence. A large crowd had gathered in a tightly packed circle. Several individuals could be heard shouting taunts over the general clamor.

As they grew closer they saw two men in the center of the crowd. One was a tall, older man with a hooked nose and ruffled, slick black hair. Clad in expensive blackened leather, from the gauntlets worn on his hands to the shiny boots upon his feet, he stood with burning hazel eyes and a vengeful grin as he glared at the other man.

The man across from him was younger by far, with pale skin and short blond hair. His hand was upon his face, which had reddened on one side, presumably from an earlier strike. He scowled at the man with the hooked nose and shouted over the crowd.

"Just as I supposed! The barbarians of Raedelle have no composure at court. You, sir, are no better than the tribal scum that threaten our very civilization. Have you come to the Pyramid to steal our food?"

The dark-haired man brushed his hair back and made a show of yawning. Actaeon recognized him as the Lord Gunther Arcady from his own homeland of Shore – the Overseer of the Conclave of Shore. It was strange to find him outside of Raedelle, thought the Engineer. The Lord was a staunch isolationist and had often voiced his public disapproval of the Prince's policies of interdominional relations.

Arcady pointed a leather-clad finger at the man. "Care to back up your words, young man? Or is that all they are – just words? I'm no swooning Lady from your fancy Niwian courts. You'll have to back up your words or I'll paddle you back to your nurse mother where you can be taught some manners."

The young man flinched at Arcady's finger but stepped forward despite that and smacked it out of the way.

"I am Lord Terchin vor Steubick, of the Sunken City Lords, Nephew of His Eminent Lordship Garizo Forthrakas. You will speak to me with the respect that I deserve!"

The smack to the other side of his face took the young Niwian off guard and brought him to his knees.

Wave drew to a halt to watch the event unfold.

Actaeon shook his head and scratched his right arm before he tugged on the mercenary's sleeve. "Let us go, Wave. This is no place for us."

The mercenary shook his head, sparing a glance at the Engineer with his single eye. "No, Act," he insisted. "I've gotta watch this. The proceedings must be done honorably."

The Engineer shrugged. "If you insist."

Terchin drew to his feet once more, his hand falling to the hilt of his rapier.

The Lord Arcady's voice carried clearly along the Avenue of Glass. "My poor child. We shall have to bring you back to your wet nurse after all. You've yet to learn that respect is earned, not inherited. And a hand on sword, too. You've many lessons to learn – are you sure that you want to start there?"

The Niwian Lord drew his sword and pointed it at Arcady, the tip of it shaking in his grip. "Gunther Arcady, Lord of Barbarians! I have suffered your insults long enough," he declared. "You are hereby challenged to a duel. If you refuse, then you shall lay your sword down upon this Avenue and return back to your prisoner-kin people. Though I plead with you – give me the satisfaction of turning the Avenue red today."

Wave smacked his forehead and muttered, "Idiot."

Arcady took a step back and let his hand rest upon the filigree basket hilt of his dueling sword. The smile he leveled upon the younger Lord was positively malevolent.

"I accept your challenge, boy. Is there an Arbiter present to oversee this duel?"

A young Arbiter that had arrived at the commotion shoved his way through the crowd and shouldered his way between the two men.

"I will oversee this duel. I'm Knight Arbiter Trello sof Allyk. The duel will proceed by the standard rules of the land. I'd ask the participants as to the limit of the competition."

"Blood," said Arcady.

"Death," countered Terchin.

A hushed silence drew over the crowd at the young Niwian's word, followed by a low murmur and a cry or two of anguish.

Wave glanced over at Actaeon, his face pale as he whispered in a hushed tone. "That dumb boy doesn't know who he's messing with."

Arcady threw his head back and laughed. "The outcome would be the same either way. I'm glad that you said that. I won't feel as bad now when I bleed you dry."

"Are both participants in agreement?" asked the Arbiter.

The Niwian Lord nodded eagerly, lifting his rapier into a high stance. Lord Arcady shrugged at the Arbiter and nodded as well, one hand still resting easily on the basket hilt of his undrawn sword.

"Then the matter will be settled as requested by the participants involved – to the death. The proceedings will commence."

The Arbiter motioned the crowd of onlookers back to a safe distance before he signaled for the participants to begin.

Actaeon glanced at Wave. "Why would the Arbiter condone this?"

"He's young. He could've invoked power of arbitration and forced them to fight to just blood. We're outside the Pyramid, however. It's allowed. Unfortunately."

The younger man had begun to circle the older, feinting thrusts occasionally with his rapier. Arcady seemed rather unimpressed, leaning to his left or right to avoid the feints – his sword still in its scabbard. He stepped back and started to yawn once more, enticing the young man to thrust his blade in towards his face. Arcady's blade was out in a barely visible flash. Terchin's blade spiraled loose from his hand to skitter along the elderglass off to his left. The Raedellean finished his yawn and gestured with the blade for the younger man to go retrieve his own.

Terchin turned to get his blade, but at the last moment spun about with his companion dagger drawn to slash beneath the older man's chin. The slash was easily parried and a firm kick sent the boy sliding away on his backside. The Niwian took a deep breath and collected his weapon before taking another stance with both rapier and dagger ready as he faced the Lord Arcady again.

The Niwian Lord stomped an appel before he erupted in a flurry of feints, lunges, and slashes with both sword and dagger. Each was parried easily by his Raedellean opponent, who backed away a step on each parrying action. The blur of blades came to a sudden stop however, as both Niwian sword and dagger were knocked to one side in a single parry and the forward momentum of the attacker brought the riposte of his opponent's blade up between his left ribs to puncture his chest wall.

Terchin staggered to the side but took another stance, with both sword and dagger poised to attack. He coughed once, turning the front of his white tunic red with the blood that was now filling his pierced lung. The Niwian staggered again and pointed the tip of his sword toward Arcady's throat.

The Lord of Shore batted the blade aside like a cat playing with a captive mouse and thrust quickly to the other side of his opponent's chest, bringing him to both his knees.

"No!" came a scream from the crowd and a much younger version of Terchin came running out to lunge at the Raedellean Lord with a dagger.

Arcady spun wide of the dagger and slashed downward, separating Terchin's younger brother's hand from his arm. Another kick sent the boy down onto his back to lie beside his kneeling brother. Terchin raised his sword and opened his mouth to say something, though nothing came out but more blood, pouring down his chest.

"The consequences to interfering in an authorized duel is death," said Arcady, stepping forward with a smile.

His downward slash would have disemboweled the younger vor Steubick, were it not blocked by Wave's quickly deployed blade.

"Leave the lad out of this. You've got yer duel here with this man, not the boy. Finish it!"

Wave glared at Arcady with his single eye, their blades locked together above them. He had leapt forward to block the killing blow faster than Actaeon could even realize. The Engineer blinked in surprise that his man was no longer beside him.

Gunther Arcady bit back another laugh and pushed Wave's blade away.

"You shouldn't be here, Gavid. Haven't you done enough to set back this realm?"

The next few slashes and thrusts were a blur to Actaeon, but even lacking an eye, Wave parried them all and did not lose a sliver of ground to the Lord Shore.

"This isn't about me," said Wave. "This lad isn't part of the duel. You'll let him go. It's enough he lost his sword hand."

Wave backed up and grabbed the collar of the young boy's tunic. The boy wept and clutched the bleeding stump where his hand used to be. The mercenary dragged the lad back to the circle of the crowd, his flamberge rapier still held high as he faced the Lord Arcady. When Wave exited the dueling circle, the Arbiter nodded in satisfaction that the man-at-arms left the area he had entered unbidden.

Terchin's eyes had begun to flutter as he continued to lose blood through his chest wounds, but the proud young lord actually drew to his feet one last time to face his opponent.

The Shorian Overseer's blade flashed forward and opened an efficient chasm along the Niwian's throat to empty him of the remainder of his lifeblood. Terchin collapsed like a rag doll to the Avenue of Glass. Behind Wave, his brother wailed at the sight.

After cleaning his dueling blade on the corpse of his opponent, the Lord Arcady smirked and started off. The crowd parted to let him through.

"Ironic that they always hold the Monsoon Festival in the Sun Chamber," Actaeon said, as he cast a glance up at the maze of winding staircases that comprised the Skyspiral above.

The Monsoon Festival was an annual celebration that was sponsored and organized by a different Dominion each year, as selected by the Altheans. It was largely used by that Dominion to put on displays of grandeur and skill that would prove their culture superior. This year Thyr had been chosen to direct the festivities and appropriately the Sun Chamber was bedecked in all sorts of representations of ships and the sea.

In the center of the vast chamber stood the centerpiece of the festival – a mock ship that had been constructed by the Thyrians over the several weeks prior. It was comprised of several tiered decks, with each one bearing a different purpose. The lower decks supported acrobats and other entertainers. On one side of the ship, two duelists were engaged in a slow battle with ornamental sabres. On the other side, two musicians each played a fiddle, switching to and fro in a musical bout.

Mid-tier decks held tables with some of the select chosen nobility and the topmost deck held a grand table with Pyramid's upper echelon seated at it. The Supreme Captain of Thyr was seated at the head of the table where he could look out over the entirety of the Sun Chamber. Faux sails made from netting rose from the three giant masts and towered over the rest of the chamber, with a plethora of different colored luminaries affixed throughout the net 'sails'.

The rest of the chamber was filled with smaller tables designed to look like gigs and dinghies. It was at one of these that Actaeon, Trench, Wave and Caider sat. The giant grinned.

"From the looks of it they expect the chamber to flood with monsoon water."

"That wouldn't be quite so unusual given recent events, would it?" asked Wave.

"Especially not with the three of you about, that's for certain!" said the Companion, before he flagged a server down and acquired several tankards of ale for them.

Trench took a deep drink from his and slammed it down on the wooden table. "Ne'er a dull moment with Master Rellios, here."

Caider raised his glass. "That's right. I'll make a toast to the raising of your new workshop, Act. It's done soon, no?"

Actaeon grinned and raised his glass as well. "It should be complete in the next week, as long as we have a few breaks in the rain. There are only a few more final touches to be completed. I will drink to that."

They all lifted their tankards then and drank in unison.

Trench's gaze wandered back up to the highest tier of the centerpiece stage. "I don't see Raj Mujarba. 'Tis odd for him not to show his face at the height of the festival."

The Companion's eyes widened and he leaned forward. "You mean you haven't heard the news yet? Hang on, you'll need another tankard after hearing this." Caider flagged down another server and got them another round of drinks. "Best to finish the first one too. It'll help digest the –"

The two mercenaries yelled at him, causing revellers nearby to look over.

"Out with it, ya fool Companion!"

"Spit it out – what're ya jabbering on about?"

"Alright, alright," Caider said. "Well, don't you come blaming me later that I didn't try and prepare you! Alcohol heals the soul after all. The Raj Fenrik Mujarba died in his sleep last night. The Ajmani are in an uproar over his loss. He's been the Raj for longer than I can remember. Back even during the Wars."

"I know that, man! How'd he die though? What are they saying?" demanded Trench, lifting the scorched remains of one brow.

"Depends on who you listen to," began Caider. "The Raj's nephew was the closest to him at the time – Viyudun sil'Mujarba al-Arshad is his name. He's the closest of kin since the Raj's own children died in the Invasion War. Al-Arshad vows that his uncle passed away peacefully of natural causes and the House healer agreed with him. The religious leadership is arguing otherwise, of course. They say that the Raj was murdered – poisoned in his sleep. On top of all that they claim that the High Priestess Nadiya Ajman is the true heir to Ajman, since she is directly descended from the Ajman line. Either way, everyone else is pretty damned worried about it. Nothing will be the same with the old Raj dead."

"Wow. Especially with Ajman being located directly in the center of Redemption. The stability of borders, trade routes, the isolation of certain regions, and the security of Pyramid itself could be in question depending on the disposition of the next Raj, or Raja, for that matter," said Actaeon thoughtfully.

"Well, we've all gotta die sometime," said Wave, glancing sidelong at Trench. "Anyway, here's to good ol' Mujarba. May he soon be comfy in the ground along with other old legends."

The one-eyed mercenary took one last drink from his tankard before he stood up and smiled.

"That said, gentlemen, I'd best make my rounds. There are many fine ladies here and the night is too young."

When Wave moved off, the music stopped. Amodeus Jarval, the Supreme Captain of Thyr, stepped forward upon the prow of the mock ship, one foot up on the railing triumphantly.

The Supreme Captain was a handsome man, in the middle of his years, with a chiseled jaw and a neat mustache. He ran a hand through his shock of red hair and shrugged off his epauleted white jacket, which he tossed to someone behind him before speaking. "Hail, ladies and gentlemen of Redemption! I hope you are enjoying the fine festivities provided to you by the capable hands of Thyr. The monsoons this year have been exceptional, and are sure to bring all Dominions a bountiful harvest. May we all prosper."

Someone behind him thrust a tankard into his hand and he held it high before drinking to his toast. The festival-goers all drank of their respective drinks and let out a cheer.

When the cheer died down, Captain Jarval spoke again, his tone grave. "While there is much to celebrate, let us not forget the tragedy that befell those in the Sea Lounge just one day past now. Twenty-five men and women lost their lives – seven of them Thyrian. Let us take a moment to remember them now. They were taken from us too soon – all of them."

The Captain took another long swig from his tankard before he snapped his fingers and stepped down from the prow. The pair of fiddlers began to play a mournful, slow melody. The sad sounds of the strings echoed up into the cavernous Sun Chamber. Far above, in the Skyspiral, attendants with drip pails hung them from the staircases and for a time, it rained inside Pyramid.

When the last of the water had fallen, the fiddlers gradually picked up the pace of their rhythm, dueling back and forth once more. And soon, the Monsoon Festival was again alive with celebration.

The rest of the festivities wound by quickly that night. Caider tried to outdrink Trench and eventually needed to be hauled back to Saint Torin's to sleep off the night. Knight Arbiter Eisandre passed through the Sun Chamber on patrol at one point and Actaeon approached her to say hello.

"Greetings, Knight Arbiter. It is good to see you here," Actaeon said.

"Hello, Actaeon Rellios of Shore," said Eisandre stoicly. "Please excuse me, I must continue my patrol."

The Engineer grinned and nodded. "Of course, Eisandre. I hope your night is calm and uneventful."

She nodded simply and continued on her way.

Actaeon returned to his seat, thoughtful. At times it seemed like his new friend existed in two different states.

During the night several people approached Actaeon to ask for his assistance with projects or just to thank him for what he'd done in the marketplace. Most of the people he turned away after offering some advice, occasionally giving them a quick sketch to help them along. Others he would meet with at the workshop to discuss more details at a later time.

"Wave said that this would be a distraction from my work. It seems like I will be distracted indeed, by more work," said the Engineer to a victorious-looking Trench.

"That's given that half of them even remember they'd spoken to you come morning," said the giant.

"Aye. I suppose that I should depart before I accidentally overbook myself for the next few days," Actaeon said.

Just then, Wave arrived, an elegantly dressed Niwian Lady on his arm.

"Not yet my friend," said Wave. "Allow me to introduce the beautiful Lady Agarine Lartigan to you. Lady Lartigan, this is the Master Engineer Actaeon Rellios – the hero of the marketplace. And beside him don't mind my friend Trench. He might not be easy on the eyes, but he does make your beauty stand out that much brighter."

Agarine glanced down at them, and Actaeon could see the ever so brief look of disgust cross her expression as Wave introduced Trench. She hid it quite quickly though, a skill that must come in handy often at court. Summoning a fake smile, she held out her hand for Actaeon to take.

Before he could react, Trench stood and took the lady's hand, towering over her. He grinned down at the young woman, the expression yanking at the brutal line of his scar. Lifting the Niwian Lady's hand to his mouth, he kissed it lingeringly.

"Any friend of Wave's is a friend of mine. I hope to be seeing a lot more of you, pretty Lady Lartigan."

Impressively, the young woman maintained her composure, though Actaeon saw her face grow three shades paler.

A shrill whistle blew and the music stopped, a hush falling over the festivities. A low murmur began on the other side of the centerpiece ship and the nobles all stood from their seats to watch. The susurration advanced toward the ship and then around it, revellers craning their necks to see what was happening.

"This is most unfortunate," said the Engineer as the object of attention finally came into view around the side of the massive ship.

It was a gigantic slug, ten feet long and as high as a man, squirming its drunken way over, directly toward them.

"By the Gods, I've seen enough of these damned things," growled Trench, dropping the Niwian woman's hand.

It wasn't a real slug though, and as it grew nearer they could recognize the stuffed and dyed fabric and see the tips of men's boots sliding out from beneath the fringes. It was a very realistic costume. Someone had clearly done some research into it. How though, Actaeon could only guess at.

The monstrosity ambled up to Actaeon and came to a halt. There was silence as the crowd strained to hear and see what would happen.

The Engineer stood.

"Begone, sir slug!" he called. "You are not welcome here. Return to the depths where you belong!"

After he had spoken, arms emerged from either side of the slug, carrying buckets. They heaved the buckets and hurled liquid at the group that left the three of them and the Lady Lartigan thoroughly soaked in a thick green liquid with the consistency of gelatin.

"All hail the heroes of the marketplace!" cried out many voices in unison, from inside the costume. Before they could react, the slug turned and the fringes lifted while a half dozen feet ran from the Sun Chamber.

Trench went to pursue them but slipped on the slime and fell heavily onto his back.

Wave laughed at his friend, but the laughter was drowned out by the piercing scream of Lady Lartigan, as it dawned on her what had happened.

"My outfit! It is ruined! How dare you!" Her slap caught Wave off guard and made him slip in the slime as well, sending him to sprawl beside his friend. Lady Lartigan ran off in embarrassment, slipping and sliding her way from the Sun Chamber as she left a trail of slime in her wake.

Actaeon laughed at the two mercenaries and he tried to flee when they both lunged at him, but they grabbed him and dragged him down into the pool of slime with them.

Cheers started from the top deck and then spread throughout the chamber. The music resumed and Wave slid his way back to the table. He handed his friends their tankards before he took his own and leaned heavily against the table. He wiped some of the greenish liquid from above his remaining eye.

"I should know better than to introduce a nice lady to my friends."

They all shared in a good laugh at that.

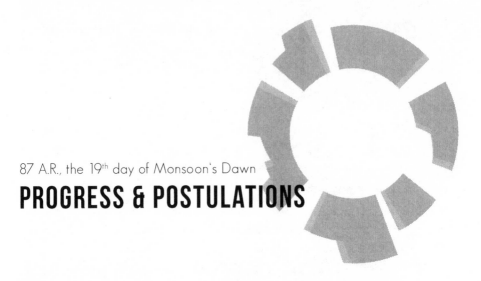

PROGRESS & POSTULATIONS

THE NEXT MORNING, THE SHIELDIAN escort arrived outside the completed workshop to bring Wave to Lazi's Tomb. When Actaeon opened the door at their knock he was amused to find the slug costume from the previous evening's entertainment pinned to the outside of the door. On it was a note which read:

In case you court another slug.

Actaeon grinned and shot an accusatory look at the Shieldians. "I should have known that Shield was behind the uproarious entertainment last night."

The escort leader's eyes widened and she took a step back, waving her hands. "Assuredly, sir, it was here before we even arrived."

"Quick to protest, are we? Well, anyway, I understand you are here for Wave. Allow me a moment to rouse him."

Trench helped load up pack mules that the escort brought with supplies that the Engineer had selected for help with measurements and survey of the region. Actaeon gave some last minute instructions to Wave and then the mercenary was off. There was a rare gap in the rains and the travelling party hoped to make the most of the opportunity to cover some distance quickly.

For the remainder of the morning, Actaeon experimented with the slime he had acquired from their slain slug adversary. Subjecting the material to heat, fire, and exposed luminary surfaces did not appear to have any effect, nor did Trench striking the material between his maul and an anvil.

"It exploded, did it not? Why wouldn't it explode now? It makes no sense," asked the giant as he worked to clean the stinky goo from the face of his maul. He lifted his free hand to the fresh burns on his face, remembering the explosion in the tunnels.

"We have, as yet, made no determination as to the exact mechanism of the explosion," explained Actaeon as he held a half-through bottle of the substance before his eyes. "Duplicating all of the factors involved may not be as simple as we initially thought. Remember, there were many details that we cannot replicate in this laboratory environment. The biggest of all being that the slime material was part of a living creature at the time of explosion. Being separate now, it may have lost its efficacy in this matter. As I recall, one of the tendrils around the creature's mouth caught the thrown luminary and surrounded it before the explosion – perhaps it even exerted pressure upon it. If we had a container that was slightly larger than a luminary, we could duplicate the encapsulation of luminary material and pressurization of the combination of artifact and slime."

"Whatever ya say, boss. Whaddaya want me to do while you work on that?" asked Trench.

"I have been thinking of that actually. Take a look at these drawings," he said, gesturing toward two parchments on one of the nearby workbenches. "It is a modified trap, designed to trap some of the smaller slugs instead of maiming or killing them as before. See how the wooden panels of the top portion interlock with the bottom base to encapsulate the creature? It works on the same principle as before minus the spikes. Could you handle putting those together and setting a few throughout the market tunnels?"

"Aye, I'll do it. But don't expect me to fight one of those big ones again. I ain't seen anything so terrifying in decades of bloody war," said the big man as he scratched his short beard thoughtfully.

"If we can figure out the key to this riddle, Trench, then maybe we will hold the answer to preventing bloody war in the future."

The search for the container he had described brought the Engineer back to the now vibrant Open Market. The multicolored awnings that sheltered the shopkeepers and their customers from the worst of the sun and rain flapped violently in the wind creating a cacophony that heralded the coming of yet more rain being blown in. A river of humanity wound its way along between the stalls as most of Pyramid's denizens came out to make the most of the break in the downpour.

It had been weeks since the unbearable stench had disappeared from the marketplace and though things were returning to normal, many stand were still boarded up and abandoned, awaiting reclamation by their owners.

Actaeon strode from stand to stand, as he browsed the wares. He paused at one stand full of various scavenged artifacts and lifted one of the half-through bottles to inspect it more closely. The cloudy bottles were referred to by that name – half-through, because they let about half of the light from a luminary through. In fact, most people in Redemption used them to cover and dim their luminaries in the evening hours.

While useful for a variety of tasks, the half-through bottles found throughout Redemption's ruins came in only a few standard sizes. He often thought that they must have been manufactured en masse by some sort of machine, such was the consistency from one to the next. A process similar to his own metal-casting, only infinitely more repeatable. His efforts to melt the bottles in a mold and cast them were always in vain though, since the material just crumbled to ash.

He set the bottle back down. Unfortunately, they were not found in a size that he required for this experiment. He needed something just slightly larger than a small handheld luminary so as to be able to surround it by just a small amount of the slug slime. It would also be beneficial, he thought, if the cross section of the bottle could be standard throughout, so he could push a piston into it and compress the material if required. The half-through bottles were made with an inward curve halfway up, perhaps to be more easily held. A simple cylinder with one end closed or capped off would be better for his needs.

Actaeon came to a stop at a woodcarving stand and let his halberd rest on his shoulder so he could lift up a finely crafted wooden bowl with elaborate details and a constant diameter. He turned the bowl over in his hands, carefully examining the workmanship. He set the bowl down and lifted the slender shape of a short bow from a barrel to take a closer look.

"It is about time that we had some fine Raedellean bows in this market," said the Engineer with a grin to the shopkeeper. The small, freckled girl had long brownish-red hair held up with carved wooden combs in the shape of three pointed leaves. She wore a brown linen dress with a simple white chemise beneath the bodice.

"Thank you. Is it really the first you've come across?" the girl asked, eyeing him suspiciously.

"I have seen none since I left Shore. Indeed, this is good news. If my bow ever breaks, I will be sure to enlist your services to carve a new one. Alas, I have little time these days to remake my own should the need arise." He set the bow back down in its stand. "Just be sure not to sell them to our enemies, lest they skewer us with the fine instruments of our own making."

"Be assured, my bows will only find their way into the most honorable of hands," said the girl with a laugh. "So you are from Shore then? Have you been here long?"

"Aye, from Shore. Arrived here during Arrival, appropriately enough – though it seems like longer with all of the goings on. A busy place, this Pyramid. And yourself? Have you been here for long? I hope you have not had to deal with the noxious stench that recently plagued this area."

"I arrived just as Hunger's Spur began. It is remarkably busy, not at all like home. I'd thought I would have more time to keep up with my craft after opening this stand, but it seems that I am doomed to spend much of my day setting up and breaking down the shop. Things aren't as secure as they were in Raedelle. You can't leave things out here. Dare I ask what happened with this stench you speak of?" she asked, a mischievous gleam in her eye.

"Creatures down in the tunnels beneath this marketplace clogged up the outflow. Things have returned to normal since they were slain. An Arbiter and two mercenaries killed them. Hopefully things will remain normal now for the foreseeable future," Actaeon said.

"And you expect me to believe such a silly story? I happened to be there, and I *do* recall you going in with them," said the young shopkeeper in mock accusation. A mirthful smile lit her face.

"You are correct," said Actaeon, his face flushing red. "They are the ones that defeated the creatures though. In fact, without them –"

But the Engineer was interrupted from his thought as his feet were swept out from under him. He crashed atop the table and shattered the fine bowl before he tumbled to the ground and rolled onto his back.

An ancient figure stepped astride him and pointed a walking stick at his nose. At the end of the walking stick was some sort of green crystal shard, though it was tough to focus on while the old man poked it in his face. The man was bald, with a tremendous grey beard that reached his waist. There a silver belt fastened crimson red robes woven with detailed silver ropework about his body. Attached to the robes and belt was an assortment of artifacts that would have put the walls of The End to shame.

"You had best watch yourself, young man. Aren't I fragile enough as it is? You tripped me up and nearly sent me down upon my head. Think of the loss of a lifetime of knowledge! Think of all the experiences yet to be passed along! Could you mindfully condone such a waste? And yet there you lie, prostrated upon the ground under my legs as though you intend to trip me again! How long have you been following me this time, great impeder of progress? What will you try next?"

After every nonsensical sentence, the man jabbed the walking stick at Actaeon's face.

Actaeon pulled his goggles down to protect his eyes and gently pushed the stick with its shard aside to climb back to his feet.

"Indeed, the audacity is astounding! How someone could have tripped you up so thoughtlessly and then fled into the crowd is beyond comprehension. Did you get a good look at them?"

The old man stood looking at Actaeon for a long moment, mouth agape, before speaking once more.

"Of course I did not! I was barely able to prevent myself from falling! I see that he knocked you over as well by the look of your clothing." He spun Actaeon and began patting the dust and dirt from his jacket. "We can't have this, not for one of the heroes of the market. Trust old Sol on that. And what of you, young lass?" he said, turning to the shopkeeper. "What is your name? I see that the vagrant who assaulted us also succeeded in destroying one of your wares. Now now, that's not a problem – nothing ol' Grandfather Sol can't fix."

Before she could answer, the old man swept the shards of the bowl into one of the large pockets of his robe and just as quickly withdrew the same bowl now perfectly constructed with no signs of having been broken. He dropped it carelessly upon the table where it spun in a circle as it settled.

The girl looked outraged after seeing her work shattered so, though confusion at the events that just took place before her dominated her expression now.

"I'm... I'm Lauryn of Lakehold," she managed.

"Well, Lauryn, nothing to cry about dear. I see you have met Actaeon Rellios here. The hero of the marketplace! Well then, both of you, I'll let you get back to your storytelling. Don't let ol' Sol continue to interrupt. Perhaps I will see you again, above the Sea Lounge." With that the old man swept past Actaeon and off into the crowd with the agility of a man much younger.

The Engineer lifted his goggles to his forehead and watched the man disappear into the crowd, letting out a low whistle.

"That reeked of Travail. If that man is who I believe him to be then I am in the wrong people's sights."

"I... I don't understand what just happened," said Lauryn. She turned the bowl over and over in her hands.

"Well, you see, I dabble and study in technology and artifacts of a nature that is of utmost interest to the Loresworn. I have managed, thus far, to keep from attracting the attention of their leaders. Not only do the Loresworn study the technology of the Ancients, but it is by my experience that they also enjoy holding that knowledge close to their chest and aim to keep it all for themselves. There is power in such information. It seems that in solving the dilemma of the Open Market, I have also succeeded in achieving the notice that I strove so hard to avoid. Unfortunately, I think it was a necessity, as —"

"That's not what I mean!" exclaimed Lauryn as she continued to turn the bowl over in her hands. "I meant, what sort of mechanism could possibly reassemble a broken wooden bowl, leaving no seams, no sign of the mended crack?"

Actaeon's eyes widened as she lifted the bowl high above her head and smashed it soundly upon the table, shattering the thin wood into a half dozen wooden shards.

"See, look at this," she said, lifting a shard for inspection. "These were not the original pieces. I've fixed many a broken bowl. If wood breaks and is mended and then breaks again, it always breaks in the same location. Whatever he used to do this — it's amazing!"

Actaeon couldn't help but grin at the girl's fascination with the Loresworn elder's machination.

"Amazing indeed. May I ask what made you decide to leave Lakehold?"

"To be honest, I'm not quite sure myself. It is almost as if there was some drive within me. I have been making these things for friends and family in my hometown for so many years. I'm good at it, but there has to be something more. There must be something more for me to learn – an entire world to see. You must think me a fool."

"Well, if foolishness it is, then I am as much a fool as you are. I came here also in search of knowledge and new things to learn. And I must be frank in telling you that I have found that here and much more in the process. The Pyramid is an intriguing place indeed," said the Engineer. "Shore was different... calmer, more secure, easier. However, any difficulties here seem to be met with reward if one is willing to persist."

"Persistence is something I've got," said Lauryn. "My family called me stubborn. Once I'm set on a task, I'm not one to give up easily." She looked up at him then. "So was there something I could help you with, Actaeon Rellios of Shore, Hero of the marketplace?"

"It is a softwood that you're looking for, for such a thing. Any other type of wood is porous and will absorb the liquid or goo that you're working with. I can get you some, and, yes, I can carve them into the shapes you need, easily," said Lauryn.

They were in Actaeon's workshop. Trench was busy hauling wood and materials up into the loft for the construction of cots, bookshelves and desks – a priority request from the Engineer. The giant slug costume hung from several large hooks above the workbench that they stood at. Upon the bench's surface sat several dozen half-through containers filled with the brownish-green slime, carefully arranged and with caps in place.

With a charcoal stick, Actaeon hastily sketched a dimensioned shape on a roll of vellum pinned to the workbench surface. "You can take this sketch so that they are made to careful specification. I shall need several different diameters where shown, but I am sure that is no issue for someone of your skill."

"This place is amazing! Is it really your workshop?" asked Lauryn as she watched the giant mercenary coming back down the steps.

"It is indeed. You are, of course, welcome to drop in at any time. In fact, we are in the middle of constructing some more furniture as it is, so a woodcarver such as yourself would be most welcome here."

"I'll certainly be doing so. Thank you for the work, Actaeon of Shore. I will return as soon as I've finished your parts," Lauryn said. She accepted the rolled drawing from him and smiled brightly as she spun about to survey the workshop. "You'll certainly need more furniture – that I can do! And some finishing touches on the windows. And that door looks quite plain, if you don't mind my saying. Any reason the whole building is stone? Seems like wood would be a perfectly workable material for such a place."

"Aye, there is a very good reason. We shall have to talk more very soon. I think I will be calling upon you more for your craftsmanship."

Later that evening, Actaeon and Trench returned to Pyramid, where they paid a visit to the Sea Lounge. On their way up through the western tunnels, they passed a confident-looking old man garbed in a crimson red robe that Actaeon failed to recognize until, having passed them, the man began to chuckle.

"May all doors open before the Great Engineer of Shore!" called the old man over his shoulder – his walking staff thrust into the air above his head as though to emphasize his words. Without a pause to his step, the man continued on.

Both Mercenary and Engineer halted and turned in unison to catch a flash of the man's red robe as he disappeared around the bend.

"Another friend of yours?" asked Trench as he brought a hand to rub at the itchy spot on his face where stubble was growing through the scar of his burn.

"Of course, what else? And this time it seems I have caught the watchful eye of the Loresworn," he replied.

"You'd best be wary. I don't suppose they like you stealing their subjects of research," said the giant.

"That is why I need you, Trench. You are wary for me while I concentrate on stealing subjects," he said with a laugh. "Stolen subjects – you would think that we did not live within a giant artifact itself the way that the Loresworn infer possession of all technology unknown. I am not sure what is more arrogant: that, or the Keepers' flawed fundament that it is their right to keep us from exploring Redemption's secrets."

"The Keepers' flawed fundament!" repeated Trench with a laugh of his own. "I like the sound of that for the next time we have to kick one of their like out of The End and onto their arse."

When they arrived at the Sea Lounge they found Knight Arbiter Kylor sof Haringar conferring with another of his Order. The man turned to regard him through the reflective goggles that covered his eyes.

"How surprising. The Engineer, so soon after Master Sollemnis' departure and the arrival of the others. If you wish to join us we are about to examine the door more closely."

"I fail to understand how you have concluded that it is in fact a door. Has it opened for you or otherwise indicated such?" asked Actaeon, arching a brow. "It could conceivably be a variety of alternate mechanisms. It may perhaps be dangerous to assume that something which we clearly do not understand is something that shares such a similarity to a familiar thing as a door."

"Only because it has been referred to as such by the Loresworn, Master Rellios," explained Kylor. "Come within and perhaps he can explain more." The Knight Arbiter led the way into the Sea Lounge.

Actaeon cast a warning glance at Trench and then shrugged before heading in himself.

The sight within left both of them speechless.

A man was there, dressed in simple cloth trousers, hemp sandals and a tunic, with an overstuffed satchel that hung over one shoulder. Attached to him were all manner of artifacts. A string of half-through bottles was worn as a bandolier across his other shoulder and atop his head sat what appeared to be a shell helmet made from the same material as the bottles. A writheblade dagger sat in a sheath at his side, its eerie hum of it audible even so encapsulated. And, even stranger, his left arm appeared to itself be a sort of mechanical artifact – metal joints that culminated in a metal hand. Upon the man's satchel was sewn a patch with a blue bolt shooting from the tip of a writheblade, the sigil of the Loresworn.

And if that wasn't unusual enough, beside him stood an imposing woman dressed in full plate armor, with a broadsword scabbarded at her side. Her sweeping blond hair, soft features and sparkling tan eyes stood in beautiful contrast to the brutal efficiency of the armor. Even if the long blue cape worn on her shoulders was not a giveaway, the symbol of the blazing sun, the universal sign of the Allfather, etched upon her breastplate, made it undeniable that this was a Keeper Knight standing before them.

The Keepers were mortal enemies of the Loresworn and strove to destroy all of the artifacts that the Loresworn studied. The pair of them together, and not trying to kill one another, was amazing in itself.

On top of that, both of them were smiling.

"By the Fallen, now I've seen it all!" exclaimed Trench. "I've seen strange things in my day, but a Keeper shacking up with a Loresworn. Does your Father know about this?"

The smile disappeared from the woman's face and she stepped forward toward the mercenary, her broadsword drawn from the scabbard in a flash of light. Just as quickly, the blade lay in two upon the ground. The woman recoiled, gripping her wrist in pain.

"Hammer beats blade. Care to play again?" asked Trench, spinning his maul slowly in his hands. He shot the Keeper Knight a big smile that stretched his cheeks, bunching up his burnt flesh and tugging at his old scar.

The woman went pale and took another step back, away from the big man. She suddenly looked very young.

"Well then, if I can trust everyone to remain orderly from hereon in, we can proceed," said Kylor, looking between the mercenary and Keeper Knight with apprehension. "Master Actaeon Rellios of Shore, this is Adept Fauntin Comeris of the Loresworn. Trench, you have already met Keeper Knight Atreena Covellet. Try not to meet anyone else today in quite that manner."

The Arbiter then led the way up a ladder that had been placed at the bottom of the opening in the ceiling.

"Do try to keep up," Fauntin said to Actaeon with a smirk. He turned and bounded up the ladder after the Arbiter.

Atreena hesitated, eyeing the hole before glancing nervously back at Trench and Actaeon.

"After you, Lady Covellet. I shall ensure that Trench brings up the rearguard," said Actaeon, dipping his head politely as he gestured the woman ahead of him with the point of his halberd.

The Keeper Knight glared and climbed the ladder, having some difficulty in her full plate armor.

Once the Keeper was up and out of earshot, the Engineer grinned back at his comrade. "Flawed fundament indeed, Trench. Was so soon an example of that really required?"

"Depends on how many more blades she has hidden. Though so far it seems her fundament's still intact to me," Trench said with a chuckle.

As soon as all of them had ascended into the cylindrical corridor, they started forward. Actaeon put his baffled luminary into his goggle strap. Fauntin and Kylor had their own that they used to light the way at the front of the group. Fauntin was struggling to move past Kylor along the rounded bottom of the corridor. After the Adept jostled him a few times, the Arbiter paused and let him pass.

Once past, Fauntin jogged ahead and reached the end of the corridor first. When he arrived there, the ring of symbols lit up in the curved wall before him. Without waiting for the others, Fauntin began to push the different symbols, seemingly at random.

"Halt that at once, Adept Comeris!" Actaeon called ahead, scratching a sudden itch on his right arm. "Have you studied those symbols? What is your intent?"

Fauntin let out a cackle of a laugh, which echoed down the corridor.

"Have I studied the symbols? What is it you think I do, Shorian? Stand back and observe. Perhaps you'll learn how to be a real Loresworn one day, since you clearly were unable to attain Travail."

"Your insults fail to offend me, Adept Comeris. However, your blatant disregard for both our safety and the safety of the residents of Pyramid has me quite concerned. Unless you have discerned the import of these symbols, then I suggest you forego tampering with them as you cannot know what effect, dangerous or otherwise, will result."

"If it is the baths you're concerned about, then rest assured they've been evacuated for the duration of this excursion, not that anyone would want to spend much time in the chill waters there anyway. As for the rest of the details, you'll have to observe quietly. It is not my concern that you lack the knowledge needed to understand the language of the Ancient ones."

That said, Fauntin continued pressing his hand against the lit symbols.

When he had pushed the ninth symbol a red circle lit up in the center of the ring and the entire corridor shuddered and threw them all to the floor.

Actaeon used his halberd to regain his feet. "See what you are doing, Comeris? You are playing with systems and mechanisms which are beyond your understanding. If you continue with this, someone will be hurt. This must be studied further until a reasonable course of action is discerned." It seemed to Actaeon as though the Loresworn was just pushing random symbols and hoping for any result.

Fauntin was up though, and pushing symbols again. "Study all you want, Engineer," he said the word with a sneer, "but progress is won through action, not through study and evaluation and reevaluation." The red light lit again and the corridor shook once more.

The Knight Arbiter fell and caught the back of his head against the side of the corridor.

Atreena stepped over him and accosted the Loresworn. "By the Allfather, I demand you step back from that artifact at once! I will not allow you to harm another person of this world with such evils of the past!"

She reached out and grabbed his bottle bandolier, tugging him away from the symbols.

"Hands off me, you uneducated bitch!" snarled Comeris, lashing out with the hand of his artificial arm.

The Keeper Knight lifted her arm to block it, but the mechanical hand dented her vambrace plate, pushing her arm aside and catching her across the face, which sent her to the ground. He followed up with a kick to her face, breaking her nose and sending a spray of blood down her breastplate.

Actaeon strung his recurve bow and nocked an arrow, aiming it down the corridor at Fauntin. "That is quite enough. You are finished meddling with things that you have no knowledge of."

"No!" said Kylor with a groan, as he recovered. He pulled his sword free and pointed the blade at Actaeon, his voice booming down the corridor, "You will remove your arrow from the string, Master Rellios! The Loresworn are our allies and endeavour to repair the damage that has been done to the Pyramid. If there is knowledge that they don't wish to share with you, then that is their right. Adept Comeris will continue as he sees fit."

Actaeon lowered the bow and returned his arrow to its quiver.

"Let us depart, Trench. I will not abide such unnecessary risk in the guise of progress." That said, he turned and they both started on their way back toward the ladder.

Comeris was already activating the different symbols again. The corridor rumbled once more. He pressed more symbols, more frantically this time, and a low tone resounded down the corridor's length.

When Actaeon glanced back over his shoulder, he stopped in his tracks and grabbed Trench. A blue circle had lit now in the center of the ring of symbols. It flashed several times and then all of the symbols disappeared. The surface before the Adept appeared to change subtly. Fauntin leaned in toward it, fascinated.

"It is moving! Back away from it!" shouted Actaeon, running back toward them with Trench right on his heels. As he ran, he felt the beginning of a cool breeze at his back. It increased quickly to a steady wind and then a gale-force wind. He braced himself with the butt of his halberd and pointed at the walls of the corridor. "Trench, can you chip away some material there and there?"

A crack resounded through the air followed by another as the sharp end of Trench's maul knocked a chip out of the corridor's rounded walls on either side. At the end of the corridor, a hole had appeared and grew larger by the lifebeat, dilating like the pupil of an eye.

Atreena got up and pushed her way past Kylor. Streams of blood gushed from her nose and flew back toward Adept Comeris, who was struggling to push himself back from the enlarging hole that was sucking him in.

Actaeon jammed either end of his halberd into the notches that Trench had created for him and felt himself being pushed against it heavily by the rushing winds from behind him.

"I am not sure how long this will hold, but everyone get behind me!"

Atreena reached back to pull Kylor, who was staring dumbfoundedly at the end of the corridor. When he felt her tug, he snapped out of it, and the Arbiter and Keeper, shoulder to shoulder, stayed low and crawled their way back to the halberd, where they joined Actaeon and Trench to cling for dear life.

As the four of them were pushed against the halberd, the hole opened more and the force of the wind increased so greatly that Fauntin could not hold himself off from it even with the extra strength of his artifact arm. They watched as his right arm snapped and he was forcibly sucked into the hole. If he screamed, they couldn't hear him over the rush of air. His torso crumbled and compacted in order to fit into the smaller orifice. His neck bent backward horrifically under the tremendous pressure until it broke. Gouts of blood were ejected from his ruptured neck and just as quickly sucked away. In an instant he was gone completely.

The force of the wind began to increase to the point where Actaeon felt he might black out under the pressure. As blackness crept in along the edges of his vision, he noticed that the hole had begun decreasing in diameter once more. As it gradually grew smaller, rotating like an iris, the wind followed suit and began to die down. When it closed, the four survivors dropped in a pile beneath the jammed halberd, their ears ringing.

It took a long time for anyone to say anything. The Loresworn, with his arrogance, had risked all of their lives.

Actaeon scowled and searched for something good to say about the man, and when he finally spoke, he could only manage, "Well, that was a most unfortunate loss of a perfectly good arm."

Some time later, Trench and Actaeon were seated at a table in the Tea Lounge, one of the Pyramid's many places of respite. It was the closest place to the Sea Lounge and, after their ordeal, they needed to find a nice, quiet place to recover.

A hodgepodge of widely varying tables and chairs that had been appropriated throughout Redemption served as the main decor in the small lounge. An array of various kettles of tea sat upon a metallic surface toward the back of the room. The surface kept the tea warm. A lone server in the lounge made periodic rounds with a kettle in each hand, filling up people's cups, not two of those identical.

They sat across from each other sharing a companionable silence, Actaeon leaning back in his chair and Trench hunched over the table as he took long sips of his tea from a comically small cup.

It was the giant who finally broke the silence. "Now, why, by a god's sphincter, would he give me this damned, tiny cup? As though any man that came into this cluster of junk wouldn't want more tea than this!"

"Perhaps he knows that he has to slow down your rate of intake,"

Actaeon suggested with a chuckle. "A man your size could put a place like this out of business if you put it away like you would a tankard of ale."

A heavy hand came down on the big man's shoulder from behind.

"Nobody'd want you to need to piss either, brother. We've had enough flooding on this side of the Pyramid," said Caider, from behind the mercenary.

"Caider! Sit yer arse down if you plan on chiming in like that." Trench growled a laugh and nearly threw the Companion into a chair next to him, grabbing a fistful of the man's tunic. He set his tiny cup down loudly on the table, causing it to ring in its emptiness. "Perhaps the Companion here's worried I'll pour him a cup o' tea!" The big man made a show of reaching for his belt.

"Aye, I'd much prefer the server pour me one," said Caider with a grin. He received a fresh cup and thanked the server while the mercenary's was being refilled. "Honestly, I'd much prefer a cup of strong ale. It doesn't feel all that safe to be inside the Pyramid anymore. Did you guys feel all the rumbling before?"

"Aye, you could say that," Actaeon said with a shudder at the gruesome scene from earlier. He was still angry with the arrogant Loresworn that had risked them all. But still, nobody should have to die in such a manner.

"You could also consider leaving the Pyramid if you're so afraid. Feel free to wallow in the filth of the marketplace. I hear it is the appropriate place for the sort of crudity that seems to be your wont, or rather... I smell it is the appropriate place," said a man several tables over. He sat before a steaming cup of tea with his eyes closed, letting the fair aroma of his drink waft to his nostrils. Judging by the look of his rough cut garb and the woad markings on both of his arms, he was Raedellean – a warbander, by the look of the heavy warbow on the table before him.

Trench's grip tightened on the tiny cup, threatening to shatter it. Instead, he took another long sip.

"Well, you heard the man, gentlemen. Back to the market tunnels for us!" Actaeon said with a grin, in an attempt to diffuse the situation.

The three men erupted in laughter at the thought and it took some time for their laughter to die down so that the Engineer could speak again, "If you like, we can take our tea and leave. I do not wish to bother you any more than we already have as you attend to your important tasks, good sir."

One edge of the man's mouth curled into a crude smirk, temporarily balancing out his crooked hawkish nose. When he spoke again, it was with a sneer.

"On the other hand, I could just settle for an explanation on who in shattered Redemption would let the likes of you three into the political center of the land. And secondly, why a Raedellean would carry a giant toothpick as a weapon and spend his time with a Companion of questionable repute and a giant freak of a Czerynian brute that should probably be tending to his slave whores instead of hanging around our Tea Lounge!"

"You'd better watch it, warbander," growled Caider under his breath.

Actaeon held up his hand to forestall his friends.

"Perhaps we can start with introductions, since you are so interested in our backgrounds. I must admit that I have quite the curious mindset myself, though it tends to apply more to other thoughts, rather than who is sitting beside me in the Tea Lounge. Admittedly, such curiosity can become quite preoccupying at times and is best dealt with by offering knowledge to satiate such avid inquisitiveness. In that spirit, I am Actaeon Rellios of Shore and, as I am not a soldier, I have seen to it that most of my weapons double as tools. In that way I do not waste effort in carrying them. For example, my halberd also serves as an excellent lever arm and pry bar. As for my friends here, the faux Czerynian is named Trench and he does a poor job as a slave owner as they all seem to have deserted him. It seems you are already familiar with Companion Caider, though I doubt the veracity of your conclusions on his rapport as I have been with him to the Hold and his reputation has not been questioned before me."

The man regarded the three of them with open disgust, eyes lingering upon each in turn. When he was finished, he lifted his cup for the first time and took a deep draught of his tea before setting it down delicately.

"How about a little game? It's been some time since I've encountered such a lively and boisterous crowd. You, Trench, can go make me another pot of tea and if it is acceptable, then I will honor you with my birth name. Companion Caider can tell his friends here the story of his questionable reputation for my surname. And you, Actaeon Rellios of Shore, you can explain to me why I shouldn't take that halberd and crack it over your thick head for treating it like a tool instead of with the respect a weapon deserves, and perhaps I'll tell you a bit about who I am."

"I don't play games," growled Trench as he spun to regard the warbander more closely.

"I had not realized that your name held such extraordinary value," said Actaeon. "Something tells me that you will be hard pressed to have Trench brew your tea, so we shall have to make do without your first name. Perhaps we could decide upon a fitting nickname for you despite this. My personal recommendation in the sake of brevity would be Vain, though I suppose you could convince us to call you Vanity if you would do us the favor of ceasing this interruption into our conversation. As for the other information you offer, I believe your words have told me all that I need to know about your character and I sincerely doubt that a surname would change that opinion at this point. Although, once again, ending this undue waste of our time would potentially help in that matter. The choice lies with you, though be warned that my friends' patience wears thin much more quickly than my own."

The warbander laughed at the Engineer's words and wiped his nose on his sleeve. He closed his eyes once more and breathed in deeply, ignoring them. After a few moments of quiet, the three men turned back to their conversation.

"Have you heard about the disappearance?" asked Caider, changing the subject.

"There are many things that have disappeared or had their state augmented in other ways. It is becoming difficult to keep track. What disappearance do you speak of?" asked the Engineer.

"The Niwian Lady. Lady... Angrin Lartigan, I think. She disappeared the night of the Monsoon Festival. The Arbiters have been scouring for clues on whereabouts. Supposedly she hadn't been seen since several festival-goers spotted her rushing off that night. Niwian's screaming abduction. They want somebody held responsible for it. That on top of the unrest that's been going on in Ajman has people worried that there might be another war in the cards. Perhaps one of the factions in Ajman is trying to pin the abduction on the other to gain support."

Trench's eyes widened at Caider's words.

"Do ya mean Agarine Lartigan?"

"Oh yeah, that's right! So you've heard about it then? It's got the Hold worried. Us Companions are working double time to make sure that our higher-ups are well protected."

"That the same Lartigan that Wave was fooling around with that night?" Trench asked Actaeon.

"Yes, that is correct," replied the Engineer. "And we know why she left in a hurry, do we not?"

Trench opened his mouth to speak again, but his head was slammed against the table so loudly that it echoed in the chamber. The warbander stood over the giant with a grin, one hand on Trench's neck. His blade was in his other hand.

"You should've just made my cup of tea, friend," said Vain.

A normal man would've been knocked unconscious by such an impact. But Trench was no normal man. The giant mercenary blinked and shook his head in amazement.

"Some people never learn."

Trench cast an apologetic look toward Actaeon. In one fluid motion, he grabbed the man's arm and yanked it over his shoulder, at once drawing to his feet to lift Vain into the air. A well placed elbow sent the warbander to sprawl like a rag doll behind him, though he recovered quickly to lift his blade in defense.

Without missing a beat, Trench lifted the heavy table before him, one of the larger ones in the establishment, and slammed it down atop the man Actaeon had nicknamed Vain. Nearby chairs were scattered and sent splintering in all directions.

Arbiter whistles sounded from the hallway at the sounds of the clash. Vain pushed the table off of him and pulled his blade loose from the surface. He wiped blood from his freshly broken nose on his sleeve and shook his head at the big man.

"Looks like you'll get to spend the evening in an Arbiter cell with me then. They'll certainly want you to cover the damages, since you cannot contain yourself from destroying the poor proprietor's furniture. And all you had to do was pour me tea. This type of behavior would have had you killed in a war, boy."

"Here's your damned tea," roared Trench, raising the tiny cup that was still clutched in one hand to smash it down upon the man.

"Are you kidding?" said Caider, his sword in hand as he stood beside

Trench. "This man has killed more men in battle than ants you've stepped on. Just get out of here!"

Actaeon gestured toward the exit with his halberd.

"I suggest you be on your way, Vain. You have crossed the line. Learn your lesson and take a walk."

The man snarled and dragged himself to his feet to dust himself off and sheathe his blade.

"You have crossed the wrong man, Trench. Pray you don't find yourself on the opposing side of battle from me. I will be the one to fell the giant."

"By the Fallen, I pray I do. I'll feed you to the wardogs after I'm through with you," said Trench, grinning at the thought.

The man they called Vain made his way out, but not before he shoved the server and sent him flying backwards. The tray he'd been holding tumbled to the floor and the kettles upon it shattered.

The three friends helped the server up and helped him clean up the mess. Actaeon made sure that he was well compensated for the damages.

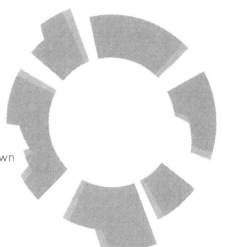

87 A.R., the 24th day of Monsoon's Dawn

FIGHTING FOR LIFE

THE DOOR SLID OPEN HALFWAY with the torturous shriek of metal on metal and, as soon as the cross-decorated face came into view, the Engineer released the string and let the arrow fly. It appeared to float toward the raider as it spun heavily through the air with its unbalanced center of gravity, the critical load throwing it off balance. Actaeon winced as the arrow seemed about to miss completely, but, at the last moment, the arrow pulled to the right to bury itself firmly in the raider's neck.

The raider opened his mouth in a silent scream as blue flame erupted from his neck and poured down his body, setting his flesh and clothing afire. Unable to hold the door open, the man toppled backward, blue flame tips shooting from his nostrils and open mouth.

The door slammed shut with a screech that Actaeon felt resonate in his teeth. Struggling raiders could be heard from the other side.

"Now they will be angry, though I will hope there will be less of them when that door opens again," he said with a nervous grin as he put another arrow to the string. "Six," he muttered under his breath in his usual mantra that helped him keep track of his arrows. "How many do you think are back there? Judging by the commotion and the racket from earlier, I would estimate that ten or so men made it to that door."

Beside him stood Eisandre, sword drawn and in her left hand. Her right arm – her sword arm – was in a sling at her side. She was pale but steady as she replied.

"Ten seems like a reasonable estimate. You will fire your six arrows, or as many of them as you can before they get into melee range. Then, as per your plan, if there are more than a few left standing, we will close this door and then cut them down as they try to force their way in. You will allow me to protect you for once, yes? Just keep thinking of the beach, alright? We'll bring some food and drink. It will be peaceful."

Actaeon grinned over at her before he turned back to the door and drew, sighting down the length of the arrow. This one a normal shaft.

Six arrows, an Arbiter without a sword arm, and an Engineer with limited combat training against ten of the cross-faced raiders – the most relentless, dogged pursuers that he had ever faced amongst the ruins. With those odds, that stormy day on the beach when the both of them sheltered from the storm may well be their last memory in that special place. Actaeon couldn't help but to let his thoughts wander to how they got into this situation in the first place – a peaceful jaunt through the ruins, cut short by a fall...

Earlier that day, with Wave off in Shield and Trench busy setting traps to catch more slug creatures, Actaeon and Eisandre walked together through a relatively well-explored area of the Boneyards. A small flock of birds flew noisily overhead through the clear blue sky, the morning unusually cool for the time of year. The air carried the fragrance of metallic dew, mingled with moss and dirt.

There were a few common artifacts that he wanted to find on this excursion. Glass string in particular, would be useful for a reusable trigger line, especially given its resistance to flame. He could cast most of the parts required to make his explosive contraption, but he often was inspired to create even better mechanisms from components that he found in the rubble of the Ancients.

They passed beneath the fractured remnants of great arches that caught the light of the rising sun as they walked along upon overgrown patches of what once must have been a magnificent tiled floor.

Actaeon used his halberd to pick his way through the detritus-strewn ground. He had learned through years of exploration in these ruins that it always paid to have three points of contact – you never knew when a surface would give way under your weight. He pointed at one of the great arches.

"Too bad I could not have had arches of that size in my workshop. I could fit some incredible mechanisms in such a large workspace."

"There are ruins in other places that remain partially intact. Some of them with rather large chambers. Perhaps you will one day find a place that suits your expanding needs," said the Knight Arbiter with amusement.

Eisandre turned to glance up toward the arch that they had passed beneath, admiring the intricate features crafted somehow into the elderstone. As she stepped forward, something felt wrong. There was a loud crack and a rumble along the ground as she committed her weight to that foot. Quickly, she shifted her weight and threw herself to the side, but it was too late and she fell.

Actaeon heard the crack just behind him and spun to grab Eisandre, but he was too slow – a crash came from somewhere below. A hole emerged where his friend stood just moments before and fracture lines spread in multiple directions from that point – some beneath his very feet.

"Eis!" he cried out as he made the agonizing decision to leap away from the hole. More crashes followed behind him, telling him that he'd made the right decision to jump away. His fist came down beside him in frustration at his own negligence – in a more unstable area of the ruins they might have been tethered together. It was no use thinking of that now though and he set his mind to work on the problem at hand.

The key to approaching the hole safely would be to distribute his weight as much as possible. A quick survey of his surrounds told him that there was nothing available that would do that without adding much more weight to the fractured surface of the ruin. He would have to spread his weight out on his own. The larger the area he spread his body across, the lower the chance of catastrophic failure.

He stuck his luminary into the strap of his goggles and lowered himself to the ground. Gingerly, he shimmied up towards the edge of the hole on his belly, all the while keeping his halberd's shaft across his chest before him to help spread out his weight. Once he slid to the edge, he dipped his head over to survey the scene below.

"Eisandre! Can you hear me?" he called down from above.

The Knight Arbiter lay two stories below at the bottom of a large chamber in a bed of dirt, rocks, corroded metal and broken glass. Several large insects rushed across her body and scattered into the shadows, disturbed by the collapse. The light of Actaeon's luminary scattered in a thousand different directions by countless mirrors positioned seemingly at random throughout the chamber. He found himself momentarily distracted as he tried to identify a pattern in the mirrors' positions but he shook his head and brought his thoughts back to the task at hand.

"Eisandre! Knight Arbiter! Speak to me!"

Below, she stirred a bit and groaned in pain. Thank the Ancestors, she was alive! He noted that a pillar to his left supported the ceiling of the chamber below and was likely the only reason that more hadn't come down.

"Eisandre," he called down to her. "Hold tight. I will be down in a moment."

The Engineer slid carefully back from the hole and only stood after he was twice the distance of the fracture lines from the hole. He pulled the spool from the big pocket of his jacket and unraveled the coil of thick glass rope from it. The length of the artifact rope was enough to reach Eisandre from the hole, but not to reach any substantial objects to tie off on. After scouring the debris around him, he located two long metal rods and brought them back over to the coil. He placed each of the rods' ends on a block and stomped on the middle so that each one had a small bend in the middle – that way they wouldn't roll while they supported his weight. A figure eight knot in the glass rope allowed it to be slid over the halberd's metal-reinforced length, which would act as the anchor point to lower him down. Those things done, he pulled his goggles down over his eyes and laid down to slide forward to the edge of the hole again, pushing the halberd and rods in front of him.

When he peeked over the edge he found that Eisandre had pushed herself up to a seated position and was assessing herself for injuries. She brushed some rather large spiders from her clothing and pulled a small shard of mirror glass from her arm with a muffled cry.

While Actaeon carefully laid the two bars across the opposite edges of the hole, she squinted up into the sunlight.

"Wait! Act, you cannot think to come down here. Just... toss down a rope and... now why are you grinning?" She tried to lift herself with her right arm, but the pain when she put weight on it brought tears to her eyes. Instead, she clutched her arm to her chest and winced. When she looked back up at the Engineer, he could see a bruise and blood on her forehead as well.

"Just glad that you are alright. It looks like your arm might be hurt. You will not be able to pull yourself up like that. See if you can move aside."

He put some weight on one of the rods and used it to get a better vantage around the room below, his luminary shining over the hidden depths. "Is there enough material down there? Perhaps we can pile it up and climb out. Or maybe there is another way out?"

"I see a lot of mirrors. And spider webs. And, ugh – some kind of slippery algae all over the place. I don't see any obvious exits, other than the big hole I so gracefully discovered," called up the Arbiter as she made her way from atop the fallen pile and out from beneath the hole. Broken glass clattered aside and bugs skittered out of her way. "You should move to a safe distance. You know better than I how unstable this place is. If the whole ceiling comes down when I try to climb up this rope of yours, I want you well away from here."

"I need to stabilize the halberd or it may spin and fall while you are climbing up. Besides, you will need my help to pull you up. We will both get out of this together, Eisandre."

"I will be very unhappy if you are injured for my sake," said Eisandre, shooting him a stern look.

"Well, I will be unhappy if you die down there without my trying to help."

Birds wheeled in the sky far above the Engineer. They shrieked as they dove lower, fighting over some hidden treasure.

Actaeon glanced up. He could've sworn he'd heard something more. He bit his lip and listened carefully. The birds sped away to the west as they shrieked and fought over their prize, leaving that part of the ruins quiet again.

"So, what's the plan? I should just try to climb up?" asked Eisandre, bringing Actaeon's attention back down to his fallen friend.

"Or I can lower down and help you pile up things to climb out with. Or you can search for an alternate exit out of there. I would bring more objects over to help us, but the ground around me will not support much weight. As it is, I am keeping my own body spread out. What are you capable of trying?"

"I think we need more information," she responded after a moment of thought. "Give me some time. I'll have a look around." She saluted him sharply before she disappeared into the shadows of the chamber.

A few moments later, he could barely make out her voice as she gave a report.

"Mirrors. Thousands of them. The Pyramid has something like this as well, to somehow distribute natural light through interior rooms, only larger I think. Ugh, I just stepped in something very wet and... there are spider webs, with resident spiders. Here's a ladder that goes down through a hole in the floor. I can't see how far."

Actaeon could hear the crunching of broken mirror shards under her boots as she searched the chamber. He directed the light of his luminary after her and craned his neck to see what she was looking at.

"Eisandre, see if you can drop something down the –"

There it was again, and this time he had definitely heard a noise. He shimmied back from the hole and drew to his knees before he pulled the recurve from his back and strung it, cringing at the action as it concentrated his weight on the fractured ruin. He nocked an arrow and thumbed down the scope to peer through it and scan the ruins in the direction of the noise.

More than a dozen men crested a rubble pile in the distance. Upon their faces were the familiar crosses that he had seen in the past, forming four equal quadrants on each of their faces. The lead man looked up and met his eye.

As an afterthought, Actaeon reached up and lowered the baffle on his luminary, but they had already seen him and streamed down the hill in pursuit.

The Engineer cursed and drew back the arrow. Adjusting his angle and neglecting windage, he let loose at the lead raider. A sharp twang resonated from his bow and the raider fell. Even so, they would be upon him in moments.

"Nine. Not enough arrows."

He made a hasty decision and dropped his bow into the hole before he wrapped the glass rope around his waist, bringing both ends to his front to squeeze together and control his descent. He rolled into the hole and lowered himself down the rope, still swinging from the initial drop. Toward the bottom he lost control and fell the last several feet, slamming into the pile below. He hurried to his feet and pulled the rope to one side, which moved the halberd off of one of the bent bars to fall at his feet.

Hastily, he strapped the halberd to his back after wrapping the coil around it. His bow was in his hands then and he put another arrow to the string.

"Isn't this the perfect place for a summer home? We'll put the dining table over there, and maybe, yes, that would be a lovely corner for a water garden," jested Eisandre, unaware of the complications topside as she knelt to peer down along the ladder. "I tossed a pebble down the hole with the ladder, Act. It landed in water, I don't know how deep it is. You should've left while you had the chance. Did something happen up there? You couldn't wait until I finished my search?" She seemed surprised at his sudden arrival, and curiously, hadn't noticed his quick descent and fall down the rope. Perhaps her own fall had given her a concussion.

"I have a feeling we will find out how far that ladder –"

A face poked down into the hole and Actaeon's arrow buried itself deep into the center of the painted cross. The raider tumbled down into the chamber and landed with a crash.

Eisandre rushed to his side and drew her sword with her off hand.

"Eight. It seems we have our first visitors," Actaeon said with a grin. He stepped briskly over to her and wrapped her in a hug. "I would never leave you behind." She didn't return his hug, sword still at the ready. Actaeon released her and put another arrow to the string. "Well, you had better show me to our storage cellar. I did not bring enough arrows for all of our guests."

"I don't think it's a cellar. If this room is what I think it is, then we're at the top of another one of the old buildings, and all these mirrors were meant to redirect sunlight below, just like in the Pyramid. We have no idea what's down there, how stable it is, or if there's any other viable exit. This could be really bad, Act. I'd almost rather stay here and fight."

He was impressed with her recognition of the similarities between the different buildings of the Ancients. "Do not worry. In these ruins, there is almost always another way out. I have been in very bad spots before."

Movement could be heard from above and dust and loose debris began to rain down steadily from the ceiling above them. Thinking the same thing, Actaeon and Eisandre backed up toward the ladder and away from the hole in the ceiling.

When they reached the rusty ladder against the chamber wall, the ceiling above fell apart in a roar, and brought down with it a half dozen bodies. A billowing cloud of dust enveloped them and loose fragments pelted their bodies as they sheltered against the wall and covered their faces.

Actaeon knelt beside the ladder and aimed his arrow into the dust cloud.

"Go on ahead, and call me when it is clear down there. I will finish off any that are able to walk." He met her eyes through the haze. "I will be right behind. I promise."

"You're kidding, right? I'm not leaving you, Act. We fight together," she insisted.

A large mirror fell from the ceiling and landed before them, throwing a cloud of shattered glass particles over them. Eisandre turned and took cover near the wall while Actaeon pulled the collar of his jacket to cover his mouth, his goggles already protecting his eyes.

"Agreed," he said. "Let us stay back here near the wall. The ceiling overhead is less likely to collapse on us that way, since it is well supported."

As the glass dust cleared, he watched one figure scrabble out from beneath the rubble and draw shakily to its knees. Actaeon released the string and his arrow shot forward, sealing the man's eye shut forever, mid-blink. The raider tumbled over silently as the Engineer put another shaft to string.

"Seven," he muttered.

There was no movement from the rest of the newly arrived rubble; either they were all dead or any survivors were smart enough not to move. It was only a matter of time before the raiders above would figure out a way down and if his past experiences were any sign, they wouldn't stop their pursuit.

"We should search for another way out now. They will descend to look for us."

"One day, when we're not in such dire circumstances perhaps you will tell me what you did to earn the ire of these raiders," said Eisandre as she tested the ladder under her weight. "Wait until I'm all the way down and call up that it's safe. I don't think this will hold both of us at once."

The ladder creaked as she worked her way down with one hand. Before long, Actaeon could hear water sloshing below. He maintained his vigilance on the hole before him as he waited.

"Oh, you're not going to like it down here very much," called the Arbiter from below. "The flooding isn't too deep – just past my waist. But it's freezing. We're going to have to move quickly. But, otherwise, it looks remarkably clear. Come on down. Just watch the fourth rung from the bottom – it's broken."

On her order, Actaeon returned his arrow to the quiver and started down the ladder. He reached the bottom quickly and lifted the baffle on his luminary to take a look around. They were inside a rusted metal corridor. Years of water dripping down from above had left parts of the walls and ceiling covered in calcified stone. Some of the stalactites that hung from above reached the water that they waded in.

"They seem to have an interest in me or my abilities," he began to explain. "I have encountered them several times before, as you know. For a while I thought them imagined – a product of madness caused by my wanderings in the ruins. I have heard of other such cases, where something in the ruins causes such hallucinations. But, before I arrived at Pyramid this last time, they caught me, though I escaped." He tested the ground around the ladder carefully. "Best not to move too fast. We should check for holes in the floor ahead of us lest we suffer the same misfortune as before."

"And if we move too slowly, we'll start to suffer detrimental effects from this cold," countered Eisandre. "At least there are no insects down here – that we can see. Do you think they'll try to follow us down? Should we remove the ladder?"

"I am rather certain that will not prevent the insects from following us," Actaeon replied with a grin. "Besides, removing it might attract the cross-faced raiders and besides, we may need to retrace our steps."

The water was indeed quite cold. As they sloshed their way down the corridor, the frigid water quickly filled their boots and soaked into their clothing.

They walked a long way in silence, their way lit by their luminaries as they checked the floor before them with every step. At some point they noticed a dim light that radiated from separate luminaries overhead. Curiously, their presence or perhaps the presence of their handheld luminaries seemed to activate the luminaries of this ancient structure. The Engineer paused a moment to look at one, but it did not appear to change in brightness while he watched it.

Farther along the corridor, the ceiling had collapsed. Eisandre shined her luminary over the debris and located a small gap in the rubble to the right.

Actaeon wasted no time in climbing up onto the pile and began to free loose detritus in an attempt to widen the hole. He moved slowly to ascertain that any piece he removed did not bear weight of the collapse above. When he pulled at a heavier stone, it rolled past him to splash into the water below.

Splashes could be heard from where they had come, along with the clanging of metal.

The Engineer closed the baffle on his luminary and gestured for Eisandre to cover hers.

"It would seem we have little time left."

"These people really want to get at you, Actaeon," Eisandre said, cupping her hand over her luminary to shine light for Actaeon to work by. "Badly enough to risk their own deaths. You cannot fathom why?"

"Not sure, though I have a suspicion. The first time I was out near Pyramid, there was a man named Markor that asked me to the Warrens to activate some strange artifact. I refused him and shortly after that was the first time I ever saw the cross-faced raiders. It might have just been a coincidence though." The hole was wide enough now and he scrambled through and used his halberd to check the floor on the other side. The room on the other side was dry. After helping Eisandre through the narrow hole, he knelt to dump the water from his boots.

"We're going to have to figure it out eventually, Act. Either that or kill them all. Ah, it really does look like our summer home now!" she said as Actaeon helped her dump the water from her boots.

"Yes, the dining hall. Perhaps we can find a heavy object or twenty to pile atop the hole we just made and make it impossible for them to lift."

The room they were in was a great hall of some sort, a place that had been opulent in its time. The walls were cracked and rusted, but one of them seemed like it might once have been one of the flickering screens found throughout the ancient city, only bigger. There was a large table in the center of the room, covered with dust and place settings of astonishing beauty, each pearlescent cup, plate and bowl perfectly arranged as if for a meal. Old cobwebs hung from a large and elaborate luminary fixture overhead. Two archways led to other parts of the hall and a partially calcified door led somewhere beyond.

"Anything we can lift, they can lift too," Eisandre said as she jumped up and down to warm up. "We can keep running or we can make a stand here. Personally, I think running through these ruins is dangerous. I'd rather kill them here, as they try to crawl out of that hole while half numb from the cold, than further endanger our lives by moving too hastily through these ruins."

"We only need to hold them off for a bit. After awhile they will be forced to retreat from the cold. And they do not have the same lifting leverage that we... or, I do. Anything that they lift, they need to do with a single man who is on his belly in the process of squeezing through a small hole. If we place this table over the hole, then pile everything we can atop it, they should never be able to lift it. Then we can search the ruins more carefully for a way out."

Actaeon quickly removed the dishes from the heavy table and then knelt to lift and flip it onto its top. Eisandre used her left hand to help him maneuver the table into position. They lifted it together and jammed it at an angle so that the surface was covering the hole that they had come through. Then they stacked as many pieces of heavy Ancient furniture as they could find on the underside of the table.

"I think I preferred the evening when we watched the rainstorm and the sunset on the beach," said Eisandre as they worked.

"Well, I would love to accompany you back there after we get out of this mess," Actaeon said, pausing to squeeze her hand gently.

After the weight was piled atop the table, they jammed several chairs between the wall and table to further lodge it in place. Actaeon fashioned a rough sling out of his bandage roll for Eisandre's injured arm, and they explored the other passageways in search of a way out.

The first archway yielded what might have been a kitchen, with preparation surfaces everywhere and many strange devices set into the wall, some of them still lit with the strange characters of the Ancients. Dishes and assorted cutlery lined several shelves at head height. Through a door in the kitchen, there was another chamber with a bathing pool in the center, long dry, and a large shattered luminary that had landed at the bottom of the pool. Curved benches surrounded the pool and a mosaic on the wall beyond showed a cluster of flowers, sparkling even through a layer of dust.

Through the next doorway they found a chamber with a wide central platform and a narrow compartment behind it. The archway on the opposite side of the room led back into what Actaeon now thought of as the great hall. At the edge of the platform there lay a faceted clear stone, sparkling in their luminary light. After Eisandre passed it by, Actaeon picked it up and pocketed it – he'd have to study it later, if they survived this.

Eisandre made her way through the archway and back into the great hall. She shone her luminary through the crack in the partially calcified door.

"Actaeon, there is a draft here. Fresh air."

A loud knock sounded from the other side of the table, followed by several more successive bangs. The table shuddered but held. After several more blows that failed to move the table, they could hear a scraping sound that Actaeon guessed was a dagger on the table surface.

"Nice place we have here, though I am not certain about the location," he said, before joining her at the door. The big door was split down the middle and when open, slid into a pocket on either side of the opening, he guessed, as there was no evidence of exterior hinges and the door was partially open already.

"Well, you know what they say – location is everything. We'll have to keep looking, I suppose," said Eisandre with a weak smile.

He tested the door with his hand and it did not budge. He placed the end of his halberd through the opening and used it to lever the doors the rest of the way open, cracking the thin calcified stone that held it in place. As they stepped into the dark and damp corridor beyond, they could both feel the fresh air on their faces.

"Good find, Eis. The airflow in here is palpable. We may be nearing an exit."

"That's good. We need a nice front entrance," said Eisandre as she leaned against the wall next to the doorway, and squeezed her eyes shut.

"Do not worry. We are almost out of this, Eisandre. We can go visit our shelter on the beach after this is over. I know it is much smaller, but I do feel the location suits us better," he said, placing his hands on her shoulders.

When her blue eyes flicked open he could see the weariness there, and her skin was beginning to pale. Her injury from the fall was beginning to catch up with her after the initial adrenaline burst from the pursuit. He would have to keep her motivated and moving.

They were interrupted by a much louder bang from the table which sent one of the chairs wedged into the pile tumbling to the floor. A battering ram, he thought – stupid, that he hadn't thought of that eventuality.

"I would like that, but I think there may be some competition over the pleasure of your company," she said, leaning on him as they started down the musty corridor. After they passed it, Actaeon helped her over to a wall and pushed the doors shut. Beyond, they had to be careful with their footing as the floor was slippery with some sort of black mold. Many-legged creatures scurried out from underfoot as they trudged onward.

"It could be an air vent," she said, fatigue in her voice. "This is our most... our most exciting adventure yet, don't you think? Think of the... story we'll be able to tell, somewhere nice and warm, with something nice to eat and a good stout drink."

They came to an open door on their right and entered. Inside was a colorfully-painted room, furnished with child-sized tables and chairs. A small object on one of those tables caught the Engineer's eye with its rainbow luminance, but he ignored it as he lead his friend over to a longer orange table where he gently guided her to lay down.

Actaeon lifted her legs and placed one of the small chairs underneath them. He suspected that she was entering a state of shock. A combination of the blood loss and the cold, most likely. He would have to remedy this first, before they continued on.

"Here, drink this. It should make you feel better," he said, handing her an opaque flask from his jacket. "Lay with your legs elevated for a few minutes and you should start to feel better." He examined the door, searching for possible ways to close it.

"I don't want to lie down. We want to get out of this place, not settle in for a nap. I suppose you're a healer now as well as an Engineer. Full of surprises, you," she murmured, though she followed his instructions and drank from the flask.

"It is just water. It will help you recover your blood volume. I am not really a healer, I just picked up a few things as a young lad when my mother grew ill. The body is just a complex series of mechanisms that function together to create the system we know as a human being – it is quite simple when you look at it that way. Just keep sipping that water. You will feel better in this position, but the weakness will return if you try to stand. The blood in your body will flow to your head this way, but away from it and into your legs if you stand," said Actaeon with a concerned glance back at her.

"Hey, now. I'm feeling better already. Quit looking so worried. And please place my sword near my hand, if you will. We should be off again in but a moment, but if your friends show up, I'd rather not greet them empty-handed."

Actaeon placed a hand on her shoulder and smiled down at her gently. "I am trying not to worry, but with you, I... I need you to get better for me." Reaching over, he retrieved the rainbow, luminescent object and handed it to her. "Here, see if you can figure out what this is. I will try to get that door closed to buy us some time." He touched her cheek lightly and then rested his hand on her forehead to check her temperature – she felt cold. He frowned and left to better examine the door. A quick analysis found some small pebbles jammed one side of the door in its track. He cleared the track and slid the door closed onto one of the miniature chairs.

Stepping back to inspect his work, he then slid a large cabinet over to the door and laid it on its side at an angle in front of the doorway, allowing them enough space to kick the chair out of the doorway. If their attackers made it this far, they would be forced to climb over the cabinet before attacking them hand to hand.

And so they stood now, in the hall just outside the door held open by a chair belonging to a child of the Ancients.

Six arrows, an Arbiter without a sword arm, and an Engineer with limited combat training against ten of the cross-faced raiders, the most relentless, dogged pursuers that he had ever faced amongst the ruins.

"Just keep thinking of the beach, alright? We'll bring some food and drink. It will be peaceful," said the Arbiter, her voice grounding him in reality.

Yes, there was life beyond this dark, moldy corridor with the faint breeze at his back. There was life beyond the horrific sounds of cross-faced raiders burning to death that came from beyond the door at the end of the corridor. And, by the Fallen, they were going to survive this, if Actaeon had anything to do with it!

The door that hid their enemies slid open with a shuddering shriek, the smell of burnt human flesh wafting into the corridor. This time two pairs of hands yanked each side of the door open and four men came running past them at full sprint into the corridor, swords raised in the air. They ran in silence – no battlecries uttered, an unnerving force to face down.

Unlike the unwieldy blue fire arrow he had fired several long moments ago, Actaeon's next arrow lodged itself nicely in the first man's chest, splitting the facets of a corroded mail coat. "Five." He nocked another arrow and let fly hastily, sending the arrow skittering along the wall of the corridor past the three men who had to slow to step over their fallen comrade. "Four."

He took a deep breath while aiming the next arrow and it struck another raider right in the center of the cross on his face, punching through the bridge of his nose. "Bullseye," said the Engineer with a grin, though he wasted no time in putting the next arrow to the string. "Three."

Those final three arrows he fired in quick succession. The first arrow caught the lead man in the bicep of his off-hand arm, barely even slowing him. The second entered the man's thigh, which did stop him. The third bounced harmlessly off the raider's crudely hammered plate.

Behind the two remaining men in the corridor came those that had held the doors open for the first wave.

"Retreat may be optimal at this point," stated Actaeon, as he tossed the recurve bow into the room and pulled Eisandre back into the room after him.

They climbed over the furniture that had been arranged on the other side of the door and with his halberd, Actaeon hooked the chair in the door and yanked it away. The metal door slammed shut and the chair tumbled aside. They took up defensive positions on the other side of the furniture; their assailants would have to bypass several obstacles into their waiting blades. The Knight Arbiter took the lead, her gleaming longsword held in the easy grip of a practiced swordswoman. The Engineer stood behind her and to the right, ready to assist with the reach of his halberd.

"Six of them left, I think. You can have the rest of them," said Actaeon with a wry grin.

"Thanks."

Three loud clangs came from the other side of the door, followed by silence.

If they listened carefully, they could hear a low scraping sound on the other side.

The Engineer tilted his head to listen. "What now?"

"Be ready. They are about to strike."

True to the Arbiter's words, two blades slid in through the door seam and both sides of the door were pulled open with a gut-wrenching squeal.

At the same moment, two daggers were thrown into the room, one at each of them before the door slid shut once more.

Actaeon instinctively ducked and blocked with his halberd, deflecting the dagger over his shoulder to strike the ceiling. A spray of blood spattered the room behind him from where the blade cut through the back of his left hand.

Eisandre easily sent the other dagger spinning aside harmlessly with the sweep of her blade, though the sudden movement sent an icy sharp stab of pain along her right arm, draining the color from her face.

"Look, dear," she stated in a tone of mock cheerfulness, giddy with pain. "They brought us presents. Are you okay?"

Actaeon nodded, but he could feel the rivulets of blood running down his sleeve from the gash.

The blades remained in position to pull the door open again and allow two more daggers into the room.

They were ready this time, and one of the daggers was deflected by the blade of Actaeon's halberd while Eisandre whirled aside to avoid the other.

"Now they will come," whispered the Engineer.

"It's about time. I was starting to get bored."

She shifted her position so that she stood directly to the side of the door.

When the doors were pulled open again, two of the raiders rushed in.

The lead man rushed at Actaeon and promptly stumbled over one of the cabinets. A halberd blade swept across the back of his neck severed the spine neatly.

The second man was caught unaware with the Arbiter's blade in his belly. It took her two tries to pull the blade free from the man as he fell, which nearly caused her to miss the slash of the third man that was right behind him. She got it free though, and knocked his blade upward to the ceiling. She thrust forward, her sword splitting mail and biting into the man's shoulder as he tried to dodge.

A fourth raider leapt atop the cabinet and began to rain blows down upon the Engineer with a heavily gouged two-handed blade. Actaeon blocked the blows with the metal-shod shaft of his weapon, but was driven to his knees.

Actaeon kicked the cabinet solidly with his boot, knocking the raider off balance. While the man flailed in an attempt to recover, the Engineer crouched and thrust upwards to drive the wedge of the halberd's endcap up through the raider's lower jaw. With a jerk, he lifted and pulled the shaft free, snapping the man's neck. The greatsword clattered to the floor as the man's body crumpled down beside it.

The raider with the gut wound fell back against the last two that had held the door open, which slowed their forward momentum as they struggled to work their way past him. One of their blades was raked across his throat as they passed by and shoved him aside.

They leapt the cabinet to attack Actaeon, raining blows down upon him so fast and hard that he was forced deeper into the room and separated from Eisandre, desperately parrying with his halberd to keep their blades at bay.

Eisandre parried another blow and lithely slid under her attacker's arm and behind him. A firm kick sent him face first into the wall and her blade's tip found the gap in his mail under his arm and slid home into his heart. Bright red blood poured out of his mouth.

Actaeon continued to frantically parry both of the raider's swords as he retreated. Blade and shaft of his halberd were a blur as they swept to and fro in short, concise arcs. He knew he wouldn't be able to keep up this pace for long. With the halberd's long reach, he could keep them at a distance from him, but they were starting to work their way inside his defenses, nicking the arms of his jacket on either side. And there wasn't much room left to work with.

When he bumped into one of the child-sized chairs, he reached back and hurled it at the assailant on his left. The man promptly ducked, revealing the pale and bloody figure of Eisandre behind him. She painted a terrifying figure, and despite being struck in her injured right arm by an errant tiny chair, closed the distance between them and inserted her blade efficiently between neck and clavicle to dispatch one of Actaeon's attackers.

"One left," muttered the Arbiter as they both turned to corner the final raider against the back wall of the room. "You want to try to find out why they were after you?"

"Aye, let us take him alive."

In a move of desperation, the raider threw his sword at Eisandre, which forced her to dodge backward. The raider pulled a dagger free from his boot and smiled emptily at Actaeon as he stood tall and drew the blade across his own throat.

Actaeon leapt at the man and kicked the dagger out of his hand, but it was too late. The body spasmed violently once, then twice – the left side of his neck gouged open in a pulsing red fountain. The raider continued to gaze at the Engineer, even as the lifeblood poured from him and he fell to the ground.

"You are a coward and will never be anything more," shouted Actaeon. "Your people will never have me." As the last of the light faded from the man's eyes, Actaeon's boot ended it even faster as it came down on the man's face with a thud. "What could possibly be worth this much sacrifice?" He spun about, surveying the carnage of the room. Six men lay dead amidst shattered furniture meant for the long-gone children of the Ancients, with more dead out beyond the door. "Insanity!"

"You are, evidently. In the future, I'm thinking that we will not enter the Boneyards without a larger escort. Your hand is bleeding badly, let me see it," instructed Eisandre.

He let his halberd fall to the floor with a clatter and sat down upon one of the childrens' tables, dazed. A tear welled up at the corner of one eye and he reached up to wipe it, which left a streak of blood along the side of his face. Eisandre ripped off a piece of her tunic and began to tie it over his wound.

"Saints, what was I thinking? If... if you had been hurt –"

"This is not your fault," said Eisandre. "This isn't like what happened with Allyk. We're both okay. Well, we probably both look like we've been dipped upside down in a swamp and gnawed by rats, but other than that..."

"Well, that is quickly becoming the new style. We can go back to the workshop and apply some noxious goo from the slug creature to complete the look," said Actaeon with a thankful smile.

As she finished tying the bandage off, he stood and pulled her into an embrace, careful not to put any pressure on her injured arm. She returned the hug and rested her head against his cheek.

"We make a good team I think," said the Engineer with a grin. "We should sell this house though."

"A good team, sure. You have all the brains. I'm just the girl waving the sword. And I agree about the house. We'll just have to keep looking, I suppose."

"But you are so much more than the girl waving the sword. You are also the girl that knows how to use that sword, and with the wrong hand at that. I am quite impressed with your skill."

He placed a light kiss upon her forehead before he let her go.

"I've never killed anyone before," said Eisandre, in a conversational tone. "I thought... maybe I should tell you that."

"It never gets any easier. Though it helps to realize that they effectively caused their own demise in making their decisions today."

"We are taught to be able to use deadly force when necessary, and also how to refrain from doing so when it is not. I wouldn't want it to be easy. But, at least, in this case, there wasn't any question of it being necessary. I'm just glad you didn't have to face this alone."

"And I am glad of that fact as well. Had I faced them without you, I would not have succeeded. You are a valuable companion to have around, in more ways than one. Shall we find our way out of here?"

"Did you want to search the bodies before we go?"

"We can search the ones at the entrance when I retrieve the arrows, I suppose. I do not wish to search them all," he replied after considering the bodies with a grimace. They made their way from the room.

While Actaeon pried open the door once more, she withdrew the rainbow luminescent artifact.

"I believe this is yours, sir."

"Perhaps I can set that in the sword of my defender in thanks for my life."

"It doesn't seem like that kind of artifact – it's way too big," she decided. "Besides, at this point, you are my savior as well. We're working together, and all the thanks that I need is that you are still walking at my side. And smiling too. Here. Take it."

The Engineer accepted it graciously and turned it over in his hand once before slipping it into his jacket.

A quick search of the bodies as Actaeon retrieved his arrows turned up nothing except for a small copper bit with a cross etched upon it. They left it there.

"Rest in peace, angry warriors," spoke the Arbiter softly as Actaeon closed the final raider's eyes. "I wonder what causes a man to run from all traces of civilization, to become 'wild', for lack of a better term. And to think, some of the other Dominions liken Raedelle to this."

"In some ways they are no different than the Dominions. The strong dominate the weak and send them on quests that they do not fully understand or agree with. Wars are fought by soldiers that must fight to provide for their own security at home, to make sure their families continue to be fed – all at the call of the powerful, the strong. People say that raiders and outcasts benefit from freedom from rules of civilization, but they will never be free from the forces of nature or the whim of man."

They walked the silent corridors, forging ahead into new parts of the ruin as they searched for an exit. They traversed slimy puddles filled with algae and piles of debris in places where parts of the ceiling had given way. Many-legged insects and spiders scurried out of their way, disappearing into crevices and under fragments. Numerous doors along the halls were long sealed shut, concealing innumerable secrets within. The fresh air continued to draw them onward, past many interesting artifacts and rooms that would've tempted Actaeon in any other situation.

One day, he would have to come back to this place and explore more. There were so many areas left unseen, with the promise of so much within. He'd already found two intriguing artifacts, and there were likely countless more among the ruins of this ancient building. Eisandre was his main concern right now, however; she had lost too much blood and was utterly exhausted from the effort of the fight. He pushed the thoughts of exploration to the back of his mind and concentrated on their progress as they made their way toward fresh air.

Eventually the maze of corridors ended in a large, open chamber. The chamber itself was in bad condition – its ceiling on one side entirely caved in, leaving a mountain of rubble that stood on display before them, like a frozen waterfall of ruin. Beyond it and above they caught tantalizing glimpses of bright sunlight. The light air current they had followed was now a palpable breeze on the back of the Engineer's neck. Through one of the bigger gaps, nearly six inches in diameter, a portion of the sky was visible like a blue jewel sitting just beyond their reach.

"Great," said the Arbiter with a dejected sigh.

"We are almost there, Eis. Do not lose heart. We shall find our way out of here. There – this!" He pointed and made his way over to a long bench along one of the walls. "We can use this to climb the debris so we do not slip on our ascent."

Actaeon knelt and pushed the bench until one end was against the base of the rubble slope. He then lifted the far end and walked the bench upwards hand over hand until it was lying bottom up against the pile. He found several pointy shards of elderstone amidst the rubble and wedged them beneath the end of the bench and the ground, kicking them into place with his boot before he stepped back to survey his work. The top of the bench nearly reached the largest of the holes that led to fresh air and open sky.

"This whole place looks likely to fall on our heads. We can still turn back and look for a different way out." Eisandre leaned against the wall and watched, casting a doubtful glance up at the cave-in before them.

"Listen, Eis, we are going to make it out this way," said Actaeon, taking her shoulders and looking into her eyes. "You are the best friend I have ever had, and I am not going to let that end in this dark ruin. Whatever challenge lies in getting out of here, well, we are both its equal. Ready to get out of here?"

"I'm guessing you already have some kind of plan. What can I do?" she responded with a look of amazement – the confident tone of an Arbiter behind her words once again.

"Just stay back for now, maybe you can foot the bottom of this bench for me."

That said, he made his way delicately up the bench, climbing using the feet on the underside. Halfway up, he noticed, with a grimace, that the cut on the back of his left hand had started to bleed through the bandage. When he made it to the top, he wedged his halberd in between the bench and where the ceiling met the rubble pile. Once that was firmly in place, he stepped onto the haft of the weapon gingerly and used his elbows to squirm up over to the hole on his belly.

He methodically removed one piece of debris at a time from the perimeter of the hole. Each piece he checked to make sure there was no load-bearing weight upon it before carefully removing it and finding another secure place for it at the top of the pile. The process was painstaking, and during it blood started to run down along his left arm, soaking his jacket. After several long minutes he had managed to double the size of the opening to their freedom.

"There's a big spider on your left arm," warned Eisandre from below.

The Engineer turned and watched an arachnid the size of a tankard crawl down his left arm. It paused to look him in the eye and then calmly sunk its fangs into the thick leather of his jacket. Actaeon pulled the dagger from his belt with his other hand and stabbing the wretched thing clean through and into the rubble below.

It sent some of the looser rubble scattering downwards, but Eisandre was vigilant and sidestepped the falling debris.

Actaeon wiped the spider halves from his blade, before returning it to its scabbard. He pulled down the thick material of the jacket from its collar to inspect his upper arm and breathed a sigh of relief when he verified that the fangs had not passed through the thick leather.

Not long after, he had enlarged the hole enough for a person to squeeze through.

"Alright, I think that should be adequate. Want to climb up here?"

"You should go first," she said. "The weight of both of us standing on the rubble may or may not make a difference when it comes to stability, but it doesn't seem like a risk we need to take. Go. I will follow. Besides, then you can advise me about where I should and shouldn't step, right?"

Without brooking argument, he removed his halberd and pushed his way up and through. After reaching the other side and assessing the stability, he motioned for Eisandre to follow. She made her way carefully up to the hole. He held the halberd out to help her the last of the distance until he could reach her and pull her up beside him.

As he lifted her through the constricted opening, she let loose a breath of relief and wrapped her good arm around Actaeon to hug him fiercely. "Thank you," she whispered, fervently.

Caught off guard, Actaeon grinned and returned the embrace.

"Thank you as well. I told you we would get out of there."

He glanced up at the beautiful blue sky and about them. They were standing upon a span of flat surface, probably the roof of the structure they had been within. It stood midway up one of the many huge and tentatively stable heaps of ancient disaster in the area. The sky overhead was every bit as dazzling blue as it had promised from below, cloudless and radiant with the greatness of the sun – a notably long break in the rains now.

As in the beginning of their unexpected adventure, a flock of small birds flew overhead, calling to one another as their flight shifted and dipped and soared. There was a good vista of the Boneyards from here, the graveyard of Ancient civilization glittering with a haunting beauty all its own. The Pyramid stood tall in the distance above it like some great guardian.

Actaeon turned to look at Eisandre's bruised, dirty, and beautiful face and placed a gentle kiss upon her cheek.

"Now you shall have to owe me that day at the beach," Actaeon said.

"And we will make time to go to the beach, where hopefully neither of us will fall into a hole or get dragged out by the tide or experience any other sort of life-threatening disaster," said Eisandre, still clutching him against her.

They lingered for several long moments, just enjoying the sun on their faces and the closeness of their embrace. Eisandre was the one to speak finally.

"Shall we head back now? You'll be okay to walk?"

"Ha! I just thought I should not let you go so that you cannot go falling into any more holes. I thought you lost to me for a moment there."

Before letting go, he gave her another squeeze and then drew to his feet and offered her his hand, which she accepted and held. "I am quite alright to walk. And yourself?"

"We've been through so much, Act. I can handle a walk back to the Pyramid. Hopefully our appearance in this state will not cause too much of a fuss."

Hand in hand, they made their way back to the Pyramid before night fell.

ACT TWO: BUILDING THE FOUNDATION

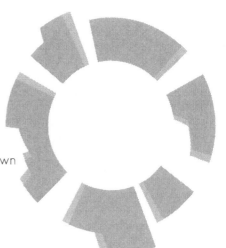

87 A.R., the 33rd day of Monsoon's Dawn

ONGOING ANALYSIS

"**H**OW DO YOU LIKE THE door?"

The young Raedellean woodcarver stood before the new door to the workshop, proudly rocking back and forth on the balls of her feet. Lauryn had been hard at work in the corner of the workshop for days now, first hacking away at something with an adz, and then whittling away with a knife – or at least 'hacking' was what Trench had called it from up in the loft while he was trying to catch an early night's rest.

Lauryn had arrived at the close of the market on the day following their first meeting, hauling a wagon filled with heavy timber. She returned each subsequent evening and settled into one corner of the big workshop. There she hung sheets up to block the view of her work and hadn't allowed either of them to see what she was working on.

Until now.

Actaeon appraised the new door, lifting a hand to shield his eyes from the rising sun's rays. The door was a work of art, with intertwined Raedellean knot patterns weaving their way in low relief over the thick outer face of the entire door. A pierced relief at the top of the door had been carved with a pair of crossed halberds set over a particularly intricate Raedellean knot. Topping it all off, in the center of the door was a high relief that depicted the Engineer and the two mercenaries locked in battle with the tremendous slug. He wondered why Lauryn had felt it necessary to drag the big slug costume behind her curtains, and now it was clear. He grinned and let his halberd fall against his right shoulder as he regarded it.

"There appears to be no discernable difference in functionality versus the previous door. However, it is good to see that you are versed in the creation of doors. Should I need one in the future, I now have no doubt to whom I should turn. I must note, however, that there are many other items of furniture, specifically in the loft, that have yet to be created. Proof that you can create these would be dually advantageous since it would highlight your ability and also offer increased functionality to our workshop," said the Engineer, tilting his head to the side and running a hand through his hair.

The girl's jaw dropped. She regarded Actaeon as she stood there, lips quivering, before she was distracted by the roaring laughter coming from the loft. Recognition dawned in her eyes and she grinned herself, before grabbing Actaeon's jacket and shoving him through the doorway.

"Increased functionality – noted, Master Rellios. I've a couple of ideas already. In fact, one of them involves a technique for the storage of said furniture. You'd best be off to wherever you are going before I conscript you into testing."

Another laugh came from Trench, up in the loft, and this time the girl was laughing along.

"It is an amazing door, Lady Lauryn," said Actaeon with a smile. "In all seriousness, I hope we shall get to see more of your handiwork. Nicely done."

She would get along just fine working with them, thought the Engineer as he traced a bow to her before heading out.

Kylor and the Arbiters had brought the materials that he'd recommended and piled them in the center of the ruined Sea Lounge amidst puddles of water and smashed furniture. He was pleased to see that they included the long lengths of glass rope that he requested. It would serve to have a backup safety mechanism in the plan. After seeing what had happened to Adept Comeris, he wasn't keen on taking any chances.

Less pleased was he to see the Keeper Knight, Atreena Covellet, standing beside the stack of materials. Clearly the Keepers were taking more than just a passive interest in this problem with Pyramid.

"Good day, Master Rellios," said Kylor, with a respectful dip of his head. "We have gathered the materials you requested. I hope you can make some better progress today. The Dominion officials are getting anxious about the loss of the baths and the danger to their officials."

"As do I, Kylor," said Actaeon as he nodded in return. "I see the Keepers are still interested in helping. And that the Loresworn have not sent anyone today – I suppose things will be substantially less exciting." He wouldn't miss having to deal with the risky and impulsive behavior of Fauntin Comeris, even though he'd have preferred the man to have a kinder ending.

"Perhaps you will suffer a similar fate," the Keeper suggested ominously. "I'm just here to make sure you don't use these artifacts to harm the people of Redemption. Fauntin did not treat the evils of the Ancients with seriousness and thus he is no more."

The Engineer grinned and knelt to retrieve one of the hammers, which he handed to her. "In that case, you may as well make yourself useful."

Atreena grunted her annoyance, but she accepted the hammer.

It took about an hour to build what he had in mind: A folding scaffold, made from the metal and wood supplies, that could be carried up and wedged into place before the end of the corridor, with its strange symbols. They chiseled deep notches into the cylindrical corridor just before the end in places that Actaeon marked with his charcoal stick. The scaffold unfolded and fit neatly into the notches, anchoring it in place. He then placed several wedges to prevent it from folding back on itself and stepped back to inspect his work.

It would allow space for at least one person to press forward against it and, while reaching both arms forward, still manage to manipulate the symbols at the corridor's end. If the end of the corridor opened up and sucked in the air again, the scaffold would bear his weight and prevent him from being pulled into the aperture. At least that was the plan.

Lengths of metal and wood were bound into a solid cross on the far side of the scaffold. Attached to a shorter length of glass rope, it could be lowered in place to jam the opening that had sucked in Comeris.

Satisfied with his arrangements, Actaeon fashioned a harness from the end of the long glass rope, tying off the other end down in the Sea Lounge. He instructed Kylor to stay with it in case he needed to be hauled back by hand. After donning the harness, he climbed back up into the corridor.

"I'll be coming with you. You're not to be trusted alone," said Atreena. Her tone brooked no argument.

"Very well. I would hate to be left to my lonesome in the swallowing corridor of doom."

"Quite the comedian, Shorian. Though notice, I'm not laughing. Proceed and I will follow."

They started down the corridor – Engineer and Keeper. When they reached the scaffold again, Actaeon stopped.

"Allow me to tie a harness around you as well. If the scaffold fails, it will be our only hope at survival."

Atreena glared at him and shook her head. "I will do naught to restrict my movements. As I've said, Shorian: proceed."

"You are sure? The scaffold was only designed for myself... Very well, I can see that you are determined, Lady Covellet. I do hope that you like Adept Comeris – you may meet him today."

Her response was the scraping of steel on steel as she drew her longsword from its heavy scabbard and pointed its tip at him.

"Just get it over with. I don't want to be here, so let's not draw this out."

"As you wish, Lady Covellet."

Actaeon took his place up against the scaffold, and, as the blue symbols flared to life on the corridor's end, he pulled his notes out from his jacket pocket and reviewed them. Once satisfied, he began double checking all of his equipment to be sure it was secure. He took special care to tighten his goggle strap after pulling them over his eyes – the luminary in the strap would be especially important not to lose.

Sparing a glance back at Atreena Covellet, he found her observing closely from several meters behind him, sword still drawn.

"I would advise you to put your sword away now, Lady Covellet. I assure you, I will perform no action requiring such weaponry."

The Keeper Knight stared at him, making no move to return sword to scabbard. He shrugged and began to press symbols methodically, with a pause after each one to recheck the notes. When he reached the tenth one, he folded the vellum carefully and slid it back into his jacket pocket.

"Ready yourself," he said, hoping the Keeper would brace herself beside him, but there was to be no such luck.

He pushed the final symbol.

The blue circle at the center blazed to life and flashed several times before it disappeared. Hairs on the back of his neck rose as air rushed forward before he could even see the aperture appear. The cool breeze increased to a whipping gale, followed by the gusts of a gale. His body was buffeted by the wind and pressed heavily against the upright scaffold platform, which helped stabilize it further against the anchor grooves.

Behind him, Atreena exclaimed in surprise as the wind swept her from her feet and slammed her into the platform beside him. The entire scaffold shook with the force of the impact and the Keeper's sword was ripped from her hand and spun wildly through one of the gaps in the scaffold, nearly catching the side of Actaeon's head as it passed by.

Annoyed with his failure to realize the hazard of the drawn sword, he watched it slam across the enlarging aperture. He slid down so that only his eyes peeked out over the scaffold platform. After watching what the forces had done to the Loresworn, he didn't need to break his neck.

As the aperture grew, so did the force of the wind behind him. It ripped at his clothing and pushed him harder and harder against the scaffold. The pressure made the aperture appear to blur and blackness crept in along the fringes of his vision. Beside him, he thought he could hear Atreena screaming – barely audible over the roar of wind. The entire scaffold shuddered violently under the buffeting force of the wind. Blinking to clear his vision, he concentrated on the aperture. It was almost large enough – just a little more. The longsword bent at the hilt and was gone – sucked through.

He fought the blackness seeping in as he watched the opening. Only a moment more, a little bit – there! He worked his arm over to the slipknot for the cross and yanked it. The big support cross fell free of the scaffold and flew forward a predetermined distance along the glass rope that held it. It stopped sharply, jarring the entire scaffold. As he'd planned, it fit neatly within the width of the opening and a moment later the aperture began to close, jamming on the metal-reinforced cross. Actaeon watched the bars shudder as the aperture tried to close, but they held fast.

The rush of air went on for much too long before it finally started to peter out. After what felt like an eternity, he felt his weight begin to release from the scaffold and return to the floor of the corridor. He collapsed and drew in a deep breath that brought attention to fresh pain in his ribcage.

Atreena fell down beside him, clutching her left arm, which was broken at an obscene angle. She looked over at him, her gaze containing a mixture of awe and defeat.

The Engineer grinned at her and climbed to his feet, twisting to stretch his sore back. After ducking beneath the scaffold assembly, he approached the jammed aperture. It held steadily with no sign of bending or fatigue in the support cross.

"Bastard..." gasped Atreena behind him, as she regained her breath.

He ignored her and continued forward, past the support cross. On the other side was another end to the tunnel and a similar ring of symbols lit up as he approached. There was also fresh air, coming from above. A glance up showed another circular tunnel, leading directly upwards to a chamber far above. Sunlight shined in through a jagged hole in the ceiling of the chamber. Little else was discernable up there.

"Well then, we have learned enough for one day," he said as he stepped back through the aperture and approached the scaffold, where Kylor had arrived beside the injured Keeper. "We will require additional supplies for the next stage of this investigation, and I will need Wave for this. He has some skills that we may require. Be sure to set a guard so that nobody enters the area without our supervision. The situation is tenuous for certain. Thank you for your help. Both of you."

The Keeper grumbled something under her breath and struggled to stand, trying to right herself with one arm on the curved floor of the corridor. Kylor reached down and tugged her to her feet.

"What should I relay to the Dominion leaders about the state of the baths? They will not be happy about their continued malfunction," said Kylor, any emotion hidden behind the reflective goggles that covered his eyes.

"There are other hygiene options in the city. Perhaps you could suggest the pools in the Warrens?"

The comment drew a chuckle even from the Keeper.

A letter from Wave awaited Actaeon back in the workshop. It was a lengthy letter and within were a dozen more drawings and sketches showing the Lazi's Tomb area and the structures around it. The details were all there and the course of action was clear to Actaeon based on Wave's information.

Lazi's Tomb was too open to defend as it was. Options such as building a wall, or digging a trench would take more manpower than Lord Zar had available to him for such a task. No, there was a much easier option. There were two places where the Shieldian holdings of Rust and Amphis' Ledge were closest together – roughly in the middle and at their eastern bounds.

There were two towers in the eastern region that were of the appropriate height. Actaeon had taught him how to measure tall structures by comparing shadow lengths. The towers were tall enough that if they fell in the correct directions, they would leave only a few defensible choke points between them and the other Holds.

So they would dig.

He drew forth two fresh sheets of vellum and drafted two letters. The first would be sent to Wave with detailed instructions. Wave would instruct the Lazi's Tombsmen, as Actaeon fancied them, and once he oversaw the start of efforts would return to the workshop. Along with the letter he included detailed sketches of the plan for their scrutinization. The second, shorter letter was for Lord Enrion Zar himself and detailed how many Tombsmen and what other supplies would be required. Both he sent immediately to the Shieldian Hold.

The rest of the day he spent in and around the workshop. There were many projects that he wanted to make progress with and he hadn't been able to concentrate on them sufficiently with everything that was going on.

"One of the best techniques to help me come up with a solution for a problem, is to work on a different problem," he explained to Trench and Lauryn as he toyed with the luminescent rainbow globe that he and Eisandre had found in the ruins. "The more you concentrate on a problem to be solved, the greater the difficulty in seeing all of the factors involved."

"If you say so, boss. I'll just stick to concentrating on what I'm working on. I'd rather not burn up the other half of my face," spoke Trench with a grin that tugged at the twisted burn scar on his face.

Lauryn stood quietly off to the side near the foundry and watched the giant man-at-arms intently while he worked to create castings of various parts for the Engineer. Actaeon had wasted little time in introducing the two mercenaries to his metal-casting process and both had picked up the basics very quickly. He found that having them melt and pour the molten metal into the mold saved him a lot of time to work on more things. Trench was especially skilled at the foundry and had even started building his own molds at the Engineer's direction.

With one hand, Actaeon slowly rotated the globe upon the heavy wood of the workbench. It was a fascinating artifact – a smooth sphere with different colored rainbow blotches that moved and shifted past one another like a desert mirage. When he tried to roll it, the globe curiously rolled back to the place it had been originally. Some sort of mechanism must be shifting inside of it, he thought, helping to right it and keep it in place. He gave it a bigger push and the globe rolled and nearly tumbled from the table.

When he reached out with both hands to stop it from falling, the device came to life.

The entire workshop was suddenly filled with stars, similar to those in the night sky; some were upon the walls and ceiling while others yet floated in midair. It was like he stood, not under, but amidst the stars in the night sky. When he reached out to touch one, his hand passed directly through it. And when he placed his hand between the device and a select star, the star persisted. This indicated to him that the artifact was not simply shining these star lights throughout the workshop as a luminary's light would, but rather generating the points of light in place. Also, the stars did not fill the entire workshop, merely the side he was on. He could find no stars on the far walls and ceiling, which meant that the device must have a range within which it could make stars appear.

"Interesting," he said, unaware of the fascinated gazes of Trench and Lauryn, who had paused to watch the star show.

It reminded him of such images he had seen throughout the ruins. They existed in various states of function – sometimes displaying an object or set of objects, and sometimes even one of the lost Ancients themselves – humanoid beings that appeared identical to the current residents of Redemption. Most of those, however, flickered and played as though in a haze. None were tangible and all that he'd seen always disappeared in the Darkest Hour. He believed that such projections were recordings of the Ancients and that, with their high technology, they were able to record clearly captured images in three dimensions and replay them at will. Those images that remained were inconsequential and incomplete, and, though many cultures throughout Redemption drew guidance and religious insight from them, Actaeon found it to be quite ridiculous to draw any conclusions from such incomplete data.

These stars though – they did not flicker or appear hazy. They were sharp and clear illusions that appeared more realistic than any other projection he'd seen in his travels. The device might serve as an excellent distraction if he ever needed it. There was no other use that he could think up. Perhaps it was a device for the entertainment of Ancients, children probably, given that they found it in some sort of school room. Perhaps it was for learning the positions of different stars – he would have to compare them to the night sky. It might even be possible to decipher how old the contraption was if he could relate it to any existing star formations!

When the stars began to rotate after he tapped it again, his theory of an entertainment artifact seemed to be the most likely explanation. Chimes played in the background, as though a distant sound, even though he knew the device was generated the sound.

Grasping the globe with both hands turned it off once more and he returned it to his pocket. It was an artifact that required further study.

"You could compare the current positions of the stars to it, you know," said Lauryn shyly.

Actaeon looked over at her in surprise. "Assuming they are accurate, you mean to date the artifact?"

"Of course! Then wouldn't we know how old they are? Or maybe how long they've been gone?" suggested Lauryn.

"That is a great idea, Lauryn! We shall have to look at it in further detail." The thought that they could potentially determine how long ago the Ancients had lived in Redemption was an exciting prospect.

When the castings were complete and polished, he started with the testing of the Arbiter's whistles first. There were several promising candidates and he had both Trench and Lauryn stand inside and outside the workshop and down in the cellar with the door closed to judge how audible the different whistles were from various locations. After that was done, he did the same while they blew the whistles, which also helped him to decide how simple the whistle was to blow. On one hand, it would be best if an Arbiter under stress could blow the whistle easily, yet on the other hand, if the whistle got into the wrong hands, it might be best if it was more difficult to blow.

In this way he narrowed the collection down to two choices: one an elongated whistle that blew air across the hole in an acoustic chamber at one end and the other a straight but short, fluted whistle that had several notches in the body.

The pipe whistle was more difficult to blow well, but once done correctly was incredibly loud. It could generate different tones by cupping one's hand around the chamber in different ways. Louder, but it would take more skill to use well.

The fluted whistle was not quite as loud, though it was still easily audible in the situations he had tested. However, it was easier to blow and the notches along the body could be covered to generate different tones.

Both options were considerably louder than the sample whistle that Eisandre had lent him.

He was pleased. The next step would be to have the Arbiters test the whistles in the field and decide on their preferred option.

The continuation of the slug slime experiments brought him behind the workshop and onto the plains of the Windmoor. There stood a haphazard cluster of stones far from the rest of the Outskirts. This experiment he did on his own – it would not do to put the others at risk. He prepared the wooden canisters that Lauryn had made for him and carefully inserted the various triggering mechanisms along with the slug slime and luminaries in accordance with the configurations in his notes. He worked late into the afternoon on these tests, with many failures and a few mixed successes. There were no explosions, but in a few cases he had managed to cause some more volatile reactions – some of which even burnt up the canister in the process.

Once Actaeon completed the tests he started back to the workshop. With the limited amount of slug slime, every experiment needed to be well thought out – at least until they managed to catch or kill another slug. The traps they had set out had no luck in catching slugs big or small, however. And the marketplace had no smells other than the normal tanning, perfume, animal dung, forges, and human sweat that the shoppers there found acceptable.

When he got back to the workshop, there was a Shieldian soldier waiting for him.

At first he mistook Adjutant Shar Minovo for a young girl. With her short stature and petite build, she seemed a child playing – dressed as she was in the plate-covered red tabard of a soldier. Her sharp features were unmistakably Shieldian and the only clue to her age lay within her dispassionate expression. Two single-edged swords were crossed upon her back and on her left arm was a brace of throwing knives. She stood at the entrance to the workshop, leaning against the outer wall with her arms folded across her chest.

"Good evening, young lady. Are you a friend of the Lady Lauryn? You can wait inside for her."

The knife that thudded into the open door of the workshop answered the Engineer's question as it stood there shuddering in what was left of one of the slug's eyes.

"Well then, that is no way to make introductions. Lady Lauryn worked very hard on that slug carving. Let us try again – I am Actaeon Rellios of Sh–"

"I know who you are, you foolish man!" spoke the girl-soldier, clenching her fists and taking several steps towards him in effort to intimidate. "I am no young lady! You will address me as Adjutant Shar Minovo of Shield. I was dispatched here by His Most Venerable Grace Indros Zar, himself, and you will heed what I have come to say!"

"On the contrary, I will do nothing of the sort so long as you continue to throw blades in and around my home. This is my workshop, and you will follow my rules, lest you want to explain to Prince Zar why I sent you away with a bill of damages instead of whatever else you may have come for," said Actaeon with a grin. Unperturbed, he continued into the workshop, knocking the knife from the door with a tap of his halberd.

He set his supplies down on one of the nearby workbenches and began to doff his jacket. Trench approached and eyed the soldier that now stood in the doorway cautiously.

"Any progress on the tests, boss?"

"Aye, Trench. I think I am getting close to something. I will be up in the loft doing some research. Please be sure that I am not distracted needlessly," said Actaeon before starting up the loft stairs.

"That won't be a problem, Master Rellios," said the giant. He stepped forward and began to swing the large door closed.

The tiny soldier surprised him as she pushed the door out of his hands and stepped quickly past him.

"Wait, Master Rellios... my apologies. I should've given more courtesy, but the news I bring is dire, and I have suffered somewhat already. I really... I really need your help with something."

She stood there waiting for his reply, her fists balled up and eyes narrowed upon him.

Actaeon paused on his way up the stairs and glanced over his shoulder.

"Ah, Lady Minovo," Actaeon said in a friendly tone. "Do come in. What might I assist you with?"

Though she cringed at the word Lady, some of the tension went out of the Adjutant's shoulders.

"The sewers beneath the marketplace have been invaded. There is a creature most foul that has been running amok and killing more denizens. I've been down there myself with my entire unit. I return alone."

Actaeon walked back down the stairs and gestured for her to join him at one of the workbenches as he pulled up a stool.

"Have you seen this creature? Is it another giant slug?"

"No, not one of the slugs. It was something even worse. The soldiers call it a deathcrawler. I've not seen anything like it in my life."

Over tankards of ale that Trench poured them, the young Shieldian soldier related to them the details.

After several Shieldian artifact hunters had not returned from the market tunnels, a unit was dispatched to investigate the disappearances. However, that unit did not return either. So Adjutant Minovo's elite unit was sent to follow up. It was not long into their excursion before they were attacked.

The creature that attacked them had been, from what she could make out during the melee, a giant insectoid creature with an elongated, hard, brown and black carapace with dozens of long, thin legs protruding from either side of its body. "They almost looked like waving hairs, they were moving so fast," Shar recalled, with subdued horror. "It seemed to glide along on them." It stood two feet tall and about eight feet long. She expressed some doubt about the exact size of the creature because it had moved with such speed that some of the fastest warriors in her unit could not even bring their blades to bear. Long tendrils that appeared to be longer versions of the legs extended in either direction from both the head of the creature and the rear of the long carapace.

"In mere lifebeats, my unit was completely cut to pieces. Devastated. I managed to cut several legs from one, but my sword only glanced off its main body," said the young soldier while she stared blankly into her tankard. "It was... horrible."

"By the Fallen, lass! How'd you survive such a thing?" asked the giant man-at-arms, perched atop a stool which he dwarfed.

"It stabbed me with something – I... I couldn't move. I tried to scream, but I couldn't. It was unbearable. I finally passed out and when I awoke, I was in a small chamber with no light. After I found my backup luminary, I found that there were two others in there. One of them was dead – one of the artifact hunters, I think. He was several days dead and had been ripped open, from the inside, it looked like. The other was one of the soldiers from my unit. He was badly mangled and barely breathing. His legs and one arm had been completely amputated and were cauterized somehow. He was too far gone – I helped him on his journey to meet his Ancestors. I didn't stay long to look around then, I just ran and ran toward fresh air and made it out alive."

The young Shieldian took a deep swig from her tankard and set it down heavily upon the workbench.

"A paralyzing agent. Interesting. And they kept your fellow soldier alive. Perhaps they wanted you for food in the future," Actaeon suggested. "For their young maybe. That would explain why the artifact hunter looked like that. Perhaps the young crawled in through his –"

Trench's big hand on Actaeon's arm stopped that thought from finishing aloud. Actaeon frowned and bit his tongue, reaching over to scratch the back of his right hand through the fingerless glove.

"In any case, I will need a few days to devise a plan. I think we want to capture one of these creatures and study them more closely, but I will need some time to come up with something. Go recuperate and return in three days time. I will have something ready for you then."

DEATHCRAWLERS

T TOOK ACTAEON, TRENCH AND Lauryn several days to prepare the traps for the deathcrawlers. They modified the dimensions of the slug trap and built an appropriately sized one for the task. The deadfall box was so large, that they would have to build it for onsite assembly using mortise and tenon joints that Lauryn expertly crafted for them. Metal angle brackets that they hammered into proper shape at the foundry were also prepared to reinforce the trap.

Wave returned on the day they were showing the Adjutant how to assemble the traps. He reeked of some sort of sweet odor and strode into the workshop with an uncharacteristic aloofness. The swordsman stopped in front of the wide open door and rapped his knuckles loudly upon it before he strode nonchalantly into the workshop.

"Hey, nice door you had put in. Whoa! You two've been busy since I left. I hope you brought one for me, or at the very least intend to share," he said, oogling the two young women with his single eye.

A guffaw from Trench was the only thing that stopped Minovo from going for her brace of knives. Lauryn set aside a wooden mallet and gave Wave a bemused look.

"This must be the Wave I've heard so much about. I see he wastes no time making good impressions," said Lauryn.

"Mind yer tongue, Wave, or our young Shieldian friend is like to put a blade between yer balls! Welcome back," said Trench as he reached out to give Wave a clap on the back, but before he could complete the action he pulled away, wrinkling his burn-scarred nose in disgust. "What in a god's sphincter is that smell?! Been missing the slug reek too much and find the local Shieldian equivalent?"

"God's sphincter is right! A ripe description of the hole in the ground that Master Rellios sent me off to. There wasn't much to do there but smoke some root decoction that a farmer there made. Pierxon Hyk's his name – the Fallen know he's got some farm! Aside from that, I don't know what Lord Zar sees in that place. I guess it's a rite of passage for the brown-nosing nobles over there. Manage the ass crack of the Dominion and prove yourself to Daddy."

Wave laughed and pulled out a thin brown paper roll. The Adjutant closed the distance between them and smacked it out of his hand before he could light it.

"Guaraja root? You should be ashamed of smoking that mind-bending trash and be glad as well – for if you didn't have a good excuse for speaking of Shieldian nobility with such derision, I'd gladly hone my blades on your carcass," said Minovo, standing nose to nose with the swordsman.

"I'd love to see that, little gi–"

"Welcome back Wave," interrupted Actaeon, placing a hand on the swordsman's shoulder. "I see you have met the Lady Shar Minovo. She is an Adjutant of Shield sent here by Indros Zar himself. We are helping her solve a deathcrawler problem that I will bring you up to speed on later." He gestured to Lauryn. "And this is the Lady Lauryn of Lakehold. She has come on as my apprentice and another associate that will be helping us with our projects. She has a sharp eye and a steady hand for woodworking. You can let her know what items you will need up in the loft for your bunk area. In the meantime though, please get your equipment ready. We will be departing shortly for the Sea Lounge. There has been some significant progress in the matter, but we shall require your climbing expertise."

"Aye, boss," said Wave before lighting his guaraja stick. He puffed on it once and winked at Minovo with his single eye before turning to head upstairs.

Minovo turned back to the others and marched over, her face flushed with restrained anger, and something else – desire perhaps?

"Are you alright, Adjutant? You look a bit distracted," said Lauryn, exchanging a smirk with Actaeon.

"I'm just fine. Continue. My time is valuable."

They finished showing Minovo how to set up the trap and when old Vez showed up some time later all of the supplies were loaded onto his cart for deployment. The Adjutant left shortly thereafter with the carter to deploy the first trap.

Wave lit another guaraja stick as he and Actaeon strode along down the Avenue of Glass towards the Pyramid. His coil of climbing rope and other gear was draped over one shoulder.

"She's a cute one, that Adjutant. Not as young as she seems though, but I like that – sort of like myself."

"You had best be careful with your women, Wave. The last one you were spending time with disappeared, you know."

"The last one? Magdalena? I heard she married some Niwian sop from that owns a plantation down in the colonies. She always wanted to be rich and well off. Though I guess even a Lady has to work down there. Not as easy on the frontier. Hey, the Niwians have doubled their colony assets now that the Keepers are joining them – the Niwian colonies vastly outsize the others down there. Hopefully they don't try to take over that whole area, eh? That'd throw off the balance of power and resources down there."

"I was speaking of the Lady Agarine Lartigan," said Actaeon, coming to a stop. "She disappeared after the Monsoon festival and has not been seen since. The Arbiters were asking about your contact with her, but Trench and I vouched that we saw you at the workshop later that night, so you were not suspect. I think the fact that we mentioned you were on Shieldian business helped to alleviate suspicion."

"Ah, that's unfortunate. I think she'd of been fun to show a few things. It isn't too often you get a shot at a porcelain blond like that."

"Is that your goal then, Wave?" asked the Engineer as he resumed walking. "To amass a vast list of ladies with whom you have shared a bed with? Many of the women in Pyramid lack intellect or wisdom of any kind; in fact it is often that their only skills are the sort of elitist sophistry that is common of the nobility. It seems like a waste of time to conduct intercourse with the majority of them and to endure the frivolous courtships that lead up to such engagements."

"Not at all, my friend. There is far more to the intricacies of inter-Dominion politics than just negotiation, talk and power. There is much that can be both gained and learned through sex as well. It is also a means of picking up work – though we haven't had such a need for that of late."

"Fine – I shall humor you then. What, if anything, did you hope to gain from sleeping with the Lady Lartigan?" asked the Engineer.

"I'm glad you asked. The Lady Lartigan was an old prospective conquest of mine. You see, her cousin is none other than Garizo Fothrakas, the Lord Protector of Memory Keep himself. When he and I were just lowly officers in our respective militaries, he called into question my character. I challenged him to a duel, and he instead tried to frame me for a theft. You see, he knew he would lose and did not want to be made a fool of. He said he would not honor a thief with the right of a duel. So I told him that I would either see him in the dueling ring or I would bed his beloved cousin. So you see, it was an old goal."

"Ah, so you are a man who holds grudges then, Wave."

"Not so much. Age and time soothes all those things. But I'll tell you what – I never forget a lady!"

When they arrived at the Sea Lounge, Kylor and Atreena were already there waiting for them. The Keeper Knight had a new longsword sheathed on her off-hand hip. Her broken sword arm was splinted and in a sling around her neck.

Kylor stepped forward and regarded them both with his goggle-covered eyes.

"I am glad that you could make it, Master Rellios. The nobles are ever anxious."

"Of course, Arbiter Kylor. I would not pass up the opportunity to learn more. Wave has returned and with any luck, will help us to ascend to the open chamber today." Actaeon grinned and turned towards Atreena. "I am beginning to think that you live here, Lady Covellet. I do not believe you have met my companion. This is Wave. He is a man-at-arms in my employ."

The Keeper Knight dipped her head ever so slightly to Wave before she replied.

"I am here to make sure that you don't use any Artifact of the Ancients in a way that will harm the denizens of the Pyramid. I will be here until I am completely satisfied on that account."

"I do not understand. Is it not true that the Keepers hope to destroy the Artifacts at the direction of the Allfather? Why would you be here monitoring Pyramid and not trying to destroy it?"

"Would I be given the opportunity, I would destroy this structure in a moment – but not with all of the people that live here. My first and foremost oath to the Allfather is to protect the civilized peoples of Redemption. The people that live in this Pyramid must be taught the ways of the Allfather. Only then will they choose to abandon this source of evil and demolish it. That is the answer. Show me a writhe-blade or a luminary and it will be destroyed."

"And what of our artifacts? Why is it that you do not try to destroy them?" asked Actaeon, with the heft of his halberd and a gesture to the equipment worn by him, Wave and Kylor.

"I am no fool, like that Loresworn Comeris. I realize there are limits and times when we must cooperate with others. Ask me again though, amidst the ruins, and when my arm has healed, and I assure you that you will not have time to ask these questions before your artifacts have been eliminated."

"Brave words from a brave lady," said Actaeon, and he meant it. "You ascend through the tunnels of this evil structure to watch evil men and make sure their deeds are not ill. I am amazed that you would even cede to the possibility that those such as we could do anything that is not malign."

"You are not evil men. You are simply misinformed – all of you. When you turn to the ways of the Allfather and hear his words, it will be clear that the way you have chosen can only result in ruin."

At that, Wave couldn't resist. He stepped forward and waggled a finger in front of the Keeper Knight. "Now, now, Lady Knight. Now that you are a Niwian, you need to show more respect for your fellow Redemptionites. I don't think the Lord Protector would be very happy with you pushing all that 'Allfather' nonsense."

"Niwian is but a nation-state, as are all the Dominions. I am and will always be a Keeper, just as you are a Swordsman, and he is an Engineer, and he is an Arbiter – but even more than that. If you lose your sword arm, you might stop being a swordsman; if he loses his mind, he might stop being an Engineer; and if he loses his sight he might retire as an Arbiter. However, being a Keeper runs to one's very soul. I could be a Czerynian, or a Raedellean, or a man instead of a woman, or a Priest instead of a Knight or a Tailor or anything, but I would never stop being a Keeper. It is simply what I am. When you accept something like that as a part of you, there is no Dominion or power that can change that. I hope that one day you are blessed enough to discover that for yourself."

"Well put, but I think Master Rellios might disagree with you. Poke out his eyes or cripple his hands and I think he'd still be an Engineer. Might not be as fast as one, but it'd stay as much a part of him as my sword is for me. And speaking of poked out eyes, how's that eye you owe me coming along, Act?" asked Wave, casting a skeptical look toward his employer.

The Arbiter interrupted them with the low clearing of his throat. "I would be content to listen to this longer, but as Atreena pointed out, I am an Arbiter and I have important duties to attend to. Can we proceed?"

They made their way up into the corridor and Actaeon led Wave to the area in the corridor where the vertical shaft lead straight up toward the chamber. Wave stood there for a long while, glancing about and muttering under his breath. After a time, he spoke.

"Seems like you made good progress here, Act. Do you have something that can throw my grapple up that high? I can't swing it here – there isn't enough space in the corridor."

Actaeon turned to examine Atreena with an arched brow. After looking her over for a moment, he grinned. "You don't need two splints for that arm, do you?"

A few minutes later, Atreena sat at the side of the corridor while Kylor re-splinted her arm. Meanwhile, Actaeon put the grapple, to which he had bound the Keeper's splint, against the shelf of his bow. He pulled his goggles down over his eyes and surveyed the span of the shot.

"Might as well give it a try. Everyone stand clear."

The Engineer pulled the splinted grapple back against the string and lined up his shot, holding his breath. When he let loose, the grapple/splint combination went flying upward, taking from the coil of rope that stood by his right side. He could hear the echoed clattering of the grapple as it landed on the floor of the chamber above. Wave then took over and tried to slowly pull the grapple into a fixed position.

It took them three tries before Wave tugged at the line and announced that he had hooked something substantial. He tugged on his harness and hooked the line into it before he started on his way up the rope using ascender clamps. The small mercenary climbed nimbly and was quickly up top. He tied off the rope and lowered the slack back down.

"Alright, head on up."

Knight Arbiter Kylor climbed up first and Actaeon followed. The Keeper Knight tugged at Actaeon's pant leg as he started up.

"How am I supposed to get up there?" she asked, shrugging her broken arm.

"Perhaps you should have thought about that before you decided not to listen to me last time, Lady Covellet. Do not worry though, I will only be reconnoitering this time. I do not make hasty decisions."

The Engineer pulled free and started back up the rope, ignoring the aggravated yells of the Keeper below.

When he reached the top, Kylor and Wave pulled him up and he had his first chance to look around.

The room was absolutely tremendous and reminded him of the Sun Chamber, but without the criss-crossing stairwells. Instead there were large pillars, both horizontal, vertical, and diagonal, criss-crossing the room and intersecting with one another in various places. Some of the pillars were as large as the corridor they had ascended from, and Actaeon figured they must be large conduits – for water most likely. Other pillars were thinner, some as narrow as the shaft of his halberd. The pillars were painted a multitude of different colors which did not appear to be related to their size. He followed several of the pillars' paths throughout the chamber and found that they would always exit and enter the chamber. There were none that simply terminated, though several intersected with three enormous spheres held in place at the top of the chamber with some sort of blue translucent material. One of the three spheres was fractured on the northern side of the chamber and it looked like the contents of it had spilled to the floor below long ago and left a sort of solidified silvery metal on the ground that covered a significant portion of the room there.

The ceiling was fractured in that location as well and allowed light to stream in from above – it was part of the ruined northern face of Pyramid. The slope of the western face was also present, which would put the room against the northwest corner of Pyramid, Actaeon thought. It was notable that there were very few luminaries in the room, but there were some along the floor in a line extending from beneath the solidified metal and deep into the chamber where they took a turn upwards to follow a square column. At the top of the square column was a large cube with clear windows. The inside of it was also lit by luminary light.

The hole that they had emerged from had been a large hollow pillar, but had shattered somehow above the floor. Huge pieces of it lay upon the floor around them.

"This is where it all comes together," said the Engineer.

Wave and Kylor just looked at each other and shrugged as Actaeon led the way towards the lit column. He stopped before it and knelt to inspect the ground, running his hands along it and wiping centuries of dust away. With his hand he wiped dust away in a wide line to form a large rectangle adjacent to the base of the lit column. When he was satisfied, he stood and turned to the others.

"Gentlemen, would you please join me inside the rectangle?"

Kylor stepped forward into the rectangle.

Wave quirked a brow, "This reminds me of a game we used to play as children."

"I can assure you it is much more interesting," Actaeon replied.

When Wave stepped within the rectangle, the Engineer turned to inspect the face of the column. As his hands approached it a circular symbol flared to life. He pushed it and the entire floor started to move. Wave and Kylor flinched back and bumped into Actaeon as parts of the floor rotated up and seemed about to crush them before coming to a stop at right angles.

Actaeon turned around and grinned at the men, "Not to worry, it is just a railing. I have seen this sort of thing before."

As the floor they were standing on began to rise farther and farther from the ground, the need for the railing became apparent. They rose swiftly as they were carried away by the section of floor and all three men felt an unfamiliar lurch in their stomachs, as if they were falling.

"I think I prefer my rope," said Wave.

As the lifted floor took them higher they were able to see the room from a better vantage point. Most of the columns appeared to have a lit symbol or set of symbols upon them and each one was different. Something else became clearer as well as they continued to ascend.

"Fascinating. It appears that something large crashed through the wall into this chamber. See how the walls around the hole are curved inwards? Whatever caused that was from the outside, and it was substantial. It also did not remain afterwards, unless it accounts for the melted mess down below. Something might have been launched at Pyramid. Or maybe many things. It came from somewhere north. It must have been the event that obliterated the Northern Descent."

A hiss of air blew from behind them and they turned away to see dozens of symbols flicker to life in the small room behind them. The lift had halted its ascent.

The Engineer led the way into the room and paused in the center. From his location, you could see through the windows to nearly all of the symbols on the pillars in the room outside. In fact, some of the windows were slanted so that you could even see symbols far below. There was a semi-circular desk in the center of the room in front of him with a plethora of symbols and changing images. A glance about the room found more images and symbols in the walls and ceiling above the windows.

Another hiss of air sounded as the wall slid shut behind Wave and Kylor after they both walked in.

"What is this place? It seems to be of great import," said the Arbiter.

"I believe this is where everything in Pyramid comes together and this room holds the machine that controls it all. See how the symbols on the desk before me correspond to the symbols on those pillars? We came out of a pillar that carried water, so it is a good assumption that many of these pillars – especially ones of the same diameter, are also carrying water. Perhaps there are other things that are carried as well in these conduits. Air, energy, other fluids? We cannot be sure, but I am certain that this is the crux. The unexplained aspects of Pyramid: the Baths, the dancing water in the Terrace Gardens, the Sea Lounge, the Rainbow Lounge – I would hypothesize that they are all controlled here and much more. More than perhaps we will ever understand."

"So what in shattered Redemption are we supposed to do here, Act?" asked Wave.

"I agree with your man-at-arms. What can we hope to accomplish in this room? It would appear to be beyond our understanding," said Kylor.

"It may be, but that will not stop us from trying. This room is the key to fixing the Baths, I am certain of it."

The Engineer withdrew a roll with several sheets of vellum along with his sharpened charcoal stick. There was a clear area on the desk before him that had no symbols, and he unrolled the sheets there and began to draw.

"We may be here awhile."

They didn't arrive back at the workshop until late that night. But, when they finally did, Adjutant Shar Minovo was waiting for them, along with a most horrid smell.

"Your trap didn't work," she said disdainfully from where she sat, tilted back on one of the stools at a workbench that she sat at with Trench. Tankards of ale sat in front of both of them. The Shieldian looked worse for wear, her hair covered in some sort of gunk and scratches upon her face and both arms. She folded her arms and looked critically at the returning Engineer.

Wave leaned against the door frame and lit yet another of his guaraja sticks.

"How did the trap malfunction?" asked the Engineer as he approached the bench. He set his halberd down on the adjacent bench and pulled off his jacket before pouring his own tankard and joining them.

"The gods' damned floor fell apart underneath us," she recounted angrily. "We fell into some sort of underground lake. It smelled like piss and burned my eyes. I managed to crawl to another tunnel and lift myself out. Three others made it with me, but we lost the others in the collapse, or they drowned."

"I am sorry that you lost your comrades, but hold on a moment," said Actaeon. "The floor fell apart underneath you? I thought that you said the trap malfunctioned?"

"It did! It made the floor collapse!"

Actaeon shook his head. "I would think that to be very unlikely. Please tell me more about the circumstances."

"It happened! We tested it like you said, and it collapsed the moment the trap triggered. The unit I brought in the first time went the same route last time and that didn't happen. Your damned trap nearly killed us all!"

"Let us not jump to conclusions prematurely. What were the differences between the unit you brought last time and the unit you brought this time?"

The Adjutant took a long swig from her tankard and set it down heavily.

"Well, I can tell you that most if not all died both times!" she said, fighting to keep down her anger. It took her a long moment and another two swigs from the tankard, but she was able to bite down her emotion enough to speak. "The first group was five of us. This time I brought more to be safe. Fifteen! Fifteen warriors of Shield died! We cannot afford to lose more people down in that miserable cesspit!"

Actaeon's eyes widened and he set his own tankard down.

"Fifteen people? Bringing so many people through an old and untested ruin is extremely hazardous. The tunnel likely collapsed from their weight. The trap only weighed as much as a few men at the most. Also, I thought I instructed you clearly to place the traps at locations near the entrances to the tunnels – not to delve deep into the depths where you would be vulnerable to attack. It –"

Minovo interrupted him and drew to her feet.

"I was the leader of the expedition, and I made the decision to go there. We could not wait for months, so I decided to place the trap close to where we'd encountered them before. It was your poorly made trap that ruined my plan! It was your f– f–"

Trench's fist slammed down on the bench, the sound echoing beneath the workshop vault, bringing her to a stuttering halt. His voice was an ugly roar. "Sit yer ass down, lass, or I'll sit it down for you! Open yer ears, and listen to the man. He's telling you you brought too many people too deep into the tunnels. You were the leader of the expedition, and you led those men to their deaths. Taking a risk that didn't need to be taken and not following the instructions of someone that has real experience taking down creatures in the market tunnels. You want someone to blame? Well then, by the Fallen, find yourself a damned mirror! But for now, shut yer yap, and tell Master Rellios the rest of the story."

Wave, who had been quiet until then, spoke up. "How can she shut her yap and tell the story at the same time? Make up your mind, Trench."

The giant shot a glare at his friend.

"Go ahead," said Wave with a smirk. "Tell me to shut up and tell a story. I'll try to pantomime the entire damned thing!"

The giant burst into laughter. The Shieldian soldier was not so amused. Her face had gone red and she had retaken her seat as instructed. She seemed even more shaken than she had been earlier.

"I'm sorry," said Minovo, bowing her head. "You're right in this. It was my fault. I didn't think of it – that the extra soldiers had caused the collapse. It was just that... your trap triggered and the collapse happened. I had thought... no, but I see now that I made a mistake.

"Correlation does not infer causation," said the Engineer. "I would say it is more likely that the number of soldiers you brought into the tunnels caused the collapse, though it is always possible that the triggering mechanism could have caused the collapse somehow. I am afraid that we will never know for sure given that the section of tunnel has collapsed."

"Um... as you say. Though I should have listened. It is true, what Trench says: the deaths are my fault. I will bear the responsibility and I will see this through – correctly."

"I am glad to hear you say that. And all of us make mistakes, do not be too hard on yourself. Without knowledge of the stability of the tunnels, you made an intelligent decision in bringing more warriors. Please do continue with your story," spoke Actaeon.

"Aye. So we started out, the four of us that survived the fall, traveling through a maze of tunnels. We kept following the ones that seemed to lead upwards. We only had one luminary and it had been somewhat damaged, so we had to feel our way along in some places. One turn that we took, we found those... those slugs," she said, shuddering. "Small ones though. They ripped into Bin and killed him instantly. I had one in my hair but I smashed it quickly. Then they were all around us, springing left and right and dropping from above.

"I thought we were dead, but then all of the slugs started to leave. They started heading back down the incline of the tunnel to where we had come from. A moment later three deathcrawlers arrived, and we ran for our lives. I felt the slugs squishing under my boots, and after a few minutes of hard running, I realized that I was alone."

Actaeon stood and retrieved a large half-through bottle and stick. He approached Minovo and began to scrape the slime from her hair and into the bottle. She just sat there and allowed him to do so, not wanting Trench to yell again.

"Were the slugs fleeing the deathcrawlers?" asked Actaeon. "Of course! It would make sense why we were unsuccessful in the capture of additional slugs. When we destroyed the giant slug, we may have disrupted the entire ecosystem down there. We paved the way for the deathcrawlers to arrive with nothing to keep them at bay and with all of the smaller slugs as their prey they are able to feed and grow to a very large size. The slug supply must be dwindling though to cause the deathcrawlers to prey on humans."

"What happened then, Adjutant?" asked Wave as he joined them after finishing his smoke.

"Yes, please continue," said Actaeon.

"Yes, they were moving away from the deathcrawlers," Minovo continued. "Maybe they were fleeing. I don't know. I just kept running and didn't stop. I finally arrived in a big open room. There was a glowing symbol there and I touched it. The floor moved around me and I felt this sick feeling in my stomach. Eventually I was blinded by light and collapsed. Two Arbiters helped me up. Whatever it was took me to the Sun Chamber in the Pyramid. They told me the floor opened. After that I came back here."

Actaeon met Wave's eye. "Sounds familiar, does it not?"

"Aye, another lifting floor."

Trench downed the rest of his tankard and set it down roughly.

"You're one lucky lass. The gods must be watching out for you," said the big scarred man.

The Engineer reached over and withdrew a charcoal stick and a sheet from his jacket. These he passed to the Adjutant. "Quite intriguing. Do you think that you can draw a map of your travels to the device that brought you to the Sun Chamber? If you reached the Sun Chamber from there then there could be a direct threat to the heart of Pyramid."

"I don't know. I just kept running away. I don't think there were too many options. It was just one way or back to the deathcrawlers. Maybe there were splits in the passage, but I just don't recall."

"Just try to sketch the route that you took until you fell through the floor. It would be a great help. And also sketch where in the Sun Chamber the lifted floor brought you to. This way we can return to investigate it more thoroughly in the correct location. It seems that having floors fall out from under adventuring parties is quite the common trend these days," said Actaeon, thinking back to his recent experience with Eisandre.

Adjutant Minovo took the charcoal stick and began to sketch.

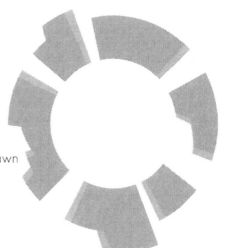

87 A.R., the 43rd day of Monsoon's Dawn

LOST & LEAVING

T HE SUN WAS ON ITS ponderous journey downward, past the midpoint of its daily adventure. On the Blacksands Beach, waves crashed noisily and assorted debris and artifacts stood in stark contrast to the absorptive black sand – remnants of a major storm that passed through two days prior.

The pair walked slowly out to their spot, their moods high as they arrived at a long sought after moment together following their adventure weeks earlier.

Actaeon wore his usual grin, his halberd balanced over his shoulder with a small bundle tied to its end. Beside him, the Knight Arbiter Eisandre looked much recovered since he'd seen her last. Her various wounds were beginning to heal and the color had returned to her face, but she would be wearing the splint and sling on her sword arm for quite some time to come.

As they arrived upon the beach, the Engineer closed his eyes and basked in the warmth of the sun.

"Is Wave back yet?" asked the Arbiter.

"Wave has returned with the information that I need. I must depart soon to complete that project. He did a fine job out there. I hired Trench and Wave as men-at-arms, not as engineering apprentices, though they are doing quite well – to my pleasant surprise. Wave brought back very detailed information for me to use."

"Those two are becoming more than men-at-arms in many ways," she observed as they walked along, sand crunching under their boots. "You've referred to them as family before – to me as well, for that matter. Although you may have meant that more in the sense that we simply work toward common purposes. They do seem talented and helpful and devoted to you, Act. I'm glad that you have them as friends."

"Me too. I am glad to have you as a friend as well, Eis. By the way, how have you been coping with your injury?" he asked. "Perhaps when you are recovered we can do some sparring to help the rejuvenation of your injured arm. The Fallen know that I could certainly use the practice."

"I'm bored," admitted the Arbiter, honestly. "And I'm having a hard time dealing with not being at my best, on multiple levels. I've been jogging the empty corridors of the Pyramid to try to keep in shape, but I'll be happy to spar as soon as I'm able. Preferably before I practice with the Arbiters again."

"Well, I would be honored to be beaten up in a sparring match by one of the finest of the Order of Arbiters."

"Don't worry," Eisandre reassured him. "If we spar, I'll be gentle about beating you up." She hesitated for a moment, her gaze upon the sea, before she spoke again. "I've missed you, you know. This might sound absurd, but everyone else seems so cold in comparison."

Actaeon reached out to rest his free hand companionably on the small of her back. "Not in the least," he assured her. "I have missed you as well. When I am with you I feel complete somehow, like I never have before," he said, blushing.

"Why does it make you blush to say such things?" she asked, studying his face with genuine fascination.

"Did I blush?" laughed Actaeon, lifting his hand to his face. "I do not know. Perhaps because it is not my wont to say such a thing." He met her gaze. "Wanted you to know that though. It is important to me," he said, trailing off.

As they continued along the vast shore they spotted the large weather-carved rock formation in the distance. Wordlessly, they adjusted their trajectory to head in that direction.

"Ah! There's the place we dreamt of in darker times. Is it not wonderful that we are actually here?" said Eisandre with excitement.

"Truly wonderful," Actaeon agreed. "And I am thankful that we are mostly hale and together in this place."

"We are alive," Eisandre said. "And we are here together. I am glad we take the time to say the things that are important. Life seems to be too fragile to do otherwise. How are you feeling? You look well and you sound happy, but then you almost always sound happy."

"How could I not be happy when I am always in such fine company?" Actaeon replied, as they drew closer to the shelter. "Aside from some aches and pains, I feel wholly myself. A good thing, as there is more than ever going on of late that requires my attention."

"You do realize that most people wouldn't consider me to be 'fine company'. They would find me rather boring," Eisandre informed him. "Or at the very least, strange."

"Well that makes two of us," said Actaeon with a grin. "Most people would rather doze off than listen to me drone on and speculate about how things work. I have never met anyone that really enjoys my company, excepting maybe Trench and Wave, who like making fun of my eccentricities. Besides, if you were not at least a slight bit strange, then I imagine I would not find you as interesting as I do."

They arrived at the stone structure and Actaeon stuck his halberd bundle up inside the rocky nook. He ran his fingers along the sun-warmed stone before lightly scratching his right arm through his sleeve.

"Unlike most people, you truly see the world around you," said Eisandre softly. "And when you talk about your observations, I don't get lost in my own thoughts. I can be here. With you. It... makes me feel almost like a normal person."

The Engineer pulled himself up to sit upon the ledge facing the water and smiled down at the Knight Arbiter. He was beginning to feel something for her that he could not explain. He canted his head to the side, regarding her with interest, and arched a brow before speaking once more. "Do you often have that happen? Become lost in your own mind? It bothers you?"

Eisandre looked down at the sand, a briefly troubled expression touching upon her features. "Ever since I was very young. It became worse, however, after my father, the Duke Branwyn, and my oldest brothers, Gawyn and Owayn, were killed. Why do you think that my mother and Aedwyn allowed me to leave?"

The Engineer knew what she was getting at. There were many children born in Redemption that were not considered normal – they were social outcasts and an embarrassment to their line. Those who could function at the higher levels were sent to give service in the ranks of the Arbiters, or to the Altheans as healers or tenders of the herbal gardens. And those were the lucky ones. Others who could not function on any productive level because they were so Lost in their thoughts were more often simply put to death – most people didn't have the resources or time to support such people that were considered failures from the start.

Actaeon recalled a scene from his childhood where he watched a man throw his infant granddaughter to her death down Incline's Steep Road. He had later learned that the grandfather had knocked the father out and ripped the baby from the arms of his own daughter – the woman had been wailing nearby as her father hurled the infant to its death. The baby had not smiled or reacted to any family members even after many months had gone by.

Afterward, during weapons practice, his father had taken him aside and squeezed his shoulder. He still remembered his words, echoing out of the distant past, "Remember that baby, son. It didn't die for naught. It died so that you would see the error of hasty judgement. When we judge an individual thusly, we draw the curtain on all of the potential that they might ever have." He could still recall the momentary doubt in his father's eyes though, and it was not the last time he had seen it expressed toward him while his father had lived.

Legends told that when the first people of Redemption, or at least the first newcomers, had passed through the portals into different places amongst the ruins of the ancient city, they were all bereft of memory of their past. They were sent to this place, with its own lost memories – a place that had been left behind for people that had been sent away. Some of them wore fetters and others had staves – the Prisoners and the Wardens - their only identifying features. Though their memory of the past was gone, many did retain their knowledge, or at least a good deal of it. How to start a fire, how to fix a weapon, how to splint a broken bone, how to hunt and how to cook – these skills kept them alive in the first days.

However, some of those that passed through the portal had been diminished somehow. Some simply sat down and stared blankly as though at something that no one else could see. Others spoke in some indiscernible otherworldly language, or gibberish, or both – holding a conversation with no one. A madness seemed to punctuate many of the affected's behaviour and they would spend their days endlessly screaming, or worse, they would lash out and hurt those that would try to care for them. In an unforgiving world where the elements and strange creatures and forgotten technology were constant threats to life, such people quickly became a burden. In some places in the city they were simply put to death and in other places, they were sent away into the wilds to fend for themselves. It was a choice of practicality in those early days and most historians considered it to be a necessity.

As the years went on though and the population grew and expanded, there would be the occasional child who was born diminished in the same ways as the first. The Lost, as they came to be known, were reviled and rejected by their own people, cast off into the shadows of the world.

Actaeon frowned and hopped back down to help her up into the stone shelter. "Now that was not thoughtful of me. I should be helping you up first. How is it when you are lost in there? Sometimes I could describe my condition similarly, but, on the contrary, I quite enjoy being lost in a problem or design. I could not imagine it being undesirable."

"That's probably because you are accomplishing something productive with your thoughts. I just... get entangled in mine. I've never tried to explain it before. No one's ever asked." Eisandre paused a moment to accept his help up to the ledge, flinching as she accidentally put some weight on her injured arm. With his help though, she was able to find a perch up on the ledge. "What was I saying? You likely get lost in a problem or quandary because you are thinking, reflecting, and considering – letting all the pieces of a puzzle rearrange themselves in a vision of clarity or answer to a question. For me it's just feeling... lost. Like being drawn into a labyrinth of thoughts that are only half mine and too loud, sparkling and beckoning, but sometimes haunted and dark. Before I joined the Arbiters, there were times when I could barely discern reality from dreams."

Actaeon hopped up to join her and took her hand gently in both of his own. Her fingers curled around his and he met her brilliant blue gaze as he spoke. "You need not be lost, Eisandre. I am here with you, and will always be there when you need someone to talk to or to pass the time with."

"You cannot always be with me, Actaeon," she pointed out, logically.

"But, when you are here, I am... happy, to not be alone. You may ask me any question, sir, about my past or future," she said, sensing that he was curious. "I told you so the very first day we met."

"There I feel that you are wrong," Actaeon insisted. "I can always be with you, in thought and spirit alike. And I thank you for your openness. Though discretion is sometimes a valid course of action, I do believe that the truth is the best path in all things. Thank you for sharing your truths with me. I admit to being curious about what you describe. Ever since you were younger, you felt lost inside your mind? Can you describe how it feels? Do you hear thoughts, feel emotions, experience memories that are not your own?"

He wrapped an arm around her shoulders as they watched the waves roll in to crash against the black sand to let her know that his feelings for her wouldn't change regardless of her answer.

"I believe you're asking if I am Lost," she murmured, her voice barely audible beneath the sounds of the crashing surf. "As in one of the people who are shunned from their families and Dominions. Untrusted, disliked, because they are not quite in the present world and nobody can understand them. And I think you already know the answer. Do you really wish to hear more of the details?"

The Engineer squeezed her in reassurance, smiling before he replied, "Well, I am not entirely convinced of your description. Especially since you are one of the only people in this world that I trust and one of the few that I truly like. Whatever world you happen to be in, suffice it to say that I am glad you exist in this one at least partially so that I might know you. You are always most welcome in my family, Eisandre. I would love to hear all of the details. In fact the phenomena interests me greatly, but I will not press you for any details if you do not wish to speak about it."

"People normally fear what they do not understand. But then, you are different," she said, as she relaxed a bit against him and interlaced her fingers with his. "My family didn't... didn't *not* love me. Even now, they love me very much. But I am not a great beauty like Eshelle, a dashing hero like Aedgar, or the sharp leader that Aedwyn is. They all sheltered me, protected me, and mostly hid me from the public due to my 'fragile health'. It was the best they could do for me.

"I wanted something more though. The Arbiters helped me to hone my mind and body into someone who could be useful to society – someone who could walk in public with honor and be respected. I have hidden this part of myself for so long, Actaeon, that I feel I don't even know how to talk about it. But I will give it some thought, if you wish, so I can describe it to you better in the future. You never make me feel Lost," she declared, turning to face him. "I don't know why or how that is. My brother Aedwyn can do that as well, in a way. I see him filled with golden light that warms my heart and lightens my spirit. He used to stay with me at night, when I was small and frightened by my nightmares, and I would never be afraid when he was there. But you don't have a light. It's strange. I just see you clearly. Like you are more real than anything else – even me. Will you run yet? Do you think I'm crazy?" she asked with genuine curiosity.

At her turn of thoughts, the Engineer laughed aloud and gave her hand another squeeze.

"I think you are amazing. If I do any running, it will not be away from you. Fear of the unknown is not useful in my field of work. I am glad that you feel like you fit in with me. I also feel like I finally found someone that I can feel normal around as well. Most people in Redemption do not understand or accept me for my strange viewpoints and speculations. You, however, have been understanding and supportive of me ever since we first met. If you wish to describe that part of yourself to me in the future, then I would be most interested. And you do not need worry, for I already know who you are, Eis. I am not going to change my mind simply because you are gifted or cursed with visions – however you might think of it. I just want you to be sure that it will not hurt you to discuss these things. In other words, do not do it for me, do it for yourself if you need to... or want to."

"I don't know if it will hurt me or be helpful to discuss this aspect of myself. As I have said, I've never done so before, not even in general terms. There's been every reason not to, after all. I will think on the matter, however. You change many things in my world of shadows and light. I even think you might truly admire me because of who I am, rather than despite it. It's... I don't even know what to say..." Clearly moved, Eisandre lapsed into silence for a long time before speaking again. "It's harder for me when there are more people around – when there are more distractions. If I address you formally or if I seem cold, it's because I fall back on Arbiter discipline, propriety, etiquette, duty and such to keep me from... from drifting away in a way that would be socially unacceptable. It's how I focus.

It would displease me greatly however, if I offended you or hurt you in some manner by appearing to push you away. I want to explain this while I can – while it is clear to me. Arbiters are supposed to be distant to a certain extent, you know," she said, noting the disparity as she rested her head upon his shoulder.

"Well sometimes it is best to get these deep and brooding secrets out," Actaeon insisted. "Hiding them away takes a lot of effort at times. And you are quite right to imagine that I admire you, even more so knowing that you have overcome our culture's expectations to rise to success as a finely skilled Knight Arbiter. Do not worry about my feelings, I understand your need for focus."

"It has taken the effort of my lifetime," she replied, matter-of-factly. She lifted her head from his shoulder then and turned to look at the bundle tied to his halberd. "What did you bring?"

Actaeon grinned mischievously and withdrew something from his jacket. He placed the object in the palm of her hand still held within his own. "I brought this for you. I made it for you, Eis."

Eisandre stared down at the object in her hand for a long moment, startled. The object he had deposited in her hand was a necklace of wrought gold. Hanging upon it was a pendant that was crafted to look like a flower, the petals sculpted from small slivers of the translucent blue material that they had found in the Boneyards – the edges curled inward back on themselves so as not to cut the wearer. In the center was the large faceted stone that he had found during their most recent adventure. She tilted her hand slightly, scattering dozens of tiny rainbows about walls and ceiling of their rocky enclosure.

She stared at it, frozen in a sudden maelstrom of thoughts, past and future – echoes and strikes of lightning across a black, empty sky. Such jewelry was a rarity in the starkness of Redemption. The practical or the functional, but rarely the decorative. Most resources needed to go toward the one all-consuming goal that all Redemptionites shared: survival. Only the political and social elite, mostly of Pyramid, could afford to waste resources on such frivolities. The piece in her hand, however, was one fit for royalty.

Her thoughts swarmed and coalesced into one word, because she knew she had to reply and that it was right to do so.

"Why?"

Actaeon touched one of the blue petals. Until that moment he had not known the reason he had made it himself. It was indeed extremely unusual for him to craft such a thing: completely devoid of utility and failing to solve any problem. However, it was the same inspiration that he drew upon in order to make the necklace, was it not?

"When I saw that at first..." he began, struggling for the right words, "I thought of you. The design came to me shortly thereafter. I suppose I find different uses for things in various situations that are applicable at a given time. And this time I wanted to show you how much I care about you for some time now. This design seemed able to accomplish that. It is something I have never tried before. I understand if you do not wish to keep it. My designs do not always work, after all!" he concluded with a nervous laugh and a smile. He reached over to scratch his right arm through the sleeve of his jacket.

"When my sister received gifts of jewelry, it was from men who desired to court her. No one has ever given me anything of the sort, for any reason. And I find myself wondering, all the same, how such an ornament that would be a fitting gift for a Princess could, in your mind, be linked to someone so plain and unadorned as myself. How must I be in your eyes, I wonder? You amaze me sometimes. Please don't be so nervous. Look, I am here and still me," she said with a faint smile.

"Will you run yet? Do you think I'm crazy?" the Engineer echoed her words from earlier with a chuckle. "In my eyes, you shine as bright as the sun. You always seem to underestimate yourself. You are an amazing person, Eisandre. A tremendously skilled swordmaiden, the kindest and most caring person I have ever met, the descendant of a strong line of Raedelleans, and possessing wisdom unequaled by many. I understand that pride can be a negative aspect, but in fairness, so can excessive humility. Do not let your own feelings of shortcoming limit how far you might soar in this life."

"It depends on one's perspective," she responded. "I was also cut off from that strong line of Raedelleans, in name and heritage, because as a Lost I was unfit to be a Companion or to marry into a political alliance. Or even to be a productive citizen, much less be in line to rule. And now I am not a Raedellean at all, but an Arbiter who has short hair and wears men's clothing, who sleeps in a dormitory with forty other Arbiters and who has taken a vow not to own anything beyond what is necessary for survival or for the effective performance of her duties. I am one of many now. Nothing remarkable, nothing special – except, it seems, to you."

"Well, you can tell the other Arbiters that the necklace is mine and I asked you to hold it for me," replied Actaeon, always looking for a solution to every problem. "If you ask me, your family made a great mistake in cutting you off. However, everything that happens in this world has led us to where we are now. In the least, everything that has happened enabled us to meet, and that I am glad for. Just remember that the events that shape a person's life need not define the person as well. Had I let that happen in my own life, I would be living among the outcasts, in truth. In this world you need to carve your own path, and anyone who wants to stop you be damned."

"I think that sometimes my family feels that they made a mistake too," noted Eisandre with a sad ghost of a smile. "But in any case, I am not discontent to be an Arbiter. I believe in the Oaths and the Vow, that I will live a good and useful life by following them. We are not much into carving our own paths, however, unless you look upon the Order as a whole. Ours is a very different world than the struggle of living in the Dominions.

"Here," she said. "I will wear the necklace now, because you have made it for me. And because it is beautiful for all that it is and for all that it means. But I cannot take it with me, or I will have to give it to my superiors. Even if I am merely holding it for you. Will you help me put it on?"

The Engineer smiled and took it from her hand. He carefully hung it about her neck to allow the flower to fall upon the front of her tunic.

"Thank you for wearing it, albeit briefly," he said before he returned his gaze to the waters. Eisandre leaned against him again and they watched the sun setting as it began to descend down toward the water, the sky turning a myriad of colors. He pulled her close, her body warm against his own.

"Thank you for thinking me worthy of such a gift," said the Arbiter softly. She reached up then, to touch a finger lightly to his lips. "Before you protest that I'm being too modest, please accept that this is a first for me. Everything here is a first for me. And, thus, allow me to marvel."

"And me," he spoke, almost inaudibly as her finger fell away. Together they watched as vibrant colors spiraled out into the darkening sky, heralding the sun's descent into night.

They stayed like that for a long while, watching the sun disappear and the stars emerge, sheltered by the stone and by the awareness of something new within themselves, neither wanting the moment to end.

Much later, as the sounds of night came out, a blanket of stars covered them, and the crash of the waves seemed to amplify, the Engineer said, "You make me feel complete."

"Did you feel incomplete before?" She sat beside him still, listening to the waves crash upon the shore.

"I think so, though perhaps I had not realized it at the time, never having experienced that part of me that was lacking. I brought some food for us to enjoy," he said, gesturing towards the bundle tied to his halberd.

"I am glad that you thought to bring food. We'll be able to stay here awhile longer. I'm not at all ready to go back."

"Neither am I. I think we can stay for quite awhile out here if we so find the need."

Actaeon gave her a hug and crawled farther back under the overhang. He untied the bundle and spread out an assortment of fruits, cheeses, bread and a small jug of light wine with two small wooden cups. Then, with a grin, he looked up at her and withdrew the small crystal sphere from one of his pockets. He set it down in the center of their rocky hideaway and grasped it with both hands.

Suddenly the chamber was filled with its own stars, the pinpricks of light spreading out in a canvas underneath the rocky ledge. The stars seemed to match up with the night sky outside their hideaway, spreading the infinite blanket into the stone shelter to cover them as well. Toward the edges of the stone enclosure and in the center, many of the stars floated in midair.

Eisandre drew to her knees and reached out to try and touch one of the floating stars, her blue eyes wide. "What? How?"

"Unsure of exactly how, though some of the behavior is similar indeed to focused light. There are some characteristics that are essentially different, however. For example, you can notice how they do not project beyond a certain distance. If there is no object between the source and the extent to which it was designed to travel, then it will simply hang in midair," he explained, waving his hand through one of the floating stars himself. "The only thing I have seen similar to this are the voluminous projections that we have seen from some of the larger artifacts around Redemption. There are many hidden in the Boneyards, some of people, others of objects, or even otherworldly places. I have never seen one in such a small form before – quite brilliant. I will have to figure out what makes it work. In fact, I already have some practical ideas for it."

After he finished, he handed her some slices of cheese and fruit.

"Here, Eis. Do not worry, this is all pretty inexpensive, but very good. Some of the best tasting fare among the humble market stands. I put it all together myself earlier today with a little advice from Trench," he explained, then lifting the small jug of wine. "Care for some of this? Rice wine I picked up from The End. There is some sort of honeyed fruit at the bottom that Oril assured me was quite good. I have not tried it myself yet."

"I wasn't worried," she assured him in response to his figure of speech. "But I am appreciative. We'll try at least a small cup, yes? It seems like a special occasion. How often do we eat supper together among the stars?"

Actaeon laughed and poured them each a cup. "Well, if I continue to carry this little sphere around, then we can eat supper under the stars whenever we like." He lifted his cup and smiled, "Shall we drink to our continued health and friendship?"

"To our continued health and friendship – and to not falling into dangerous holes," she added before they both drank.

They sat side by side with their backs against the stone wall, where they could gaze out into the starry darkness beyond the glittering black beachhead. He passed her slivers of different cheeses and fruits on slices of bread. After a time they were getting full and there was still quite a bit of food left.

"Perhaps I went a little overboard," said Actaeon as he nudged her good shoulder companionably with his own. "But I really was looking forward to this. When you are staring at death's hand, money does not ever seem to be a concern."

"I could argue with you about that, were I so inclined, but I'm really not. There were times in the ruins there when I could feel the darkness closing in, when the pain and the incessant obstacles made it difficult to believe we would ever see the stars again and eat dinner and feel happy. But you were there, with me, every moment. I could see you clearly, and you were my hope. I think perhaps I can understand why money is less important than simply being here together and celebrating our life. Thank you, Act. For this lesson, and so much more."

"Thank you for celebrating with me. It means a lot," said Actaeon as he passed some strawberries over to Eisandre for her to enjoy. "Sometimes I wonder what is out there, in the great sea and beyond," he said, with a gesture at the waves. "Something tells me there is more to this land than just Redemption, much more. Perhaps even more information on the Fallen. One of these days I think, I would like to find out."

She took a sip of her wine before replying, "As if there isn't enough for you to study in Redemption alone."

"Just think of the answers that might be found!" said Actaeon with a wondering smile. After a long moment of silent consideration, he spoke again, "I will go forth into Shield soon. With Wave returned from the preparations, I want to see the results."

"Shield," she repeated with concern in her tone. "I... I will worry for you. You will go where I cannot follow."

"I will be fine," he reassured her, placing a hand atop her own. "My mind is my shield. I will keep safe and will return before you know it. Redemption needs my aid there."

"I have the utmost confidence in your intellect and cleverness both, but some dangers can't be outsmarted. You will have Trench and Wave with you when you travel, yes?"

"Most dangers can be anticipated or thought through. Some just might need bearing the risk in order to accomplish one's goal. Of course they will accompany me. That's half the reason I hired them, to intimidate people enough to stay away from me during travels and explorations. Besides, I have been in and about that region in the past. It is not so bad as some other places."

"There are many kinds of dangers. Physical, political, emotional – and don't forget random holes. My fellow Arbiters and also my siblings deal with danger every day of their lives and I do not worry so for them. I wonder why this is different. And it is not, before you suggest it, a matter of me not having faith in your abilities."

Actaeon gazed deeply into her starlit eyes and when he spoke, there was a certain mirth to his tone, "I think there is more between us. I have found myself wondering the same. Why would I worry about an Arbiter whose skill and prowess in combat so greatly exceeds my own? Even my other friends, I do not worry about them. I think that I find myself concerned with your safety because I have strong feelings for you. I could not imagine life without you there to spend it with."

Eisandre didn't know how to reply to such a statement, but she realized the need for a reply, so she took his hand in hers, their fingers intertwining. They sat together in companionable silence for a long time.

When she finally spoke, it was but a whisper in his ear, "I am not afraid of the unknown, Actaeon. But it is unknown. I do not know how to define certain emotions nor how to decide what is to be done about them. But I am relatively certain that if something were to happen to you, when you go away from me to do whatever it is you must do, that I would lose a very real part of myself and there would be cold and darkness where there is now the most beautiful warmth I have ever known."

"That is the kindest thing anyone has ever said to me," he said, amazed. "It is unknown for me as well. We can learn how to define and act on these emotions together. I understand if it is difficult, but I know we shall have each other to lean upon along the way."

"They were the best words I could find to hold my truth," she replied, the faint flush of her cheeks hidden in the darkness of night. They were both feeling the wine now. "I have known myself for many years as Eisandre the little sister, and Eisandre the Arbiter, but with you, I am different in some way. I like the Eisandre who sits with Actaeon, drinking wine and surrounded by stars. Logically, the first step of anything after this point is that you must come back safely from your upcoming journey. And by safely, I also mean to include not getting into trouble with Eshelle Caliburn of Raedelle. Trust me, you do not want to see her mad."

"Well, I hope 'Eisandre who sits with Actaeon' stays around for a long time, I quite enjoy having her to sit with," said Actaeon. "As for Eshelle, I would not think that she would become angry with me unless there is a misunderstanding. I hope to help Redemption as a whole through this project with Shield, so she should have nothing to worry about despite the usual political tensions. If she wishes to speak to me, then I can only give her the truth, for that is all that matters."

"Politics can be complicated but I need not tell you that. And I dare not advise you further, beyond my simple wish that you will remain well. You do have your mind to protect you, in addition to your general affability. I imagine those must be great advantages." She stopped abruptly, and said, "We have said what must be said, and I wish you the very best for your journey. But you are not gone just yet, so I will enjoy what remains of this portion of our time together. Perhaps, when we part, this necklace will bring you good fortune."

"Politics is the most dangerous creature in all of Redemption. It can bring great rewards, but must be treated with the utmost caution," agreed the Engineer. "I will return sooner than you know, and I shall keep your necklace with me as a reminder of the good fortune of our friendship. As for my trip, I must finish what I have started. If I do not show up to advise and check to be sure things go well and were done properly, many people may well be hurt. We are bringing one of the great structures to its knees. There is much to learn there – whatever the outcome."

"I understand," she said, sounding worried. "It sounds like a very large and dangerous project, this one."

"A tremendous project. In fact, the biggest that I have ever undertaken," said the Engineer, excitement in his voice. "I believe we have taken the proper precautions though, and if everyone pays attention, then no one should be harmed."

"It is no wonder you wish to be there," she said, reaching her hand up to touch his face, tracing his jaw and the shape of his smile on his lips. "The sobriety and routine of an Arbiter like me must be stifling for you in some ways. There is much excitement in your work that is far more compelling."

Actaeon's laughter stood in stark contrast to the rest of the conversation. He shook his head and met her gaze, his own eyes sparkling with mirth in the starlight.

"Oh yes! It has been nothing but dull duty and boredom with you, Eisandre! In fact, you would be the most dry and uninteresting person I have ever met if it was not for the fact that you are the most interesting, compassionate and wonderful person I have ever met. And that is not even counting all of our adventures and excitement together. If all the Arbiters are anything like yourself, I would do well to get to know them all!"

The Engineer's jovial tone brought forth a grin of her own. "Alright. I will eventually be able to accept that I'm not dull in your eyes, Master

Rellios! But to most people, I really am. Really. Really!" she insisted merrily. She brushed his cheek with her thumb. "You make me a better person, I'm sure of it. But it would be no sacrifice to get to know the other Arbiters better, if you feel so inclined. They are all fine and dedicated people. My partner Garth, like many of our Order, believe that it is not possible to build true friendships that are not with other Arbiters. That no others could ever truly understand our commitment and our vows. But I'm not sure I agree. You already know me better than almost anyone. I felt like we knew each other from the first moment that we met."

"I think it certainly helps that I accept and appreciate the Arbiters' purpose here in Pyramid. Many of the politicians and warriors have trouble understanding the value of neutrality and understandably so. However, neutrality, or the illusion thereof, is essential to my work since I do not wish to limit my opportunities or enrage any Dominions. In general, I hope that my work will help Redemption as a whole as well, so I can understand your sense of duty.

"To be honest, I was thrilled and surprised that you wanted to join me that first time we met in the Boneyards, despite my incredibly long name," said Actaeon, joking about their first encounter. "Finding a beautiful Knight Arbiter out there in the Boneyards was intriguing, and I wanted much to get to know you more. I am glad to have had that opportunity. Though I knew little about you at the time, I did feel immediately that I had a sense... a sense of your soul, perhaps. That you were a good person, and I took an immediate liking to you."

"I do recall the day of our first real meeting quite clearly," she said, the memory bringing a smile to her lips. "I asked for your name and you waved your halberd about menacingly as you challenged me to a fight, and threatened to... what was it? Spontaneously combust? I remember that you burst out laughing at my reply. I liked you from that moment on."

"I liked you from the moment that you did not try to skewer me with your sword," he replied with a chuckle. "Though the first time I ever saw you was in Saint Torin's Hold when you caught my eye. The way you looked at me... I was hoping to meet you eventually. Though the circumstances of our meeting were certainly unanticipated."

"You must like a lot of people," said Eisandre, eyeing him suspiciously. "Since you are not suffering from any obvious sword wounds. And I remember Saint Torin's as well. I do not know who I am there anymore, so it can be difficult for me at times. And there were so many people on that particular evening, all a blur. You were clear, even then: Green eyes. Goggles. Polite words. All that strange equipment. That everpresent grin. I'm glad we found each other in a quieter moment and that I didn't skewer you with my sword and that you didn't spontaneously combust." She lowered her gaze then, smiling shyly. "We give each other many flowers in the form of compliments, I observe."

"Well, you certainly stood out to me clearly among many that day. Your wonderful blue eyes, obvious beauty, the air of confidence about you – how could I not give you bouquets of compliments?"

Then beneath the sparkling stars, both real and artificial, Actaeon leaned forward and kissed Eisandre lightly upon the cheek.

She was startled by the action and was silent for a short time after, absorbing the moment. But then she picked up the conversation from where they left off.

"I would protest, as I usually do, that Eshelle is the beautiful one: the confident leader, who everyone admires. But I am not talking to everyone. You are Actaeon Rellios and you evidently like me just as I am." She smiled then, and he felt his heart leap in his chest.

"Well you are right at that, indeed. I am Actaeon Rellios and to me you stood out like the glittering jewel upon your plain grey tunic stands out now, when I first saw you. Yes, Eshelle is quite beautiful as well, but you shine more brightly than the sun to me."

And eventually, their heads touching as they leaned against the back of the stone shelter, they drifted off into contemplation and, much later, sleep as they listened to the crash of the waves and the patter of rain that began to fall upon the sand.

FELLING THE GIANT

"You're late, Master Engineer!" called an annoyed voice as Actaeon trudged up to the workshop in late morning. The Outskirts were abustle with activity outside the Engineer's workshop. Thirty or so Shieldian soldiers were busy packing up a half dozen large handcarts from supplies that were being unloaded from a large drawn cart. Old Vez was there, supervising as they offloaded the supplies he had brought.

A young girl looked out of place as she yelled and waved a scabbarded sword to and fro to give directions to the soldiers. Actaeon grinned to himself when he realized that the young girl was Adjutant Minovo, bristling with knives and swords as usual, but still so small as to be easily mistaken for a child.

Lord Enrion Zar stormed up to him, and the young nobleman did not look pleased. "We could have left at dawn but for your galavanting! Wave tells me that you were away all last night on some project or another."

Actaeon dipped his head politely as the Lord drew near. "Aye, some important research needed to be conducted by myself, Lord Zar," he said, telling a half truth. He and Eisandre *had* investigated the starsphere, as he now thought of it, after all. "We may now depart and besides, it will give the team working in Lazi's Tomb the time to conduct secondary checks on everything even before we arrive."

"If you say so. Don't forget that every moment extra that we delay is another moment that the domain I am responsible for is at risk of incursion from the Ruinic barbarians. Plus, in case you haven't heard, Adhikara is severely flooded to the point where Ajmani refugees are fleeing along the caravan road, which kills my hope of a quick march into Rust. Instead we'll have to hoof it through Stormstair, and I'm sure you hold the same opinion as me about that Czerynian cesspool. Why do you think I have so many soldiers? I'm not taking any chances there," said Enrion, crossing his arms impatiently.

"That would seem to be fortuitous timing for al-Arshad and his Kendran allies. The disarray there will not help the Lady Ajman in asserting her claim as Raja," said Actaeon, considering.

"Yes, so I suppose it is worth our little detour. Viyudun would be an easy pawn for my father to keep under his thumb. Too bad it had to be right at this time. Are you ready to depart?" asked Enrion as he adjusted his formal tunic.

"Aye. Allow me to close up the workshop, and I shall be ready," Actaeon said.

Inside the workshop Trench, Wave, Lauryn and another man sat around one of the workbenches. Each had a tankard in hand and appeared to have been making a toast before Actaeon walked in.

"Ah! Loverboy! To young love – may it never fail to distract even the most complicated minds!" said Wave before downing the contents of his cup.

Trench roared a laugh and drank as well before speaking, "Welcome home, Act. One for the road?"

"No, thanks. I have already caused the Lord Zar to grow impatient enough. We should depart immediately. Oh, and Wave... if my business with the Arbiters is young love, then sending you to Shield resulted in fierce addiction," said the Engineer with a broad grin, admitting nothing.

"I'll second that! Thank the Fallen he ran out of that Guaraja trash," said Trench, lifting his tankard.

"Ha! If that was *business* you were conducting with the Arbiters then I am running entire goddamn Dominions from the beds of young noble ladies," said Wave, his words bringing a chuckle from Lauryn. "And that's right, Trench! I should be able to restock some Root while we're there."

"If that is the case, then you can stay, and we shall bring the Lady Lauryn instead," said Actaeon with a smirk.

"Oh please!" chirped Lauryn, hopping up from her stool. "I mean, I'd love to see what you are up to there."

Actaeon approached the Shorian girl and placed a hand gently on her shoulder. "I know that you would – but right now you are the best person to continue running the projects in the workshop. Can I count on you for that?"

Lauryn looked down at her feet before nodding reluctantly. "Yes, Act. I'll take care of it. But you'd better take me next time!" She withdrew a small cloth-wrapped item from a pocket in her skirts and handed it to him, "Oh, and you'd better take this. It should clip over your goggles."

"You got it," said the Engineer, accepting the gift with a smile. He unwrapped the cloth to reveal a finely carved wooden frame. In it were pressed two darkened lenses that had been lying around the workshop. "Thank you, Lauryn. This will be useful."

It was then that the young man who was seated at the workbench stood and offered a respectful bow of his head, "Master Rellios, I am Inditrovalis Jem, newly appointed Adept of the Order of Loresworn. I hope you don't mind, but Lord Zar has invited me to travel with you on this journey."

The young Adept couldn't have been more than sixteen or seventeen. Roughly cut brown hair partially obscured brown eyes that were wise beyond their years. His face was punctuated in the center by a long nose that canted radically to the right – the result of a poorly set break, no doubt. He wore rough traveling garb along with a tabard with the common sigil of the Loresworn upon it: a blue bolt shooting from the tip of a writheblade. Across one shoulder was a bandolier of small half-through bottles and at his hip was an empty ceramic scabbard.

The Loresworn caught Actaeon's glance at the scabbard and smiled, "The Lord Zar dislikes the writheblade and so I don't wear it around him."

"Well met, Inditrovalis," said the Engineer with a nod. "How much do you know about the plan?"

"Oh, very little, but enough to know that I can't miss seeing this. I know that you plan to modify the very structure of the city on a scale never before seen." Inditrovalis was unable to hide the excitement in his voice.

"Yes, that is correct. You are most welcome to come along. It is the Lord Zar's project, after all. You will learn everything that you are willing to see," said the Engineer. That said, he turned to the others. "Alright, gentlemen. Let us proceed."

Trench hefted a large pack while Wave slung a smaller pack and a heavy crossbow over his shoulder.

"'Gentlemen'... now that's a first for you, Trench!" said Wave, earning him a rough smack in the back of his head.

It took them two days to reach Stormstair. On the way eastward, along the Avenue of Glass, there were already dozens of Ajmani refugees and caravans arriving. They were all sodden, weary and short-tempered. On several occasions they shouted at the Shieldian party for taking up too much of the road.

With Adjutant Shar Minovo leading them, they made their way northeast and along the southern fringes of the Boneyards. The main trade route led them on a winding course around several partially collapsed structures, beneath a grand arch of the Ancients that towered over them, and wound through the main rubble pile of the Boneyards itself in several places.

On the second day they came upon Redoubt and broke for lunch just as it began to downpour.

Redoubt was one of the few intact Ancient buildings in that part of the city, and it jutted from the ruin like an imposing sentry. A stubby, hexagonal elderstone tower was punctuated at the bottom by a wider four-sided base. At each corner of the base jutted forth a massive pillbox with loopholes set in the walls facing every cardinal direction. Inset into the southern wall was a large door, the only entrance - also of the Ancients, the mechanism of which was only accessible from the inside.

The red shield pair of the Order of Arbiters was painted high on each face of the tower and Arbiters patrolled the battlements above the lower level. Some appeared to be very young – only boys. After a brief exchange between Shar Minovo and one of the older Arbiters up on the battlements, it was agreed that they could take their lunch under the cloth canopy that had been erected just outside the entrance. The possibility of the Shieldian party entering the structure was not broached by either side.

The fortress had been claimed by the Arbiters during the Sustenance

Wars. Until then, Czerynian and Shieldian traders had used it as a waypoint shelter. With the instability of the time, it was a strategic decision for the Arbiters to claim the impenetrable fortress in order to assure the continuation of their Order even if one of the Dominions decided to wipe them from Pyramid itself. The Arbiter presence in Redoubt proved to be priceless in the defense of the Pyramid during the Invasion Wars, as it gave the defenders a steadfast emplacement from which to assault the tribal forces that had besieged Pyramid from the rear.

"Make friends with the rain. The sun won't be coming out again on this journey," said Wave with a grin as he bit into a peach and wiped the juice from his chin.

"Always the positive one, eh Wave? I've seen worse rain in this place," replied Trench with an ugly scowl.

"Aye, but that rain was redder and stickier, as I recall," said the smaller man-at-arms, his hand brushing the hilt of his sword reflexively.

"Do these two always talk so much without saying anything of actual import?" the Lord Enrion asked Actaeon, arching a brow.

Actaeon glanced over from some drawings he had pulled out and was showing to Inditrovalis. He shrugged and was about to answer when Wave interrupted.

"Not often. We'd fit right in among the nobility, wouldn't we?"

"Speak for yerself. I ain't no noble – never will be. I'd prefer to wipe my own ass 'n shave my own whiskers," said Trench, before popping an entire peach into his large mouth and chewing it whole.

"Isn't that the truth," agreed Enrion.

"I'm not sure there is anyone in the realm who could shave your whiskers, my friend. All those peaks and valleys!" said Wave with a laugh.

Trench grunted and spit the pit from the peach at Wave's feet, drawing laughter from several nearby soldiers.

The Shieldian Lord shook his head in disgust and turned to walk away. Just as he did, he bumped into Minovo, who glanced up at him and promptly vomited on his shoes.

Even the two jovial mercenaries knew to bite down their laughter as Enrion positively glowered at the young soldier. She knelt down in her own bile and proceeded to clean the Lord's shoes with a cloth that she pulled from her pocket. All of the color had drained from her face, but Actaeon realized that such had been true even in the late morning part of their journey. The young woman hadn't looked well for some time. It was likely that she had caught one of the common illnesses of the monsoon season.

Once the Lord Zar's shoes were cleaned to his satisfaction, the group set out once more.

Actaeon cast a concerned glance back at Shar Minovo as they began moving, but she was already shouting orders, some of the color having returned to her face.

The journey through Stormstair and Rust took four more days, though three and a half of those involved a dangerous slippery ascent along the cracked surfaces of Stormstair. Hampered by mud and pouring rain, the going was slow, especially with the soldiers that hauled the big handcarts with supplies. At one point, one of the haulers slipped and in his efforts to grab the cart, he was pulled with it over an embankment. His broken leg was set and splinted, but the party was forced to leave him there with two others to help him make it back, so they could continue their pace. The cart was repaired quickly and the supplies resecured before the party continued on.

Halfway through Stormstair, they were confronted by a Czerynian battle group that approached them from the north.

"Halt! You pass through Czerynian lands. Your goods are subject to search and your passage fees must be paid," spoke the leader of the band, a young man with a seedy smile.

"This party is enroute to Rust at the behest of His Most Venerable Grace, Prince General Indros Zar. You will let us pass unharried. Here is your payment," spoke Minovo in a commanding voice as she tossed a coin purse past the man's right shoulder. Most of the color had returned to her face by that point.

"Your coin is not enough," said the man with a cackle. "We will take one of those two." He pointed to Actaeon and Inditrovalis who were walking along together. "In the name of Kergon!" he added the name of the Warlord of all Czeryn as an afterthought.

Minovo's blades came out in a flash as she took several quick steps forward and brought them together at the man's neck. The Czerynian's head tumbled neatly end over end, away from his body, spewing a spiraling stream of blood, some of which caught the young Shieldian Adjutant in the face.

The other Czerynians stepped back in shock and raised their weapons.

Minovo looked unfazed as she stepped back and licked a drop of blood from the edge of her lips. When she spoke, her commanding tone left no doubt in Actaeon's mind as to why this young woman had risen to such a high rank so quickly.

"Do not be foolish! Who is now the warlord of this pathetic band?" she demanded as she glanced from Czerynian to Czerynian, her deadly blades poised to strike again.

The men all hesitated until one finally sheathed his blade and stepped forward. "I am now warlord, unless one would challenge my command?" He waited for a moment, as though expecting a challenge, before continuing, "My name is Berk."

"Very well, Berk. You heed this: No man or ally of Shield will now or ever be a slave to Czeryn. If you or your friends ever deign to suggest such or to use Kergon's name to justify such behavior again, our Prince will speak with your Kergon and both of our Dominions will meet to wipe you from the blasted face of this city. Is that understood?" said Minovo, her deadly eyes focused on the new, self-appointed warlord.

"Yes, it is. I'm sorry for this. That one was a poor warlord and will not be missed," ceded Berk, his eyes at his feet.

"Let that be a lesson for you. Do not leave such a poor warlord unchallenged again. Now return to us our coin. After this insult, we will pass for free. And you would do your best to make sure we reach Rust with no further delays, lest the Prince General hear of it."

Berk hesitated for only a moment before he walked over and retrieved the coin purse. He hefted it and tossed it back to Minovo.

After they started out again, Enrion caught up to Minovo and placed a hand upon her shoulder, "Excellently done, Adjutant. You have redeemed your honor in that action."

"Thank you, Lord Zar. I hope that I will continue to please you with my deeds," came her reply in a tone that sounded meek compared to the commanding voice from earlier.

Behind them came a loud commotion of voices once they were out of sight of the Czerynians.

Actaeon glanced at Trench and raised a brow.

"They will now challenge his command. Some warlords are only warlords for but a moment before they die by a sword held by another ambitious hand. Only the best will stay warlord," explained the giant.

"Pretty good system, I'd say. If only they didn't have slaves," said Wave.

When they arrived at Rust, several beasts of burden drawing carriages were there waiting for them and helped them to quickly traverse the holding to their destination. They were taken to one of the long bridges that ran across Lazi's Tomb enroute to Amphis' Ledge. Lazi's Tomb itself was a deep valley set between the massive structural elevations of Rust and Amphis' Ledge. The superstructures of the Ancients rose out of the jungle like giant corroded sentinels that rivaled the height of some of the tallest buildings in Redemption, pitted and corroded as they were. The colors of lush green jungle growth and brown mud stood in stark contrast to the sickly reddish hues that gave Shield's holding of Rust its name. Far below and to the east, there was evidence of ongoing skirmishes – foliage that shook with the passage of warriors and distant figures locked in combat.

Two towers jutted from the jungle to the east. One was to the north, closer to Amphis' Ledge, and the other was south, nearer to Rust's superstructure. Between them was an enormous rectangular pool that would play a huge role in the defenses they were about to create.

The bridge itself was just wide enough for four men to walk abreast and not more. Thin glass rope ran along on either side as a sort of handrail, but with a wide open gap between it and the deck of the bridge. The bridge itself sagged in the middle under its own weight, but seemed otherwise sound from a structural perspective, especially if one considered the greater strength of materials that the Ancients used. The surface seemed to be coated with a sort of rough, hardened tar that didn't seem to be an original part of the structure. Whenever a particularly big gust of wind struck up, the bridge swayed. Despite the handrails, everyone stayed toward the center, away from the edges, and many of the soldiers crouched, their fearful gaze kept to the bridge's surface before them.

"This is the spot where Matenko Lazi fell to his death," explained Enrion as he gestured to one of the rails of the bridge that had a multitude of colorful ribbons tied to it. "After all of his great deeds – reclaiming Amphis' Ledge, pushing the enemy back through the Valley of Blood and Tears with heavy losses, and even then conquering what is now Holdfast. Despite all of that, it was this bridge that did him in." He pulled a small ribbon from his belt and tied it beside the others. "It serves to remind us that despite all of our accomplishments and skill, we must never fail to let our guard down. For just a hard rain, and a slippery bridge is all it might take to fell even the greatest warrior."

The Engineer kicked at the surface of the bridge with his boot and spoke, "So that is why the surface of the bridge is coated like this – to prevent people from slipping to the jungle floor below." Actaeon had to admit that even though the rain had diminished to just a drizzle at the moment, it was reassuring to have a higher friction surface beneath his feet.

"As I said, Master Rellios, we must never fail to let our guard down," said the Shieldan Lord with a smile, before he turned to continue on the way.

"Hey, there it is! Hyk's farm," said Wave excitedly. He gestured toward the northern tower. There wasn't anything too discernable in the jungle at the foot of the tower – they would just have to take his word for it. "We should stop in and say hello. I think you'd like him, Act. He's a businessman like yourself."

"I would not really consider myself a business–" started Actaeon, only to be interrupted by Minovo's commanding voice.

"How appropriate for you to run right off for the source of your Root. You should show your master what you've been doing out here all this time while derelicting your duties to him," barked the small soldier.

Trench laughed and nudged his friend, who grabbed the giant's sleeve, glancing nervously at the edge of the bridge.

"Now now, Adjutant. Do you really expect that I would tolerate such behavior in my service? Even were they hired through someone like the Master Engineer? I asked Wave to try some of Pierxon Hyk's product. His desire for more is a testament to the quality of it," said Enrion with a scrutinizing glance back at Minovo.

It stopped her dead in her tracks and Trench nearly bowled her over. "But... but... your father would be –"

"My father is my master in many things, but I must make a name for myself. If I am to one day lead Shield, then the people must see that I can make my own decisions for the benefit of our people," explained the Lord.

"If Prince Zar were to find out –" Minovo began again, only to be interrupted once more.

"If my father were to find out, then it would tell me much about the people around me, would it not? Besides, my father won't have me flayed for a simple Guaraja root farm."

That silenced her for good and the party continued along in silence across the rest of Lazi's Tomb, watching the distant activity and trying to stay as close to the center of the bridge as possible.

Once they arrived at Amphis' Ledge, they made their way down rickety wooden steps that descended into the valley of Lazi's Tomb far below. In most places, the stairs were only wide enough to allow one man down at a time. The steps took them down into a dense jungle that reminded Actaeon of the Underforest.

At the bottom was a small wooden guard shack and a wide dirt road that had been beaten out along the jungle floor by many passersby. They made their way along the well beaten path that took them past the northern tower. There the Shieldian delegation stopped and made camp so the Engineer and his men could do their job.

Wave led Actaeon, Trench, Inditrovalis and Enrion through the site, pointing out the details as he went. The lush green jungle had been torn away at the southeast and southwest faces of the tower, revealing the dark brown of the moist earth. Jutting from the disturbed soil around it was a complex assemblage of framework that extended quite some distance to the south from the structure and a dozen levels below the ground to the base of the building's footing. The framework was constructed around supports of heavy timber that had been hewn from the jungle trees and placed at regular intervals along the tower, set deeply into the earth so as to wedge up against the building and support it. These had been hammered into place with great weights as the excavation had continued downward. The group proceeded down to inspect the footing and as they descended, the passageways became narrower and the heavy timber supports had grown shorter.

Actaeon found that for the most part, the Shieldians had done excellent work under Wave's guidance. He pointed out a few things, mostly pertaining to the release mechanisms that they had created. The plan had been that a large counterweight would fall and pull wedges from the midpoint of each support beam to allow them to fold up and give way to the weight of the building.

Several of the wedges were placed at the tops of the support beams, which would cause them to drive farther down into the earth. Most of them were correctly placed on the underside, but the incorrectly placed top wedges would have to be pulled first before the rest of the support wedges were released. Actaeon gave some instruction to the workers on the framework and continued along.

At the bottom, Wave grinned and touched the elderstone corner, "So this is the lowest point, right here. Once we go below this point, we're standing beneath the weight of the behemoth itself. Follow at your own risk."

They followed him under and saw that a massive amount of earth had been removed from beneath the tower footing. Water had pooled down there and filled most of the area beneath the tower. The Engineer waded into the water and measured the distance with his footsteps once before immediately repeating it again. Once he finished, he grinned and spoke, "Yes, this will be perfect, I think."

"I don't understand. Why does the distance matter?" asked the Loresworn, with a genuine look of perplexion.

"Well, as you can see, the undermining has taken place well past the fulcrum, or the center of the building. With the material removed, quite a bit of weight rests upon the support beams that we inspected in our framework. And also, hidden beneath the water, the earth has been undermined deeper at the distant edges of the footing to allow for rotation," explained Actaeon, gesturing with the blade of his halberd.

Inditrovalis followed the Engineer's gestures and stood for a moment in silent contemplation. When he finally spoke, it was with a certain satisfaction at his realization of what was being described, "Ah! I understand. So the weight of the tower above us still rests upon the earth, but not in this section that has been excavated. But shouldn't the supports crack under the weight of such a massive structure?"

"That would seem the logical conclusion, however a significant portion of the weight still rests upon the portion of earth that had not been excavated. The lateral supports simply transmit the other half of the weight into earth that is not directly below the tower. Once they are removed, the tower will rotate about its fulcrum and will topple," Actaeon explained with a grin.

When they were back up upon the solid structure of Amphis' Ledge, the group assembled on an overlook built out over the edge, high above Lazi's Tomb. Beside the Engineer and the Shieldian Lord stood the Loresworn to one side and the Adjutant to the other. Pierxon Hyk, the farmer that Wave had lauded, leaned back against the rail of the overlook, smoking one of his guaraja root sticks as he idly smiled at the others.

To the rear of the overlook, a large crowd from Amphis' Ledge had gathered to see the proceedings.

Down upon the steps below, but still in earshot, Trench stood with a dozen strong Shieldian men. A thick glass rope cable was tied to an anchor beside them that had been set deep into the wall of the superstructure. The cable ran down to the jungle floor below and off toward the tower.

Wave arrived along with the final group of soldiers that had been evacuated from the jungle depths of the Tomb. When he approached the group he smiled at Actaeon and lit his own guaraja stick. "They're all ready, boss. Ready and waiting. You have but to give the signal."

"Your Engineer is about to achieve something never seen before," spoke the Lord Zar, a look of certainty upon his face. He gestured for the others to wait and stepped forward to address the people of Amphis' Ledge. Actaeon was surprised at how Enrion's tone changed to one that silenced the crowd immediately.

"Proud people of Amphis' Ledge, you have come here to bear witness and witness you shall! This is the moment where all Redemption will know the power of Shield. Until now, we have but dwelt among the ruins of the Ancients – as though ants in an abandoned hill. Today though, today marks the day that the power of Shield reshapes that hill. We reshape it to suit our needs and to better defend our great Dominion! None other in Redemption can claim such power. That power belongs to Shield and Shield alone. May all of Redemption watch and see for themselves what our people can accomplish and bow before our superiority! Now I ask you, witness! Master Engineer, you may signal the teams below."

That said, Enrion Zar turned and approached Actaeon, turning his critical gaze upon him as he spoke, this time in a low tone, "Do not fail me, Master Rellios."

The Engineer grinned and withdrew an arrow from his quiver. "Had I known you were bringing an audience, I would have practiced beforehand. No matter the outcome, what we learn from this will not be a failure – of that, I assure you." He then pulled a long, bright red ribbon from his pocket and tied it to the arrow shaft just forward of the vane. After hefting his recurve bow and nocking the arrow, he aimed high, pulled and released.

The red streamer chased the arrow across the sky high above Lazi's Tomb before it disappeared into the jungle far below. As they watched, whistles could be heard sounding from the valley floor below.

After a moment, several men climbed out from the framework and ran westward as fast as they could, away from the tower. Wave stepped forward and leaned over the rail to watch, the guaraja stick falling from his mouth and drifting down to the floor of Lazi's Tomb far below.

"How many, Wave?" asked Actaeon calmly.

"Not yet, Act. Not yet. Two more!" responded the mercenary, wiping sweat from his brow.

It seemed to take forever as they waited. The Engineer watched the tower where it stood defiantly since the time his people had arrived in this strange land, and perhaps for hundreds or even thousands of years before that. While the Lord Zar stood behind him, worrying whether or not the tower would fall, Actaeon was not concerned with that. It would be even worse if the building fell at the wrong time and killed the workers still below. Or worse yet, if it fell in the wrong direction and shattered Amphis' Ledge. A support structure had been added to the northern side to help to prevent that, but it might not be enough.

The tower continued to stand there – its ancient face staring back at Actaeon. Then finally, two tiny figures could be seen far below as they scurried out from the framework and sprinted toward the jungle.

Wave waited until they had a bit of a head start before he turned and gave the word, "All clear."

"Ready phase two, Trench!" Actaeon called down to the steps below.

The big man grinned and gave a sharp salute in return before he turned to grasp the cable. With help from the others he worked the cable through a pulley. That complete, they untied it from the anchor and started down the stairs in a column, taking the free end of the rope under their arms and hauling as they marched down the steps.

Actaeon raised the recurve's scope to his eye and gazed through it towards the base of the tower. There he watched while Wave stood nearby counting aloud the number of steps they had descended aloud. When Wave reached eighty in his count, he saw the puff of smoke and the licks of blue flame visible amidst the framework structure. At the count of one hundred, Actaeon lowered the scope and grinned broadly.

"Commence phase three," he said levelly, so Wave could hear him.

"Phase three!" Wave called down to Trench and the team below. "Phase three, get yer arses outta there!"

Trench and the others wasted no time – they dropped the glass cable and sprinted up the stairs back toward Amphis' Ledge, allowing the rope to run back through the pulley and down to the valley floor.

Along the railing, beside a bored Pierxon Hyk, Inditrovalis of the Loresworn stood rapt, watching everything unfold.

Enrion stepped forward and looked at Actaeon, spreading his hands expectantly.

It took him a moment to realize what the Lord wanted.

"Ah yes, that is blue fire. It is an invention of mine. It will burn hotly through the final supports to allow a free fall," the Engineer explained. "You see, the final supports are physically beneath the far side of the building and in remov–"

"Yes, yes. Thank you for the explanation. We will have to talk about this blue fire later. Is everything going according to plan then?"

"That is correct," spoke the Engineer.

The valley held its breath in silent stillness as though all the jungle life knew that something tremendous was about to occur. The Engineer watched the top of the tower, searching for any signs of movement there that would indicate it was tipping. After several long minutes passed and it seemed like nothing was going to happen, murmuring could be heard from the crowd behind them.

"Damn it all. Nothing happened," said Wave with a disappointed shake of his head.

Hundreds of birds took off at once into the air from the jungle floor of Lazi's Tomb. A low moan like that of a massive, wounded beast began, and brought the onlookers to silence. The moan increased in volume to become a wail and then abruptly, a scream.

Actaeon pulled his goggles down over his eyes and tilted his head as he continued to watch.

"You did it," said the Lord Zar beside him, looking on in disbelief.

"You may wish to shield your eyes," was Actaeon's simple reply.

As the tower began to waver and then slowly, to tilt, a woman in the crowd screamed. Several lifebeats later a raucous cheer went up, with cries of 'Shield' mixed in beneath the screaming agony of the tower. The ancient edifice resisted for a moment, but then came a loud crack and the tower gave way and started to lean heavily to the south. All of the glass in the tower shattered at once and fell to the earth.

A second crack, louder than the last, echoed across Amphis' Ledge and the top quarter of the tower broke free and fell to the north, away from the main tower.

"No, not there!" Enrion cried out, with the realization that he was about to lose Hyk's farm beneath the massive weight of the destroyed tower.

Hyk took a deep drag from his guaraja stick and looked on dispassionately.

In a couple of lifebeats, the rest of the tower toppled and fell to the south, broken glass, dust and fragments showering the jungle beneath. All three hundred meters of the massive tower came down in mere moments, the lower three quarters falling neatly across the jungle in a generally southward direction and the top quarter falling down between the foundation and the wall of Amphis' Ledge.

As the northern segment of the tower slammed into Amphis' Ledge, the ground rippled beneath them and sent many of the onlookers reeling. The force of the tower hitting the jungle floor sent out a shockwave that killed a nearby group of tribal attackers instantly and knocked down every tree within thirty meters. It could be heard across the entirety of the ancient city, by the people of every Dominion – even as far off as Raedelle, far to the south.

The felled tower threw up a massive cloud of billowing dust that expanded outwards from the collapse rapidly toward the onlookers.

Actaeon pulled a long bandage roll from his jacket and cut it into strips before he passed them out to the others. He wrapped one over his mouth and nose, tying it behind his neck. As Trench arrived, he handed him a strip as well and started off toward the stairs back down to Lazi's Tomb.

"Come gentlemen, let us go inspect our work," he said. Trench and Wave followed him as he led the way down.

Inditrovalis considered following them but hesitated for a moment too long. The dust cloud expanded and swallowed up the three men before engulfing everyone else.

The plume of dust from the collapse could be seen all across Redemption and in the tribal lands beyond, a sign for all of what had been done. Dirty grey dust fell from the sky for days after that and coated everything. When the heavy monsoon rains resumed after an inordinate pause, the people welcomed them.

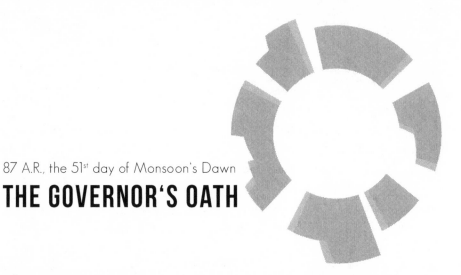

87 A.R., the 51ˢᵗ day of Monsoon's Dawn

THE GOVERNOR'S OATH

AFTER THE FALL OF THE tower, Enrion insisted that the Engineer and his men accompany him to Holdfast, to meet Prince General Indros Zar himself. Actaeon hadn't wanted to linger, with so many projects to return to at the workshop, but he figured it would be best to maintain good relations with the Shieldians, so he conceded and they continued north toward Holdfast.

Only Inditrovalis Jem, the young Loresworn Adept, had departed, insisting that he needed to return to his duties at Travail immediately. Undoubtedly, he would rush there to report the events to his superiors. Actaeon suspected that he had not heard the last from them on this matter.

"The Loresworn keep their knowledge close to the chest. That we have succeeded in toppling one of the structures of the Ancients is not something that they will be happy to know that others have knowledge of. They barter in knowledge – without it they are nothing more than any other man or woman of Redemption," explained Actaeon as he walked, the metal tip of his halberd clicking upon the rusted metal surface of the walkway.

"And what of you, Master Rellios? What makes you different from any other man or woman of Redemption? You share your knowledge. My workers now know enough to bring down the second tower without your help if it be necessary. Why not hold it close to the chest like the Loresworn?" asked the Lord Enrion as he walked along beside the Engineer.

"You see, that is the crux of the matter. I *am* just like any other man or woman of Redemption. My accomplishments could be anyone's accomplishments if they only put their minds and hearts to it. To question the intricacies of our world instead of blindly accepting them. To try to see things differently than our preconceptions demand. To have the courage to try and fail and try and fail again and again, until a solution is revealed. Every man, every woman, has this ability within them if only they choose to accept it. Many choose not to use this aspect to their great disservice. Content with the status quo, with the state of their mind and the knowledge of what is around them. Perhaps it is that there is a yearning within all of us to become the masters of our reality in our lifetimes. It leaves oneself prone to accept quick and easy conclusions while refusing to examine things more deeply. After all, one would not wish to shatter the illusion of understanding that they had worked so hard to achieve."

"Yes, yes," said Enrion, interrupting. "But you've yet to answer my question. Why not hold that information close to the chest? If so many are blinded by their preconceptions like you say, then why not keep your discoveries to yourself that you might continue to profit from them?"

"Ah, but it is not just that, is it? There is judgement as well in all of these things. My experience – my objectivity – allows me to avoid mistakes and make adjustments for minute differences in each specific situation. Blindly learning these things that I have demonstrated is no better than not learning them at all. In fact, it is even more dangerous to exercise such discoveries without the discipline that comes from experience and an open mind," said the Engineer. "It is objective learning that must be exercised. And that is what I hope to show others. We just felled a tower that was built by a people whose technology we cannot even begin to understand, Lord Zar. If everyone thought in that manner and cooperated, could you imagine the things that we could accomplish? The Loresworn would cut us out from all of that and use that knowledge as a brokerage for power."

"Oh, I think you'll get along famously with my father, Master Rellios."

"Is there a reason he is in Holdfast? I would have thought he would be interested in your project in Lazi's Tomb," inquired Actaeon with a glance over at the Lord.

"Of course he is interested. He's just busy... and he trusts me to carry out my responsibilities. There have been incursions by the Ruinic Tribals. He is there to see to the issue. Our people lead on the front lines, just as your people do. It is the main reason that the Pact of Princes between your

Prince Aedwyn and my father was able to survive even after the fall of the Pyramidal League. You see, the Pyramidal League made sense from an economic and stability standpoint, but when you looked at culture... that was the shortcoming," Enrion explained. "The Niwians rely upon secrecy and misdirection. They lack completely in the most important of qualities: honor. That is something that the people of Raedelle share with the people of Shield. And so the alliance persists in the Pact of Princes – absent the impertinence of the Niwian Dominion."

"I seem to recall Prince Aedwyn speaking about that at the time and hinting that Niwian had been complicit with some of the hostile Keeper activity at the time that had been directed at Raedelle," said Actaeon.

"That was a small part of it. I'm still not sure if it is true, but it now seems the case with the talk that the Keepers might become a Niwian protectorate. It never made sense to me that the Niwian people would associate with the Keepers willingly. Not with Memory Keep and other technological resources of the Ancients in their Holding. The collapse of the Pyramidal League had more to do with Niwian buying off the Thyrians to run goods. They were charging us exorbitant fees for transporting goods along the Poisoned Coast between Raedelle and Shield. Trying to drive a wedge between us and isolate us so that they could play us off one another and control the Pyramidal League. That was the real reason behind it. Maybe they also helped the Keepers. I'm not sure, but that's for your Prince to decide."

As they passed between two rusted monolithic buildings along a rusty avenue, they came to an open square amongst the structures. Many of the Ancient structures were still used by the residents of Holdfast, though others had been destroyed in a time long gone and stood in eternal disrepair – vines and jungle plants reclaimed them. Above the buildings to the north and west were the westernmost craggy ridges of the Iron Mountains.

They saw the pillars of light first – radiant streaks that extended from the top of the tower and through the sky in several distinct directions. Some of them appeared to match the color of the clouds as they shot through the clear blue of the sky. Others shot in different directions and were different colors – blue and yellow and purple. Actaeon had seen the Suntower of Holdfast once before, but this was something different, more pronounced and more spectacular. The beams of light seemed to ascend all the way into the heavens, riding the dust that still hung in the air from the collapse of the great tower the day before. The base of the tower jutted from a location about a quarter of the way up the nearest mountain slope and rose to a great height that surpassed the mountains themselves.

"Fascinating. Have you seen such formations of light before from the Suntower?" asked the Engineer. He lifted his goggles from his eyes for the first time that day to get a clearer look.

Enrion had paused beside him and shook his head, "No, it's a first for me. Perhaps the Gods rejoice at our success."

"I think it unlikely. I would hazard to guess that the dust in the air is enhancing the light somehow. Reflecting it, like a thousand tiny mirrors. I would love to have a closer look at the structure at the top of that tower that can cause such light formations."

"Well, you're in luck, Engineer. That's where we're headed. Let's go."

At the top of the Suntower, Indros Zar, the Prince General of Shield awaited them. He was a tall man with a long beard of thin black hair shot through with grey. Clutched in his withered hand was an iron shod staff culminating in an arc that had the sun on one side, and the moon on the other in juxtaposition. His narrow, obsidian eyes peered at the arriving party from beneath the black and red mitre that perched in an unlikely manner upon his head. The blade upon his hip was a writheblade, and, despite being sheathed in its proper scabbard, it seemed to hum and crackle with energy and radiate the smell of ozone.

At his side stood a gorgeous young woman with narrow, angular Shieldian eyes, a confident smile and long black hair that hung over the front of her shoulder in a tight braid. She stood regally, with one hand against her father's arm as she carefully appraised the new arrivals. Her gaze was drawn in particular to the Engineer with his outlandish appearance and the strange contraptions he carried with him. She wore a form-fitting, sleeved dress that fanned out below her hips to allow for a better range of motion, no doubt so she could use one or both of the thin swords that were strapped over her left shoulder.

Actaeon was preoccupied with the inside of the structure though, and didn't notice the woman's lingering gaze. The top of the tower was a gigantic open chamber that was covered in many places with thick, blackened hides that hung all about the room. Around the circumference of the chamber and in the ceiling above were several dozen circular openings, one of which contained a tremendous lens. Several more lenses were placed behind the first, supported by iron brackets. He guessed that each element must weigh as much as a man, judging by their diameter and thickness. Many more elements lay about the room, pushed to the side and covered with cloths. Above them, through any gaps in the patchwork of blackened hides, shone a bright ambient light that was difficult to even glance at.

"Well well, little brother, who have you brought to meet us? New friends?" asked the woman standing beside the Prince General. Her tone was condescending but curious nonetheless.

Enrion Zar stepped forward and traced a courtly bow before his father, eyeing the writheblade with obvious discomfort. "Father, I am glad to see you again. Allow me to introduce Master Engineer Actaeon Rellios and his associates, Trench and Wave. With their help we have succeeded in toppling one of the towers of the Ancients in the defense of Lazi's Tomb."

Indros ignored his son and walked past him while leaning heavily on his iron shod staff. The young lord recoiled in a mixture of fear and dismay. The Prince General approached the Engineer and gestured to the lenses around him. "I have heard stories of you, Engineer. How do you find my Suntower?"

Enrion straightened, his face bright red. His mouth hung open in silent protest.

Actaeon turned to face the Prince and grinned. "It is fascinating, Your Grace," he said, then remembering to bow his head respectfully. "May I ask, have you found use for the lenses that I see lying about?"

"Yes, indeed I have. Will you take a look through that lens array and tell me what you find?" asked Indros with the hint of a smile. He gestured towards the row of lenses supported by the iron brackets behind the larger element affixed in the opening to the northeast.

The Engineer nodded and started over to do just that.

Enrion cleared his throat and spoke, "Father, as I was saying, something of tremendous import to Great Shield has –"

"There is more afoot in our Dominion than your little project, Enrion," spoke the Prince, his son's name a sneer. "Engineer, tell me, what do you see in the glass?"

Actaeon had to do a double take as he leaned forward upon his halberd to gaze through the lenses, "A valley full of tribals. Organized... It appears they have created a large encampment. Pickets at the fringes of their main body. Over a thousand if I had to estimate. The –"

"Very good, Engineer," Indros interrupted. "As I was trying to explain to my son, there are more important matters afoot. The Ruinic Tribals saw that we were concentrating major efforts in Lazi's Tomb. They saw it as an opportunity to flank us and invade Holdfast. Very clever leaders, they have this time..." He trailed off, looking toward the northeast thoughtfully. "I shall have to kill them all. You will leave at once Enrion, and lead Shield in glorious battle with these heathens. Our brothers-in-arms from Raedelle are here with a warband under Aedgar Caliburn – he will also report to you in the field of battle."

"Fa... I would be honored, Father. You have my apo–" spoke Enrion before his father interrupted him with a booming voice.

"Have I taught you nothing? I need no apologies, only improvement. Go prepare the men of Holdfast for immediate battle," commanded the Prince, pointing his iron shod staff toward the northeast.

"Yes, Father. At your command," said Enrion. He turned to Adjutant Minovo and nodded. She hurried off back down the stairs.

"Wait," said the Engineer. He straightened and turned to face the others in the room.

Everyone paused and spun to face Actaeon. Indros' eyes were wide with surprise.

Actaeon stepped forward and lifted his halberd, pointing at the darkened hides above them. "The elements in this tower can grasp the light of the sun, can it not? If we arrange the lenses properly then we can direct and focus the sun's light to ignite the tents in their encampment. If we wait until the early morning, they will be distracted by the fires and your soldiers will take them unprepared. Give me one day, and I will do my best to prepare a diversion."

The tension in the room was palpable as Actaeon and Indros stood across the chamber staring at one another. The old Prince narrowed his eyes upon the Engineer.

After several long moments, Indros spoke, his voice echoing loudly across the chamber. "You can do this thing?"

"I believe it is achievable, so long as the sun is not obscured – perhaps even with the elements in this room. It is a matter of the proper ordering of the concavities and convexities to focus the light at a specific point. We will need to devise some sort of rail mechanism for at least one of the elements to slide along. This way we can control the distance that the light is focused at. We may need to shift some of the elements as well, to direct the focused light. If we can do this successfully, then, come morning, I can start lighting their encampment aflame. I will need any mirrors and other lens elements that you have stored brought up here for our effort," Actaeon said with conviction.

Indros tilted his head thoughtfully and then nodded, "Very well, Engineer. Do not fail me. Enrion, you heard the Engineer. The attack will be postponed until the morrow's rise of the sun. Send out some light Shieldian troops to harry them in the night and have them break off their attacks well before morning. They will think that we are trying to scare them off, but they will be tired and slow to wake in the morning. It will make the diversion that the Engineer is planning more effective. You have your instructions. Carry them out."

That said, the Prince turned and walked from the chamber, nearly bowling over Minovo, who had paused in the stairwell to listen to the conversation.

"Act, with your permission, I would fight with Lord Zar's soldiers," growled Trench.

"You're not going out there alone. I'll be by your side as well," seconded Wave.

Actaeon arched a brow, "You are your own men and free to make those decisions as you need. Who will help me move the lenses without you both?"

"I will," said Enrion's older sister. "You will have to forgive my father and little brother. They are poor at introductions. I am Endira Zar, daughter of Indros, the Steel Rose of Shield. I can help you with whatever you need here."

"You appear to be a Shieldian Lady to me, not a metal flower," Actaeon observed with a grin.

"I hope you never have to encounter me with my swords at the ready, Master Engineer, or else you will see the true meaning of my name," she replied with an alluring smile.

"I see. Well, either way, it is nice to meet you," he said before turning back to the mercenaries. "Very well. You gentlemen had best be off. Do not be reckless on your foray. I shall continue to require your services."

"Aye, boss. We'll be safe," said Wave.

"It's the rest of them bastards that won't be," added Trench.

Trench and Wave both saluted the Engineer and followed Enrion and Minovo from the room.

"What sort of weapon is that which you carry? It does not seem like it would be effective in battle," said Endira as she stepped forward and ran a hand along the shaft of his halberd, allowing her fingers to brush lightly against his hand.

"It is a halberd, a type of polearm," said Actaeon, unfazed by her provocative touch. "Doubtless, someone with your background has seen such a weapon before. I like to keep my opponents at a distance since I am no soldier." He wiggled one of the lens brackets with one hand to assess it.

"Yes, but I have not yet seen one so unique. May I see it?"

"Of course," he said, handing it to her absent-mindedly. He used the opportunity to grasp the metal bracket with both hands, this time rotating it slightly. "Very clever. They thought of these issues already. This will save us much time."

Endira accepted the halberd and ran one hand slowly, seductively, along the length. She held the weapon delicately in her hands and then spun it about and proceeded with a series of slashes and thrusts, testing the weapon's weight and feel.

As she was busy with that, the Engineer dug inside his jacket pocket and withdrew a small cloth-wrapped item. He unwrapped it and clipped the darkened wooden goggles that Lauryn made for him to the goggles atop his head, before pulling them down over his eyes. It was a fortuitous gift – he'd have to thank her again when he got back to the workshop.

Endira halted and tapped the butt of the halberd against the ground, eliciting a sharp click. "A finely crafted weapon but a very strange design. What's the purpose?"

"The back end of the blade is designed so as to function as a hook.

The butt of the shaft is a wedge, so that the entire shaft can serve as a lever. I carry limited equipment with me so I like for it to serve multiple functions," he said while glancing up at the ceiling full of blackened hides. "May I have it back?"

She smiled at him brazenly and spun the weapon in two half arcs before returning to his side. She touched his shoulder gently and ran her fingers down his arm before she grasped his hand and turned his palm outward. In it she placed the shaft of the halberd, her fingertips tracing along his leather clad palm teasingly as she continued to hold the weapon in her hand. All the while, she stared into the darkened lenses of his goggles.

The Engineer was amused at Endira's forward behaviour, his lips curling into a smirk. "Lady Zar, while I am flattered, I must inform you that my heart belongs with another."

Endira's lips curled into a smile. "I assure you, Master Rellios, it isn't your heart I am looking for."

Actaeon put his other hand atop hers and gently pried her fingers from his weapon. When she released her hold on it, he stepped away from her to the center of the chamber. "I would advise you to shield your eyes. It is about to get much brighter in here." That said, he lifted the halberd high and hooked several of the blackened hides before pulling down.

The action brought down the hides that had been hung at the ceiling level and flooded the chamber with the collected light of the sun.

The seductive Shieldian screeched and lifted her hands to shield her eyes, "You!"

"Alright, I am ready for those lenses to be brought up. Since you are the clear authority here, I would appreciate your help in directing others to gather and bring here any of the other lenses and mirrors that you have stored in Suntower. It is absolutely essential for us to collect as much of the light as we can to focus it on a central receiving element."

Endira opened her mouth to protest and tried to glare at the Engineer, though the bright light forced her to continue shielding her eyes. After a moment's hesitation, she grunted in annoyance and headed downstairs.

It was several hours before Endira returned to the upper chamber of the Suntower. By the time she arrived, Actaeon had already made significant progress in collecting, focusing and reflecting several significant areas of sunlight from the overhead opticks. They all returned to a clustered array of mirrors that then directed the light through a large double convex lens and into a dozen subsequent lenses. The lenses were focused upon one of the blackened hides that had been pulled down from the ceiling. Steam rose from a place as the center of the hide and an attendant stood beside it, occasionally pouring water down the face of the hide to keep it from igniting.

The optical element overhead was a tremendous artifact of the Ancients that pulled much of the sun's energy from the sky and sent it downward in seven zones. Actaeon didn't yet understand how it worked and for the moment he didn't have the time to study it.

"It seems you have made significant progress, Master Engineer," said Endira from the top of the stairs, one hand upon her hip as she looked over the setup critically. On her eyes were her own pair of darkened goggles. She had changed her outfit as well, opting for something much more revealing – a tight fitting jerkin that was cut away on either side to reveal the tender flesh of her chiseled chest and even part of her ample breasts. The close-fitting skirt she wore upon her legs was slitted well above the knee to reveal one powerful but slender leg as she walked farther into the room.

Actaeon took one glance at her and his hand went up sharply to stall her. "Hold, Lady Zar. Be careful as you move about in this chamber, there are three highly focused light sources so far. I do not wish you to burn your skin if you accidentally step into one of the focused beams of light. Your outfit from earlier had less exposed skin – perhaps you should change back into it."

The Shieldian noblewoman stared at him abjectly, her mouth hanging open at his reaction – clearly not what she had anticipated. After a moment, she regained her composure and smiled determinedly. "As you say, Master Rellios. I shall be careful. Point out the areas that I should stay clear of."

She only burned herself once as they worked, in a location beneath her underarm as she held a lens in position. She had gritted her teeth and suppressed a yell, hoping that Actaeon hadn't noticed. He was polite enough to pretend that he hadn't. Endira had no issue with getting her hands dirty and moving the lenses and brackets about the chamber to help the Engineer. Though mostly, she directed the attendants that her father had spared for the project.

By the time the sun had set, they had five of the light zones from the ceiling focused and reflected onto the central collector lens and had successfully devised a system to shift the lenses in order to change the distance and location at which the light was focused. They also managed as a test to light a bush afire that stood near the tribal encampment. On Indros' long range scope, they watched as some of the tribals ran over to stomp it out, looking about afterward in confusion.

They worked late into the evening, and, by the time they called it a night, six of the seven zones had been set to transmit light to the collector lens which focused the light into the main row of lenses. Actaeon was excited and happy with their progress. Endira, on the other hand, was so exhausted that she retreated down into the tower to collapse in her cot, any previous desires forgotten in a haze of lenses, mirrors, blinding sunlight, and a man seemingly impervious to her charms.

Early the next day, Actaeon awoke Endira with a knock upon her door. "Dawn approaches, Lady Zar. We must prepare."

When she opened the door, she was wearing naught but a short black shift with red accents. She smiled at him seductively and ran a hand along her leg. Strapped to the bare flesh of her opposite thigh was a long, thin dagger. "Surely you have time to join me inside for a cup of rice wine, Master Rellios? Trust me. It wouldn't take too long."

The Engineer spread his hands apologetically. "Alas, although I would undoubtedly enjoy a cup of wine, I have spent the the remaining darkness of the morning making final adjustments. The sun will not wait for us, and, in order to coordinate with the Lord Zar and his forces, and we must needs be prompt. Please get dressed and meet me atop the tower. You are the only one versed well enough in the adjustment of the elements. I will need your help. Oh," he said, remembering. "Be sure not to wear something with too much exposed skin. I do not wish for you to burn yourself like you did yesterday."

Her face scrunched up at the mention of her brother and she positively scowled when he mentioned her clothing. "You really love your gods' damned lenses!" she blurted out and slammed the door in his face, her plans thwarted once more.

Actaeon chuckled to himself and headed upstairs.

A short while later, everyone was in place. Actaeon stood by the telescope lens array and gazed at the Ruinic encampment, which was still as all the warriors slept after a harrowing night that Enrion provided for them. Only a few Ruinic tribals stood watch.

Endira stood beside the main lens, wearing yet another tight fitting outfit, this one with dark leather breeches that left little to the imagination. She had, however, taken his advice and covered much of her bare skin, even including her hands. Several other Suntower attendants stood by at different elements, awaiting Actaeon's orders.

Beside the Engineer stood the old Prince General, leaning heavily upon his iron shod staff. When Actaeon glanced at him, he nodded.

"Alright. It is time. Remove the sun veil," directed the Engineer.

One of the attendants pulled the darkened hide from the front of the mirror array and focused sun poured forth and entered the lens array. Actaeon leaned forward and searched the image of the encampment magnified through the large lens. After a moment, he stepped back and lifted his own scope, mounted upon his unstrung bow, to his eye. Looking through the big lens array with it, he attained an even greater magnification of a location within the lens' image, and there he found it.

The faint circle of sunlight illuminated the ground directly in front of one of the larger tents.

The Engineer grinned at the sight of it and turned to smile back at Indros. "By the Ancients, it is aimed nearly exactly where we want it. And the sun is out and shining brightly. The Shieldian gods must be watching over you today, Your Grace," he said, unmasked excitement in his tone.

"I've learnt over the years never to rely upon the gods. They've already destroyed this land once – we will not allow that to happen again. If the aim is true, it is by your skill and your sight," said the Prince slowly. He took a sip of his morning tea before setting it down on a small table beside him.

"I could not agree more, though I had much help in this case. Lady Zar, rotate element one up by one half degree," said Actaeon as he returned his attention to the scope. Angular marks had been etched into the brackets of the critical lenses the evening before. "Too far. Rotate down by one eighth degree. Yes, yes – perfect! It is ready, Your Grace. By your command."

"Destroy them, Engineer. I give you my command."

"Aye aye. And so we will. Remove the aperture."

One of the attendants pulled free another blackened hide with a circular aperture in it that limited the amount of light that entered the array. There was a bright flash of light in the image of the encampment and Actaeon could see that the tent had ignited instantaneously.

"Excellent! It is alight! Rotate element one to right by one degree. Yes, now up by one half degree. That's three of them! And one quarter degree to the right."

As he called out the commands and lit more and more of the enemy tents ablaze, he watched the tribesmen awaken in a panic as they moved to wake others and extinguish the flames. He could hear them blowing horns in the far distance to alert the whole camp. The Ruinic tribals emerged from their tents with weapons drawn and readied, but they soon realized that it was fire they were dealing with and they ran to help extinguish the field of blazing tents. The Engineer's mouth dropped open in dismay as he watched several of the tribals spill from one tent, their flailing bodies engulfed in flames. He could see them screaming through the scope, though they were much too far away for their screams to be heard. They struggled in agony for but a moment before they lay still, the fire flaring up as their bodies continued to burn.

He'd just burned those men to death – he hadn't realized that the tents would catch fire so quickly. It was only supposed to serve as a distraction. Even though he knew many of the tribals far off in the distance were destined for death by sword and spear, it didn't subtract from the savage fact that he had caused those deaths by fire.

"Very good, Engineer. He will wait until they are the most preoccupied and disorganized," said the Prince, his voice snapping Actaeon out of his horror.

As if on cue, in the bottom left corner of the image arrived the Shieldian troopers, led by Enrion, his sword held high. Adjutant Minovo was at his side, her two swords out and flashing in a blur as she reached the first Ruinic lookout, sending his head spiraling aside. At their flank were Trench and Wave. The duo was unmistakable with their disparity in height. As they neared the panicked tribals, Wave let loose a bolt from his crossbow and slung it over his shoulder, his own rapier a blur that sent enemies reeling to either side of him as they fell while he dodged and weaved between their spear thrusts. Trench stood behind him with his heavy maul and took care of anyone that the swordsman couldn't handle, shattering them each in a single blow.

Indros placed a hand on Actaeon's shoulder and spoke in a low voice that only the Engineer could hear: "Do not fail me now, Engineer. War is Death. If not theirs, then ours. Continue your work. Our countrymen are down there fighting."

Actaeon shuddered and scratched his right arm before he continued to call his commands to Endira, lighting more and more of the encampment on fire and even using the light to blind enemy troops that turned to face the attacking Shieldians. Many tribals could be seen fleeing toward the distant forest at the foot of the mountains. A group of the tribals had begun to organize at the right side of the camp, their shields held high to block the light that swept over them from the Suntower.

"Your Grace! Master Rellios! A storm arrives!" cried out one of the attendants. A crack of thunder confirmed the arrival of another monsoon storm, masked by the dust that remained hanging in the air from the collapse of the tower now two days past.

"Curse it! We could not see it coming with so much dust floating about!" complained Endira with a huff.

"It is amazing that Suntower can collect so much light even despite all the dust. Do not let it distract you. We are still needed. One degree down, one quarter degree to the left. Sweep back and forth and up and down one eighth of a degree," Actaeon called out.

As the focused sunlight swept in a broad arc across the rallying Ruinic tribals, a dozen or so fell to the ground clutching their eyes. Many tribals had their clothing and shield hides catch fire. It was a fleeting victory, however, as the sky went dark and the light from the Suntower dimmed significantly, until it could no longer affect the enemy forces.

As Actaeon watched, the tribals patted out their clothing, helped those that were blinded to their feet and stood ready to face the Shieldian troops. A heartbeat later, the Shieldians crossed the remaining distance and smashed into the tribals. The two forces stood toe to toe and fought for a minute until the Raedelleans arrived.

The warband's roar could be heard as far as the Suntower as they charged onto the battlefield, led by Aedgar Caliburn, Prince Aedwyn's young brother. He was a huge bear of a man and would have dwarfed all the others on the battlefield if it wasn't for the presence of Trench. He wasn't as tall as Trench, but he was wider in both directions and he charged forward like a battering ram, greatsword held high over his head, with the Raedelleans rallying behind him.

The first tribals that faced him were smashed and sent flying to the side as he barreled his way through them with his shoulders down.

The arrival of the warbanders ended the battle quickly as most of the Ruinic tribals, now caught between the two units, turned to flee. Those foolish enough to remain were quickly cut down and dispatched by the joined Shieldian and Raedellean pincer. The sky let loose, and it began to pour as the battle drew to a conclusive victory for the Dominions in the Pact of Princes.

"See that, Engineer?" said Indros. "Watch how they give up and run. That is their resolve. That is their conviction. They come to take something for nothing – to take things that we have given blood and sweat to create. They have no values but that of their greed and lust. The men of Shield and Raedelle will not simply turn and flee. Do you know why?"

"They are the defenders, in this case, defending their homeland. I imagine one will more steadfastly defend their home than continue an invasion," suggested Actaeon.

"That is true, Engineer, but not the real reason. The real reason is because our mission is the very heart of who we are and our vision is true. Our peoples know that we fight to defend civilization itself. They defend our values, our culture, and the beneficence that makes us civilized humans. These barbarians would throw that away in a moment for one meal to eat or one woman to rape. They have no values, and so they break and run. A child with values and the conviction to stand by them is more dangerous than a dozen men like those barbarian scum.

"Do not forget what you see here today, Engineer. Do not forget how easily men with no values turn and run."

Later that day, after the soldiers had returned and the light began to fade from the cloudy sky, a celebration took place at the top of the great Suntower.

The battle had been a decisive one and the invaders were thwarted with a minimum of casualties to the Shieldians and their Raedellean allies.

The great lens system that Actaeon had devised had been dismantled and stored away to make room for the celebration, but not before Indros had one of the attendants record all of the details of the design on a large vellum sheet. "I will send payment to your workshop for your services here," said the Prince General, almost as an afterthought before descending into the tower below.

A circle of tables was set up around the perimeter of the chamber so that everyone seated would face the center. One of the tables was raised higher than all the others. It was at this one that Indros sat, his children flanking him on either side.

Beside Enrion, at a lower table, sat Actaeon, Trench and Wave – a position of honor. At the other side, adjacent to the Prince's daughter, was Aedgar Caliburn and his warband captains. Adjutant Minovo also sat at the table beside the brother of Prince Aedwyn. Not all of the men who fought were present, Actaeon noticed. This seemed to be a celebration for the higher ranking men and women involved in the battle. By the raucous sounds from below, he guessed the lower ranking soldiers had already gotten started with their own celebrating.

"If you hit Trench with his own hammer, you'd end up getting an Aedgar Caliburn – shorter and wider. Whaddaya say, Trench? Want to confuse the Prince a bit?" said Wave with a grin. He had been hitting the rice wine hard, and, judging by the sweet odor that accompanied his presence, that had not been all.

"I've got a better idea for ya. How about I grab yer arms and give a good tug? Then you'll be wide as Aedgar. Keep filling up on that rice wine – it'll help!" responded Trench.

Actaeon joined in their laughter at that, waiting until it died down to speak. "You both seem in good spirit. Why did you decide to fight in the battle? You seemed to feel quite strongly about it. Even had I tried to stop you, I doubt it would have made a difference."

Trench grinned down at him, the scar bisecting his face scrunching unnaturally, "Aye, 'tis true at that! You'd not have stopped us. It's too much a part of who we are."

"I'll second that, old friend. You see, Act, our past is full of those who have fought and died. Some for noble causes and some for – well, not so noble. But it was during the most noble cause that has ever been fought for that we lost the most friends," Wave explained.

"The Invasion War," said Actaeon. "So if you did not try to repel the tribals, it would cast a shadow over everything that was hard won all those years past."

"Correct. Though it isn't really a question for us. We are here so we fight. To do otherwise would be –"

Wave's words were interrupted as several servants standing along the walls began to ring bells. The room grew silent as Prince Indros Zar slowly drew to his feet. Actaeon noticed that the noise from below had quieted as well.

"Victorious Shield," he said simply, in his commanding tone, undershot with the frailty of his age. He lifted his staff in the air and brought it sharply down to the floor. The sound was drowned out by dozens of Shieldian fists striking the tables before them. It ceased instantaneously when the Prince raised his other hand in the air. "We have won a great victory today. One that now has become part of Shield's great destiny to cement civilization throughout Redemption along with our brothers and sisters in Raedelle. Only eight brave warriors of Shield and Raedelle fell today, but the Ruinic barbarians have lost hundreds!"

He brought his staff down again and fists once again fell upon the tables. This time he left it unchecked, though it died out quickly as he spoke.

"Lord Enrion Zar, son of Shield, will you stand up?"

His son, beside him, stood up, his face a strange mixture of pride and nervousness. The young Lord made his way around the table and stood before his father.

"Enrion, my son, you have commanded a great victory this day upon the field of battle. Holdfast is secure for the time being. Your leadership was instrumental in this achievement. You have proven yourself a man and a warrior of Shield, and it is time for you to do even more. Who will speak for my son?" asked Indros, making a show of looking about the chamber.

"I will," called out one voice, without hesitation. It was the Adjutant, and she stood and walked around the table to stand beside Enrion. "I am Adjutant Shar Minovo and..." she trailed off, a sudden look of surprise upon her features as the color drained from her face. She grimaced and gagged a few times before she cleared her throat and started over with determination. "I am Adjutant Shar Minovo, and I will speak for my Lord Enrion Zar!"

Several moments later, Aedgar Caliburn stood and quietly walked over to Enrion. He stood beside him in silence.

Enrion glanced around the room until his expectant gaze fell upon Actaeon. The Engineer was caught off guard and pointed at himself in confusion. He figured it out quickly though and drew to his feet to join the others beside Enrion.

"Good evening, Prince Zar. As you know, I am Actaeon Rellios of Shore. I will also speak for Lord Enrion Zar. During the time that I have worked for him, he has shown a seemingly unceasing concern for the people of Lazi's Tomb and Shield as a whole. His comm–" He was interrupted by Enrion clearing his throat. "Ah yes, so as I was saying, I speak for your son," he concluded with a grin and the polite bow of his head toward the Prince.

"An Adjutant," continued Indros, "a great Lord of Raedelle, and a Master Engineer that has taught me things I didn't know about my own tower. These three speak for you, my son. And they do you great honor in doing so. And so it is time! You have shown your fortitude as a leader and are hereby named Governor of Lazi's Tomb, with all of the responsibility and authority to protect, lead, and grow your new charge. Do not fail us, Governor."

Enrion stepped forward and took a knee before his father, "I will not fail you, father. Thank you for your faith in me."

Beside Indros, Endira laughed and spoke, "How appropriate, for you to be nestled safely between your father and your older sister. Don't worry, little one, we won't let you fail." Most of those present knew that Endira held the Governorship of Amphis' Ledge.

Enrion's face turned a bright shade of red at his sister's words, but he bit his tongue on any response. He stood and took several steps back to rejoin the three behind him.

When Indros' staff touched the ground again, there was the pounding of fists upon the tables and also a cheer that went up, resounding throughout the tower. The sound wiped any embarrassment from the new Governor's face as he revelled in his accomplishment.

What happened next would be spoken of in Shieldian legend for generations to come.

When the Governor turned to faced those who had stood with him, pride written upon his features, the Adjutant wretched and emptied the bloodied contents of her stomach upon his boots. At their table, Trench and Wave laughed as the event from days earlier repeated itself.

It was much worse than they could know, though. When Minovo opened her mouth again to scream, pincers emerged and scissored desperately at the air. A pair of eyes emerged along with two long tendrils.

Actaeon reacted the instant he realized what it was and tackled the new Governor to the floor just as the creature launched itself from Minovo's mouth toward where Enrion had stood. Aedgar's greatsword was out in a lifebeat and when he cleaved the footlong creature in half it curled into two little writhing balls of death. It was a deathcrawler.

Minovo staggered back. Her piercing scream echoed throughout the Suntower, bringing everyone in the tower to silence. Another creature emerged from her lips, and she drew one of her knives from her throwing brace, pinning the creature's face to the back of her throat. She angled the blade to miss her spine. She staggered back yet again and the right side of her neck bulged. The Adjutant buried another knife in her neck, deftly avoiding her own carotid and jugular.

There was another bulge at the front of her neck and she slid another blade carefully into place right above her clavicle. The sudden inrush of air into her lungs when her blade opened her throat was the last she would ever have.

She fell to her knees then, as another creature struggled its way free from the hole that she had created in her throat. Two more blades she slid into her belly, where more creatures were gnawing their way out from the inside. Then she was out of knives.

She knelt there for several interminable moments while the creatures continued to devour her from the inside. She looked up at Aedgar Caliburn with pleading eyes. The hulking Raedellean towered over her with his greatsword, unsure of what to do. Finally, after what seemed like an endless amount of time, she raised both of her hands, almost in supplication, and gestured for him to end it all.

The big Lord's face paled at the nightmare before him, but he wasted no more time. He stepped forward and with one clean sweep of his blade, cleaved the small warrioress in half. Several people in the room screamed, and a few soldiers fainted where they stood.

The blow killed many of the creatures inside the ill-fated Adjutant, but many more inside her still lived. With her body cavity open, they spilled free in a writhing mass before scattering in every direction. Soldiers rushed forward with weapons out, stomping and slashing at the things until they all lay in many pieces.

Lying where Actaeon had tackled him, the Governor Zar recovered from his horror. He shook the Engineer's shoulders in a wholly uncharacteristic manner. "Whatever it takes, Actaeon. I don't care. You kill all of those things. Whatever it takes."

Actaeon settled his stunned gaze on the new Governor, nodding slowly before his eyes returned to the horrid remains of Adjutant Minovo. "Amazing. They were with us the entire time."

That horribly fated day came to be known as the Day of the Governor's Curse.

RETURNS WITH A BANG

O UT ACROSS THE VAST PLAINS of the Windmoor lay a cluster of stones, far south from the settlement of the Outskirts. In the center of the haphazard stone cluster, stood the lone figure of Actaeon, surveying an apparatus that stood a foot taller than him, made from wood, stone, and metal. The outline of a recurve bow upon his back was silhouetted in the late afternoon sun.

He lifted an object in his right hand, turning it over and over as he considered it, his mind elsewhere.

Wind in her short hair and purpose in her stride, Eisandre approached from the northeast, lifting a hand to shield her eyes from the sun. She wore her armor and weapons once more, and though her right arm was out of its sling now, it hung stiffly at her right side as she walked.

Actaeon knelt to set some sort of mechanism at the base of the apparatus. When he stood again, he lifted a large stone and placed it on a support above the mechanism he just set.

Eisandre paused at the edge of the cluster of stones to watch him as he made some minute adjustments to the mechanism and the stone above it. "You look busy. Did I come at a bad time?" she asked. Actaeon had sent word for her to join him out on the Windmoor, but he was clearly hard at work with one of his experiments.

"Not at all," said Actaeon, offering her a warm smile. "This is one of my side projects. It is good to see you again, Eis. I have missed your company."

"I am glad you have returned, Actaeon. Was your project in Shield a success? Did Wave and Trench come back safely as well? What is your side project?" she asked a flurry of questions before she hesitated and glanced away shyly.

Actaeon grinned. As an asker of many questions himself, he found her long list of inquiries endearing. "The project was certainly a success. We managed to fell the tower there to provide Shield with a means to defend Lazi's Tomb against invaders. Nobody involved in the project was hurt during the fall." He thought about telling her about what had happened to Minovo, but he didn't want to bring that horrible memory up after he hadn't seen Eisandre in so long. "For this apparatus here, as you may recall, when we battled the slug beast beneath the markets, it was eventually killed by a luminary thrown by Trench, which somehow caused it to explode. Just before the explosion, I saw one of the creature's tentacles wrap around it and crush it. Ever since, I have been trying to recreate the explosion. The uses for such a controlled phenomena are endless. I think I may have finally figured out the missing ingredient." He gestured toward a small wooden canister that lay near the mechanism.

Eisandre looked confused. "You wish to recreate the explosion of the slug beast? Right here?"

Actaeon took her hand in his to lead her closer to the mechanism, indicating the different parts as he spoke. "Well, this is a controlled environment that I selected for this experiment. As you can see, the rocks are set deeply into the ground to act as a blast barrier and contain any potential explosion."

He pointed toward a larger cluster of rocks furthest away from the apparatus, "Behind there are the front viewing seats. Of course, we will not be looking directly at anything. At the bottom here, we have a clamp for our concoction: a small handheld luminary sealed in one of Lady Lauryn's wooden canisters along with a sample of the slime taken from the ill-fated giant slug. As you can see, that stone wedge is suspended above it and can be hauled higher. The release mechanism may be pulled with that thin rope that goes behind our safety barrier. Basically, it drops the stone so that the edge falls across the canister and the luminary to crack it in half, thereby releasing the entirety of its energy into the slime, and, with any luck, causing the reaction we desire. I have run many such experiments to no avail, but I do believe I have finally deciphered the last missing component.

The creature's slimy by-products are incredibly noxious, which indicates a vaporous emission. I believe that, contrary to the original thought, the vapor is what caused what I witnessed down in the market tunnels, not the slime itself." The Engineer pointed to the canister again, his eyes sparkling with excitement as he continued, "This latest container should hold the fumes within and help keep them close to the luminary when it is broken. Of course..." he paused, as though in afterthought. "You need not stay for the experiment if you do not feel comfortable. However, it may be something that you are interested in reporting to your superiors."

She listened intently to his words, though many of the concepts he spoke of were alien to her. "You feel this experiment has a high chance of success. Of course I will stay – for you, as much as for the information I may acquire for the Order."

"I am glad that you will stay," he said. "How have you been Eisandre? I must say, you look much better. I am glad to see you on your way toward full recovery. Would you like to practice beating me up in a sparring practice soon?"

"I have been well, Actaeon," she replied. "In truth, the days blur together when I feel devoid of real purpose. The moment the Healer removed the splint, I felt the sun shine once again. I am not allowed to fight just yet. First I must do some exercises to regain my strength. But, soon – it will be soon, I think. And then we will spar. I do feel much better. And here you are again," she said, meeting his gaze with her brilliant blue eyes.

When Actaeon smiled and opened his arms, she stepped forward and hugged him tightly, her eyes closing as they basked in one another's energy. Despite the bulk of her armor and his bulky jacket, they held each other in that way lingeringly, with no desire for it to end.

It was Actaeon that finally loosened his embrace and stepped back, offering her a cheerful smile. "I should finish setting this up," He grabbed a rope that ran through a pulley to the mechanism that held the stone wedge. He hoisted it into place and then locked it into position with a pin. That done, he gestured back to the nearby cluster of rocks that he thought of as the front viewing seats, and said, "You should take shelter while I finish this."

"Be careful," she advised, before moving behind the large stones, where she watched the Engineer work.

Actaeon waited until she was safe behind the stones before he continued. After checking the suspended wedge shaped stone once more, he locked the canister into place with the clamp at the bottom of the apparatus. That done, he moved quickly to where Eisandre stood and pulled his goggles down over his eyes.

He handed the Knight Arbiter an extra pair of goggles, and she put them on.

"There may be some debris," he explained.

"Are we going to smell awful for days?" she asked, remembering the foul odor in the marketplace caused by the slug creature.

"That is a good question. I should not think so. The amount is small and we have this barrier protecting us – quite unlike last time when the lot of us were essentially showered in the substance."

The Engineer placed one arm companionably around Eisandre and held the rope in the other hand. He glanced over at her, grinning in excitement. "Are you ready?"

"All I have to do is stand here, so I suppose I am as ready as I can be!" she declared, grinning back at him. Actaeon's grins could be infectious.

He wrapped both arms around her and guided her down to sit beside him so that they had their backs to the rock.

Then he pulled the cord.

A click sounded and then a crack, immediately followed by a deafening blast. Bluish yellow flames ripped past them around the perimeter of their blast shield and the entire stone shuddered against their backs. Shards of stone, wood, and chunks of metal scattered about, skittering against the surrounding rocks and raining down around them.

All sound faded from the world for both Engineer and Arbiter. All they could hear was a ringing echo of the blast.

With a yell that went unheard, Actaeon raised a fist into the air in triumph and turned to kiss Eisandre on the cheek. At the same moment she turned to face him, and his lips brushed against the corner of her own. He said something that was drowned out by the ringing in her ears, and then took her hand to lead her back around the stone.

As the smoke cleared and the afterimages of the blast cleared from their vision, it revealed that the hefty drop point fixture that Actaeon had built was completely demolished. A fragment of the metal clamp was buried deeply into the bottom of a small crater left by the explosion. The stone wedge had split into two halves, and each had been cast in opposite directions against one of the larger stones as if it were naught but a children's toy. Several pieces of wood from the apparatus still burned with a low flame and one of the metal chunks had actually lodged deep into the face of one of the surrounding stones.

Actaeon said something inaudible and pointed to the center of the blast radius. He released her hand and knelt in the center of it, pulling his goggles back to scrutinize the details before he grinned in satisfaction and returned to Eisandre's side.

He leaned in towards her, as though for another kiss but instead spoke loudly into her ear. She could hear fragments of what he was saying as her hearing began to return incrementally: "...too dangerous. ...do not trust..... ....hands... ... ...Domin..." He paused and gestured to the site of the explosion once more, "I want the Arb... ...control this technol..."

That said, he reached up to cover both nostrils and blew out to equalize the pressure in his head.

Eisandre gave him a delirious look as she pulled back her goggles. She opened her lips to reply, but stopped when she heard nothing that she had spoken. She looked about frantically, searching for a way out of the situation. The absence of sense felt as though something were ripped from her that she'd never been fully aware was there. She needed to get away from there and felt a panic building in her chest that threatened to undermine all her control.

Actaeon took her arm gently and led her to a seat upon a flat stone. He knelt before her and made an exaggerated motion of breathing in and out slowly and deeply. He placed one hand on his chest and the other on her own, "Breath slow... ...eath easy..."

With no small effort, she brought her breathing into rhythm with his own, and it calmed her. As her wits came back about her, she realized that he was cradling her in his arms and rocking to and fro. She blinked and looked up at the striking sky with its billowing clouds, then at his face.

She smiled at him and tested her voice, "...at. That... was amazing..."

"You are amazing," came the Engineer's reply. "The explosion was terrifying, its ramifications at least... But I am glad you were here to share this with me. Perhaps you understand better why I am driven to my work."

He released her and knelt before her once again, taking her hands into his own before speaking once more, "I hope you understand why I asked you here, besides the fact that I wanted desperately to see you again. The Arbiters are the only ones I would trust with this technology. If they are interested, I will help them harness this power as a weapon to safeguard Pyramid further. If not, then the invention will not leave my side."

"It is an interesting question," she said. When she looked into his emerald eyes, her amazement tinged with a certain sadness. "Will the Arbiters be better able to keep the peace with the secret to causing explosions of this magnitude? Imagine, Actaeon – look around you. What could this do to people? I... I believe we should think about this very carefully. I agree that the Arbiters, above all others, will be most likely to use such information responsibly, but I can't help but be concerned, even so, at the prospect of such a weapon in anyone's hands at all.

"I know that you want to understand our world, as clearly as your own spirit shines. I cannot even imagine the extent of the amazing and beautiful and terrifying things you have the potential to create and accomplish, Actaeon Rellios of Shore." She paused and lifted one of his hands to kiss his ash-covered knuckles. "But please be careful. I think, in understanding our world, you will change it. May those changes always be for the better."

The Engineer knelt in unusual silence as he considered her words before he spoke. "Careful will I be, that I do not ever change things for the worse. Ever since I have come to this place and been confronted with knowledge and projects that I could never fathom, I have been slowly coming to the realization that my work can be used to help the people of Redemption or to truly imperil them. You can rest assured that I will do my utmost to protect the people of this ruined, yet hopeful city, lest we meet the same terrible fate as the Ancients."

"I trust you, Actaeon. You have always protected me, since we first met. And all those concerns aside, I think congratulations are in order, yes? Your experiment is a dramatic success. You are brilliant. Thank you for allowing me to be here with you – to see this."

The Engineer flushed red and shook his head. "Not brilliant. Just good at finding the right connections. And you are always welcome to witness my experiments, Eis. Though most will be less interesting than this one, I think. So here I am," he said, changing the topic. "You gave me two demands when we last spoke – to return in a single piece and to avoid the wrath of your sister." He glanced down at himself and brushed some of the dust from the explosion from his jacket. "I seem to be in one piece and I had a brief, friendly exchange with your sister yesterday where she did not appear to be upset with me. Of course, I offered to give her a detailed report, but she was not interested."

"Mission successful, then," said the Arbiter, pleased at his words. "In both our eyes, it seems. And while you have been out doing grand things and helping the Dominions, I have been doing paperwork and jogging the empty corridors of the Pyramid in an attempt to return to optimal physical shape. It has been quite dull, in truth. Nothing compared to all this. And you're blushing again, I see," she noted with a smile. "Just because I think you're brilliant at making the right connections."

Actaeon laughed at himself, lifting a hand to his cheek. "Well, you keep showering me with compliments. I am not very good with those. In any case, if you had not kept us both alive in the Boneyards, I would never have been able to accomplish any of these things. Although you may feel things have been dull, you have done just as much to ensure the accomplishment of these tasks as I have and I greatly appreciate it."

"We both just speak the truth as we see it and we seem to hold each other in high regard," said Eisandre, bluntly. "And you were saving my life. It is only reasonable that I would do my best to protect yours, in turn. I suppose now, in a way, everything we both do is connected with the fact that we continue to exist only because of each other's efforts. Also, it occurred to me that my first taste of true combat was by the side of a Raedellean Engineer and not my fellow Arbiters with whom I have trained and served all these years."

"I hope I proved worthy of fighting at your side. Though admittedly, I have little experience fighting such a large group when cornered. Typically, diversionary tactics and rapid retreat are preferable for me, especially with such a large force. That and not being seen."

"I couldn't have done it without you," the Knight Arbiter replied simply as her gaze drifted over the destructive scene beside them.

Actaeon took a seat upon the stone beside her, laying his arm across her shoulders naturally. "Since I accomplished your mission and we both sit here together today, I should like to continue to explore our emotions for each other together," he said, facing her.

Eisandre's thoughts seemed lost in the crater and the other smoking remains of the explosion. His words gently brought her out of her reverie and she turned to meet his gaze. "You do not have more work to do here?" she asked.

Actaeon laughed lightly and gestured to the crater. "There is not much left to do. I may need to build a new fixture, though I think the next step is to try and create a smaller device that will crack the luminary inside the sealed environment. A device that can be carried easily. The results however, are here before us and I have nothing more to do with this experiment today."

"I suspect that the most difficult part of the work to come will be attempting to understand the implications of your discovery, and how it might be used to achieve good and prevented from causing great harm. As we discussed already." She trailed off then, before she admitted, "I do not know how to explore emotions."

"I am probably the wrong person to teach you. When it comes to those things, I admit to being lost as well. But when I am around you, I feel that I want to learn about them. I am just afraid of hurting you... and us – our friendship."

"You have never hurt me. You have always protected me. Why are you afraid? For us? For our friendship? I don't understand," said Eisandre, genuine confusion in her eyes.

Actaeon considered carefully before replying. "I am afraid that I will overstep my bounds. Perhaps make you upset with me." He reached over to scratch his right elbow roughly through his jacket before he continued. "This entire thing is just unfamiliar to me. I just do not want to ruin everything that we have together. Do you understand why I feel that way?"

"No, I really don't. Do you... wish to define boundaries? I do not want you to be afraid. How can I help you to feel safe?" Eisandre asked. She still didn't understand, but she was trying.

Actaeon reached up to pull the goggles free from the tousled, ash-covered spikes of her short blond hair. "I need to understand better what *you* want. And you can certainly take your time to let me know, if you are not sure." The Engineer drew silent then, leaning back to run a hand through his own smoky hair.

"I suspect that this is going to be an interesting challenge for us both, and not subject to the logic and reason of your usual experiments. Not that our friendship is an experiment," she said quickly, then taking his hand in both of hers as he had done to hers earlier. "I am an Arbiter. You are an Engineer. I am Lost. You are brilliant. There are no rules, no precedence for us to follow as we discover the shape that our friendship will take. It is a new path, and a strange one in several ways. But we like spending time in each other's company, because we are comfortable, because we trust each other, because we admire what we come to see in each other's hearts. I don't ever want you to feel afraid with me, Actaeon. That much I know for certain. If there is something you know you want, then I would ask you to tell me. We will do best, I think, if we are as honest as we know how to be." She chose her words carefully. They were very important.

"Yes, it will be a challenge, but one that I hope we can enjoy. And I certainly do not want this to be an experiment. You are too important to me," said the Engineer with a laugh. "I agree, and I will only tell you the truth of my heart, for that is what I believe in. I would like to be with you, Eisandre – to court you, as they say. I can ask your family's permission if you would consider that appropriate," he offered.

"Nobody has ever wanted to before," she stated quietly, startled and rather amazed. "I never even thought it a possibility. I'm broken, you realize?" She lifted one of her hands to tap the side of her own head as though in indication of her words. "And I am an Arbiter. Perhaps it will help me if you define 'courtship' as you see it?" she suggested. Arbiters did not marry or have children – at least none that were spoken of. Such behavior would be considered a dereliction of their duty to their Order and the people of Redemption. Relationships were tolerated for Knight Arbiters so long as it did not interfere with their political neutrality, but it was not encouraged.

He smiled and reached over to caress her face. "You do not seem broken to me. And *I* should know how to tell whether something is broken. It is lucky for me that no one has ever wanted to before, because if anyone had yet seen the side of you that I have seen, you would have been swept away a long time before I ever met you. Courtship... yes, courtship," he continued, his eyes drifting up to ominous clouds that approached. "When two people in love spend time together to learn more about each other and to enjoy life through each other's eyes. The eventual goal being to determine one another's suitability for a life partnership. Those are my thoughts on it, anyway. Others may well disagree."

"Other people's thoughts don't matter here," she replied, her face aglow where he'd caressed her. She let out a sharp chuckle that ended in a sob, "I feel like such a hopeless idiot, Actaeon. I have my life so clearly mapped. If I could not be a Lady of Lakehold, then I would be a Knight Arbiter, and that is what I am and all that I know how to be. I was so uncertain about even being able to be an acceptable friend to someone that I didn't even consider the possibility that I could ever be something more. It's not the first time that I have said this to you, I realize, but I wish I could see what light you see in me, how I could be worthy of such affection in your eyes. It does not make sense to me. If you maintain the current path of your work, you will likely be eligible to court many women of grace and influence," she said, as though reminding him. Though the way her fingers tightened around his hand contradicted her words.

"Aye, I could court many beautiful and venomous women who would use me for my abilities or relish in the novelty of my work before going behind my back to find comfort in men that they can actually understand. You approach me with no ambition, but, rather, as my friend – my understanding, wonderful, beautiful friend. It is with you that I can share all things. In my mind, my heart, my soul, my trust, my truth. You *are* a Knight Arbiter, and you *are* the woman I am falling in love with. A world of uncertainty cannot change that to me. You are what you are, Eisandre – regardless of anyone's opinion. And, if it does not interfere with your life's map, I would very much like to kiss you."

And so, he leaned forward and kissed her.

When Eisandre was a young girl, she had dreamt of growing up to be a normal young woman to stand beside her brothers and sister, cherished and admired for her place in this world. Later on she had even dreamt of being loved, as she watched her sister's courtship, marriage, and the birth of her child. But it was not to be for her, never for her – not for poor Lost Eisandre, sent away from the family to find a life of purpose elsewhere. At least not until this one man stepped past the shadows and wells of echoes and lost patterns of light to shine clearly and complete in her mind. She kept checking, to be certain, because she had every reason to doubt, but he kept insisting and persisting and seeing her as the person she had always dreamt of being, only now she was! It baffled her, astounded her, amazed her, and filled her heart with the strangest and loveliest warmth.

And so it was that Eisandre was not overwhelmed by thoughts of explosions and weapons and the balance of power, nor even with the social complexities of courtship and the strangeness of those thoughts in application to her. There was only Actaeon and he was kissing her! She felt her heart leap toward him, her body tingling with unexplained energy.

The entire experience, bright and new, was like a great ball of light reaching out in all directions. It began in the center of their world and expanded outwards toward the beginning of a new one. It burned through her layers of thought and left behind what could only be described as jubilation.

It was a different feeling for the Engineer as well. His mind stopped searching for answers, analyzing problems, descrying solutions. There was nothing to search for here – with Eisandre everything was right the way it was supposed to be. For the first moment in his life, he let his mind rest and just enjoyed the truth of the moment.

They kissed for what seemed like eternity – tears streaming down their cheeks, and light laughter coming easily whenever they floundered in their kissing.

It was an unheard of peace for them both, like a shelter from a storm of constant questions and seeking and searching and striving. As though one person, they touched one another's face to lovingly explore and caress during their kiss. They ran their fingers through each other's hair and wrapped their arms around one another, pulling together with fervent passion.

The crash of distant thunder rolling across the open Windmoor interrupted them and the first drops of rain began to fall.

Actaeon kissed away a raindrop from her cheek and whispered in her ear. "You make me so happy, Eis! I do not want this to end."

"Me neither," said Eisandre with barely a whisper as she caught her breath. "Are you still afraid?"

"Not anymore," he said. "You know, I hear it is a sign of good luck when two people embark on a journey like this together after an explosion."

"I hope not. It sounds like a safety hazard," said Eisandre before pressing her lips to the corner of his mouth. "I see your light now, you know. Shining with such warmth. Piercing through my fog. Making me feel beautiful. I will never quite understand it, but I feel your truth. I still don't know where to go from here," she admitted with hesitation. "Although I think I would go nowhere at all, were that a real choice and I could stay right here in your arms."

"Those words mean the world to me, Eisandre. I feel a warmth and goodness in my heart like nothing I have felt before. I do not know where to go either, but I do know that wherever I go, I want it to be with you at my side," Actaeon said decisively.

She brushed her cheek against his own. "But how can that be? You are an Engineer of Raedelle and I am a Knight Arbiter."

The Engineer's thoughts spiraled back into a plethora of possibilities, in search of the answer to her question. "Perhaps I become an Engineer of Pyramid then. I could serve the Arbiters."

"You're not thinking clearly, Act," she suggested gently. "I'm not either. It's difficult right now. Let's not try. Yet."

"You are right. We shall figure this out like any other quandary. I know not yet where my life's journey will take me, but I do know who I want to share it with. After all, every great discovery requires a certain amount of risk."

"How can you be so certain of something like that? Based on a feeling? A wish? You are always so logical, my clever Engineer. Please don't be ready to toss so much away so quickly, when there is no need. One step at a time, while we discover, while we learn. We will help each other. Remember?" she asked in seriousness, a hint of worry in her tone.

"Indeed, it is a feeling. A thing that one can never truly be logical about. Though my feelings drive me to explore, discover, and create even despite the risk to my person. I can make arguments for or against many of the things that I do, but in the end I must be driven to decision by my feelings on the matter – by who I am. In this same way I feel about you. The same feelings that drive me to do these things you call amazing even while others would call them mad. I would not be tossing everything away, but as you noted, I must think my decisions through logically even though the pursuit is driven by passion. That has always been my wont. As you said we will help and guide each other. I remember – thank you for reminding me," he assured her before kissing her again upon the lips.

Time seemed for them to freeze as raindrops fell on and around them, dissipating the cloud of dust and ash from the explosion. Cracks of thunder echoed the blast from earlier and lightning lit the darkening sky.

They stayed like that as long as they could – revelling in the closeness, the passion of their connection, the silence, the companionship. They held one another and eventually just sat quietly together upon the stone, arms wrapped about one another while Eisandre's head rested upon Actaeon's shoulder. They faced the remains of Redemption's first controlled explosion in the age of their people, plus the strange, new, wonderful and frightening feelings in both of them.

All things must end though, and the rainstorm made certain of that. They realized without words that it was time to head back to the patterns of their lives apart. Actaeon gathered up his supplies and they walked hand in hand, back towards Pyramid. As they walked it began to downpour and they began to jog, side by side.

"You were worried about hurting me," called Eisandre over the rumble of thunder, drawing to a sudden stop on the tall, wet grass. "I worry for the same," she said loudly, though she lowered her voice as the rumbling passed. "I may seem cold to you, Actaeon. Maybe I will even *be* cold. Even in our stolen moments of being away from everything, I can never know how much I will remember or understand, although, with you, I'm hoping that will be easier. But, regardless, this will not be an easy path, for either of us. We know that. I…" She ran out of words then and stepped forward to wrap the Engineer in a fierce hug as though it might be their last.

Actaeon pulled her against him and kissed her, a loving gesture that ramped up passionately as their rain-soaked bodies pressed together once more.

After some time, and with palpable difficulty, he stepped away from her and placed a reassuring hand on her shoulder. "You will never seem cold to me, Eisandre."

When it was time for them to go their separate ways, the Knight Arbiter turned to offer him the formal bow of her head. "We will have to meet again very soon, I think. To discuss how I will report the results of your experiment, if you are amenable."

"I most concur, Knight Arbiter. We shall have to think carefully on how to approach this particular discovery. My thanks for providing witness. I look forward to our next meeting. You be safe," he said, offering her a playful wink before he started back toward the workshop, his halberd clicking upon the Avenue of Glass.

And life went on.

87 A.R., the 6ᵗʰ day of Torrentfall

THE DOPPLER

A POUNDING AT THE LARGE DOOR of the workshop woke Actaeon from a deep and wonderful dream. In it he had been kissing Eisandre while they sat on the vast plain of the Windmoor, a gentle breeze caressing them. With the knock, the dream scattered to the winds of his memory, like the ashes from the day before.

"By the Fallen, it's not yet dawn!" grumbled Wave from his cot in one of the alcoves up in the loft.

"Poor Wave needs his beauty rest. Don't worry, I'll see who it is. Just let me get my – where'd I put my damned maul?" griped Trench, as he lurched out of bed. What sounded like a dozen objects toppled to the floor, and the giant mercenary cursed.

A giggle came from the direction of Lauryn's cot – the young woodcarver had moved into her own little alcove to accommodate her regular work there. Actaeon paid her well for her help.

"Yer damned right. Lest I end up looking like you," Wave poked back as Trench composed himself and lumbered down the stairs.

Actaeon opened his eyes and rubbed the sleep from them. It was still dark out, and he could see the fading twinkle of stars through the rooftop vents. He stood and pulled his trousers and vest on before stepping into his boots. Grabbing his halberd, he headed for the stairs.

Trench unlocked the door and threw it open. "Who disturbs us at this hour?" he asked, glowering down with his hideously scarred visage at the small, colorfully-dressed delegate that stood at the entrance. A half dozen

Ajmani soldiers in their brightly striped red and gold pantaloons stood at attention behind him.

The man stood on his tiptoes, trying to see into the workshop beyond Trench's hulking frame. When the giant simply stood there staring at him, he sighed and spoke, "I am Portent Gaemri Ip Monjata of the Majestic One, Raja Nadiya Ajman, herself. I come bearing the wisest of words, straight from the wise lips of our most beloved of Raja. Words for the ears of one Master Actaeon Rellios, Engineer of Repute."

Trench smirked and turned to face the Engineer who had just reached the bottom of the stairs. "Engineer of Repute, there's someone Portent here to see you."

"I see that. Come right in. What can I do for you, Portent Monjata? The last time we spoke you came in service of the Raj Mujarba. I am sorry for his untimely passing," said the Engineer, as he uncovered one of the large luminaries standing near the entrance, casting light upon the cluttered workshop.

The Portent shuffled his way in and dipped his head to Actaeon. "Yes, yes, as am I. Your condolences are appreciated. We are in a different era now though, and I am most blessed to have been chosen to serve our new Raja. Indeed, all of Ajman is blessed."

"Then it has been decided," concluded Trench. "Nadiya Ajman has been chosen over that impudent twerp, Viyudun? I am glad."

"Uhm... chosen by the gods, yes. There is... uh, well... let us say that there are those who do not follow the wisdom of our gods in these dark days," explained Gaemri, spreading his hands.

"Then it is yet undecided. Well, I wish your Raja the best of luck. She is lucky to have you by her side," said Actaeon. He sat down at one of the workbenches and gestured to one of the stools across from him.

"No, thank you, sir. Actually, I was hoping that you would join me on this morning. The Raja has requested that you appear before her," said the Portent, bristling a bit as he continued. "As for the matter of succession, it has been quite clearly decided. That some have chosen not to accept it is another matter altogether – and it will be dealt with, of course."

"Not something that I can help the Raja with, you understand," Actaeon said. "I will meet with her, of course, but I would like to know what sort of pressing matter has the Raja reaching out to me at this hour."

"Yes, of course – though the details I shall leave for the Majestic One, Raja Ajman, to explain to you herself. Your reputation precedes you in your ability to solve the many problems of the Dominions. The slaying of the malign creature in the marketplace, the felling of the great tower in Shield, and if rumor be true, you defeated a tribal army by firing beams of light from another tower. The One True Dominion requires your help now, as the fine people of Adhikara have been assailed. Please join me. The Raja requests your presence at once. Oh, and this payment is a token of our goodwill," said the Portent, gesturing toward the door. One of the soldiers placed a sizable chest upon the ground and opened it. It was filled to the brim with silver coins.

"Oh, no – I cannot accept that, Portent Monjata. You see, I do not receive payment until I have determined to take a job," explained Actaeon, his eyes widening.

"It is a token of goodwill sent from the Raja herself. It would not do at all for you to turn it down," warned the Portent, tilting his head.

"If you say so. I do not wish it to be left here while I am away. Could you please have one of your soldiers carry it with us while we seek audience?" suggested Actaeon with a grin. He would take it up with the Raja directly.

The Portent's eyes narrowed as he regarded Actaeon carefully. After a moment, he smiled thinly and nodded. "Very well, Master Rellios. Let us depart."

Just past dawn, Actaeon, Trench and Wave all stood before the Raja in the Ajman Hold within Pyramid. She sat with her legs folded beneath her upon an ornamental cushion on the multi-tiered dais before them, behind which hung a variety of multicolored, semi-translucent curtains.

The Raja herself was an example of the purest feminine beauty – her features sharp yet delicate and her silky smooth skin radiant in the dim light. The purple eyeshadow that she wore sparkled and drew the eye to her powerful gaze. She wore loosely fitting red silk fabrics about her body that seemed to highlight the curves beneath while leaving other details nicely concealed. A thin chain woven with glittering red jewels was worn between a piercing in her ear and another in the side of her nose. Atop her head of flowing dark curls was a thin crown of large, colored jewels that Actaeon imagined must have cost more than his workshop.

The Raja's Portent joined her upon the dais, where he stood several levels below her.

"Our Majestic One, the One True Raja of the One True Dominion, High Priestess of Ajman, Nadiya Ajman. Those before you have come –"

"I know who *I* am, Portent Monjata, thank you. Please do introduce to me these fine gentlemen before me," said the Raja, interrupting him with a gentle smile.

The Portent took the comment in stride and continued speaking without missing a beat. "Allow me to introduce, Master Actaeon Rellios, Engineer of Repute and his two companions that go by the sobriquets Trench and Wave. Contrary to what you would expect, the taller of the two goes by the former name."

Trench stood there transfixed, his eyes drawn to those of the Raja. His mouth hung open as though searching for the words to say. He failed to notice as Wave followed the Engineer's lead and dropped to a knee before the Raja, as they had been instructed to do earlier by the Portent. A sharp jab from Actaeon's elbow brought him back to his senses.

"Oh, er.. right," he mumbled, and dropped to a knee beside them. When he glanced up again, he found the Raja staring at him. When she offered him a forgiving smile, he dropped his eyes to the floor, his face flushing brightly.

"Alright then, enough with the formalities, gentlemen. I thank you for meeting with me on such short notice. The matter is of the utmost import, I assure you. Come join me behind the dais for some tea," she said, before she rose gracefully to her feet and stepped behind the curtains.

The Portent smiled and gestured for them to follow. Actaeon stood and led the others up the dais. He handed his halberd to one of the guards before he parted the curtains and headed through.

Inside, the Raja sat upon a raised cushion at the head of a rectangular table with a row of cushions on either side.

Behind her and off to the side stood a stern looking warrioress dressed in thick leather armor. Her hair was tied back in a tight queue, and her eyes also had a touch of the purple eye shadow that her Raja wore. Worn at her side was a wide-bladed falchion with the hilt curved downward toward the pommel in an ornate pattern.

When the Raja gestured for the men to take seats upon the cushions, they attempted to sit with their legs folded beneath them, but only Wave seemed able to achieve such a posture. Trench and Actaeon were a jumble of legs, but they did their best to find a comfortable position.

The Raja smiled warmly down at them and poured four cups of tea from a finely wrought tea kettle. These she passed over to them. As they took tentative sips from their cups, the Raja's Portent joined them on the opposite side of the table and poured his own cup of tea.

"No doubt Gaemri has explained the details of what we need done," spoke the Raja, after taking a sip of her tea. "How soon can you begin on this project, Master Rellios?"

"My apologies, Raja. The details of the project you speak of are not known to me. I feel compelled to warn you that I do not wish to place myself in the middle of the struggle between yourself and your rival. I have not the resources to manage the risk that such positioning would place me in. I hope you can understand," said Actaeon with the dip of his head and a slight grin.

The Raja glanced sharply at her Portent before replying. "Yes, yes. And with Viyudun sil'Mujarba al-Arshad, my predecessor's unfortunate nephew, you are right to be nervous. He has helped free people of their heads for much less. Fortunately, I do not anticipate that this project will cause issues in that regard. It is not a matter of politics that I ask you for help with. I ask you for help with my people. As you know, Adhikara has experienced significant flooding as a result of this year's heavier than usual monsoon season. In truth, it is the worst flooding in the history of our Dominion. Between us, eighty percent of the Ajmani living there have had to evacuate –"

"Wise Raja, is it best to tell them such detail?" interrupted the Portent.

"If the Engineer is to solve the problem that I place before him, then I must trust him. The One True Dominion will not rely on subversiveness and conspiracy under my reign. We have the will of the gods on our side," she said. "As I was saying, Adhikara has been rendered nearly uninhabitable at this moment, and, with the Pools of Light under constant harrassment from the Ruinic Tribal forces, I dare not place more than a third of the Adhikaran refugees among those communities. This leaves more than half of the population of Adhikara homeless until the rains stop and the water recedes. This problem is the one that I ask you for help with, Master Rellios. I have heard reports of your accomplishments throughout Redemption, and I believe that yours is the expertise we need in this moment of trial."

"I understand. Do you believe that the drainage in Adhikara has been compromised? Perhaps there is a mechanism similar to the one that caused the marketplace smell situation. It would require extensive surveys of the region. Of course, there is also the possibility of sabotage. Drainage might have been disrupted by one of your enemies," suggested the Engineer.

"We have thought of that possibility as well. However, my advisors assure me that the usual sources of drainage have not been hindered. Instead we have seen an unprecedented rise in the levels of the Great Pools in both Adhikara and Pools of Light. The rising water has inundated many of our communities to the point where entire abodes are beneath the water. We have measured rainfall during the monsoon season for several decades now, and the rainfall this year has exceeded the greatest level we have yet recorded by ten fingers," she explained, tracing the edge of her cup with her finger as she spoke.

"If I understand correctly, you do not expect that I will be able to solve the issue of flooding," concluded Actaeon.

"On the contrary, I suspect that you may well solve that issue if given enough time, but that is exactly what we do not have. We have too many Adhikarans with no home right in this moment and those that are managing to endure the elements are at risk of thieves and raiders. It is this problem which I need you to solve more rapidly, if you are willing," she said.

"You require my services to find a place for the refugees?" asked Actaeon. "It is not exactly my specialty. Surely, Ajman has people more qualified in the matter?"

"Not in a matter of this scale. There are six thousand people that must be accommodated. You do not need me to explain to you the logistical complications of such an undertaking. If done wrong, people will catch illness, food will run short, waste will stagnate and death will follow," she said, shaking her head. "No. You are the one that we need to solve this crisis. Will you do it? I ask you not for myself, but for my people. The people of Ajman need your help."

"Might I ask about the most obvious of solutions that would present itself?" asked Actaeon, arching a brow.

The Raja bit her lip and looked down at the table, her face a flush of shame. The Portent also seemed to be unable to find the correct words.

It was the warrioress behind her who broke the silence. "The infidel in the north would have our Raja delivered to Kendra so he can take her head before he offers his own countrymen refuge. No, we will not allow it. The people of Ajman would sooner drown than live under such tyranny."

The Portent shot the warrioress a look and she returned his gaze unfazed.

"Forgive me for not introducing her," said the Raja. "This is my personal guard, Calisse T'ra Coletka. She is correct. Viyudun will accept refugees in the Ajman Hold of Kendra only if I deliver myself to him as his prisoner. It is something that I would readily agree to in order to protect the lives of our displaced Adhikarans. But my advisors are correct. Even if we were to concede to his demands, at the loss of my own self, our people would still eventually be lost in the face of tyranny. Calisse was right in saying this, and that is why we have asked you here."

Actaeon looked from Calisse to the Raja and then back before he replied. "I could not even begin to imagine having to make such a decision, Raja. I know enough about this world and its difficulties to commend you on your willingness to sacrifice your own self in order to help your people. You have my respect and I hope that you can succeed in solidifying your hold on Ajman. I will help you in any way that I am able to find a place for the refugees. I only ask one thing, if you will, Raja."

"Make your request, Master Rellios," she said, unflinching.

"You will take your coin back and keep all credit for whatever solution we manage to devise. Though I can sympathize and even admire the sacrifice you would make for your people, I am, whether fortunately or unfortunately, more self-serving than you. And as such, I do not wish to risk any connection to this endeavor. Though I do hope that the political climate alters soon so that we may work together more openly in the future," he said with a grin.

"You... would not take any credit, even?" spoke the Portent, looking genuinely bemused.

"May you always have the freedom to be self-serving, Master Rellios," said the Raja, ignoring her Portent. "I will accept your service on your terms, though in your efforts you will earn my friendship and respect."

"The friendship of a woman who is willing to die for her people is no matter to be taken lightly. Please give me a day or two, Raja. I will submit to you my ideas as soon as I am able."

"Isn't this the wrong direction, Act?" asked Wave, as they wound their way down the stairwells of the Skyspiral toward the Pyramid's Northern Descent.

"No, it is the correct direction, Wave. The task that the Raja gave me is tremendous. I need some time to clear my mind. Let us go and finally find that mechanical man," said the Engineer with a broad grin. He hadn't had time to conduct the search for the mechanical man in some time and the diversion would be welcome given that he had no idea where to start with the Ajman crisis. Perhaps the answer would come to him while he explored the Boneyards – answers often did.

"Haven't we spent enough time looking for that mechanical man? It is clearly naught but a hallucination," said Wave, biting down a scowl.

"Nay, we have not. It is no hallucination. I have seen it now from several different vantages. It is worth our effort to find and study, of that I am sure," Actaeon said, decidedly.

Behind them, the big mercenary walked in silence, his mind a world away.

"It seems that Trench was quite taken by the Raja. Hopefully I do not have to find another mercenary. Perhaps he has finally found the right woman," said Actaeon with a chuckle.

Wave nudged him sharply in reply and shot him a warning look. Actaeon frowned, dropping the subject.

A long moment later, the giant roared in laughter. "Well, if ya do lose me to the Raja, you could hire the warrior woman that Wave was making eyes at – or should I say, making eye at? I bet he'd like that!"

Wave grinned and turned around to give his friend a playful shove.

It took them the better part of the morning to locate the mechanical man, and it was not at all what they had expected to find. Why it had been so difficult to locate also became apparent – for it was completely covered by the shattered segment of a large transparent panel. At least it was transparent when they looked at it from afar. When the men drew near it, the panel began to grow opaque incrementally, darkening entirely when they arrived beside it so that it appeared as just another piece of debris in the strewn mess of the Boneyards. It was only by chance that Actaeon had noticed one of its shoulders protruding from beneath the panel.

Trench unslung his maul and hefted it in his hands, considering.

"Hold, Trench. Before we damage it, let us consider keeping it intact. Although we may not readily understand the function or intent of the Artifacts that we find out here, let us also consider the merit of the mechanism we just witnessed. It is evident that this object can detect the presence of our persons as we approach, and from a considerable distance. I am certain that we could utilize it as a detector, to see if someone approaches," explained the Engineer. He knelt beside the panel and ran his hand along its surface.

"I don't get it, Act. It just turns dark. If you were close enough to see it change color, then you'd be close enough to see people standing near it, right?" asked Wave.

"That is correct. However, there are other things which might travel farther, such as a focused beam of light. Or, as has been demonstrated to us in this circumstance, it could be used to secret something away," said Actaeon.

Trench simply shook his head and reslung his maul. "I don't even know why you bother asking. Ya know he'll find a use for most anything. He hired you, didn't he?" That said, he knelt and grasped one side of the shattered panel and lifted it off of the mechanical man before carefully laying it aside.

"I may not be able to lift big things like you, Trench, but I do have my own talents – what in shattered Redemption is that thing?" asked Wave, kneeling to examine the object that Trench had uncovered.

"Unanticipated," said Actaeon simply as he knelt on the other side.

It was indeed not what they had expected. From his previous sightings of the Artifact, the Engineer had thought for certain that it would be an automaton of sorts, perhaps a servant of the Ancients. It was nothing of the sort.

The Artifact before them was indeed a man, but not mechanical in nature. It was instead a statue of a man, twice the size of a normal man and carved of earthsbone – one of the hardest and most durable materials of the Ancients. The outer surface of the statue was a glossy, translucent material that appeared to be covering the earthsbone like a thin shell. The man depicted by the statue was shaped in stunning detail, draped in long robes with wide sleeves and hands clasped before him. About his neck was worn an amulet, upon which was the relief of a tiger and a dragon, both curving in upon one another to form a circle.

The most striking part of the statue was its face, however. Although lacking the deep scar, poorly healed burns, and short beard, it was undeniably, patently, and incontrovertibly, the face of Trench.

"Darkest Hour take me..." mumbled the big man as he reached up to run a hand over his face.

They all stared, speechlessly, for what seemed like an eternity.

It was Actaeon who broke the silence. "We had best rig up a way to transport this back to the workshop."

"Oh no... by the Fallen, Act, I don't want that thing anywhere near me. It needs be destroyed. I mean..." Trench trailed off as he failed to find the proper words.

"The mechanism is unexplained. I think it may be no mere coincidence that an object that can replicate the facial features of a nearby person be found near an object that can become opaque when people are nearby. It is something that we must study. I have never before seen such a technology amongst the Artifacts of Redemption," explained the Engineer with wonderment. "Try walking away now," he instructed Trench. "Wave and I will remain behind to see if the facial features change from yours. Then we can return to the workshop to build something with which to transport this."

With a grunt, the giant mercenary trudged away, but not before pausing to cast one last glare back at the strange thing that wore his face.

"There we go – now it'll start to get prettier," said Wave with a laugh.

But the face on the statue did not change.

With Lauryn's expert help back at the workshop, they quickly constructed a dolly that Actaeon estimated would be large enough to move both the statue and panel to carry them back through the Boneyards. They made the wheels very large and spiked to more easily traverse the debris strewn environment of the ruins.

"It should hold together for such a short journey. Go slowly and choose your route carefully," said Actaeon.

He sent Trench and Wave off with the dolly, ample rope and several large prying poles that could be used to lever the statue into place.

Once the two mercenaries had departed, Actaeon turned his attention to a completely different problem.

He still found himself unready to tackle the problem of the Ajman refugee problem, but there was another issue at hand that could not escape his thoughts.

Parts of the memory were as clear as yesterday in his mind: Shar Minovo stabbing herself in the throat, the way dozens of creatures had burst free after she had been cleaved in two, the horror in the new Governor's eyes when he told him to do whatever it takes to kill the creatures.

It was all horrendously morbid, but it had given him an idea. In their previous attempt at trapping the deathcrawlers, the traps had all been baited with meat, vegetables and slug slime. Minovo was evidence of the one thing that had been missing: live bait. The deathcrawlers needed living hosts in which to lay their young. It was foolish that he hadn't used chickens again to catch the vile things. Perhaps more than one creature down in those tunnels liked chicken.

After drawing up some basic plans for the alteration of the existing traps, Actaeon sent Lauryn to the market to fetch more chickens.

As the day grew long, the two mercenaries sweated and grunted while they muscled the cumbersome apparatus across the shattered landscape back toward the Outskirts of Pyramid. After some difficulty, they had managed to secure both the statue and the shattered panel to the dolly with rope.

Wave stood on one side of the apparatus, struggling to reach the handle and keep up with his friend. "If you weren't so damned tall, we'd not have a problem here. As it is, I can barely reach this p-kin handle!" he complained.

Trench grunted his reply between heavy breaths. "Yer the problem, my friend. A man in the body of a boy. If ya had a man's body, you'd be at the correct height for the handle and I wouldn't be hauling this damned thing by my lonesome. It's a wonder you can please a woman, with that boy's body."

Wave grinned and jerked the handle down. "What I lack in stature, I compensate with in other places."

"Keep tellin' yerself that, Wave. Life ain't just about women and waving your tiny sword around!"

"You're one to speak, big guy! Or should I call you Raj Big Guy? Yeah, don't think I didn't miss you making googly eyes at the Raja. Don't worry, old friend, I'll teach you a thing or two about swordsmanship, and you'll be seated beside that beauty in the Ajman Hold in no time!"

They reached a stretch of flat, packed dirt near the fringes of the Outskirts where Trench grinned and took off at a full run, hauling the dolly after him.

Wave's eyes widened, and he stumbled, clutching desperately to his handle. His legs pinwheeled ineffectively below him. He almost managed to keep his footing – almost, but then he slipped and fell forward. The wheels of the giant-powered statue dolly threatened to roll over him, and he rolled quickly out of the way.

When Wave recovered his feet, he brushed the dirt from his leathers and glared at Trench. Trench didn't seem to notice his friend's look however, for he had come to a stop and stood leaning against the statue as he pointed and laughed at Wave. Tears of mirth made little trails through the day's worth of grime that had built up on the giant's face.

The swordsman folded his arms and tapped his foot impatiently. When Trench's laughter died down, he smirked and strolled forward. "How about we both just agree that it's all the Engineer's fault?"

"You have to take some responsibility for your own size, my friend," said Trench, with an ugly grin.

"Cracked Redemption, Trench! Not my size! The design of this damned dolly. He knew who was going to haul it and yet he made both handles the same height! I'll bet he and Lauryn are sitting around with a few mugs of ale and laughing at us right this very moment!"

Trench stepped back and considered the 'damned dolly' for a moment before he burst into laughter. He put an arm around Wave. "Aye, Wave. Yer right. Height was not considered properly. You can't go too hard on him though. After all, you still need him to make you a new eye!"

Wave gave Trench a friendly shove that actually moved the man. "C'mon, let's get moving. You're right. By the Fallen, I want my eye!"

That said, he retook his handle. Trench joined him and they started along again, through the Outskirts on their way back to the workshop as the sun began to fall below the edge of the sky.

From the porch of a distant shack on the fringe of the Outskirts, a pair of crestfallen eyes watched with disinterest as two men of extremely disparate size argued. The smaller man gave the larger a shove that sent the latter reeling. Other eyes would have been impressed by such a display of strength, but not these – for there was nothing left in the world worth feeling for. The spark had gone out and only time lay before them – endless time, a sentence worse than death.

Yet the eyes watched nonetheless, for that was all there was – time. And any diversion, even a momentary one, would be better than retreat into the thoughts that lay behind that despondent gaze.

The two men began once again to push the statue of a large man across the Outskirts. Unbidden, feet found their unlikely way beneath the melancholy man behind those eyes and moved one before the other, to shuffle him along on the legs of a cripple. A distant thought came from far behind those eyes, wondering one simple thing: Why? It was replaced, banished even, by a voice that resonated inside his mind. The voice uttered one word, concise and absolute: Follow.

And so the man behind the eyes did.

And watched, unfeeling, as he hobbled along far behind. Watched, with indifference, the two men draw close to one of the newest buildings on the other side of the Outskirts. Watched, detachedly, as another man, taller than the short one, yet shorter than the tall one, came from the building to meet them and pointed with a long, pointed staff toward the entrance to the building. Watched, with cold dispassion, as the three men seemed to banter back and forth before they once more began to push the big statue toward the open entrance of the building.

As the statue rolled towards that entrance, the sun finished its downward descent to disappear from the day once and for all. And in the instance the sun retreated from the world to make way for night, something incomprehensible happened that sparked life into those old, dead eyes – something that cast light where naught but shadows had resided for as long as the mind could recall. It not only sent the shadows reeling, but banished them forever as life and hope and amazement flooded through the body, mind, and soul of the man behind those eyes.

And ever-so-slightly, he straightened, unleashing an agony in his back that brought tears of pain to his eyes.

Eyes that saw.

Saw, fully humbled and reverent, the statue as it began to glow with a gentle light that filled his heart with warmth and sent his mind reeling.

Saw, with the greatest of awe and open admiration, the very Face of Light itself. Light that cast all doubt from his mind and left him with a newfound purpose in this life.

He fell to his knees in supplication, the pain gone from his crippled legs and crooked back.

He fell to his knees and he cried – his heart filled with joy.

87 A.R., the 7th day of Torrentfall

SUCCESS

T HE NEXT DAY THE ENGINEER found more diversions as he sought to free his mind from the Ajman refugee problem. He often found that by concentrating his thoughts elsewhere, he would arrive at some of the best solutions to problems that were in the back of his mind. The solution for the Ajman issue still eluded him. And so, in the meantime, he kept his attention from it, as he worked the problem in the fringes of his mind. He was confident that he could devise a solution. All he needed was time.

The summons from Pyramid was the perfect distraction.

After helping Trench and Lauryn with the final touches to the deathcrawler traps, he left them to help Old Vez load up his rickety cart. Actaeon paid him handsomely.

"Make sure that you get your cart fixed up, Vez. We shall have need of your services for some time I imagine."

"Aye, young master – that I shall. Thank ye much!"

Actaeon then set out then for Pyramid with Wave.

There was a group of three waiting for them when they arrived.

Knight Arbiter Kylor stepped forward, regarding them from behind his reflective goggles with his usual stoicism. "Allow me to introduce Knight Arbiter Corvin sof Haringar. He is our expert in Artifact and artifice. He will be joining us for this expedition. Master Sollemnis awaits us inside as the representative of the Loresworn. And, of course, you remember Knight Covellet of the Keepers."

Atreena stepped forward silently. Her arm appeared to have mended, and she carried a rope ladder slung over one shoulder.

"Indeed. And nicely met, Knight Arbiter Corvin. I am Actaeon Rellios of Shore," he said with a dip of his head. He leaned forward upon his halberd. "So, why the sudden summons, Kylor? We have been working on this dilemma for many weeks. Has something happened that required immediate attention?"

"That is correct," said Kylor with a frown. "Three noble ladies are dead – two Niwian and one of Thyr. They attempted a quick bath in the cold waters and were caught off guard when the temperatures changed quickly. We found them all dead – badly scalded. The one attendant that was there had gone to retrieve fresh towels and managed to escape the rush of steam by diving into the bin of towels."

"Shattered Redemption..." cursed Wave under his breath.

"That is terrible," said Actaeon with a frown. "Was anything of note reported by the attendant?"

"Nothing, we interviewed him at length. He heard the screams and saw the rush of steam – that is all. He hadn't noticed any changes to the water temperature tracker."

"Alright then. Lead the way. We shall have to do our best to understand this and end these hazards," said the Engineer.

They climbed up into the tunnel and made their way along it until they passed through the opening where Fauntin had died. There Wave used his grappling hook to climb up to the chamber above and set Atreena's rope ladder in place.

While climbing, the Keeper glanced down at Actaeon and spoke. "The Loresworn must've taken his own rope with him. Typical."

"Somehow, I do not imagine Old Sol climbing a rope to get up here. He must have used some other method. I doubt, however, that he would be willing to share that with us either, knowing the Loresworn," said Actaeon.

Atreena looked at him in surprise and actually smiled. A mistrust for the Loresworn was something they could both agree on.

The gigantic chamber was unchanged from the last time they had visited, with one notable exception: the lift for what Actaeon thought of as the control cube was already up in the elevated position. A figure with a long gray beard and crimson red robes stood within before one of the consoles. It was undoubtedly Sollemnis the Gray.

Kylor started toward the cube on its thin column, his voice echoing in the chamber as he called out. "Master Sollemnis! It is I, Knight Arbiter Kylor sof Haringar! Please lower the lift so that we might ascend."

"Yes, yes, one moment... there's much to prepare... ...just one final adjustment!"

Kylor frowned and continued forward. "We agreed previously that we would not try to solve the problem with the baths without agreement between yourself, Knight Arbiter Corvin and the Engineer."

"Yes, yes, of course we did. Not to worry! I'm doing something completely different!"

That said, the robed man stepped out from the control room and onto the lift. Both of his hands stroked his thick gray beard as he descended.

Actaeon placed a hand on Kylor's shoulder. "Be careful, friend. He has no walking stick. Something is off." He felt the Knight Arbiter's shoulder tense beneath his hand.

"Yes, yes, the Engineer is right. I *have* forgotten something. No – not my walking stick. It was something else entirely. Something up in that room. What was it?"

As the old Loresworn spoke, the sound of cascading water erupted from behind them. They turned and were confronted with a deluge of water from one of the larger pillars that had opened somehow and was dumping its contents onto the floor of the large chamber.

With a yelp, the Keeper Knight ran back to the shattered pillar that they had emerged from and descended the rope ladder and out of sight. Almost as soon as she had descended, the deluge followed her down into the hole in the floor. Not a lifebeat later, Atreena was spit back out as the water filled the hole to the brim and flowed over.

The Keeper Knight sputtered and struggled to regain her feet. The two Arbiters pulled her away from the hole. She sputtered and coughed up water, bent over at the waist, "He closed... ...closed the way we came in."

"A test for the young Engineer has arisen. Will he be able to figure a way out of it?" echoed the voice of Sollemnis throughout the chamber, as though he were narrating some story.

Cold water washed across their boots as the chamber began to fill up. Wave ran toward the Loresworn with lightning speed, and his fist flashed out at the old man's face – and passed straight through it. The mercenary fell off balance and stumbled past.

The Arbiters reached for their swords but were stayed as the Engineer raised his hand. "That is not Sollemnis the Gray, it is naught but a projection. Controlled by him, likely, but a projection nonetheless. Sollemnis," said Actaeon, addressing the projection. "We are not amused by your manipulations. Tell us what to do to reverse this. You are playing games with our lives and those in all Pyramid."

The projection took no notice, but appeared to be distressed by Wave's punch, despite the lack of connection. The old Loresworn made a show of straightening his robes. "Cold... so cold – the people here are."

"Oh, you'll be plenty more cold than this when we're done with you, old man," said Wave, spitefully.

"So cold – a touch blue, I feel. Spiraling away. Take me home, Kryo."

The gray bearded man in the crimson robe began to flicker and was gone.

Actaeon waded over to the lift. The water was already up to his thighs. He was not surprised when the lift walls didn't raise and it failed to activate for him.

"Wave! Can you throw your grapple over that room up there and hook the other side? There is a small lip that it might hold onto," Actaeon said, his mind racing.

Wave nodded and unslung the rope from his torso, prepping the grapple for a throw.

In the meantime, Actaeon rushed over to a solidified hunk of melted, silvery metal at the north end of the room. It was stuck to one of the horizontal pillars and drooped over both sides. When he reached it, he jammed the wedged endcap of his halberd between it and the pillar. Using the curvature of the pillar, he pried with his halberd until it cracked and a chunk fell free.

The Arbiters were right beside him. "What do you need, Master Rellios?" asked Kylor. Atreena stood behind them, still coughing up water and trying to catch her breath.

"Move this chunk of metal directly below the cube. We can use it to gain entry," said Actaeon.

The four of them moved the heavy hunk of material over to the lift, using the buoyancy of the freezing water that was now up to their waists to help them with it.

Wave had already begun his hand over hand ascent of the rope. By the time they moved it over to the lift, Wave was atop the control cube. "What now, Act?" he called down.

"Drop the grapple end down, and we will send this up as a weight. You will need to use it to break one of the windows once it reaches the correct height."

Wave dropped the grapple end and Actaeon secured the rope around the metal piece while the others held it up. Once it was secure, Wave began to haul it up. As soon as it left the water, Wave had trouble lifting it farther. He dropped the other end of the rope down the other side of the cube as he hauled.

The water at their necks at this point and they were all beginning to shiver uncontrollably.

Corvin helped Atreena atop his shoulders and they were able to reach the other end of the rope after Wave managed to haul the chunk high enough out of the water. Once Atreena had a hold of the rope, they were able to haul the big piece of metal up quickly as a team.

Actaeon moved to the other side of the cube while the other three hauled and he stopped them once the metal chunk was at the height of the control cube's windows. They tied the rope off on a thin pillar nearby. Wave pulled it up the rest of the way, and, once everyone was clear, he hefted it with difficulty.

"By the Fallen, should've been Trench up here," he muttered, before throwing the mass. He slipped and fell flat against the roof of the cube.

The metal chunk fell to the end of the rope with enough momentum to carry it inward and crash through one of the windows on the side of the cube. The rope tied around the pillar slipped and the big chunk fell inside the cube.

Wave climbed back to his feet and whooped victoriously. He then climbed through the shattered window to enter the cube. Once the rope was cut below, he began to haul the others up.

Actaeon was first, and immediately went to the console. There he found what he was looking for: a blue spiral symbol. When he touched his finger to it, a green line appeared beside it and he used his other hand to pull down the green line until it disappeared. A look outside confirmed what he could already hear – that the water had ceased.

Once Wave finished pulling the Keeper up, Atreena crashed into the Engineer, giving him a big, wet hug.

"You did it, you clever bastard! By the Fallen!" said Wave, taking a moment to grin back at his boss.

Atreena jerked away, thinking better of the gesture. She made an attempt to appear dignified as she wrung out her hair. "The Allfather thank you for thwarting this evil, but how did you know what to do?"

"'Touch blue', Sol said. 'Spiraling away'. He pretends at the doddering old fool, but he knows exactly what he is doing. It was a test and he set it up. I would not be surprised if they set all of this up – the baths, the collapse in Sea Lounge – everything..."

The Engineer trailed off and brought his attention back to the console full of lit and flashing, cycling symbols. He pulled a soggy roll of vellum from his jacket and unrolled it upon the surface, comparing his sketches to the symbols on display. It was easy for him to pick out the changes that had been made by the Loresworn. It clicked all of a sudden and he knew the secrets of the console. It was clear by the changes in color which symbols had been changed to reroute the flow from the colder water sources to the large pillar that had been opened to try and drown them. The blue spiral controlled the opening and it matched the spiral symbol on the large pillar itself.

Now he could see more and more of the correlations – symbols on the console matching those on the pillars. And there, he spotted the one that correlated to the pillar they came through from above the Sea Lounge. He touched that symbol and was rewarded with the immediate gurgling sound as the water in the chamber began to drain out into the Sea Lounge and Pyramid below.

He found another one that had been changed that didn't match any of the pillars. When he touched it, it flared to life with bright green light.

"Have them try the lift now, Wave," he instructed.

Wave called down to the two Arbiters, and, a moment later, they were up in the control room with them.

Kylor regarded Actaeon with a neutral expression for a long moment before finally stepping forward. "You've my deepest apologies, Master Rellios. The Loresworn are trusted allies – this was wholly unexpected."

"Yes, of course. You will report this to your commanders, I am sure," said Actaeon distractedly. He held the scroll before him and seemed to be mapping it against symbols on the pillars within the room.

The Engineer considered one of the symbols and reached out tentatively.

"I will touch the symbols for you, Master Rellios. You can consult with Arbiter Corvin and instruct me with what to press," said Kylor, interposing himself calmly between Actaeon and the console. "In this way, I will bear the responsibility of the resulting effects, whatever they may be."

Wave leaned back against the sill of the shattered window and folded his arms. "Fantastic, I'm up in a room near the top of Pyramid with a bunch of nutcases pushing buttons."

"Do not be absurd, Kylor," said Actaeon, ignoring Wave's jab. "Having someone to carry out one's orders does not alleviate one from responsibility. If you want to push these keys, then be my guest – but it is not necessary."

He carefully moved the soggy sketch to an area of the console free from symbology and gestured for the others to approach. As they gathered around, he began to explain. "This room is the epicenter of liquid conduits for Pyramid. It has water, both hot and cold and perhaps with different salinity levels and potability. It clearly carried some sort of molten metal at one point, based on the damage on that side of the room. Who knows what else – but we do know what came out of the Sea Lounge conduit, and we can use that to start. These similar symbols, here, here and here, for example, I would hazard to say are all one form of water or another. Thus, we could divert water from any of these sources into the conduit that feeds the baths.

"Based on what we know of the temperatures and the associated colors indicating such, I have to conclude that this one here is the symbol for the conduit for the baths. In additional support of that hypothesis, we can see that the corresponding pillar is headed in that general direction. It is fed by what appears to be some cold water, and some hot water, but look at the symbol on the hot water feed – it is flashing rapidly. A sort of malfunction perhaps? I suggest that we reroute the water from this source here to feed the baths and we close off that feed altogether. Remember, we cannot know how long these systems have been operating. Hundreds of years? Thousands? As advanced as the Ancient's technology was, they surely expected to maintain it on occasion. Nothing is permanent after all. Your thoughts, gentlemen? Lady Knight?" asked the Engineer, raising a brow to regard the others.

"What you are saying makes sense, but it is beyond my expertise. I defer to Corvin on this issue," said Kylor, turning to his companion.

While Corvin considered, Atreena spoke. "If these abominations of the Ancients malfunctioned, then it is not meant to be used. The baths and the death that has come from the use of them are but another sign from the Allfather that the Artifacts of the Ancients are to be scorned. I say leave it as is, post a guard and never touch it again. The Keepers would be willing to help safeguard this room if need be."

"What the Engineer says, I believe, is correct," said Corvin. "I agree with his approach."

"My task has been to restore the baths, and, at the order of the Knight Arbiters, I will restore the baths, if I can," said Actaeon. "However, I do agree with the Lady Knight. A guard must be posted on this room. That – or it must be sealed off. To do otherwise is a threat to the security of all Pyramid."

"Agreed. The Pyramid is the center of Dominion negotiation and politics. The Dominion leaders meet here for convenience of location but also because of the luxuries that the Pyramid offers them. If we wish to maintain this safe center of civilized discourse on neutral ground, then we must do our best to keep such luxuries and accommodations that we can offer. That includes the baths," said Kylor with a sharp nod. "Those are my orders. Restore the baths, Master Rellios."

"Aye, Knight Arbiter Kylor. So I shall."

The Keeper stomped her foot and grunted before she stormed off back toward the lift.

The Engineer reached out to touch the appropriate symbols.

And all the lights went out.

All their candles and strikers had been too wet to light. So they all sat on the floor in the control cube, high up in Pyramid, amidst a growing ocean of darkness – stranded by the non-working lift in the Darkest Hour. Far to the other side of the room, waning sunlight cast its dim rays upon the far wall.

As the light began to fade, Actaeon poured out the contents of several half-through bottles on the floor of the control room and his blue fire sputtered and sprang to life.

Wave finally spoke after a long spell of silence, his face bathed in the cold blue light. "Helluva time for the Darkest Hour."

"You're making a mistake, you know," said Atreena. She had moved away from the others to sit in the shadows near the frozen lift.

"Mistakes are all relative to one's perspective," the Engineer responded. "There are many who would argue that drawing a definitive conclusion from the unknown would be a mistake. I happen to be one of them."

"The word of the Allfather is not unknown," she said.

"Yes, and the Allfather tells you this technology that was created by the Ancients lead to their demise and will lead to ours if we embrace it, right?"

"You have done your reading, but it clearly has done nothing to educate you... Engineer." The last word was a sneer.

"So educate me then, Lady Covellet. How did the technology lead to the demise of the Ancients?"

"It obliterated them, of course. It erased them from this world. The evidence is all around us. They are no more," she said, matter-of-factly.

"And why did it obliterate them?"

"Because. It was unnatural. The embodiment of laziness and corruption and evil. It purged them from the face of this world for their arrogance."

"Mayhaps that is true. But you misunderstand my question. Did the technology – the Artifacts of the Ancients make that decision, or did the Ancients cause their own erasure through the improper use of that technology?"

Atreena laughed then. "Ha! Improper use! Any use at all is improper!"

Actaeon stared at her across the flickering flames. "Why?"

"Why, what? Do you ever stop asking questions?"

"No, he doesn't," said Wave and Kylor at the same time. Wave burst out in laughter and the ghost of a smile at the corner of the Arbiter's mouth could be made out in the pale light.

"I do not," said Actaeon with a broad grin. "And that is my point. Allow me to ask just a few more questions of you and then we can sit in companionable darkness. What do you know about your sword?" He gestured to the longsword on her hip.

"My sword... why, I've been training with it every day since I was a little girl. I don't see what that has to do with any —"

"Hold on. We will get there. So you would say that you are proficient, learned even, in the use of your sword then?"

"Of course."

"Is everyone?"

"Is everyone, what?"

"Proficient — in the use of a sword."

"No, not at all. Though most people that aren't just get themselves killed."

"Interesting. Alright, so there are people that utilize the sword that do not know the correct usages and they get themselves hurt. Let us go even deeper: how is the sword made?"

"A blacksmith forged it. This is a ridicu—"

"Just a few questions I said, and I shall be quiet. How did the blacksmith forge it?"

"In a forge of course! He heated it up and beat it into shape."

"Okay, very good," said the Engineer. "And how did he achieve the quality of its edge? How did he ensure that it would maintain strength along its longitudinal axis during the shocks of combat?"

"Longi— what?"

"The length of the blade," said Wave with a smirk. "C'mon, even I know that."

The Keeper shot a look at Wave, then shook her head in annoyance. "He knows what he's doing. I don't know; I'm not a blacksmith."

"Excellent, so you utilize your sword, and yet you know not how to make it. How do you know that it is a good sword and will not fracture in battle?"

"A good sword can be flexed in an arc and the arc should be smooth when you bend it. Otherwise would indicate a flaw. And it should be able to hold a good edge — to cut through thick sheet under its own weight," said Atreena.

"And what about the material? You said the blacksmith heated it up and beat it into shape."

"Oh in the name of the Allfather! Just get to your damned point!" said Atreena, running out of patience.

"Fine," said the Engineer with a smile. "You are an expert swordswoman – at least by the standards that you hold yourself to as a Keeper. You are educated in the use and inspection of a sword, but not as well in the manufacture and material origin of a sword. And you have observed that many in Redemption lack even your level of knowledge and therefore could hurt themselves with a sword. Compared with the level of technology that the Ancients used – Artifacts, as we call them now – compared with that, the sword is a rudimentary tool. Yet, even at our level of technology, there are details of such technology that are lost upon many of us. Would it not be within the realm of imagination that the Ancients also found that some of the details of their Artifacts were lost upon them? Perhaps they did not realize the harm that their technology was capable of, or they failed to understand the power harnessed within – power that is so incredible that it continues to feed Artifacts with the energy they need to function hundreds or even thousands of years after the Ancients themselves.

"What I am saying, is that it may well have been the Ancients' lack of knowledge itself that led to whatever demise they faced. Would it not therefore be our responsibility to learn and share all truth among ourselves, lest we face the same fate?"

"You know not what you speak of, Engineer," said the Keeper, stepping out of the shadows into the eerie light of the fire. Her sword was drawn, and the Arbiters and Wave leapt to their feet and placed hands upon their own hilts. Actaeon remained seated and watched her with curiosity.

She sat down opposite the fire from Actaeon, however, and laid the sword across her knees. The Arbiters relaxed and returned to their seats, though they were considerably more alert than before. Wave remained standing, hand on the hilt of his rapier.

Atreena continued. "The Allfather has said otherwise. He has told us that without a doubt, the Ancients were destroyed by their Artifacts."

"I have never met the man, but I shall take your word for it. Even if he said that, it still does not cut to the reason, which may well be the root cause of why the Ancients were destroyed by their Artifacts. None of us know for sure – we may never, but I know one thing in my heart and mind –and that is that truth is always the answer, we cannot hide from it, however much an Allfather or anyone else would like us to. Human nature is curiosity and advancement and drive. We are manipulators, articulators, interactors – we cannot help it. We affect our environs and in doing so we risk everything. Thus, we had better do our best to know what – by the fallen – we are doing."

Atreena tensed up at his blunt mention of the Allfather as a man and it took some obvious effort for her to compose herself. "Your words blaspheme. However, as you forgive my lack of knowledge in the manufacture of my blade, I shall too forgive your lack of knowledge in the truth of the Allfather. You see, his word is our one truth and you are correct that in lacking the knowledge of that truth, you and others like you are quite dangerous." She smiled at him thinly.

Wave couldn't help but laugh at that. "I like how she turned that around on you, Act. I hope you don't mind my saying, Lady Covellet, but you'd make an excellent politician. Perhaps it is good that Act is fixing the baths for you after all. There might be more work in Pyramid for you if you keep it up."

The lady Keeper chuckled at that, and color could be seen in her cheeks even in the cold light.

When the Darkest Hour ended, Actaeon punched in the sequence to fix the baths. Wave and Corvin left to check the status of the baths and came back to report good news: the baths were warm again, but a touch too warm.

After several more adjustments, they settled on a temperature that the bath attendants were happy with, and the wet and exhausted party went in their separate directions with little ceremony.

While Actaeon and Wave returned to the workshop along the Avenue of Glass, the answer clicked inside Actaeon's head and he grinned victoriously. He tossed his halberd up and caught it, bringing it down to click against the surface of the Avenue before he started off to the north.

"Come Wave, I believe I have an idea."

Wave blinked and rubbed his lone eye with the palm of his hand. "I believe you've had enough of those for the day." When he realized that Actaeon would continue off either way, he shrugged. "Alright, fine. But that's the last one!"

Actaeon led him to the barren strip of land just north of the Outskirts.

There he found a seemingly arbitrary location and he grinned and thrust his halberd into the dirt, "This is it!"

He sat down there before he withdrew a damp sheet of vellum along with his charcoal stick, and began to sketch. As he drew on a mostly dry section of the paper, the plans for a refugee encampment began to resolve: bunkhouse residence rows with long trenches behind them for latrines – the slope of the terrain would carry waste away down to the edge of the Felmere. While prioritizing runoff, waste management and access issues, he gradually began to lay the groundwork for the camp. It took him all evening and the better part of the next day, but, when he was finished, he had laid out the plans for a refuge community that prioritized the number of refugees the Raja had mentioned and still managed to fit in a hospital, a community hall, farming space, mess hall and a water collection apparatus to collect rainwater for drinking.

Not a day past the completion of the plans did the refugees begin to relocate and start the construction of their encampment.

COUPLES AND THEIR FIGHTS

"THAT'S IT! I'M MOVING THIS damned ugly thing out of here right now!" announced the mercenary with a roar that reverberated under the vaulted ceiling of the workshop. The blanket of night still lay heavy upon the Outskirts, though it was nearly dawn if one could judge by the tentative songs of the birds outside – though even those few songs came to an abrupt halt at Trench's roar.

If the others that slept up in the loft did not all awaken at his words, they certainly did when the giant tipped the big statue and dragged it across the stone floor. The friction between the base of the statue and the floor sent up a horrendous grinding sound that lanced through their eardrums. Actaeon cringed and threw back his sheet before sitting up to observe the shifting shadows that the luminescent statue cast upon the walls and ceiling as it was dragged along.

"Go easy, Trench! I know that you're not exactly glowing, but don't forget that there's a striking similarity there," called out Wave from his bed. Actaeon could picture the mischievous grin on the other mercenary's face as he taunted his friend.

"I'll show you ...similarity. If ya... don't shut up, I'll drag ya out ...here too," grunted Trench between huffs and puffs as he hauled the massive object. The earthsbone was dense and heavy, and the statue was twice his size. It was amazing that he could move it.

The door below crashed open, and Lauryn cried out. "Hey, careful! That's quality craftsmanship."

The grinding ceased, and several long moments later the door thumped closed.

"There. Much better. It's like a damned beacon out there. And if the craftsmanship is so great, then it can survive some abuse, lass!"

Actaeon couldn't help but grin when he heard Lauryn's harrumph of indignation over in her sleeping alcove.

Wave couldn't help himself. "Well, Trench – look at the positive side: at least people'll know where to find you."

Everyone but Trench dissolved into laughter.

"Wave!" bellowed the giant, but a moment later he joined in the laughter and returned to his cot.

Later that day Actaeon had the workshop to himself while the others were out taking care of various projects and tasks. He had cleared a large space near the still foundry by pushing the workbenches up against one wall. Glass rope formed a large ring on the floor, and several wooden training weapons lay atop the tables nearby, including a few weighted swords, a sledge with a big log as its head, and a few staves, one modified to hold a mock blade at the tip – his practice halberd. With the high clearance to the stone vault overhead, it would make an excellent sparring circle.

Actaeon stood in the center of the ring with his weapon, practicing with it in the air. It was not something he did often, but he wanted to warm up a bit before Eisandre would undoubtedly wipe the floor with him. He alternated between some broad sweeping motions and quick jabs and thrusts with the halberd's blade as he kept imaginary foes at bay. Although his sloppy movements showed his lack of formal training, there was a measure of calculation to his style. Every movement carried a reason behind it – to draw the opponent in or drive them back, distract defenses, destabilize balance, allow retreat, or just to confuse.

There was a great degree of unpredictability to Actaeon's style that Eisandre found unnerving as she stood nearby to watch him warm up. It seemed as though the halberdier did not know himself what he would do until he acted.

He came to a stop, catching his breath. "It really has been a long time since I have trained. I used to practice daily for at least a little while, if only to appease my father. And a good thing that I did, for I have needed those skills desperately at times in my life. I am glad you decided to take me up on my offer to spar, though I am sure I will come to regret it," he concluded with a grin.

"Why would you wish to do something you are sure you will regret?" wondered Eisandre, missing the humor in the statement. When he didn't immediately respond, she returned to the topic at hand. "I have been training for many hours a day, almost every day for the past five – nearly six years of my life, now. If an Arbiter falters, it could mean the death of their comrades, or the harm of innocent civilians. We must remain physically strong and mentally capable of fulfilling our duties. It requires constant focus. If you do not wish to spar, we can do something else. I must admit I have never practiced with a non-Arbiter before. Your lack of discipline would be an educational experience, but I would not wish to inadvertently cause you harm."

As though in example of such a lack of discipline, he laughed and approached to kiss her lightly upon the lips, a belated greeting that brought no reaction from the Arbiter, who was too focused on the conversation. Drawing back, he said, "When my father was alive he made me train with him regularly. It was his wish that I one day undergo The Trials. Although I chose quite the disparate path, I am still quite versed in safe sparring and experienced with my weapon. I should in the least provide for you a nominal challenge and hopefully serve as a stepping stone for you to use in your recovery before moving on to face your Arbiter brethren again. Please do not hold back, for I will gain much more if you do not."

"I did not undergo the Trials either," Eisandre admitted. "We both traveled different paths. And I have seen you fight, Actaeon. I do not doubt your skill. We shall use the practice weapons, since you have them," she decided. "And since we do not have helmets, blows to the head will not be permitted. The defender will call any strikes that hit. Anything that would result in a fatal or debilitating wound will be the end of the match. Grappling will be allowed. And either of us can call a halt at any time. Do you have any questions?"

Actaeon was genuinely surprised that she also did not undergo The Trials. It was a rite of passage for Raedellean boys and girls that had come of age, and most went on to serve in the Warbands for some time. The Trials themselves were a thing, that – despite years of preparation for – nobody spoke of the details. He had asked his father for more information about it, but his father had only replied enigmatically. "If you want to understand the Trials, then you must undergo them."

His observations had told him a few things about them: the participants left as the waning crescent faded from the night sky and did not return until the moon was full. Some children did not return at all, while others returned with scars or other injuries. Those that returned were considered adults and the occasional child that returned before the full moon was returned to their family in shame. Such shame was something that Actaeon had experienced from his own family. He learned the hard way that it was extremely difficult to earn the community's respect in other ways. It was one of the reasons he had left Raedelle the first time, and it was only caring for his dying mother and establishing his metal-casting shop that finally earned him the grudging respect of the Incline elders.

He nodded his assent. "I understand."

The pair retrieved their training weapons and loosened up with some stretches, pacing the circle several times before they squared off opposite one another.

Eisandre adopted a balanced stance as she pointed the tip of her sword at the Engineer's throat, her elbow bent and relaxed. Her intense blue eyes fixed upon Actaeon, filled with eerie calm and deadly confidence. "Are you ready?"

Across from her, Actaeon grinned and fell into a wide stance before her, one foot forward with the wooden blade of his polearm angled toward her, the shaft of his weapon held in close to his center of gravity. "Ready," came his calm reply.

The Arbiter made him wait for some time before she thrust at the Engineer's center, testing him. He batted the blade aside harshly to try to throw her off balance before lunging forward at her shoulder. The Arbiter maintained her solid stance and blocked his sloppy stab, sliding her blade back toward the blade to prevent him from withdrawing the halberd. She then stepped forward to close the distance between them.

The Engineer circled to her off-hand side and spun the halberd free of her blade, swinging the butt of the shaft at her calves. She jumped over the weapon easily and her next slash was easily blocked by Actaeon. His block pushed both weapons to the side, and he stepped forward in a risky maneuver to sweep her legs with the halberd's length. In a blur, she was clear of the sweep. He hadn't even noticed her leap over it again, and her blade slid down the shaft of his halberd to graze his elbow.

The Engineer spun free and entered a tighter stance, bringing his blade back to bear between them. "Hit my arm," he called out. "You are quick, Eis... I think I can learn a lot from you."

She grunted and lunged forward to attack – a feint toward his ankle and a quick slash at his thigh. He blocked her slash, but almost too slowly, before he thrust at her shoulder only to feel the crack of wood on wood. She riposted with a thrust at his ribcage and belted out a sharp cry to throw him off.

Despite the startling yell, Actaeon kept his composure and arched backward, rotating the shaft of the halberd across his body to knock the sword's point clear. The sword thudded lightly into the padding of his jacket, and he leapt backward to increase the distance between them.

"Another hit to my shoulder," he called.

"Then halt," instructed Eisandre, lowering her sword. "It is difficult to fight with a halberd if your arm is falling off," she noted with a quirk of her brow that suggested a lighthearted jab. "Your skills are unrefined, Actaeon, but sufficiently practical. And, as I recall, the pressing nature of actually fighting for your life makes you more accurate. I think I am a bit slower than usual, myself."

Actaeon took a moment to lean upon his halberd as he wiped sweat from his brow. "Truly you are one of the most difficult opponents I have ever faced. Had the men that attacked us possessed half your skill, then that ruin would have been my grave. My father was only a part time commander in the warband, and his skill was no equal to your own. I shall be glad that I will not have to face any Arbiters in actual combat. If this is not challenging enough for you, we need not continue," he added.

"I am but an inexperienced Knight," she replied in a quiet tone. "You should see my partner, Garth, fight. He can likely best me with his eyes closed. This practice has the potential to help us both, I think. I am willing to continue if you desire, but if that is your way of saying you wish to have lunch, that is acceptable for me as well." She looked up at him in sudden concern that she might have offended him.

The Engineer simply smiled his amusement. "I can continue for a time yet. Just wanted to make sure that I do not waste your time. I suppose you shall get some exercise for your injured arm even if it only involves hitting me with your sword. Besides, I can use all the practice I can get, especially where my forays take me. Shall we resume?"

"You never waste my time, Actaeon," she said with sincerity that brought his eyes to hers. She was already back in a fighting stance.

When he nodded that he was ready, she moved forward with brutal, elegant efficiency as she threw two easy feints at him and nimbly dodged the blade of his weapon. She spun deftly past his thrusts and unleashed a series of quick consecutive attacks.

Actaeon swung his weapon to and fro, keeping the pivot point close against his chest to speed his movements with the weapon as he skillfully blocked each attack. The shaft of his weapon was a blur as he backed away from the Arbiter. He used the mechanical advantage of the weapon's length by keeping his grip in close to his body to conserve his energy, which allowed him to rotate and sweep the shaft drastically, with minimal movement on his part.

In this way he maintained his defense under Eisandre's rapid cascade of attacks, successfully keeping her at bay.

"Good," she stated, stepping back as she began to circle him slowly.

"Thank you," came his reply and he offered her a weary smile.

She thrust toward him every so often to keep him on his toes, looking for holes in his defense. Actaeon fought with greater reserve this round, however, and he rarely countered with another attack. He recognized most of her openings as a ploy to draw him in.

They kept at this for a long while, teasing and feinting against one another. The Engineer kept on the defensive and the focused Arbiter did not give him a moment of rest. Even as they began to perspire and flush with exertion, the Arbiter did not waver in her steady stream of attacks. The only sounds in the workshop were that of their boots upon the hard floor, the occasional crack of wood against wood, and the exerted pattern of their breathing.

She was driving him into a lull, and he knew it. If they kept this up, he would be bested once she spotted a moment of inattentiveness. He had to change this pattern if he wanted to win the bout. With a grin, he feinted wide to the right and leapt to the left, before resuming his stance. Several clashes later, he thrust the blade toward her chest as he backed away. These random bursts of activity and motion he inserted into the rhythm, to break her pattern and to keep himself sharp and aware more than anything.

Eisandre nodded in appreciation and changed her movements to try to push him to the edge of the ring. Caught off guard, the Engineer neared the edge of the circle and leapt to the side. She continued to press him around the perimeter of the ring, tireless and diligent as she harried him around the circle, trying to force him out of bounds.

The Engineer's moves became sloppier as the seemingly indefatigable Arbiter continued to press him. Finally, she saw an opportunity and lunged forward, pinning him – heel against the edge of the circle. He had mass on her, but she held him there with her superior stance as he struggled to push her away. When she broke free, it was a sudden and unexpected as she burst forward to push him out of the circle and strike with her blade at his chest.

Actaeon cried out in surprise, but, rather than fall from the circle, he fell to his knees – a last second swing knocking her sword wide. In a move of desperation, he swept the halberd back low to hook her legs from behind, leaving his head and torso fully open to attack. She easily sprang over the halberd and brought her sword high. Knowing that he could not recover in time to parry, he dropped his weapon and lunged at her midsection in an attempt to lift her and pull her legs out from under her.

The Arbiter was too quick for him though, and she wrapped her arm around his shoulders and neck to pull him into a twist – a move which sent them both toppling to the floor of the ring in an awkward embrace, which brought forth a grunt of laughter from the Engineer.

She still had her sword in her hand though, and Actaeon slid his hand down her arm to grab the cross guard of her sword so she couldn't use it against him. He continued to laugh as he worked his head free of her grip, losing his goggles in the process. He wrapped his arm about her torso, pulling her toward him.

Eisandre was confused by his laughter. Why was falling against a hard floor so funny? As he continued to grapple with her – which she had said was allowed – they ended up pressed chest to chest with their limbs intertwined. She began to understand what he found so amusing as she felt his breath catch against her chest in a poignantly different manner than the exertion of sparring had brought upon. It did not mean that she would allow him to disarm her, however. She banged his hand against the floor to try to release his grip on the sword – the effort was half-hearted though.

When he laughed again, wrested her head about so they were nose to nose and peered into his sparkling emerald eyes. "What?" she asked, in annoyance.

Actaeon struggled to contain his laughter. "I was just thinking that I am in big trouble at this point. It seems that a gross change in tactics is advisable – lest I lose two matches in a row."

That said, he pulled her roughly against him and kissed her on the lips.

Oh, she thought, then *OH!* This was certainly not a tactic included in Arbiter training. Her body was telling her otherwise – that this was not a tactic, but something else entirely. It caused a torrent of confusion, the way her body reacted so naturally, melted against his, the way she returned the kiss with that same passion he had set alight out on the Windmoor four days ago. Yet her Arbiter mind was still locked in sparring mode. She refused to be distracted.

Resolutely, Eisandre used the moment of distraction to turn the situation to her advantage. She swung her leg wide over Actaeon's, immobilizing his own and shifted her weight atop so that she straddled him – effectively pinning the Engineer below her lithe frame, her lips never leaving his.

When he reached up to pull her against him, she pushed away and broke their kiss. "Call it," she whispered in a ragged breath, her eyes boring hard into his own. "Call the match," she said again, practically begging him as the conflict in her mind waged a desperate war inside her. She felt half mad with the urge to kiss him again, but, at the same time, she kept a determined grip on her sword beneath his own hand.

Below her, the Engineer smiled up into her eyes. "The Knight Arbiter wins –" he conceded, then adding, "...the Engineer's heart."

With those words, Eisandre tossed away the wooden sword, sending it clattering across the hard floor of the workshop. She took a moment to look down at him, running her fingers through his tousled black hair before she gave in and sank down against his body, her lips meeting his once more.

Were Wave or Trench or Lauryn to appear now – the Engineer and Arbiter on the floor, kissing passionately in the center of the sparring ring, would be quite the sight to see. Luckily for the two lovers, nobody arrived and they had the chance to be alone, enraptured in a world of their own creation: heat and light and the new but natural feeling of being so close.

Some time later the couple made it to Actaeon's cot, up in the loft, minus much of the clothing and armor that they had worn earlier – it lay scattered on either side of the cot. She traced the scar of the burn on his right arm with her eyes and then her hands. He ran his own hands along her bare chest and over the fresh scars on her upper arms from when she fell through the hole to land atop the mirror shards. They had spoken of love and trust and the feeling of being home together. It had been previously unimaginable for either of them, but in those moments the same thought found both of them: Has there ever been a world other than this one?

The moment seemed to hang in time forever, and neither of them wanted it to end. But then his body shifted against hers in a different way and it caused other thoughts. Words formed in place in her mind and she paused to shape them for him.

"Actaeon. I have never wanted a man before. Now I want you so much... so much that it consumes me. But, forgive me, forgive me. I do not know what it means."

Actaeon smiled into her eyes and answered her softly. "I would like that, Eisandre. I am yours if you would have me."

It was startling to Eisandre that he did not understand her in their moment of deep connection. She gazed into his eyes and felt desire. It was in that moment that something inside her also began to hurt.

"We cannot," she whispered, uncertain. "What if we create a child?" The idea sent her into a spiral of thoughts that threatened to drown her and wash away everything she was.

"Please forgive me, Eis. I should have been thinking more clearly. When I am with you, it is difficult to see beyond this world we are in." He ran his hand through her short locks of blond hair and down along the lobe of her ear.

"I forgive you for nothing – not a single moment of this beauty, of this longing, of this new bond forged between us. I didn't want to see beyond our world, but I must – I am an Arbiter. Please don't let me go," she said, her voice quavering.

"I have got you, Eisandre. I will not let you go," said the Engineer with a smile before he kissed her lightly upon the forehead. Though his body was awash with desire for this beautiful, strong, Lost woman in his bed, he knew that he must respect her concerns.

Actaeon. The man she saw so clearly from the first meeting in St. Torin's Hold and who she made laugh that second time, there in the Boneyards. He had laughed, and, after that, things had only gotten better, and he never turned away from her, never let her go – not when she had fallen down that hole and it should have been too dangerous to follow, not when they were beset upon by bandits and she thought she might be too weak to fight, not when she confided her greatest struggle of being Lost in the tangled labyrinth of her own mind, and not when she built this new wall between them, defying all instinct and nature itself, because they were from such different lives – and because of her duty.

She found that there were tears in her eyes as she held him close against her.

"Oh, Actaeon. It's all so new. I think I might need to go more slowly. I think... already I do not know how I will bear to be apart. Who am I now? Who will I be when I must leave?" she spoke softly against his ear.

"You are still the Knight Arbiter Eisandre – brave and disciplined. But you are also the woman that I love and respect more than anyone in this world. I am most happy that you are both of those things. I want to take things as slowly as you need to. I want this to be as perfect for you as it is to me," he replied in return.

"I have no words for how I love you. And I'm sorry this is not as easy as it would be for you – were I someone else," she said before kissing him once more.

"Were you someone else, this would not even be happening. The more I learn about you, the more I find myself amazed and enthralled. Know that I will always be here by your side, so long as you will have me," said the Engineer resolutely.

Eisandre was perplexed at his words and contemplated them in silence as she concentrated on the rapid beat of his heart against her chest. After a long while, she finally articulated her thoughts in three words: "What is always?"

He simply smiled and kissed her once more, a long and loving kiss that brought them both far away from all such complications. When he finally broke that kiss, he grinned. "You can leave knowing that you always have a place at my side and in my heart – for as long as I am Actaeon."

"I want to stay here," she replied in a small voice, holding him tightly to her.

"You may stay here until your duty calls you. I also wish that we could stay here forever. I do believe that I have never been so happy as when I am with you."

"Nothing lasts," she said, matter-of-factly. "We can only be sure of now. And I can remember no happier now. When you find me again, I think we may want to discuss some things after we both have time to think. I am not so Lost that I cannot discern that the path we stand on now may be a very difficult one to follow – if it is even possible."

"This path we stand upon is not straightforward, but I feel it in my heart that it is the right one... all of the pieces fit together with remarkable precision. It cannot be ignored and I stand determined to remain upon it."

The Engineer kissed the Arbiter softly, and they both closed their eyes to enjoy their shared being for as many moments as they could.

And so, as the sun rolled along in its course across the day's sky and cast its rays across the Engineer's cot – the unlikely pair found solace in one another's arms. And when, later that day, the sun set from the sky, and they stood worlds apart – the Engineer in his workshop and the Arbiter on her patrol – both of them carried with them a new fire and warmth within, created by the knowledge that they were both cherished by another in the world.

87 A.R., the 10th day of Torrentfall

FIRST OF THE FIRST

THE FOLLOWING MORNING GREETED THE inhabitants of the workshop with not one, but two visitors at the workshop. A heavy knock upon the door heralded their arrival. As Actaeon approached the door to answer it, he heard a booming voice without, and could glean the words 'Welcome' and 'Waiting Ones'.

The Engineer unbarred and pushed open the door to find old Vez standing with his back to it. The carter spun, bewildered, and pushed his way in past Actaeon. The loud voice without continued, chasing him inside the workshop: "...and the Light will guide you into the ways of truth and beauty in this world. Come, join us, fr–"

The voice was muffled as Vez slammed the door shut and barred it himself. Flustered, he turned to Actaeon and sloppily removed his well worn hat. "What sorta place're ye runnin' here, young Master? Strange folk be at yer doorstep!" The typically calm and quiet old man was ruffled in a way Actaeon had not seen since the day months ago in the tunnels.

"I thank you for the information, Master Vez." If he could be a Master Engineer, then the old man could be a Master Carter after all, thought Actaeon with amusement. "Though I imagine you did not come all this way to bring news of my doorstep. What other tidings do you bring?"

The old carter took pause when the Engineer called him Master, and though his eyes narrowed for a moment, he made no mention of it. "Ruinstalkers is why I've come. They've been caught. I've been checkin' 'em traps for ya and one've 'em's finally caught. I've brought it in my cart. Three inside by my count."

Ruinstalker was an old name for the Deathcrawler, Actaeon knew – most likely one that was used before the insectoid creatures became better known for causing human demise.

"Thank you, but you should not have handled it yourself. They are incredibly dangerous. You have not been bitten, have you?" asked Actaeon, recalling Minovo's demise with sudden horror.

"Nah, not bitten. I ain't afraid o' no Ruinstalker after I laid eye on that big slug monster ya fought. Not so dangerous as that. I used a gaff ta drag it out – hain't lived this long bein' a fool," said old Vez defensively.

"I am glad to hear that you were not bitten. Please do summon us in the future though. The deathcrawlers are much more dangerous than the slugs. Their bite can paralyze. Trench! Wave!" called the Engineer. "Master Vez here has brought one of the deathcrawler traps. Please bring it inside so we can secure the creatures. Lauryn! Bring over the container boxes you made for the deathcrawlers. We need three."

Trench and Wave came down from the loft groggily. The sun had only just begun to lighten the sky for the day ahead. The stairs creaked under Trench's heavy frame and he stormed over to the door, grumbling a sleepy good morning to Actaeon and Vez. He flung the door open and stepped out, with Wave just behind him.

"The visage! Remarkable!" announced the proselytizing voice outside. "Witness and let us pay homage, brothers and sisters of the Waiting Ones! And upon one of the Bearers themselves!"

"We pay homage!" followed a small chorus from outside.

Actaeon arched a brow and started outside to see what was happening before Trench barged in with a deathcrawler trap held before him. The Engineer quickly retreated back into the workshop, away from the writhing creature in the trap. Wave followed the other mercenary close behind, dragging the other two stacked traps by a rope threaded through the handles.

Lauryn took one look at the writhing creature in the first trap as it strained and gnashed its forward pincers against the bars of the trap, venom oozing from its unforgiving maw, and retreated hastily up the stairs to the loft, leaving the containers where she had dragged them.

The deathcrawlers were small ones, not yet a foot long. The perfect size for experimentation, thought Actaeon.

Old Vez flashed them a toothy smile and waved his hat in farewell. "Well'n I'd be off. Don't need ta be here when ya let that thing loose." He started out and was greeted outside by more of the nonsense that was going on.

"Hail the Keeper of Light, old one! Come join us in worship, for today is the day. The Keeper is among us!"

"Hail the Keeper!" repeated the chorus.

Trench slammed the door shut and barred it.

When he turned around, his face was red and the old scar aflame. Wave was chuckling.

"Oh yeah, funny 'til it happens to you! From which god's ass did those Lost ones come from?" growled Trench.

Actaeon felt his skin crawl at the mercenary's use of the word Lost. Though he had heard the word used that way many times and had never been bothered by it, it was now poignantly different.

"By the way they're going on, it sounds like you're the god. You'd better watch what you're eating! It's not healthy!" Wave returned.

A stifled giggle came from up in the loft where Lauryn hid.

"Careful, lass! Or I'll eat you next!" Trench roared up at the loft. He was smiling though.

"Alright, gentlemen. We had best contain these creatures. I will need your assistance," interrupted the Engineer with a gesture to the enraged creatures on the floor before him.

"If ya don't mind my saying, Act," began Wave. "It's damned crazy of you to bring these cursed things into our home. What if they get out in the middle of the night?"

"I understand your concern, Wave. This is not only our home, however. It is the workshop, and is uniquely equipped to run the experiments for us to discern how the deathcrawler is best exterminated. There is no better place to keep them. Also, I must point out that we know very little about these creatures, so having them close by will allow us to more closely study their behavior. It will also allow us to keep an eye on them to make sure that we maintain their healthy state until the experiments are run," explained the Engineer. "There are a variety of conditions that we will expose the creatures to, including various gasses, liquids, poisons and different physical factors. We must do this to find any weaknesses that we might exploit in order to kill them en masse."

"Gotta agree with Act on this," spoke Trench in assent. "What we saw in Shield – to that poor girl – was an abomination. We've gotta do whatever we can to prevent that from happening again. Act's right – we've a responsibility to exterminate these ugly things from the face of shattered Redemption."

"Fine, fine. Okay. I get it – keep your enemy close and all that. It makes sense. But by the Fallen, I just don't understand how we're supposed to get any sleep."

It took them nearly an hour to methodically transfer the deathcrawlers safely into separate containers. The process went smoothly though, and, after Lauryn was reassured that the deathcrawlers were safely locked in their respective containers, she came back down and the four of them each poured a tankard of ale.

After he finished his tankard, Actaeon stood and retrieved his halberd. "I am going to check on the status of the Ajman refugee camp and see about whatever is happening outside. Remember that those traps need to be reset. We may need more subjects to experiment on."

"Aye, boss. Will do," said Wave.

Lauryn smiled shyly and said, "Remind me to run away if he ever starts referring to us as 'subjects'."

Actaeon laughed along with the others and departed the workshop with a grin.

What he saw outside wiped the grin from his face.

The big statue stood outside the workshop several paces to the side of the doorway where Trench had pushed it. Arrayed around it were four figures, three men and a woman, lying prostrate upon the ground before it.

They were mumbling in low voices, repeating something over and over again. As Actaeon stepped closer, he thought it sounded like: "Light to push back the darkness."

Frowning, he cleared his throat and tapped the butt of his halberd against the ground.

The four statue worshippers, if one could call them that, did not notice him there. After a long moment though, the man directly before the statue drew slowly and stiffly up to his knees. He was an elderly fellow – his wispy grey hair in mad disarray. He wore a simple grey shift that was worn through in several places and tied about his waist with a dull rope belt. Eyes ablaze with life lifted to appraise the Engineer, contrasting with the rest of the man's dull and worn appearance.

"The Bringer has returned! Let us welcome him!" cried the old man reverentially. His voice echoed across the Outskirts.

The other three worshippers rose to their knees and spoke as one, "Welcome, Bringer of the Keeper of Light!"

"Enough with this. What is going on here? Why are you worshipping this statue?" asked Actaeon pointedly.

The man looked confused for a moment, but his gaze quickly took on clarity once more. "A test... I see. Oh, great Bringer, I am but a humble servant of the Keeper of Light. I am the First of the First of the Waiting Ones. You may call me Phyrius Ricter, if you must address me with a name. You –"

"Not a test," Actaeon interrupted. "You are well met, Phyrius Ricter of the Waiting Ones. I am Actaeon Rellios of Shore." He pointed the blade of his halberd at the statue, "That is nothing but an artifact of the Ancients. Whatever meaning you are hoping to find is not within it. You must search for that meaning elsewhere – inside yourselves perhaps." It was amazing to him that these poor decrepit souls had so quickly latched onto this artifact in such a manner that had them groveling before his workshop. Hopefully his words would bring some sense to them.

The man fell to the ground and lay prostrate before the Engineer, his forehead touching the muddy ground at Actaeon's boots. "Search for meaning inside ourselves... Yes, Bringer of the Keeper of Light! We shall do as you bid. We thank you for your wisdom and guidance!"

"Thank the Bringer of the Keeper of Light!" chorused the others.

Actaeon shook his head in dismay. "If you want to waste your time, then who am I to prevent you from doing so? I have other places to be."

With that said, he started north toward the refugee camp site. Behind him Phyrius Ricter started a chant that the others joined in with: "Search for the meaning inside!"

The refugee camp was a busy place. The construction of the main bunkhouses and mess hall was already well underway. In the meantime, tents of sun-faded colors had been erected as temporary shelter for the Ajmani that had been displaced by the flooding. As if in cruel irony, it began to rain heavily as Actaeon drew near. It was no surprise though, being well into Torrentfall.

He stayed near the fringes of the camp, not wanting to advertise his involvement with the refugee site. Notably, he found that the latrine trench was in the correct place so as to not contaminate the camp, and the water collection apparatus that he had given them plans for seemed to already be collecting rainwater even in its partially completed state.

When several Ajmani began pointing his way and staring, he turned to leave.

Halfway back to the workshop, a Shield delegation found him. They informed him that His Most Venerable Grace, Prince General Indros Zar, had summoned him. He was to meet the Shieldian Prince in the Mirrorholds within Pyramid. With a grin, he shrugged and let the delegation to lead the way.

The delegation led him to the Mirrorholds and through the Shieldian Hold, where he was thoroughly toweled off before they led him to a chamber in the back: the Prince General's private quarters.

It was a spartan room, set up for practicality, not for comfort. The Prince General was seated upon a raised settee while a nearby attendant fanned him with a large feathered fan. When the Engineer walked in, Indros waved the attendant away dismissively.

"Master Rellios, splendid of you to arrive so fast. I have a task which needs to be handled, and you are the one that will complete it," said Indros matter-of-factly.

"I am flattered that you would consider me for your task, Prince General. What is it?" asked Actaeon.

The Prince's eyes narrowed upon the man before him and he smiled thinly. "There is a work that I have commissioned before the start of the monsoon. A statue – by the Ajmani artist Maerdia Bazardjan. She has recently completed it. However, the piece is quite large and it must be transported from the Pyramid to Rust. As you well know, the flooding in Adhikara prevents us from taking any of the main roads. Though I like it not, the best way lies through Stormstair and that path is quite the difficult one."

"The Lady Bazardjan was one of the unfortunate Lady Lartigan's companions, was she not? I believe I have seen her in passing," Actaeon said.

"Indeed, she was. The disappearance of Agarine was most upsetting to her. I'd ask that you not bring it up before her."

"Of course, Prince General. It sounds like I am not required for the entirety of the project. Perhaps I can help construct a transport apparatus for you? What is the exact size of the statue and what material is it carved from? Oh yes, and the timeframe of the project is important as well."

"That will suffice. It is a limestone statue, twice the height of a tall man. I expect it to arrive in Rust before Rainbreak. And it must not be damaged – the piece is invaluable."

"Then I will be sure to construct it well to protect against drops and impacts. Your transport team will also be briefed as to its operation," explained Actaeon. He shifted the halberd to his left shoulder and tugged firmly at the glove on his right hand.

"Very well. You would do best to seek out Maerdia in the Hives – she will show you the statue. Bring your requirements for funding and material to my officials here and they will supply you with what you need."

"Understood. I will send them after I survey the details. Thank you for thinking of me for this work. I enjoy this sort of challenge," said the Engineer.

"You need not placate me, Master Rellios. We both know this is not the type of work you relish. I have seen what you can do. You will do this for me though – I am an important friend to keep."

Actaeon grinned at the Prince General. "Just so, your Grace. It is not my first choice of task, but the problem I will enjoy solving nonetheless." He changed his tone and the topic then. "How fares your campaign in the northeast? Have you any more tribal incursions since?"

"My daughter pushes northward with your Aedgar Caliburn, driving the nullifidians farther into the wilds where they will think twice on approaching our borders again. With luck, the stubborn and lazy Czerynians will join our forces in the north to help crush them once and for all and secure the region completely. You made quite the impression upon my daughter, you know."

"Aye, well I hope that the campaign will continue to solidify the alliance between our peoples. Shield has given me some very interesting work thus far, and, as such, I would like to continue helping you with projects. Motivations and cultural differences can be tricky, but at least some good might come out of this hardship in that it provides a joint purpose. If the Czerynians can realize that, then perhaps they can also build some lasting relationships," said the Engineer, pointedly ignoring the Prince's latter comment.

"True that crisis can bring people together," said Indros. "The Czerynians hold many a grudge against our people along with the Ajmani for preventing their eastward expansion many decades ago. I doubt they will even respond to my request – forget about fighting side by side."

"Well, grudges would seem to only be good for a bruised lip and a frail feeling of self worth. Forgiveness will do more for a man, so long as he does not give it ignorantly," said Actaeon, switching his weapon back to his right shoulder. "Either way, these things take time and healing to work out, but we must all continue to do what is best for the civilized people of Redemption, even if there are others that would not stand with us."

The Prince General offered another one of his thin smiles. "A philosopher and an Engineer then? I wouldn't have guessed."

Actaeon laughed and shook his head. "I would not describe myself as a philosopher, Prince General. Suffice it to say that I watch people as well as things. There is much that you can learn from the behavior of others, even though it is less predictable than that of materials and mechanisms."

"Curious that I would find people more predictable, excepting a few dangerous ones."

"Aye, and those unpredictable aspects are the ones that result in failure. Either failure of a design, or failure of political goals – it is the same thing. If I apply the same force to an iron bar, it will break at more or less the same load every time. The only unpredictabilities that arise are in defects during the manufacture or anomalies in the material itself. But these unpredictabilities can be accounted for and anticipated. Apply the same force to two different men, and, well, it is difficult to discern which will break first without knowing their disposition beforehand. And, even then, mankind has reserves of strength, conviction, and corruption that cannot be fathomed. This unpredictability is what makes man so dangerous. It is the unknowns in my work that are so risky, as well. It is indeed within my own capacity – even my own tendency – to fail in a design by missing something critical or failing to account for a variable. Therein lies my greatest risk."

"True, but failure can also bring us to new discoveries," said the Prince General. "Have you not heard it said that some of the most important inventions come about through accidents?"

"Oh, undoubtedly," said Actaeon with a grin, his mind drifting to the moment the giant slug creature squeezed the luminary and subsequently exploded, leading him to the invention of grenados. "Failure can lead to successes, but that must always be coupled with caution." He shifted the halberd to his left arm then and slid back the right sleeve of his jacket, revealing old hideous burns along his right arm, the flesh twisted and swirled unnaturally along his forearm. "Risk must always be considered carefully to determine whether the possible payoffs are worthwhile. This lesson I learned the hard way." He let his sleeve fall back into place.

"It is those that learn these lessons that can do good for this world we live in," said the Prince General in agreement. "It might interest you to know that Travail has been abandoned. Perhaps the Loresworn failed to learn the lessons we speak of. I thank you for the conversation, Master Rellios. I would like to continue our philosophical meanderings, but there are things I must attend to now. I look forward to seeing the result of your efforts in Rust."

With those words of dismissal, the Engineer excused himself with all the proper formalities and exited the room. The Prince General's last kernel of information had left his mind spinning. If Travail had been abandoned, then what had gone wrong there? And what treasures of technology still lay within? A question to be answered another time perhaps.

INVENTOR'S BLOCK

I T WAS LATE ONE AFTERNOON on a particularly rainy day in the Outskirts when the Arbiters arrived.

A saturnine Sentinel Arbiter led the way to the workshop. The door stood wide open. He wore a grey sealskin cloak over his uniform to keep off the rain, as did the others. When the Sentinel lowered his hood, revealing a short and neat grey beard and dull, emotionless eyes, the others lowered their hoods as well.

His eyes narrowed upon the chanting figures huddled in the mud around the statue against one wall of the workshop. They were paupers and infirm, all of them, but there was something strange about their eyes, something that the Sentinel Arbiter, astute though he was, could not discern. Instead he shook his head in disgust and signaled for four of the Arbiters with him to post a guard at the door. The other two he motioned to follow before stepping inside.

All four workshop dwellers were inside gathered around a table, discussing drawings that were spread upon its surface. Several tankards of ale were also present and the discussion had become quite raucous.

"There's no damned way I'm going back there! I almost fell in the stuff – I could've burnt my face off!" Wave said vehemently.

"That'd be cute. Then you'd match your best friend," said Lauryn with a laugh that Actaeon joined in on.

"Not a chance! His scars would never have the stories that mine can tell. Where'd you get that scar, they'd ask. Fell in a pit, you'd say. Sorry

Wave, even your ladies won't like that – though something tells me you're not exactly frank with them, eh?" The giant grinned exaggeratedly, which tugged at his scar in a way that made the others wince.

"Sure... Hey! I guess you haven't been taught to knock?!" exclaimed Wave, as he hand fell to his rapier.

"Friends need not knock, Wave," reminded Actaeon, who recognized Eisandre immediately and then Knight Arbiter Corvin sof Haringar beside her. The Engineer stepped forward to address the lead Arbiter but had to do a double take as he glanced at Eisandre again. Her blond hair had always been kept short, but it had been shorn even shorter and unevenly so, not more than a finger's width from her scalp. He offered her a smile, but concern was clear in his eyes. "I am –" he began, forcing his eyes back to the lead Arbiter's.

"I know who you are. We are here to talk with you about the event on the Windmoor. I am Sentinel Arbiter Phragus sof Luep. I understand you're willing to tell us everything," stated the man matter-of-factly. He shot Eisandre a hostile look that she ignored from the man that outranked her.

"And the whistles too, remember," reminded Corvin behind him. When Phragus turned to give him a reproachful look, he persisted. "I know the other matter is our priority here, but the whistles are also important. And you said that we'd tell people that's what we were here about, right? Might as well make it a truth too."

The Sentinel Arbiter was about to respond to the other Knight Arbiter, but it was the Engineer's turn to interrupt him this time.

"Yes, yes. Come sit. I think you may be interested in those findings. That is, in fact, why I wanted Knight Arbiter Eisandre to be present for the last experiment on the Windmoor. This way she could more accurately report to you on the extent of this design. We can certainly speak about the whistles as well, Knight Arbiter Corvin. It is good to see you once more. However, I do agree that the experiment results on the Windmoor are certainly of a higher priority."

"What do you mean you told people that you were here about the whistles? What people?" Trench asked, suspicion in his tone.

"It would be best to minimize talk of this experiment of yours. The last thing we need is for the common people to think there is a matter of importance going on here. Even though we suspect this might be a matter of great importance indeed," said the Sentinel.

"Right. And bringing a squad of Arbiters to the workshop on a quiet rainy afternoon won't attract any attention at all," grumbled the big mercenary.

Corvin sat down and spoke eagerly, ignoring Trench. "We're very interested in the experiments that you shared with Knight Arbiter Eisandre. I've heard about much of your accomplishments aside from just working with you to fix the baths. The encounter with the giant slug, for instance," he said with a gesture to the big slug costume hanging on the wall. "And, of course, the consequences that you suffered as a result," he added, gesturing to Wave.

Wave laughed and poked at his eyepatch roughly. "You wouldn't happen to have any replacement eyes hidden within Redoubt, would you? This guy absolutely refuses to make me one," he said, pointing to Actaeon. He stood to pour several glasses of water for the Arbiters.

Actaeon smirked at Wave and turned to Corvin. "Well, I would be happy to speak about those things in greater detail at another time. And I will gladly help with any interesting projects you have at cost of the materials involved. I most appreciate your Order's function." The Engineer then returned his sharp gaze to Phragus. "I assume you wish to hear what happened on the Windmoor first. And I shall gladly disclose all of the details to you. However, I must first have your cooperation regarding the non-disclosure of this technology. As you can imagine, in the hands of the Dominions – even my homeland of Raedelle – I have reason to expect a ghastly outcome if this technology becomes commonplace. Therefore, I must know that you will keep any information I give you here amongst those most trusted in your Order, not to be shared with any other parties – even your sister Altheans," he added.

"You have my word, Citizen Rellios. Do continue," said the Sentinel Arbiter bluntly.

"I hope we can find a mutual trust of one another through these events," replied Actaeon. "And I do appreciate your discretion. Without it, I would not be so giving in this matter." His eyes found Eisandre's and he offered her a brief smile, which she returned with an expressionless gaze. "The event that happened out on the Windmoor was the successful end to a series of experiments: an explosion that left my test apparatus in ruins, much to my delight. I assume you will have seen the site, or at least heard Eisandre's direct recount of it. In short, my findings were that the slimy residue from the slug-like creature, when allowed to loose its vapors into a sealed environment, will combust explosively when the heat from the released energy equivalent to the typical handheld luminary is set upon it. A small amount of this residue, say... filling a quarter cup." He hefted his tankard and took a sip as though to indicate the volume. "That small amount can reproduce the blast area that we created on the Windmoor." He paused to let the words sink in.

Phragus narrowed his eyes upon the Engineer and then turned to Corvin.

The technical Knight took the sign as an opportunity to speak. "Fascinating! So you are using the giant slug slime to create explosions? I have never heard of such a phenomena. We've been to the site actually. Eisandre... er, Knight Arbiter Eisandre showed it to us. She spoke of your test apparatus. Can you tell me more? She also mentioned a missing ingredient. What was that?" he asked eagerly.

"Giant slug slime, indeed," said Actaeon. "As for the apparatus, I will gladly describe it to you. A stone wedge was used as a point load source to crack through the container and the luminary within. You would have found shards of the stone about the site. And the ingredient that I missed in the initial experiments was the sealed environment to allow expelled vapors from the slime to collect and store in a container. The slime itself will not explode or combust, only the vapors. I am currently working on a more compact means to harness the technology – a portable device. It is for this that I was hoping to find some interest amongst your Order in use for defense of Pyramid. Especially since I do not trust the release of this technology to any other parties. I do think that it will increase the defensive abilities of the Arbiters considerably in the form which I intend to harness it." He scratched his right arm through his sleeve and turned to Eisandre with a smile. "What do you think, Eisandre?"

Eisandre opened her mouth to reply, but the Sentinel Arbiter interjected.

"That is absurd. The Pyramid cannot be defended."

"It is true," Eisandre agreed, unphased by the interruption. "There is no way we could defend and hold the entire Pyramid due to its many breached walls. The Northern Descent, in particular, has too many openings for us to possibly defend, although sections of the Pyramid could certainly be secured. Still, there are not many of us, so any tactical advantage might mean the difference between survival or death."

"Have you tried igniting the vapors with open flame or a spark? We have a device that –"

Corvin's line of thought was interrupted by the Sentinel's raised hand. The action brought a glare from the Engineer, who wanted to continue that line of discussion and had much to say about it.

If the Sentinel noticed the glare, he made no sign of it. "Let us not be distracted by details here. Tell us: can more of these slug creatures be captured to produce more such explosive devices?"

Actaeon took a long hard look at the Sentinel before returning his gaze to Corvin and answering the technical Knight's question. "Yes, this was my thought, as well. Though it seems I shall have to work on a specific design in a solitary manner." He lifted his tankard and took a long sip of ale before lowering it slowly and addressing the man across from him. "You know, Sentinel... I could have spoken to the Loresworn on this if I wanted the conversation to be so one-sided. I see that my decision to disclose this to you has lent no merit to my name. I can help you catch more of the slug creatures and manufacture the devices, but right now the slugs are facing the same problem that we are: the deathcrawler infestation in the market tunnels, which I am sure you have heard of. Conveniently, I am working on a way to eliminate that problem, as well. Shall I take it that this means you are interested?"

The Engineer's trenchant language brought grins to the lips of his associates. Eisandre on the other hand, stiffened in her chair, suddenly more alert. She knew that Actaeon did not address people in such a manner often, and she did not know what it meant. The gaze of the freshly shorn Knight Arbiter flicked between the Engineer and the Sentinel, as though she was torn between the two.

"We are quite interested," said Phragus, offering a rare smile, his lips narrowing thinly within his cropped grey beard. "I trust you have not shared this invention of yours with any others? Truly, if I were you, I would not mention this to anyone else." He paused for a moment to down his cup of water. When he set it down again, he fixed his firm gaze upon Actaeon.

"After all, there is no telling what... lengths," he drew that word out for emphasis, "people would be willing to go to to acquire such technology."

"Can we not offer some kind of protection?" asked Eisandre, her voice quiet, not quite understanding the ominous tone that the conversation took.

"As I've explained to Citizen Rellios, there would be many willing to do great harm for such technology. There is no possibility that the Arbiters could devote the resources necessary for your protection," said Phragus before he beckoned for Wave to fill his cup with more water.

"Perhaps we should've kept it to ourselves, *Master* Rellios," Wave said. He narrowed his eye upon Phragus and poured the water, missing the glass and splattering water over the table, some of it spilling upon the Sentinel. "Aw, sorry, I've got terrible depth perception. The one eye and all."

Phragus took his glass and stared at the swordsman while he sipped from it, looking unfazed by the spill. Trench coughed into his sleeve, clearly trying to hide a laugh.

"Well, you may be certain that I will guard this secret as readily as you have shown you guard your own motives and secrets from my person. I have not shared this with anyone else, nor do I plan to. I may be considered eccentric by many," said Actaeon. "But I assure you, Sentinel Phragus, that I am not a fool." He turned to Wave then and shook a finger at the man. "Now Wave, even if the Order of Arbiters is unwilling to provide protection and open dialogue, I still feel it will help the safety of Redemption as a whole if we share this technology with them. That is my decision on the matter. That said, I will happily continue these experiments for you to refine the technology if you can provide for simple materials funding for us. The Knight Arbiter Eisandre is correct. Protection is required as much as discretion. Luckily, I am protected by two of the best warriors in the city."

Eisandre blinked, having trouble keeping up with the conversation. At one hand, it seemed as though the men were at odds, and then at the other hand, it seemed as though they were speaking of cooperation.

"As my two Knight Arbiters know well, we have taken steps to ensure that your situation is monitored as would any matter of high security. Some of our Arbiters are about – nearby, but less conspicuously so. You may have noticed them. Our Order does have trust in your intentions, and we appreciate your bringing this to us. However, even the most honorable of intentions can be called into question given the right circumstance," said Phragus, letting his words sink in.

"I knew it!" Wave exclaimed, his eye widening. "There's no reason that all those people out there would worship a statue that looks like this guy!"

Trench grunted a laugh, his scar turning a deep red. "Well that's a relief. I won't have to uphold my image for them any longer."

"What image?" asked Wave.

"The Order of Arbiters tries its best to maintain a certain transparency with the citizens of this city," continued Phragus, ignoring the banter of the two men. "But with the Loresworn's desire to hoard their knowledge and the Keepers' desire to destroy it, we are bound to keep certain things secret – especially where Artifacts and technology are concerned."

"I certainly will not disagree with your assessment of both Keepers and Loresworn," replied Actaeon. "Both groups are cause for similar concern from myself and are threats to my well-being when one considers the fanaticism associated with their respective orders. The Keepers, so sworn to destroy lore and technology, and the Loresworn, so set on keeping everything to themselves," said the Engineer, with an emphasis on the duality of the names. "I do understand the need for selective secrets, such as the one we sit here to discuss. For the most part though, I would have technology for the betterment of Redemption shared amongst her people as a whole. Technology that can improve and even save lives should be shared with the civilized brethren of all Dominions. Technology that bears death and destruction, of course, must be more carefully considered. Everything has an effect, and it is the extent of that effect that must be considered carefully before sharing such knowledge. After all, our salvation lies in knowledge and truth, lest we share the fates of our predecessors to this world."

"Some would inarguably deserve such a fate," added Trench with a wry grin. He shot a pointed look at Wave.

Wave shook his head and chuckled. "Well, I'm taking you with me in either case. I'll need something big to break my fall wherever we end up."

"The line is blurred sometimes," Eisandre said, breaking her silence. "That technology which might cause great harm might also have the potential to bring about great good and vice versa. It is a matter of intention, of forethought and wisdom, I should think. Sentinel, we should provide Master Rellios with definitive protection," concluded Eisandre, turning her striking blue eyes upon her superior. "To do otherwise would not be prudent. We would at least need to know if he was in trouble. I volunteer for the duty myself, if it might make a difference."

The Sentinel Arbiter returned her gaze for a long while. He reached up to slowly stroke his beard before he replied, "Agreed. You will continue to interface with Citizen Rellios as a liaison between his workshop and our Order. The protection will be provided by men carefully hidden in the Outskirts."

"The Knight Arbiter Eisandre is welcome to remain, of course," agreed the Engineer. "We can have temporary quarters allocated up in the loft if need be. As far as your undercover men go, you can instruct them to simply warn us in the case of an attack. The whistles should suffice for that purpose. Shall we show you what we have done with those?"

The Engineer brought them over to a small bench against the back wall. Sudden skittering noises that came from two of the crates stacked in the corner startled both Phragus and Corvin. Eisandre remained unfazed, but she shot Actaeon a questioning look.

After some testing, they came to a consensus that the pipe and bowl model of whistle sounded best and allowed for good variations in tone. The only question would be if the Arbiters could all easily learn different and consistent tones with the whistle, which was somewhat more difficult to use. They agreed that using whistles that non-Arbiters couldn't easily replicate or use would also be of benefit.

When the three Arbiters left, Corvin brought a dozen of that model of whistle with him to distribute and test in the Pyramid.

With the Arbiters gone and the strange cult outside chanting various nonsensical phrases, Actaeon did his best to concentrate on the other projects at hand. With Lauryn's help, he moved one deathcrawler container over to the laboratory bench against the west wall of the workshop.

After they motivated the creature to move into a partial cage, they exposed it to limited amounts of various chemicals, both liquid and vaporous. While they worked, Trench pumped at a bellows, which created a vacuum and drew the vapors safely outside of the workshop through the the western chimney. Outside, Wave monitored to make sure the vapors weren't pooling in the Outskirts community. Luckily for him (or unluckily), Actaeon couldn't see that he was smoking his guaraja root at the same time – something the Engineer would have cautioned against.

The chemicals they had retrieved from the Felmere, a fetid chemical bog to the northwest of Pyramid, adjacent to the Poisoned Coast. The Felmere was one of the more dangerous places in Redemption, with pools of unknown chemicals and settled gas. An artifact hunter had taught Actaeon how to navigate the area safely when he was younger, and he'd shared his techniques with the others – keep away from dips and valleys, test each footfall, and bring something more sensitive to the deadly vapors than you. They had brought a chicken last time. The fortunate chicken had returned safely to the workshop. As a reward, they postponed its inevitable fate as a deathcrawler meal to the next day.

Following each chemical exposure, Actaeon recorded his observations of the creature's reaction in a logbook. In most cases, there was no reaction, but in several they observed retreat, agitation or lethargy.

The Engineer waited some time between each chemical administration to make sure there were no lingering effects. In a few cases they switched deathcrawlers to test a fresh one. The door to the workshop stood open to aid with airflow, and Phyrius and his nutty followers could be heard murmuring and chanting. It seemed to be interminable. Actaeon wondered how many things they could say about that cursed statue. And some people thought that *he* could be long-winded!

"I thought we tested that one already," said Lauryn, gesturing to one of the stoppered flasks in his hand.

"Really?" asked Actaeon. He set the flask down and lifted the goggles from his eyes to look again. He held the flask up to inspect it more closely before turning to check the log.

"Yes, see? There it is. Three trials ago. It didn't do anything. Were you going to do something different with it?" His young assistant looked amused.

"I was considering just hurling it this time," said Actaeon in jest. "Yes, yes. I see it now. I did not even recall that we tested this particular chemical."

"Yes, we did. Do you want to take a break?"

"No, let us continue. We need to make progress with this," said the Engineer.

"By the Fallen, can you guys either keep going or agree to stop? Just stop talking about it!" grumbled Trench as he continued to pump the large bellows.

"Aye, Trench. We shall," said Actaeon. "Let us see... There was one chemical that we had retrieved yesterday that I wanted to combine with this one anyway." He began to search through a collection of vials and flasks filled with liquids of varying colors on a shelf nearby. He picked one up and shook his head before putting it back again.

Outside, another chant began: "With the Light comes new life. With the Light there is hope of salvation. With the Light..."

"There is constant distraction!" yelled the Engineer, throwing up his hands. "These people are relentless!" He turned away from the shelf and shook his head.

Lauryn tried to suppress her giggle, but Trench wasn't quite as amused. He dropped the bellows handle and stormed off. "That's it, break time!" decided the big man.

The group outside had paused in their chant. Not a minute later, they began again, but with something different:

"Take time from constant distraction – be relentless in pursuit of the Light!"

The Engineer leaned back against the shelves and started laughing.

It was at that moment that the fully armed Keeper Knight strode in. Wave rushed in several paces behind, his hand on the hilt of his rapier. Trench paused in mid-step on the stairs to the loft, his posture tense.

"What's so funny, Master Rellios? Nothing you can't tell me!" came a vibrant female voice beneath the Knight's armor. Atreena removed her slotted helm, allowing her sweeping blond hair to fall free upon the blue cape she wore about her shoulders. She glanced back at Wave and smirked. "Very hospitable staff you have here. I hope you don't welcome all your guests so."

Actaeon grinned and stepped forward. "Only the finest of guests – or the least expected, Lady Covellet. I shall let you decide where you stand." He rubbed his right arm through the thick leather of his jacket. "Now, is there anything we may help you with? I am sure that you would not be here simply to stop in and say hello."

"You scald me with your words, Master Rellios. But you are correct. I come seeking help with something of concern," said the Knight, offering him a smile that came across as more of a grimace.

"Don't trust her, Act. She's got something up her sleeve, I'll bet," said Wave. He pulled the door shut behind him and stood behind the Lady Knight, regarding her skeptically.

"You endeavor to refute everything that I am and everything that I believe in, yet you arrive here, in the place where I do my work, asking me to help you. You need something that utilizes my abilities, no doubt. What sort of a situation would cause a Keeper Knight to ask an Engineer for help?" Actaeon asked, folding his arms.

"Your friend is right, I do have something up my sleeve," said Atreena, smiling at Wave. Her smile transformed easily to a scowl as she withdrew a small cloth pouch from her left vambrace. She tossed it to Actaeon as though it were infected with a plague, then wiping her hand on her cape in disgust.

Actaeon caught it without hesitation. Trench and Wave both cried out, though they relaxed after their friend caught the pouch and opened it so he could pull an object free. Lauryn leaned forward to get a better look.

It was an Artifact – something that the Keepers spent their entire existence trying to destroy. Yet this Keeper had brought it here and given it to a known meddler in Artifacts and technology. It made no sense, and everyone in the room knew it.

Regardless of the illogic of the situation at hand, Actaeon raised the Artifact to his face to examine it closely. It was a small translucent sphere that flexed when he squeezed it in his fingers. Suspended at the center of the sphere was a faceted green crystal. Three curved needles protruded from one side of the crystal. The Engineer noted that the needles exited the crystal at different angles, but they all curved to point in the same parallel direction. There was nothing like it that he had seen in his experience.

He lowered the sphere and regarded the Knight skeptically, waiting in expectant silence.

"Can I have a seat? I came here for business – not to threaten you," said Atreena with a frown.

The Engineer nodded and gestured to a table in the middle of the workshop. Trench and Wave joined them at the table and Lauryn brought over a pitcher of water and a few cups.

"You don't have anything... heavier?" said Atreena, looking at the water in disappointment.

"The last Knights in here preferred water," said the young girl. "I'll get some ale."

"Thanks. That'd be much preferred. Especially after having to carry that... abomination."

Wave got up to help Lauryn bring over a few tankards.

"An abomination that I notice remains intact in my hand, having been delivered by a Keeper Knight. Tell me its story?" asked Actaeon. He accepted his tankard with thanks and took a sip.

"We found it in a Keeper Initiate. He was acting strange and we took it away from him. He insists that it was a mistake and that he was not at all influenced by the evils of the Artifact, but we know not what effects it may really have had on him. We'd like you to study it... and then return it to us so we might destroy it. Tell us whether or not the evils of the Ancients have corrupted him from the path of the Allfather," explained the Keeper.

"I am uncertain how I could determine that, considering I know little of the path of the Allfather," said the Engineer truthfully. "Let us start at the beginning though. You found it *in* a Keeper Initiate? How was it in him?"

"It was jammed right in..." she paused and shuddered. "Right in his eye. He said that he saw things through it, but that everything was strange. That he couldn't make sense of anything he saw."

"He saw through it? Finally, an eye for me! Let me test it out, Act – you owe me one of those!" exclaimed Wave, who leaned across the table to take a closer look at it.

"You'd fit right in with all your bejeweled ladies," said Trench with an ugly grin.

"In due time, Wave," said Actaeon. "So he was not able to describe what he saw? What words did he use when he tried to explain it?"

"Maelstrom, he said. It was like a maelstrom of color and light," she related.

Actaeon glanced at the door and felt relieved that it was closed at this moment.

"He also used the word disembodied," she continued. "And numb... he said it made him feel numb. Disembodied and numb."

"I can analyze it for you if you wish and will give you my thoughts on the Artifact. My price is that we be allowed to keep it if we find that it is an effective replacement for Wave's eye," said Actaeon.

"I'm sorry, but we cannot allow that. We will compensate you for your time and you will be in the good favor of the Keepers for your help – but that object must be destroyed. It is Keeper property and ours to do with as we wish. You must respect that, no?" The Keeper Knight spread her hands and shrugged.

"Of course we will respect your property. If that is what you wish, it will be done. It must also be true that it would not make a difference if the Artifact was destroyed by us during the analysis. Am I correct?"

"Yes. So long as you can return to me the remnants, that would be acceptable," agreed Atreena. "And I understand that you know not the ways of the Allfather, but we simply wish to know if the boy has been corrupted or changed in any permanent way. Please let us know what you discover. There are no others that we can turn to for this. The evil of the Loresworn precludes us from approaching their ilk."

"You have my word on this, Atreena. We will endeavor to decipher the function and effect of this artifact. Thank you for coming to us with this request."

Actaeon departed some time after the Keeper Knight left, to seek out Maerdia Bazardjan in the Hives of Pyramid. On his way there along the Avenue of Glass, the second tower fell in Lazi's Tomb.

It couldn't be seen, of course – not from there. But the way the ground shuddered violently beneath his feet was a clear sign. He had expected the tower to fall any day now. However, this was wholly unexpected. Even though he had stood very near to the first tower while it had toppled, he was surprised that he could feel such strong reverberations in the ground beneath his boots from such an incredible distance away. The Engineer had heard tales of the ground shaking when the first tower fell, but he had thought them to be embellishments made by storytellers.

To actually experience it though was incredible. The thought that his plan, enacted, had caused something that shook the entire city of

Redemption gave him pause. He was reminded of something that his mother had said mere days before she had succumbed to her illness:

"I never really understood you, Actaeon, my dear son. And I am not sure how... but I can see now that you will leave your mark upon this world."

Actaeon grinned at the old, painful memory of one of his mother's final coherent moments. *I left my mark, mother. I just had to topple an Ancient tower or two,* he thought with amusement.

His suspicions were confirmed as he made his way farther along the Avenue and could see the plume of dust and smoke from the fallen tower billowing up far to the east.

The Hives were exactly what they sounded like: a honeycombed lattice of chambers and tunnels that could well be a maze to those unfamiliar with it. Those who were too low-ranking or lacking in political connections to find housing in the Mirrorholds typically found themselves residing in cramped quarters in this place on the opposite side of Pyramid. Thus, it had become a melting pot of artists, bards, political wannabes, scholars, highbrow artifacts dealers, and a variety of more successful swindlers and cheats.

Due to the complexity of the Hives, there were many signs affixed to the walls to direct people to the different sections and individual units. The same signs pointed the way out, as well. Actaeon followed those markers until he reached Maerdia's apartment.

Her unit had a particularly tall door, upon which was hung a note that said: Please Enter.

He pushed the door open with the shaft of his halberd and did just that.

The inside of her apartment was not impressively spacious, but it was impressively tall. The curved ceiling stood a full four or five men in height. It was very clearly an Ajmani's apartment, filled with expensive, colored fabrics and the gold filigree statues and furniture. In the center of the apartment stood a giant statue, dominating the room. It was hidden under a large tarp, which covered all but the carved toes of the figure's shoes that peeked out from beneath.

A petite woman with deep russet skin knelt before a small, multi-tiered table also in the center of the room. Bolts of purple and blue silk were wrapped around her delicate body, in a way which both flowed and formed against her. Upon the table were a number of lit candles and a book at the center, which stood open to a page from which she read intently.

When she heard the door creak open, she turned to the Engineer and offered him a captivating smile. Her eyes shone with joy. "Do come in, Engineer. Master Actaeon Rellios, is it? Prince General Zar told me to expect you."

"Aye, that is correct," the Engineer replied with a grin. "And I take it you are the correct Lady Bazardjan that I seek?"

"Well I'm certainly not the incorrect one!" She stood and offered him a flowing curtsey, "Please, call me Mae. It helps the conversation flow more easily. Will you please join me for a prayer?" she asked.

"Indeed, I shall. And you may call me Act in the spirit of flowing conversation."

She smiled a bright and happy smile and pulled over another pillow, which she gestured toward welcomingly. Actaeon knelt awkwardly beside her as she began to pray. He set his halberd lengthwise on the ground before him and watched her with interest.

The small Ajmani woman opened a pouch with her delicate fingers and sprinkled some dust from it over one of the candles. A sweet, fragrant scent that Actaeon couldn't quite place filled the room, and she opened a book slowly and reverently, upon the top tier of the table before her.

She murmured a few words under her breath that the Engineer could not make out before she reached out to take his hand and began to speak. He accepted her hand in his and noted with interest that her eyes were closed as she spoke – an almost musical lilt to her words.

"Gods of the old and gods of the new, we call upon you. Your blessings we do seek, your guidance we ask that you speak. Our hands are yours to guide with our spirit open wide. Foremost, I ask that you send your blessings down upon our new Raja in her consolidation of the Ajman Dominion. May the banished infidel to the north never return."

The Engineer raised his brow at this but kept his silence while she prayed.

"With smoke again rising from the northeast, I ask that you protect the people of Redemption from such destruction and the threat of the barbaric tribals. May we all learn to live in peace. And lastly, I ask that you guide this man beside me in his task to deliver my work of art to its new home in Rust. May it arrive safely and unharmed."

That said, she squeezed his hand lightly and released it to extinguish the candle flames with small pewter caps. She then bowed her head until it touched the page of the open book before she straightened and closed it carefully.

She rose to her feet and politely offered Actaeon her hand. With a grin, he took it and was surprised at the strength with which the petite artist tugged him to his feet.

"I gather that the Raja is now uncontested from Viyudun in the north?" he asked.

"Yes, the people of Kendra have deposed and banished him. They were upset with the way he refused aid to the people of Adhikara. The Raja proved her love to her people by quickly setting up the refugee encampment for them. Even though the flood is a terrible thing for those people to have dealt with, I am glad that it caused them to realize who our true leader is," she said.

"How curious," he said with a knowing grin. "I am also glad that she has solidified your Dominion. She is the better choice."

The artist smiled and gestured to the large statue in the center of the room. "I will show you my piece now? So that you may plan for the transport?"

"Yes, that would be ideal," said Actaeon.

When she pulled the tarp from the statue, he leaned forward on his halberd and smiled. He supposed he shouldn't have been surprised at the subject. It was impressively done, with the defining features such as the peering eyes and the long, thin beard carved in a way that accentuated their impact. In one of the carved stone hands was held a formidable stone writheblade that looked like a giant version of the real thing, frozen in stone. In the other hand was a staff, held as though it was casting some great spell. The look upon Indros' carved face was fearsome, and, although he'd not had to witness that look, Actaeon had no doubt that the Prince General was more than capable of it.

He regarded the statue carefully for a time as he paced in a circle around it. "Very impressive, Mae. The blade and staff are the parts we must be more careful with. They will be the weakest and we will need to be extra careful with them to avoid damage."

The artist smiled genuinely at his comment and dipped her head in gratitude. "Thank you, Act."

Actaeon reached into his jacket and withdrew a roll of thick thread. He unrolled it and began his measurements.

There was no warning.

They kicked the door aside to slam it against one of the workbenches on the side wall. The giant slug costume fell from one of the hooks near the door and was skewered by the first Knight's sword before it even hit the ground.

That moment of distraction allowed Trench time to reach forward and yank Lauryn away from the door, tossing her roughly behind him, farther into the workshop.

"Wave! To arms!" he bellowed, his own weapon already in hand. He swung the large maul wide and caught the Knight in the shoulder. It dented the plate covering the warrior's sword arm and sent the man reeling to the floor, sword clattering aside.

Five more Keeper Knights rushed through the door behind their companion, swords drawn and helms obscuring their faces. They quickly moved to surround Trench.

Out of the corner of his eye, he could see that Wave still sat exactly where he'd been sitting when he'd stuck the green crystal into his empty eye socket. His rapier was still in its scabbard and he offered Trench no more than a blank look, one human eye and one emerald crystal. Of course, Wave had insisted on trying out that stupid thing the moment the Engineer had left, in the hope that it would be a good replacement for his missing eye.

Trench cursed under his breath and blocked a backhanded slash from the center Keeper. A firm kick sent the Knight flying back out through the doorway. He backed up to keep from being surrounded by the four that remained on their feet.

The two men on opposite sides of him rushed in simultaneously with thrusts from their blades. The big man sidestepped and swung his maul, which struck the tip of one blade and shattered it lengthwise, sending a shard that separated from the main tang into the length of the man's forearm. The Keeper screamed out in pain, and Trench ended it mid-scream with another blow that crushed the man's throat.

Next he sent the head of his weapon swinging backward which knocked aside the wild slash of the Knight behind him. The other two Keepers had regained their feet though, and he faced five of them once more.

An object arced across the workshop. It struck one of them in the helm and shattered. Liquid that splattered from the ruptured container smoked and sent the Keeper warrior forward to land heavily upon his face, unconscious – or worse – from whatever fumes he had breathed in.

Trench glanced over at Lauryn and winked, moving to put one of the workbenches between him and the four remaining enemy combatants. A glance over at Wave showed the idiot still sitting, an absent smile upon his face.

"Wave! Wake the fuck up!" he shouted at his friend.

Two of the Keepers were reminded of Wave's presence at Trench's yell, and they made for the somnambulant mercenary. The other two rushed Trench and were rewarded with the wind being knocked from their lungs as the workbench that the giant kicked forward caught them in the chest.

Trench rushed past them and barely arrived in time to fend off the attacker's blades as the Keeper Knights tried to stab his friend. He grabbed Wave roughly by the neck and tossed him back against the wall. "By the Fallen! ...get yer... ass... in gear!" he bellowed between blows exchanged with his assailants.

Wave hit the wall with a shoulder and landed on his backside, before he fell over and bumped into the deathcrawler containers, which caused the creatures to awaken. They skittered around in their captivity, letting out disturbingly raspy chirping sounds as the containers shook with their violent movements.

"Allfather help us! They keep monstrosities here!" said one of the Knights, genuine fear in her tone.

Trench grinned at that, his ugly scar twisting and tugging at his old burns. "That's right, we feed people like you to them!" He surprised them as he nimbly vaulted the table and landed between the pair. Several carefully placed blows sent both Keepers staggering backward in opposite directions with fresh dents in their plate armor.

The other two were recovered though, having regained the wind that had been knocked from them. Wave was wandering directly toward the pair, his rapier still sheathed and an idiotic grin plastered across his face. It was too late for Trench to do anything, he saw. He watched as one of the Knights lifted their blade and brought it down to dispatch his best friend.

Lauryn moved like lightning as she passed between both Knights and ducked under their arms to tackle Wave to the ground a moment before the blade could take his head from its shoulders.

"Darkest Hour take you all!" yelled Trench as he rushed forward to meet them. He was angry, sure, but the relief he felt that his friend had not died was tremendous – even if the halfwit had shoved a crystal into his eye at the absolute worst moment imaginable. It was too damned close, and he wasn't going to give it a second chance.

A swing from Trench's maul knocked both blades aside and he preserved the weapon's momentum as he spun around and smashed the head of his maul into the side of one's head.

The Knight's sword fell to the floor, and he stumbled aside before falling – his metal helm grossly misshapen on one side.

Trench was outnumbered, three against one now, and there was nothing else between him and the Keeper assailants. His friends both lay upon the workshop floor behind him. He would not let them be harmed. He'd faced much worse odds than this in the past. Of course, facing a half dozen tribals was different than facing three fully armored Knights.

"Let's see how else you can die," he growled as he lifted his weapon.

At that moment, they all filed in and lined up along one side of the workshop. Each one held a sack and dropped it before them when they came to a stop.

The Keepers hesitated as Phyrius and his followers entered. There were fifteen of them now – all in tattered rags and with dirt upon their faces and hands.

It was Phyrius who stepped forward to address the Keepers. "I am the First of the First and you are standing upon sacred ground of the Keeper of Light. Those that stand before you are under His glorious protection, and you shall do them no harm!" spoke the old man, his voice booming in the workshop in contrast with his size and appearance.

One of the Keepers immediately stepped forward and addressed him,

"This is none of your concern, beggar! Begone or we will rid the Outskirts of another few roaches."

Phyrius spread his hands at the Keeper's words. He leaned forward and reached into the sack at his feet to withdraw two heavy chunks of stone. Trench watched the others do the same.

"Brothers and sisters, let us show them the way of the Light," spoke Phyrius. And when he cast the first stone at the Knight it flew true and struck the man in the forehead. Blood trickled out along the chest plate as the Knight staggered back.

When the other two Keepers turned to face Phyrius and his strange cult, the followers of the statue all began to throw their rocks, which pelted the Knights and dented their plate armor. "With the Light comes new life. With the Light there is hope of salvation. With the Light shines justice!" the cultists chanted as they threw. The Keepers lifted their arms to protect their heads and turned to face Trench.

"You heard the man! Begone!" he roared at them.

The three of them fled the workshop, and the cult followers chased them out, throwing rocks after them.

At Trench's feet, Wave pulled the emerald from his eye socket and gasped. "Cracked Redemption! You won't believe what I saw with tha... What in the name of the Fallen happened here?"

The smaller mercenary pulled himself to his feet and looked around the workshop. There were toppled workbenches, stones scattered all over the floor and what appeared to be three dead Keeper Knights.

"Wow," said Wave, gaping at the scene before him.

"Wow's right. About damned time, Wave," said Trench.

"I... I just..."

"You just what?"

"I can't believe I did all this while I had that crystal eye! And what fortuitous timing as well!"

Trench fell back against one of the workbenches and sighed.

On the floor still where she had tackled Wave, Lauryn began to laugh, and couldn't stop. It was infectious, and the three of them were all soon laughing.

CONTRIVANCES AFOOT

A SMALL ENTOURAGE OF MEN DRESSED in fine blackened leathers entered the Ajman Embassy in the Mirrorholds of Pyramid. Several of the men wore short green tabards with the intertwined crescents of Shore emblazoned upon them. The one at the lead of the group, a much older but handsome man with a hooked nose, turned and spoke to the others.

"Feel free to wait outside. I will be a few moments discussing business."

That said, he surveyed the embassy with sharp hazel eyes, waiting to be announced.

While the majority of the Shorians filed out, one of them stepped forward, cleared his throat, and announced in a resounding voice, "The Lord Gunther Arcady, Overseer of the Conclave of Shore. Here to see the Raja of Great Ajman." That done, he filed out with the others.

A short man emerged from the curtains at the back of the chamber and cracked his knuckles as he shuffled over to the Lord Shore. He smiled and made a flourishing gesture toward Arcady. "We make you welcome, Lord Gunther Arcady. I am Gaemri Ip Monjata, the Raja's Portent. Your reputation precedes you here. Please, follow me."

Arcady smiled down at the little man and nodded before following him up to the dais at the back of the chamber.

Behind the curtains, the Raja was at the head of the table, her legs folded under her where she sat upon a silken cushion. She gestured for the Lord to join her.

"Gunther Arcady of Shore. You will find friends in Ajman. Why have you honored us with your presence today?"

"Ah, Raja Ajman. The honor is all mine. As the Lord of Shore, I have come to offer you congratulations in your rise to power. Your Dominion will do well under your rule," he said smoothly as he traced a well-practiced bow to the Raja, his peering eyes regarding her intensely. He stepped over to the cushion offered to him and seated himself easily with his legs folded underneath him. "I do hope my visit finds everything well?"

"You have my thanks, Lord Shore, for your congratulations. Is everything well in Shore? It is... unusual to see you in Pyramid – you must need something," she concluded. Almost as an afterthought, she added, "Would you care for coffee?"

Arcady tugged off his leather gauntlets and offered her a thin smile, "Coffee would be just fine, thank you. I'll have it black." As a servant brought him a cup, he accepted it and took a sip. "You are quite perceptive, Raja. In truth, the difficulties lately with the Caliburn's injury have complicated matters, among other things. That, in short, is why I am here."

"Black coffee – a man after my own heart," said the Raja with the hint of a smile. "The Ajman Dominion is sorry to hear of the difficulties of its neighbors. What assistance do you come seeking from Ajman, then?"

"To the beautiful Raja's heart then," said the Shorian Lord as he lifted his cup in the air. He laughed – a melodic undertone to it, weathered by age, before taking a sip of his coffee. He set the cup down and spread his hands. "Oh, certainly no sorrow is necessary. After all, such difficulties are why people need other people, like you and I, to lead them. Woe upon us if we cannot do what is needed for our lands."

He continued as she regarded him in silence, apparently unimpressed by his toast.

"Concerning the Wall... My caravans and travelers alike have been continually harried by bandits of late. The trade routes through there and the Flamewoods have had little attention since the Tribals have proven to be a problem up north. It would seem it is in both of our interests to secure that area. For that I would propose a joint security force to escort travelers and caravans to and fro through the land. Logistically, it is the best option right now, what with some of Raedelle's main warbands off to war with the barbarians."

"The Ajman Dominion has long hoped to improve relations with our neighbors to the south. Though it seems that you are typically in favor of the contrary, am I wrong? Wouldn't you prefer to hide away in the shadows like those Tribals you speak so much about?" asked the Raja, her expression hidden behind her own cup.

"But you wound me, dear Raja. Matters of trade and friendship are entirely different than matters of war and impulsive involvement in foreign leagues that drag us into interdominional conflict," he explained with a smile. "Trade, friendship and interaction with other cultures, that is what makes us civilized. That is what separates us from the lawless barbarians beyond our borders. Raedelle stepping off to war in the north and the recent unsettlement in Adhikara has led to vulnerabilities in these areas as the opportunistic and uncivilized attempt to take what is not theirs. Not to mention the ever-present harrying on our southern fronts."

Nadiya Ajman lowered her cup to reveal her calm expression. "It is curious how things change as the balance of power flows from one to another and back again. I will not soon forget how your Lady Eshelle Caliburn approached me to offer her luck, but no real assistance. I believe it is not just in my imagination that she also approached my rival in the same manner. A wise man of my order once said, 'Better to keep your bread than to split it among baskets for it to be fought over.'"

"Sounds like a knave to me," said Arcady, folding his arms over his chest. "It is the Caliburn way, however, and not that of the Shore. Our friends are our friends and we will stand up to help them. It is why we opt to stay out of most affairs – those that we involve ourselves with, we fight fiercely for."

The Raja smiled thinly at the man from the head of the table. "Well said, Gunther Arcady of Shore. And I agree. But that stated, Shore waited conveniently to come visit until my power was consolidated on my own. You are lucky, though – for one of your people has given me direct aid even though it put them in harm's way. And for that example of the character of your people, I would hear your proposal."

Arcady resisted the urge to ask about what she meant by that, despite his curiosity. He smiled and spread his hands. "There are ways to help our friends while maintaining subtlety, of course. My people are always looking for ways to help our friends in Redemption. Perhaps this will be a stepping stone to something more? As for the defense of our trade routes, I propose a joint security force. Ajmani and Raedellean both working together to provide escorts of caravans as well as to search out and weed out problems in the region. We can organize people crossing these distances into larger and more easily defensible groups that can depart at predetermined times with the security escort along for the journey."

"That is a sound proposal, Lord Shore. And I find it acceptable. There are a few adjustments I would make: The escorts will be comprised of mixed squads with soldiery from both of our Dominions. Raedelle will command the squads when approaching a Raedellean Hold and vice versa," she concluded. The look on her face brooked no discussion.

"That will be a learning experience for all those involved. I like your ideas, Raja. It will place the soldiers on equal ground in this matter. This action in itself should encourage more trade between our Dominions as that route has always been filled with danger. It should be... very mutually beneficial. We can also make it clear that no significant property loss will be acceptable or else those commanders will be replaced. Force them to think and work together that way," said Arcady as he drained the rest of his coffee then and smiled broadly. "Excellent brew, Raja... quite excellent!"

Some of the skepticism left the Raja's expression and she chuckled, "You have a calculating mind, Lord Arcady. It is a quality I can appreciate. Have your people speak with mine and make the necessary arrangements. I'm quite pleased you enjoyed the coffee. If you like, I can have the beans ground and sent to your quarters here."

"That would be delightful. Or perhaps I can just return to visit when I am in the mood for some more," suggested Arcady with a laugh of his own. "You have my thanks, Raja."

"You are most welcome, Lord Shore. I look forward to seeing how our forces can work together." The Raja drew to her feet, indicating that the conversation was over.

Gunther stood as well, careful not to step on any of the fine cushions on the floor. "I am certain they will do well. Once again, I am glad that Ajman has proven wise in its bowing to your leadership. As a formal token of congratulations and friendship from my people, I would like to offer you this dagger."

He pulled his own companion dagger from his belt and held it aloft for her to take.

Behind the Raja, the warrioress Calisse stepped forward but was stopped with a graceful gesture from Nadiya.

"It is made from the sharpened tooth of a fearsome lion lizard – though it could not have been too fearsome, for we took its tooth," explained Arcady.

She approached him with the grace of a dancer, her robes flowing like water about her frame, and accepted the dagger. The Raja accepted it and admired it for a short moment before she placed it upon the table before her. "The lion lizard's loss is my gain," she said. "I hope to see you again soon."

Arcady echoed the well-practiced bow from earlier, his hazel eyes burning into hers the entire time. "As do I Raja," he said before rising. "It has certainly been a great pleasure to finally meet you. Thank you for your hospitality and candor."

That said, he smiled at her and spun to stride confidently from the curtained dais.

It was a busy week at the workshop as many experiments and designs began to come together. It started with a bang as Actaeon finalized his grenado design out on the Windmoor. He used the same location where he had tested the prototype that he had shown Eisandre. The final design was thrown into the stone circle and actually knocked over one of the big stones, tearing a sizable chunk free.

Lauryn helped with the grenado housing, having carved it from wood to Actaeon's specification: a cylinder the size of a large fist with a deep chamber that had a slot in the bottom to accept a standard luminary. There was a pocket adjacent to that which could be filled to the brim with the slug matter in the correct amount. The slot for the luminary stood above the slime pocket and the slime pocket was covered with some breathable fibre that was held in place with a modified tree resin. It acted as a filter that would allow the slime to outgas its explosive vapor into the rest of the chamber while keeping the slime itself away from the luminary. A fitted lid capped off the chamber and was sealed with more of the resin to create an airtight chamber. The remainder of the chamber was largely dominated by the drop trigger assembly, as Actaeon thought of it.

The drop trigger consisted of a sharpened metal spike spring-loaded against a shelf in the wall of the canister's lid with a piece of bent sheetmetal. The shelf was enough to prevent the drop spike from firing accidentally when held, but when thrown, the sheetmetal spring would jump over the shelf upon impact and fire the spike against the luminary, which would then cause the desired detonation. Actaeon, Lauryn, and the two mercenaries each tested the drop trigger hundreds of times to make sure that it never fired before a significant impact from a throw in any circumstance before the Engineer was satisfied enough to test it with a live load.

The drop trigger itself was locked into place with a pin that slid through one side of the main housing and through both sides of the lid, passing through the spike on the way. A notch in one side of the pin engaged with a key on the far side of the lid so that the pin needed to be twisted ninety degrees before it would pull free. A heavy duty string passed through a hole in the outer tab of the pin and was tied about the canister to lock the whole matter in place. A twist of the tab would loosen the string's knot and cause it to fall free.

After the initial test with the wooden grenado, they set about casting metal housings, making twelve in total. Two of these they tested right away and while Actaeon noticed that the tougher material of the housing absorbed more of the energy from the explosion, he also found that the explosion sent shards of the housing remnants flying with enough force to lodge several of them into the stones in a way that would obliterate a small force of men.

A third grenado was set aside to be tested after sitting for several weeks. Actaeon distributed one to each of them, excepting Lauryn, who insisted she didn't want to carry such a thing. The remaining grenados were hidden away behind a loose stone in the cellar wall.

After the twelve grenados and the series of experiments that brought them to that point, the slug byproduct had run out. If they were to make more of these devices, they would have to figure out a way to bring the deathcrawler population under control so that the slugs could return to be harvested for their useful slime.

The traps in the marketplace tunnels had yielded several more deathcrawlers, but no more slugs could be found – the population was kept down by the many-legged creatures. It was a delicate balance, Actaeon thought. The giant slug and its offspring must have hunted and eaten the deathcrawlers before they could grow large enough to become a threat. Once the giant slug had been killed, the deathcrawlers became the dominant species in the disturbing ecosystem of the market tunnels. Perhaps the deathcrawlers now kept the slugs from growing overly large. Actaeon was surprised that there had only been a single giant slug down there – maybe it was an alpha slug and kept all the others from growing too large to threaten it. It all begged the question of what the marketplace tunnel ecosystem was like before the giant slug clogged everything up.

"Too bad we cannot go back and see what the tunnels were like before the giant slug came to dominate," said Actaeon.

Wave almost choked on his drink and spat it back into his tankard. "Um... speak for yourself, Act. I lost enough the first time – in the name of the cursed spirits of Redemption, I'll not go back there again."

"I'll second ya that," called Trench from where he was helping Lauryn transfer one of the new deathcrawlers to a holding container.

When Actaeon grinned at Lauryn, she gave him a sidelong smirk. "Don't look at me! I'm the only one that wasn't stupid enough to go down there in the first place."

They all laughed.

The extra deathcrawlers were a blessing – if anyone could consider that of such horrid creatures. The original creatures had all died slow deaths after the numerous experiments that had been run on them. It was the end result that the Engineer was looking for, but the mechanism hadn't been fast enough. In the best case, it had taken one of the deathcrawlers three hours to die after being exposed to one green, gaseous mixture – and it had rammed itself to a violent death against the walls of its container in the process. There was no way that the creatures would remain in a location where they were exposed to such a gas for long enough to kill them. No – they needed to find something faster acting, for certain.

During the week they ran a dozen more tests on their new captives, and Actaeon had a breakthrough of sorts. It was clear that he needed to expose the creatures to chemicals that they could not simply run away from. And they were fast – absurdly fast.

They loosed one of the deathcrawlers in a long container that Lauryn had nailed together quickly and he estimated that the creature could move around twenty human strides per lifebeat at a burst. It was a tremendous rate when compared against any of the other wildlife he had encountered in Redemption.

There were two obvious ways that he could think of to expose them in a way that they couldn't escape from quickly: coat them, or inject them. And their hard carapace precluded the former from having much of an effect.

When he watched Wave bring one of the chickens over to feed a captive deathcrawler, Actaeon grinned and shook his head at the obviousness of the idea.

Thus, they began to first feed different chemicals to the sacrificial chickens before delivering them to the deathcrawlers.

"That's just terrible!" Lauryn voiced upon first hearing about the plan.

Actaeon shrugged and offered her a grin. "The chickens will die either way, but in this way they might also serve as the solution to our present problem."

"And die a hero. Not many chickens can say that!" added Wave, offering the girl a wink, or blink in his case.

Disgusted, Lauryn refused to participate, instead joining Trench at the other end of the workshop to help with the assembly of the transport vehicle for Indros' statue. She had helped Actaeon draw up the plans for the vehicle, which would be moved with four men holding support bars and straps on either side of the vehicle at any time. They designed it such so that the straps and bars could be repositioned at need depending on the ruined terrain that they traversed.

Actaeon had shown Lauryn how to empirically find the volume of a human using water displacement and after finding the volume of a stone fragment that Maerdia had lent him, how to extrapolate how much a human made from such material would weigh. They used a lever and fulcrum to determine how much more the stone weighed – they estimated that the statue was four times the size of a normal man and so they used that as a baseline weight. Considering that a good portion of the weight would be transmitted to the ground through at least two of the transport's four wheels at any given time, and considering cases where the statue was tilted or teetering precariously, they concluded that eight men would be required to conduct the transport. The statue would be transported horizontally, of course, to maximize stability.

The young woman's understanding of the principles involved impressed the Engineer, and he was happy to let her lead the manufacture and assembly of the transport device with minimal supervision.

This gave him the opportunity to run more of the deathcrawler experiments, and they were much more conclusive than the previous experiments.

In several cases, the chickens were ignored, as though the deadly creatures understood that there was something wrong with them. In just as many cases, the chickens were devoured with no discernable result. Actaeon waited several hours between each test to make sure that any lingering effects were out of the creatures' systems. Of course, to be sure, they would have to test any promising solutions on a fresh batch of deathcrawlers, but this approach allowed them to try a different chemical every time there was a feeding.

There ended up being two cases, both involving foul chemicals from the Felmere, where the deathcrawlers were affected severely. In one case, where Actaeon used a liquid that he had designated 'Shimmering Oil', the deathcrawler fell to sleep upon the ingestion of its meal – not the ideal solution, but potentially useful as an agent in their future capture.

In the second case, Actaeon used a milky liquid that he had dubbed 'Dragon's Milk' due to the burning sensations it caused if one got any on their exposed skin. The deathcrawler that time had gone into a severe seizure. After the exposure, it curled up and uncurled several times before finally unrolling and flopping onto its back, with its plurality of legs writhing spastically.

This lasted for nearly an hour before the effect petered out and the deathcrawler resumed its normal behavior.

"Quite promising, we will have to try this one again – see if we can find a lethal dosage," he said to Wave.

"Aye, it's looking good, boss. Too bad that it can't die when tiny chickens explode from its insides – that'd be more of a fitting end for the bastards," said Wave, a distant look in his gaze as he remembered what happened to Minovo.

"Aye, it certainly would. Excellent thought, Wave. We will have to work on that idea as well. It would provide the added benefit of more available food in the vicinity of Pyramid," Actaeon replied with a grin.

"So, what're your thoughts on the nutcases outside? Are they really Arbiter spies like Phragus said?"

"That would seem to go against their principles – though I would not put it past them. The Altheans, for example, claim neutrality but we all know how much they meddle with politics in Redemption. And do not even get me going about the hypocrisy of the Loresworn," said Actaeon with a pronounced sigh. "I have better hopes for the Arbiters though – better than spies, secrecy and coercion."

"Maybe that's just cause you're head over heels for one of them, eh?"

The color barely had a chance to rise in Actaeon's cheeks before there was a knock at the door. Wave's sword was out in the blink of an eye, sunlight from windows in the vault high up above gleaming off the serpentine blade.

The Engineer blinked in surprise and turned to find the Lady Keeper Knight at the door. Trench was already halfway to her, with his maul raised high.

Atreena reached down to unbuckle her swordbelt, letting her weapon fall to the floor with a soft thud.

"I simply come to apologize. I'm not here to fight with you," she said, wincing as the giant closed in on her.

"Darkest Hour take you and your apologies, woman! You came here bearing a trap to impair us and then sent your knights to assault us. In the name of all the Fallen, begone with you!" barked Trench. He drew to a stop several paces from her and pointed the end of his maul at her in accusation.

She blinked up at Trench before she turned to Actaeon with pleading eyes. "I swear that I didn't know about the assault. It was a coincidence. I should not have come here – it was a mistake!"

"You and Trench are both right," said the Engineer bluntly. "You made a mistake coming here, and you should leave at once. Whether or not you are at fault, your association with the actions of your brother knights has broken any trust we had in you."

"I know... okay, okay, I will leave. Just," and she glanced at Wave then. "Just give me back the artifact so that I can destroy it once and for all."

Trench's maul came down upon the Keeper's sword and broke it in half, causing a crack that made everyone but Wave jump.

"GET OUT!" he roared. And the Keeper ran.

They met in the late afternoon as the sun slanted through tall stone archways in long rays of luminous light, glittering on the shattered remnants of a mosaic tile floor that portrayed some ancient and complex pattern. Once there had been a ceiling between the arches, evidenced by the jagged breaks where the structure once continued. The ceiling had fallen long ago and now lay scattered upon the tile floor like the pieces on some great game board.

It was upon one of those great fallen chunks of stone, amidst the wreckage of the Boneyards, that the Arbiter sat. Her shorn hair was trimmed more uniformly now. It was much less haphazard than the last time the Engineer had seen her.

When she spotted Actaeon, she called his name and they greeted each other with an embrace. Eisandre winced when the grenado clipped to the front of his jacket pressed into her ribs. She pushed it aside and pulled him closer to murmur in his ear, "I'm so sorry."

The Engineer reached up to caress the back of her head with its freshly shaven hair that prickled his fingers. "Eis, you never need apologize to me. Are you alright?"

"I may not need to apologize, but this time I want to. I have to. I have missed you so much. There is too much to say. I don't know how..." The Arbiter trailed off, somehow bewildered but content all at once.

"I am glad that we are back in each other's arms. Seeing you here has answered most of my concerns, but I want to know that you are alright, Eis. The meeting at the workshop last week was... strained. The tension in the air was palpable, especially between you and that Sentinel Phragus. If I have caused any friction between you and your Order by asking you to be involved with the grenados, then I must be the one to apologize," said Actaeon sincerely.

"It has been a difficult last few days," she admitted. "I argued with the Sentinel twice on the day I saw you. Once before our meeting at your workshop and then again after. It is nothing that you have done, my brilliant Engineer. You share with me your work, your world, yourself, and nothing is so beautiful to me. I am being disciplined because I acted rashly, and I must take responsibility for my own behavior. An undisciplined Arbiter is a danger to all of Redemption. The initial punishment was worse, actually, but I got angry. Because it was unreasonable – and he actually backed down," she continued, enigmatically, before trailing off.

"I imagine that this makes it all the more difficult."

"What makes what more difficult?" she asked.

"Makes it that much harder to control your emotions and return to discipline when what we share is the furthest thing from that. It must be a difficult transition for you," he explained.

"It *is* difficult," she agreed. "I thought that it would be the opposite problem – that I would be so used to the order and discipline that is familiar to me, that I would not be able to remember what I am with you – what we are together. Instead, I can't ever forget." She squeezed his hand in hers. "And I must work harder to be my Arbiter self when I must. Because it is important."

"I hope that you know I am proud of you for what you do," said the Engineer. "That you are a Knight Arbiter of Pyramid. Your work is truly important, and I love you for doing it. I do not want to make things so difficult for you. Whatever I can do to make this easier for you, just let me know. If taking things slow between us will help you adjust better, then just say the word. Whatever you need. The only thing I cannot do for you is stop feeling the way I do about you. So I suppose you will just have to adjust to that either way," he said with a bright chuckle.

"Taking things slower? Faster? I don't know what it would mean, Actaeon," she replied seriously, despite his laughter. "I don't know what any of it means. If I think too much about it, I'm afraid I will get either hopelessly confused or let logic prevail when it makes no reasonable sense for us to be together in any way, despite our feelings. And that's not something I want to accept right now. You bring out the best parts of me in so many ways. You are brilliant and clever and beautiful. And you love me! As I am: Lost. Short. Stoic. Dysfunctional. Arbiter. With very short hair."

"Sometimes logic dictates to simply follow one's heart, lest they live forever in regret," said Actaeon thoughtfully. "And because of that logic, I shall love you as you are: thoughtful, empathetic, incredibly beautiful with no need to hide your features in long locks, brave, skillful, disciplined and loving, able to set my mind at ease and to free my heart, my special Eisandre..."

He leaned forward to kiss her then because he had to, his heart and mind leaving him no other choice. She returned his kiss, deeply, and he could feel the tension ease from her body – a transition from the thoughtful analytics of their relationship to the warm, radiant feelings that emanated from them both.

Their love was a thing that filled her with such brightness and warmth that she wanted nothing but to lose herself within it. His words however, brought her back to cold logic and reality as he spoke. She didn't even realize their kiss had ended before they filled her mind.

"You said that you behaved rashly. What exactly is it you were punished for? You should be allowed to stand up against unreasonable behavior, after all," said the Engineer, unaware of the difficulty he had created for Eisandre with the rapid transition from their kiss to this new thought.

The Arbiter blinked and stared blankly at his chest for a long moment before she replied. "I was punished for reckless behavior, bordering on disobeying an order by my superior. I should not have spoken against a Sentinel Arbiter. He has experience and wisdom of his own. And I... don't wish to discolor your perceptions of the Order because of one personal dispute. You might be angry too and no good will come of it. I'm not even sure I understood what happened that I might explain it fairly –"

"I am not too familiar with the inner workings of your Order, but you are not an Initiate, you are a Knight Arbiter. It would seem that if you feel the need to speak your mind to a superior, then you should be able to do so while giving the respect that their position accords. Of course, they would make any decisions in the end, but to lead blindly is worse than following blindly," said Actaeon. "The Arbiter leaders should listen to your opinions and even seek them out if need be. I am not angry. Perhaps if you talk about what happened, you might come to understand it better as well."

"You are not angry," she agreed. "But you may become angry. And I have already been angry enough for us both. Sentinel Phragus is under no illusions that I follow blindly. I'm fairly certain of it. Unfortunately, he probably thinks I am more than a little bit insane, at this point. And I have worked so very hard to be able to prove to people that I am not. It all started with my hair, of all things. I had let it grow longer than what is standard for the Arbiters. The Sentinel believed I did so intentionally. He wasn't upset that I had my hair long enough to be grabbed in close combat

– he approved of it, because as far as I can tell, he felt that my hair made me more attractive. And that I was intentionally and rightfully using this as an advantage to appear more approachable, presumably to men. At that point of the conversation, I was simply shocked. Then he mentioned your name in particular – how it was useful of me that I had earned your trust in that way. That it was useful to the Order that I had fostered our relationship so.

"That's when I got angry. Too angry, I think. He was only trying to be pragmatic, and I was furious and indignant. I've worked too hard that my primary worth should be my physical appearance. And I love you too much to bear the suggestion that I would take advantage of you in any way. I barely even remember what was said after that. I was fuming. I couldn't focus." She paused to take a deep breath then, noticeably bothered at the recollection. "When I was dismissed, I left Pyramid Command in an agitated state. Garth followed after me because he was concerned. I made him cut my hair hastily because my hands were shaking too badly and I wanted to cut it before returning to your workshop. The poor man had no idea what was going on – what had gotten into me. He still doesn't. Add to that the fact that I had acted like a spoiled child when Sentinel Phragus ordered me to accompany him to meet with you – suggesting that you might be influenced by my presence. I actually glared at him! An Arbiter cannot behave so badly. It reflects poorly on the entire Order. I deserved to be punished worse than the two weeks of Initiate duties I was given. The Sentinel was too kind with me, in the end." She stopped there, clearly still upset with herself.

"Sentinel Phragus," said the Engineer, letting the name hang in the air as he rolled his eyes. "After our long meeting the other day, I believe his mind works in quite a different way from ours, or anyone's for that matter. He fails to think about his thoughts before articulating them into words and in parallel, to think about other people's words before drawing conclusion upon them. More than once did he misunderstand me, and more than once did I fail to understand him. In fact, I do not believe he realized in the least why his words were so insulting. I would not take his words too seriously, Eis. It is clear to me that he does not take them seriously himself. The important thing about that man is what is going on inside his mind. Never worry about what others will say about us. I *know* you, Eisandre, and I know that you would not ever mean to hurt me. The

Sentinel was rightly kind to you. You were in a difficult situation where your personal involvement with me intersected with the complexities of this new technology, and, despite the poorly thought out words of your senior officer, I would hazard to say that you handled things as best as you could. Do not be so hard on yourself."

She took several long minutes to consider his words before replying. "I see now. You are right about Phragus. I just... didn't know him, and he didn't know me. I should not have been so angry. That was my own error. But I don't regret cutting my hair either, especially if it was long enough to be a problem in a fight. I have always worked so hard to control my emotions, Actaeon – to press them down beneath a tight lid of propriety and duty. You break down the prison wall and allow me to be suddenly reborn into a world of color and love. I am off balance, I fear. Not quite myself. Sentinel Phragus doesn't know the way I truly feel about you, in any case. He did not ask, so I did not say. And I was too angry at him, there in the workshop, to give him any handle on my heart. He would have seen it, had I allowed myself to look at you, you know. I thought I would be cold to you while on duty, simply because I know no other way. But, in fact, it was a terrible struggle. I felt for you then just as I do now, but I forced myself to show no sign of it. And then, afterward, when I lay alone in my bunk – I was suddenly so afraid that I had hurt you."

"You did not hurt me, my love. But I was afraid similarly that I had hurt you. Just as you say, this love has set you off balance, made things more difficult for you. More than anything, I really do not want to hurt you. Do what you need to do to cope with this. If you cannot meet my eye, then I shall understand," said the Engineer before leaning forward to kiss her forehead.

"Although I may seem cold at times or stoic by necessity, I have already learned that it does not change what's in my heart. This is beyond my experience, remember. I don't want to mess things up. I don't want to go back to being Eisandre without Actaeon's light," she said with a smile.

Actaeon was at a loss for words. His gaze wandered, taking in the vines hanging from the ancient arches and the flowers growing from cracks in the floor. When he spoke, he was grinning once more. "I am not sure that I have the words to tell you how I feel about you – how much I love you. Just suffice it to say, that you will always have my light so long as you hold it within your heart. I am so glad to be here with you now, in this place you have chosen. It must have been beautiful once," he said.

"I think it is amazing now, with all the flowers and the moss and the way the light shines through the dust that hangs in the air. I wasn't sure if my map was clear enough, but you found me. You always do," she said, leaning against him as she breathed in his presence. "Please tell me you don't have to leave very soon."

"I can stay here as long as you wish," he said.

"We have a few hours before dark, at least, just to be here. To set our minds at ease and free our hearts." She kissed the edge of his ear lightly. "It will not be as long as I wish."

"Yes," said Actaeon. "And perhaps we should find a more hidden spot so that we are not out in the open. Shall we?"

The Engineer levered himself to his feet with his halberd and offered her his hand. She took it, her eyes sparkling as she regarded him and they set out together to find it.

Birds sang their mysterious and lilting songs all around as they fluttered about amidst the foliage clinging to the ruins. Eisandre took charge and led him through golden beams of sunlight and past velvet emerald shadows. They passed beneath the last of the arches and by a series of stone benches, eventually arriving at a large crack in the wall of an intact part of the ancient structure. It was large enough for them to fit through.

She led the way inside tentatively, her other hand on the hilt of her sword.

The first thing that caught their attention as they emerged into a small circular enclosure was a multicolored mosaic wall at the back that shone translucently in the sunlight. There was a cracked dais before the wall. A single cluster of flowers grew in the dirt floor, right where a ray of sunlight shone from a narrow crack above.

Eisandre's hand relaxed and fell from her sword. "Not even a spider. I have no idea what this place might have been, but it's certainly beautiful now. Especially while the sun —"

She was interrupted as the Engineer spun her around and kissed her deeply, pulling her against him. He ran his fingers through her hair, feeling the newness of her freshly trimmed hair — he sought to memorize every detail beneath his fingers as he kissed her. She teased him with her kiss until they were both breathless. Eisandre's head spun as her heart pounded beneath her breast.

Wordlessly, they both stepped apart and helped each other free of their outer layers. Once halberd, bow, jacket with its explosive canister and bulky pockets, cuirass and sword were set aside, they found each other's arms and met in a passionate embrace once more. Of course, Eisandre left her sword where she could reach it quickly if the need arose.

After a long kiss, Eisandre pulled back and gazed up into his eyes. "You know this will not be easy, what we have, right? I'm sorry for that, my brightest jewel. You tell me not to apologize, but I only want to bring you joy – never sorrow or frustration."

"Nothing worth doing is ever easy," said Actaeon with cool confidence. "That is just the way of this world that we live in. And there is nothing more worthwhile that I have yet found than what we have together."

When he kissed her again, Eisandre felt her knees weaken and leaned heavily against the Engineer. He led her over to the dais and helped her sit before kissing her again. She ran her fingers through his hair and pulled the goggles from atop his head, which she set aside.

"Once again, I lack the right words," she said when they paused to look at one another.

"Then tell me what you want to say in other ways," was Actaeon's simple reply. "I wish I could see the things that you see in your mind."

"I'm glad that you cannot," she admitted. "You need your clarity, your focus, in order to turn your ideas into reality. To figure out the way things work and to make them work even better. You're brilliant. And you help me to see things more clearly as well. You don't need these singing songs and swirling sounds and layers of color and incessant echoes. It's a real mess inside my head, you know. But it isn't my thoughts that challenge me so right now. It's my feelings. I'm not used to feeling quite so much. There are moments when I love you so much that I wish I could just become part of you, to press into your skin and step into your soul and have not so much as a whisper to keep us apart. How can that be?"

Actaeon thought about that for a long time, as though considering a very complicated problem. "Those words are perfect," he said eventually. "They are what I feel as well. It is why I wish I could share your thoughts with you, to analyze them and marvel at them. I love you is not enough for you – your words ring truth in my heart that I could not begin to explain."

They pulled each other close once more – almost with desperation. And they spent many hours that way, alternating between passion and moments where they relaxed in each other's arms where they felt safe and whole.

In one such moment, they watched in silent admiration while an iridescent insect with six translucent wings fluttered gently into the chamber and landed quietly upon one of the flowers. It unfurled an appendage from its face and inserted it into the flower to drink its vital juices.

It was Eisandre that broke the reverie with another kiss that took the Engineer's breath away. She pushed him down and rolled atop him. More layers were removed and set carefully aside, so that fingers could explore even more and chest could press against naked chest.

In this way they explored one another, with limbs intertwined and kisses that tingled and shot flames of sensation down their bodies. Both of them had always felt the presence of others so strongly. It was always an effort – a struggle to connect and understand and sometimes even tolerate. With Actaeon and Eisandre though, it was effortless. As effortless as being in a room alone with one's thoughts. But at the same moment, it was so full of life and love and beauty and passion that it threatened to overwhelm them both. They pushed their passions to the limits that they dared, but both held back. In the end, out of respect for Eisandre's vows and despite both of their desires, they kept from being as close as they wanted.

It was dusk when they finally left. It was a struggle to pull away from that world, where all struggles ceased to exist and there was only love. But the Engineer had his projects and the Arbiter had her duty, and life must go on – even when new life, new love, is found.

The workshop was a strange sight. It was beginning to look more like a temple of worship. A large crowd stood in a semicircle outside and to the right of the entrance. They were gathered around the large statue that was just beginning to glow with an unnatural light as the sun receded from the sky. They chanted something under their breath that generated an eerie hum.

Actaeon stood just outside the entrance to the workshop and pleaded with the large crowd, though little he said was heeded. Wave stood beside him, hand on the hilt of his rapier as he regarded the proceedings with an incredulous look.

"I will drop the damned thing in the Felmere if you do not stop your cursed chanting. I cannot even hear myself think! Please, if you want to sit there like a bunch of lifeless husks with no other motivations in life, then at least be quiet!"

Wave raised his brow in surprise and turned to regard his boss – he had never before seen him so agitated. To his surprise, the murmuring finally stopped.

The crowd parted and Phyrius Ricter emerged, leaning heavily on a makeshift staff, his clothes ragged and his knees caked with mud. With much difficulty, he lowered himself to his knees and bowed before the Engineer.

"Bringer of the Keeper of Light. Long have we waited here this evening to hear your words of wisdom. Please... will you share them with the First of the First of the Waiting Ones?" he begged before lifting his gaze to Actaeon's face, eyes ablaze with light and expectation.

None noted the arrival of the artist Maerdia as the First of the First confronted the Engineer. She slipped quietly among the worshippers and approached the statue as the first rays of light began to emanate from within it. The artist's mouth dropped open and she reached out to touch it.

It was not the glow that caused her lifebeat to quicken in her chest though.

"First of the First of the First of the First... Yes, you tell me this every time I come out here! You want my words of wisdom?" asked the Engineer, shaking his halberd. "Go forth! Do something worthwhile with your lives! Stop wasting my time out here."

Phyrius' eyes widened at the words and he repeated them under his breath before he bowed again and retreated back amongst the others. There were murmurs as he spoke with the group quietly.

After a few moments, the Waiting Ones began to chant in a deep tone. "Go forth... do something worthwhile... ...stop wasting time..."

As they continued to chant, Phyrius spoke over them, "We must spread the word, my brothers and sisters! The word of the Bringer!"

Actaeon shook his head in disbelief. If he had any amusement in the beginning for the nonsense with Phyrius' cult, it had long since faded due to lost sleep and his inability to concentrate on projects with the endless chanting and ridiculousness outside.

He spotted Mae as she emerged from the crowd and lifted a hand in greeting. "Good evening, Lady Bazardjan. And welcome to this humble but incessantly obnoxious shrine."

Trench stepped into the doorway of the workshop and groaned loudly before he rubbed his eyes and let out a big yawn. "Damn – it's still not a dream, eh?"

"'Fraid not," said Wave, his one-eyed gaze wandering over Mae with curiosity.

"These are my companions, Wave and Trench," added the Engineer.

Wave smiled and traced a graceful bow before he took the artist's hand gently and placed a kiss atop it. "A pleasure to meet you. You must be the most beautiful of Phyrius' worshippers."

Trench rolled his eyes.

Mae smiled and blushed, though she withdrew her hand quickly. "It is nice to meet you both, and good to see you again, Act. In truth, I'm not one of the worshippers – though the statue is an amazing piece of work. The detail, the proportions, the emotion – all captured perfectly by the artist. I should like to study it more. I think I could learn some things from it."

"If you wish to contemplate it, I think there are more than a few people here that would be glad to help you," suggested Actaeon.

As if hearing the discussion, Phyrius Ricter rejoined them from the crowd, "Yes, yes! Listen to the Bringer of the Keeper of Light! Within his words lie the key to our understanding! Come and join us in celebration of this new age!"

"Yes, Elder. I shall do that," she said, regarding the man with a mixture of curiosity and disgust. "Act, can we discuss this further inside? I noticed something that you might be interested in."

"Oh no! Elder!? Don't encourage this," chastised Wave. "Why, Trench is nearly twice his age, and that's on a good day!"

"Oh? Is that why I could wipe the floor with you on my worst day? Because I'm an Elder?" asked the giant, slapping his friend harshly upon the shoulder.

"Indeed," agreed Actaeon, ignoring the men-at-arms. "Let us seek refuge inside the temple."

Mae marvelled at the inside of the workshop, taking in the assorted oddities such as the giant slug costume on the wall, the cages full of creatures in the far corner, the containers and bottles filled with different color liquids and the various contraptions in progress scattered about. When everyone was inside, Actaeon pushed the door shut with the butt of his halberd and sighed his relief. He could still hear them through the windows high up in the vault. They had tried to shut them for a time and that had helped, but, in truth, it had only muffled the sounds of the Waiting Ones and the inside of the workshop had become stuffy and unbearably hot. It seemed to the Engineer like the volume of their chants increased on purpose whenever they went inside. Wherever they went, it was just loud enough to be annoying. At the very least, the cultists didn't follow them on trips away from the workshop. If that were the case, Actaeon would certainly need to test out more of the grenados expeditiously.

"It is amazing in here – amazing and a bit terrifying... I came by to bring these gifts as a token of my thanks for the work that you are doing," said the artist as she held out a small basket to him.

Actaeon took the basket and glanced inside.

"Lavender soaps – my favorite," she explained. "And some perfumes, though it seems you already have your own apothecary here."

"It is much appreciated. You have my thanks for this, though there was no need for you to –"

"Oh nonsense! Enjoy them," said Mae with a sweet smile. "The statue outside – I do not recognize the sculptor. Nor the material, though it almost appears to be some sort of earthsbone?"

"Ah, yes. I agree that it is likely earthsbone, though it is coated with a sort of transparent radiant material. It functions similarly to a luminary, but somehow less... potent. The technique or method that would be used to accomplish such a thing is beyond my understanding. I was going to shatter a piece off to study it more closely, but then... well you saw what is going on out there. If I chipped off a piece of their new god, there is no telling what they would do to me. In any case, I believe it is quite old – of the Ancients, and constructed with their manufacturing techniques. We found it half buried in a fallen structure in the Boneyards."

The artist looked horrified at the prospect of Actaeon chipping a piece off of the statue. "Oh, absolutely not. You cannot chip a piece off! That would not be prudent. The amulet about its neck. Have you seen it? The tiger and dragon curved to form a circle?"

"Not be prudent? Would it not be worthwhile to attempt to discern the technique used so that we could better understand and recreate it ourselves? And yes, I have seen the amulet. Why do you ask?"

"Oh, what an awful thing to consider. You couldn't do that to such a work of art! A masterpiece, truly. I personally insist that you must not deface it in any way. Besides, the amulet is sacred to the Ajmani people. It is identical to the one that Her Holiness, the Raja Ajman, wears about her own neck. It is an amulet that is rumored to have been passed down the line from the very first Raj Ajman. And there are those who would swear that her amulet glows at times. I think you've found..." she trailed off then, directing her gaze back to the workshop door.

"Found what?" asked Actaeon with a grin. "A sign from the Fallen? That symbol is likely found all throughout the ruins if you go digging enough. I would bet that the first Ajman found that in the ruins upon his arrival in Redemption. Perhaps that unexplained artifact even helped his rise to power, just like the one sitting outside the workshop is helping another man gain a following at this very moment."

The artist shook her head, snapping out of the reverie and smiled. "Yes, of course you are right. But at the very least, the Ajman Dominion will have interest in such a thing. The timing is certainly notable – the statue being found right as the new Raja ascends. You should speak to the Raja about it; it may solve the problem of your workshop becoming a temple."

Actaeon's eyes lit up at the idea. "Now there is the solution to this problem, Mae! We shall have to speak more often if you continue to generate such excellent ideas. It would be wise to have Phyrius Ricter onboard with whatever the Raja decides though. Perhaps I shall bring him along as my emissary of the 'Keeper of Light'. After all, I am the much heralded 'Bringer of the Keeper of Light'. Perhaps it is time that I started using my powers."

Phyrius Ricter was ecstatic. He lowered himself down so low that it seemed like his crooked back might break under the weight of his head.

"Oh Bringer, I must thank you humbly for this, the kindest of gestures," said the First of the First, speaking only about being brought inside the workshop. "How may I serve you, oh venerable Bringer?"

Actaeon smiled and gestured to Maerdia, "The Lady Bazardjan comes here bearing tales of one that wears an amulet akin to the one on the statue. I think that it should be your task to seek her out and judge whether she is deserving of being shown your revered idol out there. As the First of the First of the... well, I believe that you should be the one to assess her worthiness.

"He's finally lost it," whispered Wave to Trench and Lauryn. They gathered nearby to watch the proceedings after Wave noticed that the Engineer had invited the cult leader inside.

The First of the First looked slowly up at Actaeon, his lip quavering, at a loss for words. "I... I..."

"That thing out there is naught but a statue to me. An artifact belonging to a dead civilization. If you truly worship that thing out there then *you* must make this decision," said the Engineer.

With a genuine struggle against the forces of nature and gravity, the old man lifted his bright eyes to look from Actaeon to Mae, tears streaming down his face. "I... I am most honored, oh revered Bringer of Light. H... how am I to make such a decision?"

"Well now I've seen just about damned everything," said Wave, before he strode away to go find some ale, or a guaraja stick, or the artifact to shove in his empty eye socket. Or maybe all three?

"Follow your heart, Phyrius. Do what you know is right," said Actaeon, enigmatically. After all, he had no idea how to speak to such an individual. If he gave the man some encouragement, then hopefully he would seek out the Raja and the Raja could in turn take the statue elsewhere.

The old man started to nod, slowly at first, hesitantly, but then with quick certainty. "Yes yes! I can do that! But... I know not the way. Will you... will you show me, Bringer of the Keeper of Light?"

"Yes. I will show you the way soon, but on this matter I want you to meditate in quiet solitude. If I am to bring you, you must dismiss your followers from their vigil. You have my permission to give them a much needed break," said the Engineer, mentally crossing his fingers.

Phyrius bowed his head reverently and said, "It will be done," before he turned to leave the workshop. Several minutes later, there was a truly blessed silence.

The Engineer showed Mae the progress they had made on the statue transport apparatus then. And for the rest of the day he accomplished more than he had in the entire week past.

The next day the group made for a strange sight indeed as they passed through the reflective tunnels on their way to the Mirrorholds. Several courtiers from various Dominions stopped fully in their tracks to openly stare.

The giant mercenary led the way, people clearing out of his way as he walked. He had donned his finest polished and oiled studded leather armor for the occasion, a detail that had not gone unnoticed by the crew back at the workshop. Behind him, unchanged, in his decrepit grey rags, was Phyrius. The old man limped along with determination, undeterred by the jeers and stares he received from various courtiers they passed along the way – perhaps even unaware of them. Actaeon couldn't decide whether it was the giant that was clearing the way for them or the sight or smell of the old cult leader. The latter was more likely, he supposed. The Engineer walked alongside the First of the First and his halberd clicked upon the reflective floor as he strode along. He left a good distance between them.

"Both of you are losing yer minds. I don't understand why I need to be involved in this at all. I think it is a mistake," said Trench, with a glare over his shoulder at the unusual pair.

"You have to admit, Trench, you share more than a passing resemblance to the thing. In fact if I did not know how old the thing was, I would vouch that it must have been carved in your likeness," said Actaeon.

"Yes, yes. We must have you present! For your visage is the face of light itself, flawed though it may be," said Phyrius, the dirty fringes of his tattered robe trailing behind him as he hobbled along.

Trench stopped dead in his tracks and gave the man a stern look that would've stopped most men in their tracks.

Phyrius simply strode past him, his eyes bright with the power of his faith. "Come now, we do not wish to be late," he advised Trench.

The big man seemed about to open his mouth to yell at the old man, but stopped when he saw the mirth in Actaeon's grin. Instead he turned to the Engineer and slapped his arm, "You'd better keep that to yerself, Act."

"I shall consider your suggestion," said Actaeon as he continued along with Phyrius. "...flawed though it may be."

Trench grunted but continued on with the others toward the Ajman Embassy.

When they entered, Trench took one nervous look around and exclaimed, "What in the depths of Redemption are we doing here?"

He turned to leave but Phyrius stood in his path, defiantly. "You must accompany us! You are one of the most important ones – the Visage himself!" The cult leader then leaned into Trench and shoved him bodily back one step into the embassy, nearly falling over in the process.

"You heard the man, Trench. Whatever we need to do to get r–, er... to find the truth of the statue. Besides, these sort of things is what I pay you for," said Actaeon with a grin.

Phyrius took several more steps into the embassy himself and halted. His bottom lip began to quiver and his knees faltered as he took in the grandeur of the embassy, daunted. Actaeon reached out to support his arm. "Go ahead, announce yourself. See if they will receive you."

That seemed to give the old man the courage he needed and he rose tall – as tall as he could muster with his hunched back working against him, then strode confidently forward. He addressed the nearest guard.

"I am Phyrius Ricter, the First of the First of the Waiting Ones, we who sit vigil at the Keeper of Light! Beside me stands the Bringer of the Keeper of Light, and the Visage Himself. We come seeking audience with... with the Raja, Na... Nadiya Ajman. I bear news for her," he pronounced despite some breaks in his confidence.

Despite the multitude of snickers and guffaws that could be heard throughout the chamber, the First of the First's words reached the Raja, who turned her intense gaze upon them. She excused herself from a conversation with one of her people and left the privacy of the curtains in the back to step out upon the dais. "Your news is welcome here, Phyrius. Please, come forward. Tell me what you will," said the Raja. She sat upon the great chair then, her figure folding gracefully within its red silks yet radiating power as she appraised the group.

Ricter grasped Trench's sleeve and hobbled forth in all his glory. As he tugged the ugly mercenary forward, he kept his eyes down until the last moment. As he drew to a halt, his eyes traced their meandering path up to the Raja and his jaw nearly hit the floor in awe – his eyes fixated on the pendant about her neck. At a loss for words, he regained his composure and dropped to his knees in reverence, absent-mindedly tugging Trench down in the process. "My humble apologies," he said. "Oh, Wearer of the Sign, Raja of Ajman. It is an honor to enter your presence." He gestured to the pendant about her neck, identical to that of the statue's: tiger and dragon curved inward upon one another. "It really is in sooth!"

Trench allowed the cult leader to tug him down to his knees. His face had reddened in a way that Actaeon had never seen, with the exception of the stiff flesh around the deep scar across his face. The man-at-arms looked down for a long moment in embarrassment before he shook his head and lifted his gaze to that of the Raja's. Something changed in his eyes when he met her gaze and when he spoke, his voice was filled with a gentleness that the Engineer had not thought him capable of. "I am quite sorry about this, Raja. I told them that this was a mistake."

"I assure you there is no need to apologize, Trench. If Master Rellios and yourself come escorting this gentleman, then I am sure his business is important," she said without hesitation. With a gesture to her servants, she added, "Please, have a seat and some fresh tea. We will speak of what you came to discuss."

Cushions were brought out and a pitcher of tea from which several cups were poured appeared from nowhere. Trench looked surprised at the Raja's use of his name, a realization that did not help the color in his face go down. He kept his thoughts to himself and sat on the cushion.

"Thank you, Raja," said Actaeon. "Though I am simply an escort tonight. Phyrius here is the mastermind. You have my congratulations, on the confirmation of your ascension to the charge of the Ajman Dominion." He drew silent then, taking a seat and accepting some tea, his halberd lain across his lap.

The Raja smiled at Actaeon and dipped her head in friendly greeting. She next turned to Trench and when she offered him a genuinely bright smile, he blushed a shade redder and averted his eyes. When she returned her gaze to Phyrius, he was still kneeling in prostration. "Please, Phyrius, be seated. It is undue for you to present yourself thus. Tell me about this Sign you speak of. Tell me about this Keeper of Light."

"If... if you wish," said the man in the tattered robes before he turned and struggled to find a comfortable arrangement of his ruined limbs upon the cushion. Once he was finally settled, he turned his gaze up upon the Raja, his eyes the only part of him that was not out of place there, and he spoke.

"I am the First of the First of the Waiting Ones. I was there when the Keeper of Light first arrived," said Phyrius. He continued with more confidence, the sound of his voice echoing in the chamber as he spoke. "During the first night I sat vigil and the Keeper revealed its gift to me. I have kept watch ever since and have led the Waiting Ones in vigil for a sign of what to do next. When the mysterious lady showed up and spoke of your amulet, an amulet that in truth mirrors the sigil upon our reverent Keeper of Light perfectly, I was guided by the Bringer to seek you out – to tell you of this great discovery!"

"So this Keeper of Light that you speak of? What is it, exactly?" asked the Raja, a hint of amusement in her eyes that she kept to herself.

Trench chuckled and spoke from his cushion below her, "It's a statue we found in the Boneyards."

The First of the First nodded. "Yes, the Visage speaks sooth. It is the Keeper of Light, and it gives forth its Light every evening. It has guided us, like a beacon on our vigil and has shown us the way to you, most revered Raja of Ajman. The Most Revered who shares the same sigil as the amulet of the Keeper of Light. You must come with us to see it."

"So this statue glows then? As does my own pendant at night," she said as she lifted the pendant on the string about her neck to inspect it more closely.

When Actaeon stood and approached the Raja upon the dais to inspect the pendant more closely, the warrioress that they had seen before rushed forward to stop him. The Raja stayed her with a hand and gestured the Engineer forward. He smiled and leaned forward to inspect it.

"It is indeed the same material. Elderstone coated in some sort of translucent material. I believe the translucent material is the component that causes the Artifacts to glow – a technology of the Ancients similar to luminaries," said the Engineer before returning to his cushion.

"I would like to see this statue for myself then," decided the Raja. She gestured to the warrioress. "Calisse, please assemble my guard. We will leave at once. If it is alright with you of course," she said, turning to Phyrius.

Phyrius drew to his feet and dipped his head in reverence. "Yes, you should come see it at once. Oh, and how forgetful of me! I must tell you that there is another that in sooth shares a quality with the Keeper of Light. This man carries the Visage." He gestured to Trench.

Trench turned bright red and glowered at Actaeon. "I cannot believe –"

"Oh no?" interrupted Actaeon as he drew to his feet. "We shall have to get you a mirror then, dear Trench. The resemblance is indeed striking. What without all of your stylish scars, but still most striking." The Engineer grinned mischievously.

When the motley contingent: Raja, Mercenary, Engineer, Warrioress, and the First of the First of the Waiting Ones arrived at the small clearing outside the workshop, the statue was already beginning to glow steadily in the evening's darkness. Gathered in a circle some distance away from the statue was a small crowd that chanted something inaudible. All of them were on their knees. In the doorway of the workshop, leaned Wave, puffs of smoke floating away from his mouth after he finished the drag on his smoke.

When Phyrius Ricter and his party was spotted, the group rose in frightening unison, their chants halted for the time being. It was Phyrius that addressed them first, "My friends! We have returned from our great quest to the Pyramid where we found the Most Revered Wearer of the Sign – the Keeper's own sigil! I present to you the Raja of Ajman, bearer of the tiger and dragon both." He spun on his good leg then and turned to face the Raja. "And Raja, I must now present to you, the Keeper of Light!" With that he dropped to his knees in the mud and bowed before the glowing statue.

The Raja strode directly up to the statue and paused before it. She lifted her own pendant out from beneath the folds of her cloak and held it aloft to compare it with the one on the statue. They both glowed with an equal intensity and the sight of it caused a hush among the worshippers as they held their collective breath.

"Amazing," she whispered. Behind her, Calisse interposed the Ajman guardsmen between the Raja and the worshippers. "It is truly the same pendant – the same pendant as the First Ajman. This is a holy statue," said

Nadiya in a soft tone. She reached up to caress the glowing stone face with her hand, eliciting a gasp from the cultists, and considered. After a few moments, she turned to look at Trench and smiled, "Indeed, I do see the resemblance."

In the doorway, Wave laughed and added, "Aye, and more than that: they're both glowing!"

Trench ignored Wave and approached the Raja to scrutinize the statue as well. His face was afire, but he didn't pay it any heed. "Unfortunately," he said. "Though I suppose it could be worse. They could have decided the statue was a great evil instead of this prominent Keeper of Light."

Actaeon approached on the Raja's other side and planted his halberd firmly in the ground. He offered her a grin. "So, Raja – I will sell you the statue if you would like for a very reasonable price: to take the worshippers away from here. I cannot even hear my own thoughts any longer with their interminable chanting and ambiguous sermons and lofty exclamations!"

"It all makes me wonder how my ancestor came by this pendant. I always thought he had brought it over through the portal on his arrival – but this seems to prove that he found it amidst the ruins, in a place related to the statue maybe. The technology is of the Ancients, no, Master Rellios? It means that its face cannot be that of my great great grandfather. It must be the visage of an Ancient One. If I were to buy from you, what would I do with such a thing? Have you any suggestions to that end?" she asked.

"Hear that, Trench? No need to worry! You are not the Raja's great great grandfather," said Actaeon, reaching past the Raja to slap the big man on the shoulder in a motion that made Calisse flinch and step forward.

Trench squared his shoulders and attempted to match the serious expression of the statue. "Well then. Perhaps I'm really an Ancient of Redemption!" He laughed and received a few speculative looks from cultists and Ajmani guardsmen alike.

"That'd explain more than a few things," said Wave with a smirk. "But if yer an Ancient, get going on getting me a new eye! You've no excuses!"

"The method of manufacture is indeed unbeknownst to me, Raja," said Actaeon on a more serious note. "I thought to break off a piece to try and study it further, but with all these faithful followers, First of the Whatever, always here, I was loathe to anger them. It is almost as if the Ancients learnt to cast the glowing material. Perhaps we can try something to replicate it. And the fact that it matches Trench's face, well – it might just be a coincidence that Trench was the first at the statue's side, but that certainly is a curious fact. I would not be surprised to find there is even more to this artifact's capabilities than we know. However, I digress. Perhaps you can have your priests decide what to do with it? Or maybe bring it to Adhikara as a gift or a sign or something? Admittedly, I am not the expert on these things."

The Raja looked thoughtful. Her eyes drifted from Actaeon's face to the statue's and back again. "How far are we from the refugee camp that you... that was recently established for those that left Ajman from the flooding? We will move it there, so that the people of Ajman will have a shining beacon of light in the night to keep their hopes up."

"Beacon of Light. Keep our Hopes Up," chanted the worshippers, as if on cue.

"Perfect!" exclaimed Actaeon. "That is the best idea I have heard in years. The refugee camp is quite close. It is on the way back to the Boneyards. We would have dropped it there in the first place had we known this would happen, though the image in my mind of Trench as your great great grandfather makes it all worth the hassle."

"Oh Most Revered Wearer of the Sign, you would have the Bringer move it once more? To where?" asked Phyrius, his followers silenced with a gesture.

"Not to worry, Phyrius. It is not far at all," said Nadiya before turning to face Actaeon once more. "Have you the means to move it once more? We can compensate you fully."

"Oh, absolutely, Raja," said the Engineer with a broad grin. "We have just the device to move such a statue easily. No compensation will be necessary – it will truly be our pleasure."

"Then it will be done," pronounced the Raja. "In the name of the people of Ajman."

The decrepit man turned from them and stepped forward to address his followers. "The Most Revered Wearer of the Sign has made her decision! The Bringer shall carry the Keeper of Light forth to the new settlement in the north, where it shall bring hope back to a people that have suffered much tragedy. Follow it we shall, for we are the Waiting Ones who keep vigil over the Keeper's Glory!"

"Tell me this, boss. If yer so damned smart, why didn't you tell them to do that earlier?" asked Trench.

"Like I said, Trench: I could not hear myself think," replied Actaeon with a big grin. "Come now, let us take care of this matter immediately."

87 A.R., the 41ˢᵗ day of Torrentfall

LOVE, NOT WAR

CAKED WITH MUD AND COVERED with bruises, Actaeon Rellios of Shore canted from side to side through the ruins of the Boneyards. He skimmed past debris as he meandered along, pausing only for the occasional glance back to see if they were still following him. His heavy brown trousers were torn at the knee and his quiver had only five arrows left. With a grunt and a grimace, he climbed atop another ridge of rubble and scanned the ruins below.

There was a bathing fountain near this area somewhere, out of sight from the rest of the ruins. He had camped there in the past. A glance over at the sun's position told him that he'd be staying out there for the night. He hoped that Trench and Wave were okay – they had gone off in a different direction when the attackers had arrived. The cross-faced raiders had come out in force this time, Actaeon had seen at least twenty. After he led them through an unstable area that allowed him to evade them, he circled back around to reach the location where he'd agreed to meet Eisandre. He'd never forgive himself if they captured her.

The structure was where he remembered it, overgrown with brush and half buried in the rubble. He started down an embankment, loose scree tumbling ahead of him. Once at the entrance, he shined his luminary into the recessed entryway of the archaic ruin. Satisfied, he stuck the luminary in the strap of his goggles and started forward, halberd brought to bear. Several steps inside, he stopped to listen.

There was a distant sound that sounded like it came from outside. He lowered the baffle on his luminary and walked back outside, slowly. He set the halberd against the arch of the entryway recess and pulled his recurve bow free. Kneeling to steady himself, he used the scope on the bow to sweep the distant ruins. As he scanned rapidly, the lens sped past a lone figure with a staff. He recentered his scope: shoulder badge, leather armor, grey clothing – an Arbiter. His heart leapt in his chest when he noticed the cropped blond hair. He grinned and flipped the baffle open and closed several times to signal her.

The Arbiter raised her staff to signal that she had spotted him and started in his direction.

Actaeon waved as he reclasped the bow to his jacket and stood. As she neared, he frowned and began to brush some of the caked mud from his clothing. "I am sorry. I meant to throw on a better outfit, but I suppose that this one will have to make due. How have you been? I have missed you."

"Actaeon, are you injured?" She paused to take in his ramshackle appearance.

"No, I am quite alright. Just a bit muddied up. Very happy to see you though. We should camp here for the night. I doubt we will make Pyramid before nightfall at this point."

"Yes, perhaps not. I've been looking for you everywhere," she said.

"I love you, Eisandre... been wanting to tell you again. Glad that you are here to hear it."

"You may say it as many times as you wish," she responded practically. "And I love you too, Actaeon Rellios – as if you did not know."

"Well, that works well for both of us then," he said with a grin. He thumbed over his shoulder. "Some running water back there. I have camped here before. I should wash some of this mud off. That way I do not get both of us disgusting. You are welcome to join me."

"Wouldn't getting both of us disgusting require one of us to be disgusted?" She nodded at his suggestion though. "I will join you within."

The chamber inside was wondrous and ominous all at once. Numerous pillars joined in a spiral at their ends to support a sizable dome that was hidden from without by the collapse of several neighboring structures. In the center of the room, surrounded by a low wall, was a shallow pool, half a man deep. Gentle streams of water poured endlessly out of the nearby pillars to trickle merrily upon the surface of the pool, sending steady ripples that converged in the center. A large hole in the center of the dome allowed light in – though the far edge had crumbled long ago and lay on the far side of the water. There were several other small alcoves around the perimeter of the dome with benches and tables scattered about, but the chamber stood largely open after they exited the short, winding entrance hall.

"Wow..." stated Eisandre, as she paused to take in the different color swirls that wound their way up the inside of the dome.

"Certainly not the worst place to be stuck for the night," Actaeon replied as he set his halberd down upon a bench. He peeled off the muddy jacket. Beneath, his vest was torn and missing buttons. As he kicked some of the mud from his boots against the nearest pillar, he said, "I apologize that I did not make it to our usual spot on time. I was running a tad bit late."

"Far from the worst," she agreed, eyeing him with suspicion. "You seem excessively casual about being behind schedule. Judging from your appearance and knowing your history, it seems you encountered a sizable obstacle." Her keen eyes narrowed upon his quiver. "And the fact that you are missing five of your arrows suggests to me that you were engaged in some manner of combat."

"I was just making light of it," said the Engineer with a grin. "Those raiders caught us off guard earlier. The crazies with the crosses on their faces again. There was an unstable area that I led them through to escape." He shrugged, peeling his vest off. "I am only a bit dirtied and bruised. Nothing life threatening or concerning. Not to worry." He leaned forward and kissed her firmly upon the lips.

She frowned pointedly, though she did not resist his kiss. When he broke free she spoke again. "We will have to figure this out, Actaeon – why these people are after you. Why they are willing to die to get their hands on you. It is important." Her expression as she continued was a mixture of concern and love. "You are clever and skilled and prepared and thus far, very lucky. But they are persistent. And your luck cannot go on forever."

"I would like to catch one," said Actaeon as he unlaced the ties on his undertunic. "You remember the one we would have caught that took his own life. And he was not the only one. They would rather die than be taken alive. It is insanity. There has to be a reason." He sat down heavily upon the bench, his gaze lost in the patterned ripples of the pool. "Perhaps we shall have to set a trap for them." He smirked and brushed some mud from his trousers, imagining one of the cross-faced raiders caught in a deathcrawler trap.

"Either you inadvertently did something reprehensible to them or they need you for something incredibly important. They are too determined – too willing to die in considerable numbers rather than have a simple conversation with a generally reasonable man. I don't know how to best approach the situation, in truth. I could report the matter to the Order, if you wish, but we do not have the manpower to assert authority this far from the Pyramid. My superiors may have advice."

"See, I thought about that as well," said Actaeon, his attention brought back to the Arbiter standing before him, her hand resting on the hilt of her sword. "I doubt that I did something reprehensible to them. The simplest solution in that case is just extermination. Those men were not trying to kill me, they were trying to capture me. I am not sure that I would consult the Arbiters on such a thing. I would be fearful that they would attempt to inhibit my travel in my best interest. That would not be so good for business." He rolled up his sleeves and with a wince, knelt beside the edge of the pool to wash the grit and blood from his hands and forearms – the old burn scar that wound its way like an ugly serpent up his right arm was illuminated by the fading sunlight from the top of the dome.

"You believe they want you for your skills then? And yet they choose to ask with blades and by thrusting themselves in the path of an Arbiter's sword, rather than answering a single question about their intent? I am not convinced."

"Perhaps they know that if they voice their intent I will not help them. One can never know I suppose, barring..." He splashed some water on his face. "Perhaps we could track one back to their base. Trench and Wave might have experience with such things."

Eisandre knelt beside him then. "If the water is not too cold, it would be more efficient to immerse yourself. I can clean your clothes, although they may take awhile to dry."

"Yes, that is a good idea. I should clean up, lest my cuts become infected. I suspect my clothing will have time to dry by the morrow," he agreed before he loosened the rest of the laces on his undertunic and pulled it over his head. Varied cuts, abrasions and bruises on his torso indicated a serious tumble in the ruins.

Eisandre assessed Actaeon's injuries with a clinical gaze.

"Nothing too bad," she said. She lifted her chin to meet his gaze. "But that is only the top half of you." She waited then, expectantly.

"This is an odd way to get to know me better, Eis," he jested. Though he pulled his boots off and undid his belt to let his thick brown trousers drop to the floor. He had nothing to hide from this woman and he stood before her, unabashed, in nothing but his small grey undergarment and the goggles atop his head.

"If you had something else in mind, then it is particularly unfortunate that you suffered a fall," Eisandre replied with the slightest of smiles. She walked in a circle about him then before standing before him once more, her hand still on the pommel of her sword. "You'll be alright. We'll have to get the dirt out of your cuts – your knee especially, lest they become infected. Oh, and you'll be sore in the morning."

"I am sore right now'!" responded Actaeon with a smile. "I have had worse. Besides, now I am in your expert care."

"My expert care would suggest that you immerse yourself and clean your wounds," was the Arbiter's stoic reply.

"Aye, Eis – as you instruct! Feel free to join me if you like." He pulled his recurve bow and several arrows from the jacket and reached into one of the pockets to withdraw one of the lavender soaps he had just been given. He laid the strung bow, arrows, soap, and his goggles, at the edge of the pool before he slipped out of his undergarment and slid naked into the water.

The water was surprisingly warm and he slid down to the shallow bottom of the pool, his eyes closed to enjoy the feel of warmth that surrounded his aching body. He lingered there, letting his various sores soak.

When he rose from the water he opened his eyes to find Eisandre standing near the edge of the pool. She stared blankly, lost in the white glitter of the sunlight upon the ripples of water. Her mouth hung open and she didn't notice him resurface.

He walked to the edge of the pool. "Eis... I am here. I love you." He extended a hand toward her and waited patiently.

Her eyes found his hand first, then his eyes. She stood staring at him for a prolonged moment, coping with some internal struggle, before she approached and grasped his hand tightly. "I'm sorry. It's a new situation. I'm uncertain of my place here – of what I am to do."

There was love in the Engineer's eyes as he spoke. "You never need be sorry to me. Nothing is expected of you here, never when you are by my side. Do what makes you comfortable. Do what feels right." He kissed the her knuckles gently. "Thank you for standing by my side."

"I do not have the instincts to tell me what feels right – not all the time, at least. But I do know that it feels right to be with you – to be... standing by your side, as you say." She smiled, her blue eyes sparkling in the setting sunlight as she looked down upon him, and said, "Although sometimes I wonder if you aren't a dream. If what we share isn't some curiously realistic fantasy about what I never hoped I could find. But, even if you are an illusion, I think I'm okay with that. Tell me, would you like me to help with cleaning your clothes? Would you like me to join you in the bath? Or perhaps I should stand guard?" She asked the question honestly, not sure which option would be appropriate.

"You found me, Eisandre. I am quite real and I have some stinging cuts and scrapes to prove it. If this is an illusion, then so be it – but it is the most real thing that I have ever experienced. I know though, in my heart and my mind, that this is truth and I stand ever amazed by that simple, incredible fact. I would very much like you to join me, so that I might kiss you again. But make sure you do what feels right to you. I am just happy that you are here with me."

"Doing something is vastly preferable to gazing off into reflections of memories and dream," Eisandre admitted, transfixed by his gaze. "And it feels right when you kiss me. Give me a few moments to get ready."

"Take your time," he said. He released her hand and retrieved the soap, which he used to lather himself up.

"I am an Arbiter, and I am Lost," she reminded him, feeling it was important to remind him. "I will join you soon." She walked to the nearest bench and methodically began to undress, unbuckling her swordbelt, unclasping the straps that held her thick leather cuirass in place.

Actaeon watched, captivated, as she removed the remainder of her clothing, revealing her slight breasts and curls that matched the color of her cropped head. The woman wasn't shy about her nudity – despite her uncertainty of what to do in the situation at hand. She reached down to draw her sword from its scabbard and lay it beside Actaeon's bow near the edge of the pool – in easy reach should she require it.

"You are beautiful, Eisandre," was all that he could muster.

"I am? It pleases me that you think so," she said as she lowered herself down into the pool.

"Yes, you are. You make my heart race." He took her hand and pressed her palm to his chest to show her.

Eisandre stood quietly for a time as she felt his lifebeat beneath her palm. Then she recalled the reason they were there. "Are you clean? Shall I wash your back?"

"That would be good," said the Engineer and he spun to allow her access. He revelled in the texture of her hands as she rubbed the soap along his back, and felt a stirring deep down within him.

They washed one another in that way, exploring with their hands, and then their lips – pulling one another close.

"So many people say 'I love you', tossing the words about so freely, as if they mean almost nothing," said Eisandre after a time, their bodies pressed together. "I almost rather wish to say that I know you, truly. I see the shape of your soul. And that we are a part of one another."

"Those are the words I was looking for," said Actaeon as his eyes smiled into hers. "And I could not imagine ever choosing otherwise than to be a part of you."

They kissed once more and a warmth blossomed between them on a scale they had never felt before.

"I give you my truth," she said. "I am yours as I will never be for anyone else. We are part of each other, and nothing in this changing world can ever change that."

Actaeon smiled down at her and pulled her close for another kiss, the loquacious Engineer struck silent by her words. As they slowly explored one another, their hands eventually found their most sensitive places. Her fingers wrapped gently around him and his stroked gently between her thighs.

"I'm still learning," she whispered into his ear, almost in a moan. "You will teach me? It all feels amazing, but we also... burn."

"Yes," he said with a bright smile as he explained in words that she could understand. "There is a burning and we will both glow with amazing, almost intolerable brightness, but we will be there to hold each other tightly the entire time. And when that brightness seems like it cannot possibly be allowed to grow further, it will crescendo wonderfully like the blooming of a flower. After that, we can relax in joined embrace until we burn for one another once more."

And so they did.

Flanked by two guards in the shadows at the back of the room, the intertwined crescents of Shore proudly emblazoned on their tabards, the Lord Gunther Arcady sat at a small table with a pitcher of mead and two full flagons. He leaned back slightly in his chair and read a letter, only pausing from time to time to glance at the entrance. An unoccupied chair stood directly across from him, but otherwise the room was bare, used only on rare occasions when the members of Shore's largely isolationist Conclave visited the Pyramid. The corner of his mouth twisted into a slight smirk as he crumpled the letter up and discarded it before choosing another from the table.

When his niece arrived, the elder Shorian Lord drew easily to his feet, still agile despite his age. "Little Eshelle..." he said, noting her escort of Companions that stood by to either side of the entrance. He touched her shoulder firmly and kissed her lightly upon the cheek, ignoring her involuntary flinch. There was little warmth in the expression.

"It is Lady Eshelle to you, Lord Arcady," said the acting head of state for Raedelle as she backed away several steps and took a defiant stance. "What gives us the pleasure of your thankfully rare visits to the Pyramid?"

"Please, have a seat," gestured Arcady with a wry smile. "And likewise, I am glad to have found you here. I admit to having a great many questions for you." He retook his seat and adjusted his fine leather jerkin before he met her gaze firmly. "Your brother for instance... just *how* is he?"

The Lady remained standing, though she pushed the chair in and leaned upon it, an action that amused Arcady. "He is quite fine, thank you. Do you plan to stay long?"

"Isn't that good news? You will have to encourage him to visit Shore soon. We will teach him how to hunt with a bow the correct way," said

Arcady with a chuckle at his own jest. "And your brother, your sister? What of them? Last I heard, Aedgar was out fighting Shield's wars for them. As for myself, I will not be here long – just long enough to take care of certain matters of state – one of which was to speak with you. Thus, it gladdens me that you've come to see me." His hazel eyes burned into her own as he leaned back in his chair.

"Aedgar is off fighting, as is his wont. And you know as well as I that Eisandre is doing well with the Arbiters. She always has. Cut to the chase, Uncle."

"I wish to know when my dear nephew, the Prince, will be returning to his responsibility – especially now that he is well," he asked without amusement. He lifted a copper bit from the table and rolled it back and forth between his fingers.

"He will return when he is ready. What is the problem? For now, I am the voice of Raedelle," said Eshelle, leaning forward as if to dare him to contest her.

Arcady smiled deliberately, unflinching at her words. His reply rolled off his tongue like water along the Avenue of Glass. "And why should my concern over my dear nephew be a problem? If Aedwyn's condition is to be kept a secret, then surely his Uncle would at least be told, lest he grow sick with worry."

"Ambrosius is with Aedwyn and as I said, he is fine. You should be more concerned about whether you can work with me while I lead, because if you can't, there will be a problem," she stated matter-of-factly.

"You know that Shore's loyalty to Raedelle has never been in question," asserted Arcady and he shot her a fiery look. "Always have we followed and always shall we place the needs of Great Raedelle foremost. It is Raedelle's safety and prosperity, in fact, that concerns me." He pulled off his blackened leather gauntlets and set them on the table before he gestured toward the doorway and the Mirrorholds without. "Too long have we dabbled in the affairs of other Dominions. There is a time and a place for such politics, and now is not that time. Parts of Raedelle are suffering. We must turn our gaze inward, on ourselves and our people."

"You would have me turn my back on the happenings in the Pyramid and simply trust that the other Dominions would not take advantage of our stepping out of the political arena? Don't tell me what is the priority here,

I *know* what's important. I'm making these decisions every damned day!" said Eshelle, raising her tone.

"This is not an argument, niece," said Arcady in a level tone. He drew to his feet and stood facing the wall. "This is me giving you advice. If you do not wish to heed it, then do not. Shore has suffered more than ever with the warband losses in this ridiculous war we are fighting for Shield and I *know* that Lakehold is no different, so don't try and tell me otherwise. The tribals are growing confident and have been harrying my trade caravans more and more along the Wall and farther north. Traders are afraid, the economy is suffering and certain resources are near depletion as a result. Not to mention, the people are confused and concerned. Aedwyn was always open and transparent to the people with policy and with that lacking, our fellow Raedelleans are growing suspicious. You know our people, they are independent minded – they want to be onboard with what is happening, with what the plan is."

"I am aware of the state of Raedelle!" said Eshelle in a louder tone than necessary. "And if we are hurting so much on resources, then why would it be a good idea for me to turn my back on the rest of Redemption? We may need them. Tell me, dear Uncle, since you are so wise, what would you have me do differently?"

"Well, first off, allow me to help you. I have been doing this for a very long time and I would be useful as a counsel to you," Arcady suggested before he retook his seat. "And as far as the other advice, I would start by keeping a closer tab on resources. Perhaps appointing a minister of the trade to help. Also, let us keep the interdominional military aid to a minimum – in fact, perhaps none at all unless it directly aids our territories. We need to mount a stronger offensive on the home front. It was always by keeping the tribals on their toes that we prevented invasion, and we didn't have our typical forays into their territories this year."

"It was not my decision, it was Con–" she broke off then as she realized that she had made a mistake. "My brother –"

"If you're the voice of Raedelle, then you'd best to rein him in. He's leaving his homeland vulnerable in his quest for glory," said the Lord Shore, interrupting her. "Curious that he's got so much to prove just after Aedwyn was injured. He wouldn't be vying for someone else's position now, would he?"

"He would never," she asserted. "You are right though and I will have him tone down the efforts with Shield. At the same time, Shield can aid us with their forces to help weed out some of the tribes and keep them on the run."

"They do not have the abilities nor the experience that we do. In fact, bringing them along might indeed place our own fighters at greater risk, for we have the greater skill when it comes to the deep jungle warfare needed to attack the tribes in their domain," explained Arcady. "You know my opinions, and I believe you always understood them better than your brothers. If we draw ourselves too far out of Raedelle with these useless games of court and politics, we will never be able to control the threat to our own people."

"I see your points, Uncle. And honestly, I grow weary of the politics here as well. The other Dominions are for themselves alone, it seems, and hope of a unification that some speak of seems like a distant dream. Sometimes I wonder..." she trailed off.

"Wonder what, dear niece?"

"I wonder what would happen if we struck alliances with the tribes instead. In a way, that was how Raedelle founded our Dominion in the first place. Perhaps our efforts would be better spent on the other side of the coin. The other Dominions would never disrespect us again."

The Lord Arcady's lips twisted into a thin smile and he nodded slowly, running a hand through his black hair. "I like the way you think, Eshelle. There would be a lot of prejudice and bitterness to overcome, but it is ever achievable with the right people leading the effort. Such a maneuver would put the other Dominional ambitions to rest. I think we would make an excellent team, you and I."

"I'd much prefer that we work together than stand opposed," she said. "I would do better in having the counsel of Shore behind me." She reached a hand across the table.

Arcady stood and clasped her hand firmly, winking at her across the table. "Oh, I am ever in agreement, Eshelle. And I am glad that you are willing to accept my counsel. I think that there is a lot that we may accomplish together." He lifted his flagon and slid the other across to her. "To a free and strong Raedelle. May its ideals spread like fire."

They drank and after setting down her flagon, the Lady Eshelle spoke.

"In this new spirit of cooperation, perhaps you could explain to me about this deal you've made with Ajman that we had not been able to negotiate for years?"

"As I have said, I have been doing this for a long time. Let me tell you all about it."

87 A.R., the 1ˢᵗ day of Rainbreak

UNFOLDINGS

WHEN THE RAINS OF THE Monsoon Season drew to an end, it was a time for celebration for people all over Redemption. In part to celebrate the great harvests that the rains brought and in part to celebrate the needed relief from the damage of the constant heavy rains. When the first people passed through the portals and into the ruined city, the intensity of the monsoons almost drove them to their own ruin. When the rains broke and the survivors were allowed a reprise to recover, it was said that they celebrated – each in their own way: some with prayer, some with drink and merriment, and others by simply spending time with their friends.

Thus, the Clear Skies Festival was celebrated across Redemption and legends of the early days told that wars would pause, old rivalries be set aside and some stories even told of tribals that would be invited to dine among the citizens – spear and bow set aside. There was some doubt as to whether or not such tales were true, but one thing was certain: conflict would be set aside these days, at least out in the open. Politics always had a way of getting in the way of such ideals, however, and often conflict would resume with even more fervor and intensity than before. This year's festival was no exception.

The greatest of the celebrations was held in the massive Sun Chamber of Pyramid and this year the festival was funded and arranged by the new Raja of Ajman so that she might make a show of wealth and prosperity among the Dominions. Shield was supposed to run the year's festivities and rumor had it that no little amount of coin found its way into the correct hands to change that. Notably, there were few Shield dignitaries of any rank present at the Festival. The Czerynians, who had supported the Raja's rival caused several fights and other incidents that the Arbiters brought under control.

Raised daises were constructed for delegates from each of the Dominions. They were arranged so that it would look like a six pointed star if one looked down from the stairs of the Skyspiral that wound high above. Ajman, of course, had the largest point of the star and the tallest dais. Smaller tables were scattered between the points of the star and to the periphery for others to gather. Various performers made their rounds there.

The Supreme Captain of Thyr, Amodeus Jarval, was present with a large entourage. The Niwians were also there in numbers, high ranking Keepers standing among them – their practical military garb standing in stark contrast to the colorfully ostentatious outfits of the Niwian courtiers. Eshelle Caliburn was present at the head of a Raedellean delegation that included her Uncle Arcady and several Companions and warchiefs, including the man that Actaeon recognized as Vain, who sat near the Lord Arcady. The association didn't surprise him – Vain would fit well as one of Arcady's dogs.

Despite the problems that the Czerynians in attendance were creating and perhaps because of it, Warlord Kergon of Czeryn sat upon his dais with a few trusted warriors, laughing as the Arbiters worked to quell problems that his own people had created.

Shield's dais was notably empty and there was a collective gasp when Ajman delegates escorted to that dais a group of men and women dressed in crisp, new gray robes with yellow sigils emblazoned upon the front. The sigil showed a tiger and a dragon curved inward upon one another and surrounded by rays of light. The leader of the Waiting Ones was led to the head of a table there and after he bowed in the direction of the Raja, directed the others to sit.

Wave's remaining eye looked like it was about to pop out of its socket. "Wow, is Shield gonna be pissed."

"Got that right," said Companion Caider, who sat beside him at a table just off from the center of the star. Mae, Trench, Actaeon, Balin and Lauryn were also there.

Mae frowned deeply but kept her thoughts to herself. A rift between Shield and Ajman would create difficulty for her work for the Prince General.

"Unbelievable..." said Wave, shaking his head.

"So long as he is away from my workshop, they can crown him the new Emperor of Redemption for all I care," said Actaeon with a grin.

"I'll drink to that!" said Trench, lifting his tankard.

They drank and were joined by Balin the Smith, who used any excuse to drink.

"I don't know – I think it's sort of cute. I mean, he sort of deserves it after sitting out in the mud keeping watch for all that time, don't you think? He's had life pretty hard," said Lauryn.

"Life's been hard for me too, lass, butcha don't see them powdering my sorry ass and dressing me up in finery," said Balin.

"I'll second that," said Trench with a grin that tugged at his ugly scar.

"Oh, come now, Trench. Tell me that you would not be thrilled if the Raja brought you up to sit with her on the other dais," said the Engineer with a smirk.

"Much too young for me," asserted the giant.

"Your mind's telling you that, but yer eyes spin a different tale, my friend," said Wave with a chuckle.

"And your cheeks," giggled Lauryn.

"Aye, he's got a conflict there. The mind in his head and the other one in his pants!" said Caider.

They all laughed.

"Have you considered telling her how you feel?" Mae asked Trench, her musical voice barely audible amidst the steady and gentle roar of echoed conversations in the chamber.

Trench's face was instantly a bright shade of red. He shook his head and studied his drink.

"Oh yeah, that'd go well," said Wave with a chuckle. "'Why hallo, Raja. Mename's Trench. I break skulls for a living and I think yer perty! Oh, and don't worry 'bout my face, it used to be one piece.' Not to mention that the first time he bedded her there'd be a flat Raja."

"Take a lesson, Wave," said Trench with a smile. "First off, you don't tell women they're perty – you tell them that they're lovely, or beautiful, or entrancing, or gorgeous. Second off, there's more to women than bedding. Any woman worth sharing a fling in the sheets with is worth at least ten times that in good conversation. Third off, if I am ever blessed enough to find someone that I'd care to bed and cares to bed me, it'll be a night they won't soon forget. Maybe if ya kept some of those things in mind once in awhile you'd have more than a one night stand, maybe even a two night stand!"

Wave tried to retort, but everyone laughed and clanked their tankards together before having another drink. He gave up and joined them.

They were interrupted by the bellow of a horn from atop the Ajman dais. The Sun Chamber grew quiet immediately and all eyes were on Gaemri Ip Monjata as he shuffled forward to address the crowd.

"Noble ladies and gentlemen – common folk alike. The Raja's Portent asks that you turn your full attention to Her Great Holiness, the Raja Ajman. The Raja has funded this year's Clear Skies Festival from her own coffers and she is thankful for your presence, one and all. Please open your ears and your hearts to her now, for she wishes to bestow the gift of her blessing upon you, the people of Redemption."

The Portent shuffled to the side and bowed as Nadiya stepped forward in her flowing red robes. Beside her, Calisse T'ra Coletka stood with her hand upon the pommel of her falchion. With Portent to one side and Warrioress to the other, the Raja smiled to the crowd and lifted her arms, palms upward, to the Skyspiral.

"This year has been a hard one: flooding and war, smells and machinations, death and suffering. Difficult it is to have faith in the guidance of the Ancient Ones. And yet, despite that all, there has been hope. And I task you: do not lose sight of it. We have seen great towers lain to rest to defend us. To the north, the barbarian horde has been pushed back. The great Dominion of Ajman has found unification at last. The marketplace and the baths in our Pyramid have been reclaimed. Our displaced peoples have found refuge."

Actaeon received several claps on the back and congratulatory shoves from his friends and it was his turn to have his face turn a different shade. Caider raised his tankard to toast with a 'Here here!' and caught several glares from the adjacent tables. He shrugged and drank anyway while the Raja continued.

"All are signs that the Ancient Ones guide us toward dominance, in this, our new world. And with those signs, came another miraculous sign – that of the First Ajman. Yes, the very sigil of my line has appeared once more. It stands now as a beacon of hope within the refugee encampment to the west and a sign that we as a people are the chosen successors of Redemption. As such, we are honored to have a special guest at the day's celebration: Phyrius Ricter, of the Waiting Ones that have stood watch over the blessed relic. Thank you, Phyrius."

Actaeon's eyes widened and he cast an incredulous look across the table at the others.

"The First of the Waiting Ones are blessed to be your guests on this day of light!" To Actaeon's disbelief, the old man had stood up and was addressing the entire crowd. "May the Keeper of Light's rays shine upon you all!"

"May they shine for all time!" came the answering chorus of his followers.

The Engineer counted his own blessings when Phyrius retook his chair.

The Raja's gaze found Actaeon and her eyes seemed to smile down at him though her expression showed little otherwise. She continued: "And so, I counsel you all: Drink on this day and be merry, make a new friend, reaffirm an old. Think on our bright future, and our past from which we have come so far. We are the future of Redemption. Enjoy the fruits of the year's labors and bless you all!"

An uproarious cheer went up that thundered throughout the cavernous chamber. The revelries resumed along with the conversation, food, and entertainers.

"What a curious woman," said Actaeon, speaking about the Raja.

"Aye... yes, she is," said Trench wistfully.

Wave raised his tankard, "To the Raja! I think she's a good thing for Redemption, even if she lets one of the maddest madmen I've ever seen give the big toast."

"To the Raja," they echoed at the table.

"So long as she got him away from the workshop, she can do what she wishes with mad, old Phyrius. I wish him luck. Thank the Ancients for the peaceful workshop," said Actaeon.

"To a peaceful workshop," seconded Lauryn, lifting her tankard this time.

"A peaceful workshop..." they all toasted, followed by laughter.

Trench was on his feet suddenly, his face dark with anger as he glared at someone that passed by the table.

"Speaking of breaking the peace," mumbled Wave. He stood alongside his friend.

Atreena stopped and turned to face the giant, her eyes narrowing to meet the man's own. She wore her full set of Keeper plate armor, excepting the helm. "I have as much a right to be here as you do. I offered apology. But clearly, your inability to accept it shows your complicitness in matters of evil. My brother and sister knights were right to attack you and your workshop for you will bring us all to –"

"Keep walking before I make you eat that fancy sword of yers," said Trench with a scowl.

Bravely, the Knight continued to face him when she spoke. "I will do so to avoid an interdominional incident... for now. But I know enough about what you all are doing now and mark my words, it will not go unchallenged."

Wave smirked at that and shrugged. "We like a good challenge. We'll be ready. I hope you are!"

She shook her head in dismay and strode off, leaving them alone once more. Trench and the others watched as she made her way up to the Niwian dais where she sat with the other Keepers. From time to time they glanced in the direction of the Engineer's table.

"Is everything okay here? It seemed like someone was bothering you," came a rugged effeminate voice. It was the Raja's warrioress. She stood with her hands on her hips in her fine leather armor that was traced through with gold filigree. Her eyes were on the Niwian dais and the Keepers as she spoke.

"Ah, the Lady Coletka, a pleasure," spoke Wave as he swept a polite bow in her direction. "We were just seeing off an old rival. Nothing we haven't handled before."

"Nothing *I* haven't handled before," amended Trench.

"If you require a guard for the night it can be arranged, but I doubt you gentlemen – and ladies would have much need of it," said Calisse as her eyes swept the group, lingering upon Wave.

"Well, that may be so, but it is your festival, Lady Coletka. If you like, I could brief you on the details in private. I wouldn't want to dull the conversation," suggested Wave. He winked with his remaining eye.

The warrioress shifted, her hand dropped to the hilt of her falchion and she stared at Wave for several long moments. It wasn't clear if she was going to walk away or hit him, but she finally offered the glimpse of a smile.

"Yes, I would like that. Come, let us talk," she decided.

Wave smiled and offered her his arm which, to everyone's surprise, she gladly took and they walked off together. Just as they departed, dancers in long, colorful dresses flooded into the chamber among the tables and began to dance to music that emanated throughout the chamber.

Mae smiled and pointed excitedly at the Skyspiral stairs above them, where several dozen bards stood to play music from curved horns that filled the chamber.

The dancers flowed all about them and good drink and conversation continued.

"Wow, Act! They worked those new arbiter whistles you created into the song," remarked Lauryn.

Actaeon listened and his eyes widened as he decided that he *could* hear the whistles. It was a distinct tone and it carried over the music, even past the echoes of the cavernous chamber.

"Yes, fantastic. They decided to test them in an environment with a sound volume that I could not achieve in the workshop. Excellent idea – I wish I had thought of it," said Actaeon.

Trench was pointing over their heads though and he stood to get a better vantage on something. "Not a test! Who tests out whistles at a festival?"

Indeed, there was a commotion occurring at the Czerynian dais. It seemed that Kergon had dragged one of the dancing women up onto his stage and was trying to get her to dance with him, to her consternation. She attempted to fight him off, which had ripped the straps of her dress. Kergon laughed and reached his big hands out to fondle her breasts. The Warlord of Czeryn was unfazed as the woman repeatedly slapped him and spit in his face. He spun her around and tried to wrap his arms around her from behind, but perhaps all of the ale was having an effect on him and she slipped beneath his arms and tumbled from the dais to the floor. Several of the other dancers swooped in quickly to cover her nakedness and escort her out of the Sun Chamber.

The sound of the whistles heralded the arrival of a troop of Arbiters led by Sentinel Phragus. Actaeon could see that Eisandre and her partner Garth followed closely behind him, as did another four Arbiters. As they ascended the Czerynian dais, the warlords stood. Phragus and the others must've pushed their way through because they arrived shortly at the inner point of the dais to confront Kergon.

"You will comport yourself with order so long as you are within the Pyramid, or you will leave," spoke Phragus. His voice could be heard over the music, which for some reason continued to blare on.

The Warlord leaned forward and laughed right in the Sentinel Arbiter's face. "Order! Fine then, you first, Arbiter," he said and the word 'Arbiter' was a sneer. He then lunged forward more quickly than the Arbiter could react and grabbed the man's pauldrons before he pulled him forward and over his extended knee.

The older Sentinel screamed and tumbled headfirst from the dais to land fully upon his back, his armor clattering on the floor noisily. The music halted abruptly then and the dancers all exited the room in a rainbow of retreat.

Eisandre stepped forward then and brought the Warlord to his knees with a blow to the stomach. The other Arbiters moved to draw their swords, but she stayed them with a gesture.

Actaeon could see her speaking to Kergon, but it was too low for him to make out. He failed to realize that he had gained his feet during the events and had taken several steps closer to the Czerynian dais. He calculated the distance in his head and recalculated and recalculated again as he realized that he wouldn't be able to arrive in time to help.

Kergon slowly looked up at Eisandre, his eyes lingering on her armor clad body as he did so. When his eyes finally met hers, he offered her the broad smile of a man that was imagining terrible things. "Now now... you're my kind of woman. What do ya say I take you back to Ridge and show you the real way to make a man scream?" he said, referring to the old Sentinel's scream from earlier.

If the tiny, blond Arbiter said anything in response, nobody heard it.

But everyone saw when she lifted her hand and pointed unequivocally, inarguably, and undeniably toward the exit from the Sun Chamber.

The Warlord lifted his hand and it was smacked back down by the Knight Arbiter's other hand. At the same time, three of the other Knights circled behind him. He growled and then smiled and spat at Eisandre's feet. But then he settled on his fate and stood. "You heard the lady, our kind isn't welcome here. We're too much the life of this party. Don't want to show up anyone's fancy dancers, do we? Don't worry, I'll come visit you, little lady."

The Warlord led the way off the dais then and his people followed as other Knight Arbiters arrived at the base of the stairs to escort the Czerynians out from the Sun Chamber. Other Knights arrived to aid Phragus and the Sentinel was helped to his feet and escorted out with a noticeable limp.

When the last of the Czerynians had stepped down from the dais, the Knight Arbiters stepped down behind them and ebullient applause filled the room. As if on cue, the music started up again and the dancers emerged in their colorful dresses with their flowing ribbons and began to dance once more. All at once the chamber was again filled with bright celebration, cheerful laughter, and merry conversation.

Some time later, Actaeon and Trench sat in companionable silence while they watched the goings on in the Sun Chamber. The others at the table had wandered off to various places to mingle.

"May I join you?" came a familiar voice.

Actaeon turned and grinned. "I am glad to see you, Eis. Yes, please do."

"My cue to leave," said Trench, standing. "Ya did good, lass. Real good, today," he said as he offered her a lopsided smile before starting off.

Eisandre opened her mouth at a loss for words for a moment before she spoke. "He did not have to leave."

"Aye, it is alright though. He has this idea that we have been kindling some sort of relationship together," said the Engineer with a broad grin.

"Are we not?" asked Eisandre, clearly confused as she sat down beside him.

"Oh, indeed we are, but it is amusing to keep them guessing," he replied.

"I don't see what is amusing about not being honest with them about the nature of our relationship. Also, I believe they may be more perceptive than you realize."

Actaeon laughed and gave her shoulder a playful punch. "I am lucky to have you, Knight Arbiter Eisandre. Are you on duty still, or am I even luckier?"

Eisandre returned his laugh with a stoic look. "I was told to go off duty for the rest of the night due to an incident with some Czerynians. I don't know how having me makes you lucky."

"Chance is a factor that we cannot fail to recognize. It plays a major role in every action, in every series of events and if we fail to anticipate chance, then our plans might be ruined," said the Engineer as if he had thought long about this particular topic before. "In some situations chance can offer random fortune or misfortune based on factors we could never fully anticipate. That is what I call luck. For instance, what if we had not seen each other in Saint Torin's Hold? What if we had not run into one another in the Boneyards? What if one event happened but not the other? Things might be very different. So I am lucky," he concluded.

"How can you anticipate random factors any more than that they are possible? Although, I must admit that I am grateful for our unanticipated encounters. How very different we both would be had we not met," she said, her eyes showing some warmth at her last sentence.

"Anticipating the unexpected is paramount to a good design," stated Actaeon matter-of-factly. "No one can think of every single random eventuality, but they must anticipate as many as possible, lest their design be easily failed."

"You speak like an engineer," said the Arbiter in a jestful accusation. "Or a tactician."

"The tactics of creation. Trying to make something new when nothing was there before is eminently more interesting than working with things that are there already, at least for myself. Though the things that are there already, bounded by rules and laws such as they are, are that much more difficult to make bend to one's will. Enough about me though. I saw a real tactician at work earlier. You brush off your 'incident with some Czerynians' like it was no problem, but I saw how you handled it and I was very impressed," said the Engineer with sincerity.

The Knight Arbiter's eyes found the floor quickly as she responded,

"I'm not sure the Sentinel Arbiter was very happy with my handling of it, but I was glad that it was resolved with no further injuries."

"Of course he would not have been happy. You handled the situation quite professionally and managed to defuse a potential disaster where he was thrown on his behind quite unceremoniously," he said.

"I appreciate your saying that, but the fact of the matter is that I failed my duty in letting the Sentinel Arbiter be thrown in such a manner," said Eisandre firmly.

While they spoke, several other revelers stopped nearby and were conversing in hushed tones as they gestured overtly toward Eisandre. Any discretion they may have attempted was washed away by drink.

"She's a Caliburn too," one of them could be heard saying in an unsuccessfully hushed tone.

Actaeon stood and approached them with a grin. "May I help you?"

The revelers stumbled over one another to get away and retreated to a distance that was out of earshot.

"There are quite a number of Raedellean citizens who will recognize me," said the Arbiter when he sat back down beside her. "Either because they had seen me in my younger days or because I look very much like my brother Aedwyn. Also, I do have the Caliburn eyes." She turned toward him and studied his face before she spoke, "But you have different thoughts, yes. You have from the start."

"I tend to see things differently. It is just part of who I am, I suppose. I had never met your brother, so I never had anything to compare it to. One thing I do know is that you caught my eye amongst a table full of people like a flash of bright light. If your brother has eyes anything like yours, it is no wonder that he draws people's attention," said Actaeon.

"Aedwyn is like the sun," she said quietly, a distant look in her eyes as she recalled some memory of her brother. "When I bask in his light, I shine brighter than myself. But... not everyone gets along with him. He has a very strong personality – very unyielding opinions. Perhaps you would not like him. And yet, he is a lot like me in other ways."

"Some opinions are not worth yielding. But all should be considered with critical reasoning. I should like to meet him one of these days should he return to Pyramid," he said with a smile.

The gawkers had begun to gather again in force and could be heard discussing and gesturing to Eisandre once more.

"Would you like to go elsewhere with me? We can take a walk, or relax and talk somewhere? Or if you have the need, you can beat me up in a sparring match again," the Engineer suggested with a laugh.

It took Eisandre a moment to understand the reference, but when she did, she blushed brightly. "I do not wish to spar. But perhaps we can find a quieter place somewhere, where we can..." She blushed an even deeper shade. "Where we can talk openly. And away from curious others."

"I still have that room in the Song of Sisters above us. We could go there?" he suggested, arching a brow.

"Let us go, yes," said Eisandre, eyeing the gawkers.

As they stood, he offered her an arm, which she took, and they both headed off through the crowd together to the delight of the onlookers. Actaeon led her on a weaving path through the Sun Chamber toward one of the staircases that ascended into the Skyspiral above. Eisandre tugged on his arm to lead him to a different one. "This one, it's more direct."

As they passed by a crowd of revelers near the edges of the chamber, they caught a glimpse of Wave. The Ajmani warrioress had him pinned against the wall as she kissed him deeply. Each one of them had a hand between their bodies, roaming. After a moment, the pair broke their embrace and Calisse took his hand and led him swiftly away.

Actaeon met Eisandre's gaze and rolled his eyes as they continued on their way to the stairway, which took them upward and away from the Sun Chamber floor. When they finally arrived at Actaeon's room in the Song, Eisandre was confronted with quite the sight. Assorted parchments that displayed notes, sketches, diagrams and symbols lay all over the room and atop all of the furniture, bed and in some cases even the floor. Many of the symbols were copies of those found in the room above the Sea Lounge. Various trinkets and mechanisms cluttered the areas that weren't covered with parchment. It was certainly the Engineer's room.

He shot Eisandre an apologetic look. "Well... at least there are not any prying gossipers in here – that much I can promise." He set his halberd against the wall near the door and began to clear some of the documents from the bed and floor, piling them on a table to the side as he worked.

"You do not have to reorganize your possessions for my sake. I think I can manage not to step on anything," she assured him before deftly stepping in the voids between parchments to approach the slanted window and look out on the garden terrace far below.

"I suppose I am not renowned for neatness," said the Engineer before joining her. "Beautiful view, this..."

"It's enough to make a person feel very... tall."

"Aye. Tends to make me think about bigger things, like why we were brought to Redemption and where we came from... What the world really is and what happened to the people that lived in this place. Do you ever think on such things?" he asked his love.

"We are born in the shadow of fading memories and fallen dreams, living our days within the decaying bones of an age long gone. Of course I think on such things – it is all around us, at times it is consuming. And although we may never know for certain what transpired," she said. "I do believe it important that we strive to learn as much as we can about the world around us. At the very least so that we have a fighting chance of not repeating the worst of their mistakes."

"An interesting possibility for certain and an assumption that many make, especially the Keepers. I am not sure that I am entirely convinced though," admitted the Engineer. "While such a mistake might be one explanation, there is no proof thereof. No, I think it is likely that there is something else strange going on here. The main problem with that theory is the lack of bodies. I have never seen a body of one of the Ancients, nor any physical remnant." He gestured out toward the city. "And in a city of this magnitude, how could that be possible? No, I think more likely that this place was created as is... or perhaps the Ancients chose exodus. Even then, it would be odd if they did not miss a few here or there, or that all would agree to leave. Yet another possibility and incredibly more frightening, is that something devoured every person of this ancient civilization but spared all other life. Thus, something sentient chose to eliminate and destroy all biological evidence that such a race of people ever existed." He trailed off then, retreating into such thoughts.

"If such a choice was made once," replied the Arbiter, "then it could potentially be made again. Although, I don't see that there's much we could do about it, if it came to that. This weighs heavily upon your thoughts, Actaeon. If you wish, we can discuss the various theories further."

"My thoughts are heavily weighed upon all the time," he said with a grin. "My mind is my sword, under the constant stress of practice and battle alike. There is little to be done about that, for that is who I am. The architects have left us clues below – such that we may one day be able to comprehend, it is my hope. But the answers, I fear... the answers lie in death... It is up to us to make sure that we do not find such a cruel solution to our lives."

"You cannot practice and fight all the time," said the Arbiter knowingly. "You will wear yourself down to nothing. It may be important to rest, to let your thoughts drift free. As you have described, you have some of your best ideas when you are not trying to think of them. And... why would you say that the answers lie in death? Surely, you cannot know this?"

"You are correct, of course, my love. As for the answers, there is reason to postulate that many of them either resulted in the destruction or banishment of the Ancients, or will result in ours. I hope that is not the case, but I do truly believe that knowledge and understanding will drive us toward the truth. It would be a great mistake not to try our best to learn about this world we have been thrust into."

"We cannot make that mistake with people such as you about," she said with certitude. "Seeking answers, craving knowledge, learning and searching. But some truths we may not be ready to learn. After all, the people who came before us seemed to know a great many things that we do not."

"We always must stand ready for the truth," said Actaeon. "Lest the answers pass us by undiscovered and disappear from the world entire. Some truths come when least expected."

"Which?"

The kiss that found her lips was a surprise, stealing away all conversation. The thoughts and theories and conjecture spiraled away into a bright light that erupted from deep within their cores. They kissed for a long time before they ended up holding each other in silence as they gazed out through the glass wall.

"Do you ever miss spending time with your family, in your line of work?" he asked after a time. "I imagine it must be particularly difficult, what with them being the leaders of a Dominion and your vow of neutrality."

"I used to live with my family and see them very often. I would rather be on my own and be someone useful and worthy of admiration than surrounded by them and lost in the shadow of their brightness. I do miss Aedwyn, however. And I miss when Eshelle let me braid her hair. She must be very busy lately. Aedgar too. But they do have important jobs. Why do you ask?"

"I want to learn more about you," said Actaeon. "How you feel, how you perceive the world, your history. It interests me because you are amazing to me."

"I'm fairly certain you are the only person in the world who has such an opinion of me and a desire to learn more," she noted with a smile. "Then again, you are also the only one to whom I am not broken and Lost. I wonder... why is it that you are so different in this way? What is it about you and your brilliant mind that could love a person like me? I must admit that I find myself curious about that. What of your own family? Before Wave and Trench and Lauryn, I mean. You mentioned your mother once, as being the reason you had some knowledge of healing."

A brief rain began as they spoke, the sunlit droplets cascading down the glass wall in rivulets, unaware of the irony of their arrival on this day of all days.

"My mother was an incredible woman," began the Engineer. He scratched his right arm through his jacket as he spoke. "She cared so much about me and taught me so many things about the world, at least until she ran out of answers to my questions. She was a seamstress, and taught me how to make all sorts of clothing." He tugged on the sleeve of his own jacket to indicate that it was one such case. "I hurt her a lot. Hurt both my parents, in fact, because I left home as a young man. I was supposed to undergo my Trials, but I did not want to, that was... not my path. I am no warrior, as you know.

"When I returned, my father was dead. He was a woodworker by trade and an officer in Incline's warband when needed. That's how he died — fighting tribal invaders. They told me my mother grew sick after the news of his death. I took care of her, and learned everything that I could about how our bodies function, how chemicals affect them, different poultices and herbal remedies, some legitimate and some not. I even came up with a mixture that eased her pain for a time. In the end though, I could not save her. I failed to understand what had gone wrong...

"I will remember them always in everything I do. Although they did not understand what I was trying to achieve, they always gave me their best and taught me everything they knew. I like to think that if they could see me now – see the things that I have accomplished and the people that I have met... I like to think that if they could see that, they would understand me. And be happy for me. I am lucky though, to have friends like you and Trench and Wave and Lauryn," he concluded. "And I will forever be grateful for your friendship and love."

"I did not know you could make clothing. I'm glad you had such a home growing up, that you could flourish as you have on such a strong foundation of love and support. Your parents must have been remarkable people. I would thank them, if I could, for bringing you into this world," she decided.

"My parents *were* remarkable people," agreed Actaeon. "Even if they were constantly confused and somewhat disappointed with my pursuits. I am glad that I had them to grow up with."

"I can only imagine how ashamed and embarrassed my own parents were to find they had created a Lost child. But it is a testament to their kindness that they did not cast me away as soon as they discovered this," she said.

"A testament to their kindness? How could one ever cast a child away? Especially one that they needed to raise to that point, to come that far? To not cast a child away is simply not to stoop to vileness. You are the most wonderful thing in my world, Eis. I cannot fathom the thought of you being cast aside like that." He leaned forward to kiss her forehead tenderly.

"How many Lost do you know who are part of warm and supportive families? How many Lost do you know that are loved? We are outcasts for the most part. Social anathemas. But my family, despite holding the leadership of a Dominion, kept me and educated me. I had Aedwyn to comfort me when I had nightmares, Eshelle to brush my hair and tell me stories about her admirers, Aedgar to teach me to hold a sword. And then, when I was older, they found me a place where I could go and learn to make something useful out of my life, a vocation worthy of respect. I was very, very lucky, my Actaeon. I still am. No one else thinks as you do." She reached up to touch his face.

"That is the problem," he said, meeting her gaze. "And perhaps I am wrong, Eis... perhaps I am wrong and all of Redemption is right. But in my heart and mind I know these things to hold true. This is the sickness that comes with society. Things that are unknown and unfamiliar scare people. Since they are unable to understand, they explain away and cast aside.

"It... it... it stands against everything I believe in. To cast aside the unknown, to deny that without explanation, and to close the coffin lid on the life purchased by knowledge and the quest for understanding. Truly, it is unacceptable and such persistent ignorance will destroy us all in the end if it is not readily contended with. In truth, such things are most likely what destroyed the people that lived here. Not the mechanisms and machinations of this now shattered city. No, they may have played a role in it, of course. But the thing that I believe may have gotten the better of them once and for all can only be described as a knowing denial of truth, a casting aside of knowledge. I suppose what I am trying to convey is that, if no other thinks as I do, then, by the Fallen, they are all wrong. And I shall hold you near for as long as you can bear because you are pure and true and a blessing to everyone around you, whether they see it or no."

He kissed her hard then and guided her gently to the bed. She returned his kiss and pulled him against her. Her hand slipped between them to cup him through his trousers and she pulled back from their kiss to search his eyes with her brilliant blue gaze.

"To desire, on so many levels. To want... you. To be wanted. We gave ourselves one evening to that need, to that fulfillment. Will you show me how again?" she requested, eyes searching.

Actaeon simply nodded, unable to form words. He relieved her of her armor and swordbelt before he unlaced her trousers and pulled them free.

"I have approximately three hours until my next duty shift," she murmured. "It will be..." she gasped as his fingers found their way to her most sensitive of places. "...an interesting transition."

The Engineer grinned and kissed her lips before he worked his way down her body with kisses, gently teasing all the way. When his lips finally replaced his fingers, she gasped once more. "Saints..." she whispered as she experienced things that she never thought possible, indeed perhaps that none had ever thought possible for her. And the heat within her exploded in light and joy.

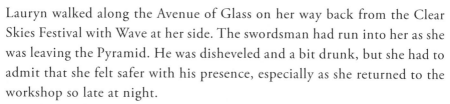

Lauryn walked along the Avenue of Glass on her way back from the Clear Skies Festival with Wave at her side. The swordsman had run into her as she was leaving the Pyramid. He was disheveled and a bit drunk, but she had to admit that she felt safer with his presence, especially as she returned to the workshop so late at night.

The brief shower had made the glass surface they walked upon very slick, but luckily the rain had been fleeting.

"Funny that..." said Wave. "I can't remember it ever raining during the Clear Skies Festival."

"Yes, it's like a mockery of the entire effort to celebrate the end of the rains. It seems like you didn't let it get in the way of your celebrating though," she said, a hint of mischievous curiosity in her tone. "What was her name? Calisse?"

"Ah, I see what you're driving at, devious lass," said Wave with a chuckle. "A gentleman never speaks of a lady outside of her own chamber."

"Oh come now, Wave. You know I know that you're no gentleman. And we're both friends, right? So did you sleep with her or not?" Lauryn prodded him in the side.

"As I said," began the mercenary. "A gentleman –"

Wave never saw the blow coming. It struck him unconscious and sent him crumpling to the wet glass.

Lauryn spun and screamed as several figures rushed up behind her. They had come from over the edge of the Avenue, and quickly. In the dim light of a distant luminary, she could make out a cross upon one man's face that divided his features into four quadrants. A lifebeat later, he had thrown a sack over her head and the blow to her gut took her wind away and cut her scream short.

The Raedellean woodcarver barely clung to consciousness as she was thrown over the man's shoulder and rushed off into the night.

SHOWDOWN

T HE DOOR OF THE WORKSHOP crashed open and in stumbled Wave, his clothing ripped and dried blood caked along one side of his face. It was late morning and Trench was helping Actaeon with another round of deathcrawler/chicken experiments.

"Wow, Calisse really did a number on you, Wave," Trench said with a chuckle. His smile faded when Wave dropped to his hands and knees.

Actaeon and Trench rushed to his side and knelt beside him.

"They took her – bastards. I didn't even see them coming. They... took... her," said the mercenary, trying to catch his breath.

"First the Lady Lartigan and now the Lady Coletka? You haven't had any luck with your love interests at festivals," remarked Actaeon.

Wave shook his head and held up his hand to stop them.

"No... not Calisse. Lauryn... they took Lauryn. Hit us on the Avenue of Glass. Knocked me out before I knew what hit me. They took her somewhere – I don't know. It was the cross-faced bastards. By the Fallen, I've lost her!" He broke down then and began to sob.

Trench lifted him by the collar of his tunic and struck him a solid blow across the face. "Pull yourself together, Wave! Every lifebeat counts now. Damnit, you know that. We need to know everything. She ain't lost yet."

Wave sniffled and straightened, "Yeah, you're right. I'm sorry. Here, help me up." He let the two men pull him to his feet. "When I came to I was in the Boneyards. It was to the northwest of where we found that glowing statue. There were six of them... no, seven – all with the crosses. One of them spoke to me. He said..." Wave hesitated and drew silent.

"Said what? Spit it out!" growled the giant.

"He said: 'Tell the Engineer to come to this place if he wants to see the girl again.' He said to come alone and if they spotted you with anyone else, then she would die. That's all. There was nothing else of note. Three of them had spears, two had a sword and two had bows. Other than that they were identical. Shaved pates, all of them. Like the others we've encountered. I'm... I'm sorry, Act. I let you down."

The Engineer grasped Wave's shoulders firmly and looked down into the man's eye. "It is not your fault, Wave. They have been pursuing me since before my arrival at Pyramid. If anyone is to blame, it is me." He turned to Trench, "Get the extra grenados. I will meet with these raiders and resolve this once and for all."

Trench shook his head. "By the Fallen, you will not. Yer not going out there on your own. You've seen those raiders, Act. If you go, I fear you'll not come back. It's our task to defend you."

Actaeon had already thrown on his jacket and was stringing his bow. "This I will not argue with you, Trench. You and Wave are in *my* employ. You heard Wave. If I fail to do this in the manner they have specified, then Lauryn will die. I know you do not want that on your conscience any more than I do. Get the grenados, there is no time to waste on this."

Trench looked at him for a long moment, the ugly scar across his face turning a dark shade. In that moment, the Engineer reminded him of someone he knew long ago. He banged his fist on a nearby workbench, but then he turned and went down the cellar stairs.

When he emerged, he carried a small crate. He set it before Actaeon and cracked it open with his dagger. Actaeon knelt and brushed aside some of the packing hay before pulling two of the canisters free. He put one in each of the big side pockets of his jacket. In addition to the one hanging from his jacket already, he now had three.

"Okay, listen up. If I fail to return in one day, no less, then I want you to let Eisandre know what has happened. Tell her I love her..."

"I knew it!" exclaimed Wave, with a weak grin.

Actaeon ignored him and continued, "Then go to the Raedellean Hold.

They should be notified. Lauryn is a Raedellean citizen. They may send a rescue party for her."

"So are you," said Wave.

"Do not try to come after me alone. You have seen these people. I do not need you both to be lost rushing headlong into battle against a force like that. I will get out of it somehow," said the Engineer.

"Darkest Hour to that!" said Trench.

"I'll second that," said Wave.

"We'll give you to sundown tomorrow, Act. And we'll do what you said until then. If you haven't figured it out by then, we're coming to get you, like it or no," said Trench, and the look on his face said that he would not be argued with.

"Very well, gentlemen. I will return."

That said, the Engineer grabbed his halberd and left, leaving the two mercenaries to do what they did worst: sit and wait.

When they pulled the blindfold off, he was in a barren, gray, cylindrical, domed room with no windows and only a sliding door with no handle on the inside. One of the cross-faced raiders stood in front of him and offered him naught but a blank stare.

"You will wait here," said the man before he exited the room. The door slid shut behind him with a loud click.

"The hospitality here is lacking," Actaeon said to the cold, closed surface of the door.

He wasted no time in reconnoitering the room. They had taken his halberd, his bow and arrows, and his dagger, but they left him his jacket and the rest of the gear in it, including – to his amusement – the grenados. The door, he found, was solid and had no give laterally. When he tested it carefully with his shoulder, he did find that it had some movement upward. The edges of the door were recessed into the walls when it was shut and there was nothing with which to grab or further manipulate it.

The wall was solid where he pushed and prodded. At the top of the room was a single hole in the center of the dome about the size of his pinky finger. Directly under it, he could feel a gentle rush of air.

If forced air entered the room, it must have a planned exit, the Engineer surmised. He knelt and felt at the seam where the floor met the wall. Sure enough, there was a small gap there all along the perimeter.

There was nothing else of note in the room, so he thought about the scene in the Boneyards when he had gone to meet the raiders. He hadn't known exactly where they wanted him to find them, but he figured they would find him if he got close enough. As he travelled through the Boneyards, a deep fog had risen from the shattered remnants of buildings and infrastructure as he carefully traversed the wreckage of the ancient city.

The visibility deteriorated to a point where he could barely make out more than an arm's length before him. It had reminded him of the time that Trench had been forced to fight some of the cross-faced raiders during their search for the mechanical man. Only this time had been worse. Much worse.

At some point while he was ascending a fallen wall, he realized that he had been surrounded. He stopped then and laughed. When the men didn't respond, he spoke, "I have come all this way. Are you going to lead the way or not?" He could make just out the dark crosses bisecting the faces of the men around him, barely visible in the fog.

He hadn't seen the blow coming, but it knocked the wind from him, the halberd from his hand and sent him to his knees. After that he was blindfolded and walked for what seemed like half an eternity.

Actaeon guessed they had taken him in a generally northwestern direction, but he couldn't be certain. Had the sun been out to warm his face, he would've known for certain, but alas, that was not to be.

As they walked, none of his captors spoke. Occasionally they would steady him, push or pull him up the rubble, but otherwise there was nothing – no communication. The silence was eerie. Especially among the foggy ruins, where speaking was a natural way to avoid getting separated.

He goaded them several times, but had received no response. In this way, he had been conducted here – wherever this was.

There was a click at the door as a mechanism cycled. It slid open and a man stepped inside. This man was different – there was no cross painted on his face. He had long, unkempt hair with ruggedly handsome features and wore a smirk like a shield. His clothing was a mishmosh of brown leathers of varying shades. Though Actaeon hadn't seen him since he was barely a young man, he recognized him immediately. He was Markor, from the Warrens – the man who claimed to be a Loresworn.

"Actaeon! Old boy! Surprised to see me?" said the man as he slapped the Engineer on the shoulder.

"Not at all, actually our last encounter correlated exactly with the beginning of my run-ins with the cross-faced raiders."

"Correlation –"

"– does not infer causation, obviously. Though, I have clearly just proven causation as well, so save it. Are you going to tell me why I am here, or are you going to continue to waste my time and threaten my friends?" The Engineer leveled an angry gaze at Markor.

"Now, now, Actaeon. You know I wouldn't hurt your friends – never, never. Come now, come now... let us walk, let us talk," said Markor. He gestured for Actaeon to follow.

When they emerged, the fog was still quite heavy. They were amidst a clearing in the ruins where several dozen hemispherical buildings stood in mostly intact clusters. The one they'd left was one of the smallest and there were several other domes of similar size grouped with it. They must be useful as cells, Actaeon figured, especially if they lacked a means to open them from the inside like his had.

"So, so, Actaeon, old boy. It seems you've been up to a lot of things since we've lasted touched base – a lot of things. Anything you'd care to share with your good friend Markor?"

"Cut the trumpery, Markor. Where is Lauryn?"

"Patience, have patience with your dear – most dear friend Markor. This is a tale I'll tell. But first you'll indulge me as I speak – yes, do indulge me," said the man, trying Actaeon's patience.

"Fine. I will indulge you for a few moments more, but then I want to know where my friend is. Without that information I can assure you that you will not have my cooperation in whatever manner you seek," said Actaeon crossly.

Markor turned to him and smiled, his eyes narrowing to small slits.

There were cross-faced raiders that stood at intervals among the buildings. They said nothing, did nothing – didn't even move.

All of their eyes followed him as he was led into one of the larger hemispheres. Inside, the building was no different from his cell, aside from the size. There was no door handle on the inside of this one either. It meant that these strange domed structures must have been used by the Ancients for some purpose that only required access from the outside. Storage of something, no doubt, Actaeon thought.

In the center of the room was a familiar object. The cylindrical device had rounded ends and various symbols alit with different colors along its body. Some of the symbols were blinking and others were not – symbols of the Ancients. The device rested upon a roughly hewn wooden stand.

Arrayed about the device were several small tables and chairs. Upon the tables there was an assortment of tools, reams of parchment and an ink fountain. Off to one side there was a larger table with two chairs.

Markor tossed his hair back and pulled a chair out at that table. "Please, please sit, old boy. I'll tell you everything... everything."

Actaeon sat and folded his arms across his chest, leaning back in the chair.

Markor sat opposite him and gave a low whistle. A scantily clad woman entered with a tray of food – the same cross as the raiders on her face. Curly blond hair cascaded down over her shoulders and her body was bruised here and there – one on her face and another on her forehead in addition to bruises on her ribcage, above her hips, and on her thighs. What she wore left little to the imagination: a leather thong tied off to cover what lay between her legs and a wider leather thong across her ample bosom. She set the tray down on the table and stepped off to the side.

"Why, thank you, thank you so much, slut. You may stand near the door," said Markor dismissively.

The woman hesitated for a moment, regarding Actaeon before she obeyed.

The Engineer's eyes lingered over her, but not due to her near nakedness. No, there was something else – some lingering familiarity. Something was very wrong here. They must be near Czeryn, where slaves were common, but there was something wrong about this one – something he couldn't quite place.

"Eat, eat! I insist. Only the finest for you, Actaeon – only the finest. Let us talk and eat, eat and talk about the most reverent task you have at hand. I'm sure you recognize the machine behind us, right? Right?" Markor paused for a moment and stuffed some cheese into his mouth. "Well, you probably guessed what we want too! You probably guessed! We want you to activate it, old boy! So it can do its trick – its little trick. You know the deal. Figure out the symbols, use the symbols, and so on. Do that and we let your little friend go. She just goes home. Refuse, and... well, refuse and I get another slut – this one smaller. She'd like that, I think."

It all came to Actaeon in a snap. He turned and his eyes confirmed the truth. Markor's slave woman was the Lady Lartigan who had gone missing from Pyramid just after the Monsoon Festival.

In one smooth motion, Actaeon stood, lifted the tray and swung it across Markor's face. The metal tray bent in his hand as the repetitive man fell back in his chair and hit the ground hard. The Engineer knelt atop him and pressed the edge of the tray to the man's throat, applying just the right amount of pressure. In his periphery, he saw two raiders enter the room.

"All of you, listen to me, right now," he said. "This is what will happen. You need something from me and I need something from you. The thing that you need from me is important enough that I know you are willing to die for it, so do not for one second attempt to feed me any of your rubbish.

"You will deliver my assistant, the Lady Lauryn, to me, presently, and in an unharmed state. I will require her aid if I am to accomplish this task. The Lady Lartigan will remain as well, in case I need her to retrieve something for me. You will also return my other gear in case I need it to do my work. I will work to activate your device. Once I have understood how to activate the device, we will negotiate the device's activation and our own release. Those are the terms."

"Now now, Actaeon, old boeaaaggh –" Markor's words were cut off in a choking sob as Actaeon applied pressure to the tray.

"Your terms are acceptable to me," said one of the raiders in the doorway. "You will commence work for the good of my city immediately. Your assistant and equipment will be brought to you."

The two cross-faced raiders marched out of the room, without addressing Markor's fate. Actaeon lifted the tray and smacked Markor across the face with it once more. "You heard the man, that will be the arrangement. And from here on in, you will call the Lady Lartigan by her name. Is that understood?"

When the man beneath him seemed about to argue, Actaeon lifted the tray again.

"Okay, okay, old boy. Lady Lartigan it is. And if you convinced the Veiled One of your bargain, it is him I serve, it is. I'll support what he says – he knows it."

Actaeon stepped away and tossed the tray aside. "Then by the Fallen, get Lady Lartigan some decent clothes, will you?"

Markor stood and brushed himself off before he spent an inordinate amount of time fluffing his hair and working to straighten it. The effort did not improve his appearance, but it seemed to make him feel better nonetheless. He sighed deeply and faced Actaeon. "You know not what you're dealing with here. Oh no, you don't!"

"Yes, the Veiled One. I am not deaf. And who, might I ask, is this Veiled One? Another deity to be blindly worshipped, like the Allfather or the Keeper of Light?"

"The city belongs to the Veiled One. You will see – yes, you will. It is his, it is! Nobody, not a one, will stop him from taking what is his," said Markor with a smirk, his eyes gleaming with madness.

"If you say so. Once you bring me my assistant, we will send out the Lady Lartigan with a list. I need that list of supplies in order to activate this device. I expect them to be brought promptly," ordered Actaeon, returning the man's smirk with a facetious grin of his own.

Markor scowled as he adjusted his leather jerkin and ran a hand through his hair again. "Fine, fine," he said at last before storming out. He slammed the door behind him and there was a click as the latch actuated.

Actaeon wasted no time in inspecting this room as well. The construction was identical to the first. A plan was forming in his mind, but he'd have to act very quickly – before the fog went away.

It wasn't long before they delivered Lauryn to the chamber. She ran forward and wrapped her arms around him. "Thank you for coming to get me. I knew you would."

"Of course, but listen to me now. We must concentrate very hard and remain focused if we wish to leave this place. Do you understand?"

"Yes, I do." She waited for him to explain, but when he didn't she followed his intentional gaze at Agarine and nodded in understanding. They didn't know what had happened to the Lady Lartigan in the hundred or so days she had been missing, and so it was best not to discuss things in front of her.

A drab grey dress and matching moccasins was brought for Lady Lartigan and she donned it without question. Along with her outfit, Actaeon's weapons were brought as well. He sheathed his knife, quivered his arrows and hung his bow from the back of his jacket. The halberd he leant upon one of the tables.

After that was done, he wasted little time in withdrawing his own vellum and charcoal stick. Upon it, he sketched the device from several different angles. In a separate area of the page, he sketched the symbols that were on the device and labeled them by color and status. He also labeled the symbols that he had seen before and their suspected meanings. Upon a separate area of the page, he made a short list. This he tore off and gave to the Lady Lartigan.

"Can you bring this to either Markor or the others?" he asked her.

"It will be done," she said, before turning to start off.

"Lady Lartigan, wait. What happened to you? Why have they brought you here?"

She did not hesitate in her reply. "The Veiled One has called me to his service. I serve him and through him, I serve the city."

Actaeon stared at her for a long moment, considering. "Lauryn and I are leaving this place soon. When we do, we can take you with us, back to your previous life in Niwian. Do you understand?"

She offered him a stiff smile and leaned in to kiss his cheek. "Yes. And thank you for that." That said, the Lady Agarine left with the list. She knocked upon the door to have them open it from without and when she slid the door shut, there was no click.

When the supplies came, Actaeon was hard at work with his assessment of the device. It was not a normal cylinder, but an elliptical one, with one end tapered more narrowly than the other. The material was warm and smooth to the touch and the symbols upon it illuminated from within the shell somehow. There were seventeen symbols in total, all in varying colors and three of them blinking in synchronization. Nine of them he recognized from his studies of the room above the Sea Lounge in Pyramid. Some of the others were familiar, but he could not be sure of their meaning. The symbols were arranged in concentric circles, with a single symbol in the center, six in the first ring and ten in the outermost ring.

He felt around the spherical ends. While one side was smooth – the narrower one, the other had a small seam that he could feel when he ran a fingernail over it; most likely, he thought, how they loaded the device with its contents.

Once he had added all the symbols to his sketch, he numbered them one through seventeen.

After the initial assessment was complete, he began to work his way through the symbols with Lauryn's help. Actaeon would touch a symbol, Lauryn would note the change, touch it again, she'd note the change, and so on. They continued with this until every symbol had been tested, and every outcome noted. Four more symbols appeared in a third ring at various stages during the process. All the while, Agarine stood in the corner quietly, her eyes traveling between the Engineer, his assistant, and the door.

"There are a few different ways that this device might be activated," postulated Actaeon. "We can press the buttons until one of several states is reached as I see it. Number one, we change them so that they are all unlit except for the center one. Number two, we make it so they are all lit, including the extra four symbols that we found. Number three, we cause them all to blink synchronously. I believe it is a puzzle with a certain code to activate it."

"There might be other possibilities," said Lauryn, uncertain.

"Indeed, there may. Those three are the most obvious though, and they are similar to other such artifact activation and deactivation processes that I have seen throughout Redemption to date," he said with a grin.

"Then... knowing what we know now, we can figure out a pattern of numbers to push so that we can achieve those three possibilities ...right?"

"Exactly, Lauryn. You have it. It may take some time. In the meantime, the gear that I requested will help us in a different way. Watch for me. We need to move quickly, before the fog dissipates. When the moment comes, I want you to help the Lady Lartigan – I suspect she might need you."

"Yes, Act. I can do that," she replied. Her gaze told him that she understood the seriousness of what was about to happen.

When Actaeon looked at Agarine, her eyes bored into his own. She said nothing.

"Lady Lartigan, we will get you out of here soon. Please, we will need your cooperation," he said.

"Yes, my cooperation. You will have it." She smiled at him. There was something strange behind that smile.

Markor slammed the door behind him when he returned, casting a glare at his Niwian slave. Two of the raiders entered behind him with bundles of supplies over their shoulders. They placed the supply bags down on one of the tables.

Lauryn helped Actaeon lay the supplies out on the table: a large chunk of soft clay, a bell, a length of glass rope, a roll of brightweave, several long lengths of wire and assorted chunks of metal from the ruins, about half the size of a man's fist.

"Whatever you're doing with that, old boy, you'd best make it quick – make it fast. The Veiled One loses his patience fast, he does. You won't like him much when he does, oh no, you won't." Markor brushed his long hair back as he regarded them.

"Let me guess, Markor, the Veiled One captured you first and you could not crack this riddle. What are you still doing here?" asked Actaeon.

"Well there's a question, there it is!" said the man. "Aye, you've got the right of it. Smart one ya are. Smart indeed. He got me and set me to the task. Was a Loresworn before that, was I. Doesn't make any sense though, that's why we found you, all those years ago, we did! A man that styled himself an Engineer, yes that was you. He insists you'll activate his device. He needs it to take back his city, for the city is his. You'll see."

"Just as you failed to unlock the secrets of this device, you have also failed to answer my question. What is it you are still doing here?" asked Actaeon with a cynical smirk.

"Let's just say we worked out an arrangement. Aye, it's great for me here. I get what I want and I step into civilization when he needs me to, because he cannot."

"Where is this Veiled One? I would like to speak with him directly."

"Why, don't you see? He's all around you, everywhere – in fact, he's been after you for years now!"

"If you say so. I would still wish to speak with him directly."

"Speak with him you can! Go ahead, he'll hear."

"If you say so. And what of Lady Lartigan, why did you kidnap her?"

"Ha! Kidnapped? Called into service the Lady was, if you can call her that. She was a dog – still is in a way. In fact, before the Veiled One –"

"Get to the point, Markor. As you said, the Veiled One is impatient."

"Right, right you are, old boy! Isn't it obvious? The Lady is Niwian, and related to Memory Keep."

Actaeon nodded, sudden understanding dawning on him. Hadn't Wave mentioned that she was cousin to the Lord Protector of Memory Keep? "I see now. Cousin to Lord Protector Fothrakas. I gather he was not so foolish as to accept your demands, like I was." He cast Lauryn a sidelong look and offered her a wink. She barely suppressed a smile at that.

"He was not, not like you. Good to your friends you are. It'll be your downfall – your death, even."

"Yeah, yeah. Do me a favor and get out of here. I cannot concentrate with your yammering. I shall send the Lady Lartigan again if I have further requirements."

Markor spat and left after knocking at the door, which he slammed shut roughly behind him.

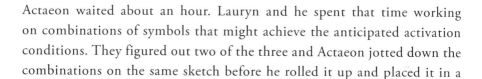

Actaeon waited about an hour. Lauryn and he spent that time working on combinations of symbols that might achieve the anticipated activation conditions. They figured out two of the three and Actaeon jotted down the combinations on the same sketch before he rolled it up and placed it in a pocket.

"It is time," he said, while Lauryn was still guessing at the third combination that would turn all of the symbols dark.

He stood and handed a folded piece of parchment to the Lady Lartigan. Upon it was written a second list of items. If he was correct, the items would be easier to find, but would give them half of an hour in which to work.

She obediently left with the list and Actaeon breathed a sigh of relief when, after she knocked, she failed to slide the door completely shut behind her. He quickly ran over to the door and placed one of the metal chunks in the small gap between the door and the pocket it fit into in case someone thought to push it all the way closed.

Actaeon molded the clay to shape while Lauryn tied the length of glass rope to the bell and laid it out in the room. He walked her through the full plan as they worked and she smiled broadly her approval.

When those two tasks had been completed, they both set about working with the brightweave. They unrolled the ancient artifact sheet and set it out upon the floor. At intervals along the perimeter, they bunched the fabric and wrapped lengths of the wire around it, then wrapping each wire around a metal chunk to provide for some weight.

For the rest, they waited for Agarine to arrive. When she did arrive, they led her to the end of the room farther from the door and had her sit. They covered her with the weighted brightweave material and left a flap open for them. The brightweave was an artifact of the Ancients, and it was invulnerable to puncture and penetration. A knight could use brightweave in place of plate armor and at only a fraction of the weight, but it would not protect against blunt force. Since it could not be pierced or cut with anything short of a writhe-blade, it was also nearly impossible to fashion into a useful set of armor.

All of the tables and chairs they laid on their sides and placed between the Niwian and the door.

While Lauryn worked to secure the rope to the outside door handle without attracting attention, Actaeon finished the final and most dangerous part of his plan. With his dagger, he pried open the endcaps of two of the grenados and carefully scooped the contents with his knife into a clay container he had fashioned. It smelled disgusting, but it was necessary. The last thing he did was place the two luminaries that had been inside the grenado housings into the new clay one. He sealed the new double grenado with a clay cap.

He walked slowly over to the door and after removing the metal chunk he had put there, he carefully and deliberately slid the deadly device into the slot that the door would recess into when fully shut. If he got it right, one of the luminaries would lie perpendicularly to the door inside the clay housing.

Once that was done, he pulled his goggles down over his eyes, grabbed his halberd and he and Lauryn both climbed over the tables. Actaeon handed them spare clay to stuff into their ears while they waited. They didn't need to wait long. A moment after they had settled in for the wait, they heard a bell ring as a glass rope was pulled across the floor.

Actaeon didn't spare a moment to look. He threw the brightweave over them and pushed both women to the floor.

The explosion itself, he didn't hear except with the absence of sound. The hemispherical room reflected all of the sound from the explosion and focused it right at the opposite end. There was a rush of air and heat that flowed under the edges of the brightweave and the tables slid against them violently, pinning them up against the wall. Debris pelted them from above.

In just a moment, it was over.

The Engineer threw back the brightweave barrier and kicked a table out of the way. Half the dome was gone. The door was there, lodged against the wall to the side; a bloody arm stuck out from underneath it.

He pulled a dazed Lauryn to her feet and pointed to Agarine's hand. He grinned at her through the smoke and haze in the air and she nodded, still dazed, but determined. He gave her his dagger.

They ran then, through the blasted open side of the dome, past what Actaeon guessed were the scattered remains of about four cross-faced raiders, give or take a raider.

He led the way past the edge of the encampment and down an embankment. Lauryn followed closely, dragging Agarine behind her with one hand, the dagger in the other.

Actaeon squatted then, and reached into an inside pocket of his jacket to withdraw his directional finder. He raised it before him and watched the needle lazily float to the right. Ears still ringing, he nudged Lauryn and started off once more, moving quickly.

The fog still hung heavy over the rubble as they ran, but he could make out silhouettes illuminated by the sun near the edge of the camp, pursuing.

The path he led was a winding one, though he kept them headed generally south. It would be obvious to head straight south, and they weren't going to make it so easy for the raiders to reacquire their prisoners.

As Actaeon's hearing gradually began to return with a ringing sound that pierced into his brain, he heard a collapse somewhere behind him and off to the east.

Suddenly one of the raider's faces was before him – thick black cross bisecting the face. His heart caught in his throat and he released Lauryn's hand to thrust his weapon forward impulsively. The blade wedged itself into the side of the man's face and jammed in the skull, which pulled

Actaeon down with him as the raider fell down an embankment. He threw his weight backward and slid painfully down on his backside. At the bottom, he placed his boot on one side of the bloody head and yanked his weapon free.

When he looked to his side, Lauryn was there, still guiding the Lady Lartigan and looking horrified. She reached out to brush his face and her hand came away with blood – not his own he hoped. Whatever she said next, he couldn't make out. He frowned and nodded forward for them to keep moving.

And so they went on, the ghosts of sounds around them, perhaps imagined, or perhaps real pursuit. One difficulty with losing their hearing was that they could not tell how much noise *they* were making either. Hopefully the raiders pursuing them had been similarly deafened by the blast.

When Actaeon thought to raise his directional finder again, he found that it was gone. A quick check of his pockets told him that he no longer had the device. Not good – he must've dropped it in the clash.

There was no choice but to continue along with all possible haste. And so they ran as fast as they could across the open terrain. Through gaps in the fog, he could make out the pursuers in the distance to either side as they fled, hopefully on a southward bearing. It did not look good at all.

But then ahead and off to one side was a sight that gave him hope. He dug into one of his pockets and withdrew several lengths of bandage. He shoved two into the hand of his assistant while he secured one over his own face, no explanation offered since none could be heard.

He led onward then, angling toward the green haze that emerged from the mist around them. The haze grew in size as they approached until they were within it. They would lose them in the Felmere.

Despite the makeshift kerchief, his nose stung when he breathed. He reached back to guide Lauryn forward. Without goggles her eyes were tearing and she was having trouble seeing her way.

Like a human snake of escaped prisoners, they wound a tortuous course through the wretched chemical bog as they sought to lose their pursuers. It was the Engineer's home advantage in this place, where he had spent so many days searching for the right chemicals for his various experiments. After what seemed like an hour of rushing around bubbling green pools, spitting red ones and staying clear of the densest concentrations of gas, Actaeon called a stop in a relative clearing so they could catch their breath and rest a moment.

"Show it to me," came a far off voice, through the ringing in his ears.

He looked up and to his dismay found that Agarine had taken the dagger from Lauryn and now held it to the young girl's throat. A trickle of blood worked its way down the Raedellean girl's neck from where the blade pressed.

"Darkest Hour take you, we helped you escape!" yelled Actaeon.

"There is much you do not understand, Actaeon Rellios of Shore. You will show it to me, now, or I will cut off your friend's head," said the woman, the words sounding outlandish on the tongue of the former Niwian noblewoman.

"Listen, Agarine... Lady Lartigan. This Veiled One, he has misled you. The same way he misled Markor, he has misled you. Just hear me –" he stopped as the blade was tightened against Lauryn's throat and more droplets of blood ran down to soak the neck of her tunic. The girl looked up at him with pleading eyes that were filled with tears.

"Okay, okay. Show what to you, show what?" asked Actaeon, desperation in his tone.

"You have deciphered the device. You will show me what you have found," said Agarine coldly.

Actaeon knew instantly that he would have sacrificed himself with no question rather then activate that Artifact for those ill-intentioned people, but this was different. Lauryn of Lakehold had nothing to do with this fight. She had made no such decisions to give her life to prevent such a thing. She was but a young woodcarver that he had dragged into this mess. It was not something he could live with, to make the decision to sacrifice her life to avoid whatever consequence the activation of that device would result in.

The Lady Lartigan's eyes bored into his own as he considered and more blood droplets fell down upon the young girl's tunic.

"Shattered Redemption," he said. "I will show it to you, but you will remove the dagger from her throat right now."

The Niwian's cold gaze didn't leave him, but the blade lowered until it was held aloft. "Bring it so that I can see it. Leave the weapon."

Actaeon set his halberd down, reached into his jacket and withdrew the roll of vellum, which he unrolled slowly in both hands as he approached. Once he was close enough, he unrolled the portion they had written the numbers down upon.

When he saw her eyes drop down to scan the numbers, he took action. With one hand he grabbed the knife arm. In the other, he had concealed his sharpened charcoal stick, which he promptly inserted into the woman's eye socket.

The fact that she didn't scream was wholly disconcerting. Instead she released Lauryn and grabbed Actaeon's wrist to prevent him from driving the stick farther into her eye. With her other hand, she fought against him in an effort to stab him with his own dagger. As he felt the cold tip of the blade slice through his jacket into his shoulder, he brought his knee up into her midsection, which allowed him to wrest the dagger from her hand. Despite this, Agarine seized his arm and began to drive the dagger back toward him.

The dagger was coming dangerously close to his neck when suddenly the woman staggered back and fell, landing face first into a reddish-brown pool of liquid. Steam came up along with the unpleasant smell of burning flesh. Behind where she had stood, Lauryn held the halberd aloft, its blade dripping with fresh blood.

The young girl stood for a long time looking at the crumpled form of the Lady Lartigan. When Actaeon touched her shoulder, she snapped out of it and they collected up the sketch of the device. He hastily bandaged her neck before they continued on.

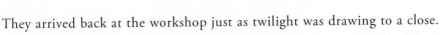

They arrived back at the workshop just as twilight was drawing to a close. They entered past Lauryn's fancy relief on the door just as Trench, Wave, Eisandre and Caider were preparing to set out.

As the four would-be rescuers stared at them, jaws agape, Actaeon grinned. "I am returned," he said. "Why such surprise? I told you I would be."

Eisandre marched up to Actaeon and tilted her head to the side as she looked into his eyes. She seemed to have some internal struggle for a short while, but she shrugged it off and wrapped her arms around the man, pulling him against her fiercely. He returned the hug with a smile.

Trench and Wave shared a knowing look.

"By the Fallen, Act! We've been prepping to mount an expedition here. What happened?" said Caider, shaking his head in disbelief.

"Well, I set out to rescue Lauryn, but it turned out that she rescued me in the end," said Actaeon, causing the young girl to blush and look at the floor. He told them the whole story then. He left the details of the escape out, so that Caider would not learn of the grenados.

When the Engineer reached the part about Agarine, Wave looked positively horrified. When he learned of her death, he let out a low wail and covered his remaining eye with one hand.

"What... what in shattered Redemption happened to her?" asked Wave, his voice shaky.

"It is hard to tell for sure, but it seemed like all of them had been brainwashed by this Veiled One. They all certainly displayed some unusual behavior," said Actaeon.

"I dunno, Act, I think they all *were* the Veiled One," said Lauryn.

"How could that be?" asked Caider.

"I'm... not sure. It just seemed like that," said the Raedellean woodworker.

"Very interesting hypothesis, Lauryn. Yes, I see how you might have drawn that conclusion. We shall have to consider it further," said the Engineer. "In either case, they did not get the end goal that they set out to achieve through my imprisonment. That much is good, for we have no idea what that artifact could do."

"Meaning that you will have to tread with even greater care," said Eisandre, pointedly.

"Aye, the lass's right, Act. They'll be after you to finish the job now," said Trench.

"We have to let the Lord Protector know that his cousin is dead," said Wave.

"No."

"Not a good idea."

Trench and Caider had spoken at once.

"And why in cracked Redemption not?" demanded Wave.

Trench gestured for the Companion to explain.

"Act said that they kidnapped Agarine to lure Garizo there. He knew she was there already – I guarantee it. If he finds out that Act and Lauryn killed her, then he might seek retaliation," explained Caider.

Trench nodded his agreement. "Aye, and the Keepers are buddies with the Niwians now. They're not necessarily our friends. Especially after what happened in this workshop."

Actaeon shook his head. "I hear your arguments, gentlemen, but it is the right thing to do. If we seek to cover this up, then we are in the wrong. In that case, retaliation would be most understandable. However, if we tell the truth, we give the Lord Protector a choice whether to believe us or not. Let us hope he makes the right one."

"I must agree with Actaeon on this," said Eisandre with a firm nod.

"We'll go with you then, boss. We're not leaving you out to dry," said Wave with a weak grin.

"I am afraid not. This I shall handle on my own. No need to drag more of us into it than strictly required," Actaeon said.

"But I should go with you too!" said Lauryn.

"It is illogical for both of us to subject ourselves to the possibility of Garizo's wrath. I will go on my own to speak with him of the death of his cousin. After all, that is why they pay me with heavier bits," said Actaeon with a grin.

Trench chuckled at that, though Caider and Wave each gave him a peeved look.

Lauryn seemed a bit relieved and simply nodded, not eager to argue the point after what she had just been through.

But when the Engineer arrived at the Niwian Hold, he was unable to speak with the Lord Protector. Garizo was unavailable – dead at the hand of an unknown assassin.

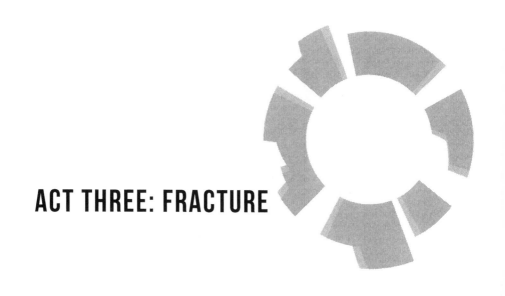

ACT THREE: FRACTURE

87 A.R., the 6ᵗʰ day of Rainbreak

TRAPPED

JINGLING ARTIFACTS ANNOUNCED THE ARRIVAL of old Sol at the workshop. The ancient figure tugged at his long beard with one hand while he pointed at the Engineer with the crystal shard at the tip of his walking stick.

"You, young man," he shouted as he thrust the staff toward Actaeon from across the workshop floor with each syllable. "We must conduct lengthy palaver now. Free yourself, and we shall do this."

Actaeon glanced up at the man and arched a brow. He set down one of the flasks he had been holding. Trench and Wave were off in the Hives helping Lauryn set up the transport vehicle to begin the long trip for Mae's statue of Indros.

"You are not going to try and drown me again, are you?" asked the Engineer with all seriousness.

"Nonsense, young man. You have already proven yourself equal to *that* task. Why should I subject you to more of the same?" asked old Sol as he sauntered farther into the workshop. He turned to examine the slug costume on the wall more closely.

"Will you bring fire then? Or gale-force winds? Perhaps bury me under layers of earth?" asked Actaeon with a grin.

"Talk, just talk," said Sollemnis the Gray. He tugged at his beard again and took a seat at one of the workbenches. When he set his walking stick on the table, Actaeon thought he saw the green crystal shard at the tip flash briefly.

"Well, you have impeccable timing. If my men-at-arms had been present, I am not sure they would have been quite as civil as I am," said Actaeon truthfully. "Something tells me you knew that already though... somehow." He sighed and joined the Loresworn at the workbench.

The old man looked across the table's surface at him with tired gray eyes. "I knew that you'd succeed in the task. Never a doubt, had I."

"Good thing you tested me in any case then, since you had no doubt. An excellent use of your time," said Actaeon.

"A young man is too smart for his own good. I like it," said old Sol. He pulled open one of the big pockets stitched into the outside of his big red robes and spoke into it. "Kryo, we are ready. Please do join us."

A small silver orb with a ring of illuminated blue dots around the horizontal circumference lifted from the pocket and floated around Actaeon's head, slowly, as though observing him. After it was satisfied, it floated to a clear area nearby and hovered there.

The Engineer watched it with curiosity, though he didn't completely take his gaze off of Sollemnis the Gray either. While he watched it, something in the bottom of the sphere opened and a dull blue light projected downward from it. Within the blue light, a figure flickered into existence. It was defocused and blurry at first, but, as it sharpened, so did all of the full details of a man.

The man was extremely short, though Actaeon wondered if it was a product of the projection or if it was his accurate height. The man wore a frame upon his face that held lenses in front of his eyes, and his head was shaved to a bald pate. He wore a full brightweave outfit, shimmering black cloth with silver edging. On his feet were shoes that were artifacts themselves, made from a similar metallic silver material as the orb that floated above his head.

"Actaeon Rellios of Shore," said the man. "Master Engineer... Toppler of Towers, Slayer of Slugs, Pyramid Problem Solver, Founder of Cults, Proliferator of –"

"Alright, enough of that," said the Engineer with a grin. He gestured to Sollemnis. "Interestingly enough, he does not require an orb to present an illusion of himself."

Old Sol laughed and said, "He refuses to use the transphasic technology."

The short man sighed and joined them at the workbench. The floating orb moved to accommodate his new location. He crossed his arms over his chest and spoke, "My name is Kryo, I am the leader of the Loresworn. We have been watching you for some time, Actaeon. Your skills would be of great use to us."

"Why am I not surprised," said Actaeon. "My answer is, of course, no. I will maintain my independence in all of my efforts."

Kryo frowned and glanced back at Sollemnis, as if silently asking for help. Sollemnis merely shrugged. "Look, I'll put it bluntly," he continued. "Travail has fallen, as you have undoubtedly heard. The Order has fractured. Many were lost during the fall. Some have defected to the Niwians. Others have set out on their own as artifact hunters. We stand at the brink of ruin, and we could use your help."

"I see," said the Engineer. "What is it that you require my help with?"

"We wish for you to join us. Your ingenuity and skill in your craft have been proven. As a member of the Loresworn, you can help us to reclaim Travail, and you can share in the knowledge that we have gained in almost a century of work by the brightest scholars our people have known," said Kryo. He spread his hands.

"I have wholehearted opposition to your wish," admitted Actaeon. "I am not sure what your motives are in approaching me in this manner. Surely, there are many others who can aid you with your troubles. Until the Loresworn is an organization that helps instead of hoards, I would never join it. Have you considered drafting an agreement with the other neutral entities of Redemption? Working with the Arbiters? Or the Altheans? Have they not a similar principle of cooperation? Contemplate the possibility – it would provide for allies that the Loresworn might have use for lacking your stronghold, and it would allow you to share the benefits of some of your technology with those that would see civilization in Redemption protected at all costs. What, may I ask, happened to Travail?"

Sollemnis and Kryo turned to face one another and seemed to come to a silent consensus before Kryo turned back to Actaeon and adjusted the lenses perched upon his nose.

"As well all know," he began, "we arrived in this city over eighty years ago when portals opened and spilled forth the Wardens and Prisoners that were our predecessors. There are few who know exactly where those portals opened: Stormstair in the north, Temple, in the Pools of Light, outside

Memory Keep, among others. Travail itself was the location of one of the great portals.

"Travail was a place of great wonders even then, and many were curious about the artifacts that were left behind. There was a problem though: many of the Prisoners from that portal fled and traveled southeast along the River of Arches. There was a great debate that night about whether to stay in the stronghold or pursue those that escaped. After all, none of the Wardens knew why they were guarding those prisoners, just that they had done something wrong. Many opted to stay, their curiosity outweighing any sense of duty they had to a life they couldn't remember.

"Eleven Wardens though, elected to pursue those Prisoners, and the next morning they left to follow them along the river. Raedelle herself was among them – the founder of your Dominion. With her were the three brothers Arandel, and Mael – who was later thrown to his death. So you see, it was in Travail that your ancestors first arrived in this land. It was home to a portal. What we didn't realize, was that it made us vulnerable as well. It opened up a weak spot in the fabric of reality, and only recently an experiment that was run caused that weak spot to tear open. Perhaps you will go and see for yourself one day, it may change your mind. As you say: contemplate the possibility. We shall do the same with your suggestion. Until then, good luck to you, Engineer Actaeon Rellios."

In the blink of an eye, Kryo was gone. The orb floated back to Sol and he opened his pocket for it to fly back inside. He stroked his beard and used his walking stick to lever himself to his feet. He then smiled at Actaeon and started out. He paused at the door, as if he had forgotten something and he smiled again, turning to face the Engineer.

"The key to Travail is a heart's blind trust," he said, and not a moment later he was gone.

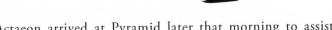

When Actaeon arrived at Pyramid later that morning to assist with the transport device, Eisandre found him first. She waved and approached him. "Good morning, Act."

"Good morning, Eis!" replied the Engineer. He stopped to allow her to catch up to him. "I was just heading to the Hives to assist with the transport of Lady Bazardjan's statue. You are welcome to join me if you wish."

"I understand. I was just looking for you after I spoke with my sister. She'd like to speak with you about some of your proposals. I believe she's reconsidered them. She's leaving this afternoon though, for Raedelle. You may wish to speak with her about it. I can join you if you like – I know her well," suggested the Knight Arbiter.

Actaeon grinned in amusement. "Everyone is more interested in a tried design, of course. Yes, let us speak with her. I would still wish to serve my Dominion in some capacity, if possible. Though, I admit I have been enjoying the freedom that comes with the pursuit of my work as I see fit. It carries many clear advantages."

"Yes, but this is something you could do again if you chose to, no? Eshelle might not always be willing to give you the opportunity to serve Raedelle directly," said Eisandre.

"Agreed. Let us meet her then. And I would much enjoy your company," said Actaeon with a bright smile that brought a tiny one from her in turn.

She made no move to take his hand and so he abstained from taking hers as well. This was her domain, after all, and he had no desire to place her in an awkward situation. Instead they walked side by side, through the Way of Pillars and into the eastern tunnels which they ascended to the Mirrorholds and finally to Saint Torin's Hold.

A man that stood inside the Hold with rough cut auburn hair and a lopsided smile spotted Eisandre and ran up to give her a hug. "Sandre!"

The Knight Arbiter stood still and tolerated his hug stiffly before she replied, "Wayd Arbrigel."

"Yes, and you look fantastic, Eisandre. But why the short hair? Are you going grow it out again? I think it looked nicer long," said the man named Wayd Arbrigel.

"No, I don't know if I'm going to let my hair grow out again. Even if you think it looked better long," she added, politely but firm.

"I see," said Wayd, his eyes shifting to Actaeon. "And who is this? I don't believe we've met."

"I am Actaeon Rellios of Shore. And you are Wayd of Arbrigel, I presume?" said the Engineer with a grin.

"Wayd Arbrigel, actually. Arbrigel's my family name. I'm with the Warbands – a specialist. I'm a Goader," said the man, looking quite proud of himself.

The Goaders were the trainers of Raedelle's lion lizards, creatures used in battle that were incredibly difficult to train. Only the Goaders of Raedelle knew the secret, which was closely guarded by the Dominion. The lion lizards themselves were rarely seen in battle, and not oft by other Dominions. They were a secret weapon of sorts and the old legends and silent threat of them was more likely to be seen on a battlefield than the actual creatures.

"Pleasantly met, Wayd," said Actaeon with a polite nod.

"Actaeon Rellios, eh? I've heard of you. You're that Engineer from Shore, right? Rumor has it you knocked the towers down," said Wayd, looking impressed.

"Rumors are full of strange things, are they not?" asked Actaeon.

The man responded with a confused look and Eisandre interjected, "I'm here to see Eshelle if that's alright?"

"Oh... oh! Of course, Sandre. Don't let me keep you! It was nice to see you. I'll speak with you again soon," said the man and they passed him by to proceed farther into the Hold. There they found her sister, seated at one of the long tables while she examined several sheafs of parchment before her. She looked positively bored.

"Ah, Sandre! And you brought Actaeon. Excellent!" she said as she stood. She looked glad to postpone her paperwork for the time being. "I was hoping to speak with you about the proposals you had suggested –"

At that moment there was a commotion and a Raedellean man stumbled into the Hold. Many there recognized him as Itarik, with his closely cropped white hair and serious demeanor – one of the Companions known to be closer to Aedwyn Caliburn. He hadn't been seen about the Pyramid since the Prince himself had gone on his hiatus after the injury.

Sweat poured down the Companion's face and had soaked well through his undertunic to his tabard. He stepped past those in the entrance and walked heavily toward the rear of the Hold. Those present grew silent as they watched the weary Companion make his way toward the Prince's sister.

"Lady Eshelle... I come bearing news of dire importance from the Wall," Itarik said. He nearly collapsed from exhaustion as he came to a halt before Raedelle's acting leader, but he managed to steady himself on a nearby chair, his gaze directed at the floor.

"Is it about the Prince?" asked Eisandre in a hard tone. She stood paralyzed before the Companion, her fists clenched and her posture tense. Beside her, Eshelle had turned white and nodded toward her sister as if to second the question.

Itarik glanced toward Eisandre and nodded gravely. "Yes... yes, the Prince." Two Companions rushed to steady him and he pushed their hands away gently, summoning some reserve of energy to straighten and regain his composure. "There is no time," he said. "We made it here as quickly as we could. He is trapped, we need to set out immediately to rescue him." He turned to the Lady Eshelle and grimaced. "We were headed back here to deal with some of the more recent... complications. The Prince insisted on stopping to investigate. Please forgive me, Lady Eshelle, I should have tried harder to deter him. The artifact... it has seized him."

Eisandre struggled to breath and stay calm as the Companion's report threatened to tear away a part of her life which she held so dear. "What do you mean seized?" she asked, well out of her realm, though that fact was the furthest from her mind with her beloved brother in danger.

"What artifact?" asked the Engineer with interest. He leaned forward on his halberd to listen intently to the man's words.

People in the Hold began to gather more closely about the Companion and the others now, interested in what they had to say. There was a low murmur from the gathering that grew in anxiety as the talk proceeded. Several Raedelleans listened for a moment before they departed quickly for the Hold exit.

"Well, Gorgrian and the others went to the Outskirts to get Rellios of Shore. They suggested that he might know how to break him free of the artifact's hold. As soon as they arrive with him we should depart," explained Itarik. He turned to Actaeon without recognition to answer his question. "It is the pillar on the way along back home. We have passed it many times, but this time it *glowed*. Aedwyn insisted on stopping to investigate it and whatever he did... well, he is stuck now. There is a wall that we cannot see. He is trapped within. Forgive me."

At once, a darkness was lifted from Eisandre's mind to be replaced by hope. "He is alive then. We can leave immediately – this is Master Rellios of Shore." She turned to Eshelle then. "He will most likely be able to assist. I will send word to Arbiter Command that I will be joining you."

Eshelle's thoughts were elsewhere though and she addressed the Companion, "What of Caliburn?"

"Aedwyn seems unharmed," explained Itarik, looking upset with himself. "He had fallen unconscious immediately, but now he is up and about. We just cannot... get to him." He glanced at Actaeon and frowned. "You say this is Rellios? Then we should depart immediately, Lady Eshelle. There is no time to waste."

"Not my brother, you idiot. I meant the sword. Our Uncle has been out here playing politics and making alliances, and this is all too convenient to have happen now. The sword, Caliburn. The bearer might seek some claim to lead Raedelle with that blade. Is it still with him? Who has it?" Eshelle's tone carried a sense of desperation with it. She grabbed the Companion's shoulders and shook him.

Itarik blinked and wiped the sweat from his eyes. "The sword is with Aedwyn. There are rations in his pack that should tide him over until our return. If what you say is true, then we must go immediately. I came straight here with my men, but I cannot account for Gorgrian and his party that split from us to seek out the Engineer."

"Companions! Prep for travel, we leave immediately," commanded Eshelle. "Wayd, assemble the warbanders and any other able bodies in the Hold. I want everyone armed and ready for battle if needed." She turned to Itarik. "I hope you are able to lead us back to this pillar."

"Of course I can, my lady. Let us go to rescue the Prince," said the Companion with determination in his voice despite his profound exhaustion from his non-stop journey to the Hold.

Eisandre took one of the sheets of paper that Eshelle had been reviewing. She tore off a section and jotted a quick note with a nearby quill. This she handed to a young girl. "Here, young lady. Bring this to Arbiter Command for me."

After a glance at Actaeon, which he met with a confident nod, the Knight Arbiter fell into step with the people of her homeland, prepared to do whatever it might take to save her beloved brother.

87 A.R., the 8th day of Rainbreak

RESCUE

AFTER A LONG TWO DAYS of hard travel over rough and treacherous terrain, the rescue party arrived at the Wall and came into sight of the pillar that Itarik had spoken of. The tireless Companion still led the way.

A half dozen or so other Companions travelled along with the party, as did a dozen warbanders and other able-bodied fighters that Wayd had managed to round up. Eshelle and Eisandre walked just behind Itarik. Actaeon trailed a bit behind and off to the side, traversing the overgrown ruins of the Wall nimbly with the aid of his halberd. As they marched, the warbanders took up position under the guidance of the Companions to defend their flanks.

Itarik halted and gestured up toward the pillar. It was tall – ten times the height of a man, and nondescript. The top of the pillar did, in fact, glow and it was very close to them, though the rest of it was hidden behind nearby ruins and rubble piles.

"We are very close," said Itarik, unnecessarily, before he continued to trudge along.

"The peak of the pillar might indeed be what forms the walls that Itarik described. I wonder if there might be a way to reach the top." Actaeon spoke mostly to himself and didn't expect an answer, especially without the presence of his two wise-cracking mercenary friends.

"We shall see," was Eisandre's simple response as they started moving again.

As the party rounded the last ruin, they came into full sight of the artifact and its surrounds. The pillar towered like a glowing giant above the figure of Prince Aedwyn, who stood in a clear area beneath the pillar with his greatsword, the Caliburn, drawn. To his side was the only other object in the clearing aside from the pillar's base – a podium of some sort, with flashing lights of different colors upon it.

Aedwyn appeared to be yelling at his remaining men from where he stood, though the sound of his voice could not be heard. The men stood in a cluster some twenty yards distant, as though some barrier stood between them and the Prince. There were over thirty of them, as would befit a Princely escort. But they were not Aedwyn's escort. No, they were men from Shore led there by the Lord Gunther Arcady, who stood with them and shook his head at the Prince. Aedwyn's original escort was nowhere to be seen.

Itarik drew his sword from its scabbard, his eyes narrowing upon Arcady. "What is the meaning of this?!"

As the rescuers drew nearer to Arcady's group, they made out about a half dozen Companions amongst his men as well, including Gorgrian, who had supposedly gone to retrieve the Engineer from the Outskirts.

Instead of drawing her sword, Eshelle drew her bow and put an arrow to the string. She seemed wholly unsurprised by Arcady's presence there. "Uncle, how am I not surprised that you have a hand in this? Care to explain this to me in a manner which won't cause me to put this arrow here through your throat?"

Two of Arcady's men reacted quickly, moving before him. They raised their shields to protect him from the arrow.

The Engineer was much less interested in the confrontation than he was the artifact. He approached the pillar's clearing with a hand out before him until he felt an invisible surface. "Fascinating," he said. "It is angled." He leaned forward, closing one eye and looked along the plane of his hand toward the top of the pillar. "As I suspected, it is inline with the angled cut atop the pillar." That determined, he waved at Aedwyn to try and get the Prince's attention.

Behind the shields, the Lord Shore spread his hands in question. His hazel eyes burned into Eshelle's from across the distance between their two forces. "Well now, that wouldn't be a very kind thing to do to family, would it?" He gestured to Gorgrian and said, "The Companion Gorgrian was wise enough to alert me to this predicament. The Prince was not travelling with adequate escort and they were chased away by bandits. Luckily, we arrived hastily to remedy the situation. Now, I suggest you put that away, young man," he said with a glare at Itarik, "before you cut someone." Indeed, some of the men in Arcady's company were bruised and spattered with the blood of battle.

Aedwyn's sharp eyes picked out Lady Eshelle's party and he moved swiftly over to where Actaeon stood beside the invisible wall. He spoke then, his gaze directed at his sisters, but although his lips moved, his words remained unheard.

"You will stand down immediately, or you'll regret it," shouted Eshelle across the field. She failed to notice as her brother approached Actaeon.

Eisandre, on the other hand, didn't. She cast a pained look in the direction of her sister and uncle before she joined Actaeon beside her brother. "Aedwyn... we're here now," she said to reassure him, her voice was a whisper beneath the shouts.

"Please, dear niece... tell your men, and indeed, your own self to stand down," came Arcady's reply. "None of the men with me have drawn their swords, you'll notice. And I am hesitant to ask these two men to lower their shields lest you make me more prickly than I already am," he said with a laugh that several of his men joined in. He gestured to Actaeon then. "I see you have brought my insightful Engineer. I would suggest you have him see about your unfortunate brother. We will do naught but guard this clearing. There is enough unrest in Redemption without placing our dear Prince's life at risk with your petty squabbles, my dear. Please do free him and tell him this time if you please... to manage the realm!" His voice was a snarl at those last words. He motioned for his men to retreat back to a safe distance to allow Eshelle's rescue party to do what they might.

With a gesture from Eshelle, the Companions and warbanders arrayed in a defensive semicircle around the royal sisters and the Engineer.

Actaeon withdrew a used piece of parchment from his jacket, which he wrote upon with his charcoal stick. When he finished writing, he pressed the paper against the barrier so that Aedwyn could read it:

Draw for me in the dirt what is on the podium. Show me what you touched.

He turned as Eshelle came to join them. "It is a barrier made somehow by the pillar, inline with the top chamfer. It would appear to be Pyramidal in shape. Wayd, if you would please confirm that by tracing a path around this barrier."

Wayd nodded and broke from his position in the defensive circle. He placed a hand upon the invisible wall and began to jog the perimeter.

Actaeon continued then. "I believe that if Prince Aedwyn touched that podium, he unknowingly activated his prison. I see no other controls or connected artifacts in the vicinity. I wonder what the purpose of such a device would be. Why would one imprison themself?"

Beside him, Eisandre stood, as though paralyzed, while she stared at her brother.

About twenty paces distant, Wayd made a turn and began to follow another side.

"By the Fallen, who gives a damn about that? Just get my brother out of there," demanded Eshelle.

Aedwyn had to crouch down to get close to his sisters under the invisible angle of the barrier. He smiled and said something to them as his eyes flicked from Eisandre to Eshelle, offering them warm and reassuring looks. His gaze then locked with Eisandre and he placed his hand against the barrier before her, his lips moving briefly in unheard words. She crouched down beside him, a mirror image of her brother, both with blond hair and blue eyes, only she smaller and female. He stared at his baby sister for a long moment before he set to drawing in the dirt before him, using the tip of his dagger.

The Prince drew a collection of shapes that contained symbols within. He then drew an arrow toward one and pointed at it before looking at Actaeon and nodding.

"That is it then," said the Engineer. "The one he pressed first." He scribbled upon his parchment again and pressed it against the barrier: *Press it again? Undo what you did.*

"Surely he tried that," said Eshelle angrily. "He hasn't been just standing around for days now and didn't try that!" She cast another angry look at her brother, unable to hide her disdain.

Aedwyn touched the barrier near Eshelle and offered her a regretful look. He then wrote his response in the dirt: *Cannot press it now. Frozen.*

Actaeon put the parchment aside and sketched the podium in the dirt on his own side of the barrier. He pointed to a tiny symbol roughly in the center, inside of a square with rounded corners. "Try this... then try the first one you touched," he said, as he slowly pointed to indicate what he meant.

The Prince nodded and pressed each one of his hands against the barrier opposite his sisters. He offered them a reassuring smile before locking eyes with Actaeon, as if to say, 'This had better work.' He stood then and trudged off toward the podium. Once there, he pressed the first button and looked back at the others. He gave an affirming nod – the original button had unfrozen.

Eshelle scowled and moved to join the others in the defensive line. Wayd joined her, having completed his rounding of the pyramidal barrier, which did, in fact, have a square footprint.

Arcady watched and smiled as Eshelle assembled the Companions on her side before he returned his gaze to Aedwyn to watch him push the buttons. Though he and his men were relaxed, the two shieldmen before him appeared nervous, as though they expected Eshelle to attack at any moment.

Actaeon stood and touched Eisandre's shoulder. "We should not be next to the barrier when it is deactivated, love," he said quietly.

Without letting her gaze leave her brother, the Knight Arbiter stood and took a reluctant step back, Actaeon's logic cutting through her fog.

Aedwyn pushed the second button and was thrown back and away from the podium. The big pillar began to flash rapidly. The Prince cursed in the silence of his encasement before he picked himself up and began to run back toward his sisters.

Eisandre pulled away from Actaeon and reached out toward her brother, touching her hand to the barrier. She cried out in surprise at the unexpected pain that lanced through her arm. "Aedwyn!" she cried out, fear in her eyes.

Eshelle spun at her sister's cry and ran forward to pound upon the barrier. She cursed at the pain that shot up her arms.

Aedwyn reached the barrier edge and knelt beside his drawing. His face and hands disappeared and reappeared in sequence with the flash of the pillar behind him which gave him a terrifying, spectre-like appearance. The inside of his clothing could be seen as his body flashed in and out of the visible in sequence with the pillar. He cast a regretful look to the others before he wiped away the arrow he had drawn. In its place he drew a new arrow to a different symbol. The resulting arrow came into being in dashed lines as the Prince phased in and out with the flash of the pillar while he drew. When he opened his mouth this time, his voice could be heard between the flashes, "...embered... ...ong... ...ymbol..."

"Fascinating," muttered Actaeon. "We have to stop this thing." He unshouldered his recurve and strung it.

Eshelle beat him to it though. She put an arrow to the string, aimed, and let it fly toward the pillar. She cursed as her arrow fell to the ground well before the pillar, cut in half.

"Aedwyn!" called Eisandre again. She touched the barrier again and again, ignoring the jolts of energy up her arm that kept pushing her back. She tried desperately to get through the impossible barrier to reach her flickering brother.

"Wayd! Get Eis away from the barrier!" cried Actaeon as he drew an arrow from his quiver and put it to the string. "The rate of flashing slows. It will be worse," he called out enigmatically as he drew back upon the string and waited.

Wayd grabbed the Knight Arbiter around her waist to pull her away from the barrier. Eisandre twisted, evading the warbander whom she knocked back with a well placed kick. She scrambled to make the barrier again but was stopped by her sister, who wrapped her arms around her tightly and pulled her to the ground.

She stopped as Aedwyn held up a flickering hand. He locked eyes with Eisandre, calm and collected, despite everything. He gave her a look that he'd given her many times – a look to still her Lost mind and give her clarity. Only once he saw that clarity did he speak, and the flashing was indeed slowing. "My sist... ...st listen." That said, he waited for their attention.

"We hear you, brother!" called Eshelle.

The Prince nodded and spoke, trying to time his words with the flashes as he moved in and out of existence, "...andre, bring them... ....together. Esh... ...ive them order." He looked from one to the other as he spoke, "Work togeth... ...omise me. ...re Raedelle's... ...ope."

At that moment, in time with the last word of Raedelle's courageous Prince, the Engineer let loose his arrow. Surprisingly, it buried itself deep into the material at the top of the pillar. Actaeon grinned at that, and was promptly hit by a concussive wave of energy that reversed the path of his arrow's arc back toward him. He flew into the air, his recurve spinning wildly out of his hand, before he landed a distance away, in a puddle of mud.

The flashing of the pillar faltered for a moment, but then continued, along with the flicker of Prince Aedwyn.

As focused as Eisandre was on her brother, the sight of Actaeon sent flying made her tense in her sister's arms. "Act!" she cried. But Aedwyn was still there, awaiting their promise and she had to answer him. "I will support Eshelle and Raedelle however I can, Aedwyn. You know I will," she promised with all the sincerity of her heart. "Please don't leave. We need you. I need you," she begged him.

"We will hold Raedelle, Aedwyn. Don't you doubt that for one moment!" said Eshelle.

"Thank you... ...oth," said the Prince. He smiled at Eisandre and said, "...ember words... ...n the swor... ...faith in yo..." With those words spoken, he stood and brushed himself off before he turned away to approach the pillar, which was flashing slower now. He made it halfway there before his clothes fell to the ground along with the legendary sword Caliburn in its scabbard. The pillar changed back to a solid glow.

The Prince of Raedelle had ceased to be.

Eisandre let out a strangled sound of anguish that echoed across the surrounding ruins. "No... no... no no no no no," she kept repeating it, over and over, her face twisted in grief. "No," her strength failed her and she fell forward, head against the dirt. "No..."

Arcady gestured to a few men and pointed to where the Engineer had landed nearby. "Go get Rellios, we'll see that he gets proper treatment and makes it back to his workshop safely," he ordered. Several men moved to follow the Lord Shore's instructions.

The others failed to notice, too distracted by the disappearance of their beloved leader. They all turned to face the artifact. Many of them had fallen to their knees, tears upon their faces. Itarik walked forward until he stood by the now steady, invisible barrier and fell to his knees. He lowered his head into his hands. "My fault... my fault."

Eshelle's face was red with anger as she shouted at the pillar, "You bastard! You leave me with this? Come back here, damn you!" She struggled to pull Eisandre to her feet, but to no avail.

Beside her, Wayd sobbed openly – the Prince had been his childhood friend.

Rough hands pulled the Engineer to his feet and collected his scattered gear before loading him into a litter and carrying him off along with Arcady's party as they withdrew.

"Raedelle will not fall to pieces in this time of uncertainty – of that I can assure you all," said Arcady to his men with confidence. "Let us depart for Raedelle, to shore up and ascertain the state of our Dominion."

Notably, half of the warriors and even three of the Companions from the rescue party joined the Lord Shore's departing group.

With a visible struggle, Eshelle released Eisandre and pulled herself together. "We cannot allow him to seek a claim to Raedelle. I must go to Lakehold to reach the Conclave first. He will return to try to claim the sword. Itarik, you have failed Aedwyn, and so you must guard Caliburn now. It is your duty. If the pillar unlocks it, bring the sword to me. Understood?"

Itarik straightened and saluted her. "I will do as you say, Lady Eshelle." He sheathed his sword and set himself to guard the artifact, his back to the barrier.

Those few who remained fractured into three groups: Two of the best warbanders joined Itarik at his post. The remaining three Companions and three more warriors joined Eshelle as she started south. And the two remaining warbanders joined Wayd as he escorted the devastated Knight Arbiter back to Pyramid.

Thus they dispersed, all save the dutiful Itarik and two others, left to watch the sword and reflect on the loss of their Prince.

Some distance away from the pillar, Arcady motioned for the vanguard to continue on its way while he drew his Warchief Beiloff off to the side of the trail that wound through the ruins of the Wall. As the litter with the unconscious Engineer made its way past, the Lord Shore glanced down and let out a chuckle. He looked back to the Warchief with his burning eyes and smiled.

"Strange how things turn about, m'lord," said Beiloff with his own smile, his eyes glittering with humor.

"Strange indeed, Warchief Beiloff. However, I am sure you will agree that we must put these events behind us now and work toward the best interests of Raedelle. My niece will run back to Lakehold and attempt to garnish support there. In the meantime, I want you to take half of this party and return to Blackstone Fortress. You are to rally the Warbands, then wait to move into Lakehold upon my order, and only my order. We will not start a civil war in Raedelle, understood?"

The Warchief nodded. "Understood, aye m'lord. I will wait upon your order."

"Excellent. You will be the lead Warchief now, Drystan. Do not make me regret this decision. This must be a political maneuver," continued the Lord Shore. "We must wrest control of the Dominion from these destructive Caliburns before they destroy us all with their neglect. Take the Engineer as well," he said with a smirk as he gestured to the litter. "Try to convince him, nicely, at first, to join our cause. We need him to unlock the pillar artifact so that we can get to the sword. It will help our claim. If you cannot convince him, then I am sure you will find other means to... coerce him."

Drystan's face lit up at that prospect and he smiled, thoughts already running through his mind about what techniques he would utilize. "Yes, m'lord. It will be done. And if my position is attacked?"

"If you are attacked, then defend, of course. If things go well, then you will be my General of Raedelle. Get the troops mobilized and wait for instruction from me. I will speak to my insiders in Lakehold and see what support we can muster." He gestured toward the line of troops again. "And when you convince Master Rellios to help our cause, take a troop back to the pillar and set him to work. Is this all understood?"

"Oh, not a problem. It'll be my pleasure, m'lord," said Drystan with a satisfied nod as he looked down the trail to the litter that was carried along.

Arcady noted the man's smirk. "Remember, we'd benefit more from having him on our side. He'd best be able to complete the task when you're finished with him. Not to worry, you will have time to exercise your heart's desire in the days to come, but right now keep your eyes on the prize, Warchief Beiloff. That is all for now. You're dismissed. Make all haste in the matters at hand."

Drystan saluted and ran to the front of the column to direct the men. Arcady jogged to catch up and issued his own commands which caused the group to split into two distinct units.

And so, both units set out. One for Blackstone Fortress under the command of Warchief Drystan Beiloff, to rally the warbands and coerce the Engineer. The other under command of the Lord Shore himself, to further their end goal elsewhere to the south. Thus set into motion events that would forever change the course of Raedellean history.

RECOVERY

TRENCH AND WAVE FOLLOWED WAYD Arbrigel out into the ruins. They took their usual positions far out on the Goader's flanks as they travelled. Both were bedecked in their heaviest battle dress – Trench in his sound-dampened chain and Wave in his finest boiled leather armor. Wave had his heavy crossbow out and loaded with a bolt. They moved through the debris with practiced ease as they approached the rundown house.

When Wayd knocked upon the door, it was unbarred from the inside and swung open. Wayd led the two mercenaries inside and the door was barred behind them by one warbander while another stood watch outside.

In the far corner of the single room within, the Knight Arbiter looked as if she had seen better days. Her sword and armor were on the opposite side of the room and she was curled into a fetal position. She gently rocked to and fro, the side of her forehead scraping against the stone wall as she rocked. One of the warbanders had tied a rag around her head to protect her, but the rag was red with blood, her skin rubbed raw beneath it. When the men entered she did not react to their arrival.

Wave regarded Eisandre with concern and paused to run a hand through his locks of hair. Trench pushed past his friend and shoved his big maul into Wave's arms. The big man moved quickly to the young Arbiter's side, tears welling up in his eyes. He knelt beside her and placed firm but gentle hands on her shoulders. He lowered his ugly face to hers to look her straight in the eyes. "It's alright, lass. Wave and I are here. We're gonna take you home, okay?" Tears that trickled down the man's face were stopped by the deep scar that ran across his features, and they pooled there.

Eisandre ceased her rocking at Trench's touch and after a long time her eyes focused on Trench's. After a time, she slowly nodded in agreement as his words sunk in.

Trench glanced back at Wave and scowled. "What're ya doin' standing at the door like that? Go fashion a litter."

Trench's harsh words snapped him out of his reverie and Wave nodded. "We're here, Eis," he called over to the young woman before he started searching the room for the proper supplies.

"See what I was saying? She's barely responded to us in the days that we've had her here. She hasn't even done so much as you've gotten her to do. There's too much that still needs to be done for Raedelle. Can you guys look after her? You were friends of Rellios," said Wayd, as he cast a hopeless look down at his childhood friend.

"Still are... though he won't be calling the rest of you the same after you let him be taken by Arcady," said Trench. "You're all welcome in the workshop. We'll do our best to get her functioning again. She may do better with the familiarity. Ready to go, lass? We'll bring ya back to the workshop. Want me to carry you?"

Wave dropped the materials he had gathered and shot Trench a look. "Why am I making a litter if you're just gonna carry her?"

Eisandre shifted on the dirty floor and tried to stand. Trench and Wave both helped steady her as she stood and walked across the room to retrieve her armor and swordbelt. They helped her don them, handing her one item at a time before the weary Knight Arbiter led the way to the door. Once outside, she stopped short, looking around in confusion.

"Come on, lass," said Trench behind her. "We're not far from home." His words grounded her back in reality despite the urgings from her mind to spiral back down into darkness and despair. She started out, with Wayd and Trench supporting her on either side. Wave took point and motioned for the two warbanders to fan out along the flanks.

When Eisandre arrived at the workshop, she immediately started to look around the building, searching – for Actaeon perhaps.

Lauryn was at the foundry, darkened goggles over her eyes and a heavy apron over her clothes as she poured molten metal into a casting block. She set the ladle aside and raised a thick gloved hand. "Eisandre. Hi!"

Wayd pointed at her. "Are you an Engineer too?"

"Um... well, not quite. An apprentice, maybe?" admitted Lauryn, though she looked positively thrilled to be asked the question. "I'm Lauryn of Lakehold," she added.

"Well met, Lauryn. Can you help me to unlock the pillar artifact that the Prince disappeared within?" Wayd asked bluntly.

The young woodcarver looked to Trench and Wave. Trench shrugged and mouthed for her to be careful. It was Wave that approached her. "It'll be dangerous, Lauryn. It'd be better to stay here where it's safe. Raedelle is in a state of civil unrest and you don't want to be caught in the middle."

Lauryn looked Wave in the eye and smiled. "Then that's precisely why I've got to go. My country needs me, and if I can help, I will!" She doffed the gloves, goggles and apron before she shouldered her longbow. "Don't you worry, I won't get into any more trouble than I do hanging around with you guys!" She leaned in and kissed Wave on the cheek before she ran up into the loft to retrieve her pack. In a few moments, Lauryn was off with Wayd and the two warbanders.

Trench closed the door and barred it after they were gone. Behind him, Eisandre still stood in the same spot, her eyes searching the workshop. He approached her and touched her shoulder. "Act isn't here, lass. We're gonna go get him though, I promise you."

"Why don't you come sit down with us? We can talk for a bit," suggested Wave.

The anxiety in Eisandre's eyes shifted to a deep sorrow at the giant's words. She realized that Actaeon was, in fact, not there and trembled as she retreated inside herself once more.

Wave regarded her vacant stare with recognition and when he looked over at his friend, he saw that Trench was thinking the same thing. Eisandre was one of the Lost. She couldn't accept the loss of her brother, the Prince, or her love, Actaeon, and so, her mind had descended back down into a spiral of madness that the firm discipline of the Arbiters must have kept at bay.

"I think I might have an idea," said Wave. He reached out and took

Eisandre's hand. "Eisandre, can you come up to the loft with me? I will show you some of Actaeon's thin—"

He was interrupted as she shrieked and pulled away from him. She spun around with her back to him and wrapped her arms around herself before she began rocking rapidly again.

Just then a loud whistle blew three sharp tones. Eisandre straightened and her hand fell to the pommel of her sword as her eyes swept the room and landed upon Trench.

Trench stood over a workbench, one of the wooden Arbiter whistles between his teeth. He spat it out into his hand.

"Wow, Trench, ya couldn't have given a warning, huh?" said Wave.

"Eisandre," said Trench, ignoring his friend, "we need you with us, lass. We need you to regain your focus. *Actaeon* needs you to do that. Do you understand?" His words were firm but compassionate and his eyes held genuine concern for her.

"Actaeon," whispered the Knight Arbiter. She said it again then, and louder: "Actaeon." She said it almost pleadingly and that was when she began to weep. Sobs racked her body as she finally allowed the emotions inside her to flow outward.

The ugly giant wrapped his arms around her while she cried. "That's it, just let it out. Take yer time." Surprisingly, the Knight Arbiter allowed herself to be held while she cried, perhaps overcome with grief. Trench offered Wave a grim look over her shoulder.

Wave grimaced back at his friend and they waited while she cried like that in the middle of the workshop while the big veteran held her. Nearly an hour passed by this way. Wave got some bread and water and set it out on one of the benches for Eisandre while they waited.

When she finally stopped, she leaned upon Trench's hulking form and whispered, her voice raspy with disuse, "Aedwyn is... gone. I didn't see what happened to Actaeon. He is... alive?"

"I know he is," said Trench, loosening his embrace. "And from what we had heard, Act was hurt and then taken by Arcady's men. We've gotta try and find out where they went with him and then go get him back." He guided her over to the workbench and poured her a cup of water. "Sit and eat, you'll need your strength back."

"Act's alive," seconded Wave. "He's been in way worse situations than that. You know that... you've been right there with him."

"I'm not with him now," she stated, mournfully. She obediently sat in the chair before she methodically began to eat her bread. She lapsed again into a troubled silence as she ate.

Trench sat down beside her and nodded grimly. "We're not with him either. Wave and me... we're going soon to get him back. We've got an idea or two about where he could be."

"That bastard Gunther needs him to retrieve the Caliburn I bet. We can stock up on supplies and journey out there to ambush them. There's rumor that the warbands are gathering in Shore. I'd stake my life that they took him there so he'd be nearer to the Wall and easier to hide away," said Wave, considered as he tapped a finger upon the bench. He turned his eye upon Eisandre. "Did you want to come, Eisandre? We could use such a skilled swordmaiden as yourself."

"That's enough, Wave," said Trench sharply. "The poor lass has been through a lot – she obviously needs to spend time recovering. Raedelle's got enough problems without us taking along someone as important as Eisandre on our half-cocked rescue mission."

"Poor lass indeed, Trench. The girl just lost her brother and her love is missing. Would you deny her the chance to save him?" asked Wave as he rapped his knuckles on the bench. "Besides, we could use an extra sword of her caliber. The two of us alone... I just don't know, Trench. Not against what we're sure to face."

"We've faced worse in the past, my friend."

The Arbiter let her bread fall to the plate and began to hum to drown out the speaking of the two men. She hugged her knees to her chest and remained like that for quite some time. Trench and Wave grew quiet, watching her.

Finally, the woman straightened and her humming ceased. "I will go to Actaeon," she declared. "Or I am worth nothing as a person. But... we will not kill my kinsmen if it can possibly be helped."

Trench glared across the table at Wave and in their locked gaze they seemed to exchange something in silence before they both returned their attention to the young woman. "It may not work that way," said Trench. "If we attempt to free Actaeon, those men may indeed misconstrue the truth to make it look as though we were attacking them for no reason. That man likes to stir unease and then sit tight and wait for others to make mistakes. No question he's already thought out this possibility." He intertwined his fingers and cracked his knuckles.

Wave grinned and leaned forward. "But there is one way to do it... and I know you might not like it, Trench, but it may be the only way for the Lady Arbiter here to avoid killing her kin." He allowed that thought to sink in for a moment, before he leaned back and met Eisandre's gaze. "We could wear the intertwined crescents of Shore and show up for the rallying of the warband that is being summoned, as though we are there to join the cause. From there, we locate Master Rellios and sneak him out subversively." He reached out to touch the Arbiter's shoulder tentatively, so as to not upset her again. "We will try to do all of the talking, Eisandre, but understand that such a plan might require you to lie... or perhaps to be clever and tell half-truths."

Eisandre blinked slowly as she processed Wave's words. "Every man and woman of Raedelle will know who I am," she said. "Even if I would agree to pretend to be someone else. Even if I would break my vows and lie – and I will not. We have insufficient information. So our first step should be to get more. Else we will all die, or worse... I will be used to facilitate the deaths of others."

"Then I'll go in alone, and you and Trench can hide nearby. Trench's height might make him stand out like a sore thumb anyway," said Wave, shooting a grin at the big man. "I can figure out if Act's there, and if so, where he is being kept. After I have the information, I'll report back to you both and we'll make our final decision from there. Sound like a plan?" he asked, looking between them.

Trench nodded slowly. "That makes a bit more sense, I think. This way we can send one person in to verify and we will not all be captured or arouse suspicion. We can still bring enough disguises so that we can sneak in in the night and break him out," suggested the veteran. He turned to Eisandre. "That way you don't need to lie to anyone. What do you think of that plan?"

Eisandre considered Wave with a speculative gaze before she replied to Trench. "I cannot lie. I told you. It would serve no purpose." She lifted a dirty hand to rub at her tired eyes. "I think it an acceptable plan. We should go soon. Actaeon is alone and likely in danger. And the Arbiters... they will be searching for me very soon, if not already." A new thought occurred to her then. "Perhaps they will punish me. But I can only be one person at a time. I can only try to do what is right. I'm doing what is right, aren't I?" she asked them, seeking approval.

"Damned right you are!" said Wave before he squeezed her shoulder. He offered her a faint smile. "Act needs all of us if he's gonna get rescued. No one else's gonna do this. Besides, you two need one another. I see the way you are together."

"Hey Wave, you remember the Thyrian command tent? How we pulled that off? Why don't we do something similar?" suggested Trench as he closed his fingers into a fist and rested it upon the bench's rough-hewn surface.

Wave's faint smile broadened at that and he nodded slowly. "Yes... yes, I still have that contact in the markets. We'll have to lay out some of Act's coin for the waythorn powder. It won't be cheap, but it'll ensure we don't have to kill anyone. And this time, we've got nothing to lose..."

Eisandre hugged her knees tightly to her chest and stared at the space before the furnace where she had once sparred with Actaeon. "With him, I am the person I always wanted to be," she admitted quietly. "I am beautiful then, did you know? I am not... this broken... fragment of a soul." She paused a moment, trembling, then asked, "When do we go and what is waythorn powder?"

"When applied to a weapon, it renders the victim unable to feel the blade and therefore unable to react. Knocks 'em clear out for an hour or so once you nick their bloodstream. Enough time for us to incapacitate them and withdraw if we need to," explained Wave.

"You ain't broken, lass," said Trench in response to her former statement. "Those hypocrites want to call you broken, but then they go around breaking everything. The people that started this whole thing, *they're* the broken ones, *they're* the ones who'll bring everyone else to ruin in order to fill up all their missing pieces, *they're* the ones that will put their own selfish desires first at the cost of all good things." He paused in his rant and took a deep breath to calm himself. "You're beautiful all the time. It's just that Act is able to shed light on the buried truths, just like he always does."

Wave nodded emphatically at those words and it was he that looked between them after a long moment of silence and extended his fist over the center of the workbench. "Well then... may the Fallen guide us to obtain the safety of our good friend, Actaeon. Steady hand and level gaze, may our strikes fall true and our enemies part before us, my brother," he said, then turning to Eisandre to add with a smile, "and sister, of course."

Trench slid his fist across the table to touch Wave's and they both turned to look at Eisandre.

Slowly and carefully, she imitated their gesture as she reached across the table to place her much smaller fist against their own. "I will drink this cup of water. Then we will go to Actaeon," decided the Lost woman who had barely slept for the past few nights. The sound of the Engineer's name and the knowledge that he needed her help were her two tenuous connections to reality. "If you need money for this... waythorn powder, there is a necklace that Actaeon gave to me that I could not keep. It might be somewhere here."

"Once you drink the water, make sure you go up and get some rest. In the meantime, I'll get the waythorn," instructed Wave, not acknowledging her suggestion. "When I return, we'll all three get geared up for the journey to come. We may need your skills, Eisandre, and if so, we'll need them at their sharpest."

That said, both men rose from their seats and walked off, Trench to get the gear ready and Wave to head off to the markets to purchase waythorn powder.

Once again, Eisandre was left alone to sit in the workshop with the chickens clucking, the creaking of the cooling furnace, and other strange sounds best left unidentified. She looked around at the dusty streaks of sunlight, the gleaming metal, the interesting shapes and colors, and the notes upon notes all over the place. All of it was empty without Actaeon's presence – their buried truths hidden away.

She remembered to drink her water and then found a basin of clean water to wash her hands and face. That done, she remembered Wave's instruction and wandered up to the loft to curl up for a time in her love's cot. It smelt like him and she dreamt of him – his piercing green eyes and perpetual grin, as he explained in words that she wouldn't quite be able to recall about how everything would be okay.

87 A.R., the 16th day of Rainbreak

MINDGAMES

T HINGS WERE BUSY IN THE main hall of Blackstone Fortress, the seat of House Arcady. Men and women reported in from all the different regions of Shore, responding to the call for muster. The purpose of the rallying was yet to be known and rumors ran rampant. One thing was for sure though – the men and women in Shore came out in vigorous support of the Lord Arcady's call to arms. Messengers rushed to bring words to and from the newly appointed Warchief of the Shorian forces.

One such man approached the new Warchief. His green tabard was emblazoned with the wedge-shaped symbol of Incline overlaid atop the intertwined crescents of Shore. Tinted goggles covered his eyes and his hair was tied back in a neat queue. He bowed his head respectfully, before speaking, "Warchief, sir, the men outside said I'd find you here. I bring word of the men of Incline. Many have mustered and are assembled outside. I need to know, do you want us to bring the other half from Incline? We are the first line of defense from the Wall, after all."

The Warchief barely glanced up at the man before he replied, "Bring half of those that remain and leave a quarter there. We'll need all the men we can muster, in case we need to bring Lakeshore in line."

"Lakeshore," repeated the man with a laugh. "I fancy the new name. Putting the Shore name in it sounds so much better. I will send word for them to leave a quarter then. Thank you, Warchief. Do you mind if I sit here for a few moments? The journey from Incline always does a number on my knees."

Drystan Beiloff grunted a brief laugh in reply, though he seemed largely annoyed at the man calling attention to his mistake. "That's right," he said. "They'll be naught but House Lakeshore of the Shorian Conclave after we put them under our heel. Say, why don't you go check on Rellios instead of lounging around on yer arse. Might as well make yourself useful, eh?"

"Uh... understood, Warchief," said the man disappointedly. He set down the mug of mead he had poured. "What is a Rellios?"

"Not you, fool. The page," said Drystan, smacking a young boy that dozed in a nearby chair in the arm with the flat of his dagger. "Get up, I said, and check on the damned Engineer. Let me know if he's awake."

"Oh, alright. I misunderstood," said the messenger as he carefully watched the page scurry off down a hallway through the tinted glass of his goggles. He took a sip of his mead and relaxed in his seat.

"And how are the men?"

"The men?"

"The warbanders. Do I have to spell everything out for you? And I thought you were the one who could write."

"I can write," said the messenger.

"I *know* that. What're you Lost? Pay attention!"

"Men're getting restless I 'spose. They don't know what's going on, but I daresay they're itching for a fight or something," said the messenger with a grin.

"Tell 'em to calm down. We're not to start nothing until the Lord Arcady sends word. In the meantime, I've gotta get Rellios working on another little problem. Shouldn't be difficult. He's from your area supposedly. Know him?" asked Drystan.

"Rellios you say?" asked the messenger, restraining from any comments on the Warchief's double negative, with some difficulty. "'Twas a Rellios boy grew up in my village. Left for Pyramid when his folks died. Not sure what you want him for, he's a general pain in yer arse, though I 'spose he meant well with all his knick-knacks and inventions and whatnot. You say he's back?"

"Aye, he came back after the incident with the Prince. Got hurt by an artifact, but I'm sure he'll help us to get the sword back," said the Warchief.

"'Bout time he came back and helped us instead of fooling around with them Pyramid folk," said the man from Incline decidedly. He took another sip of his mead before he asked, "That the same artifact that done swallowed up the old Prince that injured the Rellios boy?"

Drystan growled and stood up. "Do I have to do everything myself?" He then headed off down the hallway toward the room that Actaeon was being kept in.

The messenger called after him, the mug of mead raised in hand, "Well, send the young troublemaker my best. Been quite awhile since he's been about. Tell 'im if he ain't nice, ol' Eistenav'll show him the back of his hand. He's seen it enough to be afraid by now!" He laughed and took another sip of mead at the same time, which turned his laugh into a sputtering cough.

Drystan Beiloff scowled and ignored him.

"It's been eight days now! Is he awake?" asked Drystan as he slammed open the door to the room. The page he had sent was nowhere in sight, to his great disgust.

When the Warchief entered the room, he found the Engineer seated upright on the bed, fully dressed. Actaeon's halberd was in hand and he let it teeter to and fro where he sat. Scrapes and dull bruises covered his face from his violent landing days earlier. "I am awake alright," replied Actaeon with a mischievous grin. "And the reason I am not being allowed out of this room is?" He met Drystan's gaze squarely.

"It seems you're feeling better, Master Rellios," offered the Warchief. "I've been assigned by the Lord Arcady to watch after you after your... injury."

"Aside from the cold company and lack of fresh air, I can say that I am just great," Actaeon said with a smirk. "And Arcady could not deign to come see me himself? Why am I in Blackstone Fortress?" The Engineer cut right to the point.

"The *Lord* Arcady was generous enough to bring you back here and tend to your injuries. Your so-called friends were certainly of no mind to do so. He's off right now tending to more important things than your paltry issues," said the Warchief.

"Ah, so the Lord found you better suited to deal with the paltry issues. Excellent! And who might you be?" asked Actaeon, his eyes gleaming with amusement.

"I am Drystan Beiloff, Warchief of Shore," said the man, failing to prevent a note of pride from seeping into his tone. "Who in shattered Redemption let you have that giant toothpick in here?"

The man's words caused recognition to dawn on Actaeon. Once he had placed the man, his lips curled into a smirk. "Oh, it is Vain... I almost did not recognize you, Vain. How have you been? Still having tables thrown at you these days?"

The man threw a chair that stood between them against the wall and it shattered into pieces, his face red with anger. He raised a fist to strike the Engineer, but then thought better of it. As he recalled the words of his master, he took a deep breath and forced himself to smile. "Can I bring you a cup of mead, Master Rellios?"

"I shall pass, though I extend my gratitude for the offer," replied Actaeon, careful to make no comment on the man's tantrum. With a gesture toward the doorway, he grinned. "Mind if we take a walk outside? I could certainly use the fresh air. Unless, of course, I am being held against my will?" The Engineer drew to his feet and rolled his neck and shoulders to loosen up after his long time in bed.

"I regret to inform you that there is no time for that. I do need to ask you one thing though," said the Warchief, cutting to the chase. "The Lord Shore is quite worried about his nephew the Prince. Would you be able to join us in an excursion back to the pillar to try and bring him back? The future of Raedelle lies in your hands with this matter."

"Of course the gracious Lord Arcady would not want to let control of the artifact fall into anyone else's hands, like say, the Lady Eshelle's? I do not suppose I have a choice in the matter, and you just answered my question about my own captivity," said the Engineer. He took two steps closer to Drystan and laughed aloud. "You know, Vain, I would appreciate it if you were just honest with me. Let me know the situation and the factors involved. I can make my decision from that, then. I am not a fool, you know... not everyone is. When do we leave then, so that your clever Lord Arcady can gain the upper hand? Or does he not tell you such things?"

The Warchief grinned malevolently, and Actaeon thought he could see a gleam of pride in the man's eyes for not falling for the same trap twice. "Name calling will not win you any rewards."

Actaeon grinned at that and made a show of glancing about the room. "Oh, how lamentable! You mean I shall not win more joyous accommodations than these?" The Engineer began to laugh and at first tried to stifle it, though he could not contain his mirth. He leaned upon his halberd and laughed aloud, clutching his side with one hand. At one point, he stopped and opened his mouth as though to speak, but then lost control of his laughter once more, as he watched Drystan's face traverse the full gradient of reds.

"That's it, I've had it! Darkest Hour take you! I tried! Guards! Seize him and remove his weapons!" called out the Warchief.

The Engineer fell back several steps and lowered his weapon with calm practice, blade forward as the two guards outside the door entered the room with their swords drawn. His laughter had ceased, but he was still grinning. His eyes glowed with amusement. "Alright, alright! You want my oath or not? I apologize for my rather impolite sense of humor. You see, it is not oft that I am in these uncanny situations."

Several more men arrived outside of the room with weapons ready, in response to Drystan's call. They waited for direction from the Warchief.

"Oath? Give me your oath and hand your toothpick and other weapons over. You'll get it back when you're done helping us," assured the Warchief.

"Well, if you are nice to me, I can try to be difficult only a few times on the journey back north. As for this toothpick, I may need it in the cracking of the barrier. Everything I carry with me is a tool for my trade. Besides, I have never seen anyone so afraid of a toothpick." Actaeon shrugged. "Any specific wording you want on this oath of yours?"

"First off, hand your weapons over. Second off, I want you to swear to obey my orders and the Lord Arcady's orders in this matter until the problem is solved to the Lord's satisfaction. Now your loyalty to Raedelle is in question. What say you?" asked the Warchief, with a grin of his own.

"I so swear under the conditions that I can retain all my equipment. Besides," said Actaeon with a smile, "I will be able to crack the barrier much faster if I can avoid recreating everything I have on me now to conduct the necessary experimentation. Besides, it is not like a lowly Engineer is going to fight his way out past all of your guards with a meager toothpick."

"You'll have an even harder time getting past all my guards with your arms broken for continuing to argue with me. Hand your weapons over," ordered Drystan.

"Break my arms and you will cripple my ability to do anything productive," said Actaeon, his eyes narrowing. He was surprised he managed to put this inevitability off for so long – forget about the fact that they had left him with his weapons in the first place. For all of Lord Arcady's supposed intelligence, he sure picked an inept Warchief. "I do not imagine that Lord Arcady would be happy with that. You have my word, should you want it. My request is simple enough, even for you to understand."

"Fine, have it your way. Guards! Bind the man's arms to his little toothpick!"

The Engineer staved them off with the blade of his halberd and they kept their distance, neither wanting to get slashed. "Now hold on a moment. I need to give you a list of supplies to gather first. We will need to bring them along."

Beiloff picked up another chair and threw it at Actaeon in an effort to disrupt his stance.

Actaeon knocked the chair aside with his halberd before he spun and cracked one of the guards in the side of the head with the butt end of his halberd. The man crumpled to the floor in a heap. The other guard swung at him with the flat of a blade. The blow was hesitant. The guard didn't want to hurt him and it was easily parried by the blade of his halberd.

"I need you to allow me to *think*," said the Engineer as he readied himself to fend off more attacks. "If you do not bring the correct supplies, then you will draw this out unnecessarily."

"If you want time to think, then hand over the weapon!" yelled Drystan. "What p-kin bastard gave it to him in the first place?!" he yelled, glancing sidelong at the other guards. The one beside him shrugged and said nothing. "I'll throw every damned guard I have here at you if need be, Rellios! And forget your supplies. I'm not such a fool as you make me out to be. I'll not bring you things to aid in some escape you have in mind."

"If you will not cooperate with me in this little thing, then how can I possibly work with you to break the barrier?" asked the Engineer, quite reasonably. "You will question my every need and limit my access to equipment vital to the task. Here is my final offer: Step outside and I will pass you out a list of materials that we will need. Your men can go out and gather them – have them brought to the pillar. When the time comes, I will travel willingly with your men. Otherwise, you can explain to your

Lord Arcady how you made the otherwise cooperative Engineer completely uncooperative. I would suggest you consider this strongly, Vain."

Beiloff stared at him for a long and drawn out moment. Actaeon met his stare with open defiance, daring the man to disagree with him once more.

The Warchief turned to look at the wall and finally back to the Engineer. "Fine, we'll do it your way. But only because you're so damned..."

"Logical?"

"Shut up! You've got one hour. Get me that list. If you don't, then I'll have both of your feet lopped off. You can invent yourself peg legs then and that won't impede your work... too much. Got it? You can keep your damned toothpick."

"You will have your list," said Actaeon, with a slow nod. He neglected to inform the man that peg legs couldn't be invented, since they were already a thing that existed.

Drystan Beiloff turned and stormed out with his guards. He slammed the door behind him.

Some time later, the door opened once more and two men came in to drag the unconscious guard out of the room.

After that, Actaeon finally let himself relax and set to work on the list.

When they returned later, they took him by surprise and relieved him of his weapons.

That same day a speech was made in Pyramid. In the Mirrorholds, outside of Saint Torin's Hold, a simple podium was set up and notes were sent out to delegates from all the Dominions.

The Lord Shore stepped up to the podium in his fine black leathers and slowly removed his gloves as he regarded those present with his burning gaze. He sipped from a cup of water upon the podium and cleared his throat before speaking.

"I stand here today to confirm the news from Raedelle regarding the most unfortunate events surrounding Prince Aedwyn's recent loss. Indeed, the Prince has been lost to us, and lamentably so."

Gunther Arcady paused to allow the gasps and exclamations in the crowd to run their course. When they had, he continued.

"It is with these terrible tidings that I declare the following two weeks a period of mourning for all Raedelle and all friends of Raedelle. The loss of Prince Aedwyn indeed saddens our hearts and we must take time away from the politics of running a Dominion to reflect upon our lost leader and his contributions to this great realm.

"In his final moments, the Prince was able to speak through the barrier of the artifact that stole his life. It was then that he conveyed his wishes for a successor. I was present at the Prince's lamentable disappearance and can confirm, along with many loyal Companions and soldiers, that Prince Aedwyn Caliburn, in his final moments, wished for the Conclave of Raedelle to convene, in order to choose the next leader of Raedelle. He said that the domain needs someone to bring the people together, to give them order, and to be Raedelle's hope for the future. He put his faith in us, and we will not let him down!"

Many people in the crowd, especially Raedelleans, were distressed at this news. The succession of power in that Dominion had always fallen to the next in the Caliburn line. This new twist in the succession was news to them and caught many present off guard, which elicited a murmur of whispers and comments. Arcady didn't give them a moment to continue their thoughts though, as he kept speaking.

"As the Overseer of the Conclave of Shore, I call to council the Lords of Raedelle to come together two weeks from now in Caliburn Castle to hear and decide upon any claims made to brave Raedelle. There, we will enter conclave to decide on who will take over as the new Prince of our lands. The period of mourning *will* be observed in honor of our dearly departed leader, the Prince Aedwyn Caliburn, and this period will be a period of peace. Anyone who breaks it will have cast dishonor upon the memory of our beloved Prince. Thank you all and may the spirit of Aedwyn always remain in our hearts."

That said, Arcady made a show of brushing tears from his eyes, before he pulled his gloves back on and stepped down from the podium to retreat to Saint Torin's Hold.

87 A.R., the 16th day of Rainbreak

ASSAULT ON BLACKSTONE FORTRESS

T RENCH PACED BACK AND FORTH nervously in the low thicket where they hid on the outskirts of town. He clutched his big, twisted maul in both hands as he paced. From time to time he cast a glance toward the looming form of Blackstone Fortress in the distance. The mercenary was not used to waiting – he was more wont to action and his best friend being gone for so long created an unsettled feeling deep in the pit of his stomach.

Wave had left about two hours prior, having donned garb that they had obtained from one of Actaeon's old chests, including a green tabard with the symbol of Incline upon it and a pair of old goggles with tinted lenses. Much activity could be heard from the town as waves and waves of warbanders arrived from different areas of Shore. It was clear that this had become the gathering point for the rallying Shorians, at the seat of the House Arcady. Camps were spread out over the terrain for quite a distance from the town's limits.

"I don't like this waiting around at all," said Trench, mostly to himself. He reached up to scratch his short, stubbly beard before he stopped to stare once more at the imposing fortress.

"It is important to wait now," replied Eisandre matter-of-factly. She had dark shadows beneath her eyes from the journey, though not once had she lagged behind the two men on the way there. Instead of her usual Arbiter garb, she had donned a plain gray cloak with a wide hood that shrouded her recognizable features in shadow.

They would be an interesting pair if anyone found them: a large, scar-faced, brute of a man, and a small, athletic woman with dazzling blue eyes.

"Perhaps Wave will be here soon," offered the Arbiter in an effort to calm the big man. "This is Shore," she said, suddenly uncertain. "This is his home. What if he does not want to leave?"

"He'll leave, lass. It's not like Act to get involved in a conflict like this, but you know that," said Trench. The old, grizzled veteran stopped his pacing and approached Eisandre. When he grinned, the corners of his mouth tugged at the hideous deep scar that cut through his features. "Besides, he has no choice but to be at your side. A man's heart does such things to him. Come now, you are right," he said and he knelt before her to open his pack. "We need to wait and we should eat something to keep our strength."

"They will know that about him too. My Uncle is not stupid, although I can't speak for his men. If they offer him the chance to discover something, to study something new and fascinating, then he might want to stay. Besides, I am not the reason he should leave." She folded her arms over her chest. "If they try to lock him up or force him to do something, however, he will be angry. What if they hurt him? What if..." she trailed off.

The giant gently rested his large hand upon her shoulder and smiled. "Well, that you are wrong about, lass. You *are* the reason he should leave. Don't you worry, we're gonna get him outta there, that I promise you." He took a deep breath and nodded as if to assert his own statement. He reached into the pack to pull out some bread and jerky for them to eat, and passed some to the young Arbiter before he settled down upon the trunk of a felled tree.

The young woman accepted the food and stood there in silence. Eventually she sat down on the ground at the mercenary's feet. "Please forgive me, Trench. It is difficult for me to focus now. Let's eat and rest. We may have to move soon."

"Now yer talking sense," said Trench with a grin.

They ate in companionable silence for a time. The sound of birds chirping and the occasional cricket kept them company.

"You can't promise that," she protested, breaking the silence when she had finished her food. "There's no way you can know for sure."

"Oh, you're certain? We'll see about that then," said Trench, amused. He bit off another chunk of his bread.

"I'm not certain of anything. That's my point," she explained in a level tone.

"The only thing you can be certain of is yourself. And I know that I will always keep my promises," said the big man with another grin.

"If only I could be," she murmured before she lifted herself up and went deeper into the thicket to take care of nature's business.

Trench averted his eyes and glared up at the fortress. "C'mon, you bastard, get back here already," he said in a low tone once the Arbiter was out of earshot.

When Eisandre returned, she sat beside him, with her back against the tree trunk. She followed his gaze up toward the fortress and whispered, "Actaeon, please be okay." Trench rested a hand upon her shoulder again.

The day's sun began to set and they could hear boisterous activity picking up within the limits of Blackstone itself as nighttime approached. Torches and luminaries alit as revelry began. As the would be rescuers sat in silence awaiting their friend, the sun slowly faded over the horizon and the darkness of night came to settle around them like a chill blanket. It didn't take long for clouds to blow in, blotting out the stars and even the moon itself.

"Alright, it's done," said a voice a dozen paces behind them. Eisandre's dagger was out in an instant and Trench had his maul raised high behind her.

But it was the voice of Wave, shrouded in darkness as he picked his way through the thicket quietly until he was beside his companions. He squatted down before them and lifted the pair of tinted goggles he'd been wearing, to look at them with his single eye. Over his leather armor he wore a tabard that bore the wedge shaped symbol of Incline upon it. "He's in there, Eisandre. We have to move tonight though. They're going to take him soon to gain your brother's sword for Arcady. I know where he's being held, where the guards are, who's posted where at night. I tried to drop Act a clue we were here, but that idiot Warchief of Arcady's might not have taken that bait."

"He's being held," she said with relief, sheathing her dagger. "That means he's not here by choice. We're ready to go as soon as you give the word. Thank you, Wave. Do you think it will be possible to do this with minimal violence? Most of these people are innocent men and women, merely answering the call of their local leader. And, in addition to the moral repercussions, there is also the inevitability that whatever trouble we cause will be used to damage Eshelle's own presently tenuous political status. I know that this is not your primary concern, both of you. But the fate of a Dominion is at stake, along with the well-being of thousands of souls. I would ask that you keep this in mind."

Wave shared a look with Trench and grinned. "Someone made a grave mistake casting this one aside." He began to rummage through his pack. "Anyway, that's where the waythorn comes in. We all coat our blades and daggers with it. The entrance of the blade into the body will not be felt then, and once you strike the blood stream, the victim will fall unconscious for about an hour." He withdrew a large half-through bottle filled with liquid that had golden flakes afloat in it. "We should be able to get in and out quietly, knocking most of the guards out. Blades please, I will apply the treatment."

"We may be forced into killing someone if we are not quick enough to knock them out. We'll do our best to avoid it though," said Trench as he drew a dagger from his boot and set it down on the trunk of the tree. "If we do this, and do minimal damage, we should be able to prevent any political impact, as you say."

Eisandre pulled her sword and dagger free. She laid both of them carefully along the dead tree's trunk. "A good knock over the head can work too. Or sometimes... bribery," she said, perhaps joking. "Whatever the case, I'd best not be recognized, or there's no end to the trouble this will cause. Wave, might I borrow those goggles of yours when we go in?"

"Better this way," said Wave as he drew his wide companion dagger and then his beautifully honed flamberge rapier. He leaned both against the trunk beside the other weapons and unstoppered the bottle of waythorn. "This can knock them out with no side effects, save a small painless incision. Knocking them over the head could come with permanent damage though."

"And bribing them might cause an unhealthy bout with the conscience," said Trench with a grin. "They might never be able to live with themselves."

"Just be careful with your blade coated with this. You're used to feeling the blade edge and stopping. With this stuff, you won't feel a thing. Be attentive to where you place the blade, cause you won't feel it cutting yourself and you'll knock yourself out just like that," explained Wave with a smirk as he set to work applying the waythorn to the blades before him.

Trench nudged Wave and tilted his head toward Eisandre, pointing at Wave's goggles.

"What? Oh... sorry, Eis, I'm all distracted. Yeah, of course you can use these," he said and pulled off the goggles to hand to her. He promptly covered his empty eye socket with his black silk eyepatch before he returned his attentions to the blades.

"Thank you," said the Knight Arbiter as she slipped the tinted goggles over her eyes. "I am always attentive to where I place my blade. Is the waythorn effective for just one strike per blade?"

"You'll get quite a few out of it, if you can manage," explained Wave. "Just avoid wiping the blade on anything, cutting too deeply, or stabbing through clothing and the waythorn should mostly stay on the blades. Once we drop the first guy, we'll have an hour to get Act outta there, just keep that in mind."

"If we get split up, we circle wide and meet up back here. Understood?" asked Trench.

"Understood," said Eisandre. She pulled the goggles off and cleaned the lenses with the fabric of her cloak before she put them back over her eyes. Satisfied, she pulled her cowl back over her head.

While Wave continued with the blades, Trench dug through his pack and withdrew two more rolled up tabards similar to Wave's. One he passed to Eisandre, and the other he pulled over his head and tied over his light chain shirt. The tabard was much too small for his frame, but somehow he made it work. "There, lass. Put that on. This way nobody wonders why we're there. We're just a few Shorian warbanders responding to the Lord Arcady's call," he said with a wink.

"I am not a Shorian warband volunteer," she stated simply. "And I'm certainly not responding to Lord Arcady's call. Not everyone is wearing a tabard, anyway."

"There we go, perfect!" said Wave, stoppering the bottle. "Our blades are ready. Careful putting them in and out of their scabbards. We don't want the flakes to rub off." The mercenary sheathed his dagger before he took his rapier in hand and sliced a graceful arc through the air. He grinned and returned the sword to its sheath.

"Thank you," said Eisandre as she carefully sheathed her blades.

Trench took his own dagger and put it back into his boot sheath. "Let's go then, and quickly. There's no time to waste." That said, he led the way through the brush toward the Blackstone Fortress, which stood as an imposing figure in the night.

Wave motioned for the Arbiter to fall in first. "Stay in between us when we get there, Eisandre. Let us do the talking. Trust me."

"I trust you," she said, and fell in behind Trench, while Wave took up the rear.

They were all largely silent until they got to the town limits. There Trench grinned and exchanged banter and pleasantries with Shorian soldiers as they passed by. Most people steered well clear of the bigger man and some stared as the group passed, but mostly because of their fascination with his hideous mein and giant form, as opposed to any real suspicion. With the big man walking in front, few people paid the two soldiers that followed him any attention at all.

The group of rescuers walked through the warband encampments at the fringes of town and into the town itself. They passed soldiers in drunken revelry and celebration brought out with the fall of night – a common sight for an assembled warband, especially one with naught to do. Halfway through, on the way toward the fortress, several whores approached Trench and flashed him seductive smiles – the women were undoubtedly drawn to Blackstone by the coin associated with the gathered soldiers. "Hey there big boy, need someone to keep ya warm tonight?" asked one of the women as she batted her eyelashes.

The giant turned and growled at them, which sent them stumbling backward well out of his way. One of them cursed in disgust after she caught a closer glimpse of his face.

Behind Eisandre, Wave chuckled. "Hey big boy. You sure have a way with the womenfolk!"

Trench glanced back at them and simply grinned before he continued on toward the looming shape of Blackstone Fortress. Its dark form towered over them eerily, in the darkness of the starless night.

"Ha! You're probably jealous, because they're not approaching you," said the Arbiter in effort to join their banter.

"Oh, undoubtedly true," replied Wave, with a chuckle. As they approached a narrow section of wall on the way to the fortress entrance, he surveyed the walls above, well aware that they were now inside a gauntlet of sorts. The revelry was behind them now, though the sounds could still be heard, as they reflected off the tall stone walls.

One of the two guards that flanked the big doors held up a hand and called out to them, "Sorry, the hall is closed on order of Warchief Beiloff. You'll have to find food elsewhere. You can report in in the morning." He gestured for them to leave the way they had come.

"Oh, no no," said Trench, looking down at the two men with a serious expression. "I was told to get to the fortress immediately. We're escorting a very important person here, alright?"

"Fine, let's see your credentials then," said the other guard with a smirk. He held out a hand expectantly.

"Yeah, yeah. I got the letter right here," said Trench. He knelt to withdraw it from his boot and fumbled around a bit. When the guard impatiently waved his hand for the letter, Trench stabbed him in the hand, having withdrawn his wide dagger instead. Before the other guard could react he slashed with the same dagger and nicked the man's ear and cheek.

Trench caught the first man as he collapsed while Wave stepped forward to catch the second. They dragged their respective men into dark alcoves to the sides of the entryway.

"We've got an hour. Let's make this count," said Wave.

"Play it calm for now. Nobody knows we're intruders yet. You both ready?" asked Trench. He placed a hand on the large door handle, looking small beside the giant doors.

Wave nodded his assent.

"I'm ready," said Eisandre. "Act needs us."

Trench nodded and yanked the door open before stepping inside the fortress. When the other two followed he shut the door behind them and barred it. They entered the main hall of Blackstone Fortress together. It was an imposing room with narrow slits for windows high up in the sheer walls of black stone.

Wave took the lead and headed over to the arch that framed the hallway entrance which lead toward the western tower.

Two guards stood to either side of the arch and one nudged the other awake as the unbidden party approached them from the darkened main hall. "Eh, what's this?" asked one of the guards, looking confused.

Wave opened his mouth to reply before he fell forward against the man, his concealed dagger slicing a path along the guard's arm. He lowered the man slowly to the floor to minimize any noise.

The other guard opened his mouth to yell and Trench's elbow connected squarely with the side of his head.

As the second guard crumpled to the ground from Trench's blow, a voice behind them spoke, "By the saints, what're you doing?"

"Sorry," said Eisandre as she spun neatly on her heel and struck the source of the voice's hand with her dagger. It was a young page, and she caught him as he fell. "Do we leave the bodies here or attempt to conceal them?" she asked.

"Under the tables," said Wave.

They dragged the three hapless victims beneath the tables in the main hall. As an afterthought Wave grinned and poured a half empty tankard of mead all over them.

That done, Trench drew his dagger and let his two smaller companions lead the way. The hall through the arch lead them past many doors and other hallways, until it reached a right angle turn that lead off toward the western tower. The big man stayed a few feet behind them and kept an eye out over his shoulder, acting as a rearguard.

With a stern glance at Eisandre, Wave lifted two fingers into the air and pointed toward the bend in the hall. Quietly, he drew his beautiful, gold-flaked flamberge rapier from its leather sheath and held the weapon behind him, companion dagger in his off hand. As he approached the bend, he shimmied up to the edge and beckoned for Eisandre.

The Arbiter nodded and moved up to take a position behind him and at the center of the hallway, her weapon at ready.

Once she was in position, Wave cursed aloud and called out, "Damned page must've fallen asleep again. Would one of you guys give me a hand with this thing that obnoxious Engineer wanted?"

A faint murmur of voices could be heard from around the corner, followed by a single set of bootsteps.

As the guard rounded the corner, Wave's boot shot out to trip him toward Eisandre. Without sparing a look back at the man, he spun around the corner and sprinted down the corridor toward a second guard at the end.

The tripped guard stumbled forward, but managed to recover his footing. He seemed confused for a moment but recognition dawned on him as Eisandre reached forward to steady him. The man tensed and went for his blade, but her own waythorn-coated sword was there first to slice his hand and he slid to the floor with her guidance. "You'll be okay," she said in assurance, even as the man faded into deep unconsciousness.

She stood and raced to follow Wave – Trench behind her. His speed was surprising given his size. The giant's maul was in his hand in case someone got past the blades.

Wave reached the guard at the door and the man was prepared.

The guard knocked loudly against the door and drew his sword to meet the mercenary with the eyepatch that rushed toward him.

The guard's quick slash missed as Wave spun around the blow gracefully. A flick of his wrist and he cut the guard's leg with his rapier. The door slammed open then and Wave batted a sword aside with both of his blades before he took a kick squarely in the chest and was slammed back against the wall.

Eisandre was there though, having quickly closed the distance. She parried the guard twice before she slid the sword along the length of his blade and found the gap in his armor to stab a shallow wound in the guard's armpit.

The three of them readied themselves for more foes to attack from the open doorway.

Instead of more guards emerging, there was a loud crash from within the room, and the sound of a blade that clattered against the floor. An audible struggle could be heard along with another crash.

Wave pushed off the wall and rushed in first while the others followed.

"Please be alright," whispered Eisandre under her breath.

Inside the room, two men were grappling on the ground, a broken table beneath them. Actaeon lay on his back while he did his best to stop a dagger from entering his chest. He grimaced with effort and kneed the other man, a guard with a green tabard, in the side again and again, in an effort to drive the man from atop him.

As Wave entered the room, the guard atop Actaeon saw him out of the corner of his eye and flung a nearby pitcher at the swordsman. The limber Wave managed to duck aside, but the water within splashed him in his eye. He spun clear, reaching up to wipe the fluid from his eye with his glove.

The sight of Actaeon in danger struck immediate recognition in Eisandre and she stepped forward, her sword flashing in the dim light as it came down on the assailant's arm, harder than was strictly necessary for the poison to be effective. With her booted foot, she pushed the unconscious guard from atop the Engineer.

"Actaeon," said the Arbiter, pulling the goggles free of her eyes to better assess her love. "Are you okay?"

Actaeon looked up at Eisandre in surprise. He pulled himself to his feet and wrapped his arms tightly about her, ignoring her drawn sword. "Eisandre, my love! You came to save me!" Ecstatic at the transition from captivity to freedom and holding his loved one in his arms, he leaned forward to kiss her and half missed her mouth at first in his excitement. When he pulled back, he noticed the abrasions on her forehead. "Eis, what happened?"

Eisandre kept her blade-wielding arms wide, not willing to risk cutting the Engineer with the waythorn-coated weapons. Unbidden tears glimmered in her eyes at the realization of Actaeon's touch and the fact that he was alive and intact. "I was alone," she said. "Everyone was gone." There was no time to go into details though. "Trench and Wave came to save you as well. They have been very good to me. We have to move quickly, however. We are using waythorn, so we can try to avoid killing anyone. Wave says it lasts about an hour. Where are your weapons?"

Trench and Wave moved quickly while the lovers reunited. Trench walked out of the room and returned a few moments later with two of the guards left outside. He grunted and lowered them to the ground inside the room. Wave closed the door behind him and knelt down. He withdrew the bottle of waythorn from his belt and carefully recoated his blades with the poison. Trench handed him his dagger and stood at the door, maul to the ready.

Actaeon kissed Eisandre's injured forehead and released her from the embrace, noting her poison-coated blades with some apprehension after the fact. He scratched his right hand through its fingerless glove before speaking. "I am here for you now, Eis... we all are. My weapons are upstairs in one of the Warchief's rooms. I am not sure which one. It would be better to be armed. They will undoubtedly pursue us when we flee the fortress. They want me to try and open the barrier to retrieve Aedwyn's sword."

"I know they do," said Wave with a grimace. He glanced at Trench then, "Whaddaya say? We go up and get Act's weapons... give these two lovebirds some time to catch up?" He stoppered the bottle and took up his blades once more. He sheathed them before he handed Trench his dagger back. He clapped a hand on the Engineer's shoulder companionably. "Glad to see you're alright, my friend."

Trench nodded and shot Eisandre a look. "You'll need to guard him then, and be ready to flee. We might run into some trouble up there."

"I will guard him," she promised Trench, though she looked distinctly unhappy about the plan to split up. "And we will be ready. When you return, knock five times on the door so we will know it is you."

Trench offered her a big, ugly grin before he threw the door open. He and Wave rushed through, enroute to their goal.

After the Engineer barred the door behind them, the Arbiter pressed the hilt of her own dagger carefully into his hand. "Be careful of the blade. You will not feel if it cuts you, and the poison acts very quickly."

"I am whole again," said Actaeon with a bright grin, as he accepted the dagger. "I knew that you guys would come to get me. Even if the rest of Raedelle had forgotten about me. I am lucky to have such good friends."

They embraced again, each with one arm, while they held the dangerous weapons wide. Their foreheads touched and they soaked in one another's presence.

"Raedelle is in chaos right now, Actaeon," Eisandre said softly. "At this point, there is a real danger of things dissolving into civil war. If Eshelle had been thinking more clearly, she would not have let them take you. If *I* had been thinking more clearly..." Her voice caught in her throat. "I'm so very sorry, Act. Will you ever be able to forgive me?"

"I am being unfair. You and Eshelle both went through a lot. I know how that feels: to lose someone that you love. You have heard my own story." He placed a tender kiss upon her cheek then, before continuing, "You complete me, truly... I could never hold anything against you. And that you came out here to save me from these bastards, at risk of your service with the Order of Arbiters, and despite all the pain and loss of focus that I know you must have faced. I am so proud of you. That you would do this humbles me for certain."

"You were kidnapped and held against your will. You're not being unfair in being upset about this," said Eisandre. She pulled back from him just enough so that they could keep an eye on the door. "But I can't think about my brother now. I need to be strong. For you. For Wave and Trench. We have to get out of here and without causing a terrible mess. Trench gives nice hugs," she said then, disjointedly. She looked to him once more then, her brilliant blue eyes meeting his piercing emerald gaze. "How could I have not come to you, Actaeon?"

"Yes, I imagine he does," he said with a laugh. "I would have felt the same way as you. In fact, I wanted desperately to hold you and comfort you... had I not been trapped out here. Not to worry though, we will be out of here shortly once those two get back. Where do we go from here? Have you thought about that yet?"

The door remained quiet and undisturbed as they stood there speaking.

"You will be free," she spoke, matter-of-factly. "You can do whatever you want. I will have to go face the consequences of my decisions."

"Wherever you go, I will be at your side," said the Engineer, and the look in his eyes told her that he would brook no argument with that fact.

Rustling and footsteps could be heard outside the doorway, followed by a pause and then some whispering.

"They mustn't know who I am," whispered Eisandre urgently before she pulled the tinted goggles back down over her bright blue Caliburn eyes. She moved to the right of the door then, to catch any assailants by surprise.

Actaeon stayed in position before the door to draw their attention. He maintained his relaxed demeanor so as to throw off any attackers that might enter.

There came five solid knocks against the door. And then a sixth, fainter knock, followed by whispering again.

Actaeon glanced at Eisandre and arched a brow. The Knight Arbiter simply shrugged.

The whispers grew into louder hushed tones and then five more knocks sounded against the door.

"Here goes nothing," muttered Actaeon. He kicked the bar of the door aside and spoke aloud while readying himself, "Come on in."

The door was pushed open slowly so as not to startle anyone, and Wave walked in, his rapier still out.

"I told you it was five!" said Trench behind him. The big man carried the Engineer's halberd and a sack in one hand, his maul in the other.

"Oh shush, if I didn't have to take care of double the guards that you did, I might not have gotten the knocks mixed up!" said Wave. He grabbed the halberd from Trench and tossed it to Actaeon. "Careful, Act. Blade's coated in waythorn already."

"You had me carrying all of this gear!" argued Trench. He handed Actaeon the sack that contained his recurve bow, arrows and hooked dagger. As his boss worked to replace all his gear, the giant turned to Eisandre and said, "You did well."

"I just stood here," she informed Trench as she accepted her dagger back from Actaeon.

"'Nough talk," said Wave. "Let's get our arses outta here."

Actaeon pulled his hooked dagger from the sack and sheathed it at his belt. He then knelt down and returned all the arrows to the sewn in quiver on the back of his jacket before stringing the recurve and fastening it in place beside them. That done, he nodded at the others. "I am ready. Thank you, my friends... I will never forget this."

"Let's get out of here, first," said the Knight Arbiter. "Then we can exchange accolades and discuss memories at our leisure."

Trench led the way this time, his massive maul held over a shoulder as a threat to any who might cross them.

When Actaeon held out his hand to her, Eisandre stalled for a moment in hesitation. She had never refused his hand, but she needed it for her companion dagger. With some reluctance, she sheathed the dagger and took his hand. It stirred conflicted emotions in her – in one hand, the love and joy that could be brought by a touch, and in the other hand, the cold, unyielding steel that would bring quick death if need be.

"Let's get through this," she said.

"Yes, love. Let us go."

And so, four strong and with freshly coated blades of waythorn, the party moved back through the corridors all the way to the main hall. Trench lead the way with confidence, carrying himself as would a man who belonged there. The green tabard of Shore that he wore would give anyone a second thought, especially if they had yet to see any of their unconscious comrades.

As they walked through the main hall, a groan came from under the table that they had hidden the guards beneath. Wave moved quickly from the rear and re-administered the poison to all three men. When they reached the big doors that served as the fortress entrance, Trench pushed one open and stepped out.

As they all filed out through the doors, five more Shorians looked up with raised brows at the strange entourage from where they stood over the unconscious form of the guard that they had dragged out from the shadowy alcove.

Trench strode up to them confidently. "We came as quickly as we could. What has happened?" Before he was even done speaking, bright red blood exploded from one guard as his elbow connected with the man's nose. A well placed kick sent another guard sprawling onto her back and the mercenary's maul broke another guard's arm as she went for her sword.

Actaeon released Eisandre's hand and spun swiftly with his halberd in both hands to draw the blade across the arm of a fourth guard. As that one crumpled to the ground, the Engineer swept the endcap of his halberd between the legs of the guard with the bloodied nose, spilling him to the ground roughly.

Wave shut the door and leapt forward in time to parry aside a thrust aimed at Trench by the fifth Shorian. His riposte caught the guard across the face with a light cut from the tip of the rapier.

With both hands free, Eisandre drew her dagger and became a flurry of swiftly calculated movements. She drew blood from the guard that Actaeon had felled before the man even hit the ground and at the same moment, her dagger found the shoulder of the guard with the broken arm, sending her face first into the stone path.

The last remaining guard regained her feet after recovering from Trench's kick and her sword was a blinding flash as it cut toward the big man's face. Bright sparks flew as Trench stopped the blade with his maul.

The giant then connected with the woman's wrists using a well-placed kick. Her sword clattered to the ground loudly.

The guard leapt clear of another of Trench's swings and turned to run, but ran smack into Wave. He pulled her close against him and kissed her hard before lightly slicing her earlobe with his blade. He lowered her gently to the ground and found the others all staring at him.

"Seriously?" asked Actaeon, speaking for everyone.

Wave shrugged and offered them a wink. "Hey, when opportunity arises..."

Trench clapped him in the back of the head before leading the way swiftly into the night and away from the walls of the Blackstone Fortress. The others sheathed their weapons and hastily followed.

They moved quickly but not so fast as to arouse suspicion. They wound their way down alleys and around warband encampments in the street, through pools of orange torchlight and bluish luminary glow until they reached relative darkness at the edge of town.

Trench led the way into some heavy brush, sticking to a narrow path made by a wild animal. He lead them a long distance away to a small clearing before he held up a hand for them to stop. The sounds of the town were far behind them now. "Let's break quickly and figure out what our next step is. Don't take too long though. They should be after us shortly, I suspect."

"Way I see it, we got a few options," chimed in Wave. "Back to Pyramid to return the Lady Knight back to her duty and our good employer back to his workshop, south to Lakehold to bring report to the Lady Eshelle, or race that bastard and his men back to the Caliburn sword to have Act break the damned thing out before him." He pulled the binding from his queue of hair to let it loose. "I vote for the Pyramid if I've got a say. We don't need to get caught in the middle of this. It's been good in Pyramid – don't need to see war again if I get to choose."

"I have to return to the Pyramid," the Knight Arbiter said. "Regardless of where you decide you must go. It is possible that the Arbiters will show some clemency because I have been helping family. If I start directly interfering with politics, however, that will be a clear violation of my oaths.

I must report to Arbiter Pyramid Command as soon as possible to accept the consequences of my actions. If you feel you should go to Lakehold and warn Eshelle," she continued, turning to Actaeon, "or to the pillar to keep Caliburn out of my Uncle's hands, then you should go, Act. You know I would understand."

"It is no place for me to get involved in politics," Actaeon replied, taking her hand. "Nor do I want to do such a thing. I am an Engineer. I came out to see the artifact, to see if I could help. And, first and foremost, because it is your brother who was affected and I did what I could to help, although lamentably it was not good enough to help him. And so, I will return to Pyramid with you to stand beside you. After all, you came to rescue Pyramid's resident Engineer. A heroic endeavor, I must say. Might I suggest that we make our way toward the pillar artifact to start before we adjust our course to Pyramid. This will give Arcady's men something to rush to and keep that idiot Beiloff occupied for a time."

"I agree with returning to Pyramid. This is not our war," said Trench.

"You may not be able to stand beside me for this," warned the Knight Arbiter, though there was clear gratitude in her gaze. "But I agree. The plan is a sound one. We'll attempt to confuse the ones who try to pursue us by heading toward the pillar first." She looked very thoughtful then, and when she turned her bright gaze back to all three men, there was something in her tone that moved them all. "When strong men strive to manipulate the weak and oppress them through nefarious means, how can any of us turn our backs entirely to the sort of suffering that will inevitably cause? I cannot interfere directly. I have sworn myself to a different cause. But I am not indifferent to all the implications here. I don't think any of you are, either, when it comes to it. But I'm certain there are other ways in which we might all be able to help. Ways that don't involve rushing back to the heart of things. For now, we'd best keep moving, I think, while we still have this head start."

"I suppose if they break my kneecaps I would not be able to stand at your side, but I would sit by you at least," said Actaeon with a grin. He squeezed her hand gently.

Wave smirked and chided the Engineer, "We'll hafta break more than kneecaps if you keep going with those comments, Act." He chuckled as he drew his blade to inspect and clean it.

Trench wasn't amused with either of the men's light-hearted remarks. Instead, he replied more seriously to the Knight Arbiter's statement. "We have sworn ourselves to a different cause as well. And on our honor, we will continue to serve Master Rellios here. If he wants us to oppose your Uncle, then we shall do so without hesitation, but I would strongly advise against it, as it will place him in much danger. This man's mind is worth more than to be ruined at the whim of politics and the casting of one man's dice against another's. I've seen too much lost with such selfishness in my lifetime and I'd not happily see it again," said the giant, as he unconsciously clenched and unclenched his fist.

"I am no warrior of Raedelle," admitted Actaeon. "I have not even undergone the Trials. The three of us could not be of much use in battle. Perhaps the best approach is for us to stay around the workshop and help out as we might. However, would you have me take another course of action, Eis... I would stand up for you through anything – just say the word."

"I have no intention of placing Actaeon or his mind in danger," assured Eisandre. "And should you ever feel the need to *be* in grave danger, you know I would do what I could to protect you. This isn't about that though. I just mean to say that any situation that oppresses some people's freedom and well-being is not something that we can really say isn't our war. Even if we can't leap in and fight it directly, there are always ways to contribute, to care. For example, at the very least, I think we will have some important observations to communicate to my sister. Forgive me, please," she said with a sigh. "This is no time for lectures. I think it has been a very long week for us all. I meant no disrespect." She bowed her head to the men. "We really should keep moving."

Her words seemed to weigh heavily upon Trench. The man opened his mouth to speak but instead closed it and shook his head. "Let's go then," he said and started off once more.

As the big man barreled his way onward, the other followed, double-timing to keep up. Wave caught up to Eisandre to speak, "We know, Eisandre, we know it's important. It's just that we don't want to put our friends and loved ones at risk again... we don't need to have anything bad like that happen. It's difficult enough to go on after the first time." It was a hard admission for the man and he followed it up with a weak smile before he quickened his pace to catch his big friend.

"We are in this together, Eis," said Actaeon as he walked beside her. "Whatever needs be done, you will not have to do it alone." He parted branches with his halberd and held them aside for her as they moved along. "Those two have been through a lot. If they do not feel comfortable getting involved, then they do not need to."

They blazed a circuitous route through the brush before circling back to retrieve their packs in the thicket. From there they continued onward to leave an obvious trail in the direction of the pillar artifact.

Eisandre studied Wave as he walked ahead. "I don't know what needs to be done," she admitted. "Beyond submitting myself to the judgement of my superiors. Nothing beyond that point is clear. We will have to see. I'm just so glad you're okay, Act. I can't even imagine what... if..."

"I am not ready for that yet, Eis," said Actaeon, interrupting her train of thought. "There are too many important things left to me for completion. Such as this new phenomenon that I have only just begun to learn about with you."

"A new phenomenon," she repeated in vague amusement. "That is what I am to you?" she asked teasingly.

Actaeon laughed, though the words that followed were serious, "You have such a clear way of saying things. I am not sure whether you realize that. Hopefully we shall learn much together about this new phenomenon we now know as love. It is truly amazing what it can do to people."

"We have already learned more than I thought possible," said Eisandre honestly. "But then, we continue to learn more. About that which brings an Arbiter from her post. About a connection that makes the whole world more clear and can keep it from falling apart. About the way something can be so very real and yet defy all logic and be devoid of quantifiable characteristics. I am happy to be your partner in this discovery."

"I would not want to share in it with anyone but you," said the Engineer with a happy grin. "And I do believe that we are finding such a thing might be readily quantified through actions. Indeed, your actions these past few days have certainly quantified things for me, or at least set an impressive upper limit. As far as defiance of logic, I am not sure I can cede that point as of yet. In fact, now that I have experienced this, I would go further to say that such a thing might form the basis of human existence – to eat, to rest... to laugh, to love."

Up ahead, they could both hear Trench's burst of laughter. Actaeon laughed too, at himself, and that caused Eisandre to smile for the first time since her brother had been taken from the world by the artifact.

"Listen to me, I sound like some philosopher," said the Engineer.

"You *do* sound like a philosopher," she agreed. "Either that, or a man who is in love and... happy."

"Now that you've sounded that way, maybe you could try it quietly for a bit?" suggested Wave, casting an amused look over his shoulder.

They all laughed at that. They walked on and on, climbing in some places, circumventing impossible terrain, crossing over crevices and following trails. It was exhausting, and the night grew long as they continued onward, making steady progress.

"Do you have any idea of what sort of judgement they would come to?" asked Actaeon after a lengthy silence. "Surely, you would not be punished? I am a resident of the Outskirts and Pyramid now, and was taken against my will on a mission of good intent to rescue someone trapped."

"Does it matter how they will judge me? I would have gone to you no matter what," came her simple reply.

"You are correct, of course. It does not matter how they judge you, I will go to *you* no matter what as well," Actaeon asserted. Their eyes met and a newfound level of determined commitment passed between them, unspoken.

They travelled until the sun arrived to drive away the night sky. After they lead a winding trail toward the pillar and redoubled several times, they were now back on the trail to Pyramid. Trench found an area for them to camp in a ruin that consisted of a multitude of hollow stacked cylinders – strange remnants of the civilization past, their purpose unknown.

Trench picked one of the openings and cleared some of the debris out before he crawled in and almost immediately set to sleep on his pack. Wave smirked and called in after him, "Getting old, eh? Right to bed!" Though Wave himself wasted no time in getting situated in his own cylinder, where he lay down with his eye open.

Actaeon laughed at his two men-at-arms and leaned against the huge cylinder stack away from where the other men slept. "I have had the most sleep. I will take watch," he said.

"We should take watch in pairs," decided Eisandre. She pulled the tinted goggles from her head and shoved them in a pocket. The strap had chafed against the raw skin of her forehead and it oozed blood slowly – her probing fingers came away red with the blood. "And, in truth, I wish to stay with you."

"That is fine, so long as you let me clean and bandage your head first. And maybe use me to lean on a bit," said Actaeon. He guided her to sit in one of the cylindrical openings. "There you go, have a seat. I shall endeavor to be a decent Althean fill-in."

"It's not serious," she said, her eyes lowered in embarrassment at the nature of the injury, caused by her own inability to cope with her ordeal in a normal way.

The sing-song melodies of distant birds began out of nowhere, announcing the arrival of dawn as the sun rose, casting a splendid spectrum of color across the eastern sky.

"Do not worry about it, love. I know it is not serious. You just need to be protected against infections," he said, smiling. With water from her canteen, he cleaned her wound, then holding gentle pressure with some fabric until the bleeding stopped. He wrapped it with a bandage and secured it around her head. "There you go, that should be all healed up by the time we get back to Pyramid. No more wearing goggles for you, Lady Knight." He placed a kiss upon her lips.

"I had to conceal my eyes," said the Arbiter. "Thank you, Actaeon. We should find a good vantage point from where we can keep watch."

Actaeon grinned and gestured up towards the top of the cylinder stack. "I think I may have found just the location."

"If we can get up there, we should be able to see for quite a distance. Shall we try?" she asked, adjusting her sword belt as she stood.

"I think so," said Actaeon. He pulled her tightly against him in a firm embrace. His eyes wandered the pile while he held her, discerning the best route to the top. He kissed the top of her head and released her, pointing. "I think if I ascend on the southern side of the pile, using my halberd end as a purchase between the cylinders to climb with, I can then lower a rope to help you up."

Unable to resist, he pulled her to him once more and kissed her deeply. She melted against him and returned the kiss, her heart pounding heavily.

She clutched him desperately, feeling a longing awaken inside her that she hadn't felt in some time now.

When he broke the kiss and stepped back, she felt every inch of her body protest the separation. But then he spoke again, "We can continue this up there, where we can see an enemy approaching from farther off."

Eisandre stood there for a moment, dazed – her cheeks flushed red. "We should not be distracted while keeping watch," she pointed out, her breathing heavy. "I, for one, cannot be mindful of potential threats while we are kissing." But then a thought occurred to her and she said it aloud, "But perhaps... when our watch shift has passed?"

"Consider it a date," said the Engineer with a grin. He kissed her lips once more before he started up the south face of the pile.

"How could you allow this to happen, you incompetent fool?!" Arcady shouted at the Warchief.

They stood inside the main hall of Blackstone Fortress, where Lord Arcady had just arrived with his entourage. Before him, in throes of dejection, stood Drystan Beiloff.

"I'm... I'm... he... m'lord... he... they must've..."

Gunther Arcady calmly pulled free his black leather gauntlets and turned to the Companions in his entourage. "The fortress has been infiltrated. Secure the outer walls. No one is to go in or out," he instructed.

"Aye Lord!" said the lead Companion, and they rushed out of the Fortress. He hesitated for a moment, not wishing to leave the Lord Shore alone with the threat, but then thought better of it and left.

When the door had closed, Gunther Arcady spun and slapped Drystan across the face with the pair of gloves. The Warchief was sent spiraling to the floor and to the Lord Shore's dismay, he actually started bawling like a baby.

"Stop that immediately," said Arcady.

"I'm so... so sorry, m'lord," said Drystan, tears streaming down his face. "I'm sor—"

The kick that connected with the Warchief's face sent several teeth skittering across the floor and dislocated his jaw. Drystan reached up to feel his chin and felt the corner of his jaw as it hung loose on one side. He spit blood onto the floor before him and sobbed.

"Get up, you useless sop, or I'll skewer you where you lay," said Arcady in a low, dark tone.

Drystan was no fool. He'd seen what the Lord Shore was capable of in the past. He pulled himself to his feet and did his best to compose himself – bloody drool running from his lower lip. He wiped his face clean with the back of his sleeve and cringed at the pain. When he tried to talk, his dislocated jaw failed to move and the result was a burbling mess of barely discernable syllables.

When he looked up, he was not surprised to see the Lord's burning hazel eyes boring their way into him as he stood there. "You lost the Engineer, didn't you?"

Beiloff simply nodded, unable to do any more.

"I gave you one task, and you failed me. How do you ever expect to amount to anything, you groveling invalid?"

The Warchief knew better than to respond to that question. Instead he just stood there as Arcady stalked past him and flipped one of the tables aside. Beneath the table lay two guards and the boy page. Arcady hefted the page up by the collar and dropped him roughly onto the next table. He lifted the boy's hand and spotted a golden flake in the freshly clotted wound.

"They used waythorn. Of course. They didn't want to cause an incident. Not with their own brethren. Very smart." Arcady scowled down at the boy and shook him by the collar. The boy moaned aloud. Arcady shook him again and withdrew a flask from his belt. He released the page to fall onto the table and dumped the contents of the flask onto the boy's face.

The young page sputtered and coughed before he slowly came to. He tried to move his arms and legs to stand, but was unable to. Instead he found the burning eyes of the Lord Shore peering down into his own.

"Who attacked you, boy?"

"There were..." said the page, testing his voice. "There were three, my Lord Shore. One was huge, the other small and fast with one eye, and then a third with blond hair – a woman, I... I think. She was upon me before I could move."

"Anything else that you saw?" asked the Lord Shore.

"Nothing else, my Lord," said the page.

Arcady's dagger was a blur and took the boy by surprise. He felt a bright flare of pain as it tore through his neck, unlike the waythorn that had dulled his senses. A hot rush of blood spilled down to soak his tunic and in a moment he was gone.

Gunther Arcady wiped the blade on the boy's tunic before returning it to his belt. He returned his gaze to the Warchief and was met with a look that he could only have described as pleading.

"Oh, don't be a baby, Beiloff. I'm not going to kill you. I still need your help. Do you want your Lord's forgiveness?"

Drystan nodded emphatically, despite the pain in his jaw.

"Excellent. You're a good, loyal man. You always have been. Scour the fortress and do what I did to this boy to any man or woman that you find has been taken by the waythorn. And hurry, you likely only have a matter of minutes," commanded Arcady. "Then you will get your jaw set and lead a band to go intercept Rellios before he gets to the pillar. He'll undoubtedly return there for the sword, especially with my little niece with him. Is that understood?"

Drystan nodded feebly, but he pulled his sword free and began to skewer the other guards as his Lord had commanded. Such things didn't bother him – he'd done this sort of work many times in his life after all, sometimes for fun and other times at his Lord's behest.

"Make it quick, Beiloff. I'll go to get the men outside and when I return, I expect this to be a bloodbath they won't soon forget," said Arcady with a grin as he pulled his gauntlets back on.

"Aye," said Warchief Beiloff, but with his dislocated jaw, it came out all wrong.

87 A.R., the 19th day of Rainbreak

TRIALS & TRIBULATIONS

I T WAS TREMENDOUS.

It made the collapse of the towers in Lazi's Tomb look like a child's game.

They didn't see it at first, occupied as they were with the violent tremor that tore its way through the very bedrock of the city. It threw them all from their feet, sending them tumbling to the Avenue of Glass with the exception of Wave, who was thrown from the edge of the Avenue in its entirety.

One by one, they steadied themselves and looked up to see it. It was beautiful and terrifying, all at once. A great blue, translucent sphere that rose on the northern horizon. It grew larger and larger until it filled the entirety of the sky beyond Pyramid. And as suddenly as it had appeared, it was gone. The sphere shattered into pieces, and, in a flash of light, disappeared. Blue sparkles floated to the ground in the area where the sphere had been mere lifebeats before, twinkling on their way down.

Actaeon reached out for Eisandre and held her close as they watched the event from where they lay. A thought filled him with horror and dread – *The Lady Lartigan had seen what he had written about the device.*

She had seen it!

If she had shared the information with Markor and the other cross-faced raiders, then it was possible that they had figured out how to activate the device. Could this have been the result? She was killed in the Felmere, or at least very badly hurt. He couldn't imagine that she had survived to make it back to their encampment. But what if she had? What if she'd gotten what she needed after seeing the notes he'd written? Had they been allowed to escape after that?

"Cursed spirits, Act. What was that?" asked Trench. The big man was looking at him from where he lay. It read clear in his eyes that he had seen the recognition in Actaeon's expression.

Actaeon blinked and looked over at his friend. "I hope that we never fully know, Trench. In this case, I think that the truth may just mean our demise."

"Hey!" came a shout from farther down the Avenue. "Hey! You're back!" It was the voice of Geodric Caider as he ran to them, followed by two other Companions of Raedelle.

The Companion slid to a stop before Eisandre and offered her a hand up. She ignored it and climbed to her feet without his aid. Eisandre then reached down and helped Actaeon up.

Caider cocked his head in annoyance, but shrugged and let it go. "Lady Caliburn, I'm glad to see you're alright. I heard about what happened. We were... out, on special assignment."

"You always seem to be on a special assignment, Caider," said Actaeon, remembering the strange night when he had first encountered the man.

"Yeah, well, that's my specialty after all," said the Companion. "Anyway, it's good that you are back Actaeon, Lady Caliburn. Now you've got to get to Aedwyn's sword. Your sister headed off to Lakehold, but no word has made it back that she arrived safely at Caliburn Castle. The Lord Arcady announced that there will be a meeting there on the thirtieth of Rainbreak. That's just twelve days' time. We've got to get you, and the sword, there as well."

"I am a Knight Arbiter," said Eisandre simply.

"She's done enough, Caider. She's going back now to face her Order," said Trench as he lumbered to his feet.

"Darkest Hour take that!" said the Companion, his tone raised. "There's more important things to be done for Raedelle. By the saints, woman, you're a Caliburn!"

"I am Knight Arbiter Eisandre sof Darovin," said Eisandre firmly. "I have taken vows to my Order. This is my path, Companion Caider. It was decided for me."

She began to walk past the man then, but he grabbed her arm roughly to stop her. "Damn it, girl! Listen to me. It was decided back then, when all your siblings were alive and well. Now the Prince is gone, Aedgar's dead, and Eshelle hasn't –"

Eisandre's fist caught him off guard as it slammed into his face. One moment, the Companion was on his feet, and the next he was on his ass looking up at the Knight Arbiter, blood running from both nostrils and down his chin. He looked up at her in shock.

"What do you mean, Aedgar's dead?" demanded Eisandre.

"You bitch! Are you kidding me? I came here to help you, and you hit me?!" spat Caider, his face twisted in anger. He picked himself up and reached out to grab Eisandre.

Actaeon interposed himself between them.

"Outta the way, Act! This isn't about you," said Caider.

"Aye," said the Engineer, standing firm with his halberd held in a cross-body position. "It is."

There was a click behind the Companion and he spun to look down along the point of a bolt loaded in Wave's heavy crossbow. The mercenary smiled. "I suggest you step away from the Knight Arbiter. And while you're at it, answer her question."

Caider glowered down at Wave. "Get that thing outta my fucking face."

"Turn and answer the Lady's question, and it won't be in your fucking face," said Wave. "Also, word of advice, if you're fucking with your face, you're doing it wrong."

Trench laughed at that and the Companion turned back to face Eisandre, addressing her over Actaeon's shoulder, his face red with anger. "I'd figured you'd heard. The Shieldians brought the news. Lord Aedgar was fighting south of Rust when there was a major incursion of tribals. He didn't survive." His expression shifted to one of regret. "I'm sorry, Eisandre."

Eisandre offered him a blank expression and said nothing at all.

The silence went on that way for an unusually long time before Caider spoke, "Is she alright? She's not speaking." He turned to Actaeon. "What's up with her, Act? She just found out her brother died. She's got nothing to say?"

Actaeon frowned. "She needs some time, Caider. Please give that to her."

But the Companion grew agitated once more and shoved Actaeon. "She needs *time*? Time! *All of us* need time! She needs to take *action!* Not just sit there with a blank expression like that. By the saints —"

Trench's movement was a blur, and the clothesline sent the Companion sprawling once more to the unforgiving surface of the Avenue.

"Get walking!" yelled the giant.

Caider spit blood as the other two Companions helped him to his feet. "Cracked Redemption... we'll take action ourselves. You guys just stay here and continue wasting time." That said, Caider shrugged off the others and stormed away, back toward Pyramid. The other Companions followed, casting apologetic looks back at Eisandre.

Actaeon turned to look at Eisandre and found her still staring at the spot where Caider had stood when he had broken the terrible news. Only when he wrapped her tightly in his arms did she cry.

Eisandre paced the polished floor in one of the many empty chambers within the Pyramid of the Sun. The room she was in was likely empty due to a large hole in one of the walls that opened to the outside of the massive structure.

Actaeon leaned against the wall beside the opening, his emerald eyes shining in the light as he watched his love pace. He had never before seen her so agitated.

"I cannot do my Arbiter duties. I cannot reach Eshelle. I cannot do *anything*," she said, her hands clenching and unclenching as she spoke. "Like I am some useless piece of metal we would find along the beach and toss back into the sea." She stopped short and the look she gave Actaeon was a wild one. "But I am *not* useless. I can do many things. They are always telling me, 'Eisandre, you must learn patience.' But how can I be patient when people are dying? How can I stand aside when Raedelle is crumbling, and nobody seems to be doing anything about it?

"As a member of the Order of the Arbiters of Redemption," she had begun pacing again as she recited the words from memory, "I devote myself to the pure vision of a civilized society, in which all the people of Redemption work together toward their common goals of survival, prosperity, and happiness. I believe there is a fundamental worth in all men, women, and children. And in their collective ability to create a society in which cultural and personal differences are embraced in the light of a greater and more unified whole."

The Arbiter High Council had promptly placed Eisandre on leave after her report of the rescue in Blackstone Fortress. In the meantime, they had convened to review the incident and make a determination on the course of action they would take with the young Knight Arbiter. Afterward, Actaeon had followed her to this chamber, one that she had used in the past to clear her mind.

"Perhaps you need this more than you realize, Eis. You are conflicted right now. Your Arbiter vows would demand neutrality... your Arbiter vows also tell you that inaction, in this case, is wrong for all of the people of Raedelle – would violate their fundamental freedoms, would indeed be turning a blind eye to the destruction of the same civilized society that you are devoted to protect.

"It all comes down to enablement if you ask me," he continued. "In one position, you are constrained by the politics and prescription of an organization that must maintain neutrality and lacks the numbers to make a difference in such a situation. In the other position, you are free to make your own decisions, to lead people and to rally support to a cause that you know in your heart is right, despite any vows that you have taken. You took a vow, Eisandre, but you did not in turn vow to accept any other man's interpretation of that vow. A person's vow is their own to take, and in the end it is up to them to decide how it must be maintained, for they must live with the result. I look at the person I see before me now and I see there a Knight Arbiter, and nothing can change that. No man can take that away. Because, Eis... that is who you are at your very core. Aedwyn said your name first for a reason," he said, then quoting the Prince, "'Sandre... bring them together.'"

"Aedwyn is no longer here," Eisandre spun and snapped back at him. "And my vows *are* to the Order of Arbiters, my place within their chain of command, my actions and choices subject to the wisdom and discipline of my superiors." She continued pacing then, continuing with her recitation, "Unity of Vision for a better future. Clarity of Purpose in assisting those who are in need," she had lapsed into reciting the oath to sooth her agitation, but upon hearing those words it became more and more unclear to her whether she was doing the right thing. "Honor and Civility, that I might rightfully earn the respect of those around me. Personal Modesty, that I may remember I serve a purpose greater than myself. Purity of Focus to concentrate on the task before me.

"Where is Eshelle?" she cried out abruptly. "What is she doing? Aedwyn... Aedwyn... please come back. Raedelle needs you. I need you. We're falling apart, falling... down, down. Bright eyes, warm arms. All... gone." In effort to regain her focus she continued her recitation, "May I have the enduring strength, integrity and conviction to remain true to this difficult path, that all the people of this world might know a brighter future..." She trailed off and leaned against the wall to pull at the short remnants of her hair. The conflicting thoughts in her head threatened to drive her insane.

Actaeon gently took her in his arms and held her. "I am here for you, Eis, and I stand beside you in whatever you choose. We can accomplish *anything* together. Think of the things that we have already been through and survived to become better for it. You are a bright light in the darkness, Eisandre," he said, kissing the top of her head. "You blaze brilliantly for me and you burn steadily for Raedelle. Take that light, foster it, and let it grow and you will illuminate others in kind. Raedelle is not falling apart... is not alone. We stand here, together and strong."

She tensed in his arms. "What do I choose? What *can* I choose? The path is a difficult one. The path of Arbiter was chosen for me. I made vows. Promises. Oaths. That matters, yes?" She let out a sob. "But it hurts. It is like claws tearing my flesh, breaking my bones – to lose Aedwyn, and to not be at all certain that beautiful Eshelle is alive to do anything at all to make things right. And Aedgar – poor, stubborn Aedgar, who always wanted to fall in brave battle. How can you say Raedelle is not falling apart, when there is so little left of the Caliburns, and the Caliburns have always been the torch of hope, the noble scepter, the just and true leaders of our homeland? How can you say *I'm* a bright light?" She looked up at him with tears in her eyes. "Look at me, Actaeon. I am all in pieces. If you weren't here with me, I think I truly might go mad."

"Good thing that I am here with you then, love," said Actaeon with a grin. "That is part of what I do. I can fix things. If you are in pieces, then I shall just have to reassemble you. There is not little left of the Caliburns, for I hold the most important of them in my arms and in my heart." He wiped the tears from her cheeks. "Perhaps the only one who can bring them all together."

"You only say that because you did not know my father. You did not know Gawyn or Owayn – gone for all these years. You barely knew Aedwyn or Aedgar. And Eshelle... she lost her husband and has never been the same. All of them though, they are larger than life – heroes, champions, the sort of people you would hear the bards sing of in their epic songs. I am the one they cast aside! Unfit to undergo the Trials. Unfit to be a Companion. Unfit to marry. I am the smallest and dullest jewel in a crown of legends. I am nothing. I am no one. I am an Arbiter, one of many, and I may soon no longer be even that." She closed her eyes and leaned against him heavily. "You cannot fix this."

"The greatest heroes are the ones who can climb up from beneath all the weight of the world to overcome their shortcomings and do what is needed," said the Engineer. "Anything can be fixed. It is just the matter of finding the right components, utilized in the right way, to fix it."

"I don't believe that," protested the Arbiter. "I mean, I believe that *you* believe it, but we can't fix that Aedwyn is gone. We can't fix whatever has made Eshelle disappear. We can't fix my broken mind. I'm no hero, Act. I don't even want to be a hero. I'm just me. And I don't know what I can possibly do but pace and tear at my hair and shake my fists at all the injustice and pain."

Actaeon actually laughed aloud at that. "You are no hero? Tell that to the man you rescued from Arcady's sadistic dog. Tell yourself that all you like, I do not believe it for a moment. You want to know what to do? Let us return to the workshop and rally the rest of the Raedelleans. Let us go to the pillar and free the sword for a true Caliburn. And then, let us go to the Conclave and let that bastard uncle of yours know that we will not hand over our beloved country without a fight! Let us show every Raedellean that their freedom is worth fighting for." His tone carried an edge rarely seen in the Engineer, perhaps stoked by bitterness at his captivity. He wondered at it himself.

The Engineer's words lit a fire in Eisandre's eyes, and her fingers tightened around his arm. She drew a deep breath though, and calmed herself. "I am an *Arbiter*, Actaeon. How can you forget that? I crossed a line in going with Wave and Trench to find you in Shore. Now I must await judgement. I *must*. There is no other sensible way to go about this. If you'd have me toss my oaths to the wind, then I would be no good to anyone or to any ideal at all."

Actaeon nodded slowly as he searched her brilliant blue eyes. "No. You are not one to toss oaths to the wind. Perhaps, in the judgement, you will find the answers you seek, but perhaps you will also impede your ability to make the decision that we are talking about right now. It is a tough decision, and not one to be easily made. However, I can say that while neutrality has its usefulness, one that I exploit quite often in my work, there is also something to be said for those that take action and stand by their principles, even at the cost of neutrality and peace. Without such people, who refuse to stand back and do nothing while malice takes place... without them, evil would inherit the world."

"When I make a promise, I keep it," said Eisandre, anguish in her voice. "I don't want to talk about this anymore. I'm just turning in circles, and all that's happening is that I'm getting really dizzy." She looked up into his eyes again. "I should go back to Pyramid Command, in case they are looking for me. May I see you again soon? Tomorrow?"

"Of course, you will," said the Engineer. "Allow me to walk you back?"

She took his hand gladly, and went to meet her fate.

Actaeon did his best to keep his mind occupied while Eisandre was in the Arbiter Pyramid Command. No matter what he did though, the worry crept in. It was an unusual feeling for him that was reminiscent of his final months spent with his dying mother. He wasn't used to being so helpless.

For a time, he occupied himself in his room up in the Song of the Sisters, where he used some of his extra supplies to craft himself another makeshift metal and directional finder. He tested it on the blade of his halberd and it proved to be sufficiently sensitive. He left the room to test it out more and see if it would serve as well as his last directional finder.

After awhile, he wound up in the Tea Lounge and pored over the sketches of the device that the cross-faced raiders had forced him to study. Had that device really caused the quake and the blue sphere that followed? If so, then it was partially his fault, for letting Agarine see the information.

It was true that he hadn't expected her to betray them, but she *had* been acting quite strange.

There was also the fact that the Lady Agarine didn't have the time to relay the information to someone who could make use of it. He also doubted that she had the understanding to make sense of such a thing. Something was certainly missing – it didn't make sense.

Frustrated, he folded up the sketches and stuffed them into his jacket, leaving a few copper bits on the table in payment for his tea. He wandered the myriad winding corridors in Pyramid then, pondering the blue sphere, which had seemed to shatter in the sky as though it were glass. Were there remnants left behind that he could study? He thought back to the flexible blue shards that he'd found while with Eisandre in the Boneyards all that time ago.

The thoughts brought him back to her present situation. She had risked everything in her life to come rescue him, and now stood upon a crux in her life where things might never be the same. If only he had taken more time to ponder the symbols' meanings instead of simply asking Aedwyn to reverse them. If only he hadn't fired the arrow when he did. His actions had placed her in this situation, to a large degree – just like the artifact that the so-called Veiled One wanted him to unlock, and just like the blue fire, all those years ago, that had badly hurt someone he loved.

Eisandre was strong though – stronger than she might ever realize. He knew that she'd pull through this, whatever might happen. And no matter what, he would be by her side to help her get through it.

His wanderings brought him to the Mirrorholds to find out more about the fate of Czeryn. He had never liked the Dominion, where arguments were settled with blood and progress was forged upon the backs of slaves. Something terrible had happened though, and he feared the worst. Whatever it was, he suspected they didn't deserve it.

Outside of the Czeryn Hold a large crowd had gathered, some Czeryn citizens and many more from other cultures. The doors to the Hold were shut tight, and two warriors stood before them, their spears crossed. Actaeon stopped at the fringe of the crowd and leaned heavily on his halberd. There he waited, deep in his thoughts. The crowd carried within it a feeling of tense unrest that reminded him of a cornered animal.

When finally, the doors opened and a man stepped out, the crowd went silent, but the tension still hung palpably in the air.

"I am Warlord Berk of Stormstair. Hear me speak, for I have assumed command of those that remain, until the status of Warlord Kergon is ascertained. Reports have come in of a large crater in Ridge. Runners have told of this crater and that the Holds of Ridge, Craters and Stormstair now stand empty of our people." There was an uproar at that, but Berk put a stop to it. "Quiet! I will be heard. What has happened to them, we know not, but sightings of forces from Ajman and Shield were also seen to be invading our homeland. Warriors of Czeryn, this is our moment. I depart now to repel these invaders and secure our homeland. Join me, and we will find who did this and make them pay with their lives!"

Dozens of shouts went up at that, but many of them seemed half-hearted and even fearful. When the Warlord started on his way through the crowd, many Czerynians flooded after him and together they marched out of the Mirrorholds.

For a moment, Actaeon thought about asking one of them to look for blue shards when they arrived in Czeryn. Eisandre needed him though, and he needed to keep his mind on the matters at hand. Instead, he found his room up in the Song of the Sisters and passed the night there poring over sketches and thinking about Eisandre's situation.

Late that night a group of Raedelleans led by several Companions charged into Saint Torin's Hold. They made their way purposefully to the rear of the Hold, and there were met by several sleepy attendants.

"Companion Caider, what can we help you with?" asked one of them.

"Let us through," ordered the Companion. He motioned to one of the closed doors, the one that held all the reserve weapons in the case of fighting at the Pyramid.

"I need your authorization from a representative of the Caliburns for that," said the attendant as she glanced nervously at the large group behind him.

"Darkest Hour take the Caliburns! Outta my way, girl. We have a job to do – to save our Dominion. The Caliburns have left us out to dry."

"I'm sorry –" began the woman, but the Companion shoved her roughly aside and several of Caider's band held her down.

Caider stepped forward and kicked open the door. He waved his followers onward and they emptied the room of bows, spears and the few swords. They also claimed several barrels of ale and rolled them off.

The attendants were tied up and locked in the armory room while the band made their way out of the Pyramid. Though it was late that night, many heard them singing boisterously as they drank from tankards and carried piles of spears and arrows on their way out.

Also that evening, a messenger arrived at the Arbiter Pyramid Command with a letter. She came garbed in a green tabard that bore the intertwined crescents of Shore. The letter was penned by the Lord Gunther Arcady, and it detailed twenty-one lives that had been lost in the Blackstone Fortress, one a boy – a young page. In addition to two mercenaries that worked for the Engineer Rellios, the Knight Arbiter Eisandre was implicated.

Sentinel Phragus accepted the letter and read it with a frown. When the messenger had been dismissed, he roused his Initiate. "Wake the rest of the High Command at once. Tell them there is more information about the hearing today. We shall meet in the command chamber in one hour."

While the Initiate bowed and rushed off, the Sentinel reread the letter and shook his head.

Later the following day, Actaeon met Eisandre in another room that they had agreed upon. Eisandre stood before a tall, curved window that arched forward to overlook the myriad criss-crossing staircases in Skyspiral.

In contrast with her agitated state the day before, the Knight Arbiter carried herself with an almost eerie calm. As he entered, she approached him, and wordlessly, they embraced.

"You look like a woman that has come to terms with something," he said.

"And you look like a man that hasn't slept," returned Eisandre before she drew him into a lingering kiss. "Are you alright?" she asked after.

"Yes, I had some difficulty sleeping. I started working on a problem to help distract me a bit, but things weigh heavily upon me with all the uncertainty. I shall be alright, however – just need to learn when to head to sleep. One of the benefits of having a bed right in the same workshop is that you can head straight to sleep after a long night. Right now though, my curiosity is burning to know what is on your mind."

"I like when you look curious like that," she said with a smile. "I have not slept well myself, since Aedwyn disappeared. Perhaps we will both do better if we try to rest in each other's company... if you would be open to the idea, that is."

"Of course I am open to that idea. And if you like when I look curious, then you are in luck, for that is by far my most common expression," he replied with a grin.

"It is not your most common expression when you are with me," she reminded him, her cheeks blushing. She pushed those thoughts back though and changed the topic. "My love, I know how important your work is for you. How, in many ways, you would like nothing better than to be left to focus on your discoveries and inventions for what we hope might be a long and satisfying life. I'm afraid, however," she continued, her gaze intense as she met his eyes. "I'm afraid that my own path is about to get very complicated. I would have you know that I will love and respect you for all that you are, even should you feel that you can no longer walk with me to this new place where I must go."

"My heart demands that I go with you, you know that. You did the same to come rescue me," he said, meeting her gaze firmly. "And furthermore, the logic of my mind tells me that I must follow my heart or I shall forever be regretful." He laughed. "Now then, I shall promise to show you my 'curious look' again if you relieve my avid curiosity right now."

"I don't want you to be upset, Actaeon. Or to feel you are in any way to blame. My actions, my own choices, which led me to go after you, are not forgivable within the bounds of Arbiter rules. Understand that this does not mean they condemn what I did, nor that they oppose my noble intentions. The Paladin Arbiter who delivered my sentence did so as kindly as he could. But the Arbiter way of life is very strict," she explained. "Because it must be, so that the Order might strive to accomplish what it does. I chose to step beyond that way of life, for the very best of reasons. And I cannot go back to where I was."

Tears fell from the Engineer's eyes. "Oh Eis, I am so sorry. I know what the Order means to you." He pulled her to him once more and whispered in her ear, "You know that I will always stand beside you, whatever might happen to either of us."

The former Knight Arbiter accepted his embrace gratefully. "The Order was my life. But more important to me, always, are the Order's ideals. And it is very likely that I will be able to better fulfill my vows, in a great many ways, if I am doing all that I can to protect Raedelle from descending into darkness." She stepped back. "I will tell you, Actaeon, that the Order is very aware of the situation – of the dangers that Raedelle currently faces. As strange as it may seem, I believe, truly, that releasing me is the only way the High Command could provide assistance without breaking any of their tenets in doing so. In the end, it doesn't matter how personally difficult anything for me might be. It matters that I do what I must to better this world, with what I have, to the best of my ability." She drew a deep breath. "The High Command received a letter before they made their final decision. It was from my Uncle, and it described the deaths of twenty-one Raedelleans – the same amount, I believe, that we disabled with waythorn."

"What!? Are you serious? Then –"

"Yes, they must have been murdered afterward, by my Uncle, or his cohorts. I might've believed that we accidentally killed them, if not for some of them starting to wake as we left. We have been framed for their murder."

"Surely the Arbiters did not believe that?" asked Actaeon, giving her an incredulous look.

"Luckily, I had given my testimony the day before the letter arrived. They had time to test the waythorn on my blade and confirm my story. They were in agreement that it looked as if I had been set up. However, they also explained that the Order could not risk being tied to such events. It was quite important that they sever their ties with me. It also made it that much more important that I take this new path. If my Uncle is willing to kill our own kinsmen to win power, he must be stopped." She paused then, considering her words before she spoke once more, "You see now what is at stake. I don't want you to say that you'll always stand beside me, Act. I want you to always have that choice to make again and again, however you feel is best, however your heart leads you. I never want you to have any regrets."

"Well, you do not have to worry," he said without hesitation. "I will make that decision over and over again, and I will always come to the same conclusion. You need to know, love, that you are a part of who I am, that my place is by your side." He paused for a moment and wiped his tears away with his sleeve. "Are you happy with this path then? It will be a difficult and perilous journey, but all things worthwhile are. And more importantly, have you decided on your next course of action?"

"I am not happy, no," she replied honestly and with a frown. "I was a good Arbiter. I knew my place. I had my purpose. Now I have entered a world in which everything is much less defined and I don't know how I will manage to keep my grasp on everything crucial in this new reality. I am very afraid I will falter and fail – that I will see the last of the Caliburns fall and Raedelle lost. That all that I am will not be enough to make anything better. But I will try, and I will be strong because I must.

"As for the next course of action, we must speak with the others, to see if they will accept my return. I cannot presume that they will. Until I know more, I believe it prudent for me to lie low, especially with the bounty my Uncle has seen fit to place upon my head. Will you, perhaps, allow me to stay with you for a few days, Actaeon? I have few possessions, as you know. I will not take up much space."

"Rest assured that I will not allow you to fail, Eis," said Actaeon determinedly. He placed a hand on her shoulder. "Through my work, I have acquired connections in nearly every Dominion. Some of the leaders even owe me favors. I can give you advice on strategy and help you in discussions if you so desire. There was much that I wished to suggest to your brother and sister for the future of Raedelle, but unfortunately they were not open to hearing much about it. I think some of my ideas can help improve our Raedelle's security, safety, and prosperity." He met her eyes and Eisandre saw a fierce love and determination in his gaze that floored her. "For now and always, you can stay with me as long as you like. Wherever you go, I should like to accompany you."

"Thank you," she replied with a grateful bow of her head. "I will always value your advice and assistance, you know. I didn't really want to imagine doing this without you. You embody all the good I long to see in this world."

That brought a smile to the Engineer's face. "I love you, Eisandre Caliburn. Do not imagine life without me. Instead imagine all of the great things that we will accomplish together, all of the places we will go, and all of the things we will learn."

Stirred by his words, she pulled him against her once more and kissed him hard. For a moment the worries disappeared and there was naught but their love.

87 A.R., the 20th day of Rainbreak

DEPARTURE

T HE PAIR IMMEDIATELY RETURNED TO Saint Torin's Hold to speak
with those gathered there. Few remained, but one young woman had
taken charge. Her large frame reminded Actaeon of Trench, though he
was certain that she wasn't quite that tall. Still, she towered over the others
present as she gave orders and issued instructions. Some were repairing the
armory door, while others tended to the chafed wrists of the attendants.

The big woman wore the typical leather armor of a Raedellean warbander
and a large sharpened length of metal on her back – likely some debris from
the ruins that she had modified, wrapping leather around the base to use as
a handle. It looked large and unwieldy, but then, so was its wielder.

As Eisandre approached, her eyes sparked in recognition, then confusion.
"I am Eisandre Caliburn. What has happened here?"

"I know y'ar, Lady," said the towering woman humorlessly. "Was that
Companion Caider. He did it. Came 'n took the weapons. All've 'em. These
'ere tried stop 'em – got bound for it."

Eisandre and Actaeon shared a look, recalling their last encounter with
Caider on the Avenue of Glass. He *had* headed back toward Pyramid.

"You've done well here. What is your name, warbander?"

"Tarcy Hael, Lady. M'thanks."

"Well met, Lady Hael. I am Actaeon Rellios of Shore," said the Engineer
with a dip of his head.

"Nay. Jus' Tarcy. No Lady here," said the woman, again with no sign of
humor in her expression.

"Tarcy Hael of House Hael in Bastion," said Eisandre. "Daughter of Tridarch?"

"Aye, tho' not o' the House, no more. On me own, I am," she said, though she didn't elaborate.

"You are not on your own. You are with Raedelle," said Eisandre, matter-of-factly. "Has anyone heard from Eshelle, my sister?"

"Nay. No word, Lady. She's naw been heard from."

Eisandre frowned deeply at that. "Can you please show me the state of the rest of Saint Torin's Hold, Tarcy?" She turned to Actaeon then. "Can you look after things here for a moment, Act? I'll take inventory and return shortly."

"Of course, Eis," replied Actaeon as the women headed off.

Not ten minutes after the Engineer had sat down at one of the long tables in the Hold, did they walk right on in. It was Lauryn of Lakehold and Wayd Arbrigel.

"Lauryn!" he shouted and jumped to his feet. "You are alright! It is quite good to have you back in Pyramid."

Lauryn pulled away from Wayd and rushed to Actaeon. She embraced him and gave him a kiss on the cheek. "Act! You're alive! Are you okay? What happened?"

"Aye, I am alright," said the Engineer with a grin. "I avoided being hurt by that snake Warchief of Arcady's. Luckily, he fears the wrath of his Lord more than he enjoys hurting people, else I would not be so well right now."

"By the Fallen! Wayd told me that you'd been taken by Lord Arcady. Where were you? What happened?" she asked again, seeking further explanation.

"After I fell unconscious they took me, and I was held against my will in the Blackstone Fortress. They were going to force me to open the pillar artifact, at threat to my well-being. Luckily, Eisandre came with Trench and Wave. They used waythorn on the guards and managed to get me out of there." He paused then, his grin fading. "I think Beiloff must have killed the men afterward to frame us. Waythorn only incapacitates. It does not kill."

"There was some talk," she began. "That you'd gone with him willingly. To support your own in Shore."

Actaeon laughed at that. "Well, I did leave Shore for a reason. And I would not mind being home again, but not quite like that. Apparently, the Caliburn is more important that I ever would have guessed. Funny to think that a simple sword could hold such worth. That they would be willing to kidnap and kill for such an object – it is unthinkable. But I still have hopes that we can bring the Prince back out of there. I could use your help if you are interested. I promise I will try not to get blasted this time."

"Of course I'll help you, Act! Do you even need ask that?" she said, giving him a punch in the shoulder. "The artifact is a dangerous place though. We were forced to withdraw after a few days. The site is under continuous attack from tribal skirmishers. It wasn't safe, and... I couldn't figure it out. It seems impossible."

"Nothing is impossible. You should know that by now. It will take a creative approach to break through that barrier. It is not straightforward. I do not believe that barrier was made to be broken, even by the Ancients, and we have nowhere near their capabilities. Whatever happened to Prince Aedwyn was a particularly dangerous effect of the pillar artifact. Perhaps it was part of its purpose. We shall have to see what we can discern. Once we get the sword out, even if we cannot bring the Prince back immediately, we can bring it to the Lady Eshelle once she turns up. She can bring the Caliburn to the Conclave and assert her right to rule, until we bring back her brother."

"Eshelle's gone," Wayd interrupted with the news. "Some warbanders found her Companions on the Wall near Shore – all dead. The Lady Eshelle was nowhere to be found."

"Well then. That changes the parameters involved in this situation, does it not?" asked Actaeon. "We shall have to inform Lady Eis... Eisandre right away. And I imagine it will be much more important to recover the Caliburn sword, since her claim to rule will be even more tenuous than her sister's."

"Eisandre... c... claim to *rule*?" said Wayd, stuttering.

"Aye. She has been released from the Order. To save me, she sacrificed all that she had accomplished with them," said the Engineer with a frown.

"Then... well, then... we must –"

"Get the sword back. Of course we should," said Lauryn, cutting off Wayd. She returned her attention to Actaeon. "Wayd says that you shot the pillar?"

"That is correct," he said. "I timed the shot with the flickers and I may have interrupted the barrier briefly when it came back on. It probably drew the energy that struck me – focused it maybe. Quite curious in that effect. I have been thinking on that a bit, and it is odd, because I would have imagined that the barrier would have just cut through the arrow. Instead, it seemed to just travel down the shaft and fling itself at me. Perhaps the device was used to move someone to a different place, or perhaps it was their way of executing a person, but... no, that can't be. Not with the controls on the inside like that. It was obviously designed to affect only biological matter as it left his clothing and supplies behind. However, maybe it can transport or effect regular objects as well, depending on how it is used?"

"Or maybe it does something else altogether, and you damaged it with your arrow?" she suggested.

"Perhaps. Actually, that was the initial intent. If I did damage it, it was not enough to stop it from taking the Prince. Perhaps it is a chamber that just holds someone indefinitely until they are ready to get out? The way he flickered like that – there one moment, gone the next. It seems unlikely for him to have disincorporated and then reincorporated. Which leads one to believe that he was somewhere else entirely in the moments we did not see him. It might even have taken him back to the world our people originally came from. If we can activate it again and send through an object or device that would be highly visible from a great distance, then perhaps spotters positioned at high points throughout Redemption might see where it ended up. Though, it is a big assumption to think that the device is transporting to another location in Redemption. It could very well be deep below the city, or somewhere else entirely – in some distant land, or far out into the sea. There are rumors that the Loresworn have artifacts that are linked to one another. If that is true, then one such artifact could potentially be transported by the pillar and tracked by its counterpart. Of course, that would only hold true if the pillar could even transport non-biological matter –"

"Alright, already," said Wayd, looking exasperated at the lengthy conjecture. "Shouldn't we get going and do this thing?"

"Before we left, a bunch of Shorians showed up hauling all sorts of gear: ladders, shovels, ropes, and a bunch of other things in carts," said Lauryn, ignoring Wayd's impatience.

"Excellent. I gave Arcady's dog a list of supplies that I would need to help me break open the artifact. It sounds like he has fulfilled that request. Hopefully the gear is still there when we arrive. We may... hmm, I hope not, but we may need to fight for it if they refuse to allow us to use it," said Actaeon. He glanced around the Hold then, and failed to locate Eisandre. "We should speak to Lady Eisandre, see when she wants us to leave for the pillar. I imagine she will want to go soon."

"So what? We need *Eisandre's* permission now?" asked Wayd truculently.

Actaeon shot him a look. "*You* need not ask anyone for permission. However, I will stand by Eisandre and support her efforts to reunite Raedelle as best as I can. Thus, I will make sure that we are on the same page before I depart, in case she needs me for other things first. Let us all go. We are all in this together now, and getting the Caliburn back for Raedelle is one of Eisandre's chief priorities."

"Wait a moment," said Wayd. "I mean, she's been just an Arbiter since she was a kid! She's suddenly going to lead this effort? Plus she's a..." He trailed off, thinking better of whatever he'd been about to say. "She'll be able to handle this?"

"Eisandre is no longer an Arbiter, and moreso than that, she is my friend," said Actaeon. "I trust her. 'Just an Arbiter' would never have broken into Blackstone Fortress to come get me. When she chose to do that, she proved just how much more she is. I know her, and I have seen the emotion inside her – the deep resounding hurt at what is happening to our Raedelle. She stands for us now and that is a truth I am, at once, happy and sad to see. Happy, because we need her and sad, because she was cast out by an order that she devoted her very life to."

The Engineer met Wayd's eyes with a fierce gaze. There they stood for several long moments as Actaeon's words sunk in.

When Wayd's eyes finally lowered, he spoke, "She is my friend as well, Actaeon. I grew up with her. And, the truth is, that as a child I never doubted her potential. She was different, yes... but also something more. She had that streak of Caliburn in her. When they told me that she would be sent away to be an Arbiter, I questioned my judgement. Maybe it is time for me to question it again. This isn't the time, nor the place, for such a discussion though. I will stand with you both, Actaeon Rellios of Shore."

"I am glad to hear that," said Actaeon. "As far as the truth, I agree there can sometimes be a time and a place for it, but generally, and especially when it can do no harm, I like to be open with people. This is the only way we can become better as a people and not just individuals. And if we want to avoid the fate of the Ancients, then we had damned well better do that. Come, let us go find Eisandre Caliburn."

A knock at the door alerted Eisandre to the presence of others outside the Caliburn suite that was situated just off the Mirrorholds. The suite was clad in decor similar to that of Saint Torin's Hold, with furs and skins hung upon the walls and spread upon the floors to eliminate the reflections and create a more warm and welcoming environment. Aside from that, and a banner with the sigil of Raedelle, a golden lion lizard on a field of verdant green, the suite was sparsely furnished.

Eisandre sat at Aedwyn's spartan desk as she scoured through letters and notes that her brother and sister had left behind. She looked up at Tarcy and nodded.

When Tarcy opened the door, Actaeon led the others in and offered Eisandre a bright smile. "Eisandre, my Lady Caliburn. I have Lady Lauryn and Goader Arbrigel with me. They have just returned with a report from the pillar."

Lauryn blushed at that, but kept her tongue.

"I know who they are," said Eisandre with stoicism, though Actaeon's smile made her eyes light up. "What do you have to report?"

"I'm sorry, Eisandre. Your sister has disappeared from the Wall. Her Companions were found near Shore – dead. I'm afraid that I fear the worst for her," said Wayd.

Eisandre clenched her fist reflexively and stared at it for a long time, losing herself in her whitened knuckles.

Actaeon reached forward and gently took her fist in his hands. "I am sorry, my love. Eshelle needs you to carry on though. Raedelle needs you now, more than ever."

Her eyes found his then and she nodded. "My Uncle," she stated, leaving the rest unsaid.

"Yes, I would imagine so," Actaeon replied.

Lauryn took advantage of the opportunity to change the subject. "We weren't able to do anything to open up the pillar's invisible wall and reach the sword, but the men from Shore brought Act's supplies. You could use them to break it open, right Act?"

"We both will, Lauryn," said Actaeon before turning back to Eisandre. "We wanted to come speak with you about when you thought we should depart for the pillar. I know that the recovery of Caliburn is at the top of your list of priorities."

"I will not forget the help that you both gave to Raedelle in this matter," said Eisandre to Wayd and Lauryn before answering Actaeon's inquiries. "As soon as everyone is ready to go, we should depart. I need to leave someone in Saint Torin's, to continue to represent Raedelle's interests while we are away."

"Perhaps the Companion Itarik can be sent back to watch after the Hold?" suggested the Engineer. "Wayd says that he has loyally stood by the artifact for Eshelle since our rescue party was scattered about. He would do the same for the Hold. Perhaps Wayd could hold here and then Itarik can relieve him. It will not be a quick thing, breaking this artifact open... if it is even possible with our current knowledge."

"Last I spoke with Itarik, he and his two warbanders were going to hide nearby and keep an eye on the Shorians working with Arcady," said Wayd. "Those bastards should be working *with* us!"

"It is true," said Eisandre. "There should not be divisions between us, especially at this time, when more than ever, we need to be working together to sort everything out. But there is a natural geographical divide between Lakehold and Shore, and I'm afraid history shows a tendency for the physical separation to lend toward a separation of loyalties." She stood then and walked over to Tarcy Hael to touch the woman's elbow. "I would like you to stay and be Raedelle's representative in Saint Torin's, Tarcy." The woman opened her mouth to protest, but Eisandre continued, "Raedelle needs a reliable person here and we all can't be everywhere at once."

"Aye, that would be for the best, I believe," said Actaeon with an emphatic nod that interrupted any other protests before the big woman could speak them. "We had better keep our distance from the Shorians when we get there. They will likely vie to take hold of the sword. Especially if Warchief Beiloff is there. He is a vicious man and will fight us if we try to take it. Though if he bothers Trench again, he is likely to get hit with more than just a table."

"I'll hold the Hold, m'Lady Caliburn," said Tarcy begrudgingly when the Engineer finished speaking. She looked Eisandre in the eye and nodded sharply.

"We must make a list of items to bring with us that we may need to break into the artifact, in addition to what Beiloff's men brought," said Actaeon.

The youngest Caliburn let out a long sigh before she straightened and addressed them. "Nobody has any right to have the sword Caliburn, unless they *are* a Caliburn or are dying at the end of its blade. It is a Raedellean tradition – our heritage. Elphin's Torc, as well, must only be worn by a Caliburn." She looked between Actaeon and Lauryn. "The two of you should make a list with whatever supplies you think are both necessary and reasonable to bring along. I will do whatever I can to get you what you need."

Actaeon pulled a sheaf of paper from his jacket. "I have the list here. I can obtain the parts myself in the market." He smiled at the former Knight Arbiter. "We should get started, for there is no time to waste. I can have the items ready for departure on the morrow. And Eisandre... if I have any say in the matter, none but a Caliburn will wield that weapon. That much I can promise you."

Eisandre met his gaze and nodded. "Good. We leave tomorrow."

Later that night, Eisandre stood facing the slanted glass in Actaeon's room in the Song. The room was their momentary sanctuary, amidst the clutter and silence. It was well after midnight, and the Darkest Hour had spread its darkness across the city, which allowed the stars to emerge more prominently in the night sky. She looked up at those glittering stars in quiet reflection.

"I wonder how many there are."

"As many as you can imagine, I believe," said Actaeon as he wrapped an arm about her shoulders. "My mother used to gaze up at the stars with me when I was a young lad and tell me that each star out there was for one good thing I would accomplish in life." He laughed. "To think – a whole sky full of stars for one small boy!"

"Your mother had great expectations for you. She knew you would not always be a small boy, after all. We come from such different backgrounds," she said. She leaned against him heavily. "How many stars can you imagine? There seem to be more than we could ever count – more than we can entirely see. How can we imagine a number greater than we can fully comprehend? It makes me feel small."

"In the grand scheme of this world, we are but grains of sand on an endless beach. But it is we who must stand strong in the name of everything that is true and good," said Actaeon with a starlit grin. "And in such a world, it is comforting to know that we shall not stand alone. Not anymore."

"I am not a grain of sand," protested Eisandre as she took his words quite literally. "And sometimes I'm too tired to be strong in the name of everything worthwhile. Sometimes I need to lean on you."

"Well, when you are too tired to be strong in the name of everything, you will have me to lean upon. That much I can promise you." He leaned down then to place a kiss lovingly upon her lips. "Perhaps we should retire to bed, my love? We can gaze up at the stars and talk more if you like, but there is much to do in the morning and we should have our rest."

"Yes, let us go to bed. Please forgive me. Sometimes I lose track of time."

"Quite understandable. You have much on your mind these days. It is a stressful transition, to go from one who follows orders and enforces rules, to one that gives orders and sets down the rule. Most people would not be able to handle such a transition, but you are doing well. I am very proud of you, Eis, and seeing the way you can deal with these things makes me very happy to be by your side. Eisandre Caliburn is an amazing woman."

They both began to undress then, laying their clothes and weapons at the sides of the bed.

"You have always been happy to stand at my side," she pointed out as she unbuckled her cuirass. "Since the day that we met. We should probably leave fairly early in the morning, by the way. Wayd will be joining us as well – I spoke to him more after our conversation. He doesn't want to let me go without him. I am truly blessed to have such good people to support me."

"Keeping your trusted allies close will be most beneficial for you, I think," Actaeon said as he stripped down to his loose undershorts.

"How close?" asked Eisandre in reply as she unbuckled her swordbelt and peeled off her trousers.

Actaeon laughed as he admired her. "Shall we find out just how close works best?" he asked before he took her into his arms and pulled her down to the bed.

Eisandre tensed for a moment, but then he was kissing her and she could feel his hands on her body in all the right places. "Not for all my allies," she said, after catching her breath. "Just you."

"Well, in that case I must be sure that I do my very best. For if I do not, you will not have another option." He kissed her again, his lips gently brushing hers. "Eis, you... Knowing you, loving you, being loved by you, it is the most precious thing that I have ever or will ever have. You make my life worth living, every single lifebeat, despite its hardships and evils. When I look into your eyes, you give light to the very soul of my being."

"Not just your best, Act," she said as she wrapped her legs around him and pulled him closer against her. "You. All of you. Your best and your worst. Your good moments and bad ones – everything in between. Show your best to all the world who judges you, but I consider myself a most fortunate woman to be witness to your inner truths. Your light has always shone with the brilliance of innumerable stars, my love. Your mother told you so – she saw it too."

"Your logic is sound, my dear. The love I feel for you is so overwhelming that at times I cannot articulate into words the true nature of how I feel. In such times, rather than cast logic aside in an attempt to make a statement, perhaps I would do better to just show you how I feel."

"Ha!" She laughed at that and pulled him closer until their foreheads touched. "Take us away from words."

When they kissed again, both of them could feel it like a blazing brand throughout their bodies. In a single movement, he pulled her tunic over her head. She was naked then, beneath him, all vaguely starlit curves and a heat that reached for his own. After but a moment of admiration, he freed himself of the rest of his own clothes and was back atop her, between her legs.

As he moved against her in just the right place, he saw that there was a question in her eyes. He smiled down at her and said, "Not just yet, my love. We must first make for a safe place to live."

And for a time, their love was all that existed in the world.

Later that night, they lay awake in one another's arms, naked beneath the canopy of stars shining above them through the slanted glass.

"Have you thought about our future at all?" asked Actaeon.

"Yes, Act. Of course I have thought about our future," she answered him honestly. "Some parts are very clear: I want to be with you, as long as life and fate allows. I believe you want the same. But other parts... they may be more difficult to balance. You are a brilliant inventor, happiest when free to learn about the world at your own pace. I am, as ever, bound by duty, and there are more people depending on me now than ever before. I cannot love you and drag you into a world where you may not be happy. And yet, I'm not sure I can be who I need to be without you. It's... I just don't know. I need your thoughts now."

"As you may recall, the first time I saw you and was struck by your gaze and the life behind it, I had arrived at Pyramid and Saint Torin's with a specific goal in mind: I was to speak with your brother to offer my service to Raedelle. As we both know, that did not work out exactly as planned. I still love my country. I still love Incline and Shore. Despite the lack of acceptance I found there, that place gave me the freedom to do what I was driven to do, and I would be honored still to serve it, and even moreso to stand by your side in that. I *can* help Raedelle and continue my experiments and studies as I have before. Perhaps I will need to more strongly consider the implications of my working with other Dominions on projects. However, you know that I have always done that in either case. My relations thereof and continued aid of Dominions can, at your side, help to build trust and foster alliances that are sorely needed with the current state of Redemption." He had already put some heavy thought into the matter. "Thus, my love, at your side can I be everything I ever aspired to be – for Raedelle, for my own curious drive, and, most importantly, for you, so that you can be who you need to be."

"I trust who we are together more than I trust myself alone," admitted the former Arbiter. "And now that we can share everything with each other openly, we can always talk about our concerns or any uncertainties. Beyond that, I have always known you to carry out your work in a morally responsible manner. You have never given me any reason to fear otherwise. If you will stay at my side, always – the Engineer and the Lady of Lakehold... then I will consider myself to be the most fortunate woman alive. To know such love, to feel so happy and complete, to glimpse at the wonders of your beautiful mind... Sometimes I am struck by how very amazing it is that you would choose *me*."

"Every ounce of my being desires to be at your side. That it was a choice, I am not sure, for to deny it would be to deny my very happiness itself. It is rare, for certain, to find two things that, without modification or alteration, can fit together with a perfection that is usually only manufactured. I do suspect though, that I could never be so close to anyone as I am with you. And also, that you honor me greatly by trusting me at your side and in your arms. So, I suppose by your definition, you shall be the most fortunate woman alive – if you so desire. And I would joyfully join hands with you and declare it before all, if you would like," said Actaeon with a smile.

They turned then, to stare into one another's starlit eyes.

Eisandre responded in a pragmatic tone, "Then we will join hands, Actaeon, and we will be wed. Once we reclaim Caliburn and stabilize the leadership of Raedelle, yes?"

He answered her not with a smile, but with a kiss, and once more took her away from words for the time being, holding at bay for one night the greatest challenge that either of them might ever face.

Early the next morning, even before the sun rose from its daily slumber, they arrived in Saint Torin's Hold. To their surprise, there were no small number of gathered Raedelleans awaiting them. There was a rumble of conversation in the room and people rushed back and forth with supplies.

When Eisandre and Actaeon entered the room, everyone went quiet. Tarcy Hael and Wayd Arbrigel stood to receive them. They stood in silence and after a moment had passed, the big woman nudged Wayd forward roughly.

The Goader glanced back at Tarcy and she winked at him. He shrugged then and addressed Eisandre, "Lady Caliburn, we have assembled to support you in your mission. These were the men and women that we were able to round up in the time given."

A quick glance around told Eisandre that nearly a hundred men and women had shown up in the Hold. Instead of the typical garb of warbanders or Companions, many were dressed in the clothing of merchants. It appeared that any Raedellean in the area of Pyramid had been summoned to service. Most all Raedelleans had undergone the Trials and spent time serving in the warbands, so Eisandre knew that they all could handle themselves in combat if need be.

"What of the weapons that were stolen?" asked the Lady Caliburn. "How will we arm people?"

A familiar stocky figure stepped forward and laid his big axe upon the table. "Us in the marketplace figured you'd be good to pay us back, Lady Eisandre," said Balin with a wink. "We brought all we could: spears, blades, bows, and arrows. Not as much as that poor excuse for a man, Caider, stole, but it'll serve. We stand with you, Lady Eisandre."

Those gathered murmured their consensus.

Eisandre walked farther into the room, Actaeon at her side, until she was standing amidst those gathered. "Your support will not be forgotten – all of you. If you travel with me now, we embark on a most important task. We must be the first to win back the sword, Caliburn, for it should be born by none other than a Caliburn. From there, we will return to Lakehold to ensure that there is a peaceful transition of power. The lives of our countrymen depend on us now. Let us not fail them."

"We stand wit' ya, Lady Eisandre!" said Tarcy. "All've us. We'll not fail ya!"

A cheer went up then from all those gathered, echoing her words.

"You have my thanks," said Eisandre. She turned to Actaeon. "Do we have everything you will need?"

"Aye, we should. Lauryn, Trench and Wave were preparing the supplies that we require at the workshop," said the Engineer.

"Very good. Tarcy, you shall have charge of Saint Torin's until our return. Whatever happens, yield control to none but a Caliburn."

"You've m'word, Lady."

"Then let us depart immediately. There is no time to waste."

THE PILLAR

AS THE SUN BEGAN TO rise over the rubble strewn horizon, the large party led by the youngest Caliburn left the Pyramid to meet the Engineer's men outside the workshop.

Several handcarts were already laden with supplies and the Engineer's three associates stood at the ready, bedecked in their best armor and armament. Trench stood between Wave and Lauryn with his maul over his shoulder, dressed in his sound-dampened chain. Behind him, Wave and Lauryn wore heavy leather armor, Wave with his heavy crossbow and Lauryn with one of the finest bows of her own making. Over the armor, Wave wore an old, white leather war jacket that had long past had its sigils and decorations removed.

"A large group you have here. We're packed and ready to depart, Act," said Trench. He turned and smiled down at Eisandre. "Lady Eisandre."

Wave waved and offered Eisandre a disconcerting wink. "Quite an impressive force you have rallied, Lady. Care for some company?"

Eisandre cast Wayd a look and the Goader began shouting assignments for people to man the handcarts loaded with equipment. She stepped forward into Trench's shadow and regarded the three of them. "I cannot ask you to join me in this quest. There will be many hazards ahead. Your safety won't be guaranteed." She still wore the same grey clothes that she had as an Arbiter, though she had removed her badge and sigils.

Trench lowered his maul and grinned. "You're not asking us, and we're not asking you either. We're coming with you, come damnation or deathcrawler."

"Let us hope we need not deal with either possibility," said Actaeon with a grin. He clapped the big man on his shoulder and turned to Lauryn. "I see you have the equipment. Nice job. Anything give you trouble?"

"Just fitting it all on the three carts. Wave and Trench were a big help though!" said Lauryn, beaming at the compliment. "The ropes and pulleys you requested are all in place, as well."

"Thank you," said Eisandre to the three of them. "Your friendship won't be forgotten."

"Well, that's saying a lot given Trench's visage... flawed though it may be," said Wave, stealing a verse from Phyrius.

"And considering the sorely lacking comedy of our one-eyed friend here," rebutted Trench.

"'Nough said about that," said Wave. "Have you thought about the route we're to take?"

"Aye, and I would recommend passage through Adhikara on our way to the Wall," said Actaeon. He looked to Eisandre for confirmation.

"We will indeed stay within the borders of Ajman for as long as possible. We also want to avoid the Keeper territory, and we know they have been cavorting with the Niwians of late," said Eisandre in agreement.

Wayd Arbrigel overheard their conversation and approached. "All we're doing is admitting our fear of them if we refuse to pass through that region. It's the most direct route and time is of the essence."

"Yes, but right now we cannot risk Eisandre in Keeper territory," said Actaeon. "It would play right into her Uncle's plan if she were to fall into Keeper hands there and fail to recover Caliburn nor arrive at Caliburn Castle nine days from now. We have not the full force of the warband yet to prevent such a thing. I would not put it past him to have spoken with their leaders about just such an opportunity."

"Oh, and like he hasn't been dealing with Ajman with his little caravan guard setup. It's even more likely that he's got the Raja in his pocket," said Wayd, with a pronounced sneer.

The Engineer cocked his head to the side and raised a brow at the man's blunt belligerence in the matter. "The Raja is not that sort of person.

Besides, she owes me a favor or two. Safe passage should be little issue in this case."

"At this point, our conflict with the Keepers is clear," Eisandre said. "There is no point in exacerbating that tension right now and we shall avoid the region entirely. Ajman should not be a problem and so long as we behave like the respectful neighbors that we are, we will be able to travel through that territory as we have before, without having to call upon any favors."

Eisandre turned then and faced those assembled behind her. She closed her eyes and clenched her hands into fists – a worrisome action for those who knew her nature. A moment later though, her bright eyes opened again and her gaze was clear and serene as she spoke. "Loyal people and friends of Raedelle." Her voice resonated with calm command, much as her brother the Prince might have sounded. "Thank you. For being here. For standing at my side. We leave now on a quest to retrieve the princely regalia that is the heirloom and heritage of House Caliburn. But... it is more than that, isn't it?"

The men and women present heard their new Lady speak and drew silent to listen, those in the back shushing others around them. They inched forward to better hear her over the winds that blew through the Outskirts.

"It's the birthright of us all," she continued, "to carry on the Raedellean tradition of living lives that are good, noble, and true, under a leader you can trust. Let us promise each other that we'll do everything we can to retrieve those items peacefully and return them to Lakehold – to work with our fellow Raedelleans and not against. For we will all be stronger and better people for it.

"But if it comes to taking arms against our own brothers and sisters – and it very well might, we will try to resolve the matter with as little violence as possible. Never for a moment will we lose sight of why we are fighting and what we are trying to achieve. Raedelle, our homeland and our hope. Raedelle!"

Her last word was drowned out by a gust of wind, but the others around her took up the cry and the single word, 'Raedelle!' reverberated through the Outskirts. A rallying cheer exploded forth from those gathered and many clasped hands and embraced.

"Aye!" roared Trench, his maul raised high above his head where he stood behind Eisandre.

After a moment those gathered began to make final preparations for departure.

Wave approached Eisandre and put his hands together before her. "Well said," the veteran said sincerely before moving off to help the others.

Eisandre turned to face Actaeon and Wayd, the former wearing a proud expression while the latter wore one of surprise. "Say the word when all is ready and we will be off."

When they departed, Eisandre sent two scouts out ahead as a precaution. Trench and Wave took their usual positions on the far flanks for the journey. Actaeon stayed close to Eisandre while Wayd relayed commands from her to the rest of the warbanders. The progress was particularly slow as they could only move as fast as the handcarts could be wheeled, and those hauling them needed to be frequently rotated.

They moved quickly along the Avenue of Glass, past The End's dilapidated structure and into the ruins beyond. They skirted the edges of the Underforest on their way toward Adhikara.

Ajman officials near the border requested to know why such a large force of Raedelleans was travelling through. Actaeon drafted a note that he and Eisandre signed and sent it along with them. About halfway along in their journey, a delegation of Ajman soldiers arrived to help escort them through, dressed in their red and gold striped pantaloons. They brought words of welcome from the Raja and offered to help out the passing Raedelleans however they could on their way through. Some of the Ajmani soldiers even relieved tired Raedelleans at the handcarts during one leg of the journey.

The trade roads of Adhikara helped them cover ground quickly, and only as they neared the Wall did they need to set up Actaeon's rigging to help raise or lower the handcarts past obstacles in the rougher terrain.

At the end of their first day, the Ajmani treated them to a fine dinner in one of their merchant halls, and they all rested well that evening. It was only for a few hours though, because Eisandre roused everyone before dawn and got them moving again.

The next day they entered Pools of Light and travel became more difficult as the trade roads were sparse at the fringes of the final Hold that they needed to pass through to reach their goal.

"Brings back memories, eh?" said Wave at one point while they took a break.

"Aye, not good ones," said Trench with a grunt before he headed back off to patrol the flank.

The weather was brutally hot and the sun baked them all in their armor. They went through most of their water in just the morning, but their escort brought them to a small pool that they used to refill their water reserves.

That night they camped out in the open, for no halls there would accommodate their large party.

It was on the third day that they reached the edge of the Pools of Light. Their Ajman escort bid them farewell and Eisandre's band of Raedelleans continued alone into the no man's land of the Wall.

"Reports have arrived from Adhikara that the murderers are marching to the Wall with a large force. You are to intercept and apprehend them, preferably without violence," said the Lord.

The Captain nodded and saluted the Lord, "It will be done, Lord Arcady." Behind him stood several of his most trusted warbanders.

"Remember," said Arcady. "They took the lives of twenty-one of our brethren – including a young page. They must be brought to stand trial. If they resist you, do your best to minimize casualties. They are armed though, and will likely resist. You do what you need to do. Afterward, dead or alive, bring them to Blackstone. Is that understood?"

"Understood. Is there anything else, Lord?"

"That is all," Arcady said before he spun on his heel and left the room.

When the Shorian Lord had left, Captain Varisk Conmara ran a hand through his hair and spun to face Jezail, lifting a brow.

His friend shrugged and raised her hands. "It's beyond me. I don't know why she'd kill her own people, but she did. There's always more to things than we'll understand."

"You're right, Jez. Let's go."

On the way out of the Blackstone Fortress, they were stopped by a lone woman, in the practical green robes of a Voice – one of the religious leaders of Raedelle that led them in their worship of the Fallen. She was young, with striking brown eyes and flowing blond hair that was almost white. She strode directly up to the Captain and held up her hand for him to stop.

"Voice... we are on an important errand. Please allow us to continue," said the Captain.

"An errand that might bring death, no? And who will guide the spirits of the Fallen... you?"

The Voice regarded him levelly and waited.

"How did you... nevermind. Fine. You can join us if you want, but we know not how long we will be away. I only have supplies for my warband."

"I have my own provisions, Captain. Lead on, and I will follow and remain out of the way – at least until I am needed."

The Captain looked at her for a long while, his lips twisting into a frown. "Okay, but you will follow my orders," he hazarded.

"I will follow the orders of the Ancestors, Captain. So long as yours do not conflict with mine, you have nothing to worry about."

The Voice offered him a thin smile before falling in with the rest of his warband.

Progress became painstaking on the ruin of the Wall. A small party with light gear would have been able to make quick progress, but the Raedelleans following Eisandre were numerous. They were geared for war and each carried food and water to last the journey. In addition, the carts full of supplies hindered their travel at every step of the way.

Despite the slow progress of that afternoon, morale was high and the warbanders were excited to head to the pillar in order to free the birthright of their people. It helped that Eisandre remained steadfastly positive and confident during the journey. During stops, she walked among the troops and asked how they were making out.

At one point, Actaeon led the effort to construct a small bridge over a particularly deep crevice that could not be easily circumvented. The project took some time, even with everyone working together on it with supplies that had been hauled in with the handcarts. It brought them to their first evening in the ruins.

As the sun set, Eisandre instructed Wayd to set a rotating guard in each cardinal direction. Scouts were also sent ahead, including Actaeon and Lauryn, to decide on the best route for the following morning.

It took them another full day of travel, but they reached the artifact before sundown that day.

They found the pillar abandoned when they arrived and the tension that had been building all day left the makeshift warband. There had been worry that Gunther Arcady would await them there. None knew if that would bring battle, and worse yet, battle with their very kinsmen. Eisandre's band included a mix from both Lakehold and Shore. Many of them were terrified at the prospect of fighting their own families and friends. The unspoken thought among them all was whether the Shorians would even join in such a fight at all.

The site of the pillar artifact showed signs of recent occupation, including extinguished campfires, garbage strewn about, footprints spread all over in the dirt, and even a target with a few broken arrows scattered beside it. The site was surrounded by various large ruins and scattered debris, which created a tactical disadvantage with multiple approaches that were difficult to monitor and control. Off to the side of the pillar's field stood a big wheeled contraption that was nearly as tall as the artifact itself. It had a host of ladders, ropes, and pulleys on it and had been built on the base of an old wagon. Actaeon recognized it from one of the sketches he had drawn during his stay in the Blackstone Fortress. It would save them much time that it had already been constructed.

The warbanders and few Companions fanned out to secure the site for Eisandre and they formed a rough perimeter around the pillar, while scouts fanned out into the ruins.

Off to one side, there was a big commotion at the perimeter line that brought everyone to high alert. It quickly subsided and several men trudged into the center of the camp. They were the three men that Eshelle had left to guard the pillar, led by the Companion Itarik. All three were bleary eyed and unshaven.

Itarik marched up to Eisandre and struggled to keep his feet as he saluted her. Despite his fatigue, there was surprise in his eyes as he spoke,

"My Lady Eisandre, I am glad to see you back in the arms of great Raedelle. We need you here. Please tell me you come bearing better news than we have heard thus far." Behind him, one of the other pillar guardians hobbled over to a cracked stone and sat. He had what appeared to be an arrow wound to the leg.

The return to the site of the pillar was an emotional experience for the youngest Caliburn. It was here that she bore witness as her brother disappeared from the world. And so, she stood for a silent time and just stared at the pile of clothes that had belonged to her brother, the Prince, even as the Companion addressed her.

Just as Actaeon was about to nudge Eisandre, she spun to face the Companion and stepped forward to place a hand on the leader's shoulder. "Itarik," she said, before turning to glance at the other two men, "Davil. Matt." She knew all of their names. "I have come because I am needed. I wish I had better news to tell you, but all I can promise is that I will try to make things better. We all will try. I would hear your report of what has happened in your time here, and then you must get some rest."

Itarik dipped his head and actually cracked a weary smile. "Well, I believe that I speak for all three of us that we are so gladdened to see you have come in this time of need. You will have our loyalty and support in this endeavor. Our faithfulness to the Caliburns remains strong, and I know you will lead us into success."

The Companion reiterated the events that had transpired since last Eisandre had been there – the arrival and subsequent departure of Arcady's men and how the Shorian men had chased the three of them off into the ruins and thrown rocks at them. He told of the construction of the contraption beside the artifact and the failed attempts at getting it to work. Itarik also spoke of recent encroachments into the area by tribals, and speculated that they might be the same tribals that had been harrying merchant convoys on the Wall.

Itarik and his two warbanders could do little but conceal themselves and monitor the Caliburn sword from a distance, since they had been severely outnumbered. After Matt had been hit by a tribal arrow, they'd been forced to mostly hide, only heading out periodically to check on the status of the sword and to forage for food, water and supplies.

"You have my apologies, Lady Eisandre – that we could not do more," said the Companion. He lowered his eyes to the ground.

"You have done very well in remaining on your task despite the enormous challenges you've encountered," said the former Arbiter, ignoring his apology. "You all have my thanks. Davil and Matt, for your bravery in standing beside Itarik, I would elevate you both to Companion. I ask that you defend the Caliburns and thereby defend Raedelle. Would you accept?"

The warbander named Davil's jaw dropped, and he stared at Eisandre, lacking words. Matt struggled to regain his feet from the shattered stone.

Eisandre held up a hand to forestall Matt. "Please – do not stand. All I need is your answer."

Wayd found his way to her side and spoke with consternation, "Eisandre, are you sure about this? We know nothing of these men."

"I am sure," said Eisandre. There was no anger in her tone at his insubordination. "We know much of these men. We know they faithfully followed my sister's orders to guard the Caliburn to the best of their ability, even if it meant they would likely die here. It is men like them that we need if we are to succeed in this."

"I would... I'd be honored, Lady Eisandre. I won't let you down," said Davil, his eyes somehow brighter.

Behind him, Matt seconded, "Aye, Lady. You can count on me."

"Thank you," said Eisandre, and she stepped forward to touch their foreheads. "Please go rest now, eat food, and drink water. If we have more questions, we will come to you. And when you are feeling more like yourselves, we can decide together whether it would be better for you to stay here, return to the Pyramid, or press on toward Lakehold."

As Eisandre began to discuss the perimeter defenses with Wayd, Actaeon approached Matt on his stone. He withdrew his hooked dagger and used it to tear open the man's pantleg. After a quick examination, he frowned. "It is infected... badly." He turned and called out, "Wayd! We need a cutter for the new Companion."

An old woman that introduced herself as Gritta ran over and knelt to inspect the Companion's wound, wiping the sweat from her wrinkled features. "What do we have here, young one?"

"I was hit with an arrow," said Matt. "Tried my best to clean it, but it kept bleeding on and off."

"Of course it kept bleeding, you've gotta keep it bandaged, and keep the weight off it," scolded the old cutter.

Satisfied, Actaeon stood and turned to survey the pillar. When he was done, he turned to Lauryn and grinned. "We should set to work assembling the underminer immediately." He motioned to where the men were unpacking the handcarts, two of them full of the machine's big parts.

He took some time to brief Lauryn, Trench, and Wave on the assembly of the machine and then he went back to speak with Eisandre. She was standing at the edge of the barrier, looking inside. He placed a hand lightly on her shoulder. "We shall do our best to break through this barrier. The Caliburn will be in your rightful hands soon enough."

Without taking her eyes off the pillar, she lifted a hand to brush her fingers against his own. "I hope our best will be enough," she said simply. "How many do you require for your task? I'd like to give you only the minimum. Based on Itarik and Wayd's reports, we need everyone we can muster for the perimeter guard."

In the campground behind them they heard a sharp yell as the cutter began to do her work on Matt's leg.

"I understand, Eis. Give me four hard workers and we shall get things moving."

"They will be sent over. Do you require my assistance or shall I continue working with Wayd and the Companions?"

"I should only need assistance if you may spare it," he said, squeezing her shoulder. "This artifact is quite the challenge, and I will hear any suggestions on it. However, my team and I should be able to make headway alone, if need be."

"If no one has any dire need of me, then I will move back and forth to assist everyone as I can," Eisandre decided. She looked down at the pile of clothes where Aedwyn had stood many days ago. Even the marks he had scratched into the dirt remained undisturbed. It was as if it had only happened but moments before. She shuddered and turned her gaze back to Actaeon. "I doubt I could think of anything you have not already considered, but I will observe and assist as I can, and we will see. But first I need to make certain that Itarik and Davil have food and water and that they get some rest. Then I will check on Matt to see how he fairs with his leg. And then with Wayd about the perimeter security. Then I will come here. But, if you require me for something, you need only call, alright?"

Actaeon offered her a smile as she ran through her schedule and nodded. "Understood, Eis. It will take some time to prepare the undermining machine, and then some more time to dig below where Lauryn has dug already, to find out more about the artifact. Do let me know if you need help with anything, as well."

The process took hours and brought them deep into the night after the sun retired – unpacking the carts, sorting through all the parts, and then assembling the machine in place. But when the undermining machine was in place, the contraption, with all its pulleys, gears, and levers allowed one or more men to crank a handle to haul heavy loads of dirt up a ring-like conveyer where they were then dumped beyond the hole. While three men dug and loaded the contraption, and another cranked, the machine made short work of the job, while the men dug deep underneath the pillar artifact with luminaries to light their way.

As the four underminers worked under Lauryn's direction, Actaeon, Trench, and Wave assessed the device that was left behind. He found that the rope had been wound incorrectly through the pulleys, which had likely frustrated Arcady's men after they had tried to follow the Engineer's plans. He grinned at the thought that they must've felt he had betrayed them, but they were really betrayed by their own ineptitude.

A quick rerouting of the rope through the correct pulleys had the device operating and, with Trench and Wave's help, the Engineer wheeled the contraption close to the edge of the barrier. There they pulled on the ropes to extend the ladders up to the pinnacle of the pillar. After climbing along the ladders to the peak, Actaeon made some sketches and observations before returning to the ground. Down there he instructed the workers to shore up the edges of the artifact using lumber from the broken up handcarts so that the invisible barrier wouldn't collapse on them.

As the sun began to rise on the eastern horizon, the top of the artifact had been thoroughly assessed and the bottom had a deep hole dug alongside and underneath it to make further observations. All was reported clear by the scouts and perimeter guards as the morning watch relieved them.

Actaeon called a break for his workers and he and Lauryn sat at the edge of the trench they had created to break their fast. Wave and Trench joined them, following by Davil. The new Companion had started helping them last night in an effort to break the tedium of the guard duty that he had been serving for what seemed like an endless amount of time.

They sat and ate in silence and eventually were joined by Eisandre, who sat down on a toppled chunk of another, less efficacious pillar. She ate her own rations, chasing them down with water from her canteen.

Itarik broke the companionable silence as he arrived to bring his report. "Scouts are back in for the morning, Lady Eisandre. We've sent a fresh group out. There's a few choke points that I've pushed the line forward to. If we're attacked on any one side, we should be able to hold."

"Well, should... nevermind," said Davil before he looked back down at the chunk of bread he'd been chewing.

Itarik turned to regard him with a stoic gaze.

Wave gave him a sharp nudge. "Speak your mind, man. You're a Companion now!"

"He's right, Davil. I would hear your council. We all would," said Itarik.

Davil met Itarik's gaze and smiled. "Well, I'm just thinking – the tribals know this area pretty well. If they hit us, they'll hit us from several different spots, if they're smart. We won't be able to survive an attack for long under that sort of duress. But if we use make use of some of the choke points differently, we'll have more men."

"Traps!" blurted Lauryn through a sip of water before she covered her mouth, blushing red.

"Aye, that's right, traps!" said Davil.

"Now there's a good reason to open yer trap," said Trench with a chuckle.

"A good idea, Davil," said Eisandre. "Once you have finished your meal, please help set them up with Itarik and Wayd."

"Aye, Lady Caliburn. You've got it," said Davil with a shy smile.

"The sooner we are away from this place, the better," said Eisandre. "If only we were able to discern the secret of the artifact, then we could use the barrier as an impenetrable shield, and I would not feel so concerned. But we will be as prepared as possible for whatever might befall us. I wonder also, why Arcady's own force abandoned their attempts. Retrieving these items is of great symbolic importance. I can't imagine they would have given up easily. If there had been any major breakthroughs with your attempts," she continued, turning her attention to Actaeon, "you would have been jumping up and down with excitement, but is there anything at all new to report? Things seem as they are going well. Do you have any new ideas?"

"I'd thought of that too, Eisandre," said Wave. "We'd be sitting ducks in there. They'd just have to wait us out until we ran out of food."

"Plus if somebody bumped the wrong combination into the artifact, we'd all be swept into the arse crack of the gods," said Trench with a chuckle. After a moment, he thought better of it. "Sorry, Eisandre."

"Should we get the artifact open, we may wish to depart in any case," said Actaeon, ignoring the banter of the old veterans. "The situation in Raedelle must be stabilized quickly. Trying to bring the Prince back will be dangerous, and would cost time and lives if we tried now, although it is something that must be attempted at some point. You make a good point, Eis. Arcady should not have abandoned these attempts, it makes no sense. Unless of course he is using the artifact as bait."

"And doesn't expect us to succeed," added Itarik.

There was silence then as everyone exchanged long looks with one another, though everyone kept their thoughts to themselves.

Eisandre broke the silence. "If I were the one who had been taken by the artifact, you would try to rescue me. He could be somewhere... hungry and lost, cold, and in despair..." She trailed off then and seemed to struggle to compose herself. "I understand why we cannot linger here. Once we get the sword, there is much to be done. I *will* come back for Aedwyn, however. As soon as I reasonably can."

"If you were the best hope for Raedelle's future, I would stand by you as well. And you are, and I do," said Actaeon with a grin. "There are many things that I would do for you, specifically, and not for any other. We *will* return to work on Aedwyn's release, but we must not be rushed in the matter. The situation is delicate and I do not wish to risk losing him with a mistake."

Eisandre drew silent at that, her expression unreadable.

The Engineer began with his report. "As you can see, we are well underway. We have assessed the pillar from above and below. We have dug down past a metal rim that the invisible barrier comes down to contact.

The rim is as thick as a man is tall – a tremendous object, but it is what we find below that which is shocking."

He took a long sip of his water then, holding them momentarily in suspense.

"There is another barrier below, a reflection of the upper barrier about the plane of the ground. We dug near a corner and I measured and calculated the angles of two sides. Based on those measurements, I would approximate that the fields converge somewhere below ground at the opposite end of the pillar, which may be more of a spike in reality. The calculated point of convergence came to the same distance below ground as the tip of the pillar's height above ground. This all forms an upside down pyramid of invisible barrier below the one we already knew about. Unsurprisingly, the barrier also holds in dirt and I can get an idea of its thickness there given the proximity of the dirt to my hand. It seems to be consistently less than a thumb's width thick.

"As for the top, using the inspection apparatus that Warchief Vain was kind enough to assemble for me, I have taken several close looks and I am similarly stumped. The material at the top of the pillar is exposed and appears to be a type of differently colored earthsbone. Though, I cannot chip away a piece or scratch it with anything I have available. I can almost see under it to where I believe the barrier is cast from – it appears to shimmer oddly, but the angle and barrier prevent me from making further observations. Curiously, the arrow I fired previously protrudes from the pillar, buried inside the material, right below where the barrier starts."

The Engineer thought for a time on that description, as though taking it in for the first time himself. The others stared at him, some blankly and others in deep thought.

Finally, he spoke again, "It seems then that we have three approaches here, any and all of which may be attempted simultaneously. Firstly, we might dig down even farther to try and find a method of disabling the barrier at the base. It must receive the energy to generate the barrier from somewhere – perhaps from the bottom. Secondly, we might excavate all around the barrier to see if there is anything further we can learn from this thick metal rim, such as another method of deactivation on the outside of the barrier. Lastly, we might continue with experimentation to try and find a method to break through one of the three components to this artifact: the barrier, the rim, or the pillar."

"A writheblade," mused Eisandre. "If only we had one. They cut through nearly everything, excepting the Caliburn, of course. How did your one arrow get through, Act? What was different about that moment?"

Actaeon grinned brightly at her. He loved how she thought so critically about the problem at hand. "I timed that arrow shot. When Aedwyn and the barrier started flickering, I waited to release my shot so that it would strike at the moment the barrier was down. With the barrier down, the arrow lodged into the pillar near the pinnacle."

"Ain't never seen an arrow cleave into earthsbone like that," offered Trench.

"Maybe it isn't really earthsbone," suggested Lauryn.

"Two excellent points," said Actaeon. "If the rest of the pillar is made from the same material as the top, it indicates that perhaps the same energy which helps to form the barrier is changing the properties of the material to make it harder, or softer, as it may be. Now that the barrier is solid and steady once more, I would hypothesize that no more arrows will pass through." He scratched the back of his gloved right hand as the gears of his mind spun rapidly.

"I'm not sure what the best course of action is in this case," Eisandre thought aloud. "I cannot even imagine the purpose of such a barrier remaining in place for so long, unless it is a sort of safety mechanism that will only disengage when some unperceived danger has passed. There could be danger in piercing it at all. I don't know." She paused then, before she glanced at Itarik and frowned. "I have a bad feeling here. It's getting worse the longer we stay."

"If Master Rellios can open the barrier, we will hold this site, Lady Eisandre," said the Companion, no doubt in his voice.

Eisandre toed the ground with her boot and shook her head. "If we didn't have all this equipment, I would recommend we retreat from the area in order to find a place more easily secured. Lives are infinitely more valuable than objects. What do you think? Is it a viable option?" She asked the question generally, looking for input from everyone present.

"I agree with Companion Itarik. We'll hold it. I'll get to work on those traps," said Davil.

"Act's taken out more impressive things than this tiny little pillar," said Wave with a smirk.

"That's right! We'll get through it, right Act?" Lauryn said, though she seemed unsure herself.

"There are still many things that we can try. We have five days left before we need to be in Caliburn Castle. I would not spend longer than a day and a half here. There is a lot we could do in that day and a half though," said Actaeon as he rubbed some dust from the lenses of his goggles.

"Can ya do it, Act? She's asking... is it worth the risk? People may die holding this site," said Trench, shooting the Engineer a stern look.

"I can tell you right now it is not worth one single life. It is a damned sword – that is all. But here we are, having trudged halfway across cracked Redemption to get it. As for why it is worth so much to our people, I cannot say that I will ever understand that. A cultural icon? A spiritual relic? A token of power? All machinations of the human mind, nothing more. That is not what you are asking though. You are asking if I can do it. There is great risk in rushing as we must now. We must proceed with extreme care. That said... I will defeat the barrier."

"Then we will hold this site," Eisandre decided. She looked to Itarik and Davil. "Make your preparations. We do not know what to expect."

The first volley came in the afternoon and caught them completely off guard. Actaeon was giving instruction to one of the warbanders that was working with him when an arrow shaft erupted from her head. She fell forward into his arms and blood spurted all over his jacket as the life flew from her body.

The men and women of Eisandre's party dove for cover where they could. Davil pulled Lauryn down into the trench alongside the pillar and saved her from an arrow that lodged itself where she had stood.

Before the alarum could be raised, seven more had fallen and five more were injured by the rain of arrows that fell to the ground around the site.

It was Wayd that came to Eisandre with the report: the arrows had fallen at many different angles from enemies all around them. They were surrounded.

Eisandre ordered the erection of a roof constructed from one of the handcarts and established a central command post there. Similar structures were erected using whatever could be scavenged from the nearby ruins to protect overhead for the guard posts. Orders went out for shields to be carried at all times and several warbanders were assigned to an early warning arrow watch, including one that was placed atop the ladder apparatus whenever Actaeon was not using it for the pillar artifact.

"We should send a band to take out their positions when they least expect it," Wayd said to Eisandre.

"You said it yourself," said Itarik. "We're surrounded. Drawing us out is exactly what they'd like. Besides, they're scattered throughout the ruins all around us. You'd kill a handful, no more – and lose your entire band."

Wayd scowled. "It's that bastard, Arcady! If we catch some of his men at it, we can prove his involvement."

"We'll prove nothing if we fail to come home," said Eisandre. "We shall stand fast. Conserve your arrows. Hold this site and no more."

Six more volleys came while it was still light, and thanks to all their preparations only two more were killed in the swarms of arrows.

Despite the arrow volleys keeping everyone on edge, the afternoon was still a whirl of activity. The dead were buried and the number of injured grew to the point where they set up a makeshift field hospital in the lee of the leaning wall of some structure of the Ancients. No small number of the enemy were taken out by Raedellean arrows and the retrieval of their bodies verified that they were tribal bandits that had been seen out on the Wall before, raiding trade caravans. There was no sign of Shorian involvement.

Of course, the work continued on the pillar artifact as well, throughout the afternoon. Actaeon sent Trench and Wave out to work with Itarik and Wayd. The two Invasion War veterans were invaluable in their knowledge of battle strategy and tactics, even if they were difficult to listen to at times.

As the day's sun waned, the other new Companion, Matt, made his way on a makeshift crutch over to where Actaeon, Lauryn, and the others worked. The injured man was beginning to look sickly with infection – sweat poured down his brow and much of the color had left his face.

"Hey, Master Rellios, I'm here to see if there's anything I can do to help."

"Shouldn't you be resting?" Lauryn scolded, her hand on her hip.

"This thing'll get me either way – I've heard the cutters talking. For shattered Redemption if I don't get off my bottom and try to do something to help, instead of just lying in that makeshift cot," said Matt, though it came off more like a plea.

"Let him help Lauryn," said Actaeon. He called everyone working on the pillar over to reiterate what they had accomplished for the day.

Matt sat down heavily on a fallen tree trunk and was joined by Davil, who had returned after helping set the traps at choke points, and two warbanders that had been helping with the artifact since the night before.

They discussed everything that was done, including the continued excavation of the rim, further experimentation on both the rim and the tip of the pillar, and various trials that they had conducted with the barrier itself. All in all, it had been a long day, but they had nothing to show for it. They were still no closer to finding a way into the artifact, not after all that work.

"We've concentrated on the rim, the barrier, and the pillar, but what about the one part of it that isn't supposed to be there?" suggested Lauryn.

Actaeon grinned brightly and grasped her shoulders excitedly. "That is it, Lauryn! You have it! The arrow! You are a genius." His mind raced and he outlined a series of tasks that could help them understand the nature of the arrow's interaction with the artifact.

As the sun continued to set, they found that the arrow did indeed protrude through the barrier near the top of the pillar. After some probing, they also discovered a gap in the field the exact width of the arrow directly beneath it and all the way down to the rim.

The group paused again to discuss what they had found.

"The field is like a curtain," Actaeon explained. "It falls from top to bottom and the arrow interrupts it to create a null area underneath the shaft. The arrow that Eshelle had fired was cut into pieces by the barrier. That this one is intact correlates with the fact that it remains in direct contact with the pillar itself. Somehow, the very material of the arrow was modified such that the barrier cannot break it."

"What if we stuck something through the gap and used that to get the sword?" asked Matt.

"Like with a fishing rod, only trying to catch a sword!" Davil exclaimed.

"That would be dependant upon the gap widening enough to fit the sword through in the first place," said the Engineer. "If we can widen the gap somehow, perhaps we can just walk on through and retrieve the sword."

For several more hours then, into the gloom of night, the small group of them: Actaeon, Lauryn, Davil, and the two warbanders, all worked on using objects and techniques to widen the gap beneath the arrow. Matt sat nearby and offered suggestions. They hammered in wedges, tried to lever it open with blades, stuck a thin arrowhead through before turning it ninety degrees and pulling, all to no avail.

While they worked, many along the perimeter took the time to rest beneath their shields.

They didn't have very long.

Shouts awakened the campsite in the middle of the night as the eastern picket was attacked. There were screams as some of the attacking tribals fell prey to the deadfalls and spikes that Davil had deployed. Raedellean arrows brought down more still. Itarik took command of that force while Trench and Wave helped organize the wings under his command. On the western front, Wayd readied the troops there for an attack.

After a small skirmish, the attackers retreated quickly into the night, leaving three Raedelleans dead and one injured. Ten tribals had been killed in the brief clash.

"They're probing – testing our defenses. There'll be a few more of these, I'd guess," said Trench to Itarik and Eisandre when all was done.

"Aye, and keeping us from getting rest as well. That does its own damage," said Wave.

For the remainder of the night, they stayed on high alert, rotating men and women out for brief moments of respite to keep those on watch fresh.

The attacks that Trench predicted did come, and with similar numbers of casualties on both sides. It accomplished the mission of the enemy though – it kept the Raedelleans poorly rested and distracted from the task of opening the pillar.

Some hours past midnight, the Darkest Hour came and the tribals attacked from both east and west at once after the luminaries all went out. Several locations where warbanders had been posted had neglected to build fires or torches. Despite this, they still took a toll on the tribals, though another eleven warbanders were slaughtered in the chaos.

It was Itarik's solemn duty to inform Eisandre of the casualty count. Sixty-seven men and women were left alive, seven of them injured, out of an original count of ninety-eight. Thirty-one loyal Raedelleans were dead.

"I will speak to Actaeon," said Eisandre, pain clear in her eyes at the news.

She found the team of artifact crackers on break for another discussion beside the artifact. They had hit a wall with their progress. She interrupted them to give Actaeon the news.

"A third of us have perished. It is time that we consider retreat, no?" asked Eisandre. The Engineer could see the question in her eyes.

"By the Fallen..." he said.

"Exactly, Act. It's time we cut our losses and got out of here," said Wave, who had rushed over to join them. Wayd arrived beside him a moment later.

"There is one more thing," said Actaeon. He looked up at the pillar and leaned heavily upon his halberd.

"What? What one more thing are you going to try? You've been trying all day. You've failed! Your man Wave is right, it's time to call it quits," said Wayd. He was dirty and bleeding from the fighting.

The Engineer ignored them and took a few steps closer to the artifact. When he spoke, it was as though he was speaking to himself, considering his own thoughts.

"There is one last possibility."

"No, forget it! No last possibility. We need to leave or we'll all die here!" Wayd charged up to Actaeon but was stopped by Wave.

"During the phase of the artifact where the barrier was off, the arrow became connected to the pillar and now it is protected by the pillar's energy... somehow," said Actaeon, not responding to Wayd's rage. "Since the energy that comprises the barrier flows from one side to the other – from pillar to rim – it would seem to make logical sense that connecting the arrow to the rim might cause a direct path for the energy and, therefore, the failure of the barrier. Right now, the energy is shot across the distance between pillar tip and rim, but if we brought all that energy straight from pillar to rim, in essence, closing the gap... Yes, then how would the barrier receive the energy it needs to exist?"

"We can't give you much more time, Act. You need to do this now," said Eisandre. She touched Wayd's shoulder then and looked him in the eye.

"Find our best way out of here. Take a small group. Take Wave with you, and scout us a way out. Don't give it away though, don't let them know where we will head."

"I will, Lady Eisandre," said Wayd, appreciative of her decision. He saluted, fist to chest and rushed off. Wave followed behind him with his heavy crossbow cocked and ready.

Actaeon still stared at the pillar, seemingly unaware of the activities around him. "I must warn though, the outcome might be dangerous. Everyone else should stand aside while I make the final connection alone."

That said, they used the elevated contraption to reach the arrow again near the pinnacle of the pillar. Actaeon and Lauryn ascended to the arrow together, while Davil and the two warbanders helped operate the contraption from the ground. Matt sat beside the apparatus, atop an overturned bucket, helping however he could. Several other Raedelleans, including some of the cutters and the injured, joined Eisandre as she watched this last attempt to free Caliburn from the clutches of the artifact.

Gritta placed a frail but steady hand on Eisandre's shoulder. "Have faith, Lady Eisandre. He won't fail."

Actaeon dug into his jacket and pulled free a coil of thin glass rope. "I am not sure if it will reach the rim, but we have to try." He also pulled free some needles and thread from a different pocket. The needles he spliced into the end of the glass rope so that several were sticking out from it. Those he worked into the butt of the arrow's shaft, where a vane was attached. He felt a tingling of energy at the contact, and the hairs that raised on the back of his neck told him that it might work.

He set the coil of glass rope down carefully on the end of the ladder and pulled a bandage roll and a charcoal stick from his jacket. He placed the charcoal stick like a splint between arrow shaft and glass rope and proceeded to wrap the entire setup with the bandage to ensure the weight of the rope would not tug the needles free.

Once done, he took the glass rope coil and carefully unwound it. He lowered it to Davil below and held up his hand for the new Companion to wait.

Davil, however, was not going to let the Engineer risk his life, and so, once he received the end of the rope, he knelt down and reached into the excavated hole. There he touched the free end of the glass rope to a freshly exposed portion of metal rim.

"No!" shouted Actaeon, once he realized what the Companion was doing.

Anyone that was watching Davil was blinded for the next several hours as he erupted into a conflagration of light and flame that generated an explosion which shook the earth itself and could be felt as far away as Adhikara and Shore. The poor, brave, new Companion was instantly and utterly obliterated in the aftermath. A large chunk of the artifact's thick metal rim hurtled across the camp. It tore through the field hospital and killed most of the cutters and injured warbanders there.

As the barrier failed, the undermined ground beneath the rim caved in and with it came the ground held in place by the barrier, the elevated apparatus, anyone standing too close, and of course, the Caliburn and Prince Aedwyn's other personal effects.

Matt and the two warbanders that were operating the apparatus were caught in the trench collapse and buried as the wagon-mounted device followed them into the hole, flopping unceremoniously on its side. Actaeon and Lauryn were thrown wide from it and disappeared under the dirt.

A large dust cloud kicked up over the entire site that completely obscured the vision of any would-be rescuers that were not blinded in the flash of the explosion.

When the dust cleared to reveal a severely canted pillar, Eisandre leapt into action. Though most beside her had been blinded in the explosion, she had been watching Actaeon atop his apparatus, and despite the lingering artifacts in her eyes, she was still able to function. She quickly directed those nearby that could still see to begin digging. She started digging herself, a sick feeling in the pit of her stomach.

Wayd rushed over to help and Eisandre ordered him back over to the defensive line. Trench and Wave she couldn't stop though, and they both arrived to dig for their friend and employer.

The two mercenaries quickly pulled Lauryn from the soft dirt. She was stained red with misted blood from the vaporized Companion that had settled upon the ground. Once they saw she was breathing, they set her aside to cough up the dust and dirt from her lungs and kept on digging.

A dozen paces away, Actaeon burst free from the blood-stained dirt and shook the dust from his clothes. He pulled his goggles up from his eyes and rubbed them, unable to clear his vision. Eisandre rushed to his side and hugged him tightly. He returned the hug and grinned.

"What happened? I cannot see," he said, his words shouted to overcome the ringing in his ears.

It was Wave that answered him, "You did it, Act! You shattered the thing. The barrier's down. It –"

He was interrupted as shouting broke out around the perimeter of the site. With the blast and subsequent dust cloud that was kicked up, the tribals made the decision to attack. The clash of swords and spears and the dying cries of warriors could be heard on all sides.

Actaeon reached out and grasped Wave's sleeve. He pulled the man-at-arms down toward him. "Go and aid the defensive line! I will help Eisandre find the sword."

Trench and Wave rushed off at Actaeon's orders, weapons drawn and ready as they leapt into the fray beside Balin, who was cutting tribals down on both sides of him with his big axe.

As Eisandre helped Actaeon to his feet, Lauryn staggered over and leaned on them both. "I saw Matt... and... the others... they were swept into the trench," she said, trying to catch her breath.

"Do you recall where they were standing? Lead me over there. We will dig," said Actaeon.

"Yes, over here beside the apparatus. I'll go get some shovels."

"No. Shovel blades might kill them. The dirt should be soft. We will dig with our hands," said Actaeon.

Eisandre led him after Lauryn to the overturned elevator apparatus. Now half-buried and broken by the rim fragment that ripped past it, the remnants of the apparatus were all coated with a thin sheen of red that was all that remained of Companion Davil.

A foot was sticking out from beneath one corner of the wagon and they began to dig there. They cleared out the area around the body first, and found that there was nothing left to be saved.

While they dug, tribal forces broke through the southern defensive perimeter and rallying cries went up from fighting Raedelleans to reinforce the area. Caked in blood and dirt, Eisandre stood and drew her sword. "I must go to their aid." She gave Lauryn a pleading look.

The young woodcarver nodded and waved her off. "Go. We've got this!"

"Hurry then. We cannot hold here." Eisandre raised her sword and rushed to the southern edge of the site. She hacked down a pair of charging tribals and rallied the warbanders to push the attackers back.

As the fighting continued around them, Actaeon and Lauryn dug for the lives of the other two helpers. They pulled the soft dirt aside with their hands and unearthed another body just beneath the cart. The woman's arm and part of her shoulder were missing and they gently moved her to the side and kept digging, their hands caked with blood-soaked dirt. Below the dead woman they found a large bucket, and began digging around that.

After some frantic digging, they pulled Matt out from beneath the wreckage. He was saved by the bucket that he had been sitting on, which helped form an air pocket around his face during the collapse. When they removed the bucket and pulled him free, he sputtered as he coughed up mouthfuls of loose dirt.

The Companion clutched their arms as Actaeon and Lauryn dragged him free. Lauryn dropped to her knees and took a moment to look around her.

To the west, the troops were holding fast, despite a large onslaught of tribals that pressed them. To the south, Eisandre had successfully repelled the attackers and was holding them off for the meantime. To the east, however, things were not going as well. The eastern line had begun to disintegrate, and the Raedelleans had taken heavy losses. Itarik stood side by side with Trench and together they prevented the line from falling apart. Lauryn watched as one attacker's head disappeared under the head of Trench's maul in a cloud of red mist that reminded her, with horror, of Davil. Itarik's sword was a blur as it cut a swath through the line of attackers. She'd made fine weapons from wood all her life and knew what their purpose was, but never had she seen anything like this. It was horrible.

"Lauryn?" Actaeon's voice interrupted her thoughts. "We need to find the Caliburn. By the sound of things, they will not hold for much longer."

"Yes, yes. Sorry, Act. I think it might have been somewhere over here." She took his free hand and led him over to a spot near the crooked pillar.

"Hold on. We can use my metal detection device." He withdrew the makeshift device from his jacket and handed it to her, thankful that he'd taken the time to make a new one after he'd lost the previous one in the Felmere.

She'd seen him use the device to find things on Blacksands Beach before and understood the concept. She knelt down and attached the bracket to the bottom of his halberd.

"You will have to be my eyes for this, Lauryn. I still suffer the effects of poor Davil's demise."

He held out the halberd with one hand and she led him to walk the terrain around the canted pillar's base while he swept the halberd slowly side to side. On the third pass, Lauren watched the needle-balanced sliver tilt to one side – and shrieked as an enemy warrior rushed them.

The man made no sound, his face painted with a strange tribal pattern and there was madness in his eyes as he lunged forward with his spear.

Lauryn shoved Actaeon aside and ducked down in time to watch the man plunge to the dirt and slide up beside her, a bolt buried in the side of his neck. She turned to look at Wave as he put his foot in the stirrup of his heavy crossbow and reloaded it. He offered her his one-eyed wink and rushed back into the fray.

She helped the Engineer back to his feet and they continued their search. When the needle began to turn back to indicate they had passed the object, she stopped him. "It is here, I think."

"Let us hope you are correct," said Actaeon with a grim expression.

Lauryn knelt and began to dig through the recently displaced dirt with her hands, but stopped when he touched her shoulder.

Instead, Actaeon plunged the shaft of the halberd into the loosened dirt at a shallow angle and then lifted. Some of the Prince's clothes emerged from the dirt along the shaft of the halberd.

"That's it! His tunic. Keep going!"

Actaeon stuck the shaft into the ground at several different angles, always touching the girl's shoulder to ensure that he didn't hit her. On the fifth try, he lifted and felt more resistance. He applied more pressure and the large blade was drawn free from the ground.

"That's it!" she shouted victoriously.

"There is still the torc – Elphin's Torc. Can you find it?" he asked.

She plunged her arms in the loose dirt to look for it.

On the southern edge of the site, Eisandre fought on, leading her men and women. Bodies lay all around them, brothers, sisters, and enemies alike. Despite the constant press, they held. The way the tribals fought, perhaps the fact that they remained silent when they charged, when they clashed, and when they died, reminded her of the cross-faced raiders she had fought with Actaeon. When Wayd arrived at her side and touched her shoulder, she frowned at him.

"Tell me that you have found an escape route."

"Aye, Lady. I've found one. It is on the western front. We need to break through some of the tribals, but then we can flee south and west."

"Good. Ready your forces."

Wayd saluted and rushed off to follow her command.

The familiar tone of an Arbiter's whistle caught her attention and she left Balin in charge of the southern line. Quickly, she ran to where the Engineer was digging.

The Caliburn lay there, covered in dirt at his feet.

"Lady Eisandre Caliburn, I present your sword," said Actaeon with a grin.

Eisandre knelt beside it, bowing her head in remembrance of her brother. She knew the pillar artifact was broken – he wasn't coming back. With any hope, it had sent him somewhere that he could survive, but somehow, she knew they wouldn't see him again. She said a silent prayer to the Fallen, to watch over him.

When she stood again, she held the heavy blade in one hand and her own bloody sword in the other. She raised Caliburn slowly in the air and addressed those present, her voice carrying, despite the clash of combat around her.

"We continue south!" she called out to her people. "To heal Raedelle and reunite our people. For Aedwyn. For our brave friends who have died for this cause. For ourselves. And most importantly: For Raedelle!"

Despite their exhaustion and injury, a cheer went up among the embattled forces, echoing her own cry.

And with renewed vigor and intensity, they fought their way out through the scouted escape route, breaking through the tribal forces and making their way south as the morning's sun rose on the horizon.

87 A.R., the 26ᵗʰ day of Rainbreak

FLIGHT

I T WAS MISERABLE TRAVELING FOR the Raedellean party after they escaped the artifact site. The skies darkened with clouds, blotting out the rising morning sun, as though to mock them. The deluge of rain that came next was even worse, creating mud and loosening the terrain, which made their progress south even more difficult.

"Damned rain. It's supposed to be Rainbreak!" said Wave as he jogged south along the flank beside Balin.

"Keep yer complaints to yerself, Wave. We're part of something important here. I ain't never in my life seen a braver band than these wall breakers," said the stocky smith.

"Wall Breakers, eh? I like the sound of that," said Wave.

Three members of the rearguard were killed by errant tribal arrows as they fled south and west, away from the fallen pillar. There were skirmishes whenever their pursuers drew close, but no Raedelleans fell during those clashes. With six injured and twice that many carrying the wounded, that left only fifteen to fight. Those not bearing the wounded broke up into four groups. Wave, Balin, and another took one flank while Trench and two warbanders took the other. Eisandre and one other warbander led the way with Actaeon and Lauryn close behind. Lauryn led Actaeon by the hand since his vision had yet to return. At the rear, Itarik and Wayd kept the enemy at bay, three of the best fighters at their side.

Things looked bleak. If a large attack was mounted on any side, they would be easily overrun and slaughtered. In good weather, they were still a day's march from Shore. However, the rain and the constant onslaught that the rearguard faced slowed their pace.

And if that wasn't bad enough, at midday the man beside Eisandre slipped from a crumbled wall and broke his back. The one cutter that was left alive, Gritta, rushed to his side and began the work to immobilize him. Lauryn helped her, using lashed spears and any rope or cord that could be gathered – much of it from Actaeon's pockets.

The midday sky could've been midnight for all they were concerned. The black blanket of clouds had long wiped away any memory of sun.

While they worked, Eisandre called a stop and had everyone dig in and ready their ranged weapons. Fortuitously, the incident occurred while they were between two large, ruined buildings, and they only had the rear and the front to guard. The first tribal scouts were caught by surprise and brought down with a single volley of arrows.

Actaeon, whose vision had begun to recover, Trench, and Wave headed south to find something to use as a sled to drag the man. All such objects had already been put to use to haul Companion Matt and two of the other badly wounded warriors. Eisandre sent Wayd with them.

Caked in mud and blood and sapped of energy, the small party picked their way carefully through the ruins, first to the south, and then a distance off to the east of the temporary camp.

Actaeon led the way down along a steep, debris-covered slope, using his halberd to stay upright. He slid to a stop near a long, flat object with a large mechanism jutting from one side.

"This should work, if we can free it," he said, pulling the goggles up from his eyes to observe the object more closely.

The giant mercenary slid down the hill and landed roughly on his backside next to the Engineer. He glowered, his scar turning a deep red. "By the Fallen, I hate this damned weather. Isn't the monsoon season supposed to be done with?"

Wave slid up beside him. He nimbly kept his footing and gave the big man a playful shove. "Don't go breaking your leg. Not one of us here's going to carry your monstrosity of a frame. You'll have to take the rearguard in that case... far to the rear. Maybe we'd even see you on the way back north."

"Now now, Wave. We will not be leaving anyone behind. That is why we are out here in the first place," said Actaeon with a grin. He stooped and began to work at the mechanism in an attempt to free it.

"That's right, Trench. We're Wall Breakers now. Nothing can stop us," said Wayd with a weak grin as he echoed the name Balin had coined. The name had caught on with what remained of the ragtag warband. Before arriving at the pillar, the group had little identity – comprised only of the scattered Raedelleans that could be pulled together from around Pyramid. Since then, nearly two thirds had been killed in action and the chances of them making it off the Wall looked slim. The survivors had turned into a cohesive fighting unit, and the fact that they had broken through the pillar's barrier had invigorated them with a fresh fighting spirit. The hard part was done, now they just had to make it home alive.

An errant flash of lightning struck the nearby ruins, followed by a rumble of thunder that rattled their teeth. Trench's eyes narrowed and he unshouldered his maul. He'd seen something in the lightning flash – just for a moment, but it was there. "Trouble, Act," he said simply.

Wave unslung his heavy crossbow and used his foot to cock it and load another bolt. "More of those tribal bastards? I'm telling ya, they must've been paid off. I haven't seen 'em that persistent since the last time we saw those cross-faced raiders."

"Curious, Wave. They reminded me of them, too. Not only the persistence though, but also how quiet they are. Have you two ever come across anything like that?" Actaeon looked between the two veterans. He unslung his bow and looked through the scope.

Trench growled. "Not since the Invasion War. There were a few battles that we fought like this. I'd rather forget about them..."

Actaeon passed his scope to Wayd. "Here, take a look. My vision is still not whole. Look through the tube and let me know what you see."

Wayd gave the scope a strange look before he accepted it and stared through, as instructed. After a few moments he spoke, "They're Raedelleans. Most of them have the wedge of Incline on their tabards. Though I see a few Blackstone men as well." He handed the bow back to Actaeon.

"What are your thoughts, should we parlay with them?" asked the Engineer.

"The same bastards that captured you?" asked Wayd. "And do what?

Deliver ourselves into their hands? It was probably Arcady who sent them in the first place. To stop us."

"I think it's clear as day they're here to stop us," said Wave. "With what's going on in Raedelle, I doubt they'd be sending out warbands like this unless it has something to do with us. Especially to this location, and from Blackstone nonetheless."

Trench rubbed the stubble on his jaw and regarded the force in the distance as another lightning strike illuminated them amidst frozen drops of rain. "It's a matter of numbers, Act. If they came out here to stop us, they have an easy job ahead of them. We're already beset by tribal forces, and if you subtract the injured, they have us beat by almost two to one by the looks of it. You're from Incline, right? Maybe you know them. Maybe you can sway them. The other option is to return to the camp and make a final stand."

"And if they capture us, then what? Who warns Eisandre?" asked Wayd crossly.

"I believe I have a solution for that." Actaeon brought out his Arbiter's whistle from his pocket. He knew many of the Arbiter signals – he'd needed to learn them for the whistle redesign. He shouldered his bow and put the whistle to his lips to blow.

The notes sounded freakishly similar to one of the common Arbiter whistle patterns, but in the heavy rain and amidst the ruins, it was an eerie, dampened sound. After he finished, he raised a hand high.

In the distance, they heard shouts among the Shorian forces. Either they had yet to spot Actaeon and team, or the whistle's tones stirred them to prep for an attack.

A group broke off from the main Shorian force and made their way over.

"Eleven," grunted Trench. His eyes narrowed upon the leader of the group.

When they drew near, Actaeon waved his hand and shouted, his voice carrying along the slope toward the approaching force. "Hail friends! Be welcome!"

From the distance came a reply, "Well met!" It was swallowed in a rumble of thunder.

"Curious…" said Actaeon. "That voice sounds so familiar. Let us ascend and meet them on level ground."

Wayd looked unhappy about it, but he followed as they picked their way back up the pile.

Wave squinted at the approaching warriors. "Be careful not to knock any out, lest the blades of Warchief Vain grace their ne–" He was interrupted by a rough shove from Trench, who glared down at him, daring him to continue.

"Keep yer tongue, Wave. You know that things aren't all so black and white when it comes to war and politics."

"Yeah, yeah. There're all those shades of red in between." Wave kept his tongue though.

The two groups came to a stop at a cautious distance apart. The Shorians formed a tight semicircle behind their leader and his top warbanders. The leader, a young Captain with long brown hair and a confident gaze, raised a hand to brush the wet locks from his eyes and regarded them carefully. His eyes locked with Actaeon's. "Is that – ?"

"It is," said a young woman beside him. The woman's features were hidden beneath the cowl of her hood, though the curly locks of blazing red hair that hung down her chest raised the Engineer's suspicions. When she threw back her hood, it confirmed it – her face above her right eye was stretched and rippled from an old burn that made Actaeon cringe in remembrance. The tightly drawn skin held her right eye open wider, which only increased the drawing intensity of her gaze. She was not the little girl he remembered. "It is good to see you, Act," she said, her voice gently musical in the way he recalled from their childhood.

Suddenly, all the years wound back and Actaeon was standing with his young friend Jezail in the tiny shack that he'd called his workshop. A few years younger than he, she had idolized young Actaeon – following him around, and gathering supplies for his experiments. His little assistant. He'd loved her then, like the little sister he'd never had. She'd been his constant companion.

All that had changed though, on that one fateful day, as Actaeon poured the final bottle atop the mixture. There was a snap, and his hand was afire in blue flame that ran all the way up his arm to the shoulder. Worse yet were the screams of his little redhead assistant. The contrast of the blue fire on her red hair was shocking. He had beaten out the flames with an empty sack, but the damage was done. They would never trust him around little Jezail again. Neither would he.

One of the most beautiful gems of Incline, scarred for life.

"Well, well, then – look at what the storm blew in!" said the Captain with a broad grin that brought Actaeon out of the flashback with a jolt.

"Actually, we were washed in with an unexpected mudslide," said Actaeon with his characteristic grin as he brushed some of the mud from his sleeve. When his two childhood friends started laughing, he couldn't help but to join them. "This was certainly an unanticipated course of events. Varisk, it is good to see you again, my friend. And Jezail, look at you, all grown up now. It has truly been too long." The last time he had been in Shore, the two had been off to complete their trials and serve with Incline's warband.

Varisk looked at Jezail and his blush could be seen even through the heavy rain. "She has indeed grown up," he replied.

"This is Wayd Arbrigel," Actaeon said, introducing the others. "He helps to lead our merry band. And these two jokers are my own men, Wave and Trench. What brings you out this –"

His words were cut short as four of the men in Varisk's party drew swords and readied their spears. "Those are the two! Arrest them!" The men stepped forward and were met by the point of Wave's bolt aimed at one throat and the tip of his rapier at another. Trench held his maul before him, daring one of them to strike it.

"Surprise, surprise..." Wave murmured.

As the rain ran down everyone's face, you could cut the tension with a knife.

Wayd brought the point of his spear to bear and stepped up beside Trench.

Actaeon and Varisk remained where they stood. Neither drew a weapon. Varisk laughed.

"What're you laughing about, Conmara? Do your job and arrest these criminals already!" said one of the Blackstone men. "You've said enough – do as your Lord Arcady ordered."

With a subtle gesture from their Captain, the Incliners skillfully disarmed and restrained the Blackstoners, pulling them to the side as they spit and fumed.

Wave and Trench smirked to one another and visibly relaxed.

The Captain cleared his throat. "It is true that we have been dispatched by the Lord Shore to arrest your two men. They, along with the Lady Eisandre Caliburn, stand accused of the murder of twenty-one Raedelleans inside the Blackstone Fortress."

"Varisk, surely —"

"Quiet, Jezail. Your Captain is speaking," said Varisk sharply, though he offered her an apologetic look. "Listen, Act... we didn't know you'd be out here with them. Perhaps you were involved and perhaps not. I would hear your side of the story, and would like to speak with the Lady Eisandre, of course. I know the Caliburns are honorable people. If Lady Eisandre did something wrong, I'm sure she'll take responsibility. I'd prefer to resolve this without any fighting among brothers and sisters of Raedelle."

"I'll not be quiet, Varisk. I have been a member of this warband as long as you, Captain or no," said Jezail. Varisk rolled his eyes as she continued, "Listen, Act – whatever happened, we know that you wouldn't have committed such an atrocity, nor would you employ men who did. There is an explanation for this and we must hear it now."

"The Lord Arcady will have your head for this, you little brat!" cried out one of the Blackstone men.

One of the Incliners holding him shoved him to the dirt. "Keep yer tongue."

"Very well... she is right. I'll hear you tell it first, Actaeon. Tell it well," said the Captain.

The Engineer considered for a long moment before he started. "Yes, it seems as though the pawns are aplenty in this grand scheme. Though I imagine, knowing you both, that you will exercise judgement where this is concerned. You are here to arrest the Lady Eisandre and my two friends, no doubt, for alleged crimes committed. You should take me to your entire group so that I can tell them the true story behind what happened. I believe even the men from Blackstone would be enlightened to hear it. You both know me as a seeker of truth. If you still believe in me, then you will not doubt the veracity of my story."

"Yes, that's the Actaeon I knew as a child. We stand here adults now, with different allegiances and motivations. Even so, I've been sent by the Lord Arcady on this task, and he has entrusted me to make the correct judgements in how to proceed since he's not here himself. It will have to do," said Varisk.

"Excellent," said Actaeon. He gestured to the others then. "My friends will return to the camp for now. After you hear my full story, we can talk further about how to best proceed."

"Act, we'll go with you. I'm not liking the attitude of some of these people," said Wave.

Actaeon held up his hand to stall Wave's protest. "These are my friends, Wave. I know you are considering my safety, but this is necessary. The people of Raedelle must hear the truth. It starts here, in places like this mud pit." He grinned and met the eyes of his three companions, each in turn.

Trench nodded immediately and Wayd followed suit.

Wave cursed under his breath and shook his head. "Fine, Act, but I don't like it."

Actaeon nodded to the Captain. "My friend, let us proceed."

The Captain led the way back to the rest of the warband. They were on high alert as he approached. He put his fingers to his lips and whistled loudly to get everyone's attention. "Look what the Shore's gone and washed up. Listen up, everyone. He's got a story to tell and I'll have ya hear it."

The Engineer looked with interest at those gathered. He recognized more than one face, but none were as familiar as Varisk and Jezail. He walked to the center of the warband and leant heavily upon his halberd. As he scanned the faces of the warbanders, he found a mixture of suspicion, familiarity, and anger.

Unconsciously, he reached over and scratched his right arm through the thick leather of his jacket. The movement reminded him of Jezail again, and he looked back at the woman he had known back when she was a young girl. They shared the same horrible burn – a burn that heralded both tragedy and discovery. He offered her a sad smile.

The memory burst back into his mind, unbidden – the smell of burnt flesh, the blue flames licking up his own arm before they nearly engulfed Jezail, and the way he had to knock her to the ground and practically smother her to put out the fire. Her screams sounded in his mind and he shuddered. He had wrapped her in soaked blankets to finally put the rest of the blue fire out. When the adults had arrived, summoned by her cries, they had pulled off the blankets and he remembered how the blue fire flared up again, reigniting the screams.

"Get on with it then, we're listening."

It was one of the Blackstone warbanders, anger in her tone.

Actaeon met her gaze levelly and nodded, pushing the memory to the depths of his mind. "Starting at the beginning will make the most logical sense, so I shall begin there. I was in Saint Torin's Hold in Pyramid when the news arrived of our Prince's entrapment in the artifact just north of here. I joined the sisters Caliburn on their journey south to rescue him. We were unable to rescue the Prince, and I was blasted by the artifact and knocked unconscious in the process. When I awoke some days later, I found myself in a room in the Blackstone Fortress. A man named Drystan Beiloff came to speak with me shortly after I awoke. He made it clear to me that I would not be allowed to leave, and that I must draw up plans for them to break the Caliburn sword free from within the artifact's barrier. I truly believe that he would have hurt or tortured me, but I managed to convince him that the Lord Arcady would be displeased with my inability to work. His fear of Arcady stopped him from doing me any real harm. Despite that, I was not allowed to leave the quarters I was given, nor send out any correspondence."

"How'd you escape?" blurted out Jezail, concerned.

Actaeon rubbed the rain from his eyes and continued, "It was the Lady Eisandre who came to rescue me from captivity. She came with my own men, Trench and Wave, and they located me in the Blackstone Fortress and infiltrated it, using waythorn-coated blades to render the guards unconscious. Waythorn is a poison that temporarily renders one unconscious, and also numbs the spot where the blade enters. The person it is inflicted upon does not feel it, and it will put them under for around an hour – without killing them. They made it to the room I was being held in and freed me. All four of us then used waythorn-coated blades to fight our way free of the fortress."

There were more than a few exclamations at that, but Actaeon held up his hand.

"Not *one* of the persons we encountered was dead when we left," he said, voice raised to overcome the rumblings of the crowd. "Not a soul. The plan was enacted perfectly and did no harm to our fellow Raedelleans. This I swear to you. Every one of those men, women, and one child, were killed after we left – to frame us for the murders and discredit Lady Eisandre."

Shouts broke out across the warband – cries of outrage at Actaeon's version of the story. Others yet argued for the truth of his words. Actaeon wasn't surprised to see that the most angry individuals were from Blackstone.

"Silence!" Varisk's voice boomed over the cacophony. "Actaeon, these are serious implications you are making. Do you have any proof of this? Can you show us this waythorn? I've never heard of it."

"I have no waythorn on me," admitted Actaeon with a frown. "Wave may have some, but we shall have to verify this at a later time. As far as proof, I have none, save my story and the word of the loyal friends that stood at my side." The words were drowned out by the resumption of shouting and he shook his head. Some of the warriors were shoving each other and violence was close to erupting.

Actaeon drew the Arbiter whistle and blew on it loudly in a pattern that any Arbiter would recognize as: *all's well.*

He was about to speak again, when one of the Blackstone warbanders, a woman with blond hair and warpaint on her face, stepped forward. "Describe the waythorn. What's it look like?" she demanded.

"Wave can demonstrate it wh–"

"No, tell me now. Tell me what it looks like."

"It looks like golden flakes. It is mixed into a suspension before the application to a blade," answered Actaeon.

The young woman's breath caught in her throat. She took several more steps forward until she was up in Actaeon's face. She stared him hard in the eye for a while before she turned to face the others.

"Those of you that don't know me, I am Pollia, mother of Olli. Olli was the child who was killed. My..." she sobbed then, "my little Page." Everyone drew silent to listen to the woman. "I knew something was strange. His throat was cut – someone cut the throat of a young boy! But his hand was also cut, and this one minor, as if done by someone who held back the full force of their blade. And..." she let out a sob that racked her body. "There were golden flakes in that cut on his hand. I can't put it out of my mind."

She fell to her knees and began to cry then. Her spear fell to the muddy rubble at her feet.

"He's telling the truth then. They didn't murder them. Somebody else did," said Jezail, finding words where none of the others could. She dropped down to her knees beside the woman and held her. Pollia sobbed, her body spasming in Jezail's embrace. Jezail forced a smile up at the Engineer. "I believe you, Act. Which means that Lady Eisandre must have risked everything to come to this point – must still risk everything. What is she like? All I know is that she's an Arbiter."

"She *was* an Arbiter," explained Actaeon. "Her Order expelled her after she broke her vow of neutrality to come rescue me." He beamed with pride as he continued, "I can say with confidence that she carries a strength within her that is incredible. She is one of the truest people that I have ever met. She will guide our fellow Raedelleans justly if they decide to follow her. Before Aedwyn disappeared into the artifact, he told her to 'bring them together'. I can only assume that he meant Raedelle. And I truly believe she may be the only one who can bring us all together at this point, because she really does care about the sanctity of Raedellean freedom that we all hold dear."

Jezail's eyes were bright with hope as she listened, hanging on every word. Behind her, Varisk looked doubtful.

"Listen, Act. Of course you'd say that you were kidnapped, and that they used this waythorn stuff to knock people out instead of killing them. I'm not a moron – I can see in your eyes that your feelings for the Lady Eisandre run deep. You'd clearly say whatever you must to protect her," said the Captain. He glanced at Pollia then, and frowned. "I know that you lost Olli, but we must be careful that we are not misled here with stories. We're responsible for the future of Raedelle, and what happens in this moment may change everything. Act, you're gonna have to do more than just speak – you've got to *show* us you have proof. Short of that, I've gotta bring you to Lord Arcady."

Actaeon nodded, slowly considering, and after some thought his hand fell to the hilt of the dagger at his belt. The movement caused several present to tense, their hands reaching for weapons. He noted the tension though, and tapped the dagger gently. "I believe I still have waythorn on this." Hopefully it hadn't been wiped off when he had used it to cut open

Matt's pantleg. "Let me just finish the story and I shall use it on myself if you like, to demonstrate its efficacy."

When there was no argument, he continued, "Eisandre gained support in Pyramid and we departed soon after to return to the pillar artifact. It was there that we managed to free the Caliburn from the pillar's barrier and restore it to Caliburn hands. However, we were constantly harried by organized tribals from the moment we arrived. They killed more than fifty of our people." He let that sink in. "And even after we freed the sword and headed south, they have pursued us. Truly, such drive in tribals to bring combat to a heavily armed party is unusual to say the least – especially on the Wall. I shall let each of you draw your own conclusions there. With the imminent meeting of the Conclave of Lords in Lakehold and the disappearance of Eshelle, we must escort Eisandre to the Conclave so that she may address them and speak for the Caliburns. Having her arrested is a clever play to prevent her from making that Conclave and speaking her truths. Let the Conclave hear her words and the words of Lord Arcady. Let them judge for themselves!"

Most of those present were in thought about the words of the Engineer, considering and weighing the facts. Only a handful were still grumbling about it, discarding the story as obviously false.

"That's right, let the Conclave be the judge!" called one man from the back of the crowd.

It was the warbander Pollia that stepped forward to address Actaeon. "Alright, Engineer. We hear ya. And by the Fallen, may your words ring true." She rolled back her sleeve and extended her wrist toward him. "You'll cut me and either lay bare the truth of your words, or my comrades will lay open your throat in the name of my son, Olli."

There was a hush in the crowd at that, and two of the Blackstone men that hadn't been disarmed drew their swords and stepped forward to flank Pollia. Jezail voiced an objection, but was silenced with a touch from Varisk.

Actaeon turned slowly to scan those present, his emerald gaze moving from face to face. His eyes found Jezail's last and she looked as though she might burst into tears. He winked and shot her a grin before he turned back to Pollia and stepped forward. He looked the poor mother of the dead page in the eyes and nodded solemnly. "As a friend of mine, Phyrius, might say: My word is truth. Now let us hope the efficacy of waythorn exceeds all expectations."

"Do it," said the woman.

He drew the hooked dagger slowly, and took her hand in his own. His gesture was quick – he didn't need the rivulets of rain to wash free any of the gold flakes that might remain. He cut the woman's palm, and her blood ran together with the rain in her palm.

Lifebeats pounded away.

And then more.

Pollia looked into his eyes and he saw the hate flame up there, death in her gaze. But then, there was relief in its place and she collapsed forward into his arms.

Actaeon lowered her carefully to the ground, amidst a cacophony of shouts from those present.

One of the the Blackstone men actually dropped his sword into the mud.

The other raised his. "It means nothing!" The cry echoed across the ruins, despite the rain, and the blade was a flash, descending downward to open the Engineer's neck.

But the Captain's blade was faster and the clash of steel on steel drowned out everything else. The snap riposte removed the man's head, which landed on the ground with a thud.

There was silence then, and the rain washed the blood from Varisk's blade as he stood over Actaeon, daring anyone else to defy him.

"His words are truth," spoke the Captain. "He passed Pollia's test, and he will have our cooperation. As my friend said: may the Conclave decide from here. We are but the tip of Raedelle's sharp spear. Our duty now lies in bringing the Lady Eisandre to Lakehold. Whatever may happen there, our honor will remain intact."

Actaeon lowered Pollia's head carefully to the ground and the Blackstone man who had dropped his sword tended to her. He stood and wiped the blood splatter from his face. "Thank you, my friend. I was not yet ready to lose my head. Perhaps you will consider joining us in escort to Lakehold then. We are weary and carrying injured, and there are certain to be more attacks from the tribals that trail us. We will need your swords and spears,

Varisk, if we are to make it." He scratched the back of his right hand through its fingerless glove.

Jezail slammed into him, wrapping him in a tight hug. The rain washed her tears away.

"An escort to Lakehold will deliver you to the Lord Arcady and the rest of the Conclave. Understand that it may not go as you desire," said the Captain.

"You are correct there," said Actaeon as he hugged Jezail in return. "Please understand though, that myself and the others in our party will put our lives on the line for Eisandre, if need be. She means that much to Raedelle's future: the last bright star in the Caliburn line. She must appear at the Conclave of Raedellean Lords."

"Then we will escort you, Actaeon. And the Lady Eisandre will make it to the Conclave safely."

Thirty-two warriors marched into Eisandre's camp an hour later, led by Actaeon and Varisk Conmara, Captain of the Incline warband. Just seven of the Blackstone fighters left, to return to Shore and their Lord Arcady.

WALL BREAKERS

A CHEER WENT UP FROM THE tired men and women of the band led by Eisandre Caliburn upon seeing the fresh faces come to join them. Eisandre came forward to personally greet them all.

The Shorian warband marched into the center of camp, full of energy and well supplied. They formed a rough circle there, while the Raedelleans that had broken through the pillar gathered around them loosely. There was still suspicion in the eyes of many on both sides, and they stood there for several long moments, none knowing what to say.

It was Itarik who stepped forward first. "Ithelie?" he asked, peering into the middle of the newcomers. He sheathed his sword and stepped forward into the crowd of Shorians to wrap his arms around the Voice in her green robes. He pulled her to him tight and held her close. She returned his hug with equal ferocity before she stepped back and looked him in the eye.

"Brother – I didn't know we'd meet here."

"Aye," said Itarik with some surprise. "And what are you doing here?"

"I am here because I am needed."

That seemed to satisfy his question, and so the Companion nodded. "Then I am glad to have you here. We all are."

The Captain of the Incliners cleared his throat then and stepped forward. Itarik turned to face him, remaining beside his sister.

"We have journeyed here from Shore," began Varisk, his voice carrying, "to apprehend three wanted criminals at the orders of the Lord Arcady." Several groans went up at that. "However, I have spoken to my friend,

Actaeon, and he tells a different story than the one I was told. He tells a story of being held against his will, of the sacrifice of one person's life's work to save him, of a force of fighters led by the last Caliburn that is near to being wiped out. It is a story I have come to see for myself, and I see the truth of it before me.

"I'm not one to break my orders though, so I must escort you back to Raedelle, Lady Eisandre, to face justice. I will tell you this, though: We'll be escorting you back to Caliburn Castle, not Blackstone Fortress. The full Conclave will decide your fate, for good or for ill – not me nor any other present. I can guarantee one thing though, and that is we'll get you back alive. No tribals are going to take the last of the Caliburns from us. Not while my heart, or the heart of any man or woman in my warband still beats!"

A cheer erupted from both sides at that and the two circles became one, with hands clasped and embraces all around.

Eisandre hugged Actaeon and kissed his cheek. When she stepped back, she hefted the greatsword Caliburn from her back and raised it high until she had everyone's attention.

"Your decision on this day will not be forgotten, Captain Varisk. I will stand before the Conclave, as you said, and I trust them to decide the truth." Varisk nodded and she turned and spotted Wayd. "There is one more thing that we must do before we depart. Wayd Arbrigel, I would elevate you to Companion. I ask that you defend the Caliburns and thereby defend Raedelle. Would you accept?"

Wayd spun and shot her a stunned look. He shook his head in disbelief and stepped forward before Eisandre, dropping to his knees in the mud. "I will be your stalwart defender, Lady Eisandre."

She touched the pommel of the sword to his forehead. "Then rise, Companion Wayd. I will need your continued service."

The Lady Eisandre Caliburn turned to face the others and raised the famous sword high in the air once more. "To me, you brave Wall Breakers. We set out for Raedelle – to defend our way of life and the freedom of our people."

They departed immediately, setting on a winding path through the ruins of the Wall, guided roughly southward by advance scouts. Companion Itarik led the combined warband, with Wayd as his close second.

Itarik himself was a study in exhaustion, but somehow the man continued on, despite having been out on the Wall for eighteen straight days with hardly any rest.

The six injured were carried in the small sleds and litters that had been rigged up. They were kept in the center of the march, to be more easily defended.

Small groups of scouts were off to the east and west, flanking the group as it travelled to make sure they didn't get caught off guard. Trench joined one group and Wave the other. The two mercenaries emulated the behavior they typically showed when exploring with the Engineer. At the rear were Varisk and Jezail, leading some of the best fighters in the Incline warband. Sixty-five strong now, the Raedellean force led by Lady Eisandre had more than doubled, and marched forth with a renewed vigor and purpose.

Actaeon traveled up and down the line, talking alternatively to Matt, his Shorian friends, and checking in with Eisandre.

Matt appreciated his taking the time to speak with him, though the man lapsed periodically into unconsciousness. The infection in his leg was beginning to win the battle. At one point, when he passed out as Actaeon was speaking to him, the Voice came to say a prayer over the man.

Not one for prayer, Actaeon made his way forward to speak with Eisandre. When he arrived at her side and offered her a grin, she gave him a grim look in return.

"Things are looking up, Eis. Why the long face?" he asked.

"We're still outnumbered. If you count the number we lost, they are equal to the number we have now. I would not call that looking up," Eisandre said stoically.

"Still, outnumbered we may be, but we are moving now. And with the fresh contingent, we have a chance. As it stood, without those from Shore who joined us, it was only a matter of time before the tribals slaughtered us," said Actaeon. "Speaking of them. Have you noticed –"

"How quiet they are," said Eisandre, finishing his sentence. "Yes. Much like our encounters with the raiders that wanted to capture you. I've thought that as well."

"It makes me wonder," said the Engineer thoughtfully. "It almost seemed as though the cross-faced raiders were working as one concerted unit, without coordination. Either they were sharing thoughts between one another without words, or they were all being controlled by... something. How something like that might work, I have no idea. Some sort of projected energy, like with luminaries, only with commands. It is fascinating."

"You are fascinating," said Eisandre. "What you just described is terrifying – like something out of a nightmare. Yet you are fascinated by such a thing."

"Everything has an explanation in this world," said Actaeon. "It is just a matter of discovering said explanation." He used his halberd to pick his way past a particularly treacherous section of terrain, reaching out to steady Eisandre as they passed over it.

"If it's even possible."

"Well, I think that it is always possible. Just a matter of time and capability. There is much that we have yet to learn to fully understand the technology of the Ancients, but I believe it is all within the realm of possibility, though perhaps not within our lifetime," concluded Actaeon. "Oh," he said, remembering suddenly, "I wanted to tell you. The young page that died in Blackstone Fortress, do you remember?"

"The one who was murdered," said Eisandre, defensively.

"Yes. His mother – she is one of the warbanders from Blackstone. She has decided to join us."

"Why would she do that if she thought we killed her son," asked Eisandre, genuinely confused.

"Because I showed them the waythorn. She saw that proof, and remembered the gold flakes in the palm of her son's hand," said Actaeon.

"Oh. Then I'm glad she has decided to join us," said Eisandre, still confused.

There was a moment of silence between them then and it hung as thick as the raindrops that fell between the pair.

"It would mean a lot to her," Actaeon said, "if you offered your condolences. His name was Olli," he said, as an afterthought.

Eisandre looked at him with her brilliant blue eyes and nodded. She broke step with him and stopped, turning to face the warbanders behind her. She looked back at Actaeon, realizing that she didn't know who she was going to offer condolences to. "Who?" she asked simply.

Actaeon pointed at a woman that bore one of the sleds for the wounded. "There. Her name is Pollia."

When the last of the Caliburns started toward Pollia, Actaeon followed.

Eisandre stopped before Pollia, which forced the warbander to come to a stop as well. Once one of the litters stopped moving, the rest of the force halted. Itarik brought them to a stop once he noticed the delay.

Pollia looked up at Eisandre, who stood a head above her, and straightened.

"Actaeon told me about Olli," said Eisandre.

"Yes?"

"He should not have died. What was done to him was terrible and I'm sorry that it happened. We will do our best to find justice for him," said Eisandre, regarding the woman before her evenly.

Pollia made a study of the muddy ground at her feet. When she lifted her face to regard the Lady Eisandre once more, she nodded and reached out to take her hands in her own. "Thank you." The rain streaming down Pollia's face hid any tears that might have fallen.

Eisandre accepted her hands with some difficulty and simply nodded. She realized then, that the progress southward had halted and she released the woman's hands and stepped away, turning to Itarik. "Continue forward, Companion Itarik," she called, and the force of Raedelleans began to move once again.

The afternoon was waning, and the light began to dim as the sun set, hidden by the clouds and rain. The skies let loose once more, unleashing a torrent of rain that soaked them all to the bone.

"I thought the damned monsoon season was over!" said Trench, his voice carrying from the right flank.

"Keep your eyes sharp! I anticipate attack," called out Itarik, simply. The Companion glanced back and signaled to the rearguard to reinforce the left flank.

Varisk nodded and dispatched a group of his warriors to join the left.

When Jezail arrived nearby, Wave grinned at her and offered his disconcerting wink before checking the bolt in his crossbow. "Seems they'll attack this side first, eh? Good. With any luck I'll have bragging rights over Trench on the right. Big, ugly bastard'll owe me an ale."

Jezail smiled at him. "You'll be able to have it when everyone makes it to the Conclave."

The Raedellean line passed through a region strewn with the wreckage of ancient buildings and the ungainly terrain began to cant forward sharply, which caused several warbanders to lose their footing.

Wave smirked at her words. "Everyone? Isn't that asking al—" The man-at-arms' comment was interrupted though, and his crossbow string twanged sharply. It cast a bolt a short distance to lodge deeply into the skull of a tribal that had emerged from one of the crumbling openings in the building they passed nearest to. He quickly put his foot in the stirrup to recock the weapon as a dozen tribals charged them from the ruined structure, brandishing spears and spiked clubs.

Beside him, Jezail let loose two arrows in quick succession, then one more, before she fell back against the onrush of attackers. A man fell for each of her arrows.

Wave tried to load another bolt, but the first of the attackers was atop him already. He nimbly dodged a thrust from the man's spear and jammed the bolt into the tribal's extended forearm. To the next attacker, he tossed the heavy crossbow, which the man caught in his off hand. Wave's flamberge rapier was out of its sheath by then and it arced its way gracefully about the mercenary, leaving one man without a working throat, and the other without his spear in hand.

A slung rock caught one of the Shorians beside him in the throat, crushing it. The man went down heavily into the mud, choking on his last attempt to breath. Another Raedellean took a club to the side of his head, his skull imploding in a burst of brain matter that sprayed Wave along one side. The tribal with the club brought the weapon around to swing at Wave, but was run through and pinned to the ground by Wayd's spearpoint before the mercenary could even react.

Wave turned to watch the rest of the tribals flee. He picked up his crossbow and trudged over to one of the enemy that was trying to crawl away, an arrow through his thigh. He grinned down and brought the heavy stock of the crossbow down on the side of his head. "Two and... one captive. Beat that!" He dragged the semi-conscious man off to the center and handed him off to a warbander that had retreated from the left to get an arrow wound taken care of. "Here ya go. See what information you can get out of him. Like why are they harrying us and who paid them."

The Wall Breakers continued along at a quick pace, despite the skirmish on the left flank. The dead were left behind in their haste, though Ithelie paused to say prayers for those fallen. Eisandre and Itarik led the group onward with Trench leading the right flank and Wayd leading the left. Varisk and his force took up the rear.

At the center, Actaeon paused to sweep their surrounds with the scope of his recurve. Once done, he doubled his pace to join Eisandre and Itarik at the front of the formation. "I see a lot of movement off to the right, but the rain limits my visibility."

"We must continue forward. Stay at the fore and keep me apprised with your scope," said Itarik. Behind them, several loud protests could be heard as those at the rear realized they would be leaving their dead behind.

"Keep on forward!" shouted Varisk, at the rear. "We'll all be taken, otherwise."

Despite their grumbles and protests, the men and women listened to him and continued on. As they did, a slow, mournful melody came to life to voice their sadness as they marched. The melody did not mourn for long though, and as soon as the somber notes were played in response to the deaths of their friends, the melody shifted to one that was faster paced and hopeful. It was the sound of strings, and when Actaeon looked back he saw that it came from Jezail, who had slung her bow over her shoulder and now held a small fiddle. Her fingers flew across the strings and soon set the rhythm of the march as she plucked out a fast beat.

A shout went up through the Incliners at the music and they marched with a fresh spirit.

"Finally," said Wave. "A beat to march to in this forsaken mess. I knew something felt off." He looked across the formation and saw Trench grin at him.

"It'll draw them right to us!" exclaimed Wayd, looking appalled.

"Lad, they already know where we are. They're on all sides of us except the front if we're lucky," said Wave.

"How could you possibly know that?" asked Wayd.

"Because they ain't stupid. When we stopped, that gave them the opportunity. They're just waiting for the right moment."

The music continued, filtering through the ranks of the warriors and perhaps farther behind them to the ears of their attackers. Actaeon swept the terrain ahead with his scope.

"Ah, here we are again," he said enigmatically as he spied movement on the right, forward of their position. He tapped Itarik and pointed his halberd in that direction. "Movement out that way, as though they are preparing to hit us where the path chokes up ahead."

In response to a look from Itarik, Varisk led some warbanders up along the right flank to reinforce Trench's group. Trench offered the young Captain an ugly grin and motioned to a thin opening in the rubble. He hefted his maul and stepped inside it to find a way to circle behind the waiting attackers. The Captain sent three men in after the giant and took command of the right flank himself.

The music continued under the monotonic cacophony of rain as night drew the darkness about them like a blanket. There was tension in the notes now, bringing the Raedelleans on edge. Those in the center that remained able-bodied prepared their weapons. Beside Actaeon, Lauryn nocked an arrow and stumbled over the remnants of an old wall.

"Careful," said Actaeon, steadying her. On his other side, Eisandre drew her sword.

"Prepare for attack!" bellowed Itarik.

The right flank was immediately assailed, but despite taking several losses, managed to hold together and push the tribals back. At the same time the left flank was hit and fell to pieces as tribals emerged from the shattered remnants of a circular structure to attack them.

Wave struggled to hold the forces together, but three warbanders near him were killed, with rock, spear and arrow, respectively. His rapier flashed in successive arcs and three attackers fell before him. Others rallied to close the gap, led by Wayd, but they were too few in number to hold the left for long. As they fought, Wave took an arrow that lodged in his side, partially deflected by his thick leather armor.

Eisandre gestured and led the able-bodied men and women in the center to fill in the gaps, including Actaeon and Lauryn. The young woodcarver stuck close to, and behind, Actaeon. When he glanced over at her, he saw her rain-soaked face, white with fear. He didn't feel much better himself as he stepped up beside Eisandre and ran one tribal through the gut with his blade's long reach. Killing was not his strong suit, that was for sure.

Supported by the center and Eisandre, the left held and sent the remaining tribals on the retreat, at least temporarily.

On the right flank, Trench emerged from the growing darkness, two

Incliners at his side, the three of them caked with mud. The head of his maul replaced the head of one of the attackers, now pinned between Trench and the right flank, and a broad sweep of his weapon ended two more. From there, the Raedelleans made quick work of the rest. None escaped to regroup.

The visibility decreased rapidly in the heavy rain and the Wall Breakers reformed and began to doubletime.

Actaeon scanned the ruins around them with his scope, but it was too difficult to see much. He shouldered the bow and fell back to the center, Lauryn trailing behind him.

Wave had fallen back as well to get his arrow wound patched up. Gritta partially unlaced his armor in order to apply the suture.

The older woman did so with amazing skill as they continued marching along. She didn't skip a beat as she reached down to grab the man-at-arm's crotch hard. "Now you come by and see Gritta once we're outta this and I'll help you along with your recovery," she said, her aged eyes glittering as she looked into his.

"Um... uh, sure," said Wave, moving a hand down to cup his groin. When the cutter had retreated, he began to lace his armor back up.

Actaeon grinned and bumped into Wave's good side as they jogged along. "At a loss for words, Wave? An unusual state for you."

"Aye, well... I prefer being the teacher, not the student," he said.

"I have heard it said that the best teachers never cease to be students," said Actaeon.

"What are you talking about?" asked Eisandre as she rejoined them after ensuring the left flank was in good condition.

"Wave was just talking about his love of teaching," said Actaeon with a grin.

"I'd better go back and help Wayd," said Wave before rushing off, the redness in his face hidden by the night.

"Are you okay?" asked Actaeon, his hand finding Eisandre's and squeezing it.

With some difficulty, Eisandre squeezed his hand in return. "It doesn't matter if I am okay. I must do what is needed right now."

"It matters to me, but you are correct – we must do what needs be done now. Just know that I am here, in this, with you," he said.

"There are barely more than forty fighters left on their feet," said Eisandre soberly. "Our chances are not looking good," she added, her voice low so that only he could hear it over the rainfall.

"We are getting close, I am starting to recognize the ruins. They look familiar. We are close to home – close to Incline," he said. "They will attack us before then, will they not? One last ditch effort to stop us. There must have been some major motivation for them to lose so many men against us. I wonder if we will ever find out the truth of what happened here."

"I believe we already know the truth," said Eisandre. She might be Lost, but she was not stupid. "What you mean is that you wonder whether we will find proof that my uncle set these killers upon us."

"That is correct."

"They will not stop us. We will make Shore. These barbarians are no match for Raedelle," she decided.

Actaeon grinned and nodded his approval.

They marched for some time then in silence, and when Itarik quickened the pace even more, they followed suit, offering a hand to those carrying the wounded. Jezail's fiddle matched Itarik's pace. The melody she played was uplifting and encouraging.

When they started along a narrow chasm between two fallen structures of the Ancients, Trench led the right flank up and around the side of the small gully to make sure they weren't caught off guard from that side. The rest of the formation was forced to march through the narrow ravine of ruins.

At the front, Itarik called out orders, moving troops to different locations to anticipate possible routes of attack.

The barrage of arrows that fell among their ranks caught Actaeon off guard. He felt one of the shafts glance off the blade of his halberd and suddenly the sled he was dragging weighed twice as much. The extra weight pulled him to a stop and Gritta, who had also been hauling the sled, fell against him and knocked him from his feet. The old cutter landed atop him and coughed blood onto his vest, an arrow protruding from her skull. The odd thought that came to Actaeon in that moment of horror, was how unusual it was that the arrow was in the perfect center of the top of her skull. Her head must have been tilted at the same angle as the arrow's descent.

The thought was interrupted as more arrows thudded into her body where she lay atop him. He felt a sharp pain as one of the arrowheads tore through his trousers and nicked his thigh. Actaeon grimaced and rolled the dead cutter off of him. He stood and grabbed the leather strap of the sled with the wounded man in it, which he continued to haul, running to catch up with the others.

The music had stopped.

As he ran, he heard shouts behind him and to his left. The rearguard and the left flank had been struck by tribals as soon as they had passed out of the narrow chasm. He saw Eisandre rush over to join Varisk at the rear to hold back the attackers. It was impressive, he thought, how they could fight while still moving backward to keep up with the rest of the formation.

On a whim, he glanced down at the wounded warbander in the sled and found, instead, a body bristled with arrows. Biting back nausea, he released the strap and slid his halberd shaft into its holder on the back of his jacket. Then, he unshouldered his bow and put an arrow to string. It was just in time as several tribals broke through a gap between the rearguard and the left flank to rush the wounded in the center.

"Nine," he said as his first arrow caught an unfortunate tribal woman in the bowels. The woman didn't cry out, just coughed up blood and tried to get up. "Eight," he said, firing another that struck the next man in the heart.

As his eyes wandered the field for the next target he watched as Wave lithely stepped between the wild swings of two of the retreating attackers, his blades flashing as they neatly sliced through one man's throat and stabbed through the other's underarm to pierce the heart. At the rear, he saw two warriors rush Eisandre, with nothing he could do about it given the distance between them. She took it in stride however, and stepped away from them to use their own momentum and hasty swings against them. In a moment, she had gutted one man and beheaded another.

There was a roar behind him and he spun in time to see Trench running with a group of tribals in pursuit. The ugly giant carried a dead Raedellean over his shoulder. Trench hadn't noticed that the man's skullcap had been removed at some point and the body was a pincushion of arrows.

"They're encircling us! The right has fallen! We need to *move!*" bellowed the big man.

Actaeon let loose another arrow to knock down Trench's closest pursuer. "Seven." His next arrow went wide, but Trench spun around and shattered the tribal's ribcage with the head of his maul. "Six."

An impossible force of tribals closed in on Trench. Actaeon watched as the giant hurled something in their direction before throwing himself to the ground. The grenado's explosion tore through the large group of pursuers and Actaeon saw body parts scatter in all directions before the shockwave knocked him to the ground.

Through the ringing in his ears, Actaeon could hear someone calling his name.

"Act! Hey, Act!"

The Engineer turned to find Varisk at his side. "Tell me you've got something that can be used to send a signal into the air. If my father sees it, he'll rally the rest of the warband to our aid."

"Yes, I have something," said Actaeon, shaking his head clear. He knelt and withdrew a bandage roll. He unrolled the fabric along the wet ground, the material becoming soaked instantly in the rain.

As the Engineer worked, both Trench and Wave fell in to guard him while Varisk rejoined the lines.

Actaeon pulled a half-through bottle from his jacket and spilled the brown goo in a line onto the unfurled bandage. As he worked, the rearguard reached their position, and passed it, keeping up with Itarik's formation of march. As the rearguard passed, the wounded were left behind to guard Actaeon's effort. They formed a semicircle around the Engineer with Trench, Wave, Balin and Eisandre – fighting off the inrush of tribals.

Pollia, who had been dragging Matt, stayed to fight as well. Even after a tribal spear pinned her leg to the ground, she continued to fight on, bodies piling up before her as her spear moved back and forth in a blur.

Beside her, Matt fought on his knees to avoid putting any weight on his infected leg. The Companion fought in a feverish zeal, his sword cutting through enemy spears and laying so many enemies to rest at his knees that he needed to pull himself atop the bodies to continue fighting.

Actaeon tried not to pay attention to the deadly flashing blades of Wave and Eisandre, the dull thuds of Trench's maul, nor the cleaving slashes of Balin's axe. Instead, he tossed the empty half-through bottle aside and pulled an arrow from his quiver. To it he tied the end of the bandage just before the arrow's vane.

As he pulled another bottle from his jacket, a dead tribal landed atop him and bowled him over. He pushed the body off to the side but the bottle had been knocked from his fingers. He pulled the luminary from his jacket and stuck it in the strap of his goggles to search for it desperately amidst the death and carnage all around him.

Light reflected off the bottle and he snatched it up, uncorking it and sprinkling the contents upon the bandage roll. The foul smell of the purple crystals was pervasive even in the heavy rain and chaos. As the rain pattered against the bandage, it began to sputter and hiss violently before bursting into blue flame. The screams around him sounded like Jezail's had from so long ago, but he pushed that thought out of his mind.

As the others fought bravely around him, he drew to his feet and pulled his goggles down to cover his eyes. "Stand clear," he said, before he lifted the arrow with the flaming blue streamer. He quickly put it to string to fire it off over Shore. The string of his recurve snapped in the process and the arms of the bow flew forward violently in his hand, nearly ripping the weapon from his fingers. A spot of blue fire burned on his leather jacket, but he was too busy watching the flight of the arrow, as the arc of blue fire flew south over his hometown of Incline.

A moment later, the faint sound of watch horns could be heard to the south.

"Now we must move. And fast. Go go *go!*" shouted Eisandre. She disengaged and ran forward, tugging Actaeon after her. Trench and Wave were right on her heels.

As he was tugged forward, Actaeon saw Pollia yelling for them to come back and Matt continuing to fight on at her side. Both of them were unable to follow.

Once they caught up with the rearguard, the remaining Wall Breakers broke into a flat out run. Itarik had slowed the pace of march to make sure that they could catch up, but now they had to move fast. The tribal force pursued doggedly at their heels, hacking down anyone who paused or hesitated.

As they crested a ridge of rubble, their spirits fell when they saw a solid wall of tribals waiting for them between Incline and the Wall. Itarik pointed forward with the tip of his sword and shouted. "We're surrounded! Rally to me, you Wall Breakers! Chaaaarge!"

At the rear, Eisandre drew Caliburn and pointed. "Forward! We must break through!"

A rallying cry went up from the surviving Raedelleans as they rushed forward to join Itarik in the charge. Many of them dropped their bows on the battlefield. They wouldn't be needed from this point on.

"Shore's right past them. Don't stop. We're almost there!" cried out Itarik. Beside him, Wayd and Varisk fell in and, with others, formed a spear with Itarik as the tip. They drove into the wall of tribals and shattered them, opening a gap and driving through it. Once through, they pivoted and split, to widen and hold the gap, so that Eisandre, Actaeon, and the others could rush through it.

Actaeon burst through, Eisandre at his side, and they skidded to a stop alongside Jezail, who looked over at them questioningly.

Before them was the steep slope of Incline – elderstone worn smooth over countless years and slick with rain, down which many in history had slid to their deaths. One of the warbanders slid past them and tumbled headfirst down the slick slope. Far below they could see a line of torchlight and luminaries from the town of Incline itself, responding to the signal that Actaeon had shot off.

Actaeon looked over at Jezail and grinned. "Remember when we were kids? We would go sledding down in the rain? We can use our cloaks. Show them, Jezail. Hey, everyone, use your cloaks, tabards, whatever you have!"

"Not this far though," Jezail said skeptically. She nodded though, realizing that there wasn't much other choice, and removed the clasp from her rain cloak to spread it out before her. She sat down upon it and kicked off, leading the way down the slope, toward Incline and safety below.

Behind them, Itarik assembled a force, including Balin, Wayd, Varisk, Trench, and Wave to form a new rearguard and hold off the enemy forces until the others could escape. They formed a tight semi-circle at the edge of the slope and fought there, the mass of tribals pushing them closer and closer to the edge.

Running barbarians crashed into the new rearguard and killed a half dozen warbanders, sending others sprawling and one woman sliding down the grade. Balin jumped into the gap and single-handedly held off the attackers with his axe, giving Itarik and the others a chance to regain their feet and reform the dwindling formation. An errant stone caught Balin in the chest and knocked the wind from him before a spearpoint was rammed through his ribcage.

Still, the stocky blacksmith fought on. Balin hacked the spear shaft in half with his axe. He killed two more before he buried his blade in his killer's chest and fell flat on his face, life fled from his body.

Itarik and the others filled in behind their slain friend and held back the enemy force. A step behind them, Ithelie Faris invoked prayers to the Fallen over the dead. If there was any fear in the young Voice, she did not show it.

When Eisandre moved to join them, Actaeon grabbed her wrist firmly. Her weary gaze met his own and he shook his head. "They fight and die for you. You owe it to them to make it to safety."

The former Arbiter nodded and pulled free the crimson cape that she had once used as an Arbiter. She arranged it as best as she was able and wrapped her arms around the Engineer. "This would be a strange way to die," she murmured to him, before she pushed off and launched them both down the slippery slope and away from the enemy.

As they slid forward at a frightening speed, Actaeon braked gently with the soles of his boots and did his best to steer them around any objects jutting from the slope.

Once Eisandre was clear, Itarik dismissed more of the rearguard, including the rest of the Incliners. The survivors slid their way down the dangerous slope. He stood with just a few men now, but they fought on, holding off the enemy even as more of them died.

Trench and Wave stood on either side of him, their fighting styles a sharp juxtaposition, one brutal strength and the other a deadly graceful speed.

"Wayd, get Ithelie down the slope," Itarik ordered.

The newest Companion spun to obey. He grabbed the Voice, ignoring her protests and pulled her green robes from her. Scowling, the Voice slapped Wayd, but he ignored it, and wrapped his arms around her, using the robe for both of them to slide down to Incline.

As the bodies piled up all around Itarik, he jumped forward amidst the enemy, smashing one in the nose and cleaving another's head in half. His sword cut a swath of death through the tribals and sent them reeling.

Before a swung club could catch the Companion, Trench's maul broke the arm. On his other side, Wave's rapier flew to and fro, keeping the attackers away from the lead Companion.

And yet, Itarik continued to cut into the enemy as though a man possessed.

"By the Fallen, man! We have to get down, *now!*" cried Wave before he reached down to pull the dagger from Trench's boot. Unapologetically, he used the dagger, still coated in some waythorn, to knick the Companion and knock him unconscious.

Trench smashed in another attacker's face before lifting Itarik over his shoulder and making a run for the slope. He and Wave both hit the slope at the same time, sliding on their backs, with Trench holding the knocked out Companion atop him to prevent injury to the man.

And so, the unlikely collective of Raedelleans, led by Eisandre Caliburn, blazed a new path across the Wall to arrive back at their homeland. They slid to a stop in Incline, bearing the sword Caliburn to nurture their wounds and a new hope. There, in the small community of Incline, where the Engineer had grown up, they were met by a fresh warband, commanded by the Lord Conmara himself, ready to defend in case the tribals were foolish enough to follow into Raedelle itself.

Over one hundred men and women of Raedelle fell on that day. Only twenty-four of Eisandre's Wall Breakers, as they would come to be known, survived to set foot in their homeland once more. In Raedelle though, as the Voices say, the Fallen never really leave the living.

87 A.R., the 27th day of Rainbreak

HOME

"**I** DEFER TO YOUR JUDGEMENT, REGARDING the man's fate," said Eisandre.

Itarik stood before her, worn and exhausted. The Companion had woken an hour after Wave had knicked him with the waythorn blade. Only twenty-four men and women survived the ordeal to make it to the safety of Incline. A devastating one hundred and six people had been lost on the Wall. The rains that had harried them stopped shortly after their arrival, staying long enough to wash the blood of the dead and wounded farther down the slope.

After Itarik had found out from the others that Trench and Wave had carried him to safety, he stormed into their tent, demanding to know what happened.

"Must've passed out from the fatigue," Wave said with a smirk.

"Yer lucky we were in position to grab you," Trench added.

Itarik stood there, glaring at them. "I don't recall being close to passing out..." He looked from one mercenary to the other, meeting their eyes before he lowered his head in appreciation. "Whatever happened, thank you both for saving my life."

The Companion had given them one last suspicious look before he left the tent.

"I said, I defer to your judgement, Companion Itarik," repeated Eisandre, looking at the man with concern.

Her words snapped him out of his reverie and he nodded sharply. "Of course, Lady Eisandre. Shall I execute the enemy captive then?"

Several of the tribals had been knocked down the slope of Incline during the battle. One of them had survived to be interrogated. The captive had smiled a bloody grin and said, simply: "Gorgrian," before spitting blood at Itarik's feet.

"I leave that in your hands," Eisandre said. "When we find Gorgrian, however, I will talk to him myself."

"Aye, Lady Eisandre. It will be done."

Eisandre looked confused when the Companion continued to stand before her, saying nothing more. After a pause of consideration, she spoke. "That is all for now, Itarik. Don't hesitate to come to me when there is something I should know or something you need to ask. It'd be wise, I think, for you to get some rest now. I will need your support in Lakehold three days from now."

Itarik bowed his head. "Thank you, Lady Eisandre. Please know that you have my loyalty and allegiance in your endeavors. As I served Aedwyn, I shall now serve you – only I will do better," he said as an afterthought, haunted by the loss of his Prince.

The Companion saluted and walked off.

Actaeon watched the man walk away from where he stood beside Eisandre. Behind them stood the house that the Engineer grew up in. From the outside, it appeared unchanged from the last time he'd seen it.

"The loyalty and determination of that man is impressive. His testimony will do well to serve in your favor," Actaeon decided. "Come. Let us go inside. I want to show you where I grew up."

"I've committed no crimes," she protested. "Except against the Arbiter chain of command, and for that I have been punished."

"I did not mean it that way," said Actaeon, reaching over to squeeze her hand. "But it will do well to change the minds of people under your uncle's fold."

"I hope I will not have to kill him too," Eisandre said, her voice barely a whisper.

Her words made the Engineer wince. He wasn't used to her speaking in such a way. Not knowing what else to do, he leaned over and kissed her cheek.

Eisandre looked up at him, her blue eyes weary, but also filled with appreciation. "Thank you. For being here. With me."

"I will stand beside you, my love. Through all of this. Thank you for letting me into your life."

"I hope you will not come to regret it. You fell in love with a quiet Arbiter, which was an obstacle in itself. Now it seems that you may well end up as a leader of Raedelle, because you love me. And I know that is not what you wanted in life. It isn't what either of us wanted. But..." She trailed off. "You wanted to go inside," she said, changing the topic. "Show me your past before we lose ourselves in the future."

"I have your love and understanding – something that I never hoped to obtain in life. At this point, there is no way I can come to regret knowing and loving you," he said with a wistful smile as he glanced up at the old, abandoned house before them. "My parents would be surprised indeed, if I ended up leading Raedelle at your side. I do not suppose they ever considered that I would fall in love with a future princess and achieve such ends."

He grinned at the thought, which sounded all the more absurd when spoken aloud. He lifted the latch and toed the door open with his boot, pulling the luminary from his jacket to light their way inside the old house against the darkness of the predawn morning.

Eisandre pulled her own luminary free. "You may yet regret not having the life you desire. When politics, endless decisions, strategy, and diplomacy overtake so much of the time you crave being in your workshop, shaping your ideas, and discovering our world. I will do my best, always, to make sure you have the time and resources for your pursuits, but there will be some moments like the present, when there is just too much to do."

Actaeon led the way inside. His wet boots left footprints in the thick dust on the floor. He swept the light of his luminary across the main room. The many crates filled with packed belongings and assorted furniture piled against one wall took him by surprise. He recalled piling everything there when he left, but he better remembered the room as it was in times of use. In the back corner there was a seamstress' shop – his mother's. Wooden forms and rolls of fabric were scattered about the space. Long mechanisms and controls were built into the walls and the ceiling above the shop floor, powered by foot pedals. He smiled, the memory of working with his mother on those devices coming back to him. Some threads still wound their twisting path through the apparatus, ending at a big wooden spool.

"Home, sweet home," said Actaeon with a tired grin. "I would regret not being with you. I know that in my heart, Eis. And so, this is my path. A solver of problems is what I am. And this philosophy and methodology is what I tackle any situation with. My endeavors will continue, because that is my life – my purpose of being. Only I have found more now, and that I will not deny."

"You are never forced to follow this path. It will always be your choice. It's important to me that you know that," she insisted. "If you feel you would be happier back in your workshop, or anywhere else not at my side, you have but to say the word and I will do all in my power to grant your wish. I will not be angry."

The Engineer smiled at her and shined his luminary up at a strand of twine that was stretched taut in the device's feed. He ran a finger along it, fascinated that the gravity tensioner had lasted all this time without failing or breaking the string.

"How do you feel? Being here?" she asked him.

Actaeon paused to consider, watching dust particles drift through the light of his luminary.

"I feel... as though I have opened a door that I thought closed forever. Never did I believe I would return here. Perhaps the stigma that I carried kept the people here from taking over my house after I left. It brings back memories of my mother... but the sad ones, not the older, happier ones. This is not my home anymore. My home is at your side."

"We are together now," Eisandre assured. "And we are here. Is there anything you would like to see or do here?"

Actaeon grinned at that thought and nodded. "Yes. Let me show you the room I grew up in." He led the way down a hall and into a small bedroom. The room was lit by a half dozen strangely shaped luminaries, one of them quite large with a blanket beside it to cover the light for when it was time to sleep. The room was every bit as cluttered as his room in the Song, or the workshop itself. Old papers and sketches hung all about, tacked up on the walls – drawings of strange creatures, devices, human bodies, and assorted notes. There were still many trinkets and odd artifacts scattered about.

Several mechanisms were present as well, one of which pulled the door shut behind them when the Engineer pulled a rope beside his bed.

"Still works!" he said with a bright smile.

Eisandre offered him a faint smile of her own. She glanced about the room and touched a few of the sketches and artifacts, until an exceedingly cold, dark-hued circle of metal caused her to pull her hand back in alarm.

"There are a lot of things here," she said simply.

"Aye, plenty of things. Old ideas, failed ideas... ideas that I long ago decided were impossible, or unachievable, with my current knowledge and resources." He sat down upon the bed and leaned his halberd against the wall. "Many of these things I left up as reminders of old dreams, and old approaches. Only a few ever came to fruition. It is interesting to see the history of thought though, as concept morphs into concept and either dies or comes alive."

"Way leads unto way." Eisandre unbuckled the baldric for Caliburn and placed the legendary sword beside the halberd before sitting beside him. "I like seeing your earlier thoughts. Your mind has long been so active, so awake. It is dizzying at times for me, but... it is also very beautiful."

"That is kind of you to say." When he turned he found her eyes upon him. "Would it surprise you that my active mind often turns to thoughts to us? Way leads unto way, and as my luck would have it: led me to you." He let out a happy laugh then and leaned forward to kiss her lightly upon the lips.

"To me. Back to Raedelle," she said after the kiss. "To watching our fellows betray each other and give their lives for our cause. To your childhood home. It is a winding path you tread. And not an easy one. But, despite everything, you are always be able to focus on the clear light that is our love. It is a remarkable skill."

"It is one of the few things that I am certain of in this world," Actaeon admitted. "I can feel it – it is real, it is strong. There are not many things that I *am* certain of – the properties of materials I have explored, the knowledge that certain actions will result in specific reactions, and the happiness and safety I feel with our love."

It was an unusual thing to admit for the Engineer, dominated as he usually was by logic and empiricism. But, as he looked at the woman before him, he saw someone incredible. In her plain leather armor and her short, blond hair, in the way she sat beside him so readily, in her loving smile and in her radiant blue eyes that gazed into his own.

"The strength of your conviction pierces through the swirl of thoughts in my mind, and, with you, I find peace. I am very fortunate to know you, Master Rellios."

"And I, you, Princess Caliburn."

They embraced and held each other for what seemed an eternity. Tears spilled forth for what they had endured and the friends they had lost, their foreheads touching. Love was their shield, and they basked in the healing warmth of their embrace.

"When I was a young lad," Actaeon whispered, "I would lay in this bed, gazing up at the stars. It was a good way to dream up ideas – let my mind wander. Would you care to join me in that?"

"Itarik knows where to find us if need be. We can stay awhile," she agreed.

After removing some of their bulkier clothing, they lay in his childhood bed and held one another near.

"Let us see if this still works," Actaeon said and he kicked a lever. Two sections of the ceiling slid apart and kicked up a cloud of dust that drifted down to settle atop them. They hid their faces against the mattress and coughed, which drove them both to laughter. Once they had wiped the dust from themselves, they laid down once more and were rewarded with a clear night sky, dotted with innumerable stars. Actaeon threw the blanket over the big luminary so they could see it even better.

"Aedwyn is our Prince still," said Eisandre, correcting his earlier statement. "I am Lady Eisandre of House Caliburn. A princess, perhaps, in one definition of the term, but not by title. Not without confirmation by the Conclave of Lords."

"Lady Eisandre it is then. Though you truly act like a Princess. The way you handled our journey... I was most impressed."

"I'm not the head of my family. Although my mother, Saints watch over her, still uses the title of Dowager Duchess, as per the old ways."

"It may well be that the Conclave will agree, three days from now, that you should lead."

"If it is what they decide, then I shall accept that duty. There is much that is uncertain about what will happen though. If they decide to take the accusations against me seriously, then the outcome may be very different." She didn't elaborate on those details.

"It may well be, but your friends and allies will not cease until your name is cleared. Let us not think about that now, for there is nothing to be done," he said, caressing her short hair. "The view is much better from this vantage, no?"

"Not so practical when it rains," she said and he could sense her smile.

"Yes, that was a major consideration when I designed it. My father was not happy about my cutting a hole in the roof. The panels slide and lock together in a way that overlaps with the roof's slope and one another. I also fitted some grooves into the sides that act as funnels for the rain. Consequently, the grooves also allow the entire apparatus to slide along on matching rails. There were a few tweaks that I wanted to make, but it appears to still work well. Of course, you must remember to close it when it rains." He drew silent then, as he caught himself rambling.

"It must be particularly pleasant during the hottest months," she said, then growing silent herself.

After a time, Eisandre lifted her arm and pointed up at the glittering canvas of dazzling lights. "One for each of the good things you will accomplish in your life," she whispered and shifted so that her head touched his own.

"One for each of the good things that *we* will accomplish in a life together," he said, then kissed her ear lightly. "This is a dream come true for me, you know. To lay in this bed with my true love."

"You really dreamt that?" she asked skeptically. "I only ever wanted to be useful and not an embarrassment to my family. This is not a life I could ever have predicted. It is too beautiful and too sad, all at once. You may never know my brothers and sister, and I am sorry for that. They are all greater people than I will ever be."

"You will be hard pressed to win me over on that statement. I knew your sister well enough and I saw both of your brothers briefly. Neither of them shone so clearly with truth and beauty as you do. You may have spent all your life being told that you are lesser than others – that you are not complete. But Eis, I saw you out there, in that terrible darkness we walked through and you reached those people and guided them through. The way you led them... you *are* an incredible person. I know it is hard, that it weighs heavily upon you, but it will never be easy – not that sort of thing. Not for someone as true and caring as you," said the Engineer.

"Ah, but we both know that you see me very differently than most, my love," she said. "Regardless of what you say, they were all beautiful people – great people. Perhaps one day you will have the chance to see that, and there will be less pressure on us, and you will be able to build and explore and discover and create to your heart's content."

"I am *already* exploring and discovering to my heart's content," he said, and she could feel his smile. "And yes, I do believe you, that your siblings were all great people, but you are great as well – regardless of whether or not a lowly Engineer from little Incline loves you. You have always been strong and capable, Eis, only now you must show it to the world."

"Lowly Engineer," she repeated with a snort. "I have not always been strong or capable. The Arbiters taught me to be the person I am today." She looked over at him then. "And so did you."

When he looked back over at her, she pulled him into a kiss. They lay under the stars for the rest of that night, kissing away one another's tears and gazing up at the sky as dawn emerged.

The surviving Wall Breakers slept most of that day, and, as the following morning's sun first emerged over the horizon, they began the final leg of their journey, to Lakehold.

87 A.R., the 28th day of Rainbreak

PRINCESS

"IT'S HIM!" SOMEONE YELLED.

There was a commotion up in the front that Actaeon couldn't make out and the Incline warband rushed forward into action.

By the time Eisandre and Actaeon arrived, the shouting had subdued. In a culvert alongside the packed dirt road that led south to Lakehold, Wayd held someone down, his knee upon the small of a man's back. Sword drawn, Itarik stepped down into the culvert and grasped the man's queue of long hair to pull his face up roughly from the mud.

A look from Itarik told Wayd to move. The Companion lifted the man up by his hair and dumped him against the side of the culvert. Itarik put his foot on the man's chest and the point of his sword to his throat. "Gorgrian, who once was called Companion, tell me why we shouldn't kill you at once for betraying your Prince."

Gorgrian made a sad attempt at laughter and sputtered mud from his mouth instead. After several hacking coughs, he showed Itarik his teeth, and said nothing.

Itarik cast a questioning look up at Eisandre.

"What are you waiting for, lad? Tie him to the back of the supply wagon, and let him walk... backwards!" said the Lord Conmara, who had stopped alongside Eisandre to peer down into the culvert. The old lord chuckled and spat at the disgraced Companion.

Itarik looked to the Lord, and then back to Lady Eisandre.

"You heard the Lord Conmara," said Eisandre before she stepped away from the culvert and the group continued along.

They arrived at Lakehold a day early, after crossing the River of Arches by ferry. Lord Conmara threw the doors to the big chamber open just as the Lord Dafryl was convening the Conclave.

"Very strange," the old lord bellowed as he stormed into the circular room at the center of Caliburn Castle's main tower. The Lords and Ladies of the Conclave each sat behind raised stone podiums arranged in a circle around the room – Shore on one side, Lakehold on the other. Lesser people sat below them upon the tiered stone steps. A different raised podium with multiple seats stood off to one side for advisors and other persons of honor to sit. There sat the Dowager Duchess, the Lady Eisandre's mother, and Ambrosius the Wise, an advisor to Aedwyn and his father before him.

"I hadn't thought that my neighbors would be completely unaware of the blowing of my watch horns two nights prior and allow the Conclave to convene without sending so much as a messenger," continued Lord Conmara, casting scornful looks at Lord Blarth and the Ladies Tanderly and Fletcher.

"Is this true?" asked the Lord Dafryl, tugging at the handle of his big, white mustache as he looked across at the Shorian leaders.

"You know well that I was here since four nights ago," said the Lady Fletcher, looking impatient.

When the Lady Tanderly of Highwater refused to answer, the Lord Blarth shifted his chunky frame forward and blurted out a response, "It was the Ancestors' tears out there on that night. I'd not expect anyone heard a damned thing."

"Cathaoir, I realize you are late, and therefore unaware of recent events, but please be aware that there are much more important issues at stake than your excuses for tardiness." It was Gunther Arcady that spoke from his podium, his hazel eyes burning into the old lord below him.

"Oh, I realize that, Gunther. Since you want an excuse, I brought one. Lords and Ladies of the Conclave, I introduce to you, Eisandre Caliburn of Raedelle, now returned to us and released from her service to the Arbiters," said the old lord, gesturing to the doors.

The color drained from Arcady's face as his youngest niece led a group of twenty men and women into the room. The Engineer walked alongside her. Behind them were the Companions Itarik and Wayd, Captain Varisk and Jezail leading the other warbanders, the Voice Ithelie, and the two mercenaries taking up the rear. Lauryn and several other survivors had remained in Incline to recover from their injuries.

Eisandre wore Elphin's torc around her neck, despite its large size and upon her back was the sword Caliburn. Its ornate hilt gleamed in the cool light of the chamber. She continued inside until she stood before the Lord Dafryl's podium. Her brilliant blue eyes turned to look at the rest of the Lords and Ladies, in turn.

"With the help of Engineer Actaeon Rellios, she was able to recover our Prince's great sword from the artifact in which it had been trapped – from the artifact that took her brother from us," Lord Conmara continued. "And despite tribals that were sent by someone intent on stopping her from reaching this Conclave, one hundred and six men and women of Raedelle died out on the Wall to make sure she would make it here this day."

There was a hush from those present as they considered the loss of life.

"May the Fallen watch over us," intoned the young Voice.

"And give us their guidance," came the response from all those present.

"Welcome, Lady Eisandre. I hope you don't mind, but there are pressing matters we must discuss immediately," said the Lord Dafryl.

"Welcome? She and those two mercenaries there, are wanted by all Shore for the murder of twenty-one innocents at Blackstone Fortress. They should be in shackles!" snapped Arcady.

"Time will tell who should be in shackles," Wayd shot back at the Lord Shore.

"Silence!" said Dafryl, his voice booming down at Wayd. The young Companion shut his mouth and took a step back.

Itarik stepped forward and touched his forehead, a sign that he wished to speak.

"Yes, Companion Itarik. The Conclave will hear you."

"Please forgive Companion Wayd. We are exhausted after our long battle. Though his conduct is still inexcusable," said Itarik, the slightest hint of a smirk at the corner of his lips. Any humor was wiped from his expression for his next statement though. "I have stood watch upon the

Pillar since my Prince was locked inside it. The bravery of the force led by Eisandre Caliburn was commendable. They defied all odds in freeing our people's sacred relics and fighting to return here. Never before have I faced such a hopeless situation, but Lady Eisandre was our hope out in that battle on the Wall. I am honored to stand by her side as her protector now. If she was forced to take lives at Blackstone, then it must have been for good reason."

"Thank you, Companion Itarik, your words have been heard," said Lord Hamnin Dafryl. "Companion Wayd, you are forgiven this once. Do not speak out of turn at the Conclave again."

Wayd nodded thankfully and looked at the floor.

"Now, friends," continued the Lord. "I must change the subject to a most urgent matter, and that is the news that has arrived yesterday – brought downriver by Thyrian ship. Some of you I have spoken with already, but for all the rest of you, listen well. A massive tribal force has broken through into the heart of Redemption and, even as we speak, holds Pyramid under siege. One can only imagine that they broke through in the northeast while the Shieldian and Ajmani forces were distracted with their efforts to divvy up the remains of Czeryn's holdings after the disaster that befell them. The Dominions have called for our aid, and it is more important than ever that we send it. Shield and Ajman forces are scattered and the Czerynians have been obliterated. We must not let the city fall."

There was a murmur of voices in the chamber as everyone reacted to the news.

"I will put together a force and lead it to break the siege," said Arcady, speaking before anyone else could interject.

"Not so quickly, Lord Shore. While your haste in this matter is appreciated, there is another matter to discuss first. Lady Eisandre, I believe you must have more important news to share with us than the recovery of a sword," said Lord Hamnin with another tug at the corner of his mustache.

Arcady looked infuriated at the mustached lord, but he kept his tongue. As all the speaking went on, the Lord Conmara made his way up to Incline's podium.

Eisandre stepped forward, Actaeon beside her, and met Hamnin Dafryl's eyes firmly with her own steady gaze.

"Yes, Lord Lakeguard," she said, using the name of his seat of power.

"I must inform the Conclave that the artifact which took Aedwyn has been destroyed, with my brother within."

"And cannot our Engineer from Shore, recently rumored to have mastered so many aspects of the Ancient's technology, repair the artifact?" Lord Hamnin reasoned.

Actaeon spoke then. "While I would never preclude the possibility of repair, I must agree with Lady Eisandre in this. In my experience, the damage that was done to the pillar artifact that stole our Prince is not repairable. We have neither the technology, nor the skill to do such a thing at this time."

A cacophony of voices broke out in the chamber then, filling the room with thunderous sound. At a gesture from Lord Hamnin, a gong was rung and there was silence once again.

"Let me be the first to offer my condolences on your brother," spoke the Lord Dafryl. "And indeed for the rest of your siblings. We received news from Shield that Lord Aedgar was lost in battle far up north, and the Lady Eshelle is presumed dead after we found what remained of her party dead on the Wall."

"We must call a recess of the Conclave in order to mourn our Prince," said Jad Perth, the young lord of Lakefeed.

"There is too much at stake for such foolishness. His soul will dwell with the rest of the Fallen, as they all do, whether we use it as an excuse for inaction or not," said Tridarch Hael, the Lord of Bastion.

"I agree with Lord Tridarch," said Aethelred Ackart, the seasoned warrior Lord of Southward. "Enough tarrying. The time for action is here. We've waited long enough for a leader to organize an offensive against these increased tribal incursions. That's why the Lord Arcady should lead us forth to bring the battle to Pyramid."

"That's where we disagree, Lord Aethelred," said the Lord Hael.

"It's easy to disagree from your comfy bed in Bastion, while the warband of Southward bleeds for your safety," snapped back Aethelred.

"Agreed. Lord Gunther Arcady should be the next Prince of Raedelle. There is no longer any other that could fill such a role," said Julip Tanderly, seizing the opportune moment.

"Oh, don't be daft, Julip. The leader of Raedelle that we need to rally behind stands in the center of this very chamber." Neryl Vanora, the Lady of Whiterose, gestured down at Eisandre.

"Care to explain to us how a girl sent away in her childhood to the Arbiters stands half a chance of leading Raedelle well?" asked the Lord Blarth.

"Some of you may not recall, but Prince Aedwyn Caliburn was similarly sent to the Loresworn at a young age, and he served us well as the leader of this Dominion," said the Lord Dafryl.

"If you call his galavanting and negligence to the needs of the realm serving us well, then you and I have very different viewpoints, Hamnin," said the Lord Ackart. "Prince Aedwyn was a great leader once, and I was one of the first to offer my support. But where was he when Southward was nearly taken? Where was the organization? Where, by the Fallen, was he when my son was killed? In the end, he wasn't fit to rule, and neither was his fool of a sister, Eshelle."

A murmur arose in the chamber, as people voiced both assent and dissent. The Lord's words struck a chord with many present. Actaeon watched Gunther Arcady's mouth curl into a thin smile at his podium.

"Quiet, quiet. Keep your tongues or I'll clear the chamber for the Conclave alone," threatened Dafryl and everyone drew silent.

The Overseer of the Conclave turned to face the Dowager Duchess and smiled, twirling the end of his mustache thoughtlessly.

Gwendolyn stood then and addressed the Lord Ackart. "Your words are wholly without merit, Aethelred, and I bid you keep your tongue if you can't but speak them. Who was it that began the pre-emptive attacks on the tribals each spring? It was your Prince Aedwyn. Before that I recall a time when those in Southward turned tail each year and hid in places like Bastion. Speak no ill of my children, or may you be reminded that you can fall just as far as you have risen."

"Sorry, Duchess Gwendolyn. I stand corrected and you have my apology." The Lord Ackart knelt beside his podium and lowered his head in shame.

The Dowager Duchess ignored him and turned to her last remaining child. "I am glad you've made it here safe, my little girl. You have done well and you are home now. I know that you have no wish to lead Raedelle, and you will not have to. Your Uncle Arcady can lead."

Eisandre looked up at her mother and touched her forehead.

"Please speak freely, Eisandre Caliburn. You have a place of honor in these chambers," said Hamnin Dafryl.

Eisandre lowered her hand then and addressed her mother with sure words. "I can lead as well, mother, and with more honor and honesty than my uncle has demonstrated."

Eisandre's words were met with surprise by her mother, who looked away from her daughter's brilliant eyes and quickly retook her seat.

Varisk Conmara stepped up beside Eisandre and tapped his forehead as well, while the rest of the Lords and Ladies were at a loss for words. After the Overseer nodded, he spoke.

"My warband was sent to bring the Lady Eisandre back here by the Lord Arcady. We located her on the Wall and brought her back, but while we were out there, we met such resistance as I've never seen in my years fighting for this Dominion. And with all of the odds stacked against us, not only did she lead us, but she led us to a victorious return to Raedelle."

Cheers went up among the stands and were quickly stifled when Lord Dafryl raised both his hands to silence them.

"And lost one hundred warriors of Raedelle in the process!" said Arcady, spewing vitriol. "She's no more ready to lead Raedelle than you are to lead your warband. Your orders were to bring three known murderers to the Blackstone Fortress to stand trial and, instead, you march them into *these* chambers like they are heroes. By the saints, they've killed your brethren. Twenty-one of them! You have failed us all, Captain Conmara!"

There were shouts back and forth across the chamber as people argued.

"*That is enough!*" roared Hamnin Dafryl. "If I hear *one more word* from anyone in the sidelines, you will all be thrown out of here. Now, is this true, Captain?"

The Captain nodded somberly. "It is, Overseer. However, when we heard their side of the story, it was told quite a bit differently, and I made the call to bring them here to stand before the wise judgement of the Conclave in this time of need."

"And what of their story caused you to make that call?"

The Captain told to them the story of Actaeon's rescue from Blackstone Fortress, of the waythorn use and the demonstration on Pollia, the mother of the dead page. The Lords and Ladies listened quietly as the warbander relayed the telling, though Arcady's face was a mask of rage.

Once he was finished, the Lord Arcady shot his glare across the way to Dafryl. "Twenty-one loyal Raedelleans murdered in *my* fortress, and here you entertain these stories from a man that cannot even follow orders?"

Silent until then, Ambrosius the Wise slowly stood and touched his forehead. His grey and green robes unfolded, as he stood and he regarded the Overseer with lackluster eyes that gave one the initial impression that there was little life behind that gaze. His silver hair was cropped short and his face clean shaven.

When the Overseer recognized him, Ambrosius spoke, "I have examined the bodies and confirm that they were first assailed by waythorn – a most effective substance."

"You *what?*" exclaimed Arcady.

"Someone took their lives afterward," continued the old man, unabated, "likely to frame the Lady Eisandre and her friends. And I understand that you are mad, Lord Arcady, but I assure you we will find out who it was that took the lives in your Fortress. The Lady Eisandre has done no wrong, and in fact has done an incredible job in returning to us with Caliburn and Elphin's Torc in hand. The Lord Gunther Arcady would lead Raedelle well, but Lady Eisandre speaks truth – as long as a Caliburn of Raedelle's line shall live, a Caliburn must lead our country. Any other leader could not hope to unite the people while a Caliburn still breathes. And more than anything right now, we must be united. The peril we face abroad is greater perhaps, than any in our lifetimes. The only person that can achieve that unity is the Lady Eisandre. Prince Aedwyn spoke to me in the last days I spent with him and confided in me that of all his siblings, he felt that Eisandre was the only one who could bring us all together."

Arcady positively glowered at the old advisor, his hazel eyes burning holes into the man.

"Well said, Ambrosius. Well said. Does anyone have anything else to add to the conversation?" asked Dafryl, tugging the white hairs of his mustache. He didn't allow them much time. "No? Then I would recommend that we anoint the Lady Eisandre Caliburn as Princess of Raedelle and Lady of Lakehold, to fulfill all the duties they demand. Let us vote, so that we can respond to this great threat to Raedelle's security with haste and competent leadership.

"All those that agree Lady Eisandre shall succeed Prince Aedwyn as the Princess of Raedelle, say 'Aye'."

Several ayes sounded immediately, from the Lords Dafryl, Conmara, and Hael, and the Lady Vanora. The Lord Perth and the Lady Fletcher chimed in a few moments later. Lord Ackart looked across at the Dowager Duchess and sounded his assent as though in apology. Lady Tanderly and Lord Blarth gave their approval last and the chamber was silent as everyone watched the Lord Gunther Arcady.

Gunther looked down his hooked nose at Hamnin and shook his head in disdain. He stepped down from the podium and strode from the chamber, pulling his blackened leather gauntlets over his hands as he left.

Hamnin smiled and spread his hands. "It is unanimous then. The Conclave has spoken and all those present for the vote have agreed – Princess Eisandre Caliburn shall lead us into a new era of Raedelle. I must recommend that we conduct the ceremony now, given the nature of the threat against our country. There is but one Voice present, I see. Voice –"

"Voice Ithelie Faris," said the young woman in the green robes, discolored now with the bloodstains of dead men and women she had prayed over. She regarded the Overseer with her striking brown eyes. "I am familiar with the ceremony of anointment."

"You *are?* You are!" said Hamnin. "Excellent. Please proceed, Voice Faris."

Ithelie Faris stepped up to Eisandre and gestured for the torc. Eisandre removed it and handed it to the spiritual leader before kneeling and closing her eyes. Those present bowed their heads, save Actaeon, Trench, and Wave, who looked on in interest.

Ithelie lifted the torc high for all to see and began to recite the articles of anointment.

"Saints guide our Princess, Eisandre Caliburn.

"May the Fallen guide her hand in battle.

"Give her the strength to lead and the wisdom to command.

"By blood of Raedelle and tears of Elphin,

"See that she brings to Raedelle victory and security.

"Honor and humility will guide her in her great task,

"And the knowledge of those before will fill her with solemnity and surety.

"Eisandre Caliburn, daughter of Branwyn, Duke of Raedelle,

"Do you accept the eternal guidance of the Ancestors?"

"I accept," said Eisandre, simply.

"Then kneel a Lady and stand now a Princess. May you serve long and serve well. The Ancestor's blessings upon you."

Ithelie placed Elphin's torc around Eisandre's neck and the newly anointed Princess rose, opening her eyes to regard those around her.

The Princess nodded solemnly to the Voice before reaching out to take Actaeon's hand. From there, she led the Engineer up the steps to the one podium that had stood vacant until now. There she stood for a long moment, her eyes searching those in the chamber, perhaps searching for the right words. When Actaeon squeezed her hand, she nodded in determination.

"People of Raedelle, I will always do my utmost to serve our Dominion well as your Princess. That is what I can promise you and I now ask that you follow me. The time ahead will bring more difficulty for us all. With the Pyramid under siege, we must rally forces at once to bring to their aid. And not just that, but we must leave enough of our forces behind to defend our own borders."

Several members of the Conclave, including the Lord Ackart, nodded their approval.

"In two days time, we shall depart from Lakehold and Shore. It will allow us time to plan, to prepare ourselves, and to rally the full strength of our warbands. For in two days, we march into war. In two days, we will lead Redemption to victory against the invaders that dare put our civilization under siege."

A cheer went up from all those present and Eisandre looked at Actaeon for support. He offered her a broad grin and squeezed her hand once more. She waited until the cheer died down before she continued. While the cheering went on, Itarik approached her at the podium and whispered something in her ear. She nodded.

"A campaign of this magnitude requires the best leadership, and that is why members of the Conclave will join us on the field. Lord Arcady and Lady Fletcher from Shore, and Lady Vanora and Lord Perth from Lakehold, I will require your support on the battlefield."

"You will have it, Princess Eisandre. And I will make sure that the Lord Arcady knows your expectations," the Lady Fletcher said with a smirk.

Eisandre nodded to her and continued, turning to the Companion beside her. "Itarik, I would elevate you to First Companion. I ask that you lead all Companions to continue to defend the Caliburns and thereby defend Raedelle. Would you accept?"

Itarik blinked at her in shock and knelt. "My life for yours, my Princess."

Eisandre touched his forehead and nodded. "Then rise as First Companion Itarik."

Another cheer filled the chamber as Itarik rose to his feet, wobbly, and for the first time in a long while, it was not due to fatigue. When the sound died down again, she spoke.

"Actaeon Rellios of Shore – I would have you as my husband, if you would have me. It would be my greatest joy and blessing."

She looked up at her partner and there was only love in her eyes for him.

Actaeon knelt before her, tears falling to his cheeks, unbidden. "My Princess Eisandre, it would be my life's dream to be wed to my greatest friend and ally. I would be honored to be your husband."

She clasped his hands and pulled him to his feet, placing a tender kiss upon his forehead. It took her a moment to compose herself then, such were the feelings of relief, joy, and terror she felt. When she did, she turned from her newly betrothed and faced those in the chamber.

"Let tomorrow be a day of celebration, but also a day of planning. Eisandre Caliburn will marry Actaeon Rellios, and Raedelle will rally the warbands. In two days time, we march for the security of our future."

PRINCE ENGINEER

J UST AS THE FIRST LIGHT of the sun lit the vast ruins of Redemption the next day, the hectic activity of the mustering warbands paused so that the Princess could stand at the top of a grassy hill with the Engineer, her betrothed. The unlikely couple clasped hands before a small group of witnesses, in the traditional Raedellean style, and spoke their simple vows.

"Actaeon Rellios of Shore, I bind myself to you in truth and love, that we might walk the path of the rest of our lives together and be stronger and better for it. I honor you and declare my love for you before our people gathered here today. From this day forth, with fierce pride and greatest joy, I will call you my husband."

"Eisandre Caliburn of Lakehold, I bind myself to you in truth and love, that we might walk the path of the rest of our lives together and be stronger and better for it. I honor you and declare my love for you before our people gathered here today. From this day forth, with fierce pride and greatest joy, I will call you my wife."

A jovial cheer echoed across the hills all the way back to Caliburn Castle in the distance. Beside Eisandre stood the First Companion Itarik and Companion Wayd, while at Actaeon's side were his steadfast friends Trench and Wave. The crowd was mostly comprised of the denizens of Caliburn Castle and the Wall Breakers that had travelled with the Princess all the way from the Wall. Ambrosius the Wise was there, along with Hamnin Dafryl. Notably, Gwendolyn Caliburn stood as far away from the Lord Dafryl as possible. Actaeon had been surprised at first to see her brother, Gunther

Arcady, beside her when they'd first arrived. It made sense though, for him to be there at his niece's wedding – the conniving Lord had likely decided that it looked good to the Raedellean people.

Voice Faris stepped forward then and offered a chalice to Eisandre. The Princess accepted it and examined the cup. When she offered Ithelie a questioning look, the Voice answered formally.

"Your Grace, it is the cup of bliss. A formal ritual at any wedding. Please take a sip from it and be wed in the eyes of the Ancestors."

Eisandre glanced at Actaeon and he nodded to her, so she took a small sip from the chalice before she handed it back to the Voice.

Ithelie turned and presented it to Actaeon then. He accepted the chalice and caught a whiff of it as he held it up. It smelt like the scent of a thousand flowers all crammed into one drink – it made his eyes water. He hesitated after he raised the cup to his lips when he heard Trench and Wave chuckling behind him. A look across at his new wife made him smile though, and he took a good swig of the strange liquid before he handed it back to the Voice.

Actaeon instantly felt a warmth travel through his body to the tips of his fingers and the ends of his toes. The warmth settled in his stomach where it continued to glow like embers from a fire. He received several firm pats on the back from his friends.

Ithelie handed the chalice to a waiting attendant and then stepped closer to the couple. She placed one hand behind each of their necks and gently brought their heads together until Actaeon and Eisandre's foreheads touched.

"Ancestors young and old," spoke the young Voice, "I ask that you bear witness to these two – your kin.

"Give them your guidance and ensure they spend the rest of their days in faithfulness.

"And for this woman, our beloved Princess, we ask that our own great Raedelle watch over her and show her the path to follow.

"Eisandre Caliburn, your words have been voiced to the Ancestors. Actaeon Rellios, your words have been voiced to the Ancestors.

"May the love forged today in the eyes of all Raedelle never be put asunder."

The Voice turned then, to face the crowd, and raised her hands in overture.

"May all of Raedelle know this marriage and the love of Princess Eisandre Rellios Caliburn and Prince Engineer Actaeon Rellios Caliburn."

The cheer that followed was unrestrained and the crowd rushed forward to embrace them both. Before they realized what was happening, they were lifted from the ground by their friends and held aloft in the air, side by side, to be carried back to the castle on a sea of roaring Raedelleans.

The newlyweds were ushered into a room together. Eisandre recognized it as the main room in the suite that her late father had once occupied. The door was closed and barred behind them and beyond it they could hear the boisterous crowd as they headed off to finish the preparations for war.

In the center of the room stood a freshly made bed illuminated by a stream of sunlight that poured through one of the stone embrasures of the castle. Upon a table at the foot of the bed were two empty tankards and a pitcher of the finest mead, its lofty scent reaching their noses from there.

"Well, my wife," said the Prince Engineer, as he inspected the arrangements. "It seems that some people have already been planning and plotting behind our backs." He glanced over at his new wife and felt his face flush red. His entire body tingled from head to toe and he felt greater happiness than he could ever recall to be married to the woman before him.

In contrast, Eisandre stood in the vast space of the chamber, her thoughts divided in a way that left her mind floundering in confusion. "There is so much to be done, though. Why do they lock us in this room? I must review the supply lists and discuss tactics with Itarik. We are their leaders now, how can they make us stay here?"

Actaeon smiled at her and gently took her hand. "They feel that it is important for us to spend time together before we rush off to war. Our marriage is also a symbol of unity between Lakehold and Shore, and a happy moment for our people after a lengthy period of question and doubt at the future of their Dominion. Our friends just want us to be happy. If it is to be us who lead our people into the future, it is important to them that we get what we require. Time after marriage for two lovers like us to become one and reflect on that is quite important. They will manage the planning and other affairs for now, love. Part of being a leader is to trust in the ability of others. Let them shine for a short while as we spend time together. This is the happiest day in my life – the day I am joined to you truly. It is something I wanted since I came to know you, my Eisandre."

She stood in silence for a long moment before she spoke. "Forgive me, my love. This is all so very new for me. I find... it is difficult for me to see clearly – one of my many faults. I do understand that spending time alone is important, as we have just been wed, and I know that the others are competent and capable. And if for some reason I had been naive of what is expected of us here and now, the ribald comments of those that carried us here were more than sufficient to clarify matters, were they not?" she asked with a glimmer of amusement in her eyes. "I almost did not wish to be alone together in this moment until things have settled into some semblance of peace, but will they ever? A few brief hours will never be enough, but for all we know they might be all we have."

"No time was ever enough, Eis. We always took all the time we could together, around your busy Arbiter schedule and my engineering endeavors. If you cannot concentrate on things with us though, for now – I understand. I want our first time together to be about us, not distracted by the worries and cataclysms of Redemption. You are my wife now and we are wed. I am so happy about that. If you like, I can just hold you for awhile," said the newly proclaimed Prince Engineer, in clear contradiction with the tingling that had now spread completely throughout his body and the very different thoughts that entered his head unbidden.

"And you are my husband," answered Eisandre. "You're right. We can plan and hope for a long, happy life together, but nothing is guaranteed. It isn't logical to wait for the perfect alignment to fall into place. We can only be sure of what is here and now. And we are here now – and alone. So, I think I should like you to kiss me, if you don't mind."

The Princess gave him a smile and there was something else, that the Engineer recognized, in her eyes – an urgent need. It made his heart leap in his chest and he felt a familiar stirring deep within him. He pulled her close and kissed her deeply – a kiss which she returned happily. As they kissed, she pulled his jacket off and he unlaced her leather armor.

When they separated to remove their clothing, Actaeon said, "You make me feel complete, my Princess. You fill my soul with joy. I'm so glad that we may be together now, my beautiful Eisandre."

"You like words," she observed with amusement before she pulled him back to her. She gasped then at the sensations that jolted through her body and blinked up at him. "What I'm feeling now. There must've been something in that cup..."

"In the cup of bliss, yes. I feel it too. It makes me want you more than anything right now."

"Actaeon," she said, in sudden realization and awe, eyes meeting his, "we don't have to wait anymore. Right?"

Actaeon nodded and replied with another kiss during which he lifted her off her feet to carry her over to the bed.

And on that day, the scorned and Lost Arbiter, who at one time could barely cope with another person's touch, and the eccentric and loquacious Engineer, who had never been truly understood by another, became one.

In a world of trial and tribulation, love shone so brightly, that for a time nothing else mattered.

EPILOGUE: WORDS ON THE WIND

OUTSIDE OF THE CASTLE, WAVE took a long drag on his linreed stick and released it in a puff of smoke that hung in the air and swirled before him. A long while after they had brought the newlyweds to their room, Wave had stepped outside to enjoy the fresh air. After a long few days of rain and death, it was nice to stand outside and enjoy the presence of neither for once.

The warm breeze that blew over his neck reminded him of the breath of the lovely young warbander as she'd climaxed hard against him. Caught up in the moment, he supposed, but of course he'd been as well, and the girl hadn't provided him much other choice. She'd been riveted by the fact that he was one of the survivors of what they were now calling the Battle of the Wall.

He tried to explain to her that he'd fought in the First Battle of the Wall over twenty years ago and that the recent battle had actually been the Second Battle of the Wall, or perhaps instead should be called the Battle of the Pillar. She'd only tugged her skirts up and gone at him more aggressively.

Old Duke Macsen Caliburn had been slain on the battlefield that day fighting the invaders, and that had paved the way for his son, Princess Eisandre's father, to lead Raedelle. He remembered fighting alongside Gunther Arcady that day as well, long before the son of Myrddin had become the Lord Shore. Too bad, he thought, that Gunther hadn't died then – it would have saved them so many problems. How easy it would've been to have run the man through with his own rapier. It would've threatened to destroy the alliance of Dominions that the Invasion War had forced together, he knew. That's why, in the end he'd held his tongue and dutifully fought alongside the Raedellean.

And speaking of tongues, the things that pretty, redheaded warbander had done with hers were exquisite on a level he'd rarely seen in his many dalliances. She was likely still there. If he finished his smoke quickly, perhaps he could inspire her to a second round. Or more likely, she'd inspire him.

The thoughts were interrupted by the sounds of argument that came from the same postern door he had used to leave the castle. He casually stepped behind the trunk of a nearby tree where he watched and listened.

While he couldn't hear everything, he could tell that the two men arguing were none other than the Lord Arcady himself and Ambrosius the Wise. *Speak of the scoundrel*, he thought.

Arcady shouted at Ambrosius while the old advisor listened calmly, his hands folded into his robes. Most of the words were lost to Wave as the breeze picked up, but from what he could glean, the man was extremely angry that Ambrosius hadn't supported his claim to Raedelle at the Conclave.

Wave blinked his eye and took another drag on the linreed. He watched as Ambrosius silenced the Lord Shore with one raised hand and spoke in a level voice. Most of what he said was lost to the winds, but Wave was able to overhear one thing clearly:

"You know as well as I, the moment she showed up here there was no other choice."

THE END

ABOUT THE AUTHOR

Darran M. Handshaw is the author of The Engineer, his debut novel. In addition to writing, Darran works as an R&D Engineer at a technology company. There he designs and invents new products; he holds more than 15 patents in firefighting and data capture. Darran also volunteers as a firefighter and EMT with his local fire department, where he recently completed a two-year term as Fire Captain. Darran hails from Long Island, NY, where he lives with his wife, Stefanie, and son, Corwin, who fill his life with love, wisdom, and endless adventures.

Follow Darran below:

fb.me/ActaeonRellios/

twitter.com/Engineer7601

goodreads.com/TheEngineer

amazon.com/author/engineer

ALSO BY THE AUTHOR

The Machine in the Mountain,
A Chronicles of Actaeon Tale
A short story in The Quantum Soul: A Sci Fi Roundtable Anthology

94096927R00368

Made in the USA
San Bernardino, CA
11 November 2018